RIVER GOD
&
GOLD MINE

Wilbur Smith was born in Central Africa in 1933. He was educated at Michaelhouse and Rhodes University.

He became a full-time writer in 1964 after the successful publication of *When the Lion Feeds*, and has since written thirty novels, all meticulously researched on his numerous expeditions worldwide. His books are now translated into twenty-six languages.

He owns a farm and game reserve and has an abiding concern for the peoples and wildlife of his native continent, an interest strongly reflected in his novels.

Also by Wilbur Smith

THE COURTNEYS

Birds of Prey
Monsoon
When the Lion Feeds
The Sound of Thunder
A Sparrow Falls
Blue Horizon

THE COURTNEYS OF AFRICA

The Burning Shore
Power of the Sword
Rage
A Time to Die
Golden Fox

THE BALLANTYNE NOVELS

A Falcon Flies
Men of Men
The Angels Weep
The Leopard Hunts in Darkness

Also

The Dark of the Sun
Shout at the Devil
The Diamond Hunters
The Sunbird
Eagle in the Sky
The Eye of the Tiger
Cry Wolf
Hungry as the Sea
Wild Justice
Elephant Song
The Seventh Scroll
Warlock

WILBUR SMITH

RIVER GOD
&
GOLD MINE

PAN BOOKS

River God first published 1993 by Macmillan.
First published in paperback 1994 by Pan Books
Gold Mine first published 1970 by William Heinemann.
First published in paperback 1992 by Pan Books

This omnibus first published 2005 by Pan Books
an imprint of Pan Macmillan Ltd
Pan Macmillan, 20 New Wharf Road, London N1 9RR
Basingstoke and Oxford
Associated companies throughout the world
www.panmacmillan.com

ISBN 0 330 44378 X

1 3 5 7 9 8 6 4 2

A CIP catalogue record for this book is available from
the British Library.

Printed and bound in Great Britain by
Mackays of Chatham plc, Chatham, Kent

RIVER GOD

This book, like so many others before it, is for my wife, Danielle Antoinette.

The Nile that flows through this story has both of us in her thrall. We have spent days of delight voyaging together upon her waters and idling upon her banks. As we are, so is she a creature of this very Africa of ours.

Yet this great river runs neither so strongly nor so deeply as my love for you, my darling.

THE RIVER lay heavily upon the desert, bright as a spill of molten metal from a furnace. The sky smoked with heat-haze and the sun beat down upon it all with the strokes of a coppersmith's hammer. In the mirage the gaunt hills flanking the Nile seemed to tremble to the blows.

Our boat sped close in beside the papyrus beds; near enough for the creaking of the water buckets of the shadoof, on their long, counter-balanced arms, to carry from the fields across the water. The sound harmonized with the singing of the girl in the bows.

Lostris was fourteen years of age. The Nile had begun its latest flood on the very day that her red woman's moon had flowered for the first time, a coincidence that the priests of Hapi had viewed as highly propitious. Lostris, the woman's name that they had then chosen to replace her discarded baby-name, meant 'Daughter of the Waters'.

I remember her so vividly on that day. She would grow more beautiful as the years passed, become more poised and regal, but never again would that glow of virgin womanhood radiate from her so overpoweringly. Every man aboard, even the warriors at the rowing-benches, was aware of it. Neither I nor any one of them could keep our gaze off her. She filled me with a sense of my own inadequacy and a deep and poignant longing; for although I am a eunuch I was gelded only after I had known the joy of a woman's body.

'Taita,' she called to me, 'sing with me!' And when I obeyed she smiled with pleasure. My voice was one of the many reasons that, whenever she was able, she kept me near her; my tenor complemented her lovely soprano to perfection. We sang one of the old peasant love songs that I had taught her, and which was still one of her favourites:

1

My heart flutters up like a wounded quail
when I see my beloved's face
and my cheeks bloom like the dawn sky
to the sunshine of his smile—

From the stern another voice joined with ours. It was a man's voice, deep and powerful, but it lacked the clarity and purity of my own. If my voice was that of a dawn-greeting thrush, then this was the voice of a young lion.

Lostris turned her head and now her smile shimmered like the sunbeams on the surface of the Nile. Although the man upon whom she played that smile was my friend, perhaps my only true friend, still I felt the bitter gall of envy burn the back of my throat. Yet I forced myself to smile at Tanus, as she did, with love.

Tanus' father, Pianki, Lord Harrab, had been one of the grandees of the Egyptian nobility, but his mother had been the daughter of a freed Tehenu slave. Like so many of her people, she had been fair-headed and blue-eyed. She had died of the swamp fever while Tanus was still a child, so my memory of her was imperfect. However, the old women said that seldom before had such beauty as hers been seen in either of the two kingdoms.

On the other hand, I had known and admired Tanus' father, before he lost all his vast fortune and the great estates that had once almost rivalled those of Pharaoh himself. He had been of dark complexion, with Egyptian eyes the colour of polished obsidian, a man with more physical strength than beauty, but with a generous and noble heart – some might say too generous and too trusting, for he had died destitute, with his heart broken by those he had thought his friends, alone in the darkness, cut off from the sunshine of Pharaoh's favour.

Thus it seemed that Tanus had inherited the best from both his parents, except only worldly wealth. In nature and in power he was as his father; in beauty as his mother. So why should I resent my mistress loving him? I loved him also, and, poor neutered thing that I am, I knew that I could never have her for myself, not even if the gods had raised my status above that of slave. Yet such is the perversity of human nature that I hungered for what I could never have and dreamed of the impossible.

Lostris sat on her cushion on the prow with her slave girls sprawled at her feet, two little black girls from Cush, lithe as panthers, entirely naked except for the golden collars around their necks. Lostris herself wore only a skirt of bleached linen, crisp and white as an egret's wing. The skin of her upper body, caressed by the sun, was the colour of oiled cedar wood from the mountains beyond Byblos. Her breasts were the size and shape of ripe figs just ready for plucking, and tipped with rose garnets.

She had set aside her formal wig, and wore her natural hair in a side-lock that fell in a thick dark rope over one breast. The slant of her eyes was enhanced by the silver-green of powdered malachite cunningly touched to the upper lids. The colour of her eyes was green also, but the darker, clearer green of the Nile when its waters have shrunk and deposited their burden of precious silts. Between her breasts, suspended on a gold chain, she wore a figurine of Hapi, the goddess of the Nile, fashioned in gold and precious lapis lazuli. Of course it was a superb piece, for I had made it with my own hands for her.

Suddenly Tanus lifted his right hand with the fist clenched. As a single man the rowers checked their stroke and held the blades of their paddles aloft, glinting in the sunlight and dripping water. Then Tanus thrust the steering-oar hard over, and the men on the port bank stabbed their backstroke deeply, creating a series of tiny whirlpools in the surface of the green water. The starboard side pulled strongly ahead. The boat spun so sharply that the deck canted over at an alarming angle. Then both banks pulled together and she shot forward. The sharp prow, with the blue eyes of Horus emblazoned upon it, brushed aside the dense stands of papyrus, and she lanced her way out of the flow of the river and into the still waters of the lagoon beyond.

Lostris broke off the song and shaded her eyes to gaze ahead. 'There they are!' she cried, and pointed with a graceful little hand. The other boats of Tanus' squadron were cast like a net across the southern reaches of the lagoon, blocking the main entrance to the great river, cutting off any escape in that direction.

Naturally, Tanus had chosen for himself the northern station, for he knew that this was where the sport would be most furious. I wished it was not so. Not that I am a coward, but I have always the safety of my mistress to consider. She had inveigled herself aboard the *Breath of Horus* only after much intrigue in which, as always, she had deeply involved me. When her father learned, as he surely would, of her presence in the thick of the hunt, it would go badly enough for me, but if he learned also that I was responsible for allowing her to be in the company of Tanus for a full day, not even my privileged position would protect me from his wrath. His instructions to me regarding this young man were unequivocal.

However, I seemed to be the only soul aboard the *Breath of Horus* who was perturbed. The others were simmering with excitement. Tanus checked the rowers with a peremptory hand-signal, and the boat glided to a halt and lay rocking gently upon the green waters that were so still that when I glanced overboard and saw my own reflection look back at me, I was struck, as always, by how well my beauty had carried over the years. To me it seemed that my face was more lovely than the cerulean blue lotus blooms that framed it. I had little time to admire it, however, for the crew were all abustle.

One of Tanus' staff officers ran up his personal standard to the masthead. It was the image of a blue crocodile, with its great coxcombed tail held erect and its jaws open. Only an officer of the rank of Best of Ten Thousand was entitled to his own standard. Tanus had achieved such rank, together with the command of the Blue Crocodile division of Pharaoh's own elite guard, before his twentieth birthday.

Now the standard at the masthead was the signal for the hunt to begin. On the horizon of the lagoon the rest of the squadron were tiny with distance, but their paddles began to beat rhythmically, rising and falling like the wings of wild geese in flight, glistening in the sunlight. From their sterns the multiple wavelets of their wakes were drawn out across the placid waters and lay for a long while on the surface, as though moulded from solid clay.

4

Tanus lowered the gong over the stern. It was a long bronze tube. He allowed the end of it to sink below the surface. When struck with a hammer of the same metal the shrill, reverberating tones would be transmitted through the water, filling our quarry with consternation. Unhappily for my equanimity, I knew that this could readily turn to a murderous rage.

Tanus laughed at me. Even in his own excitement he had sensed my qualms. For a rude soldier he had unusual perception. 'Come up here in the stern-tower, Taita!' he ordered. 'You can beat the gong for us. It will take your mind off the safety of your own beautiful hide for a while.'

I was hurt by his levity, but relieved by the invitation, for the stern-tower is high above the water. I moved to do his bidding without undignified haste, and, as I passed him, I paused to exhort him sternly, 'Have a care for the safety of my mistress. Do you hear me, boy? Do not encourage her to recklessness, for she is every bit as wild as you are.' I could speak thus to an illustrious commander of ten thousand, for he was once my pupil and I had wielded the cane on more than one occasion across those martial buttocks. He grinned at me now as he had in those days, as cocky and impudent as ever.

'Leave that lady in my hands, I implore you, old friend. There is nothing I would relish more, believe me!' I did not admonish him for such a disrespectful tone, for I was in some small haste to take my place in the tower. From there I watched him take up his bow.

Already that bow was famous throughout the army, indeed throughout the length of the great river from the cataracts to the sea. I had designed it for him when he had grown dissatisfied with the puny weapons that, up until that time, were all that were available to him. I had suggested that we should try to fashion a bow with some new material other than those feeble woods that grow in our narrow riverine valley; perhaps with exotic timbers such as the heartwood of the olive from the land of the Hittites or of the ebony from Cush; or with even stranger materials such as the horn of the rhinoceros or the ivory tusk of the elephant.

No sooner had we made the attempt than we came upon a

myriad of problems, the first of which was the brittleness of these exotic materials. In their natural state none of them would bend without cracking, and only the largest and therefore the most expensive elephant tusk would allow us to carve a complete bowstock from it. I solved both these problems by splitting the ivory of a smaller tusk into slivers and gluing these together in sufficient girth and bulk to form a full bow. Unfortunately it was too rigid for any man to draw.

However, from there it was an easy and natural step to laminate together all four of our chosen materials – olive wood, ebony, horn and ivory. Of course, there were many months of experimentation with combinations of these materials, and with various types of glue to hold them together. We never did succeed in making a glue strong enough. In the end I solved this last problem by binding the entire bowstock with electrum wire to prevent it from flying apart. I had two big men assist Tanus in twisting the wire on to it with all their combined strength, while the glue was still hot. When it cooled, it set to an almost perfect combination of strength and pliability.

Then I cut strands from the gut of a great black-maned lion that Tanus hunted and killed with his bronze-bladed war spear out in the desert. These I tanned and twisted together to form a bowstring. The result was this gleaming arc of such extraordinary power that only one man out of all the hundreds who had made the attempt could draw it to full stretch.

The regulation style of archery as taught by the army instructors was to face the target and draw the nocked arrow to the sternum of the chest, hold that aim for a deliberate pause, then loose on command. However, not even Tanus had the strength to draw this bow and hold his aim steadily. He was forced to develop a completely new style. Standing sideways to the target, addressing it over his left shoulder, he would throw up the bow with his left arm outstretched and, with a convulsive heave, draw back the arrow until the feathered flights touched his lips and the muscles of his arms and chest stood proud with the effort. In that same instant of full extension, seemingly without aiming, he would loose.

At first, his arrows flew at random as wild bees leave the hive, but he practised day after day and month after month. The fingers of his right hand became raw and bleeding from the chafing of the bowstring, but they healed and toughened. The inside of his left forearm was bruised and excoriated where the bowstring slashed past it on the release of the arrow, but I fashioned a leather guard to protect it. And Tanus stood at the butts and practised and practised.

Even I lost confidence in his ability to master the weapon but Tanus never gave up. Slowly, agonizingly slowly, he gained control of it to the point where, finally, he could launch three arrows with such rapidity that they were all in the air at the same instant. At least two of the three would strike the target, a copper disc the size of a man's head set up at a distance of fifty paces from where Tanus stood. Such was the force of those arrows that they would fly cleanly through the metal which was the thickness of my little finger.

Tanus named this mighty weapon Lanata which was, quite coincidentally, the discarded baby-name of my mistress. Now he stood in the bows with the woman at his side, and her namesake in his left hand. They made a marvellous couple, but too obviously so for my peace of mind.

I called sharply, 'Mistress! Come back here immediately! It is unsafe where you are.' She did not even deign to glance over her shoulder, but made a sign at me behind her back. Every one of the crew of the galley saw it, and the boldest of them guffawed. One of those little black vixens that were her handmaidens must have taught Lostris that gesture, which was more appropriate to the ladies of the riverside taverns than to a high-born daughter of the House of Intef. I considered remonstrating with her, but at once abandoned such an imprudent course, for my mistress is amenable to restraint only in certain of her moods. Instead, I applied myself to beating the bronze gong with sufficient vigour to disguise my chagrin.

The shrill, reverberating tone carried across the glassy waters of the lagoon, and instantly the air was filled with the susurration of wings and a shade was cast over the sun as, from the papyrus beds and the hidden pools and open water, a vast cloud of water-fowl rose into the sky. They were of a hundred varieties: black and white ibis with vulturine heads, sacred to the goddess of the river; flights of honking geese in russet plumage, each with a ruby droplet in the centre of its chest; herons of greenish-blue or midnight black, with bills like swords and ponderous wing-beats; and ducks in such profusion that their numbers challenged the eye and the credibility of the beholder.

Wild-fowling is one of the most ardent pursuits of the Egyptian nobility, but that day we were after different game. At that moment, I saw far ahead a disturbance upon the glassy surface. It was weighty and massive, and my spirits quailed, for I knew what terrible beast had moved there. Tanus also had seen it, but his reaction was altogether different from mine. He gave tongue like a hunting hound, and his men shouted with him and bent to their paddles. The *Breath of Horus* shot forward as though she were one of the birds that darkened the sky above us, and my mistress shrieked with excitement and beat with one small fist upon Tanus' muscled shoulder.

The waters roiled once more and Tanus signalled to his steersman to follow the movement, while I hammered upon the gong to bolster and sustain my courage. We reached the spot where last we had seen movement, and the vessel glided to a standstill while every man upon her decks gazed around eagerly.

I alone glanced directly over the stern. The water beneath our hull was shallow and almost as clear as the air above us. I shrieked as loudly and as shrilly as my mistress had and leapt back from the stern-rail, for the monster was directly under us.

The hippopotamus is the familiar of Hapi, the goddess of the Nile. It was only with her special dispensation that we could hunt it. To that end Tanus had prayed and sacrificed at the goddess's temple that morning, with my mistress close by his side. Of course, Hapi is her patron goddess, but I doubted that alone was the reason for her avid participation in the ceremony.

The beast that I saw beneath us now was an enormous old bull. To my eye, he seemed as large as our galley, a gigantic shape that lumbered along the bottom of the lagoon, his movements slowed down by the drag of the water so that he moved like a creature from a nightmare. He raised puffs of mud from beneath his hooves the same way that a wild oryx stirs the dust as it races across the desert sands.

With the steering-oar Tanus spun the boat about and we sped after the bull. But even at that slow and mannered gallop he rapidly drew away from us. His dark shape faded into the green depths of the lagoon ahead of us.

'Pull! By Seth's foul breath, pull!' Tanus howled at his men, but when one of his officers shook out the knotted lash of the whip, Tanus frowned and shook his head. I have never seen him ply the lash where it was not warranted.

Suddenly the bull broke through the surface ahead of us and blew a great cloud of fetid steam from his lungs. The stink of it washed over us, even though he was well out of bowshot. For a moment his back formed a gleaming granite island in the lagoon, then he drew a whistling breath and with a swirl was gone again.

'After him!' Tanus bellowed.

'There he is,' I cried, as I pointed over the side, 'he's doubling back.'

'Well done, old friend,' Tanus laughed at me, 'we'll make a warrior of you yet.' That notion was ridiculous, for I am a scribe, a sage and an artist. My heroics are of the mind. None the less, I felt a thrill of pleasure, as I always do at Tanus' praise, and my trepidation was, for the moment, lost in the excitement of the chase.

To the south of us the other galleys of the squadron had joined the hunt. The priests of Hapi had kept a strict count of the number of these great beasts in the lagoon, and had given sanction for fifty of them to be slaughtered for the coming festival of Osiris. This would leave almost three hundred of the goddess's flock remaining in the temple lagoon, a number that the priests considered ideal to keep the waterways free of choking weed, to prevent the papyrus beds from encroaching upon the arable lands and to provide a regular supply of meat for the temple. Only the priests themselves were allowed to eat the flesh of the hippopotamus outside the ten days of the festival of Osiris.

So the hunt spun out across the waters like some intricate dance, with the ships of the squadron weaving and pirouetting while the frenzied beasts fled before them, diving and blowing and grunting as they surfaced to dive again. Yet each dive was shorter than the last, and the swirling breaches at the surface became more frequent as their lungs were emptied and could not be fully recharged before the pursuing ships bore down upon them and forced them to dive again. All the while the bronze gongs in the stern-tower of each galley rang out to blend with the excited cries of the rowers and the exhortations of the helmsmen. All was wild uproar and confusion and I found myself shouting and cheering along with the most bloodthirsty of them.

Tanus had concentrated all his attention on the first and largest bull. He ignored the females and younger animals that breached within bowshot, and followed the great beast through all his convolutions, drawing inexorably closer to him each time he surfaced. Even in my excitement I could not but admire the skill with which Tanus handled the *Breath of Horus* and the manner in which his crew responded to his signals. But then, he always had the knack of getting the very best out of those he commanded. How otherwise, with neither fortune nor great patron to sustain him, could he have risen so swiftly to exalted rank? What he had achieved he had done on his own merit, and that despite the malignant influence of hidden enemies who had placed every obstacle in his way.

Suddenly the bull burst through the surface not thirty paces from the bows. He came out gleaming in the sunshine, monstrous black and awful, clouds of steamy vapour spurting from his nostrils like that creature from the underworld that devours the hearts of those who are found wanting by the gods.

Tanus had an arrow nocked and now he threw up the great bow and loosed it in the same fleeting instant. Lanata played her dreadful shimmering music, and the arrow leaped out in a blur that deceived the eye. While it still hissed in flight, another followed it and then another. The bowstring hummed like a lute, and the arrows struck one after the other. The bull bellowed as they buried themselves full-length in his broad back, and he dived again.

These were missiles that I had devised especially for this occasion. The feathered flights had been removed from the

To me it seemed that she fell for ever, and my own anguished cry blended with her despairing wail.

'My baby!' I cried. 'My little one!' For I was certain that she was lost. It seemed that all her life, as I had known it, replayed itself before my eyes. I saw her again as a toddling infant and heard the baby endearments that she bestowed on me, her adoring nursemaid. I saw her grow to womanhood, and I remembered every joy and every heartache that she had caused me. I loved her then in the moment of losing her even more than I had done in all those fourteen long years.

She fell upon the vast, blood-splattered back of the infuriated bull, and for an instant lay spread-eagled there like a human sacrifice upon the altar of some obscene religion. The bull whirled about, mounting high out of the water, and he twisted his huge deformed head backwards, trying to reach her. His bloodshot piggy eyes glared with the insanity of his rage, and his great jaws clashed as he snapped at her.

Somehow Lostris managed to gather herself and cling to a pair of the arrow-shafts that protruded from the bull's broad back as though they were handles. She lay with her arms and legs spread wide. She was not screaming now, all her art and strength employed in staying alive. Those curved ivory fangs rang upon each other like the blades of duelling warriors as they gnashed in air. At each bite they seemed to miss her by only a finger's-breadth, and any instant I expected one of her lovely limbs to be pruned away like a delicate shoot from the vine, and to see her sweet young blood mingle with those brutish effusions that streamed from the bull's wounds.

In the prow Tanus recovered swiftly. For an instant I saw his face and it was terrible. He tossed aside the bow, for it was useless to him now, and he seized instead the hilt of his sword and jerked the blade free of its crocodile-skin scabbard. It was a gleaming length of bronze as long as his arm, and the edges were honed until they could shave the hair from the back of his hand.

He leaped up on to the gunwale and balanced there for an instant, watching the wild gyrations of the mortally wounded bull in the water below him. Then he launched himself outwards

13

and dropped like a stooping falcon with the sword held in both hands and pointing downwards.

He dropped across the bull's thick neck, landing astride it as though he were about to ride it into the underworld. The full weight of his body and the impetus of that wild leap were behind the sword as he struck. Half the length of the blade was driven into the hippopotamus's neck at the base of the skull, and, seated upon it like a rider, Tanus worried and worked the keen bronze deeper, using both arms and the strength of those broad shoulders. At the goad of the blade the bull went berserk. His strivings up to that point seemed feeble in comparison to this fresh outburst. The bull reared most of his enormous bulk out of the lagoon, swinging his head from side to side, throwing solid sheets of water so high in the air that they crashed down on the deck of the galley and, like a curtain, almost obscured the scene from my horrified gaze.

Through it all I watched the couple on the monster's back tossed about mercilessly. The shaft of one of the arrows that Lostris was holding snapped, and she was almost thrown clear. If this had happened she would surely have been savaged by the bull and chopped into bloody tatters by those ivory fangs. Tanus reached backwards and with one arm seized and steadied her, while with his right hand he never ceased working the bronze blade deeper into the nape of the bull's neck.

Unable to reach them, the hippopotamus slashed at his own flanks, inflicting terrible gaping wounds in his sides so that for fifty paces around the galley the waters were incarnadined, and both Lostris and Tanus were painted entirely crimson from the tops of their heads to the soles of their feet by the spurting blood. Their faces were turned to grotesque masks from which their eyes whitely glared.

The violent death-throes of the bull had carried them far from the galley's side, and I was the first aboard to recover my wits. I yelled to the rowers, 'Follow them! Don't let them get away,' and they sprang to their stations and sent the *Breath of Horus* in pursuit.

At that instant it seemed that the point of Tanus' blade must have found the joint of the vertebrae in the beast's neck and

14

slipped through. The immense carcass stiffened and froze. The bull rolled on to his back with all four legs extended rigidly, and he plunged below the waters of the lagoon, bearing Lostris and Tanus with him into the depths.

I choked back the wail of despair that rose in my throat, and bellowed an order to the deck below. 'Back-water! Do not overrun them! Swimmers to the bows!' Even I was startled by the power and authority of my own voice.

The galley's forward way was checked, and before I could reflect on the prudence of what I was doing, I found myself heading a rush of hulking warriors across the deck. They would probably have cheered while they watched any other officer drown, but not their Tanus.

As for myself, I had already stripped off my skirt and was naked. Not the threat of a hundred lashes would have made me do this in any other circumstances, for I have let only one other person ever see those injuries that the state executioner inflicted upon me so long ago, and he was the one who had ordered the castrating knife used upon me in the first place. But now, for once, I was totally oblivious of the gross mutilation of my manhood.

I am a strong swimmer, and although in retrospect such foolhardiness makes me shudder, I truly believe that I might have dived over the side and swum down through those blood-dyed waters in an attempt to rescue my mistress. However, as I poised myself at the ship's rail, the waters directly below me opened and two heads bobbed out, both of them streaming water and as close as a pair of mating otters. One was dark and the other fair, but from both of them issued the most unlikely sound I had ever heard. They were laughing. They were howling and shrieking and spluttering with laughter as they floundered towards the ship's side, locked so firmly in each other's arms that I was certain that they were in real danger of drowning one another.

All my concern turned instantly to outrage at this levity, and at the thought of the dreadful folly which I had been on the point of committing. Like a mother whose first instinct on finding her lost child is to thrash it, I heard my own voice lose all its previous deep authority and turn shrill and querulous. I was still

15

berating my mistress with all my famous eloquence as she and Tanus were dragged by a dozen willing hands from the water on to the deck.

'You reckless, unbridled little savage!' I railed at her. 'You thoughtless, selfish, undisciplined little hoyden! You promised me! You swore an oath on the maidenhead of the goddess—'

She ran to me and threw both arms around my neck. 'Oh, Taita!' she cried, still bubbling with laughter. 'Did you see him? Did you see Tanus spring to my rescue? Was it not the noblest deed that ever you heard of? Just like the hero of one of your very best stories.'

The fact that I had been on the point of making a similar heroic gesture was quite ignored, and this only increased my irritation. Added to which I suddenly realized that Lostris had lost her skirt, and that the cold, wet body she pressed to mine was entirely naked. She was displaying to the rude gaze of officers and men the neatest, tightest pair of buttocks in all Egypt.

I snatched up the nearest shield and used it to cover both our bodies while I shouted at her slave girls to find another skirt for her. Their giggles only increased my fury, and as soon as both Lostris and I were once again decently covered, I rounded on Tanus.

'As for you, you careless ruffian, I shall report you to my Lord Intef! He will have the skin flogged from your back.'

'You will do no such thing,' Tanus laughed at me, and threw one wet muscled arm around my shoulders to hug me so soundly that I was lifted off my feet, 'for he would have you flogged just as merrily. Nevertheless, thank you for your concern, old friend.'

He looked around quickly, with one arm still encircling my shoulder, and frowned. The *Breath of Horus* was separated from the other ships of the squadron, but by now the hunt was over. Every galley but ours had taken its full share of the bag that the priests had sanctioned us.

Tanus shook his head. 'We did not make the most of our chances, did we?' he grunted, and ordered one of his officers to hoist the recall signal to the squadron.

Then he forced a smile. 'Let us broach a jug of beer together, for now we have a while to wait and this has been thirsty work.'

He went to the bows where the slave girls were fussing over Lostris. At first I was still so angry that I would not join their impromptu picnic on the deck. Instead I maintained an aloof dignity in the stern.

'Oh, let him sulk a while,' I heard Lostris' stage-whisper to Tanus as she recharged his cup with foaming beer. 'The old darling gave himself an awful scare, but he will get over it as soon as he is hungry. He does so love his food.'

She is the epitome of injustice, is my mistress. I never sulk, I am no glutton, and at that time I was barely thirty years of age, although to a fourteen-year-old anyone above twenty is an ancient, and I admit that, when it comes to food, I do have the refined tastes of a connoisseur. The roast wild goose with figs that she was ostentatiously displaying was one of my favourite dishes, as she very well knew.

I made them suffer for a while longer, and it was only when Tanus brought me a jug of beer with his own hand and cajoled me with all his charm that I deigned to relent a little and let him lead me to the prow. Still, I was a little stiff with them until Lostris kissed my cheek and said, loud enough for all to hear, 'My girls tell me that you took command of the ship like a veteran, and that you would have dived overboard to rescue me. Oh, Taita, what would I ever do without you?' Only then would I smile at her and accept the slice of goose she pressed upon me. It was delicious, and the beer was of three-palm quality. Even so, I ate sparingly, for I have my figure to consider and her earlier jibe about my appetite still rankled a little.

Tanus' squadron was scattered widely across the lagoon, but now it began to regroup. I saw that some of the other galleys had suffered damage, as we had. Two ships had collided in the heat of the chase, while four others had been attacked by the quarry. However, they reassembled swiftly and took up their battle stations. Then, in line astern and with strings of gay pennants fluttering at the mastheads to proclaim the size of each galley's bag, they dashed past us. The crews raised a cheer as they came level with the *Breath of Horus*. Tanus saluted them with a clenched fist and the Blue Crocodile standard was dipped at the masthead, for all the world as though we had just achieved a famous victory against daunting odds. Boyish display, perhaps, but then I am still enough of a boy to enjoy military ceremonial.

As soon as it was over, the squadron resumed its battle stations and was holding its position against the light breeze that had sprung up, with skilful use of paddles and steering-oars. Of course, there was no sign of the slaughtered hippopotami as yet. Although every galley had killed at least one, while some had killed two and even three, the carcasses had all sunk away into the green depths of the lagoon. I knew that Tanus was secretly lamenting the fact that the *Breath of Horus* had not been the most successful boat, and that our protracted encounter with the bull had limited our score to only that single animal. He was accustomed to excelling. Anyway, he was not his usual ebullient self and he soon left us on the prow and went to supervise the repairs to the hull of the *Breath of Horus*.

The bull's charge had sprung the underwater planking and we were taking enough water to necessitate constant bailing of the bilges with leather buckets. This was a most inefficient procedure which diverted men from their duties as rowers and warriors. Surely it could be improved upon, I thought to myself.

So while we waited for the carcasses of the dead beasts to rise, I sent one of the slave girls to fetch the basket that contained my writing instruments. Then, after a little further thought, I began to sketch out an idea for mechanically removing the water from the bilges of a fighting galley in action, a method which did not demand the efforts of half the crew. It was based on the same principle as the shadoof water buckets. I thought that two men might operate it instead of a dozen at the buckets, as was now the case.

When I had completed the sketch, I pondered on the collision that had caused the original damage. Historically, the tactics used in battles between squadrons of river galleys had always been the same as those of land engagements. The ships would lie alongside each other and exchange volleys of arrows. They would then close and grapple and board, and finish the business with the sword. The galley captains were always careful to avoid collision, as this was considered sloppy seamanship.

18

'But what if—' I thought suddenly, and I began a sketch of a galley with a reinforced bow. As the idea took firm root I added a horn like that of the rhinoceros at the water line. It could be carved from hardwood and clad with bronze. Angled forwards and slightly downwards, it could be driven through the hull of an opposing vessel to rip out her belly. I was so engrossed that I did not hear Tanus come up behind me. He snatched the papyrus scroll from me and studied it avidly.

Of course, he understood instantly what I was about. When his father had lost his fortune, I had tried everything in my power to find a rich patron to sponsor him to enter one of the temples as a novice scribe, there to continue his studies and his learning. For I truly believed that, with my tutelage, he had every prospect of developing into one of the great minds of Egypt, perhaps in time a name to rank with that of Imhotep who, one thousand years before, had designed those first marvellous pyramids at Saqqarah.

I had been unsuccessful, naturally enough, for the same enemy whose spite and guile had destroyed Tanus' father had set out to bar the way to Tanus himself. No man in the land could prevail against such a baleful influence. So instead I had helped Tanus to enter the army. Despite my disappointment and misgivings, this had been his own choice of career ever since he had first stood upright and wielded a wooden sword on the other infants in the playground.

'By the carbuncles on Seth's buttocks!' he exclaimed now, as he studied my drawings. 'You and that designing-brush of yours are worth ten full squadrons to me!'

Tanus' casual blasphemy on the name of the great god Seth always alarms me. For although both he and I are Horus men, still I do not believe in flagrantly offering offence to any member of the pantheon of Egyptian gods. I personally never pass a shrine without offering a prayer or making a small sacrifice, no matter how humble or unimportant the god it houses. It is, to my mind, simple common sense and good insurance. One has sufficient enemies amongst men without deliberately seeking out others amongst the gods. I am particularly obsequious to Seth, for his formidable reputation terrifies me. I suspect that Tanus knows all this and deliberately does it to tease me. However, my discomfort was soon forgotten in the warm glow of his praise.

'How do you do it?' he demanded. 'I am the soldier, and today I saw everything that you did. Why did not the same ideas occur to me?'

We were instantly immersed in a lively discussion of my designs. Of course, Lostris could not be excluded for long, and she came to join us. Her handmaidens had dried and rebraided her hair and retouched her make-up. Her loveliness was a distraction, especially since she stood beside me and nonchalantly draped one slim arm over my shoulder. She would never have touched a man like that in public, for it would have offended against custom and modesty. But then I am not a man, and though she leaned against me, her eyes never left Tanus' face.

Her preoccupation with him went back to when she had first learned to walk. She had stumbled along adoringly behind the lordly ten-year-old Tanus, faithfully trying to copy his every gesture and word. When he spat, she spat. When he swore, she lisped the same oath, until Tanus had complained bitterly to me, 'Can you not make her leave me alone, Taita? She's just a baby!' He was not doing much complaining now, I noticed.

At last we were interrupted by a hail from the lookout in the bows, and we all hurried forward and peered eagerly across the lagoon. The first hippopotamus carcass was rising to the surface. It came up belly first as the gases in its intestines expanded and the guts distended like a child's balloon made from a goat's bladder. It bobbed on the surface with all its legs extended stiffly. One of the galleys sped across to recover it. A sailor scrambled out on to the carcass and secured a line to one of the legs. As soon as this was done, the galley towed it away towards the distant shore.

By now the huge corpses were surfacing all around us. The galleys gathered them up and dragged them away. Tanus secured two of them to our stern-hawser and the rowers strained at their paddles to move them through the water.

As we approached the shore I shaded my eyes against the slanting sun's rays and peered ahead. It seemed that every man, woman and child in Upper Egypt was waiting upon the bank. They were a vast multitude, dancing and singing and waving palm-fronds to welcome the incoming fleet. The restless movement of their white robes seemed like a storm surf breaking upon the edge of the placid lagoon.

As each galley drew up against the bank, teams of men clad only in the briefest loin-cloths waded out as deep as their armpits to fasten ropes to the bloated carcasses. In their excitement they were oblivious to the ever-present threat of crocodiles lurking in the opaque green waters. Every season these ferocious dragons devour hundreds of our people. Sometimes they are so bold that they rush out on to dry land to seize a child playing near the water's edge or a peasant woman washing clothes or drawing water for her family.

Now, in the vast meat-hunger that gripped them, the people were interested in only one thing. They seized the ropes and hauled the carcasses ashore. As they slithered up the muddy bank, scores of tiny silver fish that had been feasting on the open wounds were slow to relinquish their hold and were drawn out with the carcasses. Stranded upon the mud-banks, they flopped and quivered like stars that had fallen to earth.

Men and women, all wielding knives or axes, swarmed like ants over the bodies. In a delirium of greed they howled and snarled at each other like vultures and hyenas on a lion's kill, disputing each titbit as they hacked at the gigantic carcasses. Blood and bone chips flew in sheets as the blades hacked and hewed. There would be long lines of wounded at the temple that evening, awaiting treatment from the priests for their missing fingers and gashes down to the bone where the careless blades had slipped.

I too would be busy half the night, for in some quarters I have a reputation as a medical doctor that surpasses even that of the priests of Osiris. In all modesty I must admit that this reputation is not entirely unwarranted, and Horus knows my fees are much more reasonable than those of the holy men. My Lord Intef allows me to keep for myself a third part of all that I earn. Thus I am a man of some substance, despite my slave status.

From the stern-tower of the *Breath of Horus* I watched the

pantomime of human frailty that was being played out below me. Traditionally the populace is allowed to eat its fill of the meats of the hunt upon the foreshore, just as long as none of the spoils are carried away. Living as we do in a verdant land which is fertilized and watered by the great river, our people are well fed. However, the staple diet of the poorer classes is grain, and months may pass between their last mouthful of meat and the next. Added to which, the festival was a time when all the normal restraints of everyday life were thrust aside. There was licence to excess in all things of the body, in food and drink and carnal passion. There would be sore bellies and aching heads and matrimonial recriminations on the morrow, but this was the first day of the festival and there was no check on any appetite.

I smiled as I watched a mother, naked to the waist and plastered from head to toe with blood and fat, emerge from the belly cavity of a hippopotamus, clutching a running lump of liver which she threw to one of her brood in the jostling, shrieking pack of children that surrounded the carcass. The woman ducked back into the interior of the beast, while, clutching his prize, the child darted away to one of the hundreds of cooking-fires that burned along the shore. There an elder brother snatched the hunk of liver from him and threw it on the coals, while a pack of younger urchins crowded forward impatiently, slavering like puppies.

The eldest child hooked the barely scorched liver off the fire with a green twig, and his brothers and sisters fell upon it and devoured it. Immediately it was consumed they bayed for more, with fat and juice running down their faces and dripping from their chins. Many of the younger ones had probably never tasted the delicious flesh of the river-cow before. It is sweet and tender and fine-grained, but most of all it is fat, fatter than beef or striped wild ass, and the marrow-bones are truly a delicacy fit for the great god Osiris himself. Our people are starved of animal fat and the taste of it drove them wild. They gorged themselves, as was their right on this day.

I was content to keep aloof from this riotous mob, happy in the knowledge that my Lord Intef's bailiffs would secure the finest cuts and marrow-bones for the palace kitchens where the cooks would prepare my personal platter to perfection. My precedence in the vizier's household exceeds all other, even that of his major-domo or the commander of his bodyguard, both of whom are free-born. Of course, it is never openly spoken of, but all tacitly acknowledge my privileged and superior position and few would dare challenge it.

I watched the bailiffs at work now, claiming the share of my lord, the governor and grand vizier of all the twenty-two nomes of Upper Egypt. They swung their long staves with the expertise born of long practice, whacking any bare back or set of naked buttocks that presented themselves as targets, and shouting their demands.

The ivory teeth of the animals belonged to the vizier, and the bailiffs collected every one of them. They were as valuable as the elephant tusks that are brought down in trade from the land of Cush, beyond the cataracts. The last elephant had been killed in our Egypt almost one thousand years ago, in the reign of one of the pharaohs of the Fourth Dynasty, or so the hieroglyphics on the stele in his temple boast. Naturally, from the fruits of the hunt my lord was expected to tithe the priests of Hapi who were the titular shepherds of the goddess's flock of river-cows. However, the amount of the tithe was in my lord's discretion, and I who was in overall charge of the palace accounts knew where the lion's share of the treasure would end up. My Lord Intef does not indulge in unnecessary generosity, even towards a goddess.

As for the hides of the hippopotamus, these belonged to the army and would be turned into war shields for the officers of the guards regiments. The army quartermasters were supervising the skinning-out and the handling of the hides, each of which was almost the size of a Bedouin tent.

The meat that could not be consumed on the bank would be pickled in brine, or smoked or dried. Ostensibly it would be used to feed the army, the members of the law courts, the temples and other civil servants of the state. However, in practice a large part of it would be discreetly sold, and the proceeds would filter down quite naturally into my lord's coffers. As I have said before, my lord was the wealthiest man in the Upper Kingdom after Pharaoh himself, and growing richer every year.

A fresh commotion broke out behind me, and I turned quickly. Tanus' squadron was still in action. The galleys were drawn up in line of battle, stem to stern, parallel to the shore-line, but fifty paces off it on the edge of the deeper water. On each ship harpooneers stood at the rails with their weapons poised and pointed down at the surface of the lagoon.

The taint of blood and offal in the water had attracted the crocodiles. Not only from all over the lagoon, but from as far off as the main course of the Nile, they had come swarming to the feast. The harpooneers were waiting for them. Each long harpoon pole was tipped with a relatively small bronze head, viciously barbed. Spliced to an eye in the metal head was a tough flax rope.

The skill of the harpooneers was truly impressive. As one of these scaly saurians came slipping through the green water, with its great crested tail flailing, moving like a long dark shadow, silent and deadly beneath the surface, they would be waiting for it. They would allow the crocodile to pass beneath the galley, and then, as it emerged on the far side with the harpooneer's movements screened from it by the ship's hull, he would lean out over it and stab downwards.

It was not a violent blow, but an almost delicate dab with the long pole. The bronze head was as sharp as a surgeon's needle, and its full length was buried deep beneath the reptile's thick, scaly hide. The harpooneer aimed for the back of the neck, and so skilful were these thrusts that many of them pierced the spinal cord and killed the creature instantly.

However, when a blow missed its mark, the water exploded as the wounded crocodile burst into wild convulsions. With a twist of the harpoon pole the metal head was detached and remained buried in the reptile's armoured neck. Then four men took the creature on the flax line to control its contortions. If the crocodile was a large one – and some of them were four times the length of a man stretched out on the ground – then the coils of line were whipped away smoking over the gunwale, scorching the palms of the men who were trying to hold it.

When this happened, even the hungry crowds on the beach paused for a while to cheer and shout encouragement, and to watch the struggle as the crocodile was eventually subdued or the rope parted like a whiplash and the sailors were sent tumbling backwards across the deck. More often, the stout flax line held. As soon as the crew were able to turn the reptile's head towards them, it could no longer swim out into the deep water. They could then drag it in a turmoil of froth and white water to the ship's side where another gang was waiting with clubs to crush the rock-hard skull.

When the carcasses of the crocodiles were dragged to the bank, I went ashore to examine them. The skinners of Tanus' regiment were already at work.

It was the grandfather of our present king who had granted the regiment the honorific 'the Blue Crocodile Guards' and bestowed upon them the standard of the Blue Crocodile. Their battle armour is made from the horny skins of these dragons. Properly treated and cured, it becomes hard enough to stop an arrow or turn the edge of an enemy sword-cut. It is far lighter in weight than metal, and much cooler to wear in the desert sun. Tanus, in his crocodile-skin helmet all decorated with ostrich plumes, and his breastplate of the same hide, polished and starred with bronze rosettes, is a sight to strike terror into the heart of an enemy, or turmoil into the belly of any maiden who looks upon him.

As I measured and noted the length and girth of each carcass, and watched the skinners at work, I felt not even the most fleeting sympathy for these hideous monsters as I had for the slaughtered river-cows. To my mind there is no more loathsome beast in nature than the crocodile, with the possible exception of the venomous asp.

My revulsion was increased a hundredfold when a skinner slit open the belly of one of the largest of these grotesque animals, and out on to the mud slithered the partly digested remains of a young girl. The crocodile had swallowed the entire top half of her body, from the waist upwards. Although the flesh was bleached soft and pasty-white by the digestive juices and was sloughing from the skull, the girl's top-knot was still intact and neatly plaited and coiled above the ghastly, ruined face. As a further macabre touch, there was a necklace around her throat and pretty bracelets of red and blue ceramic beads on the skeletal wrists.

No sooner was this gruesome relic revealed than there came a shriek so high and heart-rending that it cut through the hubbub of the throng, and a woman elbowed aside the soldiers and ran forward to drop on her knees beside the pitiful remains. She tore her clothing and keened the dreadful ululation of mourning.

'My daughter! My little girl!' She was the same woman who had come to the palace the previous day to report her daughter missing. The officials had told her that the child had probably been abducted and sold into slavery by one of the gangs of bandits who were terrorizing the countryside. These gangs had become a force in the land, blatantly conducting their lawless depredations in broad daylight right up to the gates of the cities. The palace officials had warned the woman that there was nothing they could do about recovering her daughter, for the gangs were beyond any control that the state could exert upon them.

For once this dire prediction had proved unfounded. The mother had recognized the ornaments which still decorated the pathetic little corpse. My heart went out to the stricken woman, as I sent a slave to fetch an empty wine jar. Although the woman and her child were both strangers to me, I could not prevent my own tears from welling up as I helped her to gather the remains and place them in the jar for decent burial.

As she staggered away into the uncaring multitude of revellers, carrying the jar clutched to her breast, I reflected that despite all the rites and prayers that the mother would lavish upon her daughter, and even in the unlikely event that she could afford the staggering cost of the most rudimentary mummification, the child's shade could never find immortality in the life beyond the grave. For that to happen, the corpse must be intact and whole before embalming. My feelings were all for the unfortunate mother. It is a weakness of mine that I so often lament, that I take upon myself the cares and sorrows of every unfortunate that crosses my path. It would be easier to have a harder heart, and a more cynical turn of mind.

As always when I am saddened or distressed, I reached for my brush and scroll and began to record all that was taking place around me, everything from the harpooneers, the bereaved mother, the skinning and the butchery of the dead river-cows and crocodiles on the beach, to the unfettered behaviour of the feasting, revelling populace.

Already those who were stuffed with meat and gorged with beer were snoring where they had fallen, oblivious of being kicked and trampled by the others still capable of remaining upright. The younger and more shameless were dancing and embracing and using the gathering darkness and the inadequate cover of the scanty bushes and the trampled papyrus beds to screen their blatant copulations. This wanton behaviour was merely a symptom of the malaise that afflicted the entire land. It would not have been thus if only there had been a strong pharaoh, and a moral and upright administration in the nome of Greater Thebes. The common people take their example from those above them.

Although I disapproved most strongly of it all, still I recorded it faithfully. Thus an hour sped away while I sat cross-legged and totally absorbed upon the poop-deck of the *Breath of Horus*, scribbling and sketching. The sun sank and seemed to quench itself in the great river, leaving a coppery sheen on the water and a smoky glow in the western sky as though it had set fire to the papyrus beds.

The crowds on the beach were becoming ever more raucous and unrestrained. The harlots were doing a brisk trade. I watched a plump and matronly love-priestess, wearing the distinctive blue amulet of her calling upon her forehead, lead a skinny sailor who was half her size from one of the galleys into the shadows beyond the firelight. There she dropped her skirts and fell to her knees in the dust, presenting him with a quivering pair of monumental buttocks. With a happy cry the little fellow was upon her like a dog on a bitch, and within seconds she was yapping as loudly as he was. I began to sketch their antics, but the light faded swiftly, and I was forced to quit for the day.

As I set my scroll aside, I realized with a start that I had not seen my mistress since before the incident with the dead child. I leaped to my feet in a panic. How could I have been so remiss?

27

My mistress had been strictly raised, I had seen to that. She was a good and moral child, fully aware of the duties and obligations which law and custom placed upon her. She was aware also of the honour of the high family to which she belonged, and of her place in society. What was more, she stood in as much awe as I did of her father's authority and temper. Of course I trusted her.

I trusted her as much as I would have trusted any other strong-willed young creature in the first flush of passionate womanhood on a night such as this, alone somewhere in the darkness with the handsome and equally passionate young soldier with whom she was totally infatuated.

My panic was not so much for the fragile maidenhead of my mistress, that ethereal talisman which once lost is seldom mourned, as for the much more substantial risk of damage to my own skin. On the morrow we would return to Karnak and the palace of my Lord Intef, where there would be wagging tongues aplenty to carry the tale of any lapse or indiscretion on any of our parts to him.

My lord's spies permeated every layer of society and every corner of our land, from the docks and the fields to the palace of Pharaoh itself. They were even more numerous than my own, for he had more money to pay his agents, although many of them served both of us impartially and our networks interlocked at many levels. If Lostris had disgraced us all, father, family, and me her tutor and guardian, then my Lord Intef would know of it by morning, and so would I.

I ran from one end of the ship to the other, searching for her. I climbed into the stern-tower and scanned the beach in desperation. I could see nothing of her or of Tanus, and my worst fears were encouraged.

Where to search for them in this mad night I could not begin to think. I caught myself wringing my hands in an agony of frustration, and stopped myself immediately. I am always at pains to avoid any appearance of effeminacy. I do so abhor those obese, mincing, posturing creatures who have suffered the same mutilation as I have. I always try to conduct myself like a man rather than a eunuch.

I controlled myself with an effort and assumed the same coldly determined mien that I had seen on Tanus' features in the heat of battle, whereupon my wits were restored to me and I became rational once again. I considered how my mistress was likely to behave. Of course, I knew her intimately. After all, I had studied her for fourteen years. I realized that she was much too fastidious and conscious of her noble rank brazenly to mingle with the drunken, uncouth throng upon the beach, or to creep away into the bushes to play the beast with two backs, as I had watched the sailor and the fat old harlot do. I knew that I could call upon no one else to assist me in my search, for that would have guaranteed that my Lord Intef would hear all about it. I had to do it all myself.

To what secret place had Lostris allowed herself to be carried away? Like most young girls of her age she was enchanted with the idea of romantic love. I doubted that she had ever seriously considered the more earthy aspects of the physical act, despite the best efforts of those two little black sluts of hers to enlighten her. She had not even displayed any great deal of interest in the mechanics of the business when I had attempted, as was my duty, to warn her, at least sufficiently to protect her from herself.

I realized then that I must look for her in some place that would live up to her sentimental expectations of love. If there had been a cabin on the *Breath of Horus* I would have hurried to it, but our river galleys are small, utilitarian fighting ships, stripped down for speed and manoeuvrability. The crew sleep on the bare deck, while even the captain and his officers have only a reed awning for a night shelter. This was not rigged at the moment, and so there was no place aboard where they could be hiding.

Karnak and the palace were half a day's travel away. The slaves were only now erecting our tents on one of the small inshore islands that had been set aside to give our party privacy from the common herd of humanity. It was remiss of the slaves to be so tardy, but they had been caught up in the festivities. In the torchlight I could see that a few of them were more than a little unsteady on their feet as they struggled with the guy-ropes. They had not yet erected Lostris' personal tent, so the luxurious comforts of carpets and embroidered hangings and down-filled mattresses and linen sheets were not available to the lovers. So where then might they be?

At that moment a soft yellow glow of torchlight farther out on the lagoon caught my attention. Immediately my intuition was aroused. I realized that, given my mistress's connections with the goddess Hapi, her temple on its picturesque little granite island in the middle of the lagoon would be exactly the place that would draw Lostris irresistibly. I searched the beach for some means of reaching the island. Although there were shoals of small craft drawn up on the shore, the ferrymen were mostly falling-down drunk.

Then I spotted Kratas on the beach. The ostrich feathers on his helmet stood high above the heads of the crowd, and his proud bearing marked him out.

'Kratas!' I yelled at him, and he looked across at me and waved. Kratas was Tanus' chief lieutenant and, apart from myself, the firmest of his multitude of friends. I could trust Kratas as I dared trust no other.

'Get me a boat!' I screamed at him. 'Any boat!' I was so distraught and my tone so shrill that it carried clearly to him. It was typical of the man that he wasted not a moment in question or indecision. He strode to the nearest felucca on the shore. The ferryman was lying like a log in his own bilges. Kratas took him by the scruff of the neck and lifted him out bodily. He dropped him on the beach, and the ferryman never moved, but lay in a stupor of cheap wine, twisted in the attitude that Kratas had dumped him in. Kratas launched the craft himself and, with a few thrusts of the punt pole, laid alongside the *Breath of Horus*. In my haste I tumbled from the tower and landed in a heap in the bows of the tiny craft.

'To the temple, Kratas,' I pleaded with him as I scrambled up, 'and may the sweet goddess Hapi grant we are not already too late!'

With the evening breeze in the lateen sail we were whisked across the dark waters to the stone jetty below the temple. Kratas secured the painter to one of the mooring-rings, and made as if to follow me ashore, but I stopped him.

'For Tanus' sake, not mine,' I told him, 'do not follow me, please.'

He hesitated a moment, then nodded. 'I will be listening for your call.' He drew his sword and offered it to me, hilt first. 'Will you need this?'

I shook my head. 'It is not that kind of danger. Besides, I have my dagger. But thank you for your trust.' I left him in the boat and hurried up the granite steps to the entrance of the temple of Hapi.

The rush torches in their brackets on the tall entrance pillars threw a ruddy, wavering light that seemed to bring to life the bas-relief carvings on the walls and make them dance. The goddess Hapi is one of my favourites. Strictly speaking, she is neither god nor goddess, but a strange, bearded, hermaphroditic creature possessed of both a massive penis and an equally cavernous vagina, and bounteous breasts that give milk to all. She is the deification of the Nile, and the goddess of the harvest. The two kingdoms of Egypt and all the peoples in them depend utterly upon her and the periodic flooding of the great river which is her alter ego. She is able to change her gender or, like many of the other gods of this very Egypt, take on the shape of any animal at will. Her favourite guise is that of the hippopotamus. Despite the god's ambiguous sexuality, my mistress Lostris always considered her to be female, and so do I. The priests of Hapi may differ from us on this view.

Her images upon the stone walls were vast and motherly. Painted in hectic primary colours of red and yellow and blue, she beamed down with the head of a kindly river-cow, and seemed to invite all of nature to be fruitful and to multiply. The implied invitation was most inappropriate to my present anxiety. It was my fear that my precious charge might even at this moment be availing herself of the goddess's indulgence.

A priestess was kneeling at the side-altar, and I ran to her, seized her by the hem of her cape and tugged at it urgently. 'Holy sister, tell me, have you seen the Lady Lostris, daughter of the grand vizier?' There were very few citizens of Upper Egypt who did not know my mistress by sight. They all loved her for her

31

beauty, her gay spirit and her sweet disposition, and they clustered around her and cheered her in the streets and market-places when she walked abroad.

The priestess grinned at me, all wrinkled and toothless, and she laid one bony finger on the side of her nose with such a sly and knowing expression that all my worst fears were confirmed.

I shook her again, but less gently. 'Where is she, revered old mother? I beseech you, speak!' But instead she wagged her head and rolled her eyes towards the portals of the inner sanctum.

I sped across the granite flags, my heart outrunning my frantic feet, but even in my distress I wondered at the boldness of my mistress. Although as a member of the high nobility she had right of access to the holy of holies, was there another in all of Egypt who would have the nerve to choose such a place for her love tryst?

At the entrance to the sanctum I paused. My instinct had been right. There they were, the two of them, just as I had dreaded. I was so obsessed by my own certainty of what was taking place that I almost yelled aloud to them to stop it. Then I checked myself.

My mistress was fully clad, more so than was usual, for her breasts were covered and she had spread a blue woollen shawl over her head. She was kneeling before the gigantic statue of Hapi. The goddess beamed down upon her, bedecked in wreaths of blue water-lilies.

Tanus knelt beside her. He had laid aside his weapons and his armour. They were piled at the door of the sanctuary. He was dressed only in a linen shift and short tunic, with sandals on his feet. The young couple were holding hands, and their faces were almost touching as they whispered solemnly together.

My base suspicions were refuted, and I was struck with remorse and shame. How could I ever have doubted my mistress? Quietly I began to withdraw, although I would go only as far as the side-altar, where I would give thanks to the goddess for her protection, and from where I could keep a discreet eye on further proceedings.

However, at that moment Lostris rose to her feet and diffidently approached the statue of the goddess. I was so enthralled by her girlish grace that I lingered a moment longer to watch her.

From around her neck she unclasped the lapis lazuli figurine of the goddess which I had made for her. I realized with a pang that she was about to offer it as a sacrifice. That jewel had been crafted with all my love for her, and I hated to see it leave her throat. Lostris stood on tiptoe to hang it on the idol's neck. Then she knelt and kissed the stone foot while Tanus watched, still kneeling where she had left him.

She rose and turned to go back to him, but then she saw me in the doorway. I tried to melt away into the shadows, for I was embarrassed at having spied upon so intimate a moment. However, her face lit with joy and before I could escape, she ran to me and seized my hands.

'Oh, Taita, I am so glad that you are here – you of all people! It is so fitting. It makes it all so perfect.' She led me forward into the sanctum and Tanus rose to his feet and came smiling to take my other hand.

'Thank you for coming. I know we can always count upon you.' I wished that my motives had been as pure as they believed them to be, so I hid my guilty heart from them with a loving smile.

'Kneel here!' Lostris ordered me. 'Here, where you can hear every word we say to each other. You will bear witness for us before Hapi and all the gods of Egypt.' She pressed me to my knees, and then she and Tanus resumed their places in front of the goddess and took each other's hands, looking full into each other's eyes.

Lostris spoke first. 'You are my sun,' she whispered. 'My day is dark without you.'

'You are the Nile of my heart,' Tanus told her quietly. 'The waters of your love feed my soul.'

'You are my man, through this world and all the worlds to come.'

'You are my woman, and I pledge you my love. I swear it to you on the breath and the blood of Horus,' Tanus said clearly and openly, so that his voice echoed through the stone halls.

'I take up your pledge and return it to you one hundredfold,'

Lostris cried. 'No one can ever come between us. Nothing can ever part us. We are one, for ever.'

She offered her face to his and he kissed her, deeply and lingeringly. As far as I was aware, it was the first kiss that the couple had ever exchanged. I felt that I was privileged to have witnessed such an intimate moment.

As they embraced, a sudden chill wind off the lagoon swirled through the dimly lit halls of the temple and fluttered the torch flames, so that for an instant the faces of the two lovers blurred before my eyes and the image of the goddess seemed to stir and quiver. The wind passed as swiftly as it had come, but the whisper of it around the great stone pillars was like the distant sardonic laughter of the gods, and I shuddered with superstitious awe.

It is always dangerous to pique the gods with extravagant demands, and Lostris had just asked for the impossible. This was the moment that for years I had known was coming, and which I had dreaded more bitterly than the day of my own death. The pledge that Tanus and Lostris had made to each other could never endure. No matter how deeply they meant it, it could never be. I felt my own heart tearing within me as, at last, they broke the kiss and both turned back to me.

'Why so sad, Taita?' Lostris demanded, her own face flooded with joy. 'Rejoice with me, for this is the happiest day of my life.'

I forced my lips to smile, but I could find no word of comfort or of felicitation for these two, the ones I loved best in all the world. I remained upon my knees, with that fixed, idiotic smile on my lips and desolation in my soul.

Now Tanus lifted me to my feet and embraced me. 'You will speak to Lord Intef on my behalf, won't you?' he demanded as he hugged me.

'Oh yes, Taita,' Lostris joined her plea to his. 'My father will listen to you. You are the only one who can do it for us. You won't fail us, will you, Taita? You have never let me down, never once in all my life. You'll do it for me, won't you?'

What could I say to them? I could not be so cruel as to tell them the blunt truth. I could not find the words to blight this fresh and tender love. They were waiting for me to speak, to express my joy for them, and to promise them my help and support. But I was struck dumb, my mouth was as dry as if I had bitten into an unripe pomegranate.

'Taita, what is it?' I watched the joy wither upon my mistress's beloved countenance. 'Why do you not rejoice for us?'

'You know that I love you both, but—' I could not continue.

'But? But what, Taita?' Lostris demanded. 'Why do you give me "buts" and a long face on this happiest of all possible days?' She was becoming angry, her jaw was setting, but at the same time there were tears gathering deep in her eyes. 'Don't you want to help us? Is this the real value of all the promises you have made to me over the years?' She came to me and thrust her face close to mine in challenge.

'Mistress, please don't talk like that. I do not deserve that treatment. No, listen to me!' I placed my fingers on her lips to forestall another outburst. 'It is not me. It is your father, my Lord Intef—'

'Exactly.' Impatiently Lostris plucked my hand away from her mouth. 'My father! You will go to him and speak to him the way you always do, and it will be all right.'

'Lostris,' I began, and it was a sign of my distress that I used her name in this familiar fashion, 'you are no longer a child. You must not delude yourself with childish fantasies. You know that your father will never agree—'

She would not listen to me, she did not want to hear the truth that I would speak, so she rushed in with words to drown out mine. 'I know that Tanus has no fortune, yes. But he has a marvellous future ahead of him. One day he will command all the armies of Egypt. One day he will fight the battles which will reunite the two kingdoms, and I will be at his side.'

'Mistress, please hear me out. It is not only the lack of Tanus' fortune. It is more, much more.'

'His blood-line and his breeding, then? Is that what troubles you? You know full well that his family is as noble as ours. Pianki, Lord Harrab was my own father's equal and his dearest friend.' She had closed her ears to me. She did not realize the depth of the tragedy on which we were embarking. Neither she nor Tanus did, but then I was probably the only person in the kingdom who understood it fully.

I had protected her from the truth all these years and, of course, I had never been able to tell Tanus either. How could I explain it to her now? How could I reveal to her the depths of the hatred that her father bore towards the young man she loved? It was a hatred born out of guilt and envy, and yet all the more implacable for these reasons.

However, my Lord Intef was a crafty and devious man. He was able to conceal his feelings from those around him. He was able to dissemble his hatred and his spite, and to kiss the one he would destroy and heap rich gifts and lulling flattery upon him. He had the patience of the crocodile buried in the mud at the drinking-place on the river, waiting for the unsuspecting gazelle. He would wait years, even a decade, but when the opportunity arose, he was as swift as that reptile to strike and drag his prey under.

Lostris was blithely unaware of the depths of her father's rancour. She even believed that he had loved Pianki, Lord Harrab, as Tanus' father had loved him. But then how could she know the truth of it, for I had always shielded her from it? In her sweet innocence Lostris believed that the only objections that her father would have to her lover were those of fortune and family.

'You know it is true, Taita. Tanus is my equal in the lists of the nobility. It is written in the temple records for all to see. How can my father deny it? How can you deny it?'

'It is not for me to deny or to accede, mistress—'

'Then you will go to my father for us, won't you, dear Taita? Say you will, please say you will!'

I could only bow my head in acquiescence, and to hide the hopeless expression in my eyes.

THE FLEET was heavily laden on the return to Karnak. The galleys were low in the water under their cargoes of rawhides and salted meat. Thus our progress against the Nile's current was slower than on our outward journey, but still too swift for my heavy heart and mounting dread.

The lovers were gay and euphoric with their newly declared love and their trust in me to remove the obstacles from their path. I could not bring myself to deny them this day of happiness, for I knew that it would be one of the very last they would share. I think that if I could have found the words or summoned the courage, I would have urged them, there and then, to seek the consummation of their love that I had so opposed the night before. There would never be another chance for them, not after I had alerted my Lord Intef with my foredoomed attempt at matchmaking. Once he knew what they were about, he would come between them and thrust them apart for ever.

So instead I laughed and smiled as gaily as they did, and tried to hide my fears from them. They were so blinded by love that I succeeded, whereas at any other time my mistress would have seen through me immediately. She knows me almost as well as I know her.

We sat together in the prow, the three of us, and we discussed the re-enactment of the passion of Osiris that would be the highlight of the festival. My Lord Intef had made me the impresario of the pageant, and I had cast both Lostris and Tanus in leading roles.

The festival is held every second year, at the rising of the full moon of Osiris. There was a time when it was an annual event. However, the expense and disruption of royal life caused by having to remove the court from Elephantine to Thebes was so great that Pharaoh decreed a greater interval between the festivals. He was always a prudent man with his gold, was our Pharaoh.

The plans for the pageant provided me with a fine distraction from the looming confrontation with my Lord Intef, and so now I rehearsed the two lovers in their lines. Lostris was to play Isis, the wife of Osiris, while Tanus would take on the major role of

37

Horus. They were both vastly amused at the idea of Tanus playing Lostris' son, and I had to explain that the gods were ageless, and it was quite possible that a goddess could appear younger than her offspring.

I had written a new script for the pageant to replace the one that had remained unchanged for almost a thousand years. The language of the ancient one was archaic and unsuitable for a modern audience. Pharaoh would be the guest of honour when the pageant was performed in the temple of Osiris on the final night of the festival, so I was particularly anxious that it should be a success. I had already encountered opposition to my new version of the passion from the more conservative nobles and priests. Only my Lord Intef's intervention had prevailed against their objections.

My lord is not a deeply religious man and would not normally have interested himself in theological arguments. However, I had included a few lines that were designed to amuse and flatter him. I read them to him out of context, and then tactfully pointed out to him that the chief opposition to my version came from the high priest of Osiris, a prissy old man who had once frustrated my Lord Intef's interest in a comely young acolyte. This was a trespass for which my lord had never forgiven the high priest.

Thus it was that my version would be performed for the first time. It was essential that the actors bring out the full glory of my poetry, or it might well be the last time it would be heard.

Both Tanus and Lostris possessed marvellous speaking voices, and they were determined to reward me for my promise to help them. They gave me of their best, and thus the rehearsal was so absorbing, their recitations so startling, that for a while I could forget myself.

Then I was brought back from the passion of the gods to my own mundane preoccupations by a cry from the lookout. The fleet was sweeping around the last bend in the river, and there lay the twin cities of Luxor and Karnak, that between them made up Greater Thebes, strung out along the bank before us and sparkling like a necklace of pearls in the stark Egyptian sunlight. Our fantastic interlude had ended, and we must face reality once again. My spirits tumbled as I scrambled to my feet.

'Tanus, you must transfer Lostris and myself to the galley of Kratas before we come any closer to the city. My lord's minions will be watching us from the land. They must not see us in your company.'

'A little late, is it not?' Tanus smiled at me. 'You should have thought of that some days ago.'

'My father will learn about us soon enough,' Lostris endorsed his objection. 'It might make your task easier if we forewarn him of our intentions.'

'If you know better than I, then you must do it your way and I will take no further part in this crazy business of yours.' I put on my most stiff and offended air, and they relented immediately.

Tanus signalled Kratas' galley alongside, and the lovers had only a few moments for their farewells. They dared not embrace before the eyes of half the fleet, but the glances and the loving words they exchanged were almost as fulfilling.

From the stern-tower of Kratas' ship we waved to the *Breath of Horus* as she turned from us, and with her paddles flashing like the wings of a dragonfly, she bore away to her moorings in front of the city of Luxor, while we continued on up-river towards the palace of the grand vizier.

 IMMEDIATELY we docked at the palace wharf, I made enquiry as to the whereabouts of my master and was relieved to learn that he had crossed the river to undertake a last-minute inspection of Pharaoh's tomb and funerary temple on the west bank. The king's temple and tomb had been under construction for the past twelve years, ever since the first day that he had donned the double white and red crown of the two kingdoms. It was nearing completion at last, and the king would be anxious to visit it as soon as the festival was over and he was free to do so. My Lord Intef was anxious that the king should not be disappointed. One of my lord's many titles and honours was Guardian of the Royal Tombs, and it was a serious responsibility.

His absence afforded me a further day in which to prepare my case and plan my strategy. However, the solemn promise that the two lovers had extracted from me was to speak out for them at the first opportunity, and I knew that would be on the morrow when my lord held his weekly assize.

As soon as I had seen my mistress safely ensconced in the harem, I hurried to my own quarters in that wing of the palace which is reserved for the special companions of the grand vizier.

My Lord Intef's domestic arrangements were as devious as the rest of his existence. He had eight wives, all of whom brought to his marriage-bed either substantial dowry or influential political connections. However, only three of these women had ever borne him children. Apart from my Lady Lostris, there were two sons.

As far as I was aware, and I was aware of everything that happened in the palace and most of what happened outside it, my lord had not visited the harem in the last fifteen years. The getting of Lostris had been the last occasion that he had performed his matrimonial duties. His sexual tastes lay in other directions. The special companions of the grand vizier who lived in our wing of the palace were as pretty a collection of slave boys as you could find in the Upper Kingdom, where over the previous hundred years pederasty had replaced wild-fowling and hunting as the favourite preoccupation of most of the nobility. This was merely another symptom of the ills that beset our lovely land.

I was the eldest of this select company of slave boys. Unlike so many others over the years whom, once their physical beauty had begun to fade or pall, my lord had sent to the auction block in the slave-market, I had endured. He had come to value me for virtues other than my physical beauty alone. Not that this had faded – on the contrary, it had grown more striking as I had matured. You must not think me vain if I mention this, but I have determined to set down nothing but the truth in these accounts. They are remarkable enough without my having to resort to false modesty.

No, my lord seldom pleasured himself with me in those days, a neglect for which I was truly thankful. When he did so, it was usually only to punish me. He knew full well the physical pain and the humiliation his attentions always caused me. Although I had still been a child when I first learned to hide my revulsion,

40

and to simulate pleasure in the perverse acts that he forced upon me, I never succeeded in deceiving him.

Strangely, my feelings of disgust and my loathing for this unnatural congress never detracted from his own enjoyment, rather they seemed to enhance it. He was neither a gentle nor a compassionate man, my Lord Intef. I have counted in the hundreds the slave boys who, over the years, were brought to me weeping and torn after their first night of love with my master. I doctored them and tried my best to comfort them. That is perhaps why they called me *Akh-Ker* in the slave boys' quarters, a name which means Elder Brother.

I might no longer be my master's favourite plaything, but he valued me much more highly than that. I was many other things to him – physician and artist, musician and scribe, architect and bookkeeper, adviser and confidant, engineer and nursemaid to his daughter. I am not so naïve as to believe that he loved me or that he trusted me, but I think that at times he came as close to it as he was capable. That was why Lostris had prevailed upon me to plead on her behalf.

My Lord Intef had no concern for his only daughter, other than to maintain her marriage value at its optimum, and this was another duty that he delegated entirely to me. Sometimes he did not speak a single word to her from one flooding of the Nile to the next. He showed no discernible interest in the regular reports which I made to him of her training and schooling.

Of course, I was always at pains to conceal from him my true feelings for Lostris, knowing that he would certainly use them against me at the first opportunity. I always tried to give him the impression that I found her tuition and her care a tedious duty that I mildly resented having thrust upon me, and that I shared his own disdain and distaste for all of womankind. I don't think he ever realized that, despite my emasculation, I had the feelings and desires of a natural man towards the opposite sex.

My lord's disinterest in his daughter was the reason why I was occasionally tempted, on the urging of my mistress, to run such insane risks as this latest escapade of ours on board the *Breath of Horus*. There was usually at least a chance that we would get away with it.

That evening I retired early to my private quarters, where my first concern was to feed and pamper my darlings. I have a love for birds and animals, and a way with them that amazes even myself. I had an intimate friendship with a dozen cats, for no one can ever claim to own a cat. I owned, on the other hand, a pack of fine dogs. Tanus and I used them to hunt the oryx and the lion out in the desert.

The wild birds flocked to my terrace to enjoy the hospitality I provided for them. They competed raucously amongst themselves for a perch on my shoulder or on my hand. The boldest of them would take food from between my lips. My tame gazelle would brush against my legs like one of the cats, and my two falcons squawk at me from their perches on the terrace. They were the rare desert Sakers, beautiful and fierce. Whenever we were able, Tanus and I would take them out into the desert to fly them against the giant bustards. I took great pleasure from their speed and aerial grace as they stooped down on their prey. Anyone else who attempted to fondle them would feel the cutting edge of those hooked yellow bills, but with me they were as gentle as sparrows.

Only once I had taken care of my menagerie did I call one of the slave boys to bring my evening meal. On the terrace overlooking the wide green expanse of the Nile I savoured the exquisite little dish of wild quail cooked in honey and goat's milk that the head chef had prepared especially to welcome me home. From there I was able to watch for the return of my lord's barge from the far bank. It came with the sunset glowing on the single square sail, and I felt my spirits sink. He might send for me this evening, and I was not ready to face him.

Then with relief I heard Rasfer, the commander of the palace guard, shouting for my lord's favourite of the moment, a sloe-eyed Bedouin lad, barely ten years old. A short while later I heard the child protesting in a terrified treble as Rasfer dragged him past my door towards the curtained entrance of the grand vizier's chambers. Although I had heard it so many times before, I never could harden myself to the sounds of the children, and I felt the familiar pang of pity. Still, I was relieved that it was not

I who would be called that evening. I would need a good night's sleep so as to look my best in the morning.

I woke before dawn with the feeling of dread still strong upon me. Even my ritual swim in the cool waters of the Nile did nothing to relieve it. I hurried back to my chamber where two of the slave boys were waiting to oil my body and comb out my hair. I detested the new fashion amongst the nobility of wearing make-up. My own skin and complexion were fine enough not to require it, but my lord liked his boys to use it, and I wanted to please him especially that day.

Even though my image in the bronze mirror reassured me, I could find no appetite for my breakfast. I was the first member of my lord's entourage awaiting his arrival in the water-garden where he held his assize every morning.

While I waited for the rest of the court to assemble I watched the kingfishers at work. I had designed and supervised the building of the water-garden. It was a marvellous complex of channels and ponds which overflowed from one into the other. The flowering plants had been collected from every part of the kingdom and beyond, and they were a dazzle of colour. The ponds were stocked with all the hundreds of varieties of fish that the Nile yields up to the nets of the fishermen, but they had to be replenished daily as a result of the depredations of the kingfishers.

My Lord Intef enjoyed watching the birds hovering in the air like jewels of lapis lazuli, then darting down to hit the water in a flash of spray, and rising again with a silver sliver quivering in their long bills. I think he saw himself as a fellow predator, a fisher of men, and that he looked upon the birds as his kin. He never allowed the gardeners to discourage the birds.

Gradually I was joined by the rest of the court. Many of them were dishevelled and yawning from sleep. My Lord Intef keeps early hours and likes to complete the bulk of the business of state before the main heat of the day. We waited respectfully in the first rays of the sun for my lord's arrival.

'He's in a good mood this morning,' the chamberlain whispered, as he took his place beside me, and I felt a tiny prickle of

43

hope. I might yet be able to escape the serious consequences of my foolhardy promise to Lostris.

There was a stirring and a murmuring amongst us as when the river breeze moves through the papyrus beds, and my Lord Intef came out to us.

His walk was stately and his manner was sumptuous, for he was mighty with the weight of his honours and his power. Around his neck he wore the Gold of Praise, that necklace of red gold from the mines of Lot which Pharaoh had laid upon him with his own hands. His praise-singer preceded him, a stump-legged dwarf chosen for his misshapen body and stentorian tones. It amused my lord to surround himself with curiosities, either beautiful or grotesque. Cavorting and prancing on his bowed legs, the dwarf chanted the lists of my lord's titles and honours.

'Behold the Support of Egypt! Greet the Guardian of the Waters of the Nile! Bow down before Pharaoh's Companion!' These were all titles granted by the king, and many of them imposed specific duties and obligations on him. As Guardian of the Waters, for instance, he was responsible for monitoring the levels and flows of the seasonal floods of the Nile, a duty which was naturally delegated to that faithful, indefatigable slave, Taita.

I had spent half a year with a team of engineers and mathematicians working under me, measuring and carving the rock cliffs at Assoun so that the height of the waters rising up them could be accurately gauged and the volume of the flood calculated. From these figures I was able to estimate the size of the harvest months in advance. This enabled both famine and plenty to be anticipated and planned for by the administration. Pharaoh had been delighted with my work and bestowed further honours and reward upon my Lord Intef.

'Bend the knee for the Nomarch of Karnak and the Governor of all the twenty-two nomes of Upper Egypt! Greet the Lord of the Necropolis and the Keeper of the Royal Tombs!' My lord was by these titles responsible for designing, building and maintaining the monuments to pharaohs long dead and the one still living. Once again, these duties were unloaded upon a long-suffering slave's shoulders. My lord's visit to Pharaoh's tomb the day before had been the first that he had undertaken since the previous festival of Osiris. It was I who was sent out in the dust and the heat to cajole and curse the lying builders and the conniving masons. I often regretted having let my master realize the extent of my talents.

He singled me out now without seeming to have done so. The yellow eyes, as implacable as those of a wild leopard, touched mine, and he inclined his head slightly. I stepped in behind him as he passed, and I was struck as always by his height and the width of his shoulders. He was an outrageously handsome man with long, clean limbs and a flat, hard belly. His head was leonine and his hair dense and lustrous. At this time he was forty years of age, and I had been his slave for almost twenty of those.

My Lord Intef led us to the barrazza in the centre of the garden, a thatched building without enclosing walls, open to the cool breeze off the river. He seated himself cross-legged on the paved floor at the low table on which lay the state scrolls, and I took my usual place behind him. The day's business began.

Twice during the morning my lord leaned back slightly towards me. He did not turn his head nor did he say a word, but he was asking my advice. I barely moved my lips and I kept my voice pitched so low that no one else could hear me and very few were even aware of the exchanges between us.

Once I murmured, 'He is lying,' and a second time, 'Retik is a better man for the post, and he has offered a gift of five gold rings to my lord's private treasury.' And though I did not mention it then, another ring of gold to me if the post were secured.

At noon my lord dismissed the congregation of officials and petitioners and called for his midday meal. For the first time that day we were alone together, except for Rasfer, who was both the commander of the palace guard and the official state executioner. Now he took his post at the gate to the garden, within sight of the barrazza but out of earshot.

With a gesture my lord invited me to move up to his elbow, and to taste the delicious meats and fruits that had been laid out before him. While we waited for the effects of any possible poisoning to manifest themselves upon me, we discussed the morning's business in detail.

Then he questioned me about the expedition to the lagoon of

Hapi and the great hippopotamus hunt. I described it all to him and gave him the figures of the profits that he might expect from the meat and hides and teeth of the river-cows. I inflated the estimate of profits a little, and he smiled. His smile is frank and charming. Once you have seen it, it is easier to understand my Lord Intef's ability to manipulate and control men. Even I, who should have known better, was once again lulled by it.

As he bit into a succulent cold cut of river-cow fillet, I drew a breath, screwed up my courage and began my plea. 'My lord should know that I allowed your daughter to accompany me on the expedition.' I could see by his eyes that he already knew this and that he had been waiting for me to attempt to conceal it from him.

'You did not think to obtain my permission beforehand?' he asked mildly, and I avoided his eyes and concentrated on peeling a grape for him as I answered, 'She only asked as we were on the point of departure. As you know, the goddess Hapi is her patron, and she wished to worship and make sacrifice at the lagoon temple.'

'Still you did not ask me?' he repeated, and I offered him the grape. He parted his lips and allowed me to slip it into his mouth. That could only mean that he was well disposed towards me, so obviously he had not yet found out the full truth about Tanus and Lostris.

'My lord was in council with the nomarch of Assoun at the time. I would not have dared disturb you. Besides, there was no harm in it that I could fathom. It was a simple domestic decision which I thought beneath your concern.'

'You are so glib, aren't you, my darling?' he chuckled. 'And so beautiful today. I like the way you have painted your eyelids, and what is that perfume you are wearing?'

'It is distilled from the petals of the wild violet,' I replied. 'I am happy that you like it, for I have a flask of it as a small gift for you, my lord.' I produced the flask from my purse and went on my knees to offer it to him. He placed his finger under my chin and lifted my face to kiss me on the lips. Dutifully I responded to the kiss until he drew back and patted my cheek.

'Whatever it is you are up to, you are still very attractive,

Taita. Even after all these years you can still make me smile. But tell me, you took good care of the Lady Lostris, did you not? You never let her out of your sight or care for a moment, did you?'

'As always, my lord,' I agreed vehemently.

'So there is nothing unusual concerning her that you wish to report to me, is there?'

I was still on my knees in front of him, and my next attempt to speak failed. My voice dried up.

'Do not squeak at me, my old darling,' he laughed. 'Speak out like a man, even though you are not.' It was a cruel little jibe, but it steeled me.

'There is indeed something I wish humbly to bring to my lord's attention,' I said. 'And it does indeed concern the Lady Lostris. As I have already reported, your daughter's red moon rose for the first time at the flooding of the great river. Since then the courses of her moon have flowed strongly each month.' ·

My lord made a small grimace of distaste, the functions of the feminine body repelled him. I found this ironic, considering his own preoccupation with those far less savoury reaches of the masculine anatomy.

I hurried on, 'The Lady Lostris is now of marriageable age. She is a woman of an ardent and loving nature. I believe it would be wise to find a husband for her, as soon as we can.'

'No doubt you have one to suggest?' he asked drily, and I nodded. 'There is indeed a suitor, my lord.'

'Not one, Taita. You mean another one, don't you? I know of at least six, including the nomarch of Assoun and the governor of Lot, who have already made offers.'

'I did mean another one, but this time one that the Lady Lostris approves of. As you recall, she referred to the nomarch as that fat toad, and to the governor as a randy old goat.'

'The child's approval or disapproval is of no interest to me whatsoever.' He shook his head, and smiled and stroked my cheek to encourage me. 'But go on, Taita, tell me the name of this lovelorn swain who will do me the honour of becoming my son-in-law in return for the richest dowry in Egypt.' I steeled myself to reply, but he stopped me. 'No, wait! Let me guess.'

His smile turned into that sly and foxy grin that I knew so well, and I realized that he had been toying with me.

'For Lostris to welcome him, he must be young and handsome.' He pretended to muse on it. 'And for you to speak out for him, he must be a friend or a protégé of yours. There must have been an opportunity for this paragon to declare his suit and to solicit your support. What would be the time and the place for that to have happened, I wonder? Could it have been at midnight in the temple of Hapi, perhaps? Am I on the right trail, Taita?'

I felt myself pale. How did he know so much? He slid his hand around behind my head and caressed the nape of my neck. This was often his prelude to love-making, and he kissed me again.

'I can see by your face that my guesses are close to the target.' He took a handful of my hair and twisted it lightly. 'Now it remains only to divine the name of this bold lover. Could it be Dakka? No, no, Dakka is not so stupid as to incur my wrath.' He twisted my hair just hard enough to bring tears to my eyes. 'Kratas, then? He is handsome and foolhardy enough to take the risk.' He twisted harder and I felt a clump of my hair come away in his hand with a tearing sound. I choked back the whimper in my throat.

'Answer me, my darling, was it Kratas?' He forced my face down into his lap.

'No, my lord,' I whispered painfully. I was not surprised to find that he was fully aroused. He pushed my face down upon himself and held me there.

'Not Kratas, are you sure?' He pretended to be puzzled. 'If it was not Kratas, then I am at a loss to guess who else might be so insolent, so insulting and so mortally stupid as to approach the virgin daughter of the grand vizier of Upper Egypt.'

Abruptly, he raised his voice. 'Rasfer!' he cried. My head was twisted in his lap so that through streaming eyes I could watch Rasfer approach.

In Pharaoh's menagerie on Elephantine Island at Assoun there was a huge black bear brought in many years ago by one of the trade caravans from the East. That vicious, scarred brute always reminded me strongly of the commander of my lord's bodyguard. They both had the same vast, shapeless body and the raw, savage power to crush a man to death. However, in loveliness of face and sweetness of disposition, the bear had been favoured far beyond Rasfer.

I watched Rasfer approach now at a trot that was surprisingly swift and agile for those heavy, tree-like legs and the swell of his hairy gut, and I was transported back over the years to the day that my manhood had been plucked from me.

It all seemed so familiar, as though I was being forced to live once more through that terrible day. Every detail of it was still so clear in my mind that I wanted to shriek aloud. The actors in that long-ago tragedy were the same. My Lord Intef, Rasfer the brute, and me. Only the girl was missing.

Her name had been Alyda. She had been the same age as me, sixteen sweet innocent years. Like me, she had been a slave. I remember her now as having been beautiful, but it is likely that my memory cheats me, for had she been so she would have gone into a harem of one of the great houses and not been relegated to the kitchen. I do know for certain that she had skin the colour and lustre of polished amber that was warm and soft to the touch. I will never forget the feel of Alyda's body, for I will never experience anything like it again. In our misery we had found comfort and deep solace in each other. I never discovered who it was that betrayed us. I am not usually a vengeful man, but I still dream that one day I will find the person who delivered us up.

At that time I had been my Lord Intef's favourite, his special darling. When he discovered that I had been faithless to him, the affront to his self-esteem was such as to drive him to the very frontier of madness.

Rasfer had come to fetch us. He dragged us to my lord's chamber, one of us in each hand, as easily as if we had been a pair of kittens. There he had stripped us naked while my Lord Intef sat cross-legged on the floor, just as he was doing now. Rasfer bound Alyda's wrists and ankles with rawhide thongs. She was pale and·shivering but she did not weep. My love for her and my admiration for her courage had never been stronger than at that moment.

My Lord Intef beckoned me to kneel in front of him and he took a lock of my hair and whispered endearments to me. 'Do

49

you love me, Taita?' he asked, and because I was afraid, and because in some dim way I thought that it might spare Alyda's suffering, I answered, 'Yes, my lord, I love you.'

'Do you love anyone else, Taita?' he asked in a voice of silk and, coward and traitor that I was, I answered him, 'No, my lord, I love only you.' It was only then that I heard Alyda begin to weep. It was one of the most harrowing sounds of my life.

He called to Rasfer, 'Bring the slut here. Place her so that they can see each other clearly. Taita must be able to see everything that is done to her.'

As Rasfer pushed the girl into my line of vision I could see that he was grinning. Then my master raised his voice slightly: 'Very well, Rasfer, you may proceed.'

Rasfer slipped a loop of braided rawhide rope over Alyda's forehead. At close intervals the rope was knotted, so that it looked like a headband such as the Bedouin women wear. Standing behind the girl, Rasfer thrust a short, stout baton of olive wood through the rawhide loop and twisted it until it came up tight against her smooth, unblemished skin. The knots of harsh leather bit into her flesh and Alyda grimaced with the pain.

'Slowly, Rasfer,' my lord warned him. 'We still have a long way to go.'

The olive-wood baton seemed like a child's toy in Rasfer's huge, hairy paws. He twisted it with careful deliberation, a quarter of a turn at a time. The knots bit in deeper, and Alyda's mouth dropped open and her lungs emptied in a gasping rush of air. All the colour drained from her skin so that it turned to the colour of dead ashes. She struggled to fill her empty lungs with air and then released it in one long, penetrating scream.

Still grinning, Rasfer twisted the baton and the line of leather knots buried themselves in Alyda's forehead. Her skull changed shape. At first I thought it was a trick of my overwrought mind, then I realized that her head was, in truth, constricting and elongating as the loop tightened. Her scream was now a single unbroken peal that plunged into my heart like a sword-blade. It went on and on for what seemed like for ever.

Then her skull burst. I heard the bone collapse with a sound like a palm-nut crushed in the jaws of a feeding elephant. That terrible, piercing scream was cut off abruptly, as Alyda's corpse sagged in Rasfer's hands, and my soul was filled to overflowing with my sorrow and despair.

After what seemed like an eternity my lord lifted my head and looked into my eyes. His expression was sad and regretful as he told me, 'She has gone, Taita. She was evil and she led you astray. We must make certain that it never happens again. We must protect you from any further temptations.'

Once again he signalled to Rasfer and he took Alyda's naked body by the heels and dragged it out on to the terrace. The back of her crushed head bumped down the steps and her hair streamed out behind her. With a heave of his massive shoulders, Rasfer threw her far out into the river. Her slack limbs flashed and tumbled as she fell and struck the water. She sank swiftly with her hair spreading out around her like trailing fronds of the river-weed.

Rasfer turned away and went to the end of the terrace where two of his men were tending a brazier of burning charcoal. Beside the brazier a full set of surgeon's instruments were laid out on a wooden tray. He glanced over them and then nodded with satisfaction. He returned and bowed before my Lord Intef. 'All is in readiness.'

My master wiped my tear-streaked face with one finger, then lifted the finger to his lips as though he were tasting my sorrow. 'Come, my pretty darling,' he whispered, and lifting me to my feet he led me out on to the terrace. I was so distraught and blinded by my tears that I did not realize my own peril until the soldiers seized me. They threw me down and held me spread-eagled on the terracotta tiles, pinning me at wrists and ankles so that I could move only my head.

My master knelt at my head, while Rasfer knelt between my spread thighs.

'You will never do this evil thing again, Taita.' Only then did I become aware of the bronze scalpel that Rasfer had concealed in his right hand. My master nodded at him and he reached

51

down with his free hand and seized me and stretched me out, until it felt as though he were plucking my entrails out through my groin.

'What a fine pair of eggs we have here!' Rasfer grinned and showed me the scalpel, holding it up before my eyes. 'But I am going to feed them to the crocodiles, just as I did with your little girl-friend.' He kissed the blade.

'Please, my lord,' I begged, 'have mercy—' but my entreaties ended in a shrill cry as Rasfer slashed down with the blade. It felt as though a red-hot skewer had been thrust up into my belly.

'Say goodbye to them, pretty boy.' Rasfer held up the sac of pale wrinkled skin and its pathetic contents. Then he began to rise, but my lord stopped him. 'You have not finished,' he told Rasfer quietly. 'I want all of it.'

Rasfer stared at him for a moment, not understanding the order. Then he began to chuckle until his belly bounced. 'By the blood of Horus,' he roared, 'from now on pretty boy will have to squat like a girl when he wants to piss!' He struck again, then bellowed with laughter as he held up the finger of flesh that had once been the most intimate part of my body.

'Never mind, boy. You'll walk a lot lighter without that weight to carry around with you.' Staggering with laughter, he started towards the edge of the terrace as if to hurl them into the river, but once again my lord called to him sharply.

'Give them to me!' he ordered, and obediently Rasfer placed the bloody fragments of my manhood in his hands. For a few seconds my lord examined them curiously, and then he spoke to me again. 'I am not so cruel as to deprive you for ever of such fine trophies, my darling. I will send these to the embalmers, and when they are ready I will have them placed on a necklace surrounded with pearls and lapis lazuli. They will be my present to you at the next festival of Osiris. Thus at the day of your burial they can be placed in your tomb with you, and if the gods are kind, you may have the use of them in the afterlife.'

Those terrible memories should have ended at the moment when Rasfer staunched the bleeding with a ladle of boiling embalming lacquer from the brazier, and I was plunged into blessed oblivion by the unbearable intensity of the pain, but now

I was trapped in the nightmare. It was all happening again. Only this time little Alyda was missing, and instead of the gelding-knife Rasfer held the whip of hippo-hide in his great hairy fist.

The whip was as long as the full stretch of Rasfer's arms and it tapered to the thickness of his little finger at the point. I had watched him whittling it himself, shaving off the coarse outer layer from the long strip of cured hide until the inner skin was exposed, periodically pausing to test the balance and the heft of it, cutting it through the air until it keened and whined like the desert wind through the canyons of the hills of Lot. It was the colour of amber and Rasfer had polished it lovingly until it was smooth and translucent as glass, but so supple that he could bend it into a perfect arc between those bear-like paws. He had allowed the blood of a hundred victims to dry upon it and to dye the thin end of it to a lustrous patina that was aesthetically quite beautiful.

Rasfer was an artist with this awful tool. He could flick out and leave on the tender thigh of a young girl only a crimson weal that never broke the skin, but stung as viciously as a scorpion and left his victim writhing and weeping with the agony of it; or with a dozen hissing strokes he could strip the skin and flesh from a man's back and leave his ribs and the crest of his spine exposed.

He stood over me now and grinned as he flexed the long lash in his hands. Rasfer loved his work, and he hated me with all the force of his envy and the feelings of inferiority that my intelligence and looks and favour engendered in him.

My Lord Intef stroked my naked back and sighed. 'You are so wicked sometimes, my old darling. You try to deceive me to whom you owe the deepest loyalty. Nay, more than simple loyalty – to whom you owe your very existence.' He sighed again. 'Why do you force this unpleasantness upon me? You should know much better than to press the suit of that young jackanapes upon me. It was a ludicrous attempt, but I suppose that I understand why you made it. That childlike sense of compassion is one of your many weaknesses, and one day will probably be the cause of your complete downfall. However, at times I find it rather quaint and endearing and I might readily have forgiven you for it, but I cannot overlook the fact that you have endangered the market value of the goods that I placed in your care.' He twisted my head up so that my mouth was free to answer him. 'For that, you must be punished. Do you understand me?'

'Yes, my lord,' I whispered, but I rolled my eyes to watch the whip in Rasfer's hands. Once again my Lord Intef buried my face in his lap, and then he spoke to Rasfer above my head.

'With all your cunning, Rasfer. Do not break the skin, please. I do not want this delightfully smooth back marred permanently. Ten will do as a start. Count them aloud for us.'

I had watched a hundred or more unfortunates undergo this punishment, some of them warriors and vaunted heroes. Not one of them was able to remain silent under the lash of Rasfer. In any event it was best not to do so, for he took silence as a personal challenge to his skill. I knew this well, having travelled this bitter road before. I was quite prepared to swallow any stupid pride and pay tribute to Rasfer's art in a loud voice. I filled my lungs in readiness.

'One!' grunted Rasfer, and the lash fluted. The way a woman later forgets the full pain of childbirth, I had forgotten the exquisite sting of it, and I screamed even louder than I had intended.

'You are fortunate, my dear Taita,' my Lord Intef murmured in my ear. 'I had the priests of Osiris examine the goods last night. They are still intact.' I squirmed in his lap. Not only from the pain, but also at the thought of those lascivious old goats from the temple probing and prying into my little girl.

Rasfer had his own little ritual to draw out the punishment and to ensure that both he and his victim were able to savour the moment to the full. Between each stroke he jogged in a small circle around the barrazza, grunting exhortations and encouragement to himself, holding the whip at high port like a ceremonial sword. As he completed the circle he was in position for the next stroke, and he raised the lash high.

'Two!' he cried, and I shrieked again.

ONE OF Lostris' slave girls was waiting for me on the broad terrace of my quarters when I limped painfully up the steps from the garden.

'My mistress bids you attend her immediately,' she greeted me.

'Tell her that I am indisposed.' I tried to avoid the summons and, shouting for one of the slave boys to dress my injuries, I hurried through into my chamber in an attempt to rid myself of the girl. I could not face Lostris yet, for I dreaded having to report my failure, and having at last to make her face the reality and the impossibility of her love for Tanus. The black girl followed me, ogling the livid weals across my back with delicious horror.

'Go tell your mistress that I am injured, and that I cannot come to her,' I snapped over my shoulder.

'She told me that you would try to wriggle out of it, but she told me also that I was to stay with you and see to it that you did not.'

'You are insolent for a slave,' I reprimanded her sternly as the boy anointed my back with a healing salve of my own concoction.

'Yes,' agreed the imp with a grin. 'But then so are you.' And she dodged the half-hearted slap I aimed at her with ease. Lostris is much too soft with her handmaidens.

'Go tell your mistress that I will come to her,' I capitulated.

'She said I must wait and make sure you did.'

So I had an escort as I passed the guards at the gate of the harem. The guards were eunuchs like myself, but, unlike me, they were portly and androgynous. Despite their corpulence, or perhaps because of it, they were powerful men and fierce. However, I had used my influence to secure both of them this cosy sinecure, so they passed me through into the women's quarters with a respectful salute.

The harem was not nearly as grand nor as comfortable as the quarters of the slave boys, and it was clear where my Lord Intef's real interest lay. It was a compound of mud-brick hutments surrounded by a high mud wall. The only gardens or decorations were those that Lostris and her maids had undertaken, with my assistance. The vizier's wives were too fat and lazy and caught up in the scandals and intrigues of the harem to exert themselves.

Lostris' quarters were those closest to the main gate, surrounded by a pretty garden with a lily pond and song-birds twittering in cages woven of split bamboo. The mud walls were decorated with bright murals of Nile scenes, of fish and birds and goddesses, that I had helped her paint.

Her slave girls were huddled in a subdued group at the doorway, and more than one of them had been weeping. Their faces were streaked with tears. I pushed my way past them into the cool, dark interior, and at once heard my mistress's sobs from the inner chamber. I hurried to her, ashamed that I had been so craven as to try to avoid my duty to her.

She was lying face down on the low bed, her entire body shaking with the force of her grief, but she heard me enter and whirled off the bed and rushed to me.

'Oh, Taita! They are sending Tanus away. Pharaoh arrives in Karnak tomorrow, and my father will prevail upon him to order Tanus to take his squadron up-river to Elephantine and the cataracts. Oh, Taita! It is twenty days' travel to the first cataract. I shall never see him again. I wish I were dead. I shall throw myself into the Nile and let the crocodiles devour me. I don't want to live without Tanus—' All this in one rising wail of despair.

'Softly, my child.' I rocked her in my arms. 'How do you know all these terrible things? They may never happen.'

'Oh, they will. Tanus has sent me a message. Kratas has a brother in my father's personal bodyguard. He heard my father discussing it with Rasfer. Somehow my father has found out about Tanus and me. He knows that we were in the temple of Hapi alone. Oh, Taita, my father sent the priests to examine me. Those filthy old men did horrid things to me. It hurt so, Taita.'

I hugged her gently. It is not too often that I have the opportunity to do so, but now she hugged me back with all her strength. Her thoughts turned from her own injuries to her lover.

'I shall never see Tanus again,' she cried, and I was reminded of how young she truly was, not much more than a child, vulnerable and lost in her grief. 'My father will destroy him.'

56

'Even your father cannot touch Tanus,' I tried to reassure her. 'Tanus is a commander of a regiment of Pharaoh's own elite guard. He is the king's man. Tanus takes his orders only from Pharaoh, and he enjoys the full protection of the double crown of Egypt.' I did not add that this was probably the only reason that her father had not already destroyed him, but went on gently, 'While as for never seeing Tanus again, you will be playing opposite him in the pageant. I will make certain that there is a chance for the two of you to speak to each other between the acts.'

'My father will never let the pageant go on now.'

'He has no alternative, unless he is prepared to ruin my production and risk Pharaoh's displeasure, and you can be certain that he will never do that.'

'He will send Tanus away, and have another actor play Horus,' she sobbed.

'There is no time to rehearse another actor. Tanus will play the god Horus. I will make that clear to my Lord Intef. You and Tanus will have a chance to talk. We will find a way out for the two of you.'

She gulped back her tears and looked up at me with complete trust. 'Oh, Taita. I know that you will find a way. You always do—' She broke off suddenly and her expression changed. Her hands moved over my back, exploring the ridged welts that Rasfer's whip had raised across it.

'I am sorry, mistress. I tried to put forward Tanus' suit, as I promised you I would, and all this is the consequence of my stupidity.'

She stepped behind me and lifted the light linen tunic I had donned to hide my injuries, and she gasped. 'This is Rasfer's work. Oh, my poor dear Taita, why did you not warn me that this would happen, that my father was so violently opposed to Tanus and to me?'

I was hard put not to gasp at this artless piece of effrontery, I who had pleaded and warned them and in return been accused of disloyalty. I managed to hold my peace, however, although my back still throbbed abominably.

At least my mistress's own misery was forgotten for the moment

57

in her concern for my superficial injuries. She ordered me to sit on her bed and remove my tunic while she ministered to me, her genuine love and compassion making up for the lack of her medicinal skills. This distraction lifted her from the utter depths of her despair. Soon she was chattering away in her usual ebullient fashion, making plans to thwart her father's wrath and to reunite herself with Tanus.

Some of these plans demonstrated her good common sense, while others, more far-fetched, merely pointed to her trusting youth and lack of knowledge and experience in the wicked ways of the world. 'I shall play such a fine role of Isis in the pageant,' she declared at one stage, 'and I shall make myself so agreeable to Pharaoh that he will grant me any boon that I ask of him. Then I shall beg him for Tanus as my husband, and he will say—' here she mimicked the king's pompous ceremonial tones so cleverly that I was forced to grin, 'and he will say, "I declare the betrothal of Tanus, Lord Harrab, son of Pianki, and of the Lady Lostris, daughter of Intef, and I raise my good servant Tanus to the rank of Great Lion of Egypt and commander of all my armies. I further order that all the former estates of his father, the noble Pianki, Lord Harrab be returned to him—"' Here she broke off in the middle of her ministrations to my wounds and flung her arms around my neck.

'It could happen like that, could it not, dear Taita? Please say that it could!'

'No natural man could resist you, mistress,' I smiled at her nonsense. 'Not even great Pharaoh himself.' If I had known then how close my words would turn out to being the truth, I think I should have placed a live coal on my tongue before I spoke them.

Her face was shining with hope once again. That was enough reward for me, and I donned my tunic again to bring to an end her too enthusiastic ministrations to my back.

'But now, mistress, if you are to make a beautiful and irresistible Isis, you must get some rest.' I had brought with me a potion of the powder of the sleeping-flower which is called the Red Shepenn. The seeds of this precious flower had first been brought into this very Egypt by the trade caravans from a mountainous land somewhere far to the east. I now cultivated the red blooms in my garden, and when the petals were fallen I scratched the seed carapace with a gold fork of three tines. Thick white milk flowed from these wounds, which I gathered and dried and treated in accordance with the formula I had evolved. The powder could induce sleep, conjure up strange dreams or smooth out pain.

'Stay with me awhile, Taita,' she murmured as she settled down on the bed, curled like a sleepy kitten. 'Cuddle me to sleep like you did when I was a baby.' She was a baby still, I thought, as I took her in my arms.

'It will all turn out all right, won't it?' she whispered. 'We will live happily ever after, just like they do in your stories, won't we, Taita?'

When she was asleep, I kissed her forehead softly and covered her with a fur rug before I stole from her chamber.

ON THE fifth day of the festival of Osiris, Pharaoh came down-river to Karnak from his palace on Elephantine Island which was ten days' travel away by swift river galley. He came in full state with all his retinue to officiate at the festival of the god.

Tanus' squadron had left Karnak three days previously, speeding away upstream to meet the great flotilla and escort it on the last stage of the voyage, so neither Lostris nor I had seen him since we had all three returned from the great rivercow hunt. It was a special joy for both of us then to see his galley come flying around the bend in the river, full on the current and with a strong desert wind abeam. The *Breath of Horus* was in the van of the fleet, leading it up from the south.

Lostris was in the grand vizier's train, standing behind her two brothers, Menset and Sobek. The two boys were comely and well-favoured, but there was too much of their father in them for my taste. Menset, the elder of the two, I particularly mistrusted, and the younger followed where his brother led.

I was standing further back in the ruck of courtiers and lesser functionaries from where I could keep an eye both on Lostris and on my Lord Intef. I saw the back of her neck flush with pleasure and excitement at the glimpse she had of Tanus' tall figure on the stern-tower of the *Breath of Horus*. The scales on his crocodile-skin breastplate gleamed in the sunlight, and the spray of ostrich feathers on his helmet floated in the draught of the galley's passage.

Lostris was hopping with excitement and waving both slim arms above her head, but her squeals and her antics were lost in the roar of the vast crowd that lined both banks of the Nile to welcome their pharaoh. Thebes is the most populous city in the world, and I guessed that almost a quarter of a million souls had turned out to welcome the king.

Meanwhile Tanus looked neither left nor right, but stared sternly ahead with his unsheathed sword held before his face in salute. The rest of his squadron followed the *Breath of Horus* in the wide vee of the egret formation, named for the pattern that those birds fly in as they return in the sunset to their roosts. All their standards and battle honours were streaming out in a fluttering blaze of rainbow colours, a noble show that set the crowds cheering and waving their palm-fronds wildly.

It was some time before the first vessel of the main convoy came wallowing round the bend behind them. It was laden with ladies and nobles of the king's entourage. It was followed by another, and then by a great untidy horde of vessels great and small. They came swarming downstream, transports filled with palace servants and slaves and all their accoutrements and paraphernalia, barges laden with oxen and goats and chickens for the kitchens, gilded and gaily painted vessels bearing cargoes of palace furniture and treasure, of nobles and lesser creatures, all uncomfortably jumbled together in a most unseamanlike fashion. In what contrast was the display put up by Tanus' squadron as it rounded-to downstream and held its geometrically spaced formation against the swift Nile current!

At last Pharaoh's state barge lumbered around the bend, and the cheering of the crowd rose to a crescendo. This huge vessel, the largest ever built by man, made its ponderous way towards where we were waiting to welcome it at the stone wharf below the grand vizier's palace.

I had plenty of time in which to study it and to muse how

aptly its size and design, and the handling of it, reflected the present state and government of this very Egypt of ours – Egypt as she stood in the twelfth year of the rule of Pharaoh Mamose, the eighth of that name and line, and the weakest yet of a weak and vacillating dynasty. The state barge was as long as five of the fighting galleys laid end to end, but its height and breadth were so ill-proportioned that they gravely offended my artistic instincts. Its massive hull was painted in the riotous colours that were the fashion of the age, and the figurehead of Osiris on the bows was gilded with real gold leaf. However, as she drew closer to the landing where we waited, I could see that the brilliant colours were faded in patches and her sides were zebra-striped in dun where her crew had defecated over the rail.

Amidships stood a tall deck-house, Pharaoh's private quarters, that was so solidly constructed of thick planks of precious cedar, and so stuffed with heavy furniture that the sailing characteristics of the barge were sadly affected. Atop this grotesque edifice, behind an ornate railing that was woven of fresh lilies, beneath a canopy of finely tanned gazelle skins skilfully sewn together and painted with images of all the major gods and goddesses, sat Pharaoh in majestic isolation. On his feet were sandals of gold filigree and his robe was of linen so pure that it shone like the high cumulus clouds of full summer. On his head he wore the tall double crown; the white crown of Upper Egypt with the head of the vulture goddess Nekhbet, combined with the red crown and the cobra head of Buto, the goddess of the Delta.

Despite the crown, the ironic truth was that this beloved sovereign of ours had lost the Delta almost ten years previously. In our turbulent days another pharaoh ruled in Lower Egypt, one who also wore the double crown, or at least his own version of it, a pretender who was our sovereign's deadly adversary, and whose constant wars against us drained both kingdoms of gold and the blood of the young men. Egypt was divided and torn by internal strife. Over the thousand or so years of our history, it had always been thus when weak men took on the mantle of pharaoh. It needed a strong, bold and clever man to hold the two kingdoms in his fists.

In order to turn the unwieldy vessel into the current and bring

61

her to her moorings at the palace wharf, the captain should have steered close in to the far bank. If he had done so, he would have had the full breadth of the Nile in which to complete his turn. However, he had obviously misjudged the strength of wind and current and he began his turn from midstream. At first the barge swung ponderously across the current, listing heavily as the height of the deck-house caught the hot desert wind like a sail. Half a dozen boatswains raged about the lower deck with their whips rising and falling, the snapping of the lash on bare shoulders carrying clearly across the water.

Under the goading of the lash the rowers plied their paddles in a frenzy that churned the waters alongside the hull to foam, one hundred paddles a side pulling against each other and none of them making any effort to synchronize the stroke. Their curses and cries blended with the shouted orders of the four helmsmen who were struggling with the long steering-oar in the stern. Meanwhile, on the poop-deck, Nembet, the geriatric admiral and captain of the barge, alternately combed his fingers through his long scraggy grey beard and flapped his hands in impotent agitation.

High above this pandemonium sat Pharaoh, motionless as a statue and aloof from it all. Oh, verily this was our Egypt.

Then the rate of the barge's turn bled away until she was no longer swinging but heading straight for where we stood on the bank, locked in chains by the pull of the current and the contrary push of the wind. Captain and crew, despite all their wild and erratic exertions, seemed powerless either to complete the manoeuvre and head her into the current, or to heave-to and prevent her from ploughing headlong into the granite blocks of the wharf and staving in her great gilded bows.

As everyone realized what was about to happen, the cheers of the crowd watching from the shore slowly died away and an awful hush fell upon both banks of the Nile into which the shouting and the turmoil on the decks of the huge vessel carried all the more clearly.

Then suddenly all the eyes of the crowd were drawn downstream, as the *Breath of Horus* broke from her station at the head of the squadron and came tearing up-river, driven by the flying paddles. In perfect unison those paddles dipped and pulled and swung and dipped again. She cut in so sharply under the bows of the barge that the crowd gasped with a sound higher than the wind in the papyrus beds. Collision seemed inevitable, but at the last possible moment Tanus signalled with a clenched fist lifted above his head. Simultaneously both banks of rowers backed water and the helmsman put the steering-oar hard over.

The *Breath of Horus* checked and paid away before the ponderous advance of the great barge. The two vessels touched as lightly as a virgin's kiss, and for an instant the stern-tower of the *Breath of Horus* was almost level with the barge's main deck.

In that instant Tanus poised himself on the bulwark of the tower. He had kicked off his sandals, divested himself of his armour, and thrown aside his weapons. Around his waist he had tied the end of a light flax line. With the line trailing behind him he leaped out across the gap between the two vessels.

As though awakening from a stupor, the crowd stirred and shook itself. If there was still one amongst them who did not know who Tanus was, he would know before this day was out. Of course, Tanus' fame had already been won in the river wars against the legions of the usurper in the Lower Kingdom. However, only his own troops had ever seen him in action. The reported deed never carries the same weight as the one that the eye sees for itself.

Now, before the gaze of Pharaoh, the royal flotilla and the entire populace of Karnak, Tanus leaped from one deck to the other and landed as lightly as a leopard.

'Tanus!' I am sure that it was my mistress, Lostris, who first called out his name, but I was next.

'Tanus!' I yelled, and then all those around me took up the cry. 'Tanus! Tanus! Tanus!' They chanted it like an ode to some newly discovered god.

The moment he landed on the deck of the barge, Tanus whirled and raced into the bows, hauling in the thin line hand over hand as he ran. The crew of his galley had spliced a heavy hawser, as thick as a man's arm, to the end of the carrying-line.

Now they sent it across as Tanus lay back against the weight of it. With the muscles of his arms and back shining with sweat, he dragged it in.

By this time a handful of the barge's crew had realized what he was about, and rushed forward to help him. Under Tanus' direction they took three turns with the end of the hawser about the barge's bowsprit, and the instant it was secured Tanus signalled his galley away.

The *Breath of Horus* leaped into the current, gathering speed swiftly. Then abruptly she came up short against the hawser, and the weight of the heavy vessel on the other end threw her back on her haunches. For a dreadful moment I thought she might capsize and be dragged under, but Tanus had anticipated the shock and signalled his crew to cushion it by skilfully backing the long paddles.

Although she was dragged down so low that she took in green water over her stern, the galley weathered it, bobbed up and came back taut on the hawser. For a long moment nothing happened. The galley's puny weight made no impression on the great ship's ponderous way. The two vessels were locked together as though a crocodile had an old bull buffalo by the snout but could not drag him from the bank. Then Tanus in the bows of the barge turned to face the disorganized crew. He made one authoritative gesture that caught all their attention, and a remarkable change came over them. They were waiting for his command.

Nembet was the commander of all Pharaoh's fleet with the rank of Great Lion of Egypt. Years ago he had been one of the mighty men, but now he was old and feeble. Tanus took over from him effortlessly, as though it were as natural as the force of the current and the wind, and the crew of the barge responded immediately.

'Pull!' He gestured to the port bank of oarsmen and they bent their backs and pulled with a will.

'Back-water!' He stabbed his clenched fist at the starboard side and they dug in hard with the pointed blades of their paddles. Tanus stepped to the rail and signalled to the helmsman of the

64

Breath of Horus, masterfully coordinating the efforts of both crews. Still the barge was bearing down upon the wharf and now only a narrow strip of open water separated the vessel from the granite blocks.

Then at last, slowly, too slowly, she began to respond. The gaudily painted bows began to swing up into the current as the galley dragged them round. Once again the cheering died away and that fateful hush fell upon us all as we waited for the enormous ship to crash into the wharf and tear out her own guts on the rock. When that happened there was no doubt what the consequences must be for Tanus. He had snatched command from the senile admiral and so must bear the full responsibility for all the old man's mistakes. When Pharaoh was dashed from his throne by the collision, when the double crown and all his dignity were sent rolling across the deck, and when the state barge sank beneath him and he was dragged from the river like a drowning puppy before the gaze of all his subjects, then there would be both the insulted Admiral Nembet and my Lord Intef to encourage Pharaoh to bring the full weight of his displeasure to bear upon the presumptuous young upstart.

I stood helplessly and trembled for my dear friend, and then a miracle occurred. The barge was already so close to running aground and Tanus so near to where I stood that his voice carried clearly to me. 'Great Horus, help me now!' he cried.

There is no doubt at all in my mind that the gods often take a hand in the affairs of men. Tanus is a Horus man, and Horus is the god of the wind.

The desert wind had blown for three days and nights out of the western desolation of the Sahara. It had blown at the strength of half a gale without a check for all that time, but now it dropped. It did not taper off, it simply ceased to blow at all. The wavelets that had flecked the surface of the river flattened out, and the palms along the waterfront that had been vigorously shaking their fronds fell still, as though frozen by a sudden frost.

Released from the claws of the wind, the barge rolled back on to an even keel and yielded to the pull of the *Breath of Horus*. Her elephantine bows turned up into the current, and she came parallel with the wharf at the exact moment that her side touched the dressed stone and the rush of the Nile killed her forward-way and stalled her motionless in the water.

One last command from Tanus and, before the ship could gather stern-way, the mooring ropes were cast on to the wharf and swiftly gathered up by eager hands and made fast to the stone bollards. Lightly as a goose-down feather floating on the water, the great barge of state lay safe and serene at her berth, and neither the throne upon which Pharaoh sat, nor the high crown upon his head, had been disturbed by her moorage.

We, the onlookers, burst out in a roar of praise for the feat, and the name of Tanus rather than that of Pharaoh was on all our tongues. Modestly, and very prudently, Tanus made no attempt to acknowledge our applause. To draw any further attention to himself that might detract from the welcome that awaited the king would have been folly indeed, and would certainly have negated any royal favour that his exploit had earned him. Pharaoh was always jealous of his royal dignity. Instead, Tanus surreptitiously signalled the *Breath of Horus* alongside. When she was hidden from our view by the bulk of the barge, he dropped overside on to the galley's deck, quitting the stage on which he had just earned such distinction, and leaving it now to his king.

However, I saw the expression of fury and chagrin on the face of Nembet, the ancient admiral, the Great Lion of Egypt, as he came ashore behind Pharaoh, and I knew that Tanus had made himself another powerful enemy.

I WAS able to make good my promise to Lostris that very evening when I put the cast of the pageant through their dress rehearsal. Before the performance began I was able to give the two lovers almost an hour alone together.

In the precincts of the temple of Osiris, which was to be our theatre for the pageant, I had set up tents to act as dressing-rooms for each of the principal players. I had purposely placed Lostris' tent a little apart from the others, screened from

66

them by one of the huge stone columns that support the roof of the temple. While I stood on sentry duty at the entrance to the tent, Tanus lifted the opposite panel and slipped in under it.

I tried not to eavesdrop on their cries of delight as they first embraced, nor to the whispering and cooing, to the muffled laughter and to the small moans and gasps of their decorous love-making which followed. Although at this stage I would not have made any attempt to prevent it, I was convinced that they would not carry this love-making to its ultimate conclusion. Long afterwards both Lostris and Tanus separately confirmed this for me. My mistress had been a virgin on her wedding day. If only any of us had known how close upon us that wedding day was, I wonder how differently we might have acted then.

Although I was acutely aware that every minute that they were alone together in the tent increased the danger for all of us, still I could not bring myself to call enough and separate them. Although the welts on my back that Rasfer's whip had raised still burned, and although deep in that morass of my soul where I attempt to hide all my unworthy thoughts and instincts my envy for the lovers burned as painfully, still I let them stay together much longer than I should have done.

I did not hear my Lord Intef coming. He used to have his sandals shod in the softest kid-skin to muffle his footfalls. He moved silently as a ghost, and many a courtier and slave felt either Rasfer's whip or his noose on account of a careless word that my lord overheard on his noiseless peregrinations through the halls and corridors of the palace. However, over the years I developed an instinct that enabled me most times to sense his presence before he materialized out of the shadows. This instinct was not infallible, but that evening it stood me in good stead. When I looked round suddenly he was almost upon me, gliding between the pillars of the hypostyle hall towards me, slim and tall and deadly as an erect cobra.

'My Lord Intef!' I cried loudly enough to startle myself, 'I am honoured that you have come to witness our rehearsals. I would be deeply grateful for any advice or suggestions—' I was gabbling wildly in an attempt to cover my confusion and to alert the lovers in the tent behind me.

In both objects I succeeded better than I had any right to expect. I heard the sudden scuffle of consternation within the dressing-tent behind me as the lovers broke apart, and then the flutter of the rear panel of the tent as Tanus ducked out the way he had entered.

At any other time I would never have succeeded so easily in deceiving my Lord Intef. He would have read the guilt upon my face as clearly as I read the hieroglyphics on the temple walls or my own characters on this scroll; but that evening he was blinded by his own wrath, and intent only on taking me to task for my latest misdemeanour. He did not rage or roar with anger. My Lord is at his most dangerous when his tone is mild and his smile silky.

'Dear Taita.' It was almost a whisper. 'I hear that you have altered some of the arrangements for the opening act of the pageant, despite the fact that I personally ordered them. I could not believe that you have been so presumptuous. I had to come all this way in the heat to find out for myself.'

I knew it was of no avail to feign innocence or ignorance, so I bowed my head and tried to look aggrieved. 'My lord. It was not I who ordered the changes. It was His Holiness, the abbot of the temple of Osiris—'

But my lord broke in impatiently, 'Yes, of course he did, but only after you put him up to it. Do you think I do not know both you and that mumbling old priest? He never had an original thought in his head, while you have nothing but.'

'My lord!' I protested.

'What devious little trick was it this time? Was it one of those convenient dreams sent to you by the gods?' my lord asked, his voice as soft as the rustle of one of the sacred cobras that infested the temple, sliding across the stone flags of the floor.

'My lord!' I did my best to look shocked by the accusation, although I had indeed given the good abbot a rather fanciful account of how Osiris in the guise of a black crow had visited me in my sleep to complain of the spilling of blood in his temple.

Up until that time the priest had voiced no objection to the realistic piece of theatre that my Lord Intef had planned for the amusement of Pharaoh. I had only resorted to dreams when all my efforts to dissuade my lord had failed. It was deeply abhorrent to me to be party to such an abomination as my lord had ordered to be performed in the first act of the pageant. Of course I am aware that certain savage peoples in the eastern lands make human sacrifice to their gods. I have heard that the Kassites, who live beyond the twin rivers Tigris and Euphrates, cast new-born babes into a fiery furnace. The caravan masters who have travelled in those distant lands speak of other atrocities performed in the name of religion, of young virgins slaughtered to promote the harvest or captives of war beheaded before the statues of a triple-headed god.

However, we Egyptians are a civilized people and we worship wise and just gods, not blood-crazed monsters. I had tried to convince my master of this. I had pointed out to him that only once before had a pharaoh made human sacrifice; when Menotep had slit the throats of the seven rebel princes in the temple of Seth and quartered their corpses and sent the embalmed fragments to the governors of each of the nomes as a warning. History still remembered the deed with distaste. Menotep is known to this day as the Bloody King.

'It is not human sacrifice,' my master had contradicted me. 'Merely a well-merited execution, to be carried out in a rather novel fashion. You will not deny, dear Taita, that the death penalty has always been an important part of our system of justice, will you? Tod is a thief. He has stolen from the royal coffers and he must die, if only as an example to others.'

It sounded reasonable, except that I knew he was not at all interested in justice, but rather in protecting his own treasure and in impressing Pharaoh, who so loved pageant and theatre. This had left me with no alternative but to dream for the benefit of the good abbot. Now my Lord Intef's lip lifted in a smile which exposed his perfect teeth but which chilled my blood and raised the hairs on the nape of my neck.

'Here is a little piece of advice,' he whispered close to my face. 'I suggest that you have another dream tonight, so that whichever god it was that visited you last time has an opportunity to countermand his previous instructions to the abbot and to endorse my arrangements. If this does not happen, I will find

some more work for Rasfer – that is my solemn promise to you.'
He turned and strode away, leaving me both relieved that he had
not discovered the lovers and miserable that I was forced to go
ahead with the vile display which he had ordered.

Nevertheless, after my master had left, the rehearsal was a
heartening success that revived my spirits. Lostris was in such a
glow of happiness after her tryst with Tanus that her beauty was
indeed divine, and Tanus in his youth and power was the young
Horus incarnate.

Naturally I was perturbed by the entrance of my Osiris to the
stage, aware as I now was of the fate that my Lord Intef had
ordered for him. My Osiris was played by a handsome, middle-
aged man named Tod who had been one of the bailiffs until he
had been caught dipping into my Lord Intef's coffers to support a
young and expensive courtesan of whom he was enamoured. I
was not proud that it was my examination of the accounts that
had brought to light the discrepancies.

My lord had released him from custody, where he was awaiting
formal trial and sentencing, to play the part of the god of the
underworld in the pageant. My lord had promised not to take the
matter further if he fulfilled the role of Osiris satisfactorily. The
unfortunate Tod was unaware of the hidden menace in this offer
and threw himself into the act with pathetic enthusiasm, believing that he was about to earn his pardon. He could not know
that, in the meantime, my lord had secretly signed his death
warrant and handed the scroll to Rasfer, who was not only the
state executioner but my choice to play Seth in our little
production. It was my lord's intention that he should combine
both roles on the following evening when the pageant was
performed before Pharaoh. Although Rasfer was a natural choice
for the role of Seth, I regretted having cast him in it as I watched
him rehearse the opening scene with Tod, and I shuddered as I
imagined how the main performance would differ from the
rehearsal.

After the rehearsal it was my most pleasant duty to escort my
mistress back to the harem compound. She would not let me
leave but kept me late listening to her excited résumé of the day's
extraordinary events and the role that Tanus had played in them.

'Did you see how he called upon the great god Horus and how the god came at once to his aid? Surely he has the full favour and protection of Horus, don't you agree? Horus will not let any evil befall us, of that I am now certain.'

There was much more of this happy fantasy, and no more talk of parting and suicide. How swiftly the winds of young love shift!

'After what Tanus did today, the way he saved the state barge from wrecking, surely he must also have earned Pharaoh's high favour, don't you think so, Taita? With favour of both the god and Pharaoh, my father can never succeed in having Tanus sent away now, can he, Taita?'

I was called upon to endorse every happy thought that occurred to her, and I was not allowed to leave the harem until I had memorized at least a dozen messages of undying love which I was sworn to carry to Tanus personally.

When, exhausted, I finally reached my own quarters, there was still no rest for me. Nearly all the slave boys were waiting for me, as excited and as garrulous as my mistress had been. They also wanted to have my opinion of the day's events, and particularly of Tanus' rescue of Pharaoh's ship and the significance of that deed. They crowded around me on the terrace above the river as I fed my pets, and vied with each other for my attention.

'Elder brother, is it true that Tanus called upon the god for his help, and Horus intervened immediately? Did you see it happen? Some even say that the god appeared in his falcon shape and hovered over Tanus' head, spreading protective wings over him. Is it true?'

'Is it true, Akh, that Pharaoh has promoted Tanus to Companion of Pharaoh, and given him an estate of five hundred feddan of fertile land on the riverside as reward?'

'Elder brother, they say that the oracle at the desert shrine of Thoth, the god of wisdom, has cast a horoscope for Tanus. The oracle divines that he will be the greatest warrior in the history of our Egypt and that, one day, Pharaoh will favour him above all others.' It is amusing now to look back on these childish prattles, and to realize the strange truths that were adumbrated

71

in them, but at the time I dismissed them as I did the children, with mock severity.

As I composed myself to sleep, my last thought was that the populace of the twin towns of Luxor and Karnak had taken Tanus to their hearts completely, but that this was an onerous and dubious distinction. Fame and popularity breed envy in high places, and the adulation of the mob is fickle. They often take as much pleasure in tearing down the idols that they have grown tired of, as they did in elevating them in the first place.

It is safer by far to live unseen and unremarked, as I always attempt to do.

 ON THE afternoon of the sixth day of the festival, Pharaoh moved in solemn procession from his villa in the midst of the royal estates in the open country between Karnak and Luxor, down the ceremonial avenue lined with statues of granite lions, to the temple of Osiris on the bank of the Nile.

The great sledge on which he rode was so tall that the dense crowds lining the avenue were forced to strain their necks backwards to look up at him on his great gilded throne as he trundled by, drawn by twenty pure white bullocks with massive humped shoulders and wreaths of flowers on their horned heads. The skids of the sledge ground harshly over the paving and scarred the stone slabs.

One hundred musicians led the procession, strumming the lyre and the harp, beating the cymbal and the drum, shaking the rattle and the sistrum, and blowing on the long straight horn of the oryx and on the curling horn of the wild ram. A choir of a hundred of the finest voices in Egypt followed them, singing hymns of praise to Pharaoh and that other god Osiris. Naturally I led the choir. Behind us followed an honour guard from the Blue Crocodile regiment led by Tanus himself. The crowds raised a special cheer for him as, all plumed and armoured, he strode past. The unmarried maidens shrieked and more than one of them sank swooning in the dust, overcome by the hysteria that his new-won fame engendered.

Behind the guard of honour came the vizier and his high-office bearers, then the nobles and their wives and children, then a detachment of the Falcon regiment, and finally Pharaoh's great sledge. In all, this was an assembly of several thousand of the most wealthy and influential persons in the Upper Kingdom.

As we approached the temple of Osiris, the abbot and all his priests were drawn up on the staircase between the tall entrance pylons to welcome Pharaoh Mamose. The temple had been freshly painted and the bas-relief on the outer walls was dazzling with colour in the warm yellow glow of the sunset. A gay cloud of banners and flags fluttered from their poles set in the recesses of the outer wall.

At the base of the staircase Pharaoh descended from his carriage and in solemn majesty began the climb up the one hundred steps. The choir lined both sides of the staircase. I was on the fiftieth step and so I was able to study the king minutely during the few seconds that it took for him to pass close to me.

I already knew him well, for he had been a patient of mine, but I had forgotten how small he was – that is, small for a god. He stood not as tall as my shoulder, although the high double crown made him seem much more impressive. His arms were folded across his chest in the ritual posture and he carried the crook and the flail of his royal office and his godhead. I remarked as I had before that his hands were hairless, smooth and almost feminine, and that his feet also were small and neat. He wore rings on all his fingers and on his toes, amulets on his upper arms and bracelets on his wrists. The massive pectoral plate of red gold on his chest was inlaid with many colours of faience depicting the god Thoth bearing the feather of truth. That piece of jewellery was a splendid treasure almost five hundred years old and had been worn by seventy kings before him.

Under the double crown, his face was powdered dead white like that of a corpse. His eyes were dramatically outlined with startling jet black and his lips were rouged crimson. Under the heavy make-up his expression was petulant, and his lips were thin and straight and humourless. His eyes were shifty and nervous, as well they might be, I reflected.

The foundations of this great House of Egypt were cracked,

and the kingdom riven and shaken. Even a god has his worries. Once his domain had stretched from the sea, across the seven mouths of the Delta, southwards to Assoun and the first cataract – the greatest empire on earth. He and his ancestors had let it all slip away, and now his enemies swarmed at his shrunken borders, clamouring like hyena and jackal and vulture to feast on the carcass of our Egypt.

In the south were the black hordes of Africa, in the north along the coast of the great sea were the piratical sea-people, and along the lower reaches of the Nile the legions of the false Pharaoh. In the west were the treacherous Bedouin and the sly Libyan, while in the east new hordes seemed to rise up daily, their names striking terror into a nation grown timid and hesitant with defeat. Assyrians and Medes, Kassites and Hurrians and Hittites – there seemed no end to their multitudes.

What advantage remained in our ancient civilization if it were grown feeble and effete with its great age? How were we to resist the barbarian in his savage vigour, his cruel arrogance and his lust for rapine and plunder? I was certain that this pharaoh, like those who had immediately preceded him, was not capable of leading the nation back to its former glories. He was incapable even of breeding a male heir.

This lack of an heir to the empire of Egypt seemed to obsess him even more than the loss of the empire itself. He had taken twenty wives so far. They had given him daughters, a virtual tribe of daughters, but no son. He would not accept that the fault lay with him as sire. He had consulted every doctor of renown in the Upper Kingdom and visited every oracle and every important shrine.

I knew all this because I was one of the learned doctors he had sent for. I admit that at the time I had felt some trepidation in prescribing to a god, and that I had wondered why he should need to consult a mere mortal on such a delicate subject. Nevertheless, I had recommended a diet of bull's testicles fried in honey and counselled him to find the most beautiful virgin in Egypt and take her to his marriage-bed within a year of the first flowering of her woman's moon.

I had no great faith in my own remedy, but bull's testicles, when cooked to my recipe, are a tasty dish, while I reckoned that the search for the most beautiful virgin in the land might distract Pharaoh and prove not only amusing but pleasurable as well. From a practical point of view, if the king bedded a sufficient number of young ladies, then surely one of them must eventually drop a male pup into his harem.

Anyhow, I consoled myself that my treatment was not as drastic as some of the others proposed by my peers, particularly those disgusting remedies dreamed up by the quacks in the temple of Osiris who call themselves doctors. If not actually efficacious, my recommendations would at least do no harm. That was what I believed. How wrong the fates would prove me, and if only I had known the consequences of my folly, I would have taken Tod's place in the pageant rather than have given Pharaoh such frivolous counsel.

I was amused and flattered when I heard that Pharaoh must have taken my advice seriously, and that he had ordered his nomarchs and his governors to scour the length of the land from El Amarna to the cataracts to find bulls with succulent balls and any virgin who might fit my specifications for the mother of his first son. My sources at the king's court informed me that he had already rejected hundreds of aspiring applicants for the title of the most beautiful virgin in the land.

Then the king was swiftly past me and gone into the temple to the keening of the priests and the obsequious bobbing of the abbot. The grand vizier and all his train followed closely, and then there was an undignified rush of lesser citizens to find places from which to watch the passion play. Space in the temple was limited. Only the mighty and the noble and those rich enough to bribe the thieving priests were allowed into the inner court-yard. The others were forced to watch through the gates from the outer court. Many thousands of the citizenry would be disappointed and would have to be content with a secondhand account of the pageant. Even I, the impresario, had great difficulty in fighting my way through the press of humanity, and I only succeeded when Tanus saw my predicament and sent two of his men to rescue me and force a path for me into the precincts reserved for the actors.

Before the pageant could begin, we were obliged to endure a succession of flowery speeches, firstly from the local functionaries and government ministers, and then from the grand vizier in person. This interlude of speechifying gave me the opportunity to make certain that all the arrangements for the pageant were perfect. I went from tent to tent, checking the costumes and the make-up of each of my actors, and soothing last-minute attacks of temperament and stage-fright.

The unfortunate Tod was nervously dreading the possibility that his performance might not please my Lord Intef. I was able to assure him that it most certainly would, and then I administered to him a draught of the Red Shepenn, which would deaden the pain that he was about to have inflicted upon him.

When I came to Rasfer's tent he was drinking wine with two of his cronies from the palace guard and, with a whetstone, laying an edge on his short bronze sword. I had created his make-up to render him even more repulsive, which was not an easy feat given the high plateau of ugliness from which we started. I realized how well I had succeeded as he leered at me with blackened teeth and offered me a cup of the wine.

'How does your back feel now, pretty boy? Have a taste of a man's drink! Perhaps it will give you balls again.' I am accustomed to his taunts and I kept my dignity as I told him that my Lord Intef had countermanded the abbot's orders and that the first act was to be played out in the original form.

'I have spoken to Lord Intef already.' He held up the sword. 'Feel the edge, eunuch. I want to make certain that it meets with your approval.' I left him feeling a little queasy.

Although Tanus would not be on stage until the second act, he was already in costume. Relaxed and smiling, he clasped my shoulder. 'Well, old friend, this is your opportunity. After this evening your fame as a playwright will spread throughout Egypt.'

'As yours has already. Your name is on every lip,' I told him, but he laughed it away with careless modesty as I went on, 'Do you have your closing declamation prepared, Tanus? Would you like to recite it to me now?'

Traditionally, the actor who played Horus would close the pageant with a message to Pharaoh, ostensibly from the gods but in reality from his own subjects. In olden times this had been the one occasion during the year when the populace, through the agency of the actor, could bring to the king's notice matters of concern which they were not able to address to him at any other time. However, during the rule of this last dynasty of kings the tradition had fallen away, and the closing speech had become merely another eulogy to the divine pharaoh.

For days past I had been asking Tanus to rehearse his speech for me, but every time he had put me off with excuses so lame that I was by now thoroughly suspicious of his intentions. 'This is the last opportunity,' I insisted, but he laughed at me.

'I have decided to let my speech be as much a surprise to you as I hope it will be to Pharaoh. That way you should both enjoy it more.' And there was nothing I could do to persuade him. At times he can be far and away the most headstrong and obstinate young ruffian I have ever encountered. I left him in not a little dudgeon, and went to find more convivial company.

As I stooped in through the entrance of Lostris' dressing-tent, I froze with shock. Even though I had designed her costume myself and instructed her handmaidens as to exactly how I wanted her powder and rouge and eye-paint applied, still I was not prepared for the ethereal vision that stood before me now. For a moment I was convinced that another miracle had taken place and that the goddess had indeed risen up from the underworld to take my mistress's place. I gasped aloud and had actually begun to sink to my knees in superstitious awe when my mistress giggled and roused me from my delusion.

'Isn't this fun? I cannot wait to see Tanus in full costume. I am sure he must look like the god himself.' She turned slowly to allow me to appraise her own costume, smiling at me over her shoulder.

'No more godlike than you, my lady,' I whispered.

'When will the play begin?' she demanded impatiently. 'I am so excited that I can wait no longer.'

I cocked my ear to the panel of the tent and listened for a moment to the drone of the speeches in the great hall. I realized that this was the final oration and that at any moment my Lord Intef would call upon my players to perform.

I took Lostris' hand and squeezed it. 'Remember the long pause and the haughty look before you begin your opening speech,' I cautioned her, and she slapped my shoulder playfully.

'Away with you, you old fuss-pot, it will all go perfectly, you'll see.' And at that moment I heard my Lord Intef's voice raised.

'The divine god Pharaoh Mamose, the Great House of Egypt, the Support of the Realm, the Just, the Great, the All-Seeing, the All-Merciful—' The titles and honorifics continued while I hurried out of Lostris' tent and made my way to my opening position behind the central pillar. I peered around the column and saw that the inner courtyard of the temple was packed and that Pharaoh and his senior wives sat in the front rank on low benches of cedar wood, sipping cool sherbet or nibbling dates and sweetmeats.

My Lord Intef was addressing them from the front of the raised platform below the altar that was our stage. The main body of the stage was still hidden from the audience by the linen curtains. I surveyed it for one last time, although it was too late to do anything further about it now.

Behind the curtains the set was decorated with palms and acacia trees that the palace gardeners had transplanted under my instruction. My masons had been taken from the work on the king's tomb to build a stone cistern at the back of the temple from which a stream could be diverted across the stage to represent the river Nile.

At the rear of the stage, hanging from floor to ceiling, were tightly stretched sheets of linen on which the artists from the necropolis had painted marvellous landscapes. In the half-light of the dusk and the flicker of the torches in their brackets the effect was so realistic as to transport the beholder into a different world in a distant time.

There were other delights that I had prepared for Pharaoh's amusement, from cages of animals, birds and butterflies that would be released to simulate the creation of the world by the great god Ammon-Ra, to flares and torches that I had doctored with chemicals to burn with brilliant flames of crimson and green, and flood the stage with eerie light and smoke-clouds, like those of the underworld where the gods live.

'Mamose, son of Ra, may you be granted eternal life! We your loyal subjects, the citizens of Thebes, beg you to draw nigh and give your divine attention to this poor play that we dedicate to Your Majesty.'

My Lord Intef concluded his address of welcome and resumed his seat. To a fanfare of hidden rams' horns, I stepped out from behind the pillar and faced the audience. They had endured discomfort and boredom on the hard flagstones, and by now were ripe for the entertainment to begin. A raucous cheer greeted my entrance and even Pharaoh smiled in anticipation.

I held up both hands for silence, and only when it was total did I begin to speak my overture.

'While I walked in the sunlight, young and filled with the vigour of youth, I heard the fatal music in the reeds by the bank of the Nile. I did not recognize the sound of this harp, and I had no fear, for I was in the full bloom of my manhood and secure in the affection of my beloved.

'The music was of surpassing beauty. Joyously I went to find the musician, and could not know that he was Death and that he played his harp to summon me alone.' We Egyptians are fascinated by death, and I had at once touched a deep chord within my audience. They sighed and shuddered.

'Death seized me and bore me up in his skeletal arms towards Ammon-Ra, the sun god, and I was become one with the white light of his being. At a great distance I heard my beloved weep, but I could not see her and all the days of my life were as though they had never been.' This was the first public recitation of my prose, and I knew almost at once that I had them, their faces were fascinated and intent. There was not a sound in the temple.

'Then Death set me down in a high place from which I could see the world like a shining round shield in the blue sea of the heavens. I saw all men and all creatures who have ever lived. Like a mighty river, time ran backwards before mine eyes. For a hundred thousand years I watched their strivings and their deaths. I watched all men go from death and old age to infancy and birth. Time became more and more remote, going back until the birth of the first man and the first woman. I watched them at

79

the moment of their birth and then before. At last there were no men upon the earth and only the gods existed.

'Yet still the river of time flowed back beyond the time of the gods into Nun, into the time of darkness and primordial chaos. The river of time could flow no further back and so reversed itself. Time began to run forward in the manner that was familiar to me from my days of life upon the earth, and I watched the passion of the gods played out before me.' My audience were all of them well versed in the theology of our pantheon, but none of them had ever heard the mysteries presented in such a novel fashion. They sat silent and enthralled as I went on.

'Out of the chaos and darkness of Nun rose Ammon-Ra, He-Who-Creates-Himself. I watched Ammon-Ra stroke his generative member, masturbating and spurting out his seminal seed in mighty waves that left the silver smear that we know as the Milky Way across the dark void. From this seed were generated Geb and Nut, the earth and the heaven.'

'*Bak-her!*' a single voice broke the tremulous silence of the temple. '*Bak-her!* Amen!' The old abbot had not been able to contain himself, and now he endorsed my vision of the creation. I was so astonished by his change of heart that I almost forgot my next line. After all, he had been my sternest critic up to that time. I had won him over completely, and my voice soared in triumph.

'Geb and Nut coupled and copulated, as man and woman do, and from their dreadful union were born the gods Osiris and Seth, and the goddesses Isis and Nephthys.'

I made a wide gesture and the linen curtains were drawn slowly aside to reveal the fantasy world that I had created. Nothing like this had ever been seen in Egypt before and the audience gasped with amazement. With measured tread I withdrew, and my place upon the stage was taken by the god Osiris. The audience recognized him instantly by the tall, bottle-shaped head-dress, by his arms crossed over his chest and by the crook and the flail he held before him. Every household kept his statuette in the family shrine.

A droning cry of reverence went up from every throat, and indeed the sedative that I had administered to Tod glittered

80

weirdly in his eyes and gave him a strange, unearthly presence that was convincingly godlike. With the crook and the flail Osiris made mystical gestures and declaimed in sonorous tones, 'Behold Atur, the river!'

Once more the audience rustled and murmured as they recognized the Nile. The Nile was Egypt and the centre of the world.

'Bak-her!' another voice called out, and, watching from my hidden place amongst the pillars, I was astonished and delighted as I realized who had spoken. It was Pharaoh. My play had both secular and divine endorsement. I was certain that from now on mine would become the authorized version, replacing the thousand-year-old original. I had found my place in immortality. My name would live on down the millennium.

Joyfully I signalled for the cistern to be opened and the waters began to flow across our stage. At first the audience did not comprehend, and then they realized that they were actually witnessing the revelation of the great river, and a shout went up from a thousand throats, 'Bak-her! Bak-her!'

'Behold the waters rise!' cried Osiris, and obediently the Nile was swollen by the inundation.

'Behold the waters fall!' cried the god, and they shrank at his command. 'Now they will rise again!'

I had arranged for buckets of dye to be added to the water as it poured out of the cistern at the rear of the temple. First a green dye to simulate the low-water period, and then, as it rose again, a darker dye that faithfully emulated the colour of the silt-laden waters of the high inundation.

'Now behold the insects and birds upon the earth!' ordered Osiris, and the cages at the rear of the stage were opened and a shrieking, chattering, swirling cloud of wild birds and gorgeously coloured butterflies filled the temple.

The watchers were like children, enchanted and enthralled, reaching up to snatch the butterflies from the air and then release them again to fly out between the high pillars of the temple. One of the wild birds, a long-billed hoopoe marvellously patterned in colours of white and cinnamon and black, flew down unafraid and settled on Pharaoh's crown.

The crowd was delighted. 'An omen!' they cried. 'A blessing on the king. May he live for ever!' and Pharaoh smiled.

It was naughty of me, but afterwards I hinted to my Lord Intef that I had trained the bird to single out Pharaoh, and although it was of course quite impossible, he believed me. Such is my reputation with animals and birds.

On the stage Osiris wandered through the paradise that he had created, and the mood was set for the dramatic moment when, with a blood-chilling shriek, Seth bounded on to the stage. Although they had been expecting it, still the powerful and hideous presence shocked the audience, and the women screamed and covered their faces, only to peer out again from between trembling fingers.

'What is this you have done, brother?' Seth bellowed in jealous rage. 'Do you set yourself above me? Am I not also a god? Do you hold all creation to yourself alone, that I, your brother, may not share it with you?'

Osiris answered him calmly, his dignity remote and cool as the drug held him in its thrall. 'Our father, Ammon-Ra, has given it to us both. However, he has also given us the right to choose how we dispose of it, for good or for evil—' The words that I had put into the mouth of the god reverberated through the temple. They were the finest that I had written, and the audience hung upon them. However, I alone of all of them knew what was coming, and the beauty and the power of my own composition were soured as I steeled myself for it.

Osiris drew to the close of his speech. 'This is the world as I have revealed it. If you wish to share it in peace and brotherly love, then you are welcome. However, if you come in warlike rage, if evil and hatred fill your heart, then I order you gone.' He lifted his right arm all draped in the gleaming diaphanous linen of his robe and pointed the way for Seth to leave the paradise of Earth.

Seth hunched those huge, hairy shoulders like a buffalo bull, and he bellowed so that the spittle flew from his lips in a cloud that was flavoured by the rotting teeth in his jaws. I could smell it from where I stood. He lifted high the bronze broad-sword and rushed at his brother. This had never been rehearsed, and it took

82

Osiris completely by surprise. He stood with his right arm still outstretched, and the blade hissed with the power of the stroke as it swung down. The hand was lopped off at the wrist as cleanly as I would prune a shoot from the vine that grows over my terrace. It fell at Osiris' feet and lay there with the fingers fluttering feebly.

The surprise was so complete and the sword so sharp that for a long moment Osiris did not move, except to sway slightly on his feet. The audience must have believed that this was another theatrical trick, and that the fallen hand was a dummy. The blood did not come at once, which lulled them further. They were intensely interested but not alarmed, until suddenly Osiris reeled back and with a dreadful cry clutched at the stump of his lower arm. Only then did the blood burst out between his fingers and spray down his white robe, staining it like spilt wine. Still clutching his stump, Osiris staggered across the stage and began to scream. That scream, high and clear with mortal agony, broke the mood of the spectators' complacency. They knew then for the first time that what they were witnessing was not make-believe, but they were trapped in horrified silence.

Before Osiris could reach the edge of the stage, Seth came bounding after him on those thick bow-legs. He seized the stump of Osiris' arm and used it as a handle to drag him back into the centre of the stage, where he threw him sprawling full-length on the stone flags. The tinsel crown tumbled from Osiris' head and the plaits of dark hair fell to his shoulders as he lay in a spreading puddle of his own blood.

'Please spare me,' Osiris shrieked, as Seth stood over him, and Seth laughed. It was a full-throated roar of genuine amusement. Rasfer had become Seth, and Seth was hugely enjoying himself.

That savage laughter woke the audience from its trance. However, the illusion was complete. They no longer believed that they were watching a play, and for all of them this terrible spectacle had become reality. Women screamed and men roared with fury as they witnessed the murder of their god.

'Spare him! Spare the great god Osiris!' they howled, but not one of them rose from his seat or rushed on to the stage to attempt to prevent the tragedy from being played out. They knew that the struggles and passions of the gods were beyond the influence of mortal men.

Osiris reached up and pawed at Seth's legs with his one remaining hand. Still laughing, Seth grabbed his wrist and pulled his arm out to its full length, inspecting it as a butcher might inspect the shoulder of a goat before he sections it.

'Cut it off!' screamed a voice in the crowd, thick with the lust for blood. The mood had swung again.

'Kill him!' screamed another. It has always troubled me how the sight of blood and violent death affects even the mildest of men. Even I was stirred by this terrible scene, sickened and horrified, it is true, but beneath it stirred by a revolting excitement.

With a casual sweep of the blade, Seth struck off the arm, and Osiris fell back, leaving the twitching limb in Seth's red fist. He was trying to rise to his feet, but he had no hands to support himself. His legs kicked spasmodically, and his head whipped from side to side, and still he screamed. I tried to force myself to turn away, but though my gorge rose and scalded the back of my throat, still I had to watch.

Seth hacked the arm into three pieces through the joint of the wrist and the elbow. One at a time he hurled the fragments into the packed ranks of the audience. As they spun through the air they sprinkled those below with drops of ruby. They roared like the lions in Pharaoh's zoo at feeding-time, and held up their hands to catch these holy relics of their god.

Seth worked on with dedicated gusto. Osiris' feet he chopped off at the ankles. Then the calves at the knees, and the thighs at the hip joints. As he threw each of these to them, the mob clamoured for more.

'The talisman of Seth!' howled a voice amongst them. 'Give us the talisman of Seth!' and the cry was taken up. According to the myth, the talisman is the most powerful of all the magical charms. The person who has it in his possession controls all the dark forces of the underworld. It is the only one of the fourteen segments of Osiris' body that was never recovered by Isis and her sister Nephthys from the far corners of the earth to which Seth scattered them. The talisman of Seth is that same part of the body that Rasfer deprived me of, and which forms the centre-piece of that beautiful necklace that was the cynical gift of my Lord Intef.

'Give us the talisman of Seth!' the mob howled, and Seth reached down and lifted the red sodden tunic of the limbless trunk at his feet. He was still laughing. I shuddered as I recognized that merciless sound that I had heard so often at my own punishment sessions. In sympathy I experienced once again the sudden fire in my groin as the short sword flashed in Seth's hairy paw, already wet and running with his victim's blood, and he lifted on high the piteous relic.

The crowd pleaded for it. 'Give it to us,' they begged him. 'Give us the power of the talisman.' The spectacle had transformed them into ravening beasts.

Seth ignored their pleas. 'A gift,' he cried. 'A gift from one god to another. I Seth, god of darkness, dedicate this talisman to the god-Pharaoh, Mamose the divine.' And he hopped down the stone stairs on those powerful bow-legs and placed the relic at Pharaoh's feet.

To my amazement the king leaned forward and gathered it up to himself. His expression beneath the powder and paint was spellbound, as though this was the true relic of the god. I am sure that at that moment he truly believed it was. He held it in his right hand through all that ensued.

His gift accepted, Seth rushed back on to the stage to complete his butchery. The thing that haunts me still is that the poor dismembered creature was alive and sensate to the very end. I realized that the drug I had given Tod had done little to dull his senses. I saw the terrible agony in his eyes as he lay in the lake of his own blood and rolled his head from side to side, the only part that remained to him to move.

For me, then, it came as an intense relief when at last Seth struck off the head and held it up by its thick plaited locks for the crowd to admire. Even then, the poor creature's eyes swivelled wildly in their sockets as he looked for the very last time on this world. At last they dulled and glazed over, and Seth tossed the head to them.

Thus the first act of our pageant ended in swelling and

rapturous applause that threatened to shake the granite pillars of the temple from their bases.

 DURING THE intermission my slave helpers cleaned away the gruesome evidence of the slaughter from the set. I was particularly concerned that my Lady Lostris should not realize what had truly taken place in the first act. I wished her to believe that all had gone as we had rehearsed it. So I had arranged that she stay in her tent, and that one of Tanus' men remain at the entrance to keep her there, and also to ensure that none of her Cushite maidens were allowed to peep out at the first act and rush back to Lostris with a report. I knew that if she realized the truth, she would be too distraught to play her part. While my helpers used buckets of water from our stage Nile to wash away the ghastly evidence, I hurried to my mistress's tent to reassure her and to satisfy myself that my precautions to shield her had been effective.

'Oh, Taita, I heard the applause,' she greeted me happily. 'They love your play. I am so happy for you. You so richly deserve this success.' She chuckled in a conspiratorial fashion. 'It sounded as though they believed the murder of Osiris was real, and the buckets of ox-blood with which you drenched Tod were truly the blood of the god.'

'Indeed, my lady, they seemed totally deceived by our little tricks,' I agreed, although I still felt faint and ill from what I had just lived through.

My Lady Lostris suspected nothing, and when I led her out on to the stage, she barely glanced at the grisly stains that remained upon the stones. I posed her in her opening position, and adjusted the torchlight to flatter her. Even though I was accustomed to it, still her beauty choked my throat and made my eyes sting with tears.

I left her concealed by the linen curtains, and stepped out to face my audience. There was no sarcastic applause to greet me this time. Every one of them, from Pharaoh to the meanest vassal, was captive to my voice, as in my lambent prose I

86

described the mourning of Isis and her sister Nephthys at the death of their brother.

When I stepped down and the curtain was drawn aside to reveal the grieving figure of Isis, the audience gasped aloud at her loveliness. After the horror and blood of the first act, her presence was all the more moving.

Isis began to sing the lament for the dead, and her voice thrilled through the gloomy halls of the temple. As her head moved to the cadence of her voice, the torchlight was reflected in a darting and flickering shaft from the bronze moon that surmounted her horned head-dress.

I watched Pharaoh attentively as she sang. His eyes never left her face, and his lips moved silently in sympathy with the words that swelled from her throat.

> My heart is a wounded gazelle,
> torn by the lion claws of my grief—

She lamented and the king and all his train grieved with her.

> There is no sweetness in the honeycomb,
> no perfume remains in the desert blossom.
> My soul is an empty temple,
> deserted by the god of love.

In the front rank one or two of the king's wives were snuffling and blubbering, but nobody even glanced at them.

> I look on death's grim face with a smile.
> Gladly would I follow him,
> if he could lead me to the arms of my dear lord.

By now not only the royal wives but every one of the women were weeping, and most of the men also. Her words and her beauty were too much for them to resist. It seemed impossible that a god should show the same emotions as mortal men, but the slow tears were cutting runnels through the white powder on

Pharaoh's cheeks, and he blinked his heavy, kohl-darkened eyelids like an owl as he stared at my Lady Lostris.

Nephthys entered and sang a duet with her sister, then hand-in-hand the two women went in search of the scattered fragments of Osiris' corpse.

Of course I had not placed the actual dismembered portions of Tod's corpse for them to find. During the intermission my helpers had retrieved these and carried them away to the embalmers on my instructions. I would pay for Tod's funeral out of my own purse. It seemed the very least that I could do to compensate the unfortunate creature for my own part in his murder. Despite the missing portion of his anatomy that Pharaoh still held in his hand, I hoped the gods might make an exception in his case and allow Tod's shade to pass into the underworld, and that there he might not think too badly of me. It is wise to have friends wherever you can, in this world and the next.

To represent the body of the god I had the funeral artists from the necropolis build for me a magnificent mummy cartonnage, depicting Osiris in his full regalia and in the death pose with his arms folded across his chest. This container I had cut into thirteen sections that fitted together like a child's building-blocks.

As the sisters retrieved each of these sections they sang a hymn of praise to the god's parts, to his hands and feet, to his limbs and trunk, and finally to his divine head.

Such eyes, like stars set in the heavens,
must shine for ever.
Death should never dim such beauty,
nor the funeral wrappings contain such majesty.

When at last the two sisters had reassembled the complete body of Osiris, except for the missing talisman, they pondered aloud how they could return it to life once more.

This was my opportunity to add to the pageant that essential element that makes any theatrical production appeal to the popular taste. There is a broad lascivious streak in most of us, and the playwright and the poet does well to bear this in mind if he hopes to have his work appreciated by the main body of his audience.

'There is but one certain way to bring our dear lord and brother back to life.' I placed the words in the mouth of the goddess Nephthys. 'One of us must perform the act of generation with his shattered body to make it whole again and to fan the spark of life within it.'

The audience stirred and leaned forward with anticipation at this suggestion. It had elements to appeal to even the most prurient of those present, including incest and necrophilia.

I had agonized over how I would represent upon the stage this episode in the myth of the resurrection of Osiris. My mistress had shocked me when she had declared herself willing to carry her role through to the end. She had even had the effrontery to point out, with that impudent grin of hers, that she might gain some valuable knowledge and experience from doing so. I was not certain if she was jesting or if she would really have gone through with it; however, I would not give her the opportunity to demonstrate her good faith or lack of it. Her reputation and the honour of her family were too valuable to trifle with.

So it was that at my signal, the linen curtains were drawn once more and my Lady Lostris quickly left the stage. Her place was taken by one of the upper-class courtesans who usually plied her trade in a palace of love near the port. I had hired this wench, from amongst several that I had interviewed, because of her fine young body that so much resembled that of my mistress. Of course, in facial beauty she could not come close to my Lady Lostris, but then I know of none who could.

As soon as the substitute goddess was in position, the torches at the rear of the stage were lit so as to cast her shadow upon the curtain. She began to disrobe in the most provocative manner. The males in the audience cheered on her shadowy gyrations, convinced that they were watching my Lady Lostris. The harlot responded to this encouragement with an increasingly lewd display that was almost as well received as the slaughter of Osiris in the first act.

Now came that action of the play that had given me, the

author, considerable pause, for how could I contrive fecundity without a stout peg to hang it on? We had just seen Osiris forcefully deprived of his. In the end I was forced to stoop to that tired old theatrical device that I so scorned in the work of other playwrights, namely the intervention of the gods and their supernatural powers.

While my Lady Lostris spoke from the wings, her shadowy alter ego on stage stood over the mummiform figure of Osiris and made a series of mystical gestures. 'My dear brother, by the rare and marvellous powers granted to me by our forefather, Ammon-Ra, I restore to you those manly parts that cruel Seth so brutally tore from you,' intoned my mistress.

I had equipped the mummy case with a device that I could raise by hauling on a length of fine linen twine that ran over a pulley in the temple roof directly above where Osiris lay. At Isis' words the wooden phallus, hinged to the god's pudenda, rose in majestic splendour, as long as my arm, into full erection. The audience gasped with admiration.

When Isis caressed it, I jerked the string to make it leap and twitch. The audience loved it, but loved it even better when the goddess mounted the supine mummy of the god. Judging by the convincing acrobatics of her simulated ecstasy, the harlot I had chosen to play the part must have been one of the truly great exponents of her art. The audience gave full recognition to her superior performance, egging her on with whistling and hooting and shouting ribald advice.

At the climax of this exhibition the torches were extinguished and the temple plunged into darkness. In the darkness the substitution was made once more and when the torches were re-lit my Lady Lostris stood in mid-stage with a new-born infant in her arms. One of the kitchen slaves had been considerate enough to give birth a few days previously, and I had borrowed her whelp for the occasion.

'I give you the new-born son of Osiris, god of the underworld, and of Isis, goddess of the moon and of the stars.' My Lady Lostris lifted the infant high and he, astonished by the sea of strangers before him, screwed up his tiny face and turned bright red as he howled.

Isis raised her voice above his and cried, 'Greet the young Lord Horus, god of the wind and the sky, falcon of the heavens!' Half the audience were Horus men and their enthusiasm for their patron was unbounded. They came to their feet in a roaring tumult, and the second act ended in another triumph for me and in mortification for the infant god, who on later examination was found to have prodigiously soiled his swaddling-cloth.

I OPENED the final act with another of my recitations describing the childhood and the coming to manhood of Horus. I spoke of the sacred charge laid upon him by Isis, and as I did so, the curtains were drawn aside to reveal the goddess in the centre of the stage.

Isis was bathing in the Nile, attended by her hand-maidens. Her wet robe clung to her body so that the pale glory of her skin shone through. The indistinct outlines of her breasts were tipped with tiny rose-buds of virgin pink.

Tanus as Horus entered from the wings, and immediately dominated the stage. In his polished armour and his warrior's pride he was a perfect counterpoint for the beauty of the goddess. The long list of his battle honours in the river wars, together with his most recent exploit in saving the royal barge, had focused the attention of the populace full upon him. For this moment Tanus was the darling of the crowd. Before he could speak, they began to cheer him, and the applause continued so long that the actors were forced to freeze in their opening positions.

While the cheering swirled around Tanus, I picked out certain faces in the audience and watched their reactions. Nembet, the Great Lion of Egypt, scowled and muttered fiercely into his beard, making no attempt to hide his animosity. Pharaoh smiled graciously and nodded slightly, so that those seated behind him were made aware of his approbation, and their own enthusiasm was encouraged. My Lord Intef, never one to fly against the prevailing winds, smiled his most silky smile and nodded his head in concert with his king. His eyes, however, when seen from my vantage-point, were deadly.

At last the applause abated and Tanus could speak his lines, not without difficulty, however, for every time he paused to draw breath another outburst of cheering broke out. It was only when Isis began to sing that complete silence fell upon them once more.

> The suffering of your father,
> the terrible fate that hangs over our house,
> all these must be expunged.

In verse Isis warned her noble son, and held out her arms to him in supplication and in command.

> The curse of Seth is upon us all,
> and only you can break it.
> Seek out your monstrous uncle.
> By his arrogance and his ferocity,
> you will know him.
> When you find him,
> strike him down.
> Chain him,
> bind him to your will,
> that the gods and all men
> will be freed for ever from his ghastly sway.

Still singing, the goddess withdrew and left her son to his quest. Like children following a well-loved nursery rhyme, the audience knew full well what to expect and leaned forward eagerly and hummed with anticipation.

When at last Seth came leaping back on stage for the cataclysmic battle, the age-old struggle between good and evil, beauty and ugliness, duty and dishonour, the audience was ready for him. They greeted Seth with a chorus of hatred that was spontaneous and unfeigned. In defiance Rasfer leered and gibbered at them, strutting about the stage, cupping his genitalia in his hands and thrusting his hips out at them in a mocking and obscene gesture that drove them wild with fury.

'Kill him, Horus!' they howled. 'Smash in his ugly face!' And Seth pranced before them, stoking their fury.

'Kill the murderer of the great god Osiris!' they roared in a paroxysm of loathing.

'Smash in his face!'

'Rip out his guts!'

The congregation's reaction to him was in no way moderated by the fact that it knew, deep down, that this was Rasfer and not Seth.

'Hack off his head!' they screamed.

'Kill him! Kill him!'

At last Seth pretended to see his nephew for the first time, and swaggered up to him, lolling his tongue out between his blackened teeth, drooling like an idiot so that silver strands of saliva slimed down on to his chest. I would never have believed that Rasfer could make himself more repulsive than nature had already accomplished, but now he proved me wrong.

'Who is this child?' he demanded, and belched full in the face of Horus. Tanus was unprepared for this and stepped back involuntarily, his expression of disgust unfeigned as he smelled Rasfer's breath and the contents of his stomach, the sour wine still fermenting in it.

Tanus recovered swiftly and spoke his next line. 'I am Horus, son of Osiris.'

Seth let out a mocking peal of laughter. 'And what is it you seek, boy child of a dead god?'

'I seek vengeance for the murder of my noble father. I seek the assassin of Osiris.'

'Then search no further,' Seth shouted, 'for I am Seth the vanquisher of lesser gods. I am Seth the eater of stars, and the destroyer of worlds.'

The two gods drew their swords and rushed at each other, to meet in mid-stage with a ringing clash of bronze as blade struck blade. In an attempt to reduce the chances of accidental injury, I had attempted to substitute wooden swords for bronze, but neither of my actors would have any of it. My Lord Intef had intervened when Rasfer had appealed to him. He had ordered that they be allowed to wield their real battle weapons, and I had

93

been forced to yield to this higher authority. At least it added to the realism of the scene as they stood now chest to chest, with blades locked, and glared into each other's face.

They made an extraordinary pair, so totally dissimilar, pointing up the moral of the play, the eternal conflict of good against evil. Tanus was tall and fair and comely. Seth was swarthy and thick-set, bow-legged and hideous. The contrast was direct and visceral. The mood of the audience was as fiery and as fiercely partisan as that of the two protagonists.

Simultaneously they pushed each other backwards and then rushed in again, thrusting and cutting, feinting and parrying. They were both highly trained and skilled swordsmen, amongst the finest in all Pharaoh's armies. Their blades whirled and glinted in the torchlight so that they seemed as insubstantial as the sunlight reflected from the wind-ruffled surface of the great river. The sound of their flight was that of the wings of the birds startled from their roosts in the gloomy heights of the temple, but when they clashed together it was with the heavy ring of hammers at the coppersmith's forge.

What seemed to the observer to be the chaos of real battle was in fact a meticulously choreographed ballet which had been carefully rehearsed. Each man knew exactly how each blow must be launched and each parry timed. These were two superb athletes engaged in the activity for which they had trained their entire warrior's lifetime, and they made it seem effortless.

When Seth thrust, Horus left his parry so late that the point actually touched his breastplate and left a tiny bright scratch on the metal. Then when Horus launched himself forward in riposte, his edge flew so close to Seth's head that a coil of his coarse matted hair was shorn from his skull, as if by a barber's razor. Their footwork was as graceful and intricate as that of the temple dancers, and they were swift as falcons and lithe as hunting cheetahs.

The crowd was mesmerized and so was I. Therefore it must have been some deep instinct that warned me, perhaps even a nudge from the gods, who knows? At any rate, something outside myself made me tear my eyes away from the spectacle and glance at my Lord Intef where he sat in the front row.

Again, was it instinct or my own deep knowledge of him, or

94

the intervention of the god who protects Tanus that placed the thought in my mind? A little of all three of these, perhaps, but I knew with instant and utter certainty the reason for that wolfish smile on my Lord Intef's handsome features.

I knew why he had chosen Rasfer to play Seth. I knew why he had made no effort to exclude Tanus from the role of Horus, even after he had found out about the relationship between him and my Lady Lostris. I knew why he had ordered the use of real swords, and I knew why he was smiling now. The massacre was not over for the evening. He was looking forward to more. Before this act was played out, Rasfer would ply his special talents once again.

'Tanus!' I screamed, as I started forward. 'Beware! It's a trap. He intends—' My cries were drowned out by the thunder of the crowd, and I had not taken a second step when I was seized by each arm from behind. I tried to struggle free, but two of Rasfer's ruffians held me fast and started to drag me away. They had been placed there for just such a moment as this, to prevent me from warning my friend.

'Horus, give me strength!' I rendered up a swift and silent entreaty, and instead of resisting them I hurled myself back in the same direction as they were pulling me. For an instant they were thrown off-balance, and I broke half-free of their grasp. I managed to reach the edge of the stage before they could control me again.

'Horus, give me voice!' I prayed, and then screamed with all my breath, 'Tanus, beware! He means to kill you.'

This time my voice carried above that of the mob, and Tanus heard me. I saw his head flick and his eyes narrow slightly. However, Rasfer heard me as well. He responded instantly, breaking the rehearsed routine. Instead of dropping back before the whirlwind of cuts and thrusts that Tanus was aiming close to his brutish head, he stepped in and, with an upward sweep of his own blade, he forced Tanus' sword-arm high.

Without the benefit of surprise he would never have made the opening into which he now launched a thrust behind which was the full weight of those massive shoulders and mighty trunk. The point of his blade was aimed an inch below the rim of Tanus' helmet and directly at his right eye. It should have skewered his eye and cleaved his skull through and through.

However, my shouted warning had given Tanus that fleeting moment of grace in which to react. He recovered his guard just in time. With the pommel of his sword he managed to touch a glancing blow to Rasfer's wrist. It had just sufficient force to deflect the sword-point a finger's-width, and at the same moment Tanus tucked in his chin and rolled his head. It was too late to avoid the blow entirely. However, the stroke that might have skewered his eye and split his skull like a rotten melon, merely laid open his eyebrow to the bone, and then flew on over his shoulder.

Instantly a sheet of blood gushed from the shallow wound and flowed over Tanus' face, blinding his right eye. He was forced to fall back before the savage onslaught that Rasfer now launched at him. Desperately he gave ground, blinking at the blood and trying to wipe it away with his free hand. It seemed impossible that he would be able to defend himself, and if only I had not been held so securely by the palace guards, I would have drawn the little jewelled dagger at my belt and rushed to his aid.

Even without my assistance Tanus was able to survive that first murderous attack. Though he was wounded twice more, a gouge across the left thigh and a nick on the biceps of his sword-arm, he kept weaving and parrying and ducking. Rasfer kept coming at him, never letting him recover his balance or his full vision. Within minutes Rasfer was blowing and grunting like a giant forest hog, and running with sweat, his misshapen torso gleaming in the torchlight, but the speed and fury of his assault never faltered.

Though no great swordsman myself, I am a student of the art. So often had I watched Rasfer at practice in the weapons-yard that I knew his style intimately. I knew he was an exponent of the attack *khamsin*, the attack 'like the desert wind'. It was a manoeuvre that perfectly suited his brute strength and physique. I had seen him practise it on a hundred occasions and now I divined by his footwork that he was gathering himself for it, for that one last effort that would end it all.

Struggling in the grip of my captors, I screamed at Tanus

again, 'Khamsin! Be ready!' I thought that my warning had been drowned and washed away by the uproar that filled the temple, for Tanus showed no reaction. Later he told me he had indeed heard me, and that with his impaired vision that second warning of mine had certainly saved him once again.

Rasfer dropped back a half-pace, the classic prelude to the khamsin, relaxing the pressure for an instant to position his opponent for the coup. Then his weight shifted and his left foot swung forward into the lead. He used his momentum and all the strength of his right leg to launch his entire body into the attack, like some grotesque carrion-bird taking to flight. As both his feet left the ground, the point of his blade was aimed at Tanus' throat. It was inexorable. Nothing could prevent that deadly blade from flying true to its mark except the one classic defence, the stop-hit.

At the precise instant that Rasfer was fully committed to the stroke, Tanus launched himself with equal power and superior grace. Like an arrow leaving the bowstring, he flew straight at his opponent. As they met in mid-air Tanus gathered up Rasfer's blade with his own and let it run down on to the pommel, where it came up hard and short, stopping it dead. It was the perfectly executed stop-hit.

The mass and speed of the two big men were thrown on to the bronze blade in Rasfer's fist, and it could not withstand the shock. It snapped cleanly, and left him clutching only the sheared-off hilt. Then they were locked chest-to-chest once more. Although Tanus' sword was still undamaged, Rasfer had got in under his guard and he could not wield it. Both Tanus' hands, the sword still held in his right fist, were locked behind Rasfer's back as the two men heaved and strained at each other.

Wrestling is one of the military disciplines in which every warrior in the Egyptian army is trained. Bound to each other by the crushing embrace of arms, they spun about the stage, each attempting to throw the other off-balance, snarling into each other's eyes, hooking a heel to trip, butting at each other with the visors of their helmets, equally matched thus far in strength and determination.

The audience had long since sensed that this was no longer a mock engagement, but a fight to the death. I wondered that their appetites had not been jaded by all they had witnessed that evening, but it was not so. They were insatiable, howling for blood and yet more blood.

At last Rasfer tore his arm free of Tanus' encircling grip. He still clutched the hilt of the broken sword in his fist, and with the jagged edge he struck at Tanus' face, deliberately aiming at his eyes and the wound in his brow, trying to enlarge and aggravate it. Tanus twisted his head to avoid the blows, catching them on the peak of his bronze helmet. Like a python shifting its coils around its prey, he used the moment to adjust his crushing hold around Rasfer's chest. The strain that he was exerting was such that Rasfer's features began to swell and engorge with blood. The air was being forced out of him, and he struggled against suffocation. He began visibly to weaken. Tanus kept up the pressure until a carbuncle on Rasfer's back was stretched to bursting-point and the yellow pus erupted in a stinking stream and trickled down into the waistband of his kilt.

Already suffocating, Rasfer grimaced at the pain of the bursting abscess and checked. Tanus felt him falter, and he summoned some deep reserve of strength. He changed the angle of his next effort, dropping his shoulders slightly and forcing his opponent backwards and upwards on to his heels. Rasfer was off-balance, and Tanus heaved again and forced him back a pace. Once he had him moving backwards, he kept the momentum going. Still locked to his opponent, he ran Rasfer backwards across the stage, steering him towards one of the gigantic stone pillars. For a moment none of us realized Tanus' intention, and then we saw him drop the point of his sword to the horizontal and press the hilt hard against Rasfer's spine.

At a full run the point of Tanus' sword hit the unyielding column. The metal screeched against the granite, and the shock was transmitted up the blade. It stopped those two big men in their tracks, and the force of it drove the hilt into Rasfer's spine. It would have killed a lesser man, and even Rasfer was paralysed by it. With the last gust of his foul breath he let out a cry of agony, and his arms flew open. The broken haft of his own sword spun from his grip and skidded away across the stone pavement.

Rasfer's knees buckled, and he sagged in Tanus' arms. Tanus thrust his hip into him, and, with a heave of his upper body, hurled Rasfer over backwards. He landed so heavily that I heard more than one of his ribs crackle like dry twigs in the flames of the camp-fire. The back of his skull bounced upon the stone flags with a sound like a desert melon dropped from on high, and the breath from his lungs whistled out of his throat.

He groaned in agony. He had barely the strength to lift his arms to Tanus in capitulation. Tanus was so carried away by battle-rage, and inflamed by the roar of the crowd, that he was a man berserk. He stood over Rasfer and lifted his sword on high, gripping the hilt with both hands. He was a dreadful sight. Blood from the wound in his forehead had painted his visage into a glistening devil mask. Sweat and blood had soaked the hair of his chest and stained his clothing.

'Kill him!' roared the congregation. 'Kill the evil one!'

The point of Tanus' sword was aimed at the centre of Rasfer's chest, and I steeled myself for the down-stroke that would impale that gross body. I willed Tanus to do it, for I hated Rasfer more than any of them. The gods know that I had reason, for here was the monster who had gelded me, and I longed for my revenge.

It was in vain. I should have known my Tanus better than expect him to skewer a surrendered enemy. I saw the fires of madness begin to fade from his eyes. He shook his head slightly, as if to regain control of himself. Then, instead of stabbing down, he lowered his sword-point slowly until it just pricked Rasfer's chest. The keen point raised a drop of blood, bright as a garnet amongst the coarse hair of Rasfer's chest. Then Tanus picked up the lines of his script.

'Thus I bind you to my will, and I expel you from the light. May you wander through all eternity in the dark places. May you never more have power over the noble and the good amongst men. I give you to rule over the thief and the coward, over the bully and the cheat, over the liar and the murderer, over the grave-robber and the violater of virtuous women, over the blasphemer and the breaker of faith. From henceforth you are the god of all evil. Get you gone, and carry away with you the curse of Horus and of his resurrected father, Osiris.'

Tanus lifted the point of his sword from Rasfer's chest and tossed the weapon aside, deliberately disarming himself in the presence of his enemy to demonstrate his disdain and scorn. The blade clattered on the flagstones and Tanus strode to the running waters of our stage Nile and went down on one knee to scoop a handful and dash it into his own face, washing away the blood. Then he tore a strip of linen from the hem of his kilt and swiftly bound up the wound on his forehead to stem the bleeding.

Rasfer's two apes released me and rushed on stage to succour their fallen commander. They lifted him to his feet, and he staggered between them, heaving and blowing like a great obscene bullfrog. I saw that he was grievously injured. They dragged him from the stage, and the crowd howled its derision and hatred at him.

I watched my Lord Intef, and his expression was for the moment unguarded. I saw every one of my suspicions confirmed there. This was how he had planned to wreak his vengeance on Tanus – to have him slain before the eyes of the entire populace – and on his own daughter: to have her lover killed before her eyes – that was to have been Lostris' punishment for flouting her father's will.

My Lord Intef's frustration and disappointment now were enough to make me feel a smug satisfaction as I considered what retribution must be in store for Rasfer. He might have preferred more of the rough treatment that Tanus had dealt out to him, to the punishment that my Lord Intef would inflict upon him. My master was ever harsh with those who failed him.

Tanus was still gasping from the exertions of the duel, but now, as he moved to the front of the stage, he drew a dozen deep breaths to steady himself for the declamation that would bring the pageant to an end. As he faced the congregation it fell silent, for in blood and anger he was an awe-inspiring sight.

Tanus lifted up both his hands to the temple roof and cried out in a loud voice, 'Ammon-Ra, give me voice! Osiris, give me eloquence!' The traditional entreaty of the orator.

'Give him voice! Give him eloquence!' the crowd responded, and their faces were still rapt with all they had witnessed, but hungry for more entertainment.

Tanus was that unusual creature, a man of action who was also a man of words and ideas. I am sure that he would have been generous enough to admit that many of those ideas were planted in his mind by that lowly slave, Taita. However, once planted, they were in fertile ground.

When it came to oratory, Tanus' exhortations to his squadrons on the eve of battle were famous. Of course, I had not been present at all of these, but they had been relayed to me verbatim by Kratas, his faithful friend and lieutenant. I had copied many of these speeches down on a set of papyrus scrolls, for they were worthy of preservation.

Tanus had the common touch, and the ability to appeal directly to the ordinary man. I often thought that much of this special power of his sprang from his transparent honesty and his forthright manner. Men trusted him and followed willingly wherever he led them, even unto death itself.

I was still overwrought by the conflict we had all just witnessed and the closeness of Tanus' escape from the trap that my Lord Intef had laid for him. Nevertheless, I was eager to listen to the declamation that Tanus had prepared without my help or advice. To be truthful, I was still a little resentful that he had declined my assistance, and more than a little nervous as to what he might come out with. Tact and subtlety have never been Tanus' most no.able virtues.

Now Pharaoh made a gesture of invitation to him to speak, crossing and uncrossing the ceremonial crook and flail, and inclining his head gracefully. The congregation was silent and intent, leaning forward eagerly so as not to miss a single word.

'It is I, Horus the falcon-headed, that speaks,' Tanus began, and they encouraged him.

'It is verily the falcon-headed! Hear him!'

'*Ha-Ka-Ptah!*' Tanus used the archaic form from which the present name of Egypt was derived. Very few realized that the original meaning was the temple of Ptah. 'I speak to you of this ancient land given to us ten thousand years since, in the time when all the gods were young. I speak to you of the two kingdoms that in nature are one and indivisible.'

Pharaoh nodded. This was the standard dogma, approved by

both temporal and religious authority that neither recognized the impostor in the Lower Kingdom, nor even acknowledged his existence.

'Oh, *Kemit*!' Tanus used another ancient name for Egypt: the Black Land, after the colour of the Nile mud brought down by the annual inundation. 'I speak to you of this land riven and divided, torn by civil war, bleeding and drained of treasure.' My own shock was mirrored on the faces of all those who listened to him. Tanus had just given voice to the unspeakable. I wanted to rush on to the stage and clap my hand over his mouth to prevent him from going on, but I was transfixed.

'Oh, *Ta-Meri*!' Another old name: the Beloved Earth. Tanus had learned well the history I had taught him. 'I speak to you of old and feeble generals, and admirals too weak and indecisive to wrest back the stolen kingdom from the usurper. I speak to you of ancient men in their dotage who waste your treasure and spill the blood of your finest young men as though it were the lees of bitter wine.'

In the second row of the audience I saw Nembet, the Great Lion of Egypt, flush with anger and scratch furiously with chagrin at his beard. The other elderly military men around him frowned and moved restlessly on their benches, rattling their swords in their scabbards as a sign of their disapproval. Amongst them all, only my Lord Intef smiled as he watched Tanus escape from one trap only to blunder into the next.

'Our *Ta-Meri* is beset by a host of enemies, and yet the sons of the nobles prefer to cut off their own thumbs rather than to carry the sword to protect her.' As he said this, Tanus looked keenly at Menset and Sobek, Lostris' older brothers, where they sat beside their father in the second row. The king's decree exempted from military service only those with such physical disability as to render them unfit. The surgeon priests at the temple of Osiris had perfected the art of removing the top joint of the thumb with little pain or danger of infection, thus rendering it impossible for that hand to wield a sword or pluck a bowstring. The young bucks proudly flaunted their mutilations as they sat gambling and carousing in the riverside taverns. They considered the missing digit a mark not of cowardice, but of sophistication and independent spirit.

'War is the game played by old men with the lives of the young,' I had heard Lostris' brothers argue. 'Patriotism is a myth conceived by those old rogues to draw us into the infernal game. Let them fight as they will, but we want no part of it.' In vain I had remonstrated with them that the privilege of Egyptian citizenship carried with it duties and responsibilities. They dismissed me with the arrogance of the young and ignorant.

Now, however, beneath Tanus' level stare they fidgeted and concealed their left hands in the folds of their clothing. They were both of them right-handed, but had convinced the recruiting officer to the contrary, with their eloquence and a dash of gold.

The common people at the rear of the great hall hummed and stamped their feet in agreement with what Tanus had said. It was their sons who filled the rowing-benches of the war galleys, or marched under arms through the desert sands.

However, in the wings of the stage I wrung my hands in despair. With that little speech Tanus had made an enemy of fifty of the young nobles in the audience. They were men who would one day inherit power and influence in the Upper Kingdom. Their enmity outweighed a hundred times the adoration of the common herd and I prayed for Tanus to cease. In a few minutes he had done enough damage to last us all a hundred years, but he went on blithely.

'Oh, *Ta-Nutri*!' This was yet another ancient name: the Land of the Gods. 'I speak to you of the wrong-doer and the robber who waits in ambush on every hilltop and in every thicket. The farmer is forced to plough with his shield at his side, and the traveller must go with his sword bared.'

Again the commoners applauded. The depredations of the robber bands were a terrible scourge upon them all. No man was safe beyond the mud walls of the towns, and the robber chieftains who called themselves the Shrikes were arrogant and fearless. They respected no law but their own, and no man was safe from them.

Tanus had struck exactly the right note with the people, and suddenly I was moved by the notion that this was all much deeper than it seemed. Revolutions have been forged and dynasties of pharaohs overturned by just such appeals to the masses. With Tanus' next words my suspicion was strengthened.

'While the poor cry out under the lash of the tax-collector, the nobles anoint the buttocks of their fancy boys with the most precious oils of the orient—' A roar went up from the rear of the hall, and my fears were replaced by a tremulous excitement. Had this been carefully planned? Was Tanus more subtle and devious than I had ever given him credit for?

'By Horus!' I cried in my heart. 'The land is ripe for revolution, and who better to lead it than Tanus?' I felt only disappointment that he had not taken me into his confidence and made me party to his design. I could have planned a revolution as skilfully and as cunningly as I could design a water-garden or write a play.

I craned to look over the heads of the congregation, expecting at the very next moment to see Kratas and his brother officers burst into the temple at the head of a company of warriors from the squadron. I felt the hair on my forearms and at the nape of my neck lift with excitement as I pictured them snatching the double crown from Pharaoh's head and placing it upon the blood-smeared brow of Tanus. With what joy I would have joined the cry of 'Long live Pharaoh! Long live King Tanus!'

Heady images swirled before my eyes as Tanus went on speaking. I saw the prophecy of the desert oracle fulfilled. I dreamed of Tanus, with my Lady Lostris beside him, seated on the white throne of this very Egypt, with myself standing behind them resplendent in the apparel of the grand vizier of the Upper Kingdom. But why, oh why, had he not consulted me before embarking on this perilous venture?

With his next breath he made the reason plain. I had misjudged my Tanus, my honest, plain and good Tanus, my noble, straight and trustworthy Tanus, lacking only in guile and stealth and deceit.

This was no plot. This was simply Tanus speaking his mind without fear or favour. The commoners, who only moments before had been clinging enraptured to every word that fell from his tongue, were now quite unexpectedly given the sharp edge of that organ as he rounded upon them.

'Hear me, oh Egypt! What is to become of a land where the mean-spirited try to suppress the mighty amongst them; where the patriot is reviled; where there is no man of yesterday revered for his wisdom; where the petty and the envious seek to tear down the men of worth to their own base level?'

There was no cheering now as those at the back of the hall recognized themselves in this description. Effortlessly my Tanus had succeeded in alienating every man amongst them, great and small, rich and poor. Oh, why had he not consulted me, I mourned, and the answer was plain. He had not consulted me because he knew I would have counselled him against it.

'What order is there in society where the slave is free with his tongue, and counts himself as equal to those of noble birth?' he blazed at them. 'Should the son revile his father and scorn the wisdom paid for in grey hairs and wrinkled brow? Should the waterfront harlot wear rings of lapis lazuli and set herself above the virtuous wife?'

By Horus, he would not spare one of them from the lash of his tongue, I thought bitterly. As always, he was completely oblivious to his own safety in the pursuit of what he saw as the right and open way.

Only one person in the temple was enchanted with what he had to tell them. Lostris appeared at my side and gripped my arm.

'Isn't he wonderful, Taita?' she breathed. 'Every word he utters is the truth. Tonight he is truly a young god.'

I could find neither the words nor the heart to agree with her, and I hung my head in sorrow as Tanus went on relentlessly.

'Pharaoh, you are the father of the people. We cry out to you for protection and for succour. Give the affairs of state and war into the hands of honest and clever men. Send the rogues and the fools to rot on their estates. Call off the faithless priests and the usurious servants of the state, those parasites upon the body of this *Ta-Meri* of ours.'

Horus knows that I am as good a priest-hater as the best of them, but only a fool or very brave man would call down the wrath of every god-botherer in Egypt upon his own head, for their power is infinite and their hatred implacable. While as for the civil servants, their lines of influence and corruption have been set up over the centuries and my Lord Intef was the chief of them all. I shuddered in pity for my dear blunt friend as he went on handing out instructions to Pharaoh on how to restructure the whole of Egyptian society.

'Heed the words of the sage! Oh, king, honour the artist and the scribe. Reward the brave warrior and the faithful servant. Root out the bandits and the robbers from their desert fastnesses. Give the people example and direction in their lives, so that this very Egypt may once again flourish and be great.'

Tanus fell to his knees in the centre of the stage and spread his arms wide. 'Oh, Pharaoh, you are our father. We protest our love to you. In return, show us now a father's love. Hear our entreaties, we beg of you.'

Up to that moment I had been stupefied by the depths of my friend's folly, but now, much too late, I regained my wits and signalled frantically for my stage-hands to drop the curtain before Tanus could do any further damage. As the gleaming folds of cloth floated down and hid him from their view, the audience sat in stunned silence, as though they did not believe all that they had heard and seen that night.

It was Pharaoh himself who broke the spell. He rose to his feet, and his face behind the stiff white make-up was inscrutable. As he swept from the temple, the congregation prostrated itself before him. Before he too went down in obeisance, I saw my Lord Intef's expression. It was triumphant.

 I ESCORTED Tanus back from the temple to his own sparsely furnished quarters close to the dock at which his squadron was moored. Although I walked beside him with my hand on the hilt of my dagger, prepared for the consequences of his foolhardy honesty to be visited on us immediately, Tanus was quite unrepentant. Indeed, he seemed oblivious to the depths of his folly and inordinately pleased with himself. I have often remarked how a man freshly released from terrible strain and mortal danger becomes garrulous and elated. Even Tanus, the hardened warrior, was no exception.

'It was time somebody stood up and said what needed to be said, don't you agree, old friend?' His voice rang clear and loud down the darkened alley, as though he were determined to summon any awaiting assassin to us. I kept my agreement muted.

'You did not expect it of me, did you now? Be honest with me, Taita. It took you quite by surprise, did it not?'

'It surprised us all.' This time I could agree with a little more enthusiasm. 'Even Pharaoh was taken aback, as well he might be.'

'He listened, Taita. He took it all in, I could tell. I did good work this evening, don't you think so?'

When I attempted to raise the subject of Rasfer's treacherous attack upon him and broach the possibility that it might have been inspired by my Lord Intef, Tanus would have none of it. 'That is impossible, Taita. You dreamed it. Lord Intef was my father's dearest friend. How could he wish me ill? Besides, I am to be his son-in-law, am I not?' And despite his injuries he let out such a happy shout of laughter that it roused the sleepers in the darkened huts that we were passing and they shouted grumpily back at us to be quiet. Tanus ignored their protests.

'No, no, I am sure that you are wrong,' he cried. 'It was simply Rasfer working out his spite in his own charming way. Well, he'll know better next time.' He threw his arm around my shoulders and hugged me so hard that it hurt. 'You saved me twice tonight. Without your warnings Rasfer would have had me both times. How do you do these things, Taita? I swear you are a secret warlock, and have the gift of the inner eye.' He laughed again.

How could I stifle his joy? He was like a boy, a big rumbustious boy. I could not help but love him all the more. This was not the time to point out the danger in which he had placed himself and all of us who were his friends.

Let him have his hour, and tomorrow I would sound the voice of reason and of caution. So I took him home and stitched the gash in his forehead, and washed his other wounds and anointed them with my special mixture of honey and herbs to prevent mortification. Then I gave him a stiff draught of the Red Shepenn and left the good Kratas to guard his slumbers.

When I reached my own quarters well after midnight, there were two summonses awaiting me: one from my Lady Lostris and the other from the vanquished Rasfer. There was no doubt as to which of them I would have responded to if I had been given the choice, but I was not. Rasfer's two thugs almost dragged me away to where he lay on a sweat-soaked mattress, cursing and moaning by turns, and calling on Seth and all the gods to witness his pain and his fortitude.

'Good Taita!' he greeted me, raising himself painfully on one elbow, 'you will not believe the pain. My chest is afire. I swear every bone in it is crushed, and my head aches as though it is bound by thongs of rawhide.'

With very little effort I was able to force back my tears of pity, but it is a strange thing about those of us who are doctors and healers that we cannot find it in our hearts to deny our skills to even the most abominable creatures that require them. I sighed with resignation, unpacked the leather bag that contained my medical equipment and set out my instruments and unguents.

I was delighted to find that Rasfer's self-diagnosis was perfectly valid, and that apart from numerous contusions and shallow wounds, at least three of his ribs were broken and there was a lump on the back of his head almost the size of my fist. I had, therefore, a perfectly legitimate reason for adding considerably to his discomfort. One of the broken ribs was seriously out of alignment and there was genuine danger that it might pierce the lung. While his two thugs held him down and Rasfer squealed and howled most gratifyingly, I manipulated the rib back into place and strapped up his chest with linen bandages well soaked in vinegar to shrink as they dried.

Then I addressed myself to the lump on the back of his skull where it had struck the stone paving. The gods are often generous. When I held a lamp to Rasfer's eyes the pupils did not dilate. There was not the least doubt in my mind as to what treatment was required. Bloody fluid was gathering inside that unlovely skull. Without my help Rasfer would be dead by the following sunset. I thrust aside the obvious temptation and reminded myself of the surgeon's duty to his patient.

There are probably only three surgeons in all of Egypt who are capable of trepanning a skull with a good chance of success, and personally I would not put much faith in the other two. Once again I ordered Rasfer's two oafs to take hold of him to control his struggles, and to hold him face down on his mattress. By the roughness of their handling and their obvious disregard for their master's injured ribs, I surmised that they were not exactly overflowing with loving feeling towards their master.

Once again a chorus of howls and squeals turned the night hideous and gladdened my labours, as I made a semi-circular incision around the lump on his scalp, and then peeled a large flap of skin away from the bone. Now not even those two strapping ruffians could hold him down. His struggles were splashing blood as high as the ceiling of the room and sprinkling us all, so that we seemed to be inflicted with a red pox. At last, in exasperation, I ordered them to bind his ankles and wrists to the bedposts with leather straps.

'Oh, gentle and sweet Taita, the pain is beyond belief. Give me but a drop of that flower juice, I beg you, dear friend,' he blubbered.

Now that he was safely bound to the bed, I could afford to be frank with him. 'I understand, my good Rasfer, just how you feel. I also would have been grateful for a little of the flower when last you took the knife to me. Alas, old comrade, my store of the drug is finished, and there will not be another eastern caravan for at least a month,' I lied cheerfully, for very few knew that I cultivated the Red Shepenn myself. Knowing that the best was yet to come, I reached for my bone-drill.

The human head is the only part of the body that puzzles me as a doctor. At the orders of my Lord Intef the corpses of all executed criminals are handed over to me. In addition Tanus has been able to bring me many fine specimens from the battlefield, suitably pickled in vats of brine. All these I have dissected and studied so that I know every bone and how it fits into its exact place in the skeleton. I have traced the route by which food enters the mouth and passes through the body. I have found that great and wondrous organ, the heart, nestling between the pale air-bladders of the lungs. I have studied the rivers of the body through which the blood flows, and I have observed the two types of blood which determine the moods and emotions of man.

There is, of course, that bright joyous blood that, when released by the cut of a scalpel or the headsman's axe, spurts out in regular impulses. This is the blood of happy thoughts and fine emotions, it is the blood of love and kindness. Then there is that darker sullen blood that flows without the vigour and the bounding joy of the other. This is the blood of anger and of sorrow, of melancholic thoughts and evil deeds.

All these matters I have studied, and have filled one hundred papyrus rolls with my observations. There is no man in the world that I know of who has gone to such lengths, certainly none of those quacks in the temple with their amulets and their incantations have done so. I doubt any one of them could tell the liver from the sphincter of the anus without an invocation to Osiris, a casting of the divining dice and a fat fee paid in advance.

In all modesty I can say that I have never met a man who understands the human body better than I, and yet the head is still a puzzle to me. Naturally I understand that the eyes see, the nose smells, the mouth tastes and the ears hear – but what is the purpose of that pale porridge that fills the gourd of the skull?

I have never been able to fathom it myself, and no man has ever been able to offer me a satisfactory explanation, except that Tanus came closest to it. After he and I had spent an evening together sampling the latest vintage of red wine, he had woken in the dawn and suggested with a groan, 'Seth has placed this thing in our heads as his revenge on mankind.'

I once met a man who was travelling with a caravan from beyond those legendary twin rivers, the Tigris and the Euphrates, who professed to have studied the same problem. He was a wise man and together we debated many mysteries over the course of half a year. At one point he suggested that all human emotion and thought sprang not from the heart, but from those soft amorphous curds that make up the brain. I mention this naïve assertion only to demonstrate how gravely even an intelligent and learned man can err.

Nobody who has ever considered that mighty organ, the heart, leaping with its own life in the centre of our body, fed by great rivers of blood, protected by the palisades of bone, can doubt that this is the fountain from which all thought and emotion springs. The heart uses the blood to disseminate these emotions throughout the body. Have you ever felt your heart stir within you and quicken to beautiful music, or a lovely face, or the fine words of a moving speech? Have you ever felt anything leaping around inside your head? Even the wise man from the East had to capitulate before my ruthless logic.

No rational man can believe that a bloodless puddle of curdled milk lying inert in its bony jar could conjure up the lines of a poem or the design of a pyramid, could cause a man to love or to wage war. Even the embalmers scoop it out and discard it when they prepare a corpse for the long journey.

There is, however, a paradox here in that if this glutinous mass is interfered with, even by the pressure of trapped fluid upon it, the patient is certainly doomed. It requires an intimate knowledge of the structure of the head and a quite marvellous dexterity to be able to drill through the skull without disturbing the sac that contains this porridge. I have both these attributes.

As I ground down slowly through the bone, encouraged by Rasfer's bellows, I paused regularly to wash away the bone chips and filings by splashing vinegar into the wound. The sting of the liquid added little to the patient's well-being, but revived the flagging volume of his voice.

Suddenly the sharp bronze drill bit cleanly through the skull, and a tiny but perfect circle of bone was blown out of the wound by the pressure within. It was followed immediately by a spurt of dark, clotted blood that hit me in the face. Immediately Rasfer relaxed under me. I knew, not without a sneaking pang of regret, that he would survive. As I stitched the flap of scalp back into place, covering the aperture in the depths of which the dura mater pulsed ominously, I wondered if I had truly done mankind a great service by preserving this specimen of it.

111

When I left Rasfer with his head swathed in bandages, snoring and whimpering in porcine self-pity, I found that I was completely exhausted. The excitements and alarums of the day had expended even my vast store of energy. However, there was to be no rest for me yet, for my Lady Lostris' messenger still hovered on the terrace of my quarters and pounced on me as I set foot on the first step. I was allowed only sufficient grace to wash away Rasfer's blood and change my soiled raiment.

As I tottered into her chamber, barely able to place one foot before the other, my Lady Lostris met me with blazing eyes and ominously tapping foot. 'Just where do you think you have been hiding yourself, Master Taita?' she lashed out at me immediately. 'I sent for you before the second watch, and it's now not much short of dawn. How dare you keep me waiting so? Sometimes you forget your station. You know full well the punishment for impertinent slaves—' She was in full flight, having let her impatience brew for all these hours. In anger her beauty is stunning, and when she stamped her foot in that adorable gesture that was so typically her own, I thought that my heart must burst with my love for her.

'Don't you stand there grinning at me!' she flared at me. 'I am so truly angry that I could order you flogged.' She stamped her foot again, and I felt the tiredness fall from my shoulders like a heavy load. Her mere presence had the power to revitalize me.

'My lady, what a wondrous role you played this night. It seemed to me and all who watched you that it was indeed the divine goddess that walked amongst us—'

'Don't you dare try your tricks with me.' She stamped for the third time, but without conviction. 'You'll not wriggle out of this so easily—'

'Truly, my lady, as I walked back from the temple through the crowded streets, your name was on every tongue. They said your singing was the finest they had ever heard, and had quite stolen every heart.'

'I believe not a word,' she declared, but she was clearly having difficulty sustaining her fury. 'In fact I thought my voice was awful this evening. I was flat at least once, and off-key on numerous—'

'I must contradict you, mistress. You were never better. And what beauty! It lit the whole temple.' She is not truly vain, my Lady Lostris, but she is a woman.

'You awful man!' she cried in exasperation. 'I was ready to have you flogged this time, I truly was. But come and sit beside me on the bed and tell me all about it. I am still so excited that I am sure I will not sleep for a week.' She took my hand and led me to the bed, babbling on happily about Tanus, and how he must have won every heart as well as Pharaoh's with his wonderful performance and fearless speech, and how the infant Horus had beshat her dress, and did I truly think that she had sung even passing well, and wasn't I just saying so?

At last I had to stop her. 'My lady, it is almost dawn and we must be ready to leave with all the court to accompany the king when he crosses the river to inspect his funerary temple and his tomb. You must get some sleep if you are to look your best on such an important state occasion.'

'I'm not sleepy, Taita,' she protested, and went chattering on, only to slump against my shoulder a few minutes later, fallen asleep in mid-sentence.

Gently, I slipped her head down on to the carved wooden headrest and covered her with a rug of colobus monkey furs. I could not bring myself to leave immediately but hovered beside her bed. At last I placed a gentle kiss upon her cheek. She did not open her eyes, but whispered sleepily, 'Do you think there will be an opportunity for me to speak to the king tomorrow? Only he will be able to prevent my father sending Tanus away.'

I could think of no ready answer for her, and while I still dithered, she fell fully asleep.

I COULD scarcely drag myself from my couch at dawn, for I seemed barely to have closed my eyes to sleep before it was time to open them again. My reflection in the bronze mirror was haggard and my eyes were underscored in purple. Swiftly I touched on make-up to cover the worst of my sorry condition, enhancing the hollows of my eyes with kohl and my pale features with a brushing of antimony. Two of the slave boys combed out my hair and I was so pleased with the result that I felt almost cheerful as I hurried down to the grand vizier's private dock where the great state barge lay moored.

I was amongst the last to join the throng upon the quay, but no one seemed to notice my late arrival, not even my Lady Lostris who was already on the deck of the barge. I watched her for a while.

She had been invited to join the royal women. These comprised not only the king's wives, but his numerous concubines and all his daughters. Of course these last were the cause of much of Pharaoh's unhappiness, a flock of them ranging in age from crawlers and toddlers to others of marriageable age, and not a son amongst them. How was Pharaoh's immortality to be maintained without a male line to carry it forward?

It was difficult to believe that, like me, Lostris had not slept more than an hour or two, for she seemed as sweet and fresh as one of the desert roses in my garden. Even in that glittering array of feminine beauty that had been hand-picked by Pharaoh's factors or sent to him in tribute by his satraps at the ends of the empire, Lostris stood out like a swallow in a flock of drab little desert larks.

I looked for Tanus, but his squadron was already lying well upstream, ready to escort Pharaoh's crossing, and the reflection of the rising sun turned the surface of the river into a dazzling silver sheet that blinded the eye. I could not look into it.

At that moment there was the steady boom of a drum, and the populace craned to watch Pharaoh's stately progress down from the palace to the royal barge.

This morning he wore the light *nemes* crown of starched and folded linen, secured around his forehead with the gold band of the *uraeus*. The erect golden cobra, with its hood flared and its garnet eyes glittering, rose up from his brow. The cobra was the symbol of the powers of life and death that Pharaoh held over his subjects. The king was not carrying the crook and flail, only the golden sceptre. After the double crown itself, this was the most holy treasure of all the crown jewels and was reputed to be over a thousand years old.

Despite all the regalia and the ceremonial, Pharaoh wore no make-up. Under the direct rays of the early sun, and without make-up to disguise the fact, Mamose himself was unremarkable. Just a soft little godling of late middle age, with a small round paunch bulging over the waistband of his kilt and features intricately carved with lines of worry.

As he passed where I stood, it seemed he recognized me, for he nodded slightly. I immediately prostrated myself on the paving, and he paused and made a sign for me to approach. I crawled forward on hands and knees, and knocked my forehead three times on the ground at his feet.

'Are you not Taita, the poet?' he asked in that thin and petulant voice of his.

'I am Taita the slave, your Majesty,' I replied. There are times when a little humility is called for. 'But I am also a poor scribbler.'

'Well, Taita the slave, you scribbled to good effect last night. I have never been so well entertained by a pageant. I shall issue a royal edict declaring your poor scribblings to be the official version.'

He announced this loud enough for all the court to hear, and even my Lord Intef, who followed him closely, beamed with pleasure. As I was his slave, the honour belonged to him more than to me. However, Pharaoh was not finished with me yet.

'Tell me, Taita the slave, are you not also the same surgeon who recently prescribed to me?'

'Majesty, I am that same humble slave who has the temerity to practise a little medicine.'

'Then when shall your cure take effect?' He dropped his voice so that only I could hear the question.

'Majesty, the event will take place nine months after you have

115

fulfilled all those conditions that I listed for you.' As we were now in a surgeon-and-patient relationship, I felt emboldened to add, 'Have you followed the diet I set you?'

'By Isis' bountiful breasts!' he exclaimed with an unexpected twinkle in his eye. 'I am so full of bull's balls, it is a wonder that I do not bellow when a herd of cows passes the palace.'

He was in such pleasant mood that I tried a little joke of my own. 'Has Pharaoh found the heifer I suggested?'

'Alas, doctor, it is not as simple as it would seem. The prettiest flowers are soonest visited by the bee. You did stipulate that she must be completely untouched, did you not?'

'Virgin and untouched, and within a season of her first red moon,' I added quickly, making it as difficult as possible to put my recipe to the test. 'Have you found one who meets that description, Majesty?'

His expression changed again, and he smiled thoughtfully. The smile looked out of place on those melancholy features. 'We shall see,' he murmured. 'We shall see.' And he turned and mounted the boarding-ladder of the barge. As my Lord Intef drew level with me, he made a small gesture, ordering me to fall in behind him, and so I followed him up on to the deck of the royal barge.

The wind had dropped during the night and the dark waters of the river seemed heavy and quiet as oil in the jar, disturbed only by those streaks and whirlpools upon the surface where the eternal current ran deep and swift. Even Nembet should be able to make the crossing in these conditions, although Tanus' squadron stood by in most unflattering fashion, as if Tanus was preparing to rescue him from error once again.

My Lord Intef drew me aside as soon as we reached the deck. 'You still have the power to surprise me sometimes, my old darling,' he whispered, and squeezed my arm. 'Just when I was seriously beginning to doubt your loyalty.'

I was taken aback by this sudden flush of goodwill, since the welts from Rasfer's lash across my back still ached. However, I bowed my head to shield my expression and waited for him to give me direction before committing myself, which he did immediately.

'I could not have written a more appropriate declamation for

Tanus to recite before Pharaoh if I had tried myself. Where that imbecile Rasfer failed so dismally, you retrieved the day for me in your usual style.' It was only then that it all fell into place. He believed that I was the author of Tanus' monumental folly, and that I had composed it for his benefit. In the uproar of the temple he could not have heard my shouted warnings to Tanus, or he would have known better.

'I am pleased that you are pleased,' I whispered back to him. I felt an enormous sense of relief. My position of influence had not been compromised. It was not my own skin I was thinking of at that moment – well, not entirely. I was thinking of Tanus and Lostris. They would need every bit of help and protection that I could give them during the stormy days that lay ahead for both of them. I was grateful that I was still in a position to be of some use to them.

'It was no less than my duty.' Thus I made the most of this windfall.

'You will find me grateful,' my Lord Intef replied. 'Do you remember the piece of ground on the canal behind the temple of Thoth that we discussed some time ago?'

'Indeed, my lord.' We both knew that I had hankered after that plot for ten years. It would make a perfect writer's retreat and a place to which I could retire in my old age.

'It is yours. At my next assize, bring the deed to me for my signature.' I was stunned and appalled by the vile manner in which it had come into my possession, as payment for an imagined piece of treachery on my part. For a moment I thought of rejecting the gift, but only for a moment. By the time I had recovered from my shock we were across the river and pulling into the mouth of the canal that led across the plain to Pharaoh Mamose's great funerary temple.

I had surveyed this canal with only minimal help from the royal architects, as I had planned virtually single-handed the whole complicated business of the transport of Pharaoh's body from the place of his death to the funerary temple where the mummification process would take place.

I had assumed that he would die at his palace on lovely little Elephantine Island. Therefore his corpse would be brought down-river in the state barge. I had designed the canal to accommodate the huge ship snugly. So now she slipped into it as neatly as the sword into its scabbard.

Straight as the blade of my dagger, the canal cut through the black loam soil of the riparian plain two thousand paces to the foot of the gaunt Saharan foothills. Tens of thousands of slaves had laboured over the years to build it, and to line it with stone blocks. As the barge nosed into the canal, two hundred sturdy slaves seized the tow-ropes from the bows and began to draw her smoothly across the plain. They sang one of the sad melodious work chants as they marched in ranks along the tow-path. The peasants working in the fields beside the canal ran to welcome us. They crowded to the bank, calling blessing on the king and waving palm-fronds, as the great barge moved majestically by.

When at last we slid into the stone dock below the outer walls of the half-finished temple, the slaves made the tow-ropes fast to the mooring-rings. So precise was my design that the entry port in the bulwark of the state barge lined up exactly with the portals of the main gate to the temple.

As the huge vessel came to rest, the trumpeter in the bows blew a fanfare on his gazelle horn, and the portcullis was raised slowly, to reveal the royal hearse waiting in the gateway attended by the company of embalmers in their crimson robes and fifty priests of Osiris in rank behind them.

The priests began to chant as they trundled the hearse forward on its wooden rollers, on to the deck of the barge. Pharaoh clapped his hands with delight and hurried forward to examine this grotesque vehicle.

I had taken no part in the conception of this celebration of bad taste. It was entirely the work of the priests. Suffice it only to say that in the naked sunlight, the superabundant gold-work shone so brightly as to offend the eye almost as painfully as did the actual design. Such weight of gold forced the priests to pant and sweat as they manhandled the clumsy ark on to the deck, and it listed even the great ship alarmingly. That weight of gold could have filled all the grain stores of the Upper Kingdom, or built and fitted out fifty squadrons of fighting ships and paid their crews for ten years. Thus the inept craftsman attempts to hide the paucity of his inspiration behind a dazzle of treasure. If only they had given me such material to work with, they might have seen something different.

This monstrosity was destined to be sealed in the tomb with Pharaoh's dead body. No matter that its construction had contributed largely to the financial ruin of the kingdom, Pharaoh was delighted with it.

At my Lord Intef's suggestion, the king mounted the vehicle and took his seat on the platform designed to carry his sarcophagus. From there he beamed about him, all his dignity and royal reserve forgotten. He was probably enjoying himself as much as he ever had in all his gloomy life, I reflected with a pang of pity. His death was to be the pinnacle to which most of his living energy and anticipation were directed.

On what was clearly an impulse, he beckoned my Lord Intef to join him on the ark and then looked around the crowded deck as if seeking someone else in the throng. He seemed to find who he wanted, for he stooped slightly and said something to the grand vizier.

My Lord Intef smiled and, following his direction, singled out my Lady Lostris. With a gesture he ordered her to come to him on the ark. She was clearly flustered, and blushed under her make-up, a rare phenomenon for one who was so seldom caught out of countenance. However, she recovered swiftly, and mounted the carriage with girlish, long-legged grace that as usual carried every eye with her.

She knelt before the king and touched her forehead three times to the floor of the platform. Then, in front of all the priests and the entire court, Pharaoh did an extraordinary thing. He reached down and took Lostris' hand, and lifted her to her feet, and seated her beside him on the platform. It was beyond all protocol, there was no precedent for it, and I saw his ministers exchange looks of amazement.

Then something else happened of which even they were not aware. When I was very young there had lived in the boys' quarters an old deaf slave who had befriended me. It was he who had taught me to read men's speech not only by the sound of it, but also by the shape of their lips as they formed the words. It was a very useful accomplishment. With it I could follow a conversation at the far end of a crowded hall, with musicians playing and a hundred men around me laughing and shouting at each other.

Now, before my eyes I saw Pharaoh say softly to my Lady Lostris, 'Even in daylight you are as divine as was the goddess Isis in the torchlight of the temple.'

The shock of it was like the blow of a fist in my stomach. Had I been blind, I berated myself desperately, or had I merely been stupid? Surely any imbecile must have anticipated the direction in which my capricious meddling must incline the order in which the dice of destiny might fall.

My facetious advice to the king must inevitably have had the effect of directing his attention towards my Lady Lostris. It was as though some malignant impulse below the surface of my mind had set out to describe her precisely to him as the mother of his first-born son. The most beautiful virgin in the land, to be taken within the first season after her moon had flowered – it was her exactly. And then, of course, by casting her as the leading female in the pageant, I had managed to display her to the king in the kindest possible light.

What I suddenly realized was about to happen was all of it my fault, as much as though I had deliberately engineered it. What is more, there was nothing I could do about it now. I stood in the sunlight so appalled and stricken with remorse that for a while I was deprived of the powers of speech and of reason.

When the sweating priests shoved the hearse off the deck and through the gateway, the crowd around me started after it and I was borne along with them willy-nilly, as though I were a leaf upon a stream without direction of my own. Before I was able to recover my wits I found myself within the forecourt of the funerary temple. I began to push my way forward, jostling those ahead of me to get past them and to reach the side of the hearse before it came to the main entrance of the royal mortuary.

As one team of priests pushed the vehicle forward, a second team picked up the wooden rollers that were left behind it and ran forward to place them ahead of the ponderous golden vehicle. There was a short delay as the carriage reached that area of the courtyard that had not yet been paved. While the priests spread straw ahead of the rollers to smooth the passage over this rough ground, I slipped quickly around the back of the row of huge carved stone lions that lined the carriageway, and hurried down this clear space until I was level with the ark. When one of the priests tried to bar my way and prevent me reaching the side of the vehicle, I gave him such a look as would have made one of the stone lions quail, and spat a single word at him that was seldom heard in the temple confines and caused him to step hurriedly aside and let me pass.

When I reached the near side of the ark I found myself directly below Lostris, close enough to stretch up and touch her arm, and to hear every word she addressed to the king. I could tell at once that she had completely recovered her poise which Pharaoh's unexpected interest in her had disturbed, and was now setting out to be as agreeable as possible to him. Miserably, I recalled how she had planned to do exactly this, and to use his favour to secure his agreement to her marriage to Tanus. As recently as last evening I had dismissed it as girlish prattle, but now it was happening, and it was beyond my power to prevent it or to warn her of the dangerous waters into which she was steering.

If, earlier in this chronicle, I have given the impression that my Lady Lostris was a flighty child with not a thought in her pretty head other than romantic nonsense and her own frivolous enjoyment of life, then I have fallen short in my efforts as historian of these extraordinary events. Although still so young, she was at times mature far beyond her years. Our Egyptian girls bloom early in the Nile sunlight. She was also a diligent scholar, with a bright mind and a thoughtful and enquiring side to her nature, all of which I had done my very best over the years to foster and develop.

Under my tutelage she had reached the stage where she could debate with the priests the most obscure religious dogma, could hold her own with the palace lawyers on such matters as the Land Tenure Acts and the extremely complicated Irrigation Act that regulated the usage of the waters from the Nile. Of course, she had read and absorbed every single one of the scrolls in the palace library. These included several hundred of which I was the author, from my medical treatises to my definitive essays on the tactics of naval warfare, together with my astrological scrolls on the names and natures of all the heavenly bodies, and my manuals on archery and swordsmanship, horticulture and falconry. She could even argue with me my own principles of architecture, and compare them to those of the great Imhotep.

Thus she was perfectly equipped to discuss any subject from astrology to the practice of war, from politics or the building of temples to the measurement and regulation of the Nile waters, all of which were subjects that fascinated Pharaoh. In addition she could rhyme and riddle and coin an amusing pun, and her vocabulary was almost as extensive as my own. In short, she was an accomplished conversationalist, with a ready sense of humour. She was articulate and had an enchanting voice and a merry little laugh. Truly, no man or god could resist her, especially if she could offer to someone without a son the promise of an heir.

I had to warn her, and yet how could a slave intrude upon the congress of persons so infinitely high above his own station? I skipped nervously beside the carriage, listening to my Lady Lostris' voice at its most enthralling as she set herself out to engage the king's fancy.

She was describing to him the manner in which his funerary temple had been laid out to conform to the most propitious astronomical aspects, those of the moon and the zodiac at the time of Pharaoh's birth. Of course she was merely repeating knowledge that she had gleaned from me, for I was the one who had surveyed and orientated the temple to the heavenly bodies. However, she was so convincing that I found myself following her explanations as though I was hearing them for the first time.

The funeral ark passed between the pylons of the inner court of the temple and rolled down the long colonnaded atrium, past the barred and guarded doors to the six treasuries in which were manufactured and stored the funerary offerings which would go with the king to his tomb. At the end of the atrium the acacia-wood doors, on which were carved the images of all the gods of the pantheon, were swung open, and we entered the mortuary where Pharaoh's corpse would one day be embalmed.

Here in this solemn chapel the king dismounted from the

carriage, and went forward to inspect the massive table on which he would lie for the ritual of mummification. Unlike the embalming of a commoner, royal embalming took seventy days to accomplish. The table had been sculpted from a single block of diorite, three paces long and two wide. Into the dark, mottled surface of the stone had been chiselled the indentation that fitted the back of the king's head, and the grooves which would drain the blood and other bodily fluids released by the scalpels and the instruments of the embalmers.

The grand master of the guild of embalmers was standing beside the table, ready to explain the entire process to the king, and he had an attentive audience, for Pharaoh seemed fascinated by every gruesome detail. At one stage it seemed that he might so far forget his dignity as to climb up upon the diorite block and try its fit, very much as though it were a new costume of linen presented by his tailor.

However, he restrained himself with an obvious effort, and instead devoted himself to the mortician's description of how the first incision would be made from his gullet to his groin, and how his viscera would be lifted out cleanly and then divided into their separate parts – liver, lungs, stomach and entrails. The heart, as the hearth of the divine spark, would be left in place, as would the kidneys with their associations with water and thus with the Nile, the source of life.

After this edifying instruction, Pharaoh minutely examined the four Canopic jars that would receive his viscera. They stood on another smaller granite table close at hand. The jars were carved from gleaming translucent alabaster the colour of milk. Their stoppers were fashioned in the shapes of the animal-headed gods: Anubis the jackal, Sobeth the crocodile, Thoth the ibis-headed, Sekhmet with the head of a lioness. They would be the guardians of Pharaoh's divine parts until his awakening in the eternal life.

On the same granite table that held the Canopic jars, the embalmers had laid out their instruments and the full array of pots and amphorae that contained the natron salts, lacquers and other chemicals that they would use in the process. Pharaoh was fascinated by the glistening bronze scalpels which would disembowel him, and when the embalmer showed him the long pointed spoon that would be pushed up his nostrils to scoop out the contents of his skull, those cheesy curds over which I had pondered so long and fruitlessly, the king was fascinated and handled the grisly instrument with reverential awe.

Once the king had satisfied his curiosity at the mortuary table, my Lady Lostris directed his attention to the painted bas-relief engravings that covered the walls of the temple from floor to ceiling. The decorations were not yet completed, but were none the less quite striking in their design and execution. I had drawn most of the original cartoons with my own hand, and had closely supervised the others drawn by the palace artists. These had been traced on to the walls with charcoal sticks. Once the tracings were in place, I had corrected and perfected them in free-hand. Now a company of master sculptors was engraving them into the sandstone blocks, while behind them a second company of artists was painting in the completed bas-relief.

The dominant colour I had chosen for these designs was blue in all its variation: the blue of the starling's wing, the blues of the sky and the Nile in the sunlight, the blues of the petals of the desert orchid and the shimmering blue of the river perch quivering in the fisherman's net. However, there were other colours as well, all those vibrant reds and yellows that we Egyptians love so well.

Pharaoh, accompanied closely by my Lord Intef, in his capacity of Keeper of the Royal Tombs, made a slow circuit of the high walls, examining every detail, and commenting on most of them. Naturally the theme I had chosen for the mortuary was the *Book of the Dead*, that detailed map and description of the route to the underworld that Pharaoh's shade must follow, and the depictions of all the trials and dangers he would confront along the way.

He paused for a long while before my drawing of the god Thoth, with his bird head and long curved ibis beak, weighing Pharaoh's disembodied heart on the scales against the feather of truth. Should the heart be impure, it would tip the scales against the feather, and the god would immediately toss it to the crocodile-headed monster that waited close at hand to devour it. Softly, the king quoted the protective mantra laid down in the book to shield himself from such a calamity, and then passed on to my next engraving.

It was almost noon before Pharaoh had completed his inspection of the mortuary temple and led the way out into the forecourt where the palace chefs had laid out a sumptuous open-air banquet.

'Come and sit here, where I can speak to you further on the matter of the stars!' Once again the king ignored precedent to place my Lady Lostris close to him at the banquet table, even moving one of his senior wives to make a place for her. During the meal he directed most of his conversation towards my mistress. She was now completely at her ease and kept the king and all those around her enthralled and merry with her wit and charm.

Of course, as a slave I did not have a seat at the table, nor could I even inveigle myself within range of my mistress to warn her to moderate her demeanour in the king's presence. Instead, I found myself a place on the pedestal of one of the granite lions, from where I could look down the length of the banquet table and watch everything that took place there. I was not the only observer, for my Lord Intef sat close to the king and yet withdrawn, watching it all with glittering, implacable eyes, like a handsome but deadly spider at the centre of his web.

At one stage of the meal a yellow-billed kite wheeled high overhead, and uttered a screech, a sardonic and mocking cry. Hurriedly I made the sign against the evil eye, for who knows what god it was that had taken the form of the bird to muddle and confuse our petty endeavours?

After the midday meal it was customary for the court to rest for an hour or so, especially at this the hottest season of the year. However, Pharaoh was so wrought up that today he would have none of it.

'Now we will inspect the treasuries,' he announced. The guards at the doors of the first treasury stood aside and presented arms as the royal party approached, and the doors were swung open from within.

I had planned these six treasuries not only as store-rooms to hold the vast funerary treasure that Pharaoh had been collecting for the past twelve years, ever since his accession to the double throne, but also as workshops in which a small army of craftsmen and artisans was permanently employed in adding to that treasure.

The hall that we entered was the armoury that housed the collection of weapons and accoutrements of the battlefield and the wild chase, both practical and ceremonial, which the king would take with him into the afterworld. With my Lord Intef's concurrence, I had arranged for the craftsmen to be at their benches so that the king would have the opportunity of watching them at work.

As Pharaoh passed slowly down the row of benches, his questions were so astute and technical that those nobles and priests to whom he addressed himself could provide no answers, and they looked around frantically for someone who could. I was summoned hastily from the back of the crowd and pushed forward to face the king's interrogation.

'Ah, yes,' Pharaoh grimaced bleakly as he recognized me. 'It is none other than the humble slave who writes pageants and cures the sick. No one here seems to know the composition of this electrum wire that binds the stock of the war-bow that this man is making for me.'

'Gracious Pharaoh, the metal is a mixture of one part of copper to five parts of silver and four of gold. The gold is of the red variety found only in the mines of Lot in the western desert. No other gives the wire the same pliability or elasticity, of course.'

'Of course,' the king agreed wryly. 'And how do you make the strands so thin? These are no thicker than the hairs of my head.'

'Majesty, we extrude the hot metal by swinging it in a special pendulum that I designed for the purpose. Later we can watch the process in the gold foundry, if Your Majesty so wishes.'

Thus during the rest of the tour I was able to remain at the king's side and to deflect some of his attention away from Lostris, but I still could not find the opportunity to speak to her alone.

Pharaoh passed down the armoury to inspect the huge array of weapons and armour already in store. Some of these had belonged to his forefathers and had been employed in famous battles; others were newly manufactured and would never be used in war.

All of them were magnificent, each a pinnacle of the armourer's art. There were helmets and breastplates of bronze and silver and gold, battle swords with ivory hilts set with precious stones, full-dress ceremonial uniforms of the commander-in-chief of each of the king's elite regiments, shields and bucklers in hippo-hide and crocodile-skin, all starred with rosettes of gold. It made a splendid array.

From the armoury we crossed the atrium to the furniture store, where a hundred cabinet-makers laboured with cedar and acacia and precious ebony wood to build the funeral furnishings for the king's long journey. Very few substantial trees grow in our riparian valley, and wood is a scarce and costly commodity, worth very nearly its weight in silver. Almost every stick of it must be carried hundreds of leagues across the desert, or shipped downstream from those mysterious lands to the south. Here it was piled in extravagant stacks, as though it were commonplace, and the fragrance of fresh sawdust perfumed the hot air.

We watched while craftsmen inlaid the head-board of Pharaoh's bed with patterns of mother-of-pearl and woods of contrasting colour. Others decorated the arm-rests of the chairs with golden falcons and the back-rests of the padded sofas with the heads of silver lions. Not even the halls of the royal palace at Elephantine Island contained such delicate workmanship as would grace the rock cell of the king's tomb.

From the furniture treasury we passed on to the hall of the sculptors. In marble and sandstone and granite of a hundred differing hues, the sculptors whittled and chipped away with chisel and file so that a fine, pale dust hung in the air. The masons covered their noses and mouths with strips of linen on which the dust settled and their features were powdered white with the insidious stuff. Some of the men coughed behind their masks as they worked, a persistent, dry cough that was peculiar to their profession. I had dissected the corpses of many old sculptors who had worked thirty years and died at their trade. I found their lungs petrified and turned to stone in their bodies, thus I spent as little time as possible in the masons' shop lest I contract the same malady.

None the less, their products were wondrous to contemplate,

statues of the gods and of Pharaoh himself that seemed to vibrate with life. There were life-sized images of Pharaoh seated on his throne or walking abroad, alive and dead, in his god form or in the shape of a mortal man. These statues would line the long causeway that led from the funerary temple on the valley floor up into the wall of black hills from which his final tomb was even at this moment being excavated. At his death the golden hearse, drawn by a train of one hundred white bullocks, was to bear his massive sarcophagus along that causeway to its final resting-place.

This granite sarcophagus, only partially completed, lay in the centre of the masons' hall. Originally it had been a single block of pink granite quarried from the mines at Assoun, and ferried down-river in a barge especially constructed for that purpose. It had taken five hundred slaves to haul it ashore and drag it over wooden rollers to where it now lay, an oblong of solid stone five paces long, three wide and three tall.

The masons had begun by sawing a thick slab from the top of it. Upon this granite lid a master mason was fashioning the likeness of the mummiform Pharaoh, with his arms crossed and the crook and flail gripped in his dead hands. Another team of masons was now engaged in hollowing out the interior of the main granite block to provide a nest into which the cluster of inner coffins would fit perfectly. Including the huge outer sarcophagus, there would be seven coffins in all, fitting one within the other like a child's puzzle-toy. Seven was, of course, one of the magical numbers. The innermost coffin would be of pure gold, and later we watched it being beaten out of the formless mass of metal in the hall of the goldsmiths.

It was this multiple sarcophagus, this mountain of stone and gold housing the king's wrapped corpse, that the great golden hearse would carry along the causeway to the hills, a slow journey that would take seven whole days to complete. The hearse would stop each night in one of the small shrines that were spaced at intervals along the causeway.

A fascinating adjunct to the hall of statues was the *ushabti* shop at the rear where the servants and retainers who would escort the dead king were being carved. These were perfect little manikins of wood representing all the grades and orders of Egyptian society who would work for the king in the hereafter, so as to enable him to maintain his estate and the style of his existence in the underworld.

Each *ushabti* was a delightfully carved wooden doll dressed in the authentic uniform of his calling and bearing the appropriate tools. There were farmers and gardeners, fishermen and bakers, beer-brewers and handmaidens, soldiers and tax-collectors, scribes and barbers, and hundreds upon hundreds of common labourers to perform every menial task and to go forward in the king's place if ever he were called upon by the other gods to work in the underworld.

At the head of this congregation of little figures there was even a grand vizier whose miniature features closely resembled those of my Lord Intef. Pharaoh picked out this manikin and examined him closely, turning him over to read the description on his back.

> My name is Lord Intef, grand vizier of the Upper Kingdom, Pharaoh's sole companion, three times the recipient of the Gold of Praise. I am ready to answer for the king.

Pharaoh passed the doll to my Lord Intef. 'Is your physique truly so muscular, my Lord Intef?' he asked with a smile just below the surface of his dour expression, and the grand vizier bowed slightly.

'The sculptor has failed to do me justice, Your Majesty.'

The last treasury that the king visited that day was the hall of the goldsmiths. The infernal glow of the furnaces cast a strange glow on the features of the jewellers as they worked with total concentration at their benches. I had coached them well. At the entrance of the royal entourage, the goldsmiths knelt in unison to make the triple obeisance to Pharaoh, and then rose and resumed their work.

Even in that large hall the heat of the furnace flames was so sulphurous as almost to stop the breath, and we were soon bathed in our own sweat. However, the king was so fascinated by the treasure displayed for him that he seemed not to notice the oppressive atmosphere. He went directly to the raised dais in the centre of the hall where the most experienced and skilful smiths were at work upon the golden inner coffin. They had perfectly captured Pharaoh's living face in the shimmering metal. The mask would fit exactly over his bandaged head. It was a divine image with eyes of obsidian and rock-crystal, and with the cobra-headed *uraeus* encircling the brow. I truly believe that no finer masterpiece of the goldsmith's art has ever been fashioned in all the thousand years of our civilization. This was the peak and the zenith. All the unborn ages might one day marvel at its splendour.

Even after Pharaoh had admired the golden mask from every angle, he seemed unable to tear himself too far from it. He spent the remainder of the day on the dais beside it, seated on a low stool while box after cedar-wood box of exquisite jewels were laid at his feet and the contents catalogued for him.

I cannot believe that such a treasure was ever before accumulated in one place at one time. To make a bald list of the items does not in the least way suggest the richness and the diversity of it all. None the less, let me tell you at the outset that there were six thousand four hundred and fifty-five pieces already in the cedar-wood boxes, and that each day more were added to the collection as the jewellers worked on tirelessly.

There were rings for Pharaoh's toes as well as his fingers; there were amulets and charms, and gold figurines of the gods and goddesses; there were necklaces and bracelets and pectoral medallions and belts on which were inlaid falcons and vultures and all the other creatures of the earth and the sky and the river; there were crowns and diadems studded with lapis lazuli and garnets and agate and carnelians and jasper and every gemstone that civilized man holds dear.

The artistry with which all this had been designed and manufactured eclipsed all that had been created over the preceding one thousand years. It is often in decline that a nation creates its most beautiful works of art. In the formative years of empire the obsession is with conquest and the building-up of wealth. It is only once this has been achieved that there is leisure and a desire to develop the arts, and – more importantly – rich and powerful men to sponsor them.

The weight of gold and silver already used in the manufacture of the hearse and the funeral mask and all the rest of this breathtaking collection of treasure was in excess of five hundred takhs; thus it would have taken five hundred strong men to lift it all. I had calculated that this was almost one-tenth of the total weight of these precious metals that had been mined in the entire one thousand years of our recorded history. All of this the king intended taking with him to the tomb.

Who am I, a humble slave, to question the price that a king was willing to pay for eternal life? Suffice it only to state that in assembling this treasure, while at the same time conducting the war against the Lower Kingdom, Pharaoh had, almost alone and unaided, plunged this very Egypt of ours into beggary.

No wonder, then, that Tanus in his declamation had singled out the depredation of the tax-collectors as one of the most terrible afflictions visited upon the populace. Between them and the robber bands that ravaged unchecked and unhindered through the countryside, we were all ruined and crushed under the financial yoke that was too heavy for any of us to bear. To survive at all, we had to evade the tax-collector's net. So as he set out to beggar us for his own aggrandizement, the king made criminals of us at the same moment. Very few of us, great or small, rich or poor, slept well at night. We lay awake dreading at any moment the heavy knock of the tax-collector upon the door.

Oh, sad and abused land, how it groaned beneath the yoke!

LAVISH quarters had been prepared in the necropolis in which the king would spend that night upon the west bank of the Nile, close to his own final resting-place in the gaunt black hills.

The necropolis, the city of the dead, was almost as extensive as Karnak itself. It was home to all those associated with the building and the care of the funerary temple and the royal tomb. There was a full regiment of the elite guard to protect the holy places, for the usurper in the north was as avaricious for treasure as was our own dear king, while the robber barons in the desert became each day bolder and more daring.

The treasuries of the funerary temple were a sore temptation to every predator in the two kingdoms, and beyond.

In addition to the guards there were the companies of the craftsmen and the artisans and all their apprentices to house. I was responsible for the records of wages and rations, so I knew exactly how many there were. On the last pay-day their number had been four thousand eight hundred and eleven. Added to this, there were over ten thousand slaves employed upon the work.

I will not weary myself by listing the numbers of oxen and sheep that had to be slaughtered each day to feed them all, nor the cartloads of fish that were brought up from the Nile, nor the thousands of jars of beer that were brewed daily to slake the summer thirst of this multitude as they laboured under the watchful eye and the ready lash of the overseers.

The necropolis was a city, and in that city was a palace for the king. It was with relief that we moved into it to spend the night, for it had been a wearying day. But once again there was little rest for me.

I tried to reach my Lady Lostris, but it was almost as if there existed a conspiracy to keep me away from her. According to her little black maids, first she was at toilet, and after that she was in her bath, and then she was resting and could not be disturbed. Finally, as I still waited in the ante-chamber of her quarters, a summons reached me from her father, and I could linger no longer, but must hurry to my master.

As soon as I entered my Lord Intef's bedchamber he dismissed all the others in the room. When we were alone, he kissed me. I was once more surprised by his benevolence and disturbed by his excited manner. Seldom had I seen him in such mood, and always before it had adumbrated calamitous events.

'How often the gateway to power and fortune is found in the most unexpected place!' he laughed at me, and caressed my face. 'This time it lies between the thighs of a woman. No, my old darling, don't play the innocent. I know just what a cunning hand you have taken in all of this. Pharaoh has told me how you cajoled him into it by promising him a male heir to his line. By

Seth, but you are the cunning one, are you not? Not a word to me of your design, but you schemed it all on your own account.'

He laughed again, and twisted a lock of my hair between his fingers. 'You must have divined my ultimate ambition all along, even though we have never discussed it openly. So you set out to achieve it for me. Of course, I should have you punished for your presumption,' he twisted the lock of hair until tears started into my eyes, 'but how can I be angry with you when you have placed the double crown within my grasp?' He released the tress of my hair and kissed me again. 'I have just come from the king's presence. In two days, at the culmination of the festival, he will announce his betrothal to my daughter, Lostris.' I felt a sudden darkness behind my eyes, and a chilly dew formed on my skin.

'The wedding will take place the same day, immediately after the closing ceremony of the festival, I saw to that. We don't want any delay in which something might happen to prevent it, do we?'

Such a swift royal wedding was unusual but not unheard of. When brides were chosen to seal a political union, or to consolidate the conquest of a new territory, the wedding often took place the very same day it was decided. Pharaoh Mamose the First, forefather of our present pharaoh, had married the daughter of a conquered Hurrian chieftain on the actual battlefield. However, such historical precedents were of little comfort to me now as I faced the bleak maturation of my worst fears.

My Lord Intef seemed not to notice my distress. He was too concerned with his own immediate interests, and he went on speaking. 'Before I gave my formal consent to the union, I prevailed on the king to concede that if she bore him a son then he would elevate my daughter to the rank of principal wife and queen consort.' He clapped his hands in unrestrained triumph.

'Of course, you realize what that means. If Pharaoh should die before my grandson is of age to rule, then I as his grandfather and closest male line would become regent—' He broke off suddenly and stared at me, and I knew him so well that I understood exactly what was running through his mind. He was bitterly regretting that indiscretion, nobody should ever have heard that thought expressed. It was purest treason. If Lostris bore a son to Pharaoh, then the father would not live long thereafter. We both understood that. My Lord Intef had given voice to regicide, and he was considering removing the only one who had heard it spoken, the humble slave, Taita. We both understood that clearly.

'My lord, I am only grateful that it has turned out the way I planned it. I admit now that I have worked deviously to place your daughter in the king's way, and that I described her to him as the mother of his future son. I used the pageant as a show-piece to focus his attention upon her. However, I could not bring myself to speak to you of such momentous affairs until they had been successfully engineered. But there still remains a great deal for us to do, before we can count ourselves secure—' and I began swiftly to extemporize a list of all that might go awry before he could gain control of the crown and the golden sceptre of Egypt. Tactfully I made it clear how much he still needed me if he were to achieve his design. I saw him relax as he followed my arguments, and I knew that at least for the immediate future I was safe.

It was some time before I could reasonably escape from his presence and hurry to warn my Lady Lostris of the terrible predicament in which I had placed her. However, before I reached her door I realized that my warning to her would serve no purpose other than to distress her to the point of dementia or even suicide. I could waste no further time if I were to prevent events from rushing to their tragic conclusion.

There was only one person to whom I could turn now.

 I LEFT the necropolis and set off alone along the tow-path of the canal, back towards the river-bank where I knew that Tanus' squadrons were encamped. The moon was only three days from full and it lit the jagged hills of the western horizon with a cold yellow radiance and threw black shadows on the plain below.

As I hurried along, I recited to myself a full list of all the possible calamities and misfortunes that might befall Tanus, my

Lady Lostris and myself in the days ahead. I was goading myself the same way that a black-maned desert lion lashes up his temper with the bony spike in the end of his tail before he charges at the huntsman. Thus I was in fulminating mood long before I reached the bank of the Nile.

I found Tanus' encampment without difficulty, hard by the bank of the Nile and the mouth of the canal. The ships of the squadron were anchored below the camp. The sentries challenged me and then, when they recognized me, led me to Tanus' tent.

Tanus was at late supper with Kratas and four other of his subordinate officers. He rose to greet me with a smile and offered me the beer tankard in his hand. 'This is such an unexpected pleasure, old friend. Sit down beside me and have a pull of my beer while my slave brings you a cup and platter. You look hot and out of sorts—'

I cut short these pleasantries by rounding on him furiously. 'To Seth with you, you great senseless oaf! Do you not understand what jeopardy you have placed us in? You and that flapping jawbone of yours! Do you have no thought for the safety and the well-being of my mistress?' In truth I had not meant to be so harsh on him, but once I had started, it seemed that I was unable to control my emotions, and all my fear and anxiety came tumbling out in a flood of invective. Not all that I accused him of was true or fair, but it made me feel better to have it out.

Tanus' expression changed and he held up one hand as though to shield himself. 'Whoa! You take me unawares. I am unarmed and unable to defend myself from such a murderous assault.' In front of his officers his tone was jocular, but his smile was thin as he seized my arm and steered me out of the tent into the darkness, and half-dragged me beyond the regimental lines into the open moonlit fields beyond. I was like a child in the grip of that right hand that was trained to wield the sword and draw the great bow Lanata.

'Now puke it up!' he ordered me grimly. 'What has happened to put you in such vile humour?'

I was still angry, but more afraid than angry, and my tongue took flight again. 'I have spent half my life trying to protect you from your own stupidity, and I am sick of it. Don't you understand

135

anything of life? Did you truly believe that you would be allowed to escape unscathed from the incredible folly into which you threw all of us last night?'

'Are you talking about my declamation at the pageant?' He looked puzzled, and released the crushing grip on my arm. 'How can you say it was folly? All my officers, and every other person I have spoken to since then, are all delighted with what I had to say—'

'You fool, don't you see that the opinions of all your officers and all your friends count for the price of a rotten fish in the scheme of things? Under any other ruler you would already be dead, and even this weak and vacillating old man of ours cannot afford to let you escape the consequences of your insolence. It is more than his throne is worth. There will be a bill for you to pay, Tanus, Lord Harrab. Horus knows, it will be a heavy bill.'

'You are speaking in riddles,' he snapped at me. 'I did the king a great service. He is surrounded by fawning toadies who feed him the lies they think he wants to hear. It was past time that he learned the truth, and I know in my heart that once he considers it, he will be grateful to me.'

My anger began to evaporate before his simple and steadfast belief in the triumph of good. 'Tanus, my dearest friend, what an innocent you are! No man is ever grateful for having the unpalatable truth rammed down his throat. But apart from that, you have played directly into the hands of my Lord Intef.'

'My Lord Intef?' he stared at me hard. 'What of my Lord Intef? You speak of him as though he were my enemy. The grand vizier was my father's dearest friend. I know that I can trust him to protect me. He swore an oath to my father as he lay on his death-bed—'

I could see that despite his sunny disposition and our friendship, he was becoming truly angry with me, probably for the first time in his life. I knew also that, although it was slow to rouse, Tanus' anger was something to fear.

'Oh, Tanus!' I curbed my own anger at last. 'I have been unfair to you. There is so much that I should have told you, and never did. Nothing was as you thought it. I was a coward, but I could not tell you that Intef was your own father's deadliest enemy.'

136

'How can this be true?' Tanus shook his head. 'They were friends, the dearest friends. My earliest memories are of them laughing together. My father told me that I could trust my very life to my Lord Intef.'

'The noble Pianki, Lord Harrab believed that, it is true. His faith cost him his entire fortune, and in the end his life which he placed in Intef's hands.'

'No, no, you must be mistaken. My father was the victim of a series of misfortunes—'

'And every one of those misfortunes was engineered by my Lord Intef. He envied your father for his virtues and his popularity, for his wealth and his influence with Pharaoh. He realized that Lord Harrab would be appointed grand vizier before him and he hated him for all these things.'

'I cannot believe you. I cannot bring myself to believe you.' Tanus shook his head in denial, and the last of my anger was snuffed out.

'I will explain it all to you, as I should have done long ago. I will give you all the proof you need. But there is no time for it now. You must trust me. My Lord Intef hates you even as he hated your father. Both you and my Lady Lostris are in danger. In danger of more than simply life itself, in danger of losing each other for ever.'

'But how is that possible, Taita?' He was confused and shaken by my words. 'I thought that my Lord Intef had agreed to our union. Have you not spoken to him, then?'

'Yes, I have spoken to him,' I cried, and I seized Tanus' hand and thrust it up under the back of my tunic. 'That was his reply. Feel the welts left by the lash! He had me flogged for even suggesting the marriage between you and my Lady Lostris. That is how much he hates you and your family.'

Tanus stared at me speechlessly, but I saw that he believed me at last, and so I was able to come to the subject that was dominating my thoughts even more than his intemperate speech, or the vendetta that the grand vizier had conducted so successfully against him over so many years.

'Hear me now, my dear friend, and brace yourself for the very worst tidings yet.' There was no other way to tell him, except as

137

directly as Tanus would have told me. 'Far from agreeing to your marriage, my Lord Intef has this very night pledged his daughter's hand to another. She is to be married immediately to Pharaoh Mamose, and after she bears his first son she will become his principal wife and consort. The king will make the announcement himself at the end of the festival of Osiris. The marriage will take place that very same evening.'

Tanus swayed on his feet and in the moonlight his face turned ghostly pale. Neither of us could speak for a long while and then Tanus turned away from me and walked out alone into the field of standing corn. I trailed behind him, keeping him in sight, until at last he found an outcrop of black rock and seated himself upon it with the weary air of a very old man. I came up softly and seated myself below him. Deliberately I remained silent until he sighed and asked quietly, 'Has Lostris consented to this marriage?'

'Of course not. As yet she probably knows nothing about it. But do you think for one moment that her objections would count against the will of her father and the king? She will have no say in the matter.'

'What are we to do, old friend?'

Even in my distress I was grateful to him that he used the plural, including me, reassuring me of our friendship. 'There is one other probability that we must face,' I warned him. 'And that is that in the same speech that Pharaoh announces his betrothal to Lostris, he will order your imprisonment, or worse still, issue your death warrant. My Lord Intef has the king's ear and he will certainly put him up to it. In truth he would have good reason. You are certainly guilty of sedition.'

'I do not care to live without Lostris as my wife. If the king takes her from me, then he is welcome to my head as a marriage gift.' He said it simply, without histrionics, so that I had difficulty in feigning anger and putting the edge of contempt into my voice.

'You sound like a weak and pitiful old woman, giving herself up to the fates without a struggle. What a fine and undying love is yours, if you will not even fight for her!'

'How do you fight a king and a god?' Tanus asked quietly. 'A king to whom you have sworn allegiance, and a god who is as remote and as unassailable as the sun?'

'As a king he does not deserve your allegiance. You set that out clearly in your declamation. He is a weak and dithering old man who has divided the two kingdoms and brought our *Ta-Meri* bleeding to her knees.'

'And as a god?' Tanus again asked quietly, as though he were not really interested in the answer, although I knew him to be a devout and religious man, as so many great warriors are.

'A god?' I made my tone derisive. 'You have more of the godhead in your sword-arm than he has in all his soft little body.'

'Then what do you suggest?' he asked with deceptive mildness. 'What would you have me do?'

I drew a deep breath and then blurted it out. 'Your officers and your men would follow you to the gates of the underworld. The populace loves you for your courage and your honour—' I faltered, for his expression in the moonlight gave me no encouragement to continue.

He was silent for twenty beats of my racing heart and then he ordered me softly, 'Go on! Say what you have to say.'

'Tanus, you would make the noblest pharaoh that this *Ta-Meri*, this mother-land, has known for a thousand years. You with my Lady Lostris on the throne beside you could lead this land and this people back to greatness. Call out your squadrons, and lead your men down the causeway to where that unworthy pharaoh lies unprotected and vulnerable. By dawn tomorrow you could be ruler of the Upper Kingdom. By this time next year you could have defeated the usurper and have reunited the two kingdoms.' I leaped to my feet and faced him. 'Tanus, Lord Harrab, your destiny and that of the woman you love await you. Seize them in both your strong warrior's hands!'

'Warrior's hands, yes.' He held them up before my face. 'Hands that have fought for my mother-land and have protected her rightful king. You do me a disservice, old friend. They are not the hands of a traitor. Nor is this the heart of a blasphemer, that would seek to cast down and destroy a god, and take his place in the pantheon.'

I groaned aloud in my frustration. 'You would be the greatest pharaoh of the last five hundred years, and you need not proclaim your godhead, not if the idea offends you. Do it, I beseech you, for the sake of this very Egypt of ours, and of the woman that we both love!'

'Would Lostris still love a traitor as she loved a soldier and a patriot? I think not.' He shook his head.

'She would love you no matter what—' I began, but he cut me short.

'You cannot convince me. She is a woman of virtue and of honour. As a traitor and a thief, I would forfeit all right to her respect. What is of equal importance, I would never respect myself again, or consider myself worthy of her sweet love, if I did what you urge. Speak of it no more, as you value our friendship. I have no claim to the double crown, nor will I ever make such claim. Horus, hear me, and turn your face away from me if ever I should break this pledge.'

The matter was closed, I knew him so well, that great infuriating oaf, whom I loved with all my heart. He meant exactly what he said, and would cleave to it at any cost.

'Then what will you do, damn your stubborn heart?' I flared at him. 'Nothing that I say has any weight with you. Do you want to face this on your own? Are you suddenly too wise to heed my counsel?'

'I'm willing to take your counsel, just as long as it has sense to it.' He reached out and drew me down beside him. 'Come, Taita, help us. Lostris and I need you now as never before. Don't desert us. Help us find the honourable way.'

'I fear there is no such thing,' I sighed, my emotions bobbing and spinning like a piece of flotsam caught in the Nile flood. 'But if you will not seize the crown, then you dare not stay here. You must sweep Lostris up in your arms and bear her away.'

He stared at me in the moonlight. 'Leave Egypt? You cannot be serious. This is my world. This is Lostris' world.'

'No!' I reassured him. 'That is not what I had in mind. There is another pharaoh in Egypt. One who has need of warriors and honest men. You have much to offer such a king. Your fame in the Lower Kingdom is as great as it is here at Karnak. Place Lostris on the deck of the *Breath of Horus* and send your galley flying northwards. No other ship can catch you. In ten days, with this wind and current, you can present yourself at the court of the red pharaoh in Memphis, and swear allegiance to—'

'By Horus, you are determined to make a traitor of me yet,' he cut across me. 'Swear allegiance to the usurper, you say? Then what of the allegiance I swore to the true Pharaoh Mamose? Does that count for nothing with you? What kind of man am I, that can make the same oath to every king or renegade that crosses my path? An oath is not something to be bartered or reclaimed, Taita, it is for life. I gave my oath to the true Pharaoh Mamose.'

'That true Pharaoh is the same one who will marry your love, and will order the strangling-rope to be twisted around your neck,' I pointed out grimly, and this time even he wavered.

'You are right, of course. We should not stay in Karnak. But I will not make myself a traitor or break my solemn oath by taking up the sword against my king.'

'Your sense of honour is too complicated for me.' I could not keep the tone of sarcasm from my voice. 'All I know is that it bodes fair to make corpses of us all. You have told me what you will not do. Now tell me what you will do to save yourself, and rescue my Lady Lostris from a hateful fate.'

'Yes, old friend, you have every right to be angry with me. I asked for your help and advice. When you gave it freely, I scorned it. I beg your patience. Bear with me a while longer.' Tanus sprang to his feet and began to prowl about like the leopard in Pharaoh's menagerie, back and forth, muttering to himself, shaking his head and bunching his fists, as if to face an adversary.

At last he stopped in front of me. 'I am not prepared to play the traitor, but with a heavy heart I will force myself to play the coward. If Lostris agrees to accompany me, and only if she agrees, then I am prepared to take flight. I will take her away from this land we both love so well.'

'Where will you go?' I asked.

'I know that Lostris can never leave the river. It is not only her life and mine, but her god also. We must stay with Hapi, the river. That leaves only one direction open to us.' He raised his right arm, gleaming with muscle in the moonlight, and pointed south. 'We will follow the Nile southwards into the depths of Africa, into the land of Cush and beyond. We will go up beyond the cataracts into the unfathomed wilderness where no civilized man has ever gone before. There, perhaps, if the gods are kind, we will carve out another *Ta-Meri* for ourselves.'

'Who will be your companions?'

'Kratas, of course, and those of my officers and men who are game for the adventure. I'll address them tonight and give them the choice. Five ships, perhaps, and the men to work them. We must be ready to leave by dawn. Will you go back to the necropolis and fetch Lostris to me?'

'And me?' I asked quietly. 'You'll take me with you?'

'You?' He laughed at me. Now that the decision was made, his mood took flight, high as the bating falcon launched from the gloved fist. 'Would you truly give up your garden and your books, your pageants and your building of temples? The road will be dangerous, and the life hard. Do you truly want that, Taita?'

'I could not let you go alone, without my restraining hand upon your shoulder. What folly and danger would you lead my mistress into, if I were not there to guide you?'

'Come!' he ordered, and clapped me on the back. 'I never doubted that you would come with us. I know that Lostris would not leave without you, anyway. Enough chatter! We have work to do. First, we will tell Kratas and the others what we intend, and let them make their choice. Then you must go back to the necropolis and fetch Lostris, while I make the preparations for our departure. I'll send a dozen of my best men with you, but we must hurry. It is past midnight, and well into the third watch.'

Silly romantic fool that I am, but I was as excited as he was as we hurried back to the regiment's encampment below the temple and the causeway. I was so elated that my sense of danger was dulled. It was Tanus who picked out the sinister movement in the moonlight ahead of us and seized my arm and drew me beneath the shelter of a stunted carob tree.

'An armed party,' he whispered, and I saw the glint of bronze spear-heads. There was a large band of men, thirty or forty, I estimated.

'Bandits, perhaps, or a raiding party from the Lower Kingdom,'

Tanus growled, and even I was alarmed by the stealthy behaviour of the armed men ahead of us. They were not using the tow-path of the canal, but creeping through the open fields, spreading out to surround Tanus' encampment on the river-bank.

'This way!' With a soldier's eye for ground he picked out a shallow wadi that ran down to join the river, and he steered me to it. We jumped down and ran doubled over until we reached the perimeter of the camp. Then Tanus sprang out of the wadi and roused the camp with a bellow.

'Stand to arms! On me, the Blues! Form on me!' It was the rallying cry of the Blue Crocodile Guards, and it was taken up at once by the sergeants of each company. Instantly the camp boiled to life. The men sleeping round the fires leaped to their feet and snatched up their stacked weapons, while the officers' tents burst open as though the men within had never slept but had been waiting, tensed and ready for Tanus' command. Sword in hand, they raced to their stations, and I saw Kratas in the forefront.

I was amazed by the swiftness of their response, even though I knew that these were all battle-tested veterans. Before I could draw a dozen excited breaths they had formed in their phalanxes, with overlapping shields and long spears thrust outwards facing the darkness. The strange band out there in the night must have been as startled as I was by this militant display, for although I could still make out the vague shapes of many men and the gleam of their weapons in the gloom, the murderous charge we were all expecting from them never materialized.

The instant that Tanus had his formations in line, he ordered the advance. We had often debated the advantages of offensive action over defence, and now the massed squadrons moved forward, poised to break into a full charge at Tanus' command. It must have been a daunting spectacle to the men out there in the darkness, for a voice hailed us with an edge of panic in its tone. 'We are Pharaoh's men on the king's business. Hold your attack!'

'Hold hard, the Blues!' Tanus stopped the menacing advance, and then called back, 'Which pharaoh do you serve, the red usurper or the true pharaoh?'

'We serve the true king, the divine Mamose, ruler of the Upper and the Lower Kingdoms. I am the king's messenger.'

'Come forward, king's messenger, who creeps around in the night like a thief. Come forward and state your business!' Tanus invited him, but under his breath he told Kratas, 'Be ready for treachery. The smell of it is thick in the air. Have the fires built up. Give us light to see.'

Kratas gave the order and bundles of dry rushes were flung on to the watch-fires. The flames leaped up, and the darkness was thrown back. Into this ruddy glow the leader of the strange band stepped forward and shouted, 'My name is Neter, Best of Ten Thousand. I am the commander of Pharaoh's bodyguard. I bear the hawk seal for the arrest and detention of Tanus, Lord Harrab.'

'By Horus, he lies in his teeth,' Kratas growled. 'You are no felon with a warrant on your head. He insults you and the regiment. Let us at them and I'll thrust that hawk seal up between his buttocks.'

'Hold!' Tanus restrained him. 'Let us hear the fellow out.' He raised his voice again: 'Show us the seal, Captain Neter.'

Neter held it aloft. A small statuette in glistening blue faience, in the shape of the royal hawk. The hawk seal was the king's personal empowerment. The bearer acted with all the force and validity of Pharaoh himself. On pain of death, no man could question or hinder him in the course and commission of the royal business. The bearer answered only to the king.

'I am Tanus, Lord Harrab,' Tanus conceded. 'And I acknowledge the hawk seal.'

'My lord, my lord!' Kratas whispered urgently. 'Do not go to the king. It will mean your certain death. I have spoken to the other officers. The regiment is behind you, nay, the entire army is behind you. Give us the word. We'll make you king before the new day breaks.'

'My ear is deaf to those words,' Tanus told him softly, but with a weight of menace in his tone more telling than any growl or bellow. 'But only this once, Kratas, son of Maydum. Next time that you speak treason, I will deliver you to the king's wrath with my own hands.'

He turned from Kratas to me, and drew me a little to one side. 'It is too late, old friend. The gods frown on our enterprise. I must trust myself to the king's good sense. If he is truly a god, then he will be able to look into my heart and see for himself that it contains no evil.' He touched my arm, and that light gesture was to me more significant than the warmest embrace. 'Go to Lostris, tell her what has happened, tell her why it has happened. Tell her I love her and, whatever happens, I will do so through this life and the next. Tell her I will wait for her, to the ends of eternity, if need be.'

Then Tanus ran his sword back into the scabbard at his side and with empty hands stepped forward to meet the bearer of the hawk seal. 'I stand ready to do the king's bidding,' he said simply.

Behind him his own men hissed and growled, and rattled their swords against their bucklers, but Tanus turned and quieted them with a gesture and a frown, then strode out to confront Neter. The king's guard closed in around him, and then at a trot they moved away along the tow-path of the canal, back towards the necropolis.

The camp was filled with angry, bitter young men when I left it and followed Tanus and his escort at a discreet interval. When I reached the necropolis, I went directly to my Lady Lostris' quarters. I was distressed to find them deserted except for three of her little black maids, who in their usual lazy and lackadaisical manner were packing the last of their mistress's clothing into a cedar-wood chest.

'Where is your mistress?' I demanded, and the eldest and most insolent of them picked her nose as she gave me an airy reply, 'Where you can't reach her, eunuch.' The others tittered at her powers of repartee. They are all of them jealous of my favour with my Lady Lostris.

'Answer me straight, or I'll whip your insolent backside, you little baggage.' I had done so before, so she relented and muttered sulkily, 'They have taken her to Pharaoh's own harem. You have no influence there. Despite your missing balls, the guards will never let you pass amongst the royal women.'

She was right, of course, but still I had to make the attempt. My mistress would need me now, as much as she ever had in all her life.

As I feared, the guards at the gate to the king's harem were intractable. They knew who I was, but they had orders that no one, not even the closest members of Lostris' retinue, was to be allowed to go to her.

It cost me a gold ring, but the best I could achieve, even with that extravagance, was the promise that one of the guards would take my message to her. I wrote it out on a scrap of papyrus parchment, a bland little attempt at encouragement. I dared not relate all that had befallen us, nor the peril in which Tanus now stood. I could not even mention him by name, and yet I had to reassure her of his love and protection. As an investment, it was not worth the price I was forced to pay. Hardest of all to bear, I learned later that my gold had been entirely wasted and that she never received the message. Is there no man we can trust in this perfidious world?

I was not to see either Tanus or my Lady Lostris again until the evening of the last day of the festival of Osiris.

THE FESTIVAL ended in the temple of the god. It seemed once more that all the populace of Greater Thebes was packed into the courtyards. We were jammed so tightly that I could scarcely breathe in the press and the heat.

I was feeling wretched, for I had slept little for two nights in succession on account of the worry and the strain. Apart from the uncertainty of the fate of Tanus, I had been further burdened by my Lord Intef with the onerous duty of arranging the wedding ceremony of the king to his daughter, a duty that ran so contrary to my own desires. Added to which, I was parted from my mistress, and I could scarcely bear it. I do not know how I came through it. Even the slave boys were concerned about me. They declared that they had never seen my beauty so impaired, or my spirits so low.

Twice during Pharaoh's interminable speech from the throne, I found myself swaying on my feet, on the very point of fainting. However, I forced myself to hold on, while the king droned out the platitudes and half-truths with which he sought to disguise the true state of the kingdom and to placate the populace.

As was only to be expected, he never referred directly to the

146

red pharaoh in the north or the civil war in which we were embroiled, except in such broad terms as 'these troubled times' or 'the defection and insurrection'. However, after he had spoken for a while it suddenly became plain to me that he was referring to every one of the issues that Tanus had raised in his declamation, and attempting to find remedies for each of them.

It was true that he was doing so in his usual inept and vacillating fashion, but the simple fact that he had taken notice of what Tanus had said braced me and focused my wandering attention. I edged forward in the press of humanity until I had a better view of the throne, by which time the king was speaking about the impudence of the slaves and the disrespectful behaviour of the lower classes of our society. This was another issue that Tanus had mentioned, and I was amused to hear Pharaoh's solution. 'From henceforth the slave-owner may order fifty lashes to the insolent slave, without recourse to the magistrate to sanction such punishment,' he announced.

I smiled when I remembered how this same king had almost wrecked the state twelve years previously with another proclamation that ran in the exact opposite direction to this latest pronouncement. Still idealistic at his coronation, he had set out actually to abolish the ancient and honourable institution of slavery. He had wanted to turn every slave in Egypt loose and make him a free man.

Even at this remove in time, such folly is still incomprehensible to me. Though I am myself a slave, I believe that slavery and serfdom are the institutions on which the greatness of nations is founded. The rabble cannot govern itself. Government should be entrusted only to those born and trained to it. Freedom is a privilege, not a right. The masses need a strong master, for without control and direction anarchy would reign. The absolute monarch and slavery and serfdom are the pillars of a system that has allowed us to develop into civilized men.

It had been instructive to see how the slaves themselves had rebelled at the prospect of having freedom thrust upon them. I had been very young at the time, but I too had been alarmed at the prospect of being turned out from my warm and secure niche in the boys' quarters to scavenge on the rubbish-heaps for my next crust of bread with a horde of other freed slaves. A bad master is better than no master at all.

Of course, the kingdom had been thrown into chaos by this folly. The army had been upon the brink of revolt. Had the red pharaoh in the north seized the opportunity, then history might have been written differently. In the end our own pharaoh had hastily withdrawn his misguided decree of manumission, and managed to cling to his throne. Now here he was little more than a decade later proclaiming increased punishments for the impudence of a slave. It was so typical of this hesitant and muddling pharaoh that I pretended to mop my brow in order to cover the first smile that had creased my face in the last two days.

'The practice of self-mutilation for the purpose of avoiding military service will in future be strongly discouraged,' the king droned on. 'Any eligible young man claiming exemption under this dispensation is to appear before a tribunal of three army officers, at least one of whom is to be a centurion or officer of superior rank.' This time my smile was one of reluctant approval. For once Pharaoh was on the right tack. I would dearly love to see Menset and Sobek displaying their missing thumbs to some hardened old veteran of the river wars. What tender sympathy they could expect! 'The fine for such an offence will be one thousand rings of gold.' By Seth's bulging belly, that would make those two young dandies pause, and my Lord Intef would have to meet the fine on their behalf.

Despite my other concerns, I was beginning to feel a little more cheerful, as Pharaoh continued, 'From this day forward it will be an offence punishable by a fine of ten gold rings for a harlot to ply for trade in any public place, other than one set aside by the magistrates for that purpose.' This time I could barely prevent myself from laughing aloud. Vicariously Tanus would make puritans and honest men of all of Thebes. I wondered how the sailors and the off-duty soldiers would welcome this interference in their sporting lives. Pharaoh's period of lucidity had been short-lived. Any fool knows the folly of trying to legislate to man's sexual foibles.

Despite my doubts as to the wisdom of the king's remedies,

still I found myself overtaken by a tremulous excitement. It was clear that the king had taken serious notice of every issue that Tanus had brought forward in his declamation. Could he now go on to condemn Tanus for sedition, I wondered?

However, Pharaoh had not finished yet. 'It has been brought to my notice that certain officials of the state have abused the trust and faith that I have placed in them. These officials, concerned with the collection of taxes and the handling of public funds, will be called upon to account for the monies placed in their care. Those found guilty of embezzlement and corruption will be summarily sentenced to death by strangulation.' The populace stirred and sighed with disbelief. Would the king truly seek to restrain his tax-collectors?

Then a single voice at the back of the hall cried out, 'Pharaoh is great! Long live Pharaoh!' The cry was taken up until the temple rang with the cheering. It must have been an unusual sound for the king to hear, that spontaneous applause. Even at the distance that I was from the throne I could tell that he enjoyed it. His lugubrious expression lightened and the double crown seemed to weigh less heavily on his head. I was certain that all of this must improve Tanus' chances of escaping the executioner's noose.

When the cheering eventually subsided, the king went on in his particular style to diminish everything that he had just achieved. 'My trusted grand vizier, the noble Lord Intef, will be placed in sole and absolute charge of this investigation of the civil service, with the full powers of search and arrest, of life and of death vested in him.' There was just the softest echo of applause to greet this appointment, and I used it to disguise a sardonic chuckle. Pharaoh was sending a hungry leopard to count the birds in his chicken-coop. What sport my Lord Intef would have amongst the royal treasuries, and what a redistribution of the nation's wealth would now take place with my master doing the counting, and milking the tax-collectors of their secret hoards of savings!

Pharaoh had a rare talent for capsizing or running the noblest sentiments and intentions on to the rocks with his blundering helmsmanship. I wondered what other folly he would manage to perpetrate before he finished speaking that day, and I did not have too long to wait.

'For some time it has been a cause for great concern to me that a state of lawlessness exists in the Upper Kingdom, placing the lives and the estates of honest citizens in the gravest jeopardy. I had made dispositions to deal with this state of affairs at an appropriate time. However, the matter was recently presented to me in such an untimely and ill-advised manner as to reek of sedition. It was done under the dispensation of the festival of Osiris. However, that dispensation does not cover treason or the crime of blasphemy, an attack on the person and divinity of the king.' Pharaoh paused significantly. It was clear that he was speaking of Tanus, and I was once again critical of his judgement. A strong pharaoh would not explain his motives to the people, or seek to win their approval for his actions. He would simply have pronounced sentence and have had done with the matter.

'I speak, of course, of Tanus, Lord Harrab who played the role of the great god Horus at the pageant of Osiris. He has been arrested for the crime of sedition. My councillors are divided on the subject of this person's guilt. There are those amongst them who wish him to pay the supreme penalty—' I saw my Lord Intef, standing below the throne, avert his gaze for a moment, and it confirmed what I already knew, that he was the chief amongst those who wished to see Tanus executed '—and there are those who feel that his declamation at the festival was indeed inspired by divine forces and that it was not the voice of Tanus, Lord Harrab, that spoke out on these matters, but the veritable voice of the god Horus. If this latter be the case, then clearly there can be no culpability to the mortal through whom the god chose to speak.'

The reasoning was fair, but what pharaoh worth the double crown would deign to explain it to this horde of common soldiers and sailors and farmers, of tradesmen and labourers and slaves, most of whom were still suffering from the ill-effects of too much wine and revelry? While I still pondered this, the king gave a command to the captain of his bodyguard who stood below the throne. I recognized him as Neter, the officer who had been sent to arrest Tanus. Neter marched away smartly and returned a moment later, leading Tanus from the sanctuary at the rear of the hall.

My heart leaped at the sight of my friend, and then with joy and hope I realized that he was unbound, there were no chains on his ankles. Although he carried no weapons and wore no badge of rank, and was dressed in a simple white kilt, he walked with his accustomed elastic step and jaunty grace. Apart from the healing scab on his forehead where Rasfer had struck him, he was unmarked. He had not been beaten or tortured, and I felt my optimism revived. They were not treating him as a condemned man.

A moment later all my hopes were dashed to pieces. Tanus made his obeisance before the throne, but when he rose to his feet again, Pharaoh looked down upon him severely and spoke in a voice without pity. 'Tanus, Lord Harrab, you stand accused of treason and sedition. I find you guilty of both these crimes. I sentence you to death by strangulation, the traditional punishment of the traitor.'

As Neter placed the noose of linen rope around Tanus' neck to mark him as one condemned to die, a groan went up from the people who watched. A woman wailed, and soon the temple was filled with cries of lamentation and the ululation of mourning. Never before had such a display accompanied the passing of the death sentence. Nothing could demonstrate more clearly the love which the populace bore Tanus. I wailed with them and the tears broke from my lids and streamed down my face to pour like a waterfall on to my chest.

The bodyguards fell upon the crowd, using the butts of their long spears in an attempt to beat the mourners into silence. It was in vain, and I screamed out over their heads, 'Mercy, bountiful Pharaoh! Mercy for the noble Tanus!'

One of the guards struck me on the side of the head, and I fell to the ground half-stunned, but my cry was taken up. 'Mercy, we beseech you, oh divine Mamose!' It took all the efforts of the guards to restore some order, but still a few of the women were sobbing.

Only when Pharaoh raised his voice again were we at last

silent, so that every one of us heard his next pronouncement. 'The condemned man has complained of the lawless state of the kingdom. He has called upon the throne to stamp out the bands of robbers who ravage the land. The condemned man has been called a hero, and there are those who say that he is a mighty warrior. If this be true, then he himself would be better suited than any other to carry out those measures he demands.'

Now the people were confused and silent, and I struck the tears from my face with my forearm as I strained to catch the next word. 'Therefore, the sentence of death is deferred for two years. If the condemned man was truly inspired by the god Horus when he made his seditious speech, then the god will assist him in the task I now place upon him.'

The silence was profound. None of us seemed able to understand what we were hearing, although hope and despair filled my soul in equal measure.

At a signal from the king one of the ministers of the crown stepped forward and offered Pharaoh a tray on which lay a tiny blue statuette. Pharaoh held it aloft and announced, 'I issue to Lord Harrab the hawk seal of the pharaohs. Under the auspice of the seal he may recruit all the men and materials of war that he deems necessary to his task. He may employ whatever means he chooses, and no man may prevent him. For two full years he is the king's man, and he answers only to the king. At the end of that time, on the last day of the next festival of Osiris, he will come before the throne once again, wearing the noose of death around his neck. If he has failed in his task, the noose will be tightened and he will be strangled to death on the spot where he now stands. If he has completed his task, then I, Pharaoh Mamose, will lift the noose from around his neck with my own hands and replace it with a chain of gold.'

Still none of us could speak or move, and we stared in fascination as Pharaoh made a gesture with the crook and the flail. 'Tanus, Lord Harrab, I charge you with the task of eradicating from the Upper Kingdom of Egypt the outlaws and robber bands that are terrorizing this land. Within two years you will restore order and peace to the Upper Kingdom. Fail me at your peril.'

Lostris was like a corpse in his embrace. Her arms hung limply at her side, and her face was pale as death. Her father released her, but kept a grip on her hand as he turned and faced the congregation to offer the ritual gift to his daughter. Traditionally, this gift was made over and above the dowry that went directly to the bridegroom. However, only the nobility observed this custom, which was designed to give the bride an independent income.

'Now that you go from my house and from my protection to the house of your husband, I bestow upon you the gift of parting, that you will remember me always as the father that loved you.' The words were inappropriate to the circumstances, I thought bitterly. My Lord Intef had never loved another living soul. However, he continued the ancient formula, as though the sentiments were his own. 'Ask any boon of me, my beloved child. I will refuse you nothing on this joyous day.'

It was the usual practice for the extent of the gift to be agreed in private between father and daughter before the ceremony. In this case, however, my Lord Intef had told his daughter unequivocally what she was entitled to ask for. He had done me the honour of discussing the matter with me the previous day, before informing Lostris of his decision. 'I don't want to be extravagant, but on the other hand I do not wish to appear parsimonious in Pharaoh's eyes,' he had mused. 'Let us say, five thousand gold rings and fifty feddan of land – not on the riverfront, mind you.'

He had, with my prompting, finally decided on five thousand gold rings and one hundred feddan of prime irrigable land as being a suitable gift for a royal wedding. On his instruction I had already drawn up the deed of grant for the land, and set aside the gold from a secret store that my master kept out of the way of the tax-collectors.

The matter was settled. It remained only for Lostris to give voice to the request before her groom and all the wedding guests. But she stood pale and silent and withdrawn, seeming neither to see nor hear what was going on around her.

'Speak up, my child. What is it that you desire from me?' My Lord Intef's tones of paternal love were becoming strained, and he shook his daughter's hand to rouse her. 'Come, tell your father what he can do to make this happy day complete.'

My Lady Lostris stirred as though coming awake from a dreadful dream. She looked about her and her tears welled up and threatened to break over her quivering eyelids. She opened her mouth to speak, but what came from her throat was the weak little cry of a wounded bird. She closed her lips again and shook her head speechlessly.

'Come, child. Speak out.' My Lord Intef was having difficulty sustaining an expression of paternal affection. 'Name your marriage gift, and I will give it to you, whatever it is that you desire.'

The effort that Lostris had to make was apparent to me, even though I stood so far from her, but this time when she opened her mouth her request rang out over our heads, clear as the music of the lyre. There could not have been a soul in the crowd who did not hear every word of it.

'For my gift give me the slave, Taita!'

My Lord Intef reeled back a pace as though she had thrust a dagger into his belly. He stared at her aghast, his mouth opening and closing without a sound escaping. Only he and I knew the value of the gift that Lostris had demanded. Not even he, with the store of wealth and treasure that he had garnered over a lifetime, could afford such a payment.

He recovered swiftly. His expression was once more calm and benign, though his lips stretched tight. 'You are too restrained, my darling daughter. A single slave is no fitting gift for Pharaoh's bride. Such stinginess is not in my nature. I would rather you accepted a gift of real value, five thousand rings of gold and—'

'Father, you have always been too generous with me, but I want only Taita.'

My Lord Intef smiled a white smile, white teeth, white lips and white rage. While he still stared at Lostris I could see that his mind was racing.

I was the most valuable of all his possessions. It was not simply my wide range of extraordinary talents that made up the full measure of my worth to him. Even more, it was that I knew intimately every convoluted thread of the intricate tapestry of his affairs. I knew every informer and spy in his network, every person whom he had ever bribed and who had bribed him. I knew which favours were outstanding on each account, which favours remained to be settled, and which grudges were still to be paid off.

I knew all his enemies, a long list; and I knew those he counted his friends and allies, a much shorter list. I knew where every nugget of his vast treasure was hidden, who were his bankers and his agents and his nominees, and how he had concealed the ownership of great tracts of land and stores of precious metals and gemstones in the legal labyrinth of deeds and titles and servitudes. All of this was information that would delight the tax-collectors and cause Pharaoh to revise his opinion of his grand vizier.

I doubted that my Lord Intef himself could remember and trace all his wealth without my assistance. He could not properly order and control his sprawling, shadowy empire without me, for he had kept himself aloof and separated from the most unsavoury aspects of it. He had preferred to send me to take care of those details which, if discovered, might incriminate him.

So it was that I knew a thousand dark secrets, and I knew of a thousand fearful deeds, of embezzlement and extortion, of robbery and bloodiest murder, all of which taken together could destroy even a man as powerful as the grand vizier.

I was indispensable. He could not let me go. And yet, before Pharaoh and the entire population of Thebes, he could not deny Lostris her request.

My Lord Intef is a man full of ire and hatred. I have seen such rage in him that must have made Seth, the god of anger, start up and take notice. But I had never seen such fury as now that his own daughter had him cornered.

'Let the slave Taita stand forward,' he called, and I saw that it was a ruse for him to gain a respite. I pushed my way as swiftly as I was able to the foot of the wedding platform, to give him as little time as possible to plan his next mischief.

'I am here, my lord,' I cried, and he stared down at me with those deadly eyes. We have been together so long that he can speak to me with a look almost as clearly as with the spoken word. He stared at me in silence until my heart was racing and

157

my fingers fluttered with fear, then at last he said in soft, almost affectionate tones, 'Taita, you have been with me since you were a child. I have come to regard you as a brother more than as a slave. Still, you have heard my daughter's request. I am by nature a fair and kind man. After all the years it would be inhuman of me to discard you against your wishes. I know that it is unusual for a slave to be given a say in his own disposal, but then your circumstances are indeed unusual. Choose, Taita. If you wish to stay in your home, the only home you have ever known, then I cannot find the heart to send you away. Not even at the request of my own daughter.' He never took his eyes off me, those terrible yellow eyes. I am not a coward but I am careful of my safety. I realized that I was staring into the eyes of death, and I could not find my voice.

I tore my gaze from his, and looked towards my Lady Lostris. There was such appeal there, such loneliness and terror, that my own safety counted for nothing. I could not desert her now, not at any price or under any threat.

'How can a poor slave deny the wish of Pharaoh's wife? I am ready to do the bidding of my new mistress,' I cried out at the top of my lungs, and I hoped that my voice had a manly ring to it and was not as shrill as it sounded in my own ears.

'Come, slave!' my new mistress ordered. 'Take your place behind me.'

As I mounted the platform, I was forced to pass close to my Lord Intef. His white, stiff lips barely moved as he spoke for my ears alone. 'Farewell, my old darling. You are a dead man.'

I shuddered as though a poisonous cobra had slid across my path and I hurried to take my place in the retinue of my mistress, as though I truly believed that I could find safety in her protection.

158

I STAYED close to Lostris during the rest of the ceremony and I waited on her personally at the wedding feast, hovering at her elbow and trying to make her eat a little of the meats and fine fare that was spread before her. She was so wan and sickly that I was certain that she had eaten nothing in the last two days, not since her betrothal and the condemnation of Tanus.

In the end I succeeded in getting her to take a little watered wine, but that was all. Pharaoh saw her drink and thought that she was toasting him. He lifted his own gold chalice, and smiled at her over the rim as he returned the toast, and the wedding guests cheered the couple delightedly.

'Taita,' she whispered to me as soon as the king's attention was diverted by the grand vizier who sat at his other hand, 'I fear that I am going to vomit. I cannot stay here another moment. Please take me back to my chamber.'

It was an impudence and a scandal, and had I not been able to adopt the role of surgeon, I could never have achieved it, but I was able to creep on my knees to the king's side, and to whisper to him without causing an undue comment amongst the wedding guests, most of whom were well along in wine at this stage.

As I grew to know him better, I found that Pharaoh was a kindly man, and this was the first proof he gave me of it. He listened to my explanations and then clapped his hands and addressed the guests. 'My bride will go to her chamber now to prepare for the night ahead,' he told them, and they leered and greeted the announcement with lewd comment and lascivious applause.

I helped my mistress to her feet, but she was able to make her obeisance to the king and leave the banquet hall without my support. In her bedchamber she threw up the wine she had drunk into the bowl that I held for her, and then she collapsed upon the bed. The wine was all her stomach contained and my suspicion that she had been starving herself was confirmed.

'I don't want to live without Tanus.' Her voice was weak, but I knew her well enough to recognize that her will was as strong as ever.

'Tanus is alive,' I tried to console her. 'He is strong and young

159

and will live for another fifty years. He loves you and he promises to wait for you to the end of time. The king is an old man, he cannot live for ever—'

She sat up on the fur bedcover and her voice became stern and determined. 'I am Tanus' woman and no other man shall have me. I would rather die.'

'We all die in the end, mistress.' If only I could distract her for the first few days of this marriage, I knew I could see her through. But she understood me too well.

'I know what you are up to, but all your pretty words will do you no good. I am going to kill myself. I order you to prepare a draught of poison for me to drink.'

'Mistress, I am not versed in the science of poison.' It was a forlorn attempt, and she crushed it effortlessly.

'Many is the time that I have seen you give poison to a suffering animal. Do you not remember your old dog, the one with abscesses in its ears, and your pet gazelle that was mauled by a leopard? You told me that the poison was painless, that it was the same as going to sleep. Well, I want to go to sleep and be embalmed and go on to the other world to wait for Tanus there.'

I had to try other persuasion. 'But what about me, mistress? You have only this day taken possession of me. How can you abandon me? What will become of me without you? Have pity on me.' I saw her waver, and I thought I had her, but she lifted her chin stubbornly.

'You will be all right, Taita. You will always be all right. My father will take you back gladly after I am dead.'

'Please, my little one,' I used the childhood endearment in a last attempt to cajole her, 'let us talk of this in the morning. Everything will be different in the sunlight.'

'It will be the same,' she contradicted me. 'I will be parted from Tanus, and that wrinkled old man will want me in his bed to do horrid things to me.' Her voice was raised so that the other members of the king's harem might hear every word. Fortunately most of them were still at the wedding feast, but I trembled at the thought of her description of him being relayed to Pharaoh.

Her voice became shriller with the edge of hysteria in it. 'Mix me the poison draught now, this instant, while I watch you do it. I order you to do it. You dare not disobey me!' This command was so loud that even the guards at the outer gates must be able to hear her, and I dared not argue longer.

'Very well, my lady. I will do it. I must fetch my chest of medicine from my rooms.'

When I returned with the chest under my arm, she was up from the bed and pacing around her chamber with glittering eyes in that pale, tragic face.

'I am watching you. Don't try any of your tricks on me now,' she warned me, as I prepared the draught from the scarlet glass bottle. She knew that colour warned of the lethal contents.

When I handed the bowl to her, she showed no fear, and paused only to kiss my cheek. 'You have been both father and loving brother to me. I thank you for this last kindness. I love you, Taita, and I shall miss you.'

She lifted the bowl in both hands as though it were a wassail cup rather than a fatal potion.

'Tanus, my darling,' she toasted him with it, 'they shall never take me from you. We shall meet again on the far side!' And she drained the bowl at a swallow, then dropped it to shatter on the floor. At last, with a sigh, she fell back upon the bed.

'Come, sit beside me. I am afraid to be alone when I die.'

Taken on her empty stomach, the effect of the draught was very rapid. She had only time to turn her face to me and whisper, 'Tell Tanus again how much I loved him. Unto the portals of death, and beyond.' Then her eyes closed and she was gone.

She lay so still and pale that for a moment I was truly alarmed, afraid that I had misjudged the strength of the powder of the Red Shepenn which I had substituted for the essence of the deadly Datura Pod. It was only when I held a bronze hand-mirror to her mouth that the clouded surface reassured me she still breathed. I covered her gently, and tried to convince myself that in the morning she would be resigned to the fact that she was still alive, and that she would forgive me.

At that moment there was a peremptory knock upon the door of the outer chamber and I recognized the voice of Aton, the royal chamberlain, demanding entrance. He was another eunuch, one of the special brotherhood of the emasculated, so I could count him as a friend. I hurried through to greet him.

'I have come to fetch your little mistress to the king's pleasure, Taita,' he told me, in high girlish tones so incongruous with such a large frame. He had been gelded before puberty. 'Is she ready?'

'There has been a small mishap,' I explained, and led him through to see Lostris for himself.

He puffed out his rouged cheeks with consternation when he saw her condition. 'What can I tell Pharaoh?' he cried. 'He will have me beaten. I will not do it. The woman is your responsibility. You must answer to the king, and stand before his wrath.'

It was not a duty that I relished, but Aton's distress was real, and at least I had my medical status to afford me some protection from the king's frustrated expectations. Reluctantly, I agreed to accompany him to the royal bedchamber. However, I made sure that there was one of the older and more reliable slave maids in attendance in my mistress's outer chamber before I left her alone.

Pharaoh had removed his crown and his wig. His head was shaved as bare and white as an ostrich egg. The effect startled even me, and I wondered how my mistress would have responded to the sight. I doubt that it would have raised either her ardour or her opinion of him.

The king seemed as startled to see me as I was to see him. We stared at each other for a moment before I fell to my knees and made my obeisance.

'What is this, Taita the slave? I sent for another—'

'Merciful Pharaoh, on behalf of the Lady Lostris I come to beg your understanding and indulgence.' I launched into a harrowing description of my Lady Lostris' condition, larding it with obscure medical terms and explanations that were intended to divert the royal appetite. Aton stood beside me, nodding in emphatic corroboration of all I had to say.

I am sure that it would not have worked with a younger and more vigorous bridegroom, ready and rearing to get to the business, but Mamose was an old bull. It would have been impossible to tally all the lovely women who over the past thirty years or so had enjoyed his services. In single file they would probably have encircled the city of Thebes of a hundred gates, possibly more than once.

'Your Majesty,' Aton interrupted my explanations at last, 'with your permission, I will fetch you another female companion for the night. Perhaps the little Hurrian with the unusual control of her—'

'No, no,' the king dismissed him. 'There will be plenty of time for it when the child is recovered from her indisposition. Leave us now, chamberlain. There is some other matter that I wish to discuss with the doctor – I mean, with this slave.'

As soon as we were alone the king lifted his shift to display his belly. 'What do you think is the cause of this, doctor?' I examined the rash that adorned his protuberant paunch, and found it to be an infestation of the common ringworm. Some of the royal women washed less frequently than is desirable in our hot climate. I have noted that filth and the contagious itch go together. The king had probably contracted the infection from one of them.

'Is it dangerous? Can you cure it, doctor?' Fear makes commoners of us all. He was deferring to me now as would any other patient.

With his permission, I went to my quarters to fetch my medicine chest, and when I returned, I ordered him to lie on the ornate gold and ivory marquetry bed while I massaged an ointment into the inflamed red circle of skin on his belly. The ointment was of my own concoction and would heal the rash within three days, I assured him.

'In a great measure you are responsible for the fact that I have married this child who is your new mistress,' he told me as I worked. 'Your ointment may cure my rash, but will your other treatment provide me with a son?' he demanded. 'These are troubled times. I must have an heir before I am another year older. The dynasty is in jeopardy.'

We physicians are always reluctant to guarantee our cures, but then so is the lawyer and the astrologer. While I procrastinated he gave me the escape I was searching for.

'I am no longer a young man, Taita. You are a doctor and I can tell you this. My weapon has been in many a fierce battle. Its

163

blade is no longer as keen as once it was. Of late it has failed me when I most had need of it. Do you have something in that box of yours that would stiffen the wilting stem of the lily?'

'Pharaoh, I am pleased that you have discussed this with me. Sometimes the gods work in mysterious ways—' we both made the sign to avert evil before I went on, 'your first congress with my virgin mistress must be perfectly executed. Any faltering, any bending from our purpose, any failure to raise on high the royal sceptre of your manhood, will frustrate our efforts. There will be only one opportunity, the first union must be successful. If we have to try again there will be the danger of your fathering yet another female.' My medical grounds for this prognosis were rather insubstantial. Nevertheless, we both looked grave, he graver than I did.

I held up my forefinger. 'Had we made the attempt tonight, and—' I said no more, but let my forefinger droop suggestively, and shook my head. 'No, we are fortunate to have been given another chance by the gods.'

'What must we do?' he demanded anxiously, and I was silent for a long while, kneeling in deep thought beside his bed.

It was difficult not to let my relief and satisfaction become apparent. Within the first day of my mistress's marriage, I was already working my way into a position of influence with the king, and I had been offered a perfect excuse for keeping her maidenhead intact for at least a little longer, long enough perhaps for me to be able to prepare her for the brutal shock of her first act of procreation with a man whom she did not love and who was, indeed, physically distasteful to her. I told myself that with clever management of the situation, I might be able to draw out this period of grace indefinitely.

'Yes indeed, Your Majesty, I can help you, but it will take some time. It will not be as easy as curing this rash.' My mind was racing. I had to wring every drop out of this sponge. 'We will have to go on to a very strict diet.'

'No more bull's balls, I beseech you, doctor.'

'I think you have had enough of those now. However, we will need to warm your blood and sweeten your generative fluids for the fateful attempt. Goat's milk, warm goat's milk and honey three times a day, and of course the special potions I will prepare for you from the horn of the rhinoceros and the root of the mandrake.'

He looked relieved. 'You are certain this will work?'

'It has never failed before, but there is one other measure that is essential.'

'What is that?' His relief evaporated, and he sat up and peered at me anxiously.

'Complete abstinence. We must allow the royal member to rest and regain its full strength and force once again. You must forsake your harem and all its pleasures for a while.' I said this with the dogmatic air of the physician that cannot be gainsaid, for it was the one sure way to ensure that my Lady Lostris would remain untouched. However, I was worried by what his reaction would be. He could conceivably have flown into a rage at the thought of being denied his conjugal pleasures. He might have rejected me, and I could have lost all the advantage that I had so newly won. But I had to take the risk for the benefit of my mistress. I had to protect her just as long as I was able.

The king's reaction surprised me. He simply lay back on his headrest and smiled complacently to himself. 'For how long?' he asked quite cheerfully, and I was struck by the realization that my strictures had come as a relief to him. For me, to whom the act of love with a beautiful woman would always be an unattainable and elusive dream, it took an immense effort to understand that Pharaoh was content to be relieved of a once pleasurable duty that, by reason of being so often performed, had become onerous.

There must have been at least three hundred wives and concubines in his harem at that time, and some of those Asian women were notorious for their insatiable appetites. I tried to sympathize with the effort that it must require to act like a god night after night, and year after year. The prospect did not daunt me as the actuality seemed to have wearied the king.

'Ninety days,' I said.

'Ninety days?' he repeated thoughtfully. 'Nine Egyptian weeks of ten days each?'

'At least,' I said firmly.

'Very well.' He nodded without rancour and changed the subject easily.

'My chamberlain tells me, doctor, that apart from your medical skills, you are also one of the three most eminent astrologers in this very Egypt of ours?'

I wondered why my friend the chamberlain had qualified his assertion. For the life of me I could not think who the other two might be, but I inclined my head modestly. 'He flatters me, Your Majesty, but perhaps I do have some little knowledge of the heavenly bodies.'

'Cast a horoscope for me!' he ordered, sitting up eagerly.

'Now?' I asked with surprise.

'Now!' he agreed. 'Why not? For on your orders there is nothing that I should rather be doing at this moment.' That unexpected smile of his was really quite endearing, and despite what he meant to Tanus and my mistress, I found myself liking him.

'I shall have to fetch some of my scrolls from the palace library.'

'We have all night,' he pointed out. 'Fetch whatever you need.'

The exact time and date of the king's birth were well documented and I had in the scrolls all the observations of the movements of the heavenly bodies made by fifty generations of astrologers before me. While the king watched avidly, I made the first cast of the royal horoscope, and before I had half finished it I saw the character of the man, as I had observed it, perfectly endorsed by his stars. The great red wandering star, that we know as the eye of Seth, dominated his destiny. It was the star of conflict and uncertainty, of confusion and war, of sadness and misfortune, and in the end of violent death.

But how could I tell him all these things?

I extemporized and put together a scantily veiled résumé of the well-documented facts of his life, and laced these with a few less well-known details that I had gathered from my spies, one of whom was the royal chamberlain. Then I followed with the usual assurances of good health and long life that every client wants to hear.

The king was impressed. 'You have all the skills that your reputation made me expect.'

'Thank you, Your Majesty. I am pleased that I have been able to be of service.' I began to gather up my scrolls and my writing instruments preparatory to taking my leave. It was very late by now. From the darkness beyond the palace walls I had already heard the first cockerel crow.

'Wait, Taita. I have not given you permission to leave. You have not told me what I really want to know. Will I have a son and will my dynasty survive?'

'Alas, Pharaoh, those matters cannot be predicted by the stars. They can give only the general inclination of your fate, and the overall direction that your life will take, without making clear such details—'

'Ah, yes,' he interrupted me, 'but there are other means of seeing into the future, are there not?' I was alarmed by the direction in which his questions were leading, and I attempted to head him off, but he was determined.

'You interest me, Taita, and I have made enquiry about you. You are an adept of the Mazes of Ammon-Ra.' I was distressed. How had he found this out? Very few knew of this esoteric gift of mine, and I wanted it to remain thus. However, I could not blatantly deny it, so I remained silent.

'I saw the Mazes hidden at the bottom of your medicine chest,' he said, and I was relieved that I had not attempted to deny my gift and been caught out in the lie. I shrugged with resignation, for I knew what was coming.

'Work the Mazes for me, and tell me if I am to have an heir and whether or not my dynasty will survive,' he ordered.

A horoscope is one thing; it requires only a knowledge of the configuration of the stars and their properties. Some little patience, and the correct procedure will result in a fairly accurate prediction. A divination by the Mazes of Ammon-Ra is another matter entirely. It requires an expenditure of the life-forces, a burning up of something deep inside the seer that leaves him worn out and exhausted.

These days I will go to lengths to avoid having to exercise this

167

gift. It is true that on rare occasions I can still be persuaded to work the Mazes, but then for days thereafter I am spiritually and physically depleted. My Lady Lostris, who knows of this strange power of mine, also knows of the effect that it has upon me, and she has forbidden me, for my own sake, to practise it, except occasionally on her behalf.

However, a slave cannot deny a king, and with a sigh I reached for the leather bag in the bottom of my chest that contained the Mazes. I set the bag aside and prepared a mixture of the herbs that are necessary to open the eyes of the soul, to enable them to look into the future. I drank the potion, and then waited until the familiar but dreaded sensation of rising out of my own body assailed me. I felt dreamy and far from reality as I brought out the leather bag which contained the Mazes.

The Mazes of Ammon-Ra consist of ten ivory discs. Ten is the mystical number of the greatest potency. Each disc represents a single facet of human existence, from birth to death and the hereafter. With my own hands I had carved the symbols on the face of each of the Mazes. Each one was a tiny masterpiece. By constantly handling and breathing upon them over the years I had endowed them with part of my own life-force.

I poured them from the bag and began to fondle them, concentrating all my powers upon them. Soon they began to feel warm as living flesh to my touch, and I experienced the familiar sensation of depletion as my own strength flowed from me into the ivory discs. I arranged the Mazes face-down in two random stacks and invited Pharaoh to take up each pile in turn, to rub them between his fingers and to concentrate all his attention upon them at the same time as he repeated his questions aloud: 'Will I have a son? Will my dynasty survive?'

I relaxed completely and opened my soul to allow the spirits of prophecy to enter. The sound of his voice began to penetrate into my soul, deeper and deeper with each repetition, like missiles from a sling-shot striking upon the same spot.

I began to sway slightly where I sat, the same way that the cobra dances to the flute of the snake-charmer. The drug took its full effect. I felt as though my body had no weight to it and that I was floating in air. I spoke as if from a great distance and my voice echoed strangely in my own head, as though I sat in a cavern below the surface of the earth.

I ordered the king to breathe upon each stack and then to divide it into halves, setting aside one half and retaining the other. Again and again I made him split each pile and then combine the remainder, until he was left with only two of the coin-shaped Mazes.

For the last time he breathed upon them and then at my instruction placed one in each of my hands. I held them tightly and pressed them to my breast. I could feel my heart pounding against my clenched fists as it absorbed the influence of the Mazes.

I closed my eyes and from the darkness saw shapes begin to emerge, and strange sounds filled my ears. There was no form or coherence to them, it was all confusion. I felt dizzy, and my senses blurred. I felt myself grow lighter still, until I seemed to float in space. I allowed myself to be carried upwards as though I were a blade of dry grass caught in a whirlwind, one of those dust devils of the Saharan summer.

The sounds in my head became clearer, and the dark images firmed.

'I hear a new-born infant cry.' My voice was distorted, as though my palate had been riven at birth.

'Is it a boy?' Pharaoh's question throbbed in my head, so that I felt rather than heard it.

Then slowly my vision began to harden, and I looked down a long tunnel through the darkness to a light at the far end. The ivory Mazes in my hands were hot as embers from the hearth and seared the flesh of my palms.

In the nimbus of light at the end of the tunnel I saw a child, lying in the bloody puddle of its own birth-waters, with the fat python of the placenta still coiled upon its belly.

'I see a child,' I croaked.

'Is it a boy?' Pharaoh demanded from out of the surrounding darkness.

The infant wailed and kicked both legs in the air, and I saw rising from between the chubby thighs a pale finger of flesh surmounted by a cap of wrinkled skin.

169

'A boy,' I confirmed, and I felt an unexpected tenderness towards this phantom of my mind, as though it were truly flesh and blood. I reached out to it with my heart, but the image faded, and the birth cry receded and was lost in the blackness.

'The dynasty? What will become of my line? Will it endure?' The king's voice reached me, and then was lost in a cacophony of other sounds that filled my head – the sound of battle trumpets, the shouts of men in mortal conflict, and the ring of bronze on bronze. I saw the sky above me, and the air was dark with flights of arrows arcing overhead.

'War! I see a mighty battle that will change the shape of the world,' I cried to make myself heard above the sounds of conflict that filled my head.

'Will my line survive?' The king's voice was frantic, but I paid it no heed, for there was a mighty roaring in my ears, like the sound of the *khamsin* wind, or the waters of the Nile boiling through the great cataracts. I saw a strange yellow cloud that obscured the horizon of my vision, and the cloud was shot through with flashes of light, which I knew were the reflection of the sun from weapons of war.

'What of my dynasty?' Pharaoh's voice tugged at my mind, and the vision faded. There was a silence in my head and I saw a tree standing upon the bank of the river. It was a great acacia in full leaf, and its branches were heavy with fruit pods. On the topmost branch was perched a hawk, the royal hawk, but even as I watched, the hawk changed shape and colour. It was transformed into the double crown of Egypt, red and white, the papyrus and the lotus of the two kingdoms entwined. Then, before my eyes, the waters of the Nile rose and fell, and rose and fell again. Five times in all I saw the waters flood.

While still I stared with burning eyes, abruptly the sky above the tree darkened with flying insects, and a dense cloud of locusts descended upon the tree. They covered it completely. When they rose again the tree was devastated and bare of the last trace of green. Not a leaf remained on the dry brown twigs. Then the dead tree toppled and fell ponderously to earth. The fall shattered the trunk and the crown was smashed into pieces. The fragments turned to dust and were blown away on the wind.

Nothing remained but the wind and the driven sands of the desert.

'What is it that you see?' Pharaoh demanded, but it all faded and I found myself once more seated on the floor of the king's bedchamber. I was gasping for breath, as though I had run a great distance, and salt sweat scalded my eyes and poured down my body in rivulets to soak the linen of my kilt and to form a pool on the tiles beneath me. I was shaking with a burning fever and there was that familiar sick and heavy feeling in the pit of my stomach that I knew would be with me for days to come.

Pharaoh was staring at me and I realized what a haggard and dreadful sight I presented to him. 'What did you see?' he whispered. 'Will my line survive?'

I could not tell him the truth of my vision, so I invented another to satisfy him. 'I saw a forest of great trees that reached to the horizon of my dream. There was no end to their number and on top of each tree there was a crown, the red and the white crown of the two kingdoms.'

Pharaoh sighed and covered his eyes with his hands for a while. We sat in silence, he in the release that my lie had given him, and I in sympathy for him.

At last I lied softly. 'The forest that I saw was the line of your descendants,' I whispered, to spare him. 'They reach to the boundaries of time, and each of them wears the crown of Egypt.'

He uncovered his eyes, and his gratitude and his joy were pathetic to watch. 'Thank you, Taita. I can see how the divination has taxed your strength. You may go now and rest. Tomorrow the court will sail for my palace on Elephantine Island. I will have a galley set aside for the safe passage of you and your mistress. Guard her with your life, for she is the vessel that contains the seeds of my immortality.'

I was so weak that I had to use the frame of the bed to lift myself to my feet. I tottered to the door and steadied myself against the jamb. However, I was not so weakened that I could not think of my duty to my mistress.

'There is the matter of the marriage sheet. The populace will expect to have it displayed,' I reminded him. 'Both your reputation and that of my mistress is at stake.'

171

'What do you suggest, Taita?' This soon he was relying on me. I told him what must be done, and he nodded. 'See to it!'

Carefully I folded the sheet that covered the royal bed. It was of the finest linen, white as the high cirrus clouds of summer, embroidered with the rare silk thread that the trade caravans occasionally bring in from the East. I carried the folded sheet with me when I left the king's bed-chamber and made my way back through the still dark and silent palace to the harem.

My mistress was sleeping like a dead woman, and I knew that with the amount of the Red Shepenn I had given her, she would sleep the day away and would probably only wake that evening. I sat beside her bed for a while. I felt exhausted and depressed for the Mazes had drained my soul. The images they had evoked still troubled me. I felt certain that the infant I had seen was that of my mistress, but then how could the rest of my vision be explained? There seemed to be no answer to the riddle, and I set the thought aside for I still had work to do.

Squatting beside Lostris' bed, I spread the embroidered sheet upon the floor. The blade of my dagger was sharp enough to shave the hair from my forearm. I picked out one of the blue rivers of blood beneath the smooth skin on the inside of my wrist, and I pricked it with the point of the dagger and let the dark slow blood trickle on to the sheet. When I was satisfied with the extent of the stain, I bound up my wrist with a strip of linen to staunch the bleeding, and bundled the soiled sheet.

The slave girl was still in attendance in the outer chamber. I ordered that Lostris was to be allowed to sleep undisturbed. Knowing that she would be well cared for, I was content to leave her, and climb the ladder to the top of the outer wall of the harem.

The dawn was only just breaking, but already an inquisitive crowd of old women and loiterers had gathered below the walls. They looked up expectantly when I appeared.

I made a show of shaking out the sheet before I draped it over the ramparts of the outer wall. The bloodstain in the centre of the cloud-white ground was the shape of a flower, and the crowd buzzed with gossip at this badge of my mistress's virginity and her bridegroom's virility.

At the rear of the crowd stood a figure taller than those around him. His head was covered by a striped woollen shawl. It was only when he threw this back and exposed his face and his head of red-gold hair that I recognized him.

'Tanus!' I shouted. 'I must speak to you.'

He looked up at me upon the wall, and his eyes were filled with such pain as I wished never to see again. That stain upon the sheet had destroyed his life. I also had known the agony of lost love and remembered every detail of it even after all the long years. Tanus' heart wound was fresh and bleeding still, more agonizing than any hurt that he had received on the battlefield.

He needed my help now, if he were to survive it. 'Tanus! Wait for me.'

He threw the shawl over his head, covering his face, and he turned from me. Unsteady as a drunkard, he stumbled away.

'Tanus!' I shouted after him. 'Come back! I must talk to you.' He did not look round, but quickened his pace.

By the time that I had climbed down from the wall and run out of the main gates, he had disappeared into the maze of alleys and mud huts of the inner city.

 I SEARCHED for Tanus half the morning, but his quarters were deserted and nobody had seen him in any of his customary haunts.

At last I had to abandon the search, and to make my way back to my own rooms in the quarters of the slave boys. The royal flotilla was preparing to sail for the south. I had still to assemble and pack my possessions if my mistress and I were to be ready for the departure. I forced aside the sense of gloom that the Mazes and my glimpse of Tanus had left me, and I set about bundling up my possessions and breaking up the only home that I had ever known.

My animals seemed to sense that something untoward was happening. They fretted and chirped and whined, each trying in his own way to attract my attention. The wild birds hopped and fluttered on the paved terrace outside, while in the corner nearest my bed, my beloved Saker falcons stretched their wings and raised the feathers along their backs, and screeched at me from their perches. The dogs and the cats and the tame gazelle crowded around my legs, trying to brush against me, and hindered my efforts to pack my possessions.

In exasperation I noticed the jug of soured goat's milk beside my bed. It is one of my favourite drinks, and the slave boys make certain that the jug is always refilled. My animals also enjoy the thickened milk, so to distract them I carried the jug out on to the terrace and filled their clay drinking-bowls. They crowded around the bowls, pushing and shoving each other, and I left them and went back to my task, closing the awnings of rush matting to keep them out.

It is curious how many possessions even a slave can gather about him over a lifetime. The boxes and bundles were piled high against one wall before I was at last finished. By this time my mood of depression and weariness was almost prostrating, but I was still sufficiently alert to be aware of the silence. I stood for a while in the centre of my room, listening uneasily. The only sound was the jingle of the tiny bronze bells on the jesses of my female falcon where she sat in the far corner and watched me with that intent, implacable gaze of the raptor. The tiercel, smaller but more handsome than she, was asleep on his own perch in the other corner, with the soft leather hood of the rufter covering his eyes. None of my other pets made a sound. Not one of the cats mewed or hissed at the dogs, nor did the wild birds chirrup or sing, none of my puppies growled or tumbled over each other in boisterous play.

I went to the rush awning and drew it aside. The sunlight burst into the room and blinded me for a moment. Then my vision returned and I cried out with horror. They were scattered upon the terrace and down into the garden every bird and animal.

They lay in the abandoned attitudes of death, every one of them where he had fallen. I rushed out to them, calling my favourites by name, kneeling to pick one of them up in my arms and hugging the slack warm body as I searched for signs of life. There was no flicker of it in any of them, though I went to each of them. The birds were small and light in my hand, their marvellous plumage undimmed by death.

I thought that my already heavy heart must now burst with the sheer weight of my grief. I knelt on the terrace with my family scattered around me and I wept.

It was some time before I could bring myself to think about the cause of this tragedy. Then I stood up and went to one of the empty bowls that lay on the tiles. They had licked it clean, but I sniffed at it to try and fathom the nature of the poison that had been intended for me. The odour of soured milk disguised any other smell; all I knew was that it had been swift and deadly.

I wondered who had placed the jug beside my bed, but it did not matter whose hand had carried the vessel to me. I knew with utter certainty who had given the order for it. 'Farewell, my old darling. You are a dead man,' Lord Intef had told me, and he had not waited long to transform the words into the deed.

The anger that seized me was a form of madness. It was aggravated by my unsteady state and sombre mood. I found that I was shaking with a rage that I had never known before. I drew the little dagger from my belt and before I realized what I was doing, I was rushing down the steps of the terrace with the naked blade in my hand. I knew that at this time of the morning Intef would be in his water-garden. I could no longer bear to think of him as my Lord Intef. The memory of every outrage he had ever visited upon me, every agony and every humiliation, was bright and clear in my mind. I was going to kill him now, stab him a hundred times through that cruel and evil heart.

I was in sight of the gate to the water-garden before I regained my sanity. There were half a dozen guards at the gate, and there would be as many more beyond. I would never get within dagger-thrust of the grand vizier before they cut me down. I forced my flying feet to check and turn back. I slipped the dagger into the jewelled leather sheath, and brought my breathing under control. I walked slowly back to the terrace and gathered up the pathetic bodies of my pets.

I had planned to plant a row of sycamore trees along the border of my garden. The holes to take them had already been dug. The trees would never be planted now that I was leaving Karnak, and the pits would serve as graves for my beloved creatures. It was the middle of the afternoon before I had filled the last grave, but my rage was unabated. If I could not yet have my full vengeance, at least I could give myself a foretaste of it.

There was still a little of the sour milk left in the jug beside my bed. I held the jug in my hands and tried to think of some way in which I could get it to the grand vizier's kitchens. It would be so fitting to pay him his own vile coin, although I knew in my heart that the idea was futile. Lord Intef was far too cunning to be taken so easily. I myself had helped him devise the system he used to keep himself secure from poison and assassination. He could not be reached without much careful planning. What was more, he would be especially on his guard now. I would have to be patient, but that was impossible. Even if I could not kill him yet, I could exact some lesser payment as a deposit against what I was determined must follow.

Still carrying the fatal jug, I slipped out of one of the side-doors of the boys' quarters into the street. I did not have to go far to find a milkman surrounded by his flock of nanny-goats. While I waited he stripped the rich milk from the swollen udders of one of them, topping the jug to the brim. Whoever had prepared the poison had used enough to murder half the citizens of Karnak. I knew that more than sufficient remained in the jug for my purpose.

One of the grand vizier's bodyguards loafed at the door to Rasfer's chamber. The fact that he had him under guard proved to me that Rasfer was still valuable to Lord Intef, and the loss of his personal lieutenant would annoy if not seriously discommode him.

The guard recognized me and waved me into the sick-room that smelled like a sty. Rasfer lay on his filthy bed, basting in his own sweat. However, I could tell at once that my surgery had been successful, for he opened his eyes and cursed me weakly. He must also be so certain of his own eventual recovery that he need no longer toady to me.

'Where have you been, you ball-less freak?' he growled at me, hardening my resolve and ridding me of the last traces of any pity that I might have felt for him. 'I have been in agony ever since you drilled into my skull. What kind of physician are you—'

There was much more in this style, which I pretended to

ignore as I unwound the soiled bandage from around his head. My interest was purely academic as I examined the small wound that the trepan had left in his scalp. It was another perfectly executed operation, and I felt a certain professional regret that it would be wasted.

'Give me something for the pain, eunuch!' Rasfer tried to seize the front of my tunic, but I was too quick for him and stepped back out of his reach.

I made a fuss of shaking a few crystals of harmless salt from a glass vial into his drinking-bowl, and then topped it up with milk from my jug.

'If the pain becomes too bad, this will relieve it,' I told him as I set the bowl near to his hand. Even at this stage, I could not bring myself to hand it to him directly.

He heaved himself up on one elbow and reached for the bowl to guzzle it down. Before his fingers touched it, I pushed it out of his reach with my foot. At the moment I thought that this was merely a desire to prolong the anticipation, and I felt satisfaction at his distress as he whined at me, 'Good Taita, give me the potion. Let me drink. This pain in my head will drive me mad.'

'First let's talk a while, good Rasfer. Did you hear that the Lady Lostris asked for me as her parting gift from Lord Intef?'

Even in his pain, he grinned at me. 'You are a fool if you think he will let you go. You are a dead man.'

'The very words Lord Intef used. Will you mourn for me, Rasfer? Will you weep for me when I am gone?' I asked softly, and he began to chuckle, then broke it off and glanced at the bowl.

'In my own way, I have always been rather fond of you,' he grunted. 'Now let me have the bowl.'

'How fond of me were you when you castrated me?' I asked, and he stared up at me.

'Surely you do not still bear a grudge for that? It was long ago, and besides, I could not disobey the orders of Lord Intef. Be reasonable, Taita, let me have the bowl.'

'You laughed as you cut me. Why did you laugh? Did you enjoy it so much?'

He shrugged and then winced at the pain that the movement

caused him. 'I am a jovial man. I always laugh. Come now, old friend, say you forgive me and let me have the bowl.'

I nudged it towards him with my foot. He reached out and seized it, his movements still uncoordinated. A few drops slopped over the rim as he raised it greedily to his mouth.

I didn't realize what I was about to do, until I had leapt forward and struck the bowl out of his hands. It hit the floor without shattering and rolled into the corner, splashing milk up on to the wall.

Rasfer and I stared at each other. I was appalled by my own stupidity and my weakness. If ever a man deserved a death by the agony of poison, it was this one. But then I saw again the contorted bodies of my pets strewn across the terrace, and I knew why I had not been able to allow Rasfer to drink. Only a fiend could commit such an act. I have too high a regard for myself ever to descend to the ignominy of the poisoner.

I saw understanding dawn in Rasfer's bloodshot eyes. 'Poison,' he whispered. 'The bowl was poisoned.'

'It was sent to me by Lord Intef.' I don't know why I told him this. Perhaps I was trying to excuse myself for the atrocity that I had almost committed. I don't know why I was behaving so strangely. Maybe it was still the after-effects of working the Mazes. I staggered slightly as I turned for the door.

Behind me Rasfer began to laugh, softly at first and then louder, until great gusty bellows of laughter seemed to shake the walls.

'You are a fool, eunuch,' he roared after me as I ran. 'You should have done it. You should have killed me, for now as surely as I have a hole between my buttocks, I will kill you.'

As I had expected, when at last I returned to her chamber my Lady Lostris was still asleep. I settled at the foot of her bed, intending to wait for her to wake on her own. However, the rigours and the exertions of the past day and night had been too much for me. I slumped down and fell asleep, curled like a puppy on the tiles.

I WOKE under attack. Something struck the side of my head such a painful blow that I was on my feet before I was properly awake. The next blow took me across the shoulder and stung like the bite of a hornet.

'You cheated me!' my Lady Lostris screamed at me. 'You did not let me die.' She swung the fan again. It was a formidable weapon, the bamboo handle was as long as twice the span of my arms, and the comb at its head that held the fan of ostrich feathers was of solid silver. Fortunately she was still groggy from the drug and from oversleeping, and her aim was erratic. I ducked under the blow, and the momentum of it swung her around so that she collapsed on the bed again.

She dropped the fan and burst into tears. 'I wanted to die. Why did you not let me die?'

It was some time before I could approach her, and put one arm around her to comfort her. 'Did I hurt you, Taita?' she asked. 'I have never beaten you before.'

'Your first attempt was a very good one,' I congratulated her ruefully. 'In fact you are so good at it that I do not think you need practise it further.' Theatrically I rubbed the side of my head, and she smiled through her tears.

'Poor Taita. I do treat you so badly. But you did deserve it. You cheated me. I wanted to die and you disobeyed me.'

I saw it was time to change the subject. 'Mistress, I have the most remarkable news for you. But you must promise to tell no one of it, not even your maids.' Not since she had first learned to talk had she been able to resist a secret, but then what woman can? The promise of one had always been enough to distract her, and it worked yet again.

Even with her heart broken and the threat of suicide hanging over her, she sniffed back the last of her tears and ordered, 'Tell me!'

Recently, I had accumulated a good store of secrets to choose from, and I paused for a moment to make my selection. I would not tell her of the poisoning of my pets, of course, nor of my glimpse of Tanus. I needed something to cheer her rather than to depress her further.

'Last night I went to Pharaoh's bedchamber and I spoke to him for half the night.'

The tears rose to the surface of her eyes once more, 'Oh, Taita, I hate him. He's an ugly old man. I don't want to have to—'

I wanted no more in that vein, in moments she would be weeping again, so I hurried on, 'I worked the Mazes for him.' Instantly I had her complete attention. My Lady Lostris is totally fascinated by my powers of divination. If it were not for the deleterious effect that the Mazes have upon my health, she would make me work them every single day.

'Tell me! What did you see?' She was riveted. No thought of suicide now, all sadness forgotten. She was still so young and artless that I felt ashamed of my trickery, even though it was for her own good.

'I had the most extraordinary visions, mistress. I have never had such clear images, such depths of sight—'

'Tell me! I declare I will die of impatience if you don't tell me immediately.'

'First you must swear secrecy. Not another soul must ever know what I saw. These are affairs of state and dire consequence.'

'I swear. I swear.'

'We cannot take these matters lightly—'

'Get on with it, Taita. You are teasing me now. I order you to tell me this very moment or, or,' she groped for a threat to coerce me, 'or I shall beat you again.'

'Very well. Listen to my vision. I saw a great tree upon the bank of the Nile. Upon the summit of the tree was the crown of Egypt.'

'Pharaoh! The tree was the king.' She saw it at once, and I nodded. 'Go on, Taita. Tell me the rest of it.'

'I saw the Nile rise and fall five times.'

'Five years, the passing of five years!' She clapped her hands with excitement. She loves to unravel the riddles of my dreams.

'Then the tree was devoured by locusts, and thrown down and turned to dust.'

She stared at me, unable to utter the words, so I spoke for her.

'In five years Pharaoh will be dead, and you will be a free woman. Free from your father's thrall. Free to go to Tanus, with no man to stop you.'

'If you are lying to me, it will be too cruel to bear. Please say it is true.'

'It is true, my lady, but there is more. In the vision, I saw a new-born babe, a boy child, a son. I felt my love go out to the infant, and I knew that you were the mother of the child.'

'The father, who was the father of my baby? Oh, Taita, tell me please.'

'In the dream I knew with absolute certainty that the father was Tanus.' This was the first deviation from the truth that I had allowed myself, but once again I had the consolation of believing that it was for her benefit.

She was silent for a long time, but her face shone with an inner glow that was all the reward I could ever ask for. Then at last she whispered, 'I can wait for five years. I was prepared to wait all eternity for him. It will be hard, but I can wait five years for Tanus. You were right not to let me die, Taita. It would have been an offence in the face of the gods.'

My relief buoyed me up, and I now felt more confident that I would be able to steer her safely through all that lay ahead.

AT DAWN the following day the royal flotilla sailed south from Karnak. As the king had promised, my Lady Lostris and all her entourage were on board one of the small, fast galleys of the southern squadron.

I sat with my mistress on the cushions under the awning on the poop that the captain had arranged especially for her. We looked back at the lime-washed buildings of the city shining in the first tangerine tints of the rising sun.

'I cannot think where he has gone.' She was fretting over Tanus as she had a score of times since we had set sail. 'Did you look everywhere for him?'

'Everywhere,' I confirmed. 'I spent half the morning scouring the inner city and the docks. He has disappeared. But I left your message with Kratas. You can be sure Kratas will deliver it to him.'

'Five years without him, will they ever pass?'

 THE VOYAGE up-river passed pleasantly enough in long, leisurely days spent sitting on the poop-deck in conversation with my mistress. We discussed every detail of our changed circumstances in great depth, and examined all that we might expect and hope for in the future.

I explained to her all the complexities of life at the court, the precedent and the protocol. I traced for her the hidden lines of power and influence, and I listed all those whom it would be in our interest to cultivate and those whom we could safely ignore. I explained to her the issues of the day, and how Pharaoh stood on each of them. Then I went on to discuss with her the feeling and the mood of the citizenry.

In a large measure I was indebted to my friend Aton, the royal chamberlain, for all this intelligence. It seemed that over the last dozen years every ship that had come down-river from Elephantine Island to Karnak had carried a letter from him to me full of these fascinating details, and on its return to Elephantine Island had carried a golden token of my gratitude back to my friend, Aton.

I was determined that we would soon be at the centre of the court and in the mainstream of power. I had not trained my mistress all these years to see the weapons that I had placed in her armoury rust with disuse. The sum of her many accomplishments and her talents was already formidable, but I was patiently adding to it each day. She had a keen and restless mind. Once I had helped her to throw off the black mood that had threatened to destroy her, she was, as always, open to my instruction. Every chance I had, I fired up her ambition and her eagerness to take up the role I had planned for her.

I soon found that one of the most effective means of enlisting her attention and cooperation was to suggest that all this would be to the eventual benefit and advantage of Tanus. 'If you have

influence at court, you will be better able to protect him,' I pointed out to her. 'The king has set him an almost impossible task to fulfil. Tanus will need us if he is to succeed, and if he fails only you will be able to save him from the sentence that the king has placed upon him.'

'What can we do to help him carry out his task?' At the mention of Tanus I immediately had all her attention. 'Tell me truly, will any man be able to stamp out the Shrikes? Is it not too difficult a mission, even for a man like Tanus?'

The bandits that terrorized the Upper Kingdom called themselves the Shrikes, after those fierce birds. Our Nile shrike is smaller than a dove; a handsome little creature with a white chest and throat and a black back and cap, it plunders the nests of other birds and makes a grisly display of the pathetic carcasses of its victims by hanging them on the thorns of the acacia tree. Its vernacular name is the Butcher Bird.

In the beginning the bandits had used it as a cryptic name to conceal their identity and to hide their existence, but since they had grown so strong and fearless, they had adopted it openly and often used the black and white feather of the Butcher Bird as their emblem.

In the beginning they would leave the feather on the doorway of a home they had robbed or on the corpse of one of their victims. But in those days, so bold and so organized had they become that at times they might send a feather to an intended victim as a warning. In most cases that was all that was necessary to make the victim pay over a half of all he owned in the world. That was preferable to having all of it pillaged, and having his wives and daughters carried off and raped, and he and his sons thrown into the burning ruins of their home to boot.

'Do you think it possible that even with the power of the hawk seal Tanus will be able to carry out the king's mission?' my mistress repeated. 'I have heard that all the bands of the Shrikes in the whole of the Upper Kingdom are controlled by one man, someone that they call the Akh-Seth, the brother of Seth. Is that true, Taita?'

I thought for a moment before I answered. I could not yet tell her all I knew of the Shrikes, for if I did so, then I would be forced to reveal how such knowledge had come into my possession. At this stage that would not be much to her advantage, nor to my credit. There might be a time for these disclosures later.

'I have also heard that rumour,' I agreed cautiously. 'It seems to me that if Tanus were to find and crush this one man, Akh-Seth, then the Shrikes would crumble away. But Tanus will need help that only I can give him.'

She looked at me shrewdly. 'How can you help him?' she demanded. 'And what do you know about this business?'

She is quick, and hard to deceive. She sensed at once that I was hiding something from her. I had to retreat swiftly and to play on her love of Tanus and her trust in me.

'For Tanus' sake, ask me no more now. Only give me your permission to do what I can to help him complete the task that Pharaoh has set him.'

'Yes, of course we must do all in our power. Tell me how I can help.'

'I will stay with you at the court on Elephantine Island for ninety days, but then you must give me leave to go to him—'

'No, no,' she interrupted me, 'if you can be of help to Tanus, you must go immediately.'

'Ninety days,' I repeated stubbornly. That was the period of grace that I had won for her. Although I was torn between these two dear children of mine, my first duty was to my mistress.

I knew that I could not leave her alone at the court without a friend or a mentor. I also knew that I had to be with her when the king finally sent for her in the night.

'I cannot leave you yet, but don't worry. I have left a message for Tanus with Kratas. They will be expecting me, and I have explained to Kratas all that has to be done before I arrive back at Karnak.' I would not tell her more, and there can be few as obtuse or as evasive as I can be when I set myself to it.

The flotilla sailed only during the day. Neither the navigational skills of Admiral Nembet nor the comfort of the king and his court would stand up to a night passage, so every evening we moored and a forest of hundreds of tents sprang up on the riverbank. Always the royal stewards chose the most congenial spot to pitch camp, usually in a grove of palm trees or in the lee of a sheltering hillock, with a temple or a village nearby from which we were able to draw supplies.

The entire court was still in festive mood. Every camp was treated as a picnic. There was dancing and feasting in the light of the bonfires, while in the shadows the courtiers intrigued and flirted. Many an alliance both political and carnal was struck during those balmy nights, perfumed with the fruity aromas of the irrigated lands along the river and the spicier desert airs blown in from further afield.

I used every moment to the best advantage of both my mistress and myself. Of course she was now one of the royal ladies, but there were already several hundred of those, and she was still a very junior wife. Lord Intef's foresight might change her future status, but only if she bore Pharaoh a son. In the meantime it was up to me.

Almost every evening after we had gone ashore, Pharaoh sent for me, ostensibly to see to the of his ringworm, but in reality to review the preparations begetting a male heir to the double crown. While he watch with interest. I prepared my tonic for potency and virility grated rhinoceros horn and mandrake root, which I mixed warm goat's milk and honey. When he had taken this, I exd the royal member and was delighted for the sake of my ss to find that it possessd neither the length nor the gt one would have expected from a god. I was of the op at my mis tress, even in her virgin state, would be able with its modest dimensions without too much discomfort lly I ould do all in my power to avoid the dread mout if she s unable to stave it off, then I was determined to ne passa ge to womanhood for her.

Having found the king ealthy is uni regions, I recommended a of cor nflour able in these oil and honey to be applied e of royal member at h olive raising, and then I went on al with the ringworm. king's intense gratification my ntment cured the condit. within the three days that I had promised, and my already considerable reputation as a physician was enhanced. The king boasted of my accomplishment to his council of ministers, and within days I was in huge demand throughout the court. Then, when it was known that I was not only a healer but also an astrologer whom even the king consulted, my popularity became boundless.

Every evening there came to our tents a succession of messengers bearing expensive gifts for my mistress from this lady or that lord and begging that she allow me to visit them for a consultation. We acceded to only those with whom we wished to make better acquaintance. Once I was in the tent of a powerful and noble lord, he with his kilt up around his waist while I examined his haemorrhoids, it was a simple matter to extol my mistress and bring her many virtues to the attention of my patient.

The other ladies of the harem soon discovered that my Lady Lostris and I sang a beautiful duet together, and that we could compose the most intricate riddles and tell even more amusing stories. We were in demand throughout the court, and especially amongst the children the harem. This gave me special pleasure, for if there is thing I love more than animals, it is small children.

Pharaoh, who was responsible for our popularity in the first place, soon had the news of it reported to him. This further spurred his interest in mistress, if it were not already sufficiently intense. At time on many mornings she was summoned on board the barge to spend the day in the king's company, while mings, at the royal invitation, my mistress dined at the board, and regaled him and the assembled company with tural wit and childlike grace. Of course J was in her attendance. When the king made no move to force her in order to force her to submit those horrible but her hazy terrors she had conjured up, her feelings towards him moderate.

Beneath him exterior Pharaoh Mamose was a kind and decent man. My Lady Lostris realized this, and like me, she became quite fond of him. Before we reached Elephantine she was treating him like a favourite uncle, and quite unexpectedly would sit on his knee to tell him a story, or would

186

play throwing-sticks with him on the deck of the royal barge, both of them flushed with the exertion and laughing like children. Aton confided to me that he had never seen the king so gay.

All this was watched and noted by the court, who very soon recognized her as the king's favourite. Soon there were other visitors to our tents in the evening, those who had a petition which they wished my mistress to bring to Pharaoh's notice. The gifts they proffered were even more valuable than those offered for my services.

My mistress had rejected her father's gift in favour of a single slave, so she had begun the journey southwards as a pauper, dependent on my own modest savings. However, before the voyage was done she had accumulated not only a comfortable fortune, but also a long list of favours owed by her new rich and powerful friends. I kept a careful accounting of all these assets.

I am not so conceited that I should pretend that my Lady Lostris would not have achieved this recognition without my help. Her beauty and her cleverness and her sweet, warm nature must have made her a favourite in any circumstances. I only suggest that I was able to make it happen a little sooner and a little more certainly.

Our success brought with it some drawbacks. As always, there was jealousy from those who felt themselves displaced in Pharaoh's favour, and there was also the matter of Pharaoh's mounting carnal interest in my mistress. This was aggravated by the period of abstinence that I had enforced upon him.

One evening in his tent after I had administered his rhinoceros horn, he confided in me, 'Taita, this cure of yours is really most efficacious. I have not felt so virile since I was a young man, way back before my coronation and my divinity. This morning when I awoke I had a stiffening of the member which was so gratifying that I sent for Aton to view it. He was mightily impressed and he wished forthwith to fetch your mistress.'

I was thoroughly alarmed by this news, and I put on my sternest expression and shook my head and sucked air through my teeth and tut-tutted to show my disapproval. 'I am grateful for your good sense in not agreeing to Aton's suggestion, Your Majesty. It could so easily have undone all our efforts. If you want a son, then you must follow my regime meticulously.'

This brought home to me the swift passage of time, and how soon the ninety days of grace would be up. I began to condition my mistress for that night which Pharaoh would soon insist upon.

First I must prepare her mind, and I set about this by pointing out to her that it was inevitable, and that if she wished to outlive the king and eventually to go to Tanus, then she would have to submit to the king's will. She was always a sensible girl.

'Then you will have to explain exactly what it is he expects of me, Taita,' she sighed. I was not the best guide in this area. My personal experience had been ephemeral, but I was able to outline the fundamentals and to make it seem so commonplace as not to alarm her unduly.

'Will it hurt?' she wanted to know, and I hastened to reassure her.

'The king is a kind man. He has much experience of young girls. I am sure he will be gentle with you. I will prepare an ointment for you that will make things much easier. I will apply it every night before you retire. It will open the gateway. Think to yourself that one day Tanus will pass through those same portals, and that you are doing this to welcome him and no other.'

I tried to remain the aloof physician and take no sensual pleasure in what I had to do to help her. The gods forgive me, but I failed in my resolution. She was so perfect in her womanly parts as to overshadow the most lovely blossom that I had ever raised in my garden. No desert rose ever bore petals so exquisite. When I smoothed the ointment upon them they raised their own sweet dew, more oleaginous and silky to the touch than any unguent that I could concoct.

Her cheeks turned rosy and her voice was husky as she murmured, 'Up until now, I thought that part of me was meant for only one purpose. Why is it that when you do that, I long so unbearably for Tanus?'

She trusted me so implicitly, and had so little understanding of these unfamiliar sensations, that it required the exercise of all my ethics as a physician to proceed with the treatment only as long as was necessary. However, I slept only fitfully that night, haunted by dreams of the impossible.

AS WE sailed deeper into the south, so the belts of green land on each side of the river narrowed. Now the desert began to squeeze in upon us. In places brooding cliffs of black granite trod the verdant fields under foot and pressed so close as to overhang the turgid waters of the Nile.

The most forbidding of these narrows was known as the Gates of Hapi, and the waters were whipped into a wild and wilful temper as they boiled through the gap in the high cliffs.

We made the passage of the Gates of Hapi, and came at last to Elephantine, the largest of a great assembly of islands that were strung through the throat of the Nile, where the harsh hills constricted its flow and forced it through the narrows.

Elephantine was shaped like a monstrous shark pursuing the shoal of lesser islands up the narrows. On either side of the river the encroaching deserts were distinct in colour and character. On the west bank, the Saharan dunes were hot orange and savage as the Bedouin who were the only mortals able to survive amongst them. To the east, the Arabian desert was dun and dirty grey, studded with black hills that danced dreamlike in the heat mirage. These deserts had one thing in common – both of them were killers of men.

What a delightful contrast was Elephantine Island, set like a glistening green jewel in the silver crown of the river. It took its name from the smooth grey granite boulders that clustered along its bank like a herd of the huge pachyderms and also from the fact that the trade in ivory brought down from the savage land of Cush beyond the cataract had for a thousand years centred upon this place.

Pharaoh's palace sprawled over most of the island, and the wags suggested that he had chosen to build it here at the southernmost point in his kingdom to be as far from the red pretender in the north as possible.

The wide stretch of water that surrounded the island secured it from the attack of an enemy, but the remainder of the city had overflowed on to both main banks. After great Thebes, west and east Elephantine together made up the largest and most populous city in the Upper Kingdom, a worthy rival to Memphis, the seat of the red pretender in the Lower Kingdom.

As at no other place in the whole of Egypt, Elephantine Island was clad with trees. Their seeds had been brought down by the river on a thousand annual floods, and they had taken root in the fertile loams that had themselves been transported by the restless waters.

On my last visit to Elephantine, when I had come up-river to do a survey of the river gauges for my Lord Intef in his capacity as Guardian of the Waters, I had spent many months on the island. With the assistance of the head gardener, I had catalogued the names and natural histories of all the plants in the palace gardens, so I was able to point them out to my mistress. There were *ficus* trees the like of which had never been seen elsewhere in Egypt. Their fruits grew not upon the branch but on the main trunk, and their roots twisted and writhed together like mating pythons. There were dragon's blood trees whose bark, when cut, poured out a bright red sap. There were Cushite sycamores and a hundred other varieties that spread a shady green umbrella over the lovely little island.

The royal palace was built upon the solid granite that lay below the fertile soil and formed the skeleton of the island. I have often wondered that our kings, the long line of pharaohs of fifty dynasties that stretches back over a thousand years, have each of them devoted so much of his life and treasure to the building of vast and eternal tombs of granite and marble, while in their lifetimes they have been content to live in palaces with mud walls and thatched roofs. In comparison to the magnificent funerary temple that I was building for Pharaoh Mamose at Karnak, this palace was a very modest affair, and the dearth of straight lines and symmetry offended the instincts of both the mathematician and the architect in me. I suppose the sprawling jumble of red clay walls and roofs canted at odd angles did have a sort of bucolic charm, yet I itched to get out my ruler and plumb-line.

Once we had gone ashore and found the quarters that had been set aside for us, the true appeal of Elephantine was even more apparent. Naturally we were lodged in the walled harem on the northern tip of the island, but the size and the furnishings of our lodgings confirmed our favoured position, not only with the king but with his chamberlain as well. Aton had made the allocation, and he, like most others, had proved completely defenceless against my mistress's natural charm, and was now one of her most shameless admirers.

He placed at our disposal a dozen spacious and airy rooms with our own courtyard and kitchens. A side-gate in the main wall led directly down to the riverside and a stone jetty. That very first day I purchased a flat-bottomed skiff which we could use for fishing and water-fowling. I kept it moored at the jetty.

As to the rest of our new home, however comfortable it might have been, neither my mistress nor I was satisfied, and we immediately set about improving and beautifying it. With the cooperation of my old friend the head gardener, I laid out and planted our own private garden in the courtyard, with a thatched barrazza under which we could sit in the heat of the day, and where I kept my Saker falcons tethered on their perches.

At the jetty I set up a shadoof to lift from the river a constant flow of water that I led through ceramic pipes to our own water-garden with lily-ponds and fish-pools. The overflow from the pools drained away in a narrow gutter. This gutter I directed through the wall of my mistress's chamber, across a screened corner of the room and out the far side, from whence it returned to the main flow of the Nile. I carved a stool of fragrant cedar wood, with a hole through the seat, and placed this over the gutter so that anything dropped through the bottom of the seat would be borne away by the never-ending flow of water. My mistress was delighted with this innovation and spent far more time perched upon the stool than was really necessary to accomplish the business for which it was originally intended.

The walls of our quarters were bare red clay. We designed a set of frescoes for each room. I drew the cartoons and transposed them on to the walls and then my mistress and her maids painted in the designs. The frescoes were scenes from the mythology of the gods, with fanciful landscapes peopled by wonderful animals and birds. Of course, I used my Lady Lostris as my model for the figure of Isis, but was it any wonder that the figure of Horus was central to every painting, or that on the insistence of my mistress, he was depicted as having red-gold hair and that he looked amazingly familiar?

The frescoes caused a stir throughout the harem and every one of the royal wives took turns to visit us, to drink sherbet and to view the paintings. We had set a fashion, and I was prevailed upon to advise on the redecoration of most of the private apartments in the harem, at a suitable fee, of course. In this process we made many new friends amongst the royal ladies and added considerably to our financial estate.

Very soon the king heard about the decorations and came in person to examine them. Lostris gave him the grand tour of her chambers. Pharaoh noticed her new water-stool of which my mistress was so proud that when the king asked her to demonstrate it for him she did so without hesitation, perching upon it and giggling as she sent a tinkling stream into the gutter.

She was still so innocent as not to realize the effect that this display had upon her husband. I could tell by his expression that any attempt that I might make to delay him beyond the promised ninety days was likely to be difficult.

After the tour, Pharaoh sat under the barrazza and drank a cup of wine while he actually laughed aloud at some of my mistress's sallies. At last he turned to me. 'Taita, you must build me a water-garden and a barrazza just like this – only much bigger, and whilst you are about it, you can make a water-stool for me as well.'

When at last he was ready to leave, he commanded me to walk a little way alone with him, ostensibly to discuss the new water-garden, but I knew better. No sooner had we left the harem than he was at me.

'Last night I dreamed of your mistress,' he told me, 'and when I awoke, I found that my seed had spilled out upon the sheets.

That has not happened to me since I was a boy. This little vixen of yours has begun to fill my thoughts both sleeping and waking. I have no doubt that I can make a son with her, and that we should delay no longer. What do you think, doctor, am I not yet ready for the attempt?'

'I counsel you most strongly to observe the ninety days, Majesty. To make the attempt before that would be folly.' It was dangerous to label the king's desire as folly, but I was desperate to contain it. 'It would be most unwise to spoil all our chances of success for so short a period of time.' In the end I prevailed, and left him looking glummer than ever.

When I returned to the harem, I warned my mistress of the king's intentions, and so thoroughly had I conditioned her to accept the inevitable that she showed no undue distress. She was by this time completely resigned to her role as the king's favourite, while my promise that there would be a term to her captivity here on Elephantine Island made it easier for her to bear. In all fairness, our sojourn on the island could not truly be described as captivity. We Egyptians are the most civilized men on earth. We treat our women well. I have heard of others, the Hurrians and the Cushites and the Libyans, for example, who are most cruel and unnatural towards their wives and daughters.

The Libyans make of the harem a true prison in which the women live their entire lives without sight of a living male apart from the eunuchs and the children. They say that even male dogs and cats are forbidden to pass through the gates, so great is their possessive frenzy.

The Hurrians are even worse. Not only do they confine their women and make them cover their bodies from ankle to wrist, but they force them to go masked as well, even within the confines of the harem. Thus only a woman's husband ever lays eyes upon her face.

The primitive tribes of Cush are the worst of all of them. When their women reach the age of puberty they circumcize them in the most savage manner. They cut away the clitoris and the inner lips of the vagina to remove the seat of sexual pleasure so that they may never be tempted to stray from their husbands.

This may seem so bizarre as to defy belief, but I have seen the results of this brutal surgery with my own eyes. Three of my mistress's slave girls were captured by the slavers only after they were matured and had been subjected to the knife by their own fathers. When I examined the gaping, scar-puckered pits they had been left with, I was sickened, and my instincts as a healer were deeply offended by this mutilation of that masterpiece of the gods, the human body. It has been my observation that this circumcision does not achieve its object, for it seems to deprive the victim of the most desirable female traits, and leaves her cold and calculating and cruel. She becomes a sexless monster.

On the other hand, we Egyptians honour our women and treat them, if not as equals, at least with consideration. No husband may beat his wife without recourse to the magistrate, and he has a legal duty to dress and feed and maintain her in accordance with his own station in society. A wife of the king, or of one of the nobles, is not confined to the harem, but, if suitably escorted by her entourage, may walk abroad in city street or countryside. She is not forced to hide her charms, but, according to the fashion of the moment and her own whim, she may sit at her husband's dinner-table with her face uncovered and her breasts bared, and entertain his male companions with conversation and song.

She may hold, in her own right, slaves and land and fortune separately from the estate of her husband, although the children she bears belong to him alone. She may fish, and fly hawks, and even practise archery, although such masculine endeavours as wrestling and swordsmanship are forbidden to her. There are, quite rightly, certain activities from which she is barred, such as the practice of law and architecture, but a high-born wife is a person of consequence, possessed of legal rights and dignity. Naturally it is not the same for the concubine or for the wife of a common man. They have the same rights as the bullock or the donkey.

Thus my mistress and I were free to wander abroad to explore the twin cities on each bank of the Nile and the surrounding countryside. In the streets of Elephantine my Lady Lostris was very soon a favourite, and the common people gathered round her to solicit her blessing and her generosity. They applauded her grace and beauty, just as they had done in her native Thebes. I was instructed by her always to carry a large bag of cakes and sweetmeats from which she stuffed the cheeks of every ragamuffin we encountered who seemed to her to require nourishing. Wherever we went, we seemed always to be surrounded by a shrieking, dancing flock of children.

My mistress always seemed happy to sit in the doorway of a poor shanty with the housewife, or under a tree in the field of a peasant farmer and listen to their woes and grievances. At the first opportunity she would take these up with Pharaoh. Often he would smile indulgently and agree to the redress that she suggested. So her reputation as a champion of the common man was born. When she passed through even the saddest, poorest quarters of the city, she left smiles and laughter behind her.

On other days we fished together from our little skiff in the backwaters of the lagoons that the inundation of the Nile had created, or we laid out decoys for the wild duck. I had made a special bow for my mistress which was suited to her strength. Of course, it was nothing like the great bow, Lanata, that I had designed for Tanus, but it was adequate for the water-fowl we were after. My Lady Lostris was a better marksman than most men I have watched at the archery butts, and when she loosed an arrow it was very seldom that I was not required to plunge overside and swim out to retrieve the carcass of a duck or a goose.

Whenever the king went out hawking, my mistress was invited to attend. I would walk behind her with my Saker falcons on my arm, as we skirted the edge of the papyrus beds. As soon as a heron rose with heavy wing-beats from a hidden pool in the reeds, she would take one of the falcons from me and kiss its hooded head. 'Fly fast and true, my beauty!' she would whisper to it, and slip the rufter to unmask the fierce yellow eyes, and launch the splendid little killer aloft.

We would watch entranced as the falcon towered high above the quarry, and then folded those sickle wings and stooped with a speed that made the wind sing over his dappled plumage. The shock of impact carried clearly to us over a distance of two hundred paces. A puff of pale blue feathers was smeared across the darker blue of the sky, and then was carried away like smoke on the river breeze. The falcon bound to its prey with hooked talons to bring it smashing to earth. My mistress shrieked in triumph and ran as fast as a boy to retrieve the bird, to lavish praise upon it and pamper it, and then to feed it the severed head of the heron.

I love all creatures of the water and the land and the air. My mistress has the same feelings. Why is it then, I often wonder, that both of us are so moved by these sports of the chase? I have puzzled over it without finding an answer. Perhaps it is simply that man, and woman also, are the earth's fiercest predator. We feel a kinship with the falcon, with his beauty and his speed. The heron and the goose were given to the falcon by the gods as his rightful prey. In the same way, man has been given dominance over all other creatures on earth. We cannot deny these instincts with which the gods have endowed us.

From the earliest age, when she had first developed the strength and the stamina to stay with us, I had allowed my Lady Lostris to accompany Tanus and myself on our hunting and fishing forays. For, perhaps to mask his hatred of his rival, Lord Harrab, my Lord Intef consented to my hunting sorties with young Tanus.

Years before, Tanus and I had taken possession of a deserted fisherman's shack which we had discovered on the fringe of the swamp below Karnak. We had made this our secret hunting-lodge. It was only a short distance from the shack to the edge of the true desert. So from this comfortable base we had the options of fishing the lagoon or of wild-fowling or of hawking that noble bird, the giant bustard, in the open desert.

In the beginning Tanus had resented the intrusion of this gawky nine-year-old girl, skinny and flat-chested as a boy, into our private world. Soon, however, he had grown accustomed to her presence and even found it convenient to have someone to run errands for him and perform the irksome little chores around camp.

Thus, little by little, Lostris had picked up the lore and the wisdom of the outdoors, until she knew every fish and bird by its proper name, and could wield a harpoon or a hunting-bow with equal skill. In the end Tanus had become as proud of her as if it had been he who had invited her to join us in the first place.

She had been with us in the black rock hills above the river valley on the day that Tanus had hunted the cattle-killer. The lion was a scarred old male with a black mane that waved like a field of corn in the wind as he walked, and a voice like the thunder of the heavens. We set my pack of hounds upon him and followed them as they bayed the lion up from the paddock beside the Nile where he had killed his last bullock. The dogs cornered him at the head of a rocky defile. The lion fixed on us as soon as we came up and brushed the dogs aside as he charged through them.

As he came grunting and roaring towards us, my mistress had stood unwavering, only a pace behind Tanus' left shoulder, with her own puny little bow at full draw. Of course, it had been Tanus who had killed the beast, sending an arrow from the great bow Lanata hissing down his gaping throat, but we had both seen Lady Lostris' courage displayed in full measure.

I think it was probably on that day that Tanus first became aware of his true feelings for her, while for my mistress, the hunt and the chase were for ever bound up with the images and memories of her lover. She had remained ever since an avid huntress. She had learned from Tanus and myself to respect and to love the quarry, but not to burden herself with guilt when she exercised her god-given rights over the other creatures of the earth, to use them as beasts of burden, to consume them as food, or to pursue them as game.

We may have dominance over the beasts, but in the same way, all men and women are Pharaoh's cattle, and none may gainsay him. Promptly on the ninetieth night the king sent Aton to fetch my mistress.

BECAUSE OF our friendship and his own feelings for my mistress, Aton had given me ample warning before he came. I was able to make my final preparations well in advance of his arrival.

For the last time I rehearsed my mistress in exactly what to say to the king and how to behave towards him. Then I applied the ointment that I had reserved for this occasion. It was not only a lubricant, but contained also the essence of a herb that I use on other patients to deaden the pain of toothache and other minor afflictions. It had the property of numbing the sensitive mucous membranes of the body.

She was brave right up to the moment that Aton appeared in the doorway of her chamber, and then her courage deserted her and she turned to me with tears brimming against her lids. 'I cannot go alone. I am afraid. Please come with me, Taita.' She was pale beneath the make-up that I had applied so carefully, and a fit of shivering took hold of her so that her small white teeth chattered together softly.

'Mistress, you know that is not possible. Pharaoh has sent for you. This once I cannot help you.'

It was then that Aton came to her aid. 'Perhaps Taita could wait in the ante-chamber of the king's bedroom, with me. After all, he is the royal physician, and his services may be needed,' he suggested in his reedy voice, and my mistress stood on tiptoe to kiss his fat cheek.

'You are so kind, Aton,' she whispered, and he blushed.

My Lady Lostris held my hand tightly as we followed Aton through the labyrinth of passages to the king's apartments. In the ante-chamber she squeezed it hard, and then dropped my hand and went to the doorway to the king's chamber. She paused and looked back at me. She had never looked so lovely or so young and vulnerable. My heart was breaking, but I smiled at her to give her courage. She turned from me and stepped through the curtains. I heard the murmur of the king's voice as he greeted her and her soft reply.

Aton seated me on a stool at the low table, then without a word set up the bao board between us. I played without attention, moving the polished round stones in the cups carved into the wooden board, and Aton won three quick games in succession. He had very seldom beaten me before, but I was distracted by the voices from the room beyond, although they were too low for me to catch the actual words.

Then quite clearly I heard my mistress say, exactly as I had coached her, 'Please, Your Majesty, be gentle with me. I beseech you, do not hurt me,' and the appeal was so moving that even Aton coughed softly and blew his nose upon his sleeve, while it was all I could do to restrain myself from leaping to my feet and rushing through the curtain to drag her away.

For a while there was silence and then a single high, sobbing cry that rent my soul, and once again silence.

Aton and I sat hunched over the bao board, no longer making any pretence at playing. I do not know how long we waited, but it must have been in the last watch of the night when I heard at last the sound of an old man's snores from beyond the curtain. Aton looked up at me and nodded, then he rose ponderously to his feet.

Before he reached the curtains, they parted, and my mistress stepped through them and came directly to where I sat. 'Take me home, Taita,' she whispered.

Without thinking about it I picked her up in my arms, and she hugged me around the neck and laid her head on my shoulder, just like she used to as a little girl. Aton took up the oil lamp and lit the way for us back to the harem. He left us at the door to my mistress's bedchamber. I laid her on the bed, and while she drowsed I examined her gently. There was a little blood, just a smear of it on those silken thighs, but it had staunched itself.

'Is there any pain, my little one?' I asked softly, and she opened her eyes and shook her head.

Then quite unexpectedly she smiled at me. 'I don't know what all the fuss was about,' she murmured. 'In the end, it was not much worse than using your water-stool, and it didn't take much longer either.' And she curled herself in a ball and fell asleep without another sound.

I almost wept with relief. All my preparations and the numbing herbs I had employed had seen her through without damage to either her body or her sweet spirit.

IN THE morning we went out hawking as though nothing untoward had happened, and my mistress mentioned the subject only once during the day. As we picnicked on the bank of the river, she asked thoughtfully, 'Will it be the same with Tanus, do you think, Taita?'

'No, mistress. You and Tanus love each other. It will be different. It will be the most wonderful moment in your entire life,' I assured her.

'Yes, I know deep in my heart that is how it should be,' she whispered, and involuntarily both of us looked northwards along the sweep of the Nile, towards Karnak far below the horizon.

Although I knew well where my duty towards Tanus lay, life on the island was so idyllic, and I so much enjoyed the exclusive company of my mistress, that I delayed my departure with the excuse that she still needed me. In truth, although Pharaoh sent for her night after night, my mistress had a tough and resilient streak in her and was blessed with the instinct of survival in full measure. Very swiftly she learned how to please the king, but at the same time to remain untouched and emotionally unmoved by it. She did not need me as much as Tanus did. Indeed, it was she who began to nag me to leave her at Elephantine and to journey down-river once again.

I procrastinated until one evening, after a full day out in the field with the king, we returned late to the palace. I saw to it that my mistress was bathed and her evening meal was laid out for her before I went to my own rooms.

As I entered my chamber the delicious odour of ripe mangoes and pomegranates filled the air. In the centre of the floor stood a large closed basket which I could tell was filled with these two favourite fruits of mine. I was not surprised to find it there, for never a day passed without gifts being sent to my mistress and me by someone seeking our favours.

I wondered who it was this time, and my mouth filled with saliva as another whiff of the fragrance filled my nostrils. I had not eaten since noon. As I lifted the woven lid and reached for the reddest and ripest of the pomegranates, the fruit spilled and rolled across the floor. There was a sharp hissing sound and a great black ball of writhing coils and gleaming scales flopped out of the basket and lashed out at my legs.

I leaped backwards, but not fast enough. The open jaws of the serpent struck the leather heel of my sandal with such force that I very nearly lost my balance. A cloud of venom was released from the curved fangs. The clear but deadly fluid drenched the skin of my ankle, but with another leap, I managed to evade the second strike that followed immediately upon the first. I threw myself back against the wall in the far corner of the room.

The cobra and I confronted each other across the width of the floor. Half its body was coiled upon itself, but the front portion of it was raised as high as my shoulder. Its hood was extended to display the broad black and white bands which patterned it. Like some dreadful black lily of death swaying upon its stem, it watched me with those glittering, beady eyes, and I realized that it stood between me and the only door to the chamber.

It is true that some cobras are kept as pets. They are given the run of the household, and they keep down the numbers of rats and mice that infest the building. They will drink milk from a jug and become as tame as kittens. There are others of these serpents that are trained by methods of torment and provocation to become deadly tools of the assassin. I was in no doubt as to which kind of cobra this was standing before me now.

I sidled along the wall, trying to outflank it and to reach safety. It launched itself at me, and the gape of its jaw was a pale sickly yellow and tendrils of venom drooled from the tips of its fangs. Involuntarily I yelled with terror as I sprang away from it and cowered in my corner again. The serpent recovered swiftly from the strike, and reared upright. It was still between me and the doorway. I knew that its poison sacs were charged with sufficient venom to kill a hundred strong men. As I watched, its lower body uncoiled slowly and it began to glide across the floor towards me, its flaring head held high and those terrible, bright little eyes fastened upon me.

I have seen one of these snakes mesmerize a fowl so that it made no move to escape at this sinuous approach, but lay before it with a patent air of resignation. I was paralysed in the same way, and found that I could neither move nor cry out again as death glided towards me.

Then suddenly I saw a movement beyond the swaying cobra. My Lady Lostris appeared in the doorway, summoned by my first terrified cry. I found my voice again, and I screamed at her, 'Be careful! Come no closer!'

She paid no heed to my warning as she took in the scene at a glance. A moment's delay or hesitation on her part, and the serpent would have struck at me for the third and last time. My mistress had been at her dinner when she heard my cry for help. She stood now with a half-eaten melon in one hand and a silver knife in the other, and she reacted with the swift instinct of a true huntress.

Tanus had taught her to forsake the awkward double-jointed manner of throwing that is natural to the female, and she hurled the melon she held with the force and aim of a trained javelineer. It struck the cobra upon the back of its extended hood, and for a fleeting instant the blow knocked it flat upon the tiled floor. Like the release of a war bow, the serpent whipped erect and turned its dreadful head towards my mistress and then sped at her across the room in full attack.

I was released from my trance at last and started forward to help her, but I was too slow. Using its tail as a fulcrum, the cobra swung forward and aimed at her with its jaws so widely distended that venom sprayed from its erect fangs in a fine, pale mist. My mistress leaped back, agile and swift as a gazelle before the rush of the hunting cheetah. The cobra missed its strike, and for an instant the impetus threw it flat at her feet, extended to its full glistening, scaly length.

I do not know what possessed her, but she had never lacked in courage. Before the cobra could recover, she hopped forward again and landed with both those neat little sandalled feet upon the back of its head, pinning it to the tiles with her full weight.

Perhaps she had expected to crush its spine, but the snake was as thick as her wrist and resilient as the lash of Rasfer's whip. Although its head was pinned, the rest of its long body whipped up and over and coiled around her legs. A woman of lesser sense and nerve might have tried to escape that loathsome embrace. If she had done so my mistress would have died, for the instant the cobra's head was freed the death-strike would have followed.

Instead, she kept both feet planted firmly upon the writhing serpent, spreading her arms to balance herself, and she screamed out, 'Help me, Taita!'

I was already halfway across the room, and now I dived full length and thrust my hands into the coils of the serpent's body that boiled around her legs. I groped along its sinuous length, down to where it narrowed into the neck, and I seized it and locked both my hands around the cobra's throat, with my fingers entwined.

'I have him!' I yelled, almost incoherent with my own horror and loathing for this cold, scaly creature that struggled in my grip. 'I have him! Get away from us! Stand clear!'

My mistress leaped back obediently, and I came to my feet clutching the creature with a frantic strength, trying to keep its gaping jaws away from my face. The tail whipped back and wound around my shoulders and my neck, threatening to strangle me as I clung to the head. With this grip upon me the snake now had purchase, and its strength was terrifying. I found that I could not hold it, even with both my fists locked around its throat. It was gradually forcing its head free, drawing it inexorably back through my fingers. I realized that the instant it broke out of my grip, it would lash out at my unprotected face.

'I can't hold it!' I screamed, more to myself than to Lady Lostris. I was holding it at arm's-length, but it was pulling itself towards my face, drawing closer to my eyes every moment as waves of power pulsed through it, contracting and tightening the coils around my throat, forcing the head back through my fingers.

Although my knuckles were white with the strength of my grip, the cobra was so close to my face that I could see the fangs flicking back and forth in the roof of its wide gaping jaws. The cobra was able to erect or to flatten them at will. They were bony white needles, and pale, smoky jets of venom spurted from their tips. I knew that if even a droplet of that poison entered my eyes, it would blind me, and the burning pain of it might drive me half-mad.

I twisted the snake's head away from my face so that the spray of poison was discharged into the air, and I screamed again in despair, 'Call one of the slaves to help me!'

'On the table!' my mistress spoke close beside me. 'Hold its head on the table!' I was startled. I had thought that she had obeyed my order and run to find help, but she was at my side, and I saw that she still brandished the silver table-knife.

Carrying the cobra with me, I staggered across the floor and fell to my knees beside the low table. With a supreme effort I managed to force the snake's head down across one edge of the table, and to hold it there. It gave my mistress a chopping-block against which to wield the knife. She hacked at the base of the cobra's neck, behind the hideous head.

The snake felt the first cut and redoubled its struggles. Coil after coil of rubbery flesh lashed and contorted around my head. Hissing bursts of air flew from its gape, almost deafening us, the awful din mingling with the spurts of venom from its fangs.

The little blade was sharp, and the scaly flesh parted under it. Slippery, cool, ophidian blood welled up over my fingers, but the blade bit down to the bone of the spine. With all her strength and with her face contorted by the effort, my mistress sawed at the bone, but now my fingers were lubricated by the cobra's blood. I felt the head slither out between them and the serpent was free, but at the same moment the knife found the joint between the vertebrae and slipped through, cleaving the spine.

Dangling by a thread of skin, the head was thrown about loosely by the cobra's death-throes. Although almost severed from the body, the fangs still flickered and oozed poison. The lightest touch would be enough to drive them into my flesh. I tore at the body with frenzied, bloody fingers and at last managed to unwind it from around my throat, and to hurl it to the floor.

As the two of us backed away to the door, the snake continued its grotesque contortions, knotting itself and coiling into a ball, scaly turns sliding over each other.

'Are you harmed, my lady?' I asked, without being able to tear my eyes away from the death-throes of the carcass. 'Is there any of the venom in your eyes or on your skin?'

'I am all right,' she whispered. 'And you, Taita?' The tone of her voice alarmed me enough to make me forget my own distress, and I looked at her face. The reaction from danger had already seized her, and she was beginning to shake. Her dark green eyes were too large to fit that glassy white face. I had to find some way to release her from the icy grip of shock.

'Well,' I said briskly, 'that takes care of tomorrow evening's dinner. I do so love a nice piece of roast cobra.'

For a moment she stared at me blankly and then she let out a peal of hysterical laughter. My own laughter was no less wild and unrestrained. We clung helplessly to each other and laughed until tears poured down our cheeks.

 I WOULD not trust our cook with it, so I prepared the cobra myself. I skinned and gutted it and stuffed it with wild garlic and other herbs, together with a dollop of mutton fat from the tail of a prime ram. Then I coiled it in a ball and wrapped it in banana leaves and covered the whole bundle with a thick coating of wet clay. I built over the lump of clay a hot fire which I kept burning all day.

That evening when I cracked open the hard-baked ball of clay, the aroma released by the succulent white flesh flooded our mouths with saliva. There are those who have dined at my table who say they have never eaten tastier food than that which I prepare, and who am I to contradict my friends?

I served the flaky fillets to my mistress with a wine of five-palm quality that Aton had chanced upon in Pharaoh's store-rooms. My Lady Lostris insisted that I sit with her under the barrazza in the courtyard and share the meal. We agreed that it was better than the tail of crocodile, or even than the flesh of the finest perch from the Nile.

It was only when we had eaten our fill and sent the rest of it to her slave maidens that we broached the matter of who it was that had sent me the gift of the basket of fruit.

I tried not to alarm my mistress, and made a joke of it: 'It must have been somebody who does not like my singing!' However, she was not to be put off so easily.

'Don't play the clown with me, Taita. It is one direction in which you have little talent. I think you know who it was, and I think I do as well.'

I stared at her, not sure how to deal with what I suspected was coming. I had always protected her, even from the truth. I wondered how far she had seen through me.

'It was my father,' she said with such finality that there was no reply or denial I could give her. 'Tell me about him, Taita. Tell me all the things I should know about him, but which you never dared tell me.'

It came hard at first. A lifetime of reticence cannot be overcome in a moment. It was still difficult to realize that I was no longer completely under the thrall of Lord Intef. Deeply as I had always hated him, he had dominated me body and soul since my childhood, and there persisted a kind of perverse loyalty that made it difficult for me to speak out freely against him. Weakly I attempted to fob her off with only the barest outlines of her father's clandestine activities, but she cut across me impatiently.

'Come now! Don't take me for a fool. I know more about my father than you ever dreamed. It is time for me to learn the rest of it. I charge you straight, tell me everything.'

So I obeyed her, and there was so much to tell that the full moon was halfway up the sky before I was done. We sat in silence for a long time afterwards. I had left out nothing, nor had I tried to deny or to excuse my own part in any of it.

'No wonder he wants you dead,' she whispered at last. 'You know enough to destroy him.' She was silent a little longer, and then she went on, 'My father is a monster. How is it possible that I am any different from him? Why, as his daughter, am I not also possessed by such unnatural instincts?'

'We must thank all the gods that you are not. But mistress, do you not despise me also for what I have done?'

She reached across and touched my hand. 'You forget that I have known you all my life, since the day that my mother died giving birth to me. I know what you really are. Anything you did, you were forced to do, and freely I forgive you for it.'

She sprang to her feet and paced restlessly around the lily pond before she returned to where I sat.

'Tanus is in terrible danger from my father. I never realized just how much until this evening. He must be warned so that he will be able to protect himself. You must go to him now, Taita, without delaying another day.'

'Mistress—' I began, but she cut me off brusquely.

'No, Taita, I will not listen to any more of your sly excuses. You will leave for Karnak tomorrow.'

 SO BEFORE sunrise the next morning I set out fishing, alone in the skiff. However, I made certain that at least a dozen slaves and sentries saw me leave the island.

In a backwater of the lagoon I opened the leather bag in which I had concealed a tom-cat that had befriended me. He was a sad old animal riddled with mange and with agonizing canker in both ears. For some time I had been steeling myself to give him release from his misery. Now I fed him a lump of raw meat laced with Datura essence. I held him on my lap and stroked him as he ate, and he purred contentedly. As soon as he slipped painlessly into oblivion, I cut his throat.

I sprinkled the blood over the skiff, and dropped the carcass of the cat overboard where I knew that the crocodiles would soon dispose of it. Then, leaving my harpoons and lines and other gear on board, I pushed the skiff out into the slow current and waded through the papyrus beds to hard ground.

We had agreed that my mistress would wait until nightfall before she raised the alarm. It would be noon tomorrow before they found the blood-smeared skiff and concluded that I had been taken by a crocodile or been murdered by a band of the Shrikes.

Once I was ashore, I changed swiftly into the costume I had brought with me. I had chosen to impersonate one of the priests of Osiris. I would often ape their stilted gait and pompous manners for the amusement of my mistress. It needed only a wig, a touch of make-up and the correct costume to make the transformation. The priests are always on the move, up and down along the river, travelling between one temple and another, begging or rather demanding alms along the way. I would excite

207

little interest, and my disguise might help to discourage an attack by the Shrikes. On superstitious grounds they were often reluctant to interfere with the holy men.

I skirted the lagoon and entered the town of West Elephantine through the poor quarter. At the docks I approached one of the barge captains who was loading a cargo of corn in leather bags and clay jugs of oil. With the right degree of arrogance I demanded free passage to Karnak in the name of the god, and he shrugged and spat on the deck, but allowed me to come aboard. All men are resigned to the extortions of the brotherhood. They may despise the priests, but they also fear their power, both spiritual and secular. Some say that the priesthood wields almost as much power as does Pharaoh himself.

The moon was full and the barge captain a more intrepid mariner than Admiral Nembet. We did not anchor at night. With the breeze and the full flood of the Nile behind us, we made a fair passage and on the fifth day rounded the bend of the river and saw the city of Karnak lying before us.

My stomach was queasy as I went ashore, for this was my town and every beggar and idler knew me well. If I were recognized, Lord Intef would hear about it before I could reach the city gates. However, my disguise held up, and I kept to the back alleys as I hurried in a purposeful and priestly manner to Tanus' house near the squadron base.

His front door was unbarred. I entered as though I had the right, and closed the door securely behind me. The starkly furnished rooms were deserted and when I searched them, I found nothing to give me any indication of his whereabouts. Tanus had obviously been gone for a long time, possibly since my mistress and I had left Karnak. The milk in a jug by the window had thickened and dried like hard cheese, and a crust of sorghum bread on the plate beside it was covered with a blue mould.

As far as I could see, nothing was missing; even the bow Lanata still hung on its rack above his bed. For Tanus to have left that was extraordinary. Usually it was like an extension of his body. I hid it away carefully in a secret compartment below his sleeping-place, which I had built for him when first he had moved into these lodgings. I wished to avoid moving around the city in daylight, so I remained in Tanus' rooms for the rest of that afternoon, occupying myself with cleaning up the dust and filth that had accumulated.

At nightfall I slipped out and went down to the riverside. I saw immediately that the *Breath of Horus* was at her moorings. She had obviously been in action since last I had seen her, and had suffered battle damage. Her bows were shattered and her timbers amidships had been scorched and charred.

I noted with a stir of proprietary pride that Tanus had made the modifications to her hull that I had designed. The gilded metal horn protruded from her bows, just above the water-line. From its battered condition I surmised that it had done fierce execution amongst the fleets of the red pretender.

However, I could see that neither Tanus nor Kratas was on deck. A junior officer whom I recognized had the watch, but I discarded the idea of hailing him, and instead set out to tour the sailors' haunts around the area of the docks.

It says a great deal for the morals and the sanctity of the priests of Osiris that I was welcomed in the dives and whorehouses like an habitué. In one of the more respectable taverns I recognized the impressive figure of Kratas. He was drinking and playing at dice with a group of his brother officers. I made no move to approach him, but I watched him across the crowded room. Meanwhile I fended off the advances of a succession of pleasure-birds of both sexes who were progressively lowering their tariffs in their efforts to tempt me out into the dark alleyway to sample their well-displayed charms. None of them were in the least deterred by my priestly collar of blue glass beads.

When Kratas at last gave his companions a hearty goodnight and made his way out into the alley, I followed his tall figure with relief.

'What is it you want from me now, beloved of the gods?' he growled at me with scorn when I hurried up beside him. 'Is it my gold or my bum-splitter you crave?' Many of the priests had taken enthusiastically to this modern vogue for pederasty.

'I'll take the gold,' I told him. 'You have more of that than the other, Kratas.' He stopped dead in his tracks and stared at me suspiciously. His bluff and handsome features were only a little flushed and befuddled by liquor.

'How do you know my name?' He seized me by the shoulder and dragged me into a lighted doorway, and studied my face. At last he snatched the wig from off my head. 'By the piles between Seth's buttocks, it's you, Taita!' he roared.

'I'd be obliged if you would refrain from shouting out my name to all the world,' I told him, and he turned serious at once.

'Come! We'll go to my rooms.'

Once we were alone, he poured two mugs of beer. 'Haven't you had enough of that?' I asked, and he grinned at me.

'We'll only know the answer to that in the morning. How now, Taita! Don't be too strict with me. We have been down-river raiding the red usurper's fleet for the past three weeks. Sweet Hapi, but that bow-horn of yours works wonders. We cut up nearly twenty of his galleys and we chopped the heads off a couple of hundred of his rascals. Although it was thirsty work, not a drop of anything stronger than water has passed my lips in all that time. Don't begrudge me a mouthful of beer now. Drink with me!' He raised his mug, and I was also thirsty. I saluted him in return, but as I put the mug down again, I asked, 'Where is Tanus?'

He sobered instantly. 'Tanus has disappeared,' he said, and I stared at him.

'Disappeared? What do you mean, disappeared? Did he not lead the raid down-river?'

Kratas shook his head. 'No. He's gone. Vanished. I have had my men scour every street and every house in all of Thebes. There is no sign of him. I tell you, Taita, I am worried, really worried.'

'When did you last see him?'

'Two days after the royal wedding, after the Lady Lostris married the king, on the evening of the day that you sailed with the royal flotilla for Elephantine. I tried to talk some sense into his thick head, but he would not listen.'

'What did he say?'

'He handed over the command of the *Breath of Horus* and the entire squadron to me.'

'He could not do that, surely?'

'Yes, he could. He used the authority of Pharaoh's hawk seal.'

I nodded. 'And then? What did he do?'

'I have just told you. He disappeared.'

I sipped at the mug of beer as I tried to think it out. Meanwhile Kratas went to the window and urinated through it. It splashed noisily into the street below and I heard a startled passer-by shout up at him, 'Careful where you spray, you filthy pig!'

Kratas leaned out and quite cheerfully offered to crack his skull for him, and the man's grumblings receded rapidly. Chortling with this small victory, Kratas came back to me and I asked, 'What mood was Tanus in when he left you?'

Kratas turned serious again. 'The blackest and most ugly temper I have ever witnessed. He cursed the gods and Pharaoh. He even cursed the Lady Lostris and called her a royal whore.'

I winced to hear it. Yet I knew that this was not my Tanus speaking. It was the voice of despairing and hopeless love.

'He said that Pharaoh could carry out his threat to have him strangled for sedition and he would welcome the release. No, he was in terrible straits and there was nothing that I could do or say to comfort him.'

'That was all? He gave you no hint as to what he intended?' Kratas shook his head and refilled his beer mug.

'What happened to the hawk seal?' I asked.

'He left it with me. He said he had no further use for it. I have it safe aboard the *Breath of Horus*.'

'What of the other arrangements that I discussed with you? Have you done what I asked?'

He looked into his mug guiltily and muttered, 'I began to make the arrangements, but after Tanus was gone, there seemed no point to it. Besides, I have been busy down-river since then.'

'It is not like you, Kratas, to be so unreliable.' I had found that with Kratas hurt disappointment was more effective than anger. 'My Lady Lostris was relying on you. She told me that she trusted you completely. Kratas is a great rock of strength – those were her exact words.'

I could see that it was working yet again, for Kratas is also one of my mistress's ardent admirers. Even a hint of her displeasure would move him.

'Damn you, Taita, you make me sound like a weak-kneed idiot—' I kept silent, but silence can be more irksome than words. 'What in the name of Horus does the Lady Lostris want me to do?'

'Nothing more than I asked you to do before I left for Elephantine,' I told him, and he slammed down his mug.

'I am a soldier. I cannot leave my duties and take half the squadron to go off on some mad adventure. It was one thing when Tanus had the hawk seal—'

'You have the hawk seal now,' I told him softly.

He stared at me. 'I cannot use it without Tanus—'

'You are his lieutenant. Tanus gave you the hawk seal to use. You know what to do with it. Do it! I will find Tanus and bring him back, but you must be ready by then. There is desperate and bloody work ahead, and Tanus needs you. Don't let him down, not again.'

He flushed with anger at the jibe. 'I'll make you swallow those words,' he promised.

'And that will be the finest meal you could set for me,' I told him. I love brave and honest men, they are so easily manipulated.

 I WAS uncertain as to how I would make good my promise to find Tanus, but I left Kratas to sleep off his debauch, and I went out into the town again to try. Once more I made the rounds of every one of his old haunts and questioned anyone who could possibly have seen him. I had no illusions as to the risk I was taking in pursuing my enquiries about Tanus, or as to just how flimsy was my disguise if I should run into anybody who knew me well, but I had to find him. I kept going through the night, until even the shebeens and whorehouses along the waterfront had thrown out the last drunken customers and doused their lamps.

As the dawn broke over the river, I stood tired and disconsolate on the bank of the Nile, and tried to think if there was some possibility I had overlooked. A wild honking cry made me look up. High above me a straggling skein of Egyptian geese was outlined against the pale gold and coppery tones of the eastern sky. Immediately they brought to my mind those happy days that the three of us, Tanus and the Lady Lostris and myself, had spent wild-fowling in the swamps.

'Fool!' I reviled myself. 'Of course that's it.'

By this time the alleyways of the souk were filled with a noisy, jostling crowd. Thebes is the busiest city in the world, no man is idle here. They blow glass and work gold and silver, they weave flax and throw pots. The merchant deals and haggles, the lawyer cants, the priest chants and the whore swives. It is an exciting, flamboyant city and I love it.

I forced my way through the throng and the hubbub of banter and bargaining as the merchants and the farmers displayed their wares for the housewives and the bailiffs of the rich households. The souk stank fulsomely of spices and fruits, of vegetables and fish and meats, some of which were far from fresh. Cattle bellowed and goats bleated and added their dung to the human contribution of excrement that trickled down the open gutters towards old Mother Nile.

I thought of buying an ass, for it would be a long walk in this hottest season of the year, and there were some sturdy beasts on offer. In the end I decided against such extravagance, not only on the grounds of economy, for I knew that once I was out in the open countryside, an expensive animal would certainly attract the attention of the Shrikes. For such a prize they might overcome their religious scruples. Instead, I purchased only a few handfuls of dates and a loaf of bread, a leather bag to carry these provisions and a gourd water-bottle. Then I set out through the narrow streets for the main gate of the city.

I had not reached the gates when there was a commotion in the street ahead of me and a detachment of the palace guards came towards me, using their staves to force a passage through the market crowds. Close behind them a half-dozen slaves carried an ornate and curtained litter at a jog-trot. I was trapped against the clay-daub walls of one of the buildings and though I recognized both the litter and the commander of the bodyguards, I could not avoid a confrontation.

Panic seized me. I might survive a casual scrutiny from Rasfer, but I was certain that even under my disguise, my Lord Intef would know me instantly. Standing beside me was an old slave woman with breasts like two great amphorae of olive oil and a backside like a hippopotamus's. I wriggled sideways until her bulk hid me. Then I settled my wig over my eyes and peeped out from behind her.

Despite my fears I felt a tingle of professional pride that Rasfer was on his feet again so soon after my surgery. He led his troop of bodyguards towards where I hid, but it was only when he drew almost level that I noticed that one side of his face had collapsed. It was as though his unlovely features had been modelled in wax and then held close to a naked flame. This condition is often the consequence of even the most skilful trepanning. The other half of his face was set in its customary scowl. If Rasfer had been hideous before, now he should cause the children to cry and their elders to make the sign against the evil eye when they looked upon him.

He passed close by where I stood, and the litter followed him. Through a chink in the embroidered curtains I caught a glimpse of Lord Intef as he sprawled elegantly on pillows of pure silk imported from the East that must have cost at least five gold rings each.

His cheeks were freshly shaved and his hair was dressed in formal ringlets. On top of his coiffure was set a cone of perfumed beeswax that would melt in the heat and trickle over his scalp and down his neck to cool and soothe his skin. One hand, the fingers stiff with jewelled rings, lay languidly on the smooth brown thigh of a pretty little slave boy who must have been a recent addition to his collection, for I did not recognize him.

I was taken off-guard by the strength of my own hatred as I looked at my old master. All the countless injuries and humiliations that I had suffered at his hands rushed back to torment me, and these were aggravated by his most recent outrage. By sending the cobra to me he had endangered the life of my mistress. If I had been able to forgive all else, I would never be able to forgive him that.

He began to turn his head in my direction, but before our eyes could meet, I sank down behind the mountainous woman in front of me. The litter was borne away down the narrow alley, and as I stared after it, I found that I was trembling just as I had after my struggle with the cobra.

'Divine Horus, hear this plea. Grant me no rest until he is dead and gone to his master, Seth,' I whispered, and I pushed my way on towards the city gate.

 THE INUNDATION was at its height, and the lands along the river were in the fecund embrace of the Nile. As she had done every season from the beginning of time, she was laying down on our fields another rich layer of black silt. When she receded again, those glistening expanses would once more bloom with that shade of green that is peculiar to this very Egypt. The rich silt and the sunshine would raise three crops to harvest before the Nile poured over its banks once more to deliver its bounty.

The borders of the flooded fields were hemmed with the raised dykes that controlled the flood and also served as roadways. I followed one of these footpaths eastward until I reached the rocky ground along the foothills, then I turned southward. As I went, I paused occasionally to turn over a rock beside the path, until I found what I was looking for. Then I struck out with more determination.

I kept a wary eye on the rough and broken ground on my right-hand side, for that was just the type of terrain that would afford a fine ambush for a band of Shrikes. I was crossing one of the rocky ravines that lay across the pathway when I was hailed from close at hand.

'Pray for me, beloved of the gods!' My nerves were so tightly strung that I had let out a startled cry and leapt in the air before I could prevent it.

A shepherd boy sat on the edge of the ravine just above me. He was not more than ten years old, but he seemed as old as

215

man's first sin. I knew that the Shrikes often used these children as their scouts and their sentinels. This grubby little imp looked perfect for that role. His hair was matted with filth, and he wore a badly tanned goat's skin that I could smell from where I stood. His eyes were as bright and as avaricious as those of a crow as he ran them over me, assessing my costume and my baggage.

'Where are you headed, and what is your business, good father?' he asked, and blew a long warbling note on his reed flute that could have been a signal to somebody hidden further up the hillside.

It took another few moments for my heart to steady its wild pace, and my voice was a little breathless as I told him, 'You are impertinent, child. What business is it of yours who I am or where I go?'

Immediately he changed his demeanour towards me. 'I am starved, gentle priest, an orphan forced to fend for myself. Don't you have a crust for me in that big bag of yours?'

'You look well-nourished to me.' I turned away, but he scrambled down the bank and danced beside me.

'Let me see in your bag, kind father,' he insisted. 'Alms, I beg of you, gentle sir.'

'Very well, you little ruffian.' Out of the bag I brought a ripe date. He reached out for it, but before his fingers touched it, I closed my hand and when I opened it again the date had been transformed into a purple scorpion. The poisonous insect lifted its tail menacingly over its head, and the boy screamed and fled back up the bank.

At the top he paused only long enough to howl at me, 'You are not a priest. You are one of the desert djinn. You are a devil, not a man.' Frantically he made the sign against the evil eye and spat three times on the ground, and then he raced away up the hill.

I had captured the scorpion from under a flat rock farther back along the path. Naturally, I had nipped the sting from the end of its tail before slipping it into my bag in readiness for just such an eventuality. The old slave who had taught me to read lips, had showed me a few other tricks while he was about it. One of them was sleight-of-hand.

At the shoulder of the next hill I paused to look back. The shepherd boy was on the crest far above me, but he was not alone. There were two men with him. They stood in a group looking down at me, and the child was gesticulating vehemently. As soon as they saw I had spotted them, all three of them disappeared over the skyline. I doubted they would want further truck with a demon priest.

I had not gone much farther when I saw movement on the track ahead of me, and I stopped short and shaded my eyes against the dazzle of the noonday sun. I was relieved to make out a small and innocent-seeming party coming in my direction. I moved forward cautiously to meet it, and as we drew together, my heart leaped as I thought I recognized Tanus. He was leading a donkey. The doughty little animal was heavily burdened. Atop the large bundle on its back sat a woman and a child, but it trotted on gamely. I saw that the woman was herself heavily burdened, her belly swelling out with her pregnancy. The child balanced behind her was a girl on the verge of puberty.

I was about to hail Tanus and hurry forward to meet him, when I realized that I was mistaken and the man was a stranger. It was his tall, broad-shouldered figure, the limber way he moved and the shining shock of gold-blond hair that had deceived me. He was watching me suspiciously and had drawn his sword. Now he pulled the donkey off the path and interposed himself between me and the precious burden it carried.

'The blessings of the gods upon you, good fellow.' I played out my role as priest, and he grunted and kept the point of the sword aimed at my belly. No man trusted a stranger in this very Egypt of ours.

'You risk the life of your family on this road, my friend. You should have sought out the protection of a caravan. There are brigands in the hills.' I was truly worried for them. The woman seemed gentle and decent, while the child was on the verge of tears at my warning.

'Pass on, priest!' the man ordered. 'Keep your advice for those who value it.'

'You are kind, gentle sir,' the woman whispered. 'We waited a week at Qena for the caravan, and could not wait longer. My mother lives at Luxor, and she will help with the birth of my baby.'

'Silence, woman!' her husband growled at her. 'We want no truck with strangers, even though they wear the robes of the priesthood.'

I hesitated, trying to fathom if there was anything that I could do for them. The girl was a pretty little thing with dark obsidian eyes, and she had quite touched my heart. However, at that moment the husband urged the donkey past where I stood, and with a helpless shrug, I watched them go.

'You cannot bleed for all of mankind,' I told myself. 'Nor can you force your advice on those who reject it.' Without looking back again, I went on northwards.

It was late afternoon before I looked down on the spur of rock that thrust out into the green swampland. Even from this vantage-point it was impossible to pick out the shanty. It was hidden deep in the papyrus beds, and the roof was of papyrus stems, so the concealment was perfect. I ran down the path, leaping from rock to rock, until I reached the edge of the water. This far from the main course of the Nile, the flood was not so significant.

I found our old dilapidated boat tied up at the landing. It was half-flooded and I had to bale it out before committing it to the water. I poled out cautiously along the tunnel through the papyrus. At low ebb of the Nile the shanty stood on dry land, but now there was sufficient water under the stilts that supported it to drown a standing man.

There was an empty boat in better shape than mine tied to one of the hut stilts. I moored mine beside it, climbed the rickety ladder and peered into our old hunting-lodge. It consisted of a single room, and the sunshine streamed in through the holes in the thatched roof, but no matter, for it never rains in Upper Egypt.

The hut had not been in such disorder since the day Tanus and I had first discovered it. Clothing and weapons and cooking-pots were scattered around like the debris of a battlefield. The stink of liquor was even more powerful than that of old food and unwashed bodies.

Those unwashed bodies were lying on an equally unwashed mattress in the far corner. I crossed the littered floor gingerly to inspect them for signs of life, and at that moment the woman grunted and rolled over. She was young and her naked body was full and enticing, with big round breasts and a thatch of crisp curls at the base of her belly. However, even in repose, her face was hard and common. I had no doubt that Tanus had found her on the waterfront.

I had always known him to be fastidious, and he was never a drinking man. This creature and the empty wine jars that were stacked against every wall were merely an indication of how far he had been brought down. I looked at him now as he slept, and hardly recognized him. His face was mottled and bloated with drink and covered with untrimmed beard. It was clear that he had not shaved since last I had seen him outside the harem walls.

At that moment the woman woke. Her eyes focused on me and in a single catlike movement she was off the mattress and reaching for the sheathed dagger hanging on the wall beside me. I snatched the weapon away before she could reach it and offered her the naked point.

'Go!' I ordered softly. 'Before I give you something in your belly that even you have never felt before.'

She gathered up her clothes and pulled them on hurriedly, all the while staring at me venomously.

'He has not paid me,' she said, once she was dressed.

'I am sure you have already helped yourself generously.' I gestured towards the door with the dagger.

'He promised me five rings of gold.' She changed her tone and began to whine. 'I have worked hard for him these last twenty days or more. I have done everything for him, cooked and kept his house, serviced him and cleaned up his puke when he was drunk. I must be paid. I will not leave until you pay me—'

I seized her by a lock of her long black hair and ushered her to the doorway. I helped her, still by means of her hair, into the more dilapidated of the two boats. Once she had poled out of my reach, she turned upon me such a stream of abuse that the egrets and other water-fowl were frightened from the reed-beds around us.

When I returned to where Tanus lay, he had not moved. I checked the wine jars. Most of them were empty, but there were still two or three that were full. I wondered how he had accumulated such a store of liquor, and guessed that he had probably sent the woman back to Karnak to find a ferryman to ship it out to him. There had been enough to keep the entire corps of the Blue Crocodile Guards drunk for a season. Little wonder that he was in such a condition.

I sat beside his mattress for a while, letting my sympathy for him run its full course. He had tried to destroy himself. I understood that, and did not despise him for it. His love for my mistress was such that without it he did not wish to continue living.

Of course I was also angry with him for abusing himself in such a fashion, and for succumbing to such self-indulgent folly. However, even in this pitiful drink-sodden state, I could still find much that was noble and admirable about him. After all, he was not alone in guilt. My mistress had tried to take poison for the very same reason as he had tried to destroy himself. I had understood and forgiven her. Could I do less for Tanus? I sighed for these two young people who were all that I had in life of any real value. Then I stood up and got to work.

Firstly, I stood over Tanus for a while, bolstering my anger to the extent that I could be really harsh with him. Then I took him by the heels and dragged him across the floor of the hut. He came half out of his stupor and cursed weakly, but I took no notice of his protests and tumbled him through the doorway. He plunged into the swamp head-first and raised a mighty splash as he went under. I waited for him to come up and flounder about groggily on the surface, still only half-conscious.

I dropped in beside him, grabbed a double handful of his hair and thrust his head back under-water. For a moment he struggled only weakly and I was able to hold him under with ease. Then his natural instincts of survival took over and he heaved up with all his old strength. I was lifted clear of the surface and thrown aside like a twig in a storm.

Tanus came out bellowing in the effort to draw breath, and

striking out blindly at his unseen adversary. One of those blows would have stunned a hippopotamus, and I backed away hurriedly and watched him from a distance.

Coughing and choking, he floundered to the ladder and hung upon it with his hair streaming into his eyes. He had obviously swallowed so much water and sucked so much of it into his lungs that I felt a tingle of alarm. My cure might have been a little too vigorous. I was just about to go to his aid, when he opened his mouth wide and a foul mixture of swamp water and rotten wine erupted out of him. I was astonished by the quantity of it.

He hung on to the ladder, gasping and gurgling for breath. I swam to one of the stilts of the hut and waited until he had vomited again before I told him, putting all the contempt I could muster into my voice, 'My Lady Lostris would be so proud to see you now.'

He peered about with streaming eyes and focused on me at last. 'Taita, damn you! Was it you that tried to drown me? You idiot, I could have killed you.'

'In your present condition the only damage you could do would be to a jar of wine. What a sorry, disgusting sight you are!' I climbed the ladder into the hut and left him in the water, shaking his head and mumbling to himself. I set about tidying up the mess and the filth.

It was some time before Tanus followed me up the ladder and sat shamefacedly in the doorway. I ignored him and went on with my work, until at last he was forced to break the silence.

'How are you, old friend? I have missed you.'

'Others have missed you also. Kratas, for one. The squadron has been fighting down-river. They could have found use for another sword. My Lady Lostris, for another. She speaks of you every day, and holds her love pure and true. I wonder what she would think of that trollop I chased out of your bed?'

He groaned and held his head. 'Oh, Taita, don't speak your mistress's name. To be reminded of her is unbearable—'

'So broach another jug of wine and wallow in your own filth and your self-pity,' I suggested angrily.

'I have lost her for ever. What would you have me do then?'

'I would want you to have faith and fortitude, as she has.'

He looked up at me pitifully. 'Tell me about her, Taita. How is she? Does she still think of me?'

'More is the pity,' I grunted disgustedly. 'She thinks of little else. She holds herself ready for the day that you two are brought together again.'

'That will never be. I have lost her for ever and I don't want to go on living.'

'Good!' I agreed briskly. 'Then I'll not waste further time here. I'll tell my mistress that you did not want to hear her message.' I pushed past him, swarmed down the ladder and dropped into the skiff.

'Wait, Taita!' he called after me. 'Come back!'

'To what purpose? You want to die. Then get on with it. I'll send the embalmers out to pick up the corpse later.'

He grinned with embarrassment. 'All right, I am being a fool. The drink has fuddled my mind. Come back, I beg of you. Give me the message from Lostris.'

With a show of reluctance I climbed back up the ladder, and he followed me into the hut, staggering only a little.

'My mistress bids me tell you that her love for you is untouched by any of the things that have been thrust upon her. She is still and will always be your woman.'

'By Horus, she puts me to shame,' he muttered.

'No,' I disagreed. 'Your shame is of your own making.'

He snatched his sword from the scabbard that hung above the filthy bed and slashed out at the row of wine amphorae that stood against the far wall. As each one burst, the wine poured out and trickled through the slats of the floor.

He was panting as he came back to me, and I scoffed at him. 'Look at you! You have let yourself go until you are as soft and as short of wind as an old priest—'

'Enough of that, Taita! You have had your say. Mock me no more, or you will regret it.'

I could see he was becoming as angry as I had intended. My insults were stiffening him up nicely. 'My mistress would have you take up the challenge thrown to you by Pharaoh so that you

222

will still be alive and a man of honour and worth in five years' time, when she is free to come to you.'

I had his full attention now. 'Five years? What is this about, Taita? Will there truly be a term to our suffering?'

'I worked the Mazes for Pharaoh. He will be dead in five years from now,' I told him simply. He stared at me in awe and I saw a hundred different emotions pursue each other across his features. He is as easy to read as this scroll on which I write.

'The Mazes!' he whispered at last. Once long ago he had been a doubter, and had disparaged my way with the Mazes. That had changed and he was now an even firmer believer in my powers than my mistress. He had seen my visions become reality too often to be otherwise.

'Can you wait that long for your love?' I asked. 'My mistress swears that she can wait for you through all eternity. Can you wait a few short years for her?'

'She has promised to wait for me?' he demanded.

'Through all eternity,' I repeated, and I thought he might begin to weep. I could not have faced that, not watched a man like Tanus in tears, so I went on hastily, 'Don't you want to hear the vision that the Mazes gave me?'

He thrust back the tears. 'Yes! Yes!' he agreed eagerly, and so we began to talk. We talked until the night fell, and then we sat in the darkness and talked some more.

I told him the things that I had told my Lady Lostris, all the details that I had kept from them both over the years. When I came to the details of how his father, Pianki, Lord Harrab, had been ruined and destroyed by his secret enemy, Tanus' anger was so fierce that it burned away the last effects of the debauchery from his mind, and by the time the dawn broke over the swamps, his resolve was once more clear and strong.

'Let us get on with this enterprise of yours, for it seems the right and proper way.' He sprang to his feet and girded on his sword scabbard. Although I thought it wise to rest a while and let him recover fully from the effects of the wine, he would have no part of it.

'Back to Karnak at once!' he insisted. 'Kratas is waiting, and the lust to avenge my father's memory and to lay eyes on my own sweet love again burns like a fire in my blood.'

 ONCE WE had left the swamp, Tanus took the lead along the rocky path, and I followed him at a run. As soon as the sun came up above the horizon, the sweat burst out across his back and streamed down to soak the waistband of his kilt. It was as though the rancid old wine was being purged from his body. Although I could hear him panting wildly, he never paused to rest or even moderated his pace, but ran on into the rising heat from the desert without a check.

It was I who pulled him up with a shout, and we stood shoulder to shoulder and stared ahead. The birds had caught my attention. I had picked out the commotion of their wings from afar.

'Vultures,' Tanus grunted with ragged breath. 'They have something dead amongst the rocks.' He drew his sword and we went forward cautiously.

We found the man first, and chased the vultures off him in a flurrying storm of wings. I recognized him by the shock of blond hair as the husband I had met on the road the previous day. There was nothing left of his face, for he had lain upon his back and the birds had eaten the flesh away to the bones of the skull. They had picked out his eyes, and the empty sockets stared at the cloudless sky. His lips were gone and he grinned with bloody teeth, as though at the futile joke of our brief existence upon this earth. Tanus rolled him on to his stomach, and we saw at once the stab-wounds in his back that had killed him. There were a dozen of these thrust through his ribs.

'Whoever did this was making sure of the job,' Tanus remarked, hardened to death as only a seasoned soldier can be.

I walked on into the rocks and a buzzing black cloud of flies rose from the dead body of the wife. I have never understood where the flies come from, how they materialize so swiftly out of the searing dry heat of the desert. I guessed that the wife had aborted while they were busy with her. They must have left her alive after they had taken their pleasure with her. With the last

224

of her strength she had taken the infant protectively in her arms. She had died like that, huddled against a boulder, shielding her still-born infant from the vultures.

I went on deeper into the broken ground, and once again the flies led me to where the bandits had dragged the little girl. At least one of them had summoned up the compassion to cut her throat after they had finished with her, rather than let her bleed slowly to death.

One of the flies settled on my lips. I brushed it away and began to weep. Tanus found me still weeping.

'Did you know them?' he asked, and I nodded and cleared my throat to answer.

'I met them on the road yesterday. I tried to warn—' I broke off, for it was not easy to continue. I took a deep breath. 'They had a donkey. The Shrikes will have taken it.'

Tanus nodded. His expression was bleak as he turned away and made a rapid cast amongst the rocks.

'This way!' he called, and broke into a run, heading out into the rocky desert.

'Tanus!' I yelled after him. 'Kratas is waiting—' But he took not the least notice and I was left with no option but to follow him. I caught up with him again when he lost the tracks of the donkey on a bad piece of ground and was forced to cast ahead.

'I feel for that family even more than you do,' I insisted. 'But this is folly. Kratas waits for us. We do not have time to waste—'

He cut me off without even glancing in my direction, 'How old was that child? Not more than nine years? I always have time to see justice done.' His face was cold and vengeful. It was clear to see that he had recovered all his former mettle. I knew better than to argue further.

The image of the little girl was still strong and clear in my mind. I joined him and we picked up the trail again. Now, with the two of us cooperating, we went forward even more swiftly.

Tanus and I had tracked gazelle and oryx, and even lion, in this fashion and we had both become adept at this esoteric art. We worked as a team, running on each side of the spurs that our quarry had left, and signalling every twist or change in it to each other. Very soon our quarry reached a rough track that led eastward from the river and still deeper into the desert. They had joined it, and made our task of catching up with them that much simpler.

It was almost noon, and our water-bottles were empty when at last we spotted them far ahead. There were five of them, and the donkey. It was clear that they had not expected to be followed deep into the desert which was their fastness, and they were moving carelessly. They had not even taken the trouble to cover their back-trail.

Tanus pulled me down behind the shelter of a rock while we caught our breath, and he growled at me, 'We'll circle out ahead of them. I want to see their faces.'

He jumped up and led me in a wide detour out to one side of the track. We overtook the band of Shrikes, but well beyond their line of sight. Then we cut in again to meet the track ahead of them. Tanus had a soldier's eye for ground, and set up the ambuscade unerringly.

We heard them coming from afar, the clatter of the donkey's hooves and the sing-song of their voices. While we waited for them, I had the first opportunity to contemplate the prudence of my decision to follow along so unquestioningly. When the party of Shrikes at last came into view I was convinced that I had been over-hasty. They were as murderous-looking a bunch of ruffians as I had ever laid eyes upon, and I was armed only with my little jewelled dagger.

Just short of where we lay, the tall, bearded Bedouin who was obviously their leader stopped suddenly, and ordered one of the men who followed him to unload the water-skin from the donkey. He drank first and then passed it on to the others. My throat closed in sympathy as I watched them swallow down the precious stuff.

'By Horus, look at the stains of the women's blood on their robes. I wish I had Lanata with me now,' Tanus whispered, as we crouched amongst the rocks. 'I could put an arrow through that one's belly and drain the water from him like beer from the vat.' Then he laid a hand on my arm. 'Don't move until I do, do you hear me? I want no heroics from you now, mind.' I nodded vigorously, and felt not the slightest inclination to protest against these very reasonable instructions.

The Shrikes came on again directly to where we waited. They were all heavily armed. The Bedouin walked ahead. His sword was strapped between his shoulder-blades, but with the handle protruding up over his left shoulder, ready to hand. He had the cowl of his woollen cloak drawn over his head to protect him from the fierce sunlight. It impaired his side-vision and he did not notice us as he passed close in front of us.

Two others followed him closely, one of them leading the donkey. The last two sauntered along behind the animal, engrossed in a listless squabble over a piece of gold jewellery that they had taken from the murdered woman. All their weapons were sheathed, except for the short, bronze-headed stabbing spears carried by the last pair.

Tanus let them all pass, and then he stood up quietly and moved in behind the last two men in the column. He appeared to move casually, as the leopard does, but it was in reality only a breath before he swung his sword at the neck of the man on the right.

Although I had intended backing Tanus up to the full, somehow my good intentions had not been translated into action, and I still crouched behind my comforting rock. I justified myself with the thought that I would probably only have hindered him if I had followed him too closely.

I had never watched Tanus kill a man before. Although I knew that it was his vocation and that he had, over the years, had every opportunity to hone these gruesome skills, still I was astonished by his virtuosity. As he struck, his victim's head leapt from its shoulders like a desert spring-hare from its burrow, and the decapitated trunk actually took another step before the legs buckled under it. As the blow reached the limit of its arc, Tanus smoothly reversed the stroke. With the same movement he struck back-handed at the next brigand. The second neck severed just as cleanly. The head toppled off and fell free, while the carcass slumped forward with the blood fountaining high in the air.

The splash of blood and the weighty thump–thump of the two

disembodied heads striking the rocky earth alerted the other three Shrikes. They spun about in alarm, and for a moment stared in bewildered disbelief at the sudden carnage in their ranks. Then with a wild shout they drew their swords and rushed at Tanus in a body. Rather than retreating before them, Tanus charged them ferociously, splitting them apart. He swung to face the man he had isolated from his mates, and his thrust ripped a bloody flesh-wound down the side of his chest. The man squealed and reeled backwards. But before Tanus was able to finish him off, the other two fell upon him from behind. Tanus was forced to spin round to face them, and bronze clashed on bronze as he stopped their charge. He held them off at sword's-length, engaging first one and then the other, until the lightly wounded man recovered and came at him from his rear.

'Behind you!' I yelled at him, and he whipped round only just in time to catch the thrust on his own blade. Instantly the other two were upon him again, and he was forced to give ground in order to defend himself from all sides. His swordsmanship was breathtaking to watch. So swift was his blade that it seemed that he had erected a glittering wall of bronze around himself against which the blows of his enemies clattered ineffectually.

Then I realized that Tanus was tiring. The sweat streamed from his body in the heat, and his features were contorted with the effort. The long weeks of wine and debauchery had taken their toll of what had once been his limitless strength and stamina.

He fell back before the next rush with which the bearded Bedouin drove at him, until he pressed his back to one of the boulders on the opposite side of the track from where I still crouched helplessly. With the rock to cover his back, all three of his attackers were forced to come at him from the front. But this was no real respite. Their attack was relentless. Led by the Bedouin, they howled like a pack of wild dogs as they bayed him, and Tanus' right arm tired and moved slower.

The spear carried by the first man whom Tanus had beheaded had fallen in the middle of the track. I realized that I must do something immediately if I were not to watch Tanus hacked down before my eyes. With a huge effort I gathered up my slippery courage, and crept from my hiding-place. The Shrikes had forgotten all about me in their eagerness for the kill. I reached the spot where the spear lay without any one of them noticing me, and I snatched it up. With the solid weight of the weapon in my hands, all my lost courage came flooding back.

The Bedouin was the most dangerous of the three of Tanus' adversaries, and he was also the closest to me. His back was towards me, and his whole attention was on the unequal duel. I levelled the spear and rushed at him.

The kidneys are the most vulnerable target in the human back. With my knowledge of anatomy, I could aim my thrust exactly. The spear-point went in a finger's-width to one side of the spinal column, all the way in. The broad spear-head opened a gaping wound, and skewered his right kidney with a surgeon's precision. The Bedouin stiffened and froze like a temple statue, instantly paralysed by my thrust. Then, as I viciously twisted the blade in his flesh the way Tanus had taught me, mincing his kidney to pulp, the sword fell from his fist and he collapsed with such a dreadful cry that his comrades were distracted enough to give Tanus his chance.

Tanus' next thrust took one of them in the centre of his chest, and despite his exhaustion it still had sufficient power in it to fly cleanly through the man's torso and for the blood-smeared point to protrude a hand-span from between his shoulder-blades. Before Tanus was able to clear his blade from the clinging embrace of live flesh and to kill the last Shrike, the survivor spun round and ran.

Tanus took a few paces after him, then gasped, 'I'm all done in. After him, Taita, don't let that murderous jackal get away.'

There are very few men that can outrun me. Tanus is the only one I know of, but he has to be on top form to do it. I put my foot in the centre of the Bedouin's back and held him down as I jerked the spear-head out of his flesh, and then I went after the last Shrike.

I caught him before he had gone two hundred paces, and I was running so lightly that he did not hear me coming up behind him. With the edge of the spear-head I slashed the tendon in the back of his heel, and he went down sprawling. The sword flew out of his hand. As he lay on his back kicking and screaming at me, I danced around him, pricking him with the point of the spear, goading him into position for a good clean killing thrust.

'Which of the women did you enjoy the best?' I asked him, as I stabbed him in the thigh. 'Was it the mother, with her big belly, or was it the little girl? Was she tight enough for you?'

'Please spare me!' he screamed. 'I did nothing. It was the others. Don't kill me!'

'There is dried blood on the front of your kilt,' I said, and I stabbed him in the stomach, but not too deeply. 'Did the child scream as loudly as you do now?' I asked.

As he rolled over into a ball to protect his stomach, I stabbed him in the spine, by a lucky chance finding the gap between the vertebrae. Instantly he was paralysed from the waist down, and I stepped back from him.

'Very well,' I said. 'You ask me not to kill you, and I won't. It would be too good for you.'

I turned away and walked back to join Tanus. The maimed Shrike dragged himself a little way after me, his paralysed legs slithering after him like a fisherman dragging a pair of dead carp. Then the effort was too much and he collapsed in a whimpering heap. Although it was past noon, the sun still had enough heat in it to kill him before it set.

Tanus looked at me curiously as I came back to join him. 'There is a savage streak in you that I never suspected before.' He shook his head in wonder. 'You never fail to amaze me.'

He pulled the water-skin from the back of the donkey and offered it to me, but I shook my head. 'You first. You need it more than I do.'

He drank, his eyes tightly closed with the pleasure of it, and then gasped, 'By the sweet breath of Isis, you are right. I am soft as an old woman. Even that little piece of sword-play nearly finished me.' Then he looked around at the scattered corpses, and grinned with satisfaction. 'But all in all, not a bad start on Pharaoh's business.'

'It was the poorest of beginnings,' I contradicted him, and when he crooked an eyebrow at me I went on, 'We should have kept at least one of them alive to lead us to the Shrikes' nest.

230

Even that one', I gestured towards the dying man lying out there amongst the rocks, 'is too far-gone to be of any use to us. It was my fault. I allowed my anger to get the better of me. We won't make the same mistake again.'

We were halfway back to where we had left the bodies of the murdered family before my true nature reasserted itself, and I began bitterly to regret my callous and brutal treatment of the maimed brigand.

'After all, he was a human being, as we are,' I told Tanus, and he snorted.

'He was an animal, a rabid jackal, and you did a fine job. You have mourned him far too long. Forget him. Tell me, instead, why we must make this detour back to look at dead men, instead of heading straight for Kratas' camp.'

'I need the husband's body.' I would say no more until we stood over the mutilated corpse. The pathetic relic was already stinking in the heat. The vultures had left very little flesh on the bones.

'Look at that hair,' I told Tanus. 'Who else do you know with a bush like that?' For a moment he looked puzzled, and then he grinned and ran his fingers through his own dense ringlets.

'Help me load him on the donkey,' I ordered. 'Kratas can take him into Karnak to the morticians for embalming. We'll buy him a good funeral and a fine tomb with your name on the walls. Then, by sunset tomorrow, all of Thebes will know that Tanus, Lord Harrab perished in the desert, and was half-eaten by the birds.'

'If Lostris hears of it—' Tanus looked worried.

'I'll send a warning letter to her. The advantage we will win by letting the world believe you dead will far outweigh any risk of alarming my mistress.'

231

KRATAS WAS camped at the first oasis on the caravan road to the Red Sea, less than a day's march from Karnak. He had with him a hundred men of the Blue Crocodile Guards, all of them carefully selected, as I had commanded. Tanus and I reached the encampment in the middle of the night. We had travelled hard and were close to exhaustion. We fell on our sleeping-mats beside the camp-fire and slept until dawn.

At first light, Tanus was up and mingling with his men. Their delight at having him back was transparent. The officers embraced him and the men cheered him, and grinned with pride as he greeted each of them by name.

At breakfast Tanus gave Kratas instructions to take the putrefying corpse back to Karnak for burial and to make certain that the news of his death was the gossip of all Thebes. I gave Kratas a letter for my Lady Lostris. He would find a trustworthy messenger to carry it up-river to Elephantine.

Kratas selected an escort of ten men, and they prepared to set off with the donkey and its odorous burden, back towards the Nile and Thebes.

'Try to catch up with us on the road to the sea. If you cannot, then you'll find us camped at the oasis of Gebel Nagara. We will wait for you there,' Tanus shouted after him, as the detachment trotted out of the encampment. 'And remember to bring Lanata, my bow, when you return!'

 NO SOONER was Kratas out of sight beyond the first rise on the westerly road than Tanus formed up the rest of the regiment and led us away in the opposite direction along the caravan road towards the sea.

The caravan road from the banks of the river Nile to the shores of the Red Sea was long and hard. A large, unwieldy caravan usually took twenty days to make the journey. We covered the distance in four days, for Tanus pushed us in a series of forced marches. At the outset, he and I were probably the only ones of all the company who were not in superb physical condition. However, by the time we reached Gebel Nagara,

232

Tanus had burned the excess fat off his frame and sweated out the last poisons from the wine jar. He was once again lean and hard.

As for myself, it was the first time that I had ever made a forced march with a company of the guards. For the first few days I suffered all the torments of thirst and aching muscles, of blistered feet and exhaustion that the *Ka* of a dead man must be forced to endure on the road to the underworld. However, my pride would not allow me to fall behind, apart from the fact that to do so in this wild and savage landscape would have meant certain death. To my surprise and pleasure, I found that after the first few days, it became easier and easier to keep my place in the ranks of trotting warriors.

Along the way, we passed two large caravans moving towards the Nile, with the donkeys bow-legged under their heavy loads of trade goods, and escorts of heavily armed men far surpassing in number the merchants and their retainers who made up the rest of the company. No caravan was safe from the depredations of the Shrikes unless it was protected by a force of mercenaries such as these, or unless the merchants were prepared to pay the crippling toll money that the Shrikes demanded to allow them free passage.

When we met these strangers, Tanus pulled his shawl over his head to mask his face and hide that golden bush of hair. He was too distinctive a figure to risk being recognized and his continued existence being reported in Karnak. We did not respond to the greetings and questions that were flung at us by these other travellers, but ran past them in aloof silence without even glancing in their direction.

When we were still a day's march from the coast, we left the main caravan route and swung away southwards, following an ancient disused track that had been shown to me some years previously by one of the wild Bedouin whom I had befriended. The wells at Gebel Nagara lay on this old route to the sea, and were seldom visited by humans these days, only by the Bedouin and the desert bandits, if you can call these human.

By the time we reached the wells, I was as slim and physically fit as I had ever been in my life, but I lamented the lack of a mirror, for I was convinced that this new energy and force that I felt within myself must be reflected in my features, and that my beauty must be enhanced by it. I would have welcomed the opportunity to admire it myself. However, there seemed to be no dearth of others to admire it in my place. At the camp-fire in the evenings, many a prurient glance was flashed in my direction, and I received more than a few sly offers from my companions, for even such an elite fighting corps as the guards was contaminated by the new sexual licence that permeated our society.

I kept my dagger beside me in the night and when I pricked the first uninvited visitor to my sleeping-mat with the needle-point, his yells caused much hilarity amongst the others. After that, I was spared any further unwelcome attentions.

Even once we had reached the wells, Tanus would allow us little rest. While we waited for Kratas to catch up, he kept his men exercising at arms, and at competitions of archery and wrestling and running. I was pleased to see that Kratas had chosen these men strictly in accordance with my instructions to him. There was not a single hulking brute amongst them. Apart from Tanus himself, they were all small, agile men aptly suited to the role that I planned for them.

Kratas arrived only two days behind us. Taking into account his return to Karnak and the time taken up by the tasks that Tanus had set for him there, this meant that he must have travelled even more swiftly than we had done.

'What held you up?' Tanus greeted him. 'Did you find a willing maid on the way?'

'I had two heavy burdens to carry,' Kratas replied, as they embraced. 'Your bow, and the hawk seal. I am glad to be rid of both of them.' He handed over both the weapon and the statuette with a grin, delighted as ever to be back with Tanus.

Tanus immediately took Lanata out into the desert. I went with him and helped him stalk close to a herd of gazelle. With these fleet little creatures racing and leaping across the plain, it was an extraordinary sight to watch Tanus bowl over a dozen of them at full run with as many arrows. That night, as we feasted on grilled livers and fillets of gazelle, we discussed the next stage of my plan.

In the morning we left Kratas in command of the guards, and Tanus and I set out alone for the coast. It was only half a day's travel to the small fishing village which was our goal, and at noon we topped the last rise and looked down from the hills on to the glittering expanse of the sea spread below us. From this height we could see clearly the dark outline of the coral reefs beneath the turquoise waters.

As soon as we entered the village, Tanus called for the headman, and so apparent from his bearing was Tanus' importance and authority, that the old man came at a run. When Tanus showed him the hawk seal, he fell to the earth in obeisance, as though it were Pharaoh himself who stood before him, and beat his head upon the ground with such force that I feared he might do himself serious injury. When I lifted him to his feet once more, he led us to the finest lodgings in the village, his own filthy hovel, and turned his numerous family out to make room for us.

Once we had eaten a bowl of the fish stew that our host provided and drunk a cup of the delicious palm wine, Tanus and I went down to the beach of dazzling white sand and bathed away the sweat and the dust of the desert in the warm waters of the lagoon that was enclosed by the jagged barricade of coral that lay parallel to the shore. Behind us the harsh mountains, devoid of the faintest green tinge of growing things, thrust up into the aching blue desert sky.

Sea, mountains and sky combined in a symphony of grandeur that stunned the senses. However, I had little time to appreciate it all, for the fishing fleet was returning. Five small dilapidated vessels with sails of woven palm-fronds were coming in through the pass in the reef. So great was the load of fish that each of them carried, that they seemed in danger of foundering before they could reach the beach.

I am fascinated by all the natural bounty that the gods provide for us, and I examined the catch avidly as it was thrown out upon the beach, and questioned the fishermen as to each of the hundred different species. The pile of fish formed a glittering treasure of rainbow colours, and I wished that I had my scrolls and paint-pots to record it all.

This interlude was too brief. As soon as the catch was unloaded, I embarked on one of the tiny vessels that stank so abundantly of its vocation, and waved back at Tanus on the beach as we put out through the pass in the reef. He was to remain here until I returned with the equipment that we needed for the next part of my plan. Once again, I did not want him to be recognized where I was going. His job now was to prevent any of the fishermen or their families from sneaking away into the desert to a secret meeting with the Shrikes, to report the presence in their village of a golden-headed lord who bore the hawk seal.

The tiny vessel threw up her bows at the first strong scent of the sea, and the helmsman tacked across the wind and headed her up into the north, running parallel to that dun and awful coast. We had but a short way to go, and before nightfall the helmsman pointed over the bows at the clustered stone buildings of the port of Safaga on the distant shore-line.

 FOR A thousand years Safaga had been the entrepôt for all trade coming into the Upper Kingdom from the East. Even as I stood in the bows of our tiny craft, I could make out the shapes of other much larger vessels on the northern horizon as they came and went between Safaga and the Arabian ports on the eastern shore of the narrow sea.

It was dark by the time that I stepped ashore on the beach at Safaga, and nobody seemed to remark my arrival. I knew exactly where I was going, for I had visited the port regularly on Lord Intef's nefarious business. At this hour the streets were almost deserted, but the taverns were packed. I made my way swiftly to the home of Tiamat the merchant. Tiamat was a rich man and his home the largest in the old town. An armed slave barred the door to me.

'Tell your master that the surgeon from Karnak who saved his leg for him is here,' I ordered, and Tiamat himself limped out to greet me. He was taken aback when he saw my clerical disguise, but had the good sense not to remark on it, nor to mention my name in front of the slave. He drew me into his walled garden, and as soon as we were alone he exclaimed, 'Is it really you, Taita? I heard that you had been murdered by the Shrikes at Elephantine.'

He was a portly, middle-aged man, with an open, intelligent face and a shrewd mind. Some years previously he had been carried in to me on a litter. A party of travellers had found him beside the road, where he had been left for dead after his caravan had been pillaged by the Shrikes. I had stitched him together, and even managed to save the leg that had already mortified by the time I first saw it. However, he would always walk with a limp.

'I am delighted to see that the reports of your death are premature,' he chuckled, and clapped his hands to have his slaves bring me a cup of cool sherbet and a plate of figs and honeyed dates.

After a decent interval of polite conversation, he asked quietly, 'Is there anything I can do for you? I owe you my life. You have only to ask. My home is your home. All I have is yours.'

'I am on the king's business,' I told him, and drew out the hawk seal from under my tunic.

His expression became grave. 'I acknowledge the seal of Pharaoh. But it was not necessary to show it to me. Ask what you will of me. I cannot refuse you.'

He listened to all I had to say without another word, and when I had finished, he sent for his bailiff and gave him his orders in front of me. Before he sent the man away, he turned to me and said, 'Is there anything that I have forgotten? Anything else you need at all?'

'Your generosity is without limits,' I told him. 'However, there is one other thing. I long for my writing materials.'

He turned back to the bailiff. 'See to it that there are scrolls and brushes and ink-pot in one of the packs.'

After the bailiff had left, we sat on talking for half the night. Tiamat stood at the centre of the busiest trading route in the Upper Kingdom, and heard every rumour and whisper from the farthest reaches of the empire, and from beyond the sea. I learned as much in those few hours in his garden as I would in a month in the palace at Elephantine.

'Do you still pay your ransom to the Shrikes to allow your caravans through?' I asked, and he shrugged with resignation.

'After what they did to my leg, what option do I have? Each season their demands become more exorbitant. I must pay over one-quarter of the value of my goods to them as soon as the caravan leaves Safaga, and half my profits once the goods are sold in Thebes. Soon they will beggar us all, and grass will grow on the caravan roads, and the trade of the kingdom will wither and die.'

'How do you make these payments?' I asked. 'Who determines the amount, and who collects them?'

'They have their spies here in the port. They watch every cargo that is unloaded, and they know what each caravan carries when it leaves Safaga. Before it even reaches the mountain pass, it will be met by one of the robber chieftains who will demand the ransom they have set.'

It was long past midnight before Tiamat called a slave to light me to the chamber he had set aside for me.

'You will be gone before I rise tomorrow.' Tiamat embraced me. 'Farewell, my good friend. My debt to you is not yet paid in full. Call upon me again, whenever you have need.'

The same slave woke me before dawn, and led me down to the seafront in the darkness. A fine trading vessel of Tiamat's fleet was moored inside the reef. The captain weighed anchor as soon as I came aboard.

In the middle of the morning we crept in through the pass in the coral and dropped anchor in front of the little fishing village where Tanus stood on the beach to welcome me.

 DURING MY absence Tanus had managed to gather together six decrepit donkeys, and the sailors from Tiamat's ship waded ashore carrying the bales that we had brought with us from Safaga, and loaded them on to these miserable creatures. Tanus and I left the captain of the trading vessel with strict orders to await our return, then, leading the string of donkeys, we headed back inland towards the wells at Gebel Nagara.

Kratas' men had obviously suffered the heat and the sand-flies and the boredom with poor grace, for they accorded us a welcome that was out of keeping with the period that we had been absent. Tanus ordered Kratas to parade them. The ranks of warriors watched as I unpacked the first bale that we had brought in on the donkey train. Almost immediately their interest gave way to mild amusement as I laid out the costume of a slave girl. In its turn, this was replaced by a buzz of speculation and argument as the bales yielded up a further seventy-nine complete female costumes.

Kratas and two of his officers helped me place one of these on the sand in front of each guardsman, and then Tanus gave the order: 'Disrobe! Put on the dress in front of you!' There was a roar of protest and incredulous hilarity, and it was only when Kratas and his officers passed down the ranks with assumed expressions of sternness to reinforce the order, that they began to obey it.

Unlike our women who dress but lightly and often leave their bosom bared and their legs free and naked, the women of Assyria wear skirts that sweep the ground and sleeves that cover their arms to the wrist. For reasons of misplaced modesty they even veil their faces when they walk abroad, although perhaps these restrictions are placed upon them by the possessive jealousy of their menfolk. Then again there is a wide difference between the sunny land of Egypt and those more sombre climes where water falls from the sky and turns solid white upon the mountain-tops, and the winds chill the flesh and the bones of men like death.

Once they had weathered the first shock of seeing each other in this outlandish apparel, the men entered into the spirit of the moment. Soon there were eighty veiled slave girls prancing and mincing about in the long skirts that reached to their ankles, tweaking each other's buttocks and casting exaggerated sheep's eyes at Tanus and his officers.

The officers could no longer maintain their gravity. Perhaps it is because of my peculiar circumstances that I have always found the spectacle of men dressed as women to be vaguely repulsive, but it is strange how few other men share my feelings of distaste, and it needs only some hairy ruffian to don a skirt to reduce his audience to a state of incontinence.

In the midst of this uproar, I congratulated myself that I had insisted that Kratas choose only the smallest and slimmest men from the squadron. Looking them over now, I was certain that they would be able to carry through the deception. They would need only a little schooling in feminine deportment.

 THE FOLLOWING morning our strange caravan passed through the little fishing village and wound its way down on to the beach, where the trading vessel waited. Kratas and eight of his officers made up the escort. Complete lack of any armed escort for such a valuable consignment would surely have aroused suspicion. Nine armed men dressed in the motley garb of mercenaries would be sufficient to allay this, but would not deter a large raiding party of Shrikes.

At the head of the caravan marched Tanus, dressed in the rich robes and beaded head-dress of a wealthy merchant from beyond the Euphrates river. His beard had grown out densely, and I had curled it for him into those tight ringlets that the Assyrians favoured. Many of these Asians, particularly those from the high mountainous regions further north, have the same complexion and skin coloration as Tanus, so he looked the part I had chosen for him.

I followed close behind him. I had overcome my aversion to wearing female garb, and donned the long skirts and veil, together with the gaudy jewellery of an Assyrian wife. I was determined not to be recognized when I returned to Safaga.

The voyage was enlivened by the sea-sickness of most of the slave girls and not a few of the officers, for they were accustomed to sail on the placid waters of the great river. At one stage so many of them were lining the rail to make their offerings to the gods of the sea, that the ship took on a distinct list.

We were all relieved to step on to the beach at Safaga, where we caused much excitement. The Assyrian girls were famous for their skills on the love couch. It was said that some of them were capable of tricks that could bring a thousand-year-old mummy back to life. It was obvious to those who watched us come ashore that behind the veils our slave girls must be images of feminine loveliness. A shrewd Asian merchant would not transport his wares so far and at such expense, unless he was certain of a good price in the slave-markets on the Nile.

One of the Safaga merchants approached Tanus immediately and offered to buy the entire bevy of girls on the spot, and spare him the onerous journey across the desert with them. Tanus waved him away with a scornful chuckle.

'Have you been warned of the perils of the journey that you intend making?' the merchant insisted. 'Before you reach the Nile, you will be forced to pay a ransom for your safe passage that will eat up most of your profits.'

'Who will force me to pay?' Tanus demanded. 'I pay only what I owe.'

'There are those who guard the road,' the merchant warned him. 'And even though you pay what they demand, there is no certainty that they will let you pass unharmed, especially with such tempting goods as you have with you. The vultures on the road to the Nile are so fat from feeding on the carcasses of stubborn merchants that they can hardly fly. Sell to me now at a good profit—'

'I have armed guards', Tanus indicated Kratas and his small squad, 'who will be a match for any robbers we may meet.' And the onlookers who had listened to the exchange tittered and nudged each other at the boast.

The merchant shrugged. 'Very well, my brave friend. On my next journey through the desert, I will look for your skeleton beside the road. I will recognize you by that blustering red beard of yours.'

As he had promised me he would, Tiamat had forty donkeys waiting for us. Twenty of them were laden with filled water-skins, and the remainder with pack-saddles to carry the bales and bundles that we brought ashore from the trading ship.

I was anxious that we should spend as little time as possible in the port, under all those prying eyes. It would take only a single lapse by one of the slave girls to reveal his true gender, and we would be undone. Kratas and his escort hurried them through the narrow streets, keeping the bystanders at a distance, and making certain that the slave girls kept their veils in place and their eyes downcast, and that none of them responded in gruff masculine tones to the ribald comment that followed us, until we were out into the open country beyond the town.

We camped that first night still within sight of Safaga. Although I did not anticipate an attack until we were beyond the first mountain pass, I was certain that we were already being watched by the spies of the Shrikes.

While it was still light, I made sure that our slave girls conducted themselves as women, that they kept their faces and bodies covered, and that when they went into the nearby wadi to attend to nature's demands, they squatted in decorous fashion and did not uncouthly spray their water while standing.

It was only after darkness fell that Tanus ordered the bundles carried by the donkeys to be opened and the weapons they contained to be issued to the slave girls. Each of them slept with his bow and his sword concealed under his sleeping-mat.

Tanus posted double sentries around the camp. After we had inspected them and made sure that they were all well placed and fully alert, Tanus and I slipped away, and in the darkness returned to the port of Safaga. I led him through the dark streets to the house of Tiamat. The merchant was expecting our arrival, and had a meal laid ready to welcome us. I could see that he was excited to meet Tanus.

'Your fame proceeds you, Lord Harrab. I knew your father. He was a man indeed,' he greeted Tanus. 'Although I have heard persistent rumours that you died in the desert not a week since, and that even at this moment your body lies with the morticians on the west bank of the Nile, undergoing the ritual forty days of the embalming process, you are welcome in my humble house.'

While we enjoyed the feast he provided, Tanus questioned him at length on all he knew of the Shrikes, and Tiamat answered him freely and openly.

At last Tanus glanced at me and I nodded. Tanus turned back to Tiamat and said, 'You have been a generous friend to us, and yet we have been less than honest with you. This was from necessity, for it was of vital importance that no one should guess at our real purpose in this endeavour. Now I will tell you that it is my purpose to smash the Shrikes and deliver their leaders up to Pharaoh's justice and wrath.'

Tiamat smiled and stroked his beard. 'This comes as no great surprise to me,' he said, 'for I have heard of the charge that Pharaoh placed upon you at the festival of Osiris. That and your patent interest in those murderous bandits left little doubt in my mind. I can say only that I will sacrifice to the gods for your success.'

'To succeed, I will need your help again,' Tanus told him.

'You have only to ask.'

'Do you think that the Shrikes are as yet aware of our caravan?'

'All of Safaga is talking about you,' Tiamat replied. 'Yours is the richest cargo that has arrived this season. Eighty beautiful slave girls will be worth at least a thousand gold rings each in Karnak.' He chuckled and shook his head at the joke. 'You can be certain that the Shrikes already know all about you. I saw at least three of their spies in the crowd at the waterfront watching you. You can expect them to meet you and make their demands even before you reach the first pass.'

When we rose to take our leave, he walked with us as far as his own door. 'May all the gods attend your endeavours. Not only Pharaoh, but every living soul in the entire kingdom will be in your debt if you can stamp out this terrible scourge that threatens to destroy our very civilization, and drive us all back into the age of barbarism.'

IT WAS still cool and dark the following morning when the column started out. Tanus, with Lanata slung over his shoulder, was at the head of the caravan, with myself, in all my womanly grace and beauty, following him closely.

Behind us the donkeys were harnessed in single file, moving nose to tail down the middle of the well-beaten track. The slave girls were in double columns on the outer flanks of the file of donkeys. Their weapons were concealed in the packs upon the backs of the animals. Any of the men needed only to reach out to lay a hand upon the hilt of his sword.

Kratas had split his escort into three squads of six men each, commanded by Astes, Remrem and himself. Astes and Remrem were warriors of renown and more than deserving of their own commands. However, both of them had, on numerous occasions, refused promotion in order to remain with Tanus. That was the quality of loyalty that Tanus inspired in all who served under him. I could not help thinking yet again what a pharaoh he would have made.

The escorts now slouched along beside the column, making every attempt to forsake their military bearing. It would seem to the spies who were certainly watching us from the hills that they were there solely to prevent any of the slaves from escaping. In truth they were fully occupied with preventing their charges from breaking into marching step and sounding off a chorus of one of the rowdy regimental songs.

'You there, Kernit!' I heard Remrem challenge one of them. 'Don't take such long steps, man, and swing that fat arse of yours a little! Try to make yourself alluring.'

'Give me a kiss, captain,' Kernit called back, 'and I'll do anything you say.'

The heat was rising, and the mirage was beginning to make the rocks dance. Tanus turned back to me. 'Soon I will call our first rest-stop. One cup of water for each—'

'Good husband,' I interrupted him, 'your friends have arrived. Look ahead!'

Tanus turned back, and instinctively gripped the stock of the great bow that hung at his side. 'And what fine fellows they are, too!'

At that moment our column was winding through the first foothills below the desert plateau. On either hand we were walled in by the steep sides of the rocky hills. Now three men stood in the track ahead of us. The one who led them was a tall, menacing figure swathed in the woollen robe of the desert traveller, but his head was bared. His skin was very dark, and deeply pitted with the scars of the smallpox. He had a nose that was hooked like the beak of a vulture, and his right eye was an opaque jelly from the blind-worm that burrows deep into the eyeball of its victims.

'I know the one-eyed villain,' I said softly, so that Tanus alone could hear. 'His name is Shufti. He is the most notorious of the barons of the Shrikes. Be wary of him. The lion is a gentle beast compared to this one.'

Tanus gave no sign of having heard me, but lifted his right hand to show that it held no weapon, and called out cheerfully, 'May all your days be scented with jasmine, gentle traveller, and may a loving wife welcome you at your own front door when at last your journey is done.'

'May your water-skins stay filled and cool breezes fan your brow when you cross the Thirsty Sands,' Shufti called back, and he smiled. That smile was fiercer than a leopard's snarl, and his single eye glared horribly.

'You are kind, my noble lord,' Tanus thanked him. 'I would like to offer you a meal and the hospitality of my camp, but I pray your indulgence. We have a long road before us, and we must pass on.'

'Just a little more of your time, my fine Assyrian.' Shufti moved forward to block the path. 'I have something which you need, if you and your caravan are ever to reach the Nile in safety.' He held up a small object.

'Ah, a charm!' Tanus exclaimed. 'You are a magician, perhaps? What manner of charm is this you are offering me?'

'A feather.' Shufti was still smiling. 'The feather of a shrike.'

Tanus smiled, as though to humour a child. 'Very well then, give me this feather and I'll delay you no longer.'

'A gift for a gift. You must give me something in return,' Shufti told him. 'Give me twenty of your slaves. Then, when you return from Egypt, I will meet you on the road again and you will give me half the profits from the sale of the other sixty.'

'For a single feather?' Tanus scoffed. 'That sounds like a sorry bargain to me.'

'This is no ordinary feather. It is a shrike's feather,' Shufti pointed out. 'Are you so ill-informed that you have never heard of that bird?'

'Let me see this magical feather.' Tanus walked towards him with his right hand outstretched, and Shufti came forward to meet him. At the same time Kratas, Remrem and Astes wandered up inquisitively, as though to examine the feather.

Instead of taking the gift from his hand, suddenly Tanus seized Shufti's wrist and twisted it up between his shoulder-blades. With a startled cry, Shufti fell to his knees and Tanus held him easily. At the same time Kratas and his men darted forward, taking the other two bandits by as much surprise as their chief. They knocked the weapons out of their hands, and dragged them to where Tanus stood.

'So, you little birds think to frighten Kaarik, the Assyrian, with your threats, do you? Yes, my fine vendor of feathers, I have heard of the Shrikes. I have heard that they are a flock of chattering, cowardly little fledglings, that make more noise than a flock of sparrows.' He twisted Shufti's arm more viciously, until the bandit yelled with pain and fell flat on his face. 'Yes, I have heard of the Shrikes, but have you heard of Kaarik, the terrible?' He nodded at Kratas, and quickly and efficiently they stripped the three Shrikes stark naked and pinned them spread-eagled upon the rocky earth.

'I want you to remember my name, and fly away like a good little shrike when next you hear it,' Tanus told him, and nodded to Kratas again. Kratas flexed the lash of his slave-whip between his fingers. It was of the same type as Rasfer's famous tool, whittled from the cured hide of a bull hippopotamus. Tanus held out his hand for it, and reluctantly Kratas handed it over to him.

'Don't look so sad, slave-master,' Tanus told him. 'I'll let you have your turn later. But Kaarik, the Assyrian, always takes the first spoonful from the pot.'

Tanus slashed the whip back and forth through the air, and it whistled like the wing of a goose in flight. Shufti squirmed where he lay, and twisted his head around to hiss at Tanus, 'You are mad, you Assyrian ox! Do you not realize that I am a baron of the Shrike clan? You dare not do this to me—' His naked back and buttocks were stippled with pox scars.

Tanus lifted the whip on high, and then brought it down in a full-armed stroke with all his weight behind it. He laid a purple welt as fat as my forefinger across Shufti's back. So intense was the pain of it that the bandit's entire body convulsed and the air hissed out of his lungs, so that he could not scream. Tanus lifted the lash and then meticulously laid another ridged welt exactly parallel to the first, almost, but not quite, touching it. This time Shufti filled his lungs and let out a hoarse bellow, like a buffalo bull caught in a pitfall. Tanus ignored his struggles and his outraged roars, and worked on assiduously, laying on the strokes as though he were weaving a carpet.

When at last he was done, his victim's legs, buttocks and back were latticed with the fiery weals. Not one of the blows had overlaid another. The skin was intact and not a drop of blood had spilled out, but Shufti was no longer wriggling or screaming. He lay with his face in the dirt, his breath snoring in his throat, so that each exhalation raised a puff of dust. When Remrem and Kratas released him, he made no effort to sit up. He did not even stir.

Tanus tossed the whip to Kratas. 'The next one is yours, slave-master. Let us see what a pretty pattern you can tattoo on his back.'

Kratas' strokes hummed with power, but lacked the finesse that Tanus had demonstrated. Soon the bandit's back was leaking like a flawed jar of red wine. The droplets of blood fell into the dust and rolled into tiny balls of mud.

Sweating lightly, Kratas was satisfied at last, and he passed the whip to Astes as he indicated the last victim. 'Give that one something to remind him of his manners, as well.'

Astes had an even more rustic touch than Kratas. By the time he had finished, the last bandit's back looked like a side of fresh beef that had been cut up by a demented butcher.

Tanus signalled the caravan to move forward, towards the pass through the red rock mountains. We lingered a while beside the three naked men.

At last Shufti stirred and lifted his head, and Tanus addressed him civilly. 'And so, my friend, I beg leave of you. Remember my face, and step warily when you see it again.' Tanus picked up the fallen shrike's feather and tucked it into his headband. 'I thank you for your gift. May all your nights be cradled in the arms of lovely ladies.' He touched his heart and lips in the Assyrian gesture of farewell, and I followed him up the road after the departing caravan.

I looked back before we dropped over the next rise. All three Shrikes were on their feet, supporting each other to remain upright. Even at this distance I could make out the expression on Shufti's face. It was hatred distilled to its essence.

'Well, you have made certain that we will have every Shrike this side of the Nile upon us, the moment we take our first step beyond the pass,' I told Kratas and his ruffians, and I could not have pleased them more, had I promised them a shipload of beer and pretty girls.

FROM THE crest of the pass we looked back at the cool blue of the sea for the last time and then dropped down into that sweltering wilderness of rock and sand that stood between us and the Nile.

As we moved forward, the heat came at us like a mortal enemy. It seemed to enter through our mouths and nostrils as we gasped for breath. It sucked the moisture from our bodies like a thief. It dried out our skin and cracked it until our lips burst open like over-ripe figs. The rocks beneath our feet were hot, as though fresh from the pot-maker's kiln, and they scalded and blistered our feet, even through the leather soles of our sandals. It was impossible to continue the march during the hottest hours of the day. We lay in the flimsy shade of the linen tents that Tiamat had provided, and panted like hunting dogs after the chase.

When the sun sank towards the jagged rock horizon, we went on. The desert around us was charged with such a brooding nameless menace that even the high spirits of the Blue Crocodile Guards were subdued. The long slow column wound like a maimed adder through the black rock outcrops and tawny lion-coloured dunes, following the ancient road along which countless other travellers had passed before us.

When night fell at last, the sky came alive with such a dazzle of stars and the desert was lit so brightly that, from my place at the head of the caravan, I could recognize the shape of Kratas at the tail, although two hundred paces separated us. We marched on for half the night before Tanus gave the order to fall out. Then he had us up before dawn and we marched on until the heat-mirage dissolved the rocky outcrops around us and made the horizon swim so that it seemed to be moulded from melting pitch.

We saw no other sign of life, except that once a troop of dog-headed baboons barked at us from the cliffs of a stark rock tableland as we passed below them, and the vultures soared so high in the hot blue sky that they appeared to be but dust motes swirling in slow and deliberate circles high above us.

When we rested in the middle of the day the whirlwinds pirouetted and swayed with the peculiar grace of dancing houris across the plains, and the cupful of water that was our ration seemed to turn to steam in my mouth.

'Where are they?' Kratas growled angrily. 'By Seth's sweaty scrotum, I hope these little birds will soon puff up their courage and come in to roost.'

Although they were all tough veterans and inured to hardship and discomfort, nerves and tempers were wearing thin. Good comrades and old friends began to snarl at each other for no reason, and bicker over the water ration.

'Shufti is a cunning old dog,' I told Tanus. 'He will gather his forces and wait for us to come to him, rather than hurry to meet us. He will let us tire ourselves with the journey, and grow careless with our fatigue, before he strikes.'

On the fifth day I knew that we were approaching the oasis of Gallala when I saw that the dark cliffs ahead of us were riddled with the caves of ancient tombs. Centuries ago, the oasis had supported a thriving city, but then an earthquake had shaken the hills and damaged the wells. The water had dwindled to a few seeping drops. Even though the wells had been dug deeper to reach the receding water, and the earthen steps reached down to where the surface of the water was always in shade, the city had died. The roofless walls stood forlorn in the silence, and lizards sunned themselves in the courtyards where rich merchants had once dallied with their harems.

Our very first concern was to refill the water-skins. The voices

249

of the men drawing water at the bottom of the well were distorted by the echoes in the deep shaft. While they were busy, Tanus and I made a swift tour of the ruined city. It was a lonely and melancholy place. In its centre was the dilapidated temple to the patron god of Gallala. The roof had fallen in and the walls were collapsing in places. It had but a single entrance through the crumbling gateway at the western end.

'This will do admirably,' Tanus muttered as he strode across it, measuring it with his soldier's eye for fortification and ambuscade. When I questioned him on his intentions, he smiled and shook his head. 'Leave that part of it to me, old friend. The fighting is my business.'

As we stood at the centre of the temple I noticed the tracks of a troop of baboons in the dust at our feet, and I pointed them out to Tanus. 'They must come to drink at the wells,' I told him.

That evening when we sat around the small, smoky fires of dried donkey dung in the ancient temple, we heard the baboons again, the old bull apes barking a challenge in the hills that surrounded the ruined city. Their voices boomed back and forth along the cliffs, and I nodded at Tanus across the fire. 'Your friend, Shufti, has arrived at last. His scouts are in the hills up there watching us now. It is they who have alarmed the baboons.'

'I hope you are right. My blackguards are close to mutiny. They know this is all your idea, and if you are wrong, I might have to give them your head or your backside to appease them,' Tanus growled, and went to speak to Astes at the neighbouring cooking-fire.

Swiftly a new mood infected the camp as they realized that the enemy was near. The scowls evaporated and the men grinned at each other in the firelight, as they surreptitiously tested the edges of the swords concealed beneath the sleeping-mats on which they sat. However, they were canny veterans and they went through the motions of normal caravan life, so as not to alert the watchers in the dark hills above us. At last we were all bundled on our mats, and the fires died down, but none of us slept. I could hear them coughing and fidgeting restlessly all around me in the dark. The long hours drew out, and through the open roof I watched the great constellations of the stars wheel in stately splendour overhead, but still the attack never came.

Just before dawn, Tanus made his round of the sentries for the last time, and then, on his way back to his place beside the cooling ashes of last night's fire, he stopped by my mat for a moment and whispered, 'You and your friends the baboons, you deserve each other. All of you bark at shadows.'

'The Shrikes are here. I can smell them. The hills are full of them,' I protested.

'All you can smell is the promise of breakfast,' he grunted. He knows how I detest the suggestion that I am a glutton. Rather than reply to such callow humour, I went out into the darkness to relieve myself behind the nearest pile of ruins.

As I squatted there, a baboon barked again, the wild, booming cry shattering the preternatural silences of that last and darkest of the night-watches. I turned my head in that direction and heard, faint and faraway, the sound of metal strike rock, as though a nervous hand had dropped a dagger up there on the ridge, or a careless shield had brushed against a granite outcrop as an armed man hurried to take up his station before the dawn found him out.

I smiled complacently to myself; there are few pleasures in my life compared to that of making Tanus eat his words. As I returned to my mat, I whispered to the men that I passed, 'Be ready. They are here,' and I heard my warning passed on from mouth to sleepless mouth.

Above me the stars began to fade away, and the dawn crept up on us as stealthily as a lioness stalking a herd of oryx. Then abruptly I heard a sentry on the west wall of the temple whistle, a liquid warble that might have been the cry of a nightjar except that we all knew better, and instantly a stir ran through the camp. It was checked by the low but urgent whispers of Kratas and his officers, 'Steady, the Blues! Remember your orders. Hold your positions!' and not a man stirred from his sleeping-mat.

Without rising, and with my shawl masking my face, I turned my head slowly and looked up at the crests of the cliffs that stood higher than the temple walls. The shark's-tooth silhouette of the

251

granite hills began to alter most subtly. I had to blink my eyes to be certain of what I was seeing. Then slowly I turned my head in a full circle, and it was the same in whichever direction I looked. The skyline all about us was picketed with the dark and menacing shapes of armed men. They formed an unbroken palisade around us through which no fugitive could hope to escape.

I knew then why Shufti had delayed his retaliation so long. It would have taken him all this time to gather together such an army of thieves. There must be a thousand or more of them, although in the poor light it was not possible to count their multitudes. We were outnumbered at least ten to one, and I felt my spirits quail. It was poor odds, even for a company of the Blues.

The Shrikes stood as still as the rocks around them, and I was alarmed at this evidence of their discipline. I had expected them to come streaming down upon us in an untidy rabble, but they were behaving like trained warriors. Their stillness was more menacing and intimidating than any wild shouting and brandishing of weapons would have been.

As the light strengthened swiftly, we could make them out more clearly. The first rays of the sun glanced off the bronze of their shields and their bared sword-blades, and struck darts of light into our eyes. Every one of them was muffled up, a scarf of black wool wound around each head so that only their eyes showed in the slits, eyes as malevolent as those of the ferocious blue sharks that terrorize the waters of the sea we had left behind us.

The silence drew out until I thought that my nerves might tear and my heart burst with the pressure of blood within it. Then suddenly a voice rang out, shattering the dawn silence and echoing along the cliffs. 'Kaarik! Are you awake?'

I recognized Shufti then, despite the scarf that masked him. He stood in the centre of the west wall of the cliff, where the road cut through it. 'Kaarik!' he called again. 'It is time for you to pay what you owe me, but the price has risen. I want everything now. Everything!' he repeated, and flung aside the scarf so that his pock-marked features were revealed. 'I want everything you have, including your stupid and arrogant head.'

Tanus rose from his mat and threw aside his sheepskin rug.

'Then you will have to come down and take it from me,' he shouted back, and drew his sword.

Shufti raised his right arm, and his blind eye caught the light and gleamed like a silver coin. Then he brought his arm down abruptly.

At his signal, a shout went up from the ranks of men that lined the high ground, and they lifted their weapons and shook them to the pale yellow dawn sky. Shufti waved them forward and they streamed down the cliffs in a torrent into the narrow valley of Gallala.

Tanus raced to the centre of the temple court where the ancient inhabitants had raised a tall stone altar to their patron Bes, the dwarf god of music and drunkenness. Kratas and his officers ran to join him, while the slave girls and I crouched on our mats and covered our heads, wailing with terror.

Tanus leaped up on to the altar, and went down on one knee as he flexed the great bow Lanata. It took all of his strength to string it, but when he stood erect again it shimmered in its coils of silver electrum wire, as though it were a living thing. He reached over his shoulder and drew an arrow from the quiver on his back and faced the main gateway through which the horde of Shrikes must enter.

Below the altar, Kratas had drawn up his men into a single rank, and they also had strung their bows and faced the entrance to the square. They made a pitifully small cluster around the altar, and I felt a lump rise in my throat as I watched them. They were so heroic and undaunted. I would compose a sonnet in their honour, I decided on a sudden impulse, but before I could find the first line, the head of the mob of bandits burst howling through the ruined gateway.

Only five men abreast could climb the steep stairway into the opening, and the distance to where Tanus stood on the altar was less than forty paces. Tanus drew and let his first arrow fly. That single arrow killed three men. The first of them was a tall rogue dressed in a short kilt, with long greasy tresses of hair streaming down his back. The arrow took him in the centre of his naked chest and passed through his torso as cleanly as though he were merely a target cut from a sheet of papyrus.

Slick with the blood of the first man, the arrow struck the man behind him in the throat. Although the force of it was dissipating now, it still went through his neck and came out behind him, but it could not drive completely through. The fletchings at the back of the shaft snagged in his flesh, while the barbed bronze arrow-head buried itself in the eye of the third man who had crowded up close behind him. The two Shrikes were pinned together by the arrow, and they staggered and thrashed about in the middle of the gateway, blocking the opening to those who were trying to push their way past them into the courtyard. At last the arrow-head tore out of the third man's skull, with the eye impaled upon the point. The two stricken men fell apart, and a throng of screaming bandits poured over them into the square. The small band around the altar met them with volley after volley of arrows, shooting them down so that their corpses almost blocked the opening, and those coming in from behind were forced to scramble over the mounds of dead and wounded.

It could not last much longer, the pressure of warriors from behind was too great and their numbers too overwhelming. Like the bursting of an earthen dyke unable to stem the rising flood of the Nile, they forced the opening, and a solid mass of fighting men poured into the square and surrounded the tiny band around the altar of the god Bes.

It was too close quarters for the bows now, and Tanus and his men cast them aside and drew their swords. 'Horus, arm me!' Tanus shouted his battle-cry, and the men around him took it up, as they went to work. Bronze rang on bronze as the Shrikes tried to come at them, but they had formed a ring around the altar, facing outwards. No matter from which side they came, the Shrikes were met by the point and the deadly sword-play of the guards. The Shrikes were not short of courage, and they pressed in serried ranks around the altar. As one of them was cut down, another leaped into his place.

I saw Shufti in the gateway. He was holding back from the fray, but cursing his men and ordering them into the thick of it with horrid howls of rage. His blind eye rolled in its socket as he exhorted them, 'Get me the Assyrian alive. I want to kill him slowly and hear him squeal.'

The bandits completely ignored the women who still cowered on their sleeping-mats, their heads covered, wailing and screeching with terror. I wailed with the best of them, but the struggle in the centre of the yard was too uncomfortable for my liking. By this time, there were over a thousand men crowded into the confined space. Choking in the dust, I was kicked and pummelled by the sandalled feet of the battling horde, until I managed to crawl away into a corner of the wall.

One of the bandits turned aside from the fighting and stooped over me. He tore the shawl away from my face and for a moment stared into my eyes. 'Mother of Isis,' he breathed, 'you are beautiful!'

He was an ugly devil with gaps in his teeth and a scar down one cheek. His breath stank like a sewerage gutter as he lusted into my face. 'Wait until this business is over. Then I'll give you something to make you squeal with joy,' he promised, and twisted my face up to his. He kissed me.

My natural instinct was to pull away from him, but I resisted it and returned his kiss. I am an artist of the love arts, for I learned my skills in the boys' quarters of Lord Intef. My kisses can turn a man to water.

I kissed him with all my skill, and he was transfixed by it. While he was still paralysed, I slipped my dagger from its sheath beneath my blouse and slid the point through the gap between his fifth and sixth ribs. When he screamed, I muffled the sound with my own lips and clasped him lovingly to my breast, twisting the blade in his heart until, with a shudder, he relaxed completely against me, and I let him roll over on his side.

I looked around me quickly. In the few moments that it had taken me to dispose of my admirer, the plight of the small group of guards around the altar had worsened. There were gaps in their single rank. Two men were down and Amseth was wounded. He had switched his sword into his left hand, while the other arm hung bleeding at his side.

With a rush of relief I saw that Tanus was still untouched, still laughing with the savage joy of it all as he plied the sword. But he had left it too late to spring the trap, I thought. The entire band of Shrikes were crowded into the square and baying around him like hounds around a treed leopard. Within moments he and his gallant little band must be cut down.

Even as I watched, Tanus killed another of them with a straight thrust through the throat, and then he jerked his blade free of the clinging flesh and stepped back. He threw back his head and let loose a bellow that rang from the crumbling walls around us. 'On me, the Blues!'

On the instant every one of the cringing slave girls leapt up and flung aside their trailing robes. Their swords were already bared and they fell upon the rear of the robber horde. The surprise was complete and overwhelming. I saw them kill a hundred or more before their victims even realized what they were about, and could rally to meet them. But when they did turn to face this fresh attack, they exposed their backs to Tanus and his little band.

They fought well, I'll give them that, though I am sure it was terror, rather than courage, that drove them on. However, their ranks were too close-packed to allow them free play with the sword, and the men they faced were some of the finest troops in Egypt, which is to say the entire world.

For a while yet they held on. Then Tanus bellowed again from the midst of the turmoil. For a moment I thought it was another command, then I realized that it was the opening bar of the battle hymn of the guards. Though I had often heard it spoken in awe that the Blues always sang when the battle was at its height, I had never truly believed it possible. Now all around me the song was taken up by a hundred straining voices:

> We are the breath of Horus,
> hot as the desert wind,
> we are the reapers of men—

Their swords beat an accompaniment to the words, like the clangour of hammers on the anvils of the underworld. In the face of such arrogant ferocity the remaining Shrikes wavered, and then suddenly it was no longer a battle, but a massacre.

I have seen a pack of wild dogs surround and tear into a flock of sheep. This was worse. Some of the Shrikes threw down their swords and fell to their knees begging quarter. There was no mercy shown them. Others tried to reach the gateway, but guardsmen waited for them there, sword in hand.

I danced on the fringes of the fighting, screaming across at Tanus, trying to make myself heard in the uproar, 'Stop them. We need prisoners.'

Tanus could not hear me, or more likely he simply ignored my entreaties. Singing and laughing, with Kratas at his left hand and Remrem on the other, he tore into them. His beard was soaked with the spurted blood of those he had killed, and his eyes glittered in the running red mask of his face with a madness I had never seen in them before. Joyous Hapi, how he thrived on the heady draught of battle!

'Stop it, Tanus! Don't kill them all!' This time he heard me. I saw the madness fade, and he was once more in control of himself.

'Give quarter to those who plead for it!' he roared, and the guards obeyed him. But in the end, out of the original thousand, fewer than two hundred Shrikes grovelled unarmed on the bloody stone flags and pleaded for their lives.

For a while I stood dazed and uncertain on the fringe of this carnage, and then from the corner of my eye I caught a furtive movement.

Shufti had realized that he could not escape through the gateway. He threw down his sword and darted to the east wall of the court, close to where I stood. This was the most ruined section, where the wall was reduced to half its original height. The tumbled mud-bricks formed a steep ramp, and Shufti scrambled up it, slipping and falling, but rapidly nearing the top of the wall. It seemed that I was the only one who had noticed his flight. The guards were busy with their other prisoners, and Tanus had his back turned to me as he directed the mopping-up of the shattered enemy.

Almost without thinking, I stooped and picked up half a mud-brick. As Shufti topped the wall, I hurled the brick up at him with all my strength. It thumped against the back of his skull with such force that he dropped to his knees, and then the treacherous pile of loose rubble gave way beneath him and he came sliding back down in a cloud of dust to land at my feet, only half-conscious.

I pounced upon him where he lay, straddling his chest, and I pressed the point of my dagger to his throat. He stared up at me, his single eye still glazed with the crack I had dealt him.

'Lie still,' I cautioned him, 'or I will gut you like a fish.'

I had lost my shawl and head-dress, and my hair had come down on to my shoulders. He recognized me then, which was no surprise. We had met often, but in different circumstances.

'Taita, the eunuch!' he mumbled. 'Does Lord Intef know what you are about?'

'He will find out soon enough,' I assured him, and pricked him until he grunted, 'but you will not be the one to enlighten him.'

Without removing the point from his throat, I shouted to two of the nearest guards to take him. They flipped him on to his face and bound his wrists together with linen twine before they dragged him away.

Tanus had seen me capture Shufti, and he strode across to me now, stepping over the dead and wounded. 'Good throw, Taita! You have forgotten nothing that I taught you.' He clapped me on the back so hard that I staggered. 'There is plenty of work for you still. We've lost four men killed, and there are at least a dozen wounded.'

'What about their camp?' I asked, and he stared at me.

'What camp?'

'A thousand Shrikes did not spring up from the sands like desert flowers. They must have pack-animals and slaves with them. Not far from here, either. You must not let them escape. Nobody must escape to tell the tale of today's battle. None of them must be allowed to carry the news to Karnak that you are still alive.'

'Sweet Isis, you are right! But how will we find them?' It was obvious that Tanus was still bemused with battle lust. Sometimes I wondered what he would do without me.

'Back-track them,' I told him impatiently. 'A thousand pairs of feet will have trodden a road for us to follow back to where they came from.'

His expression cleared, and he hailed Kratas across the length of the temple. 'Take fifty men. Go with Taita. He will lead you to their base-camp.'

'The wounded—' I began to protest. I had enjoyed enough fighting for one day, but he brushed my objections aside. 'You are the best tracker I have. The wounded can wait for your care, my ruffians are all as tough as fresh buffalo steaks, very few of them will die before you return.'

 FINDING THEIR camp was as simple as I had made it sound. With Kratas and fifty men following me closely, I made a wide cast around the city, and behind the first line of hills I picked up the broad track that they had made as they came in and deployed to surround us. We followed it back at a trot, and had covered less than a mile before we topped a rise and found the camp of the Shrikes in the shallow valley below us.

Their surprise was complete. They had left fewer than twenty men to guard the donkeys and women. Kratas' men overran them at the first rush, and this time I was too late to save any prisoners. They spared only the women, and once the camp was secure, Kratas let his men have them as part of the traditional reward of the victors.

The women seemed to me to be a more comely selection than I would have expected in such company. I saw quite a few pretty faces amongst them. They submitted to the rituals of conquest with a remarkably good grace. I even heard some of them laughing and joking as the guardsmen threw dice for them. The vocation of camp-follower to a band of Shrikes could not be considered the most delicate calling, and I doubted that any of these ladies were blushing virgins. One by one, they were led by their new owners behind the cover of the nearest clump of rocks, where their skirts were lifted without further ceremony.

New moon follows the death of the old, spring follows winter, none of the ladies showed any signs of mourning for their erstwhile spouses. Indeed, it seemed probable that new and perhaps lasting relationships were being struck up here on the desert sand.

For myself, I was more interested in the pack-donkeys and what they carried. There were over a hundred and fifty of these, and most of them were sturdy animals in prime condition which would fetch good prices in the market at Karnak or Safaga. I reckoned that I should be entitled to at least a centurion's share when the prize money was divided up. After all, I had already dispensed large amounts of my own savings in the furtherance of this enterprise, and should be entitled to some compensation. I would speak seriously to Tanus about it, and could expect his sympathy. His is a generous spirit.

By the time we returned to the city of Gallala, leading the captured pack-animals laden with booty and followed by a straggle of women who had attached themselves quite naturally to their new menfolk, the sun had set.

One of the smaller ruined buildings near the wells had been turned into a field hospital. There I worked through the night, by the light of torch and oil lamp, sewing together the wounded guardsmen. As always, I was impressed by their stoicism, for many of their wounds were grave and painful. None the less, I lost only one of my patients before dawn broke. Amseth succumbed to loss of blood from the severed arteries in his arm. If I had attended to him immediately after the battle, instead of going off into the desert, I might have been able to save him. Even though the responsibility rested with Tanus, I felt the familiar guilt and sorrow in the face of a death that I might have prevented. However, I was confident that my other patients would heal swiftly and cleanly. They were all strong young men in superb condition.

There were no wounded Shrikes to attend. Their heads had been lopped off where they lay on the battlefield. As a physician, I was perturbed by this age-old custom of dealing with the wounded enemy, yet I suppose there was logic in it. Why should the victors waste their resources on the maimed vanquished, when it was unlikely they would have any value as slaves, and, if left alive, might recover to fight against them another day?

I worked all night with only a swallow of wine and a few mouthfuls of food taken with bloody hands to sustain me, and I was almost exhausted, but there was to be no rest for me yet. Tanus sent for me as soon as it was light.

THE UNWOUNDED prisoners were being held in the temple of Bes. Their wrists were bound behind their backs, and they were squatting in long lines along the north wall, with the guards standing over them.

As soon as I entered the temple, Tanus called me to where he stood with a group of his officers. I was still in the dress of an Assyrian wife, so I lifted my blood-splattered skirts and picked my way across the floor littered with the debris of the battle.

'There are thirteen clans of Shrikes – isn't that what you told me, Taita?' Tanus asked, and I nodded. 'Each clan with its own baron. We have Shufti. Let's see if you recognize any of the other barons amongst this gathering of the fair and gentle people.' He indicated the prisoners with a chuckle, and took my arm to lead me down the ranks of squatting men.

I kept my face veiled so that none of the prisoners could recognize me. I glanced at each face as I passed, and recognized two of them. Akheku was head of the southern clan that preyed on the lands around Assoun, Elephantine and the first cataract, while Setek was from further north, the baron of Kom-Ombo.

It was clear that Shufti had gathered together whatever men he could find at such short notice. There were members of all the clans amongst those that we had captured. As I identified their leaders with a tap on the shoulder, they were dragged away.

When we reached the end of the line Tanus asked, 'Are you sure that you missed none of them?'

'How can I be sure? I told you that I never met all of the barons.'

Tanus shrugged. 'We could not hope to catch every little bird

261

with one throw of the net. We must count ourselves fortunate that we have taken as many as three so soon. But let us look at the heads. We might be lucky enough to find a few more amongst them.'

This was a gruesome business that might have affected a more delicate stomach than mine, but human flesh, both dead and living, is my stock-in-trade. While we sat at our ease on the steps of the temple enjoying our breakfast, the severed heads were displayed to us, held up one at a time by the blood-caked hair, tongues lolling from between slack lips, and dull eyes powdered with dust staring into the other world whither they were bound.

My appetite was as healthy as ever, for I had eaten very little during the last two days. I devoured the delicious cakes and fruits that Tiamat had provided, while I pointed out those heads I recognized. There was a score or so of common thieves that I had encountered during the course of my work for Lord Intef, but only one more of the barons. He was Nefer-Temu of Qena, a lesser member of the ghastly brotherhood.

'That makes four of them,' Tanus grunted with satisfaction, and ordered Nefer-Temu's head to be placed on the pinnacle of the pyramid of skulls that he was erecting in front of the well of Gallala.

'So now we have accounted for four of them. We must find the other nine barons. Let us begin by putting the question to our prisoners.' He stood up briskly, and I hastily gulped down the remains of my breakfast and followed him reluctantly back into the temple of Bes.

Although I was the one who had made clear to Tanus the necessity of having informers from within the clans, and indeed it was I who had suggested how we should recruit them, still now that the time to act upon my suggestion had arrived, I was stricken with remorse and guilt. It was one thing to suggest ruthless action, but another thing entirely to stand by and watch it practised.

I made a feeble excuse that the wounded men in the makeshift hospital might need me, but Tanus brushed it away cheerfully. 'None of your fine scruples now, Taita. You will stay with me

262

during the questioning to make certain that you overlooked none of your old friends on your first inspection.'

The questioning was swift and merciless, which I suppose was only appropriate to the character of the men we were dealing with.

To begin with, Tanus sprang up on to the stone altar of Bes, and, with the hawk seal in one hand, he looked down on the ranks of squatting prisoners with a smile that must have chilled them, even though they sat in the full rays of the desert sun.

'I am the bearer of the hawk seal of Pharaoh Mamose, and I speak with his voice,' he told them grimly, as he held the statuette high. 'I am your judge and your executioner.' He paused and let his gaze pass slowly over their upturned faces. As each of them met his eyes, they dropped their own. Not one of them could hold firm before his penetrating scrutiny.

'You have been taken in the act of pillage and murder. If there is one of you who would deny it, let him stand before me and declare his innocence.'

He waited while the impatient shadows of the vultures, circling in the sky above us, criss-crossed the dusty courtyard. 'Come now! Speak up, you innocents.' He glanced upwards at the circling birds with their grotesque pink bald heads. 'Your brethren grow impatient for the feast. Let us not keep them waiting.'

Still none of them spoke or moved, and Tanus lowered the hawk seal. 'Your actions, which all here have witnessed, condemn you. Your silence confirms the verdict. You are guilty. In the name of the divine Pharaoh, I pass sentence upon you. I sentence you to death by beheading. Your severed heads will be displayed along the caravan routes. All law-abiding men who pass this way will see your skulls grinning at them from the roadside, and they will know that the Shrike has met the eagle. They will know that the age of lawlessness has passed from the land, and that peace has returned to this very Egypt of ours. I have spoken. Pharaoh Mamose has spoken.'

Tanus nodded, and the first prisoner was dragged forward and forced to his knees before the altar.

'If you answer three questions truthfully, your life will be spared. You will be enlisted as a trooper in my regiment of the guards, with all the pay and privileges. If you refuse to answer the questions, your sentence will be carried out immediately,' Tanus told him.

He looked down on the kneeling prisoner sternly. 'This is the first question. What clan do you belong to?'

The condemned man made no reply. The blood oath of the Shrikes was too strong for him to break.

'This is the second question. Who is the baron that commands you?' Tanus asked, and still the man was silent.

'This is the third and the last question. Will you lead me to the secret places where your clan hides?' Tanus asked, and the man looked up at him, hawked in his throat and spat. His phlegm spattered yellow upon the stones. Tanus nodded to the guardsman who stood over him with the sword.

The stroke was clean and the head toppled on to the steps at the foot of the altar. 'One more head for the pyramid,' Tanus said quietly, and nodded for the next prisoner to be brought forward.

He asked the same three questions, and when the Shrike answered him with a defiant obscenity, Tanus nodded. This time the headsman mistimed the blow and the corpse flopped about with the neck only half-severed. It took three more strokes before the head bounced down the steps.

Tanus lopped twenty-three heads, I was counting them to distract myself from the waves of debilitating compassion that assailed me, until the first of the condemned men broke down. He was young, not much more than a boy. In a shrill voice he gabbled out the replies before Tanus could actually pose the three questions to him.

'My name is Hui. I am a blood-brother of the clan of Basti the Cruel. I know his secret places, and I will lead you to them.' Tanus smiled with grim satisfaction and gestured for the lad to be led away. 'Care for him well,' he warned his gaolers. 'He is now a trooper of the Blues, and your companion-in-arms.'

After the defection of one of them, it went more readily, although there were still many who defied Tanus. Some of them cursed him, while others laughed their defiance at him until the blade swept down, and their bravado ended with their very last breath that burst from the severed windpipe in a crimson gust.

I was filled with admiration for those who, after a base and despicable life, at the end chose to die with some semblance of honour. They laughed at death. I knew that I was not capable of that quality of courage. Offered that choice, I am certain that I would have responded as some of the weaker prisoners did.

'I am a member of the clan of Ur,' one confessed.

'I am of the clan of Maa-En-Tef, who is baron of the west bank as far as El Kharga,' said another, until we had informers to lead us to the strongholds of every one of the remaining robber barons, and a shoulder-high pile of recalcitrant heads to add to the pyramid beside the well.

ONE OF the matters to which Tanus and I had given much thought was the disposal of the three robber barons we had already captured, and the score of informers we had gleaned from the ranks of the condemned Shrikes.

We knew that the influence of the Shrikes was so pervasive that we dared not keep our captives in Egypt. There was not a prison secure enough to prevent Akh-Seth and his barons from reaching them, either to set them free by bribery or force, or to have them silenced by poison or some other unpleasant means. We knew that Akh-Seth was like an octopus whose head was hidden, but whose tentacles reached into every facet of our government and into the very fabric of our existence.

This was where my friend Tiamat, the merchant of Safaga, came into my reckoning.

Marching now as a unit of the Blue Crocodile Guards, and not as a slave caravan, we returned to the port on the Red Sea in half the time that it had taken us to reach Gallala. Our captives were hustled aboard one of Tiamat's trading vessels that was waiting for us in the harbour, and the captain set sail immediately for the Arabian coast, where Tiamat maintained a secure slave-compound on the small off-shore island of Jez Baquan, run by his own warders. The waters around the island were patrolled by packs of ferocious blue sharks. Tiamat assured us that no one who had attempted escape from the island had ever avoided both the vigilance of the warders and the appetites of the sharks.

Only one of our captives was not sent to the island. He was Hui from the clan of Basti the Cruel, the same youngster who had been the first to capitulate to the threat of execution. During the march to the sea, Tanus had kept the lad close to him and had turned all the irresistible force of his personality upon him. By this time Hui was his willing slave. This special gift of Tanus' to win loyalty and devotion from the most unlikely quarters never failed to amaze me. I was sure that Hui, who had buckled so swiftly under the threat of execution, would now willingly lay down his worthless life for Tanus.

Under Tanus' spell, Hui poured out every detail that he could remember of the clan to which he had once sworn a blood-oath. I listened quietly, with my writing-brush poised, as Tanus questioned him and I recorded all he had to tell us.

We learned that the stronghold of Basti the Cruel was in the fastness of that awful desert of Gebel-Umm-Bahari, on the summit of one of the flat-topped mountains that was protected by sheer cliffs on every side. Hidden and impregnable, but less than two days' march from the east bank of the Nile and the busy caravan routes that ran along its banks, it was the perfect nest for the raptor.

'There is one path to the top, cut like a stairway from the rock. It is wide enough for only one man to climb at a time,' Hui told us.

'There is no other way to the summit?' Tanus asked, and Hui grinned and laid his finger along his nose in a conspiratory gesture.

'There is another route. I have used it often, to return to the mountain after I had deserted my post to visit a lady friend. Basti would have had me killed if he had known I was missing. It is a dangerous climb, but a dozen good men could make it and hold the top of the cliff while the main force came up the pathway to them. I will lead you up it, Akh-Horus.'

It was the first time that I heard the name. Akh-Horus, the brother of the great god Horus. It was a good name for Tanus.

Naturally, Hui and our other captives could not know Tanus' real identity. They knew only in their simple way that Tanus must be some kind of god. He looked like a god and he fought like a god, and he invoked the name of Horus in the midst of battle. So, they had reasoned, he must be the brother of Horus.

Akh-Horus! It was a name that all Egypt would come to know well in the months ahead. It would be shouted from hilltop to hilltop. It would be carried along the caravan routes. It would travel the length of the river on the lips of the boatmen, from city to city, and from kingdom to kingdom. The legend would grow up around the name, as the accounts of his deeds were repeated and exaggerated at each telling.

Akh-Horus was the mighty warrior who appeared from nowhere, sent by his brother Horus to continue the eternal struggle against evil, against Akh-Seth, the lord of the Shrikes.

Akh-Horus! Each time the people of Egypt repeated the name, it would fill their hearts with fresh hope.

All that was in the future as we sat in the garden of Tiamat the merchant. Only I knew how hot Tanus was for Basti, and how eager to lead his men into the Gebel-Umm-Bahari to hunt him down. It was not only that Basti was the most rapacious and pitiless of all the barons. There was much more to it than that. Tanus had a very personal score to settle with that bandit.

From me, Tanus had learned that Basti had been the particular instrument that Akh-Seth had used to destroy the fortune of Pianki, Lord Harrab, Tanus' father.

'I can lead you up the cliffs of Gebel-Umm-Bahari,' Hui promised. 'I can deliver Basti into your hands.'

Tanus was silent awhile in the darkness as he savoured that promise. We sat and listened to the nightingale singing at the bottom of Tiamat's garden. It was a sound totally alien from the evil and desperate affairs that we were discussing. After a while Tanus sighed and dismissed Hui.

'You have done well, lad,' he told him. 'Fulfil your promise, and you will find me grateful.'

Hui prostrated himself, as though before a god, and Tanus nudged him irritably with his foot. 'Enough of that nonsense. Away with you now.'

This recent, unlooked-for elevation to the godhead embarrassed Tanus. No one could ever accuse him of being either modest or humble, but he was at least a pragmatist, with no false illusions of his own station; he never aspired to become either a pharaoh or a divine, and he was always short with any servility or obsequious behaviour from those around him.

As soon as the lad was gone, Tanus turned back to me. 'So often I lie awake in the night and consider all that you have told me about my father. I ache in every fibre of my body and soul for revenge against the one who drove him into penury and disgrace and hounded him to his death. I can barely restrain myself. I am filled by the desire to abandon this devious way that you have devised of trapping Akh-Seth. Instead, I long to seek him out directly, and tear out his foul heart with my bare hands.'

'If you do that, you will lose everything,' I said. 'You know that well. Do it my way and you will restore not only your own reputation, but that of your noble father into the bargain. My way, you will retrieve the estate and the fortune that was stolen from you. My way will not only give you your full measure of revenge, but will also lead you back to Lostris and the fulfilment of the vision that I divined for the pair of you in the Mazes of Ammon-Ra. Trust me, Tanus. For your sake and the sake of my mistress, trust me.'

'If I don't trust you, then who can I trust?' he asked, and touched my arm. 'I know you are right, but I have always lacked patience. For me the swift and direct road has always been easiest.'

'For the time being, put Akh-Seth out of your mind. Think only of the next step along the devious way that we must travel together. Think of Basti the Cruel. It was Basti who destroyed your father's trade caravans as they returned from the East. For five seasons, not one of the caravans of Lord Harrab ever returned to Karnak. They were all attacked and looted along the road. It was Basti who destroyed your father's copper-mines at Sestra and murdered the engineers, and their slave workers. Since then those rich veins of ore have lain untapped. It was Basti who systematically pillaged your father's estates along the Nile, who slaughtered his slaves in the fields and burned the crops, until in the end, only weeds grew in Lord Harrab's fields, and he was forced to sell them at a fraction of their real worth.'

'All that may be true, but it was Akh-Seth who gave Basti his orders.'

'No one will believe that. Pharaoh will not believe that, unless he hears Basti confess it,' I told him impatiently. 'Why are you always so stubborn? We have gone over this a hundred times. The barons first, and then at last the head of the snake, Akh-Seth.'

'Yours is the voice of wisdom, I know it. But it is hard to bear the waiting. I long for my revenge. I long to cleanse the stain of sedition and treason from my honour, and I long – oh, how I long – for Lostris!'

He leaned across and clasped my shoulder with a grip that made me wince. 'You have done enough here, old friend. I could never have accomplished so much without you. If you had not come to find me, I might still be sodden with drink and lying in the embrace of some stinking whore. I owe you more than I can ever repay, but I must send you away now. You are needed elsewhere. Basti is my meat, and I don't need you to share the feast with me. You will not be coming with me to Gebel-Umm-Bahari. I am sending you back where you belong – where I also belong, but where I cannot be – at the side of the Lady Lostris. I envy you, old friend, I would give up my hope of immortality to be going to her in your place.'

I protested most prettily, of course. I swore that all I wanted was another chance at those villains, and that I was his companion and that I would be seriously aggrieved if he would not give me a place at his side in the next campaign. All the time I was secure in the knowledge that when Tanus set his mind on a course of action he was adamant and could not easily be dissuaded, except very occasionally by his friend and adviser, Taita the slave.

The truth was that I had enjoyed my fill of wild heroics and people trying to kill me. I was not by nature a soldier, not some insensitive clod of a trooper. I hated the rigours of campaigning in the desert. I could not bear another week of heat and sweat and flies without even a glimpse of the sweet green waters of

Mother Nile. I longed for the feel of clean linen against my freshly bathed and anointed skin. I missed my mistress more than I could express in mere words. Our quiet, civilized life in the painted rooms on the Island of Elephantine, our music and long, leisurely conversations together, my pets and my scrolls, all these exerted an irresistible draw upon me.

Tanus was right, he no longer needed me, and my place was with my mistress. However, to acquiesce too readily to his orders might lower his opinion of me, and I did not want that either.

At last I allowed him to convince me, and, concealing my eagerness, I began my preparations for my return to Elephantine.

 TANUS HAD ordered Kratas back to Karnak, to assemble and bring up reinforcements for the expedition into the desert of Gebel-Umm-Bahari. I was to travel under his protection as far as Karnak, but taking leave of Tanus was not a simple matter. Twice when I had already left the house of Tiamat to join Kratas where he waited for me on the outskirts of the town, Tanus called me back to give me another message to take to my mistress.

'Tell her that I think of her every hour of every day!'

'You have already given me that message,' I protested.

'Tell her that my dreams are filled with images of her lovely face.'

'And that one also. I can recite them by heart. Give me something new,' I pleaded.

'Tell her that I believe the vision of the Mazes, that in a few short years we will be together—'

'Kratas is waiting for me. If you keep me here, how can I deliver your message?'

'Tell her that everything I do is for her. Every breath I draw is for her—' he broke off, and embraced me. 'The truth is, Taita, I doubt I can live another day without her.'

'Five years will pass like that single day. When next you meet her, your honour will be restored and you will once more stand high in the land. She can only love you the more for that.'

He released me. 'Take good care of her until I am able to

assume that joyous duty from you. Now, away with you. Speed to her side.'

'That has been my intention this hour past,' I told him wryly, and made good my escape.

With Kratas at the head of our small detachment, we made the journey to Karnak in under a week. Fearful of discovery by Rasfer or Lord Intef, I spent as little time in my beloved city as it took me to find passage on one of the barges heading southwards. I left Kratas busily recruiting from amongst the elite regiments of Pharaoh's guards the thousand good men that Tanus had demanded, and I went aboard the barge.

We had the north wind in our sails all the way, and we tied up at the wharf of East Elephantine twelve days after leaving Thebes. I was still dressed in the wig and garb of the priesthood, and nobody recognized me as I came ashore.

For the price of a small copper ring I hired a felucca to take me across the river to the royal island, and it put me down at the steps that led up to the water-gate to our garden in the harem. My heart pounded against my ribs as I bounded up the stairs. I had been away from my mistress far too long. It was at times such as these that I realized the full strength of my feelings for her. I was certain that Tanus' love was but a light river breeze in comparison to the *khamsin* of my own emotions.

One of Lostris' Cushite maidens met me at the gate, and tried to prevent me from entering. 'My mistress is unwell, priest. There is another doctor with her at this moment. She will not see you.'

'She will see me,' I told her, and stripped off my wig.

'Taita!' she squealed, and fell to her knees, frantically making the sign to ward off evil. 'You are dead. This is not you, but some evil apparition from beyond the grave.'

I brushed her aside and hurried to my mistress's private quarters, to be met at the doors by one of those priests of Osiris who consider themselves physicians.

'What are you doing here?' I demanded of him, appalled that one of these quacks had been anywhere near my mistress. Before he could answer, I bellowed at him, 'Out! Get out of here! Take your spells and charms and filthy potions, and don't come back.'

He looked as though he were prepared to argue, but I placed my hand between his shoulder-blades and gave him a running start towards the gate. Then I rushed to my mistress's bedside.

The odour of sickness filled the chamber, sour and strong, and a wild grief seized me as I looked down at the Lady Lostris. She seemed to have shrunk in size, and her skin was pale as the ashes of an old camp-fire. She was asleep or in a coma, I could not be certain which, but there were dark, bruised shadows beneath her closed eyelids. Her lips had that dry and crusty look that filled me with dread.

I drew back the linen sheet that covered her and beneath it she was naked. I stared in horror at her body. The flesh had melted off her. Her limbs were thin as sticks and her ribs and the bones of her pelvis stuck out through the unhealthy skin, like those of drought-stricken kine. Tenderly, I placed my hand in her armpit to feel for the heat of fever, but her skin was cool. What kind of disease was this, I fretted. I had not encountered any like it before.

Without leaving her side, I yelled for her slave girls, but none of them had the courage to face the ghost of Taita. In the end I had to storm into their quarters and drag one of them whimpering from under her bed.

'What have you done to your mistress to bring her to this pass?' I kicked her fat backside to focus her attention on my question, and she whined and covered her face, so as not to have to look upon me.

'She will not eat. Barely a mouthful in all these weeks. Not since the mummy of Tanus, Lord Harrab was laid in his tomb in the Valley of the Nobles. She has even lost the child of Pharaoh that she was carrying in her womb. Spare me, kind ghost, I have done you no harm.'

I stared down at her in bewilderment for a moment, until I realized what had happened. My message of comfort to the Lady Lostris had never been delivered. Intuitively I guessed that the messenger whom Kratas had dispatched from Luxor to carry my letter to my mistress, had never reached Elephantine. He had probably become one more victim of the Shrikes, just another corpse floating down the river with an empty purse and a gaping wound in his throat. I hoped that my letter had fallen into the hands of some illiterate thief, and not been taken to Akh-Seth. There was no time to worry about that now.

I rushed back to my mistress's side and fell on my knees beside her bed. 'My darling,' I whispered, and stroked her haggard brow. 'It is me, Taita, your slave.'

She stirred slightly and mumbled something I could not catch. I realized that there was little time to spare; she was far-gone. It was over a month since Tanus' purported death. If the slave girl had spoken the truth, and she had indeed taken no food in all that time, then it was a wonder that she was still alive.

I leaped up again and ran to my own rooms. Despite my 'demise' nothing had been changed, and my medicine chest was in the alcove where I had left it. With it in my arms, I hurried back to my mistress. My hands were shaking as I lit a twig of the scorpion bush from the flame of the oil lamp beside her bed, and held the glowing end under her nose. Almost immediately she gasped and sneezed and struggled to avoid the pungent smoke.

'Mistress, it is I, Taita. Speak to me.'

She opened her eyes and I saw the dawn of pleasure in them swiftly extinguished by the fresh realization of her bereavement. She held out her thin, pale arms to me, and I took her to my breast.

'Taita,' she sobbed softly. 'He is dead. Tanus is dead. I cannot live without him.'

'No! No! He is alive. I come directly from him with messages of love and devotion from him to you.'

'You are cruel to mock me so. I know he is dead. His tomb is sealed—'

'It was a subterfuge to mislead his enemies,' I cried. 'Tanus lives. I swear it to you. He loves you. He waits for you.'

'Oh, that I could believe you! But I know you so well. You will lie to protect me. How can you torment me with false promises? I hate you so—' She tried to break from my arms.

'I swear it. Tanus is alive.'

'Swear on the honour of the mother you never knew. Swear on the wrath of all the gods.' She hardly had the strength to challenge me.

'On all these I swear, and on my love and duty to you, my mistress.'

'Can it be?' I saw the strength of hope flow back into her, and a faint flush of colour bloom in her cheeks. 'Oh, Taita, can it truly be?'

'Would I look so joyful, if it were not? You know I love him almost as much as you do. Could I smile thus, if Tanus were truly dead?'

While she stared into my eyes, I launched into a recitation of all that had occurred since I had left her side so many weeks ago. I excluded only the details of the condition in which I had discovered Tanus in the old shack in the swamps, and the female company I had found him keeping.

She said not a word, but her eyes never left my face as she devoured my words. Her pale face, almost translucent with starvation, glowed like a pearl as she listened to my account of our adventures at Gallala, of how Tanus led the fighting like a god, and of how he sang with the wild joy of battle.

'And so you see, it is true. Tanus is alive,' I ended, and she spoke for the first time since I had begun.

'If he is alive, then bring him to me. I will not eat a mouthful until I set my eyes upon his face once more.'

'I will bring him to your side as swiftly as I can send a messenger to him, if that is what you wish,' I promised, and reached for the polished bronze mirror from my chest.

I held the mirror before her eyes, and asked softly, 'Do you want him to see you as you are now?'

She stared at her own gaunt, hollow-eyed image.

'I will send for him today, if you order it. He could be here within a week, if you really want that.'

I watched her struggle with her emotions. 'I am ugly,' she whispered. 'I look like an old woman.'

'Your beauty is still there, just below the surface.'

'I cannot let Tanus see me like this.' Feminine vanity had triumphed over all her other emotions.

'Then you must eat.'

'You promise,' she wavered, 'you promise that he is still alive,

274

and that you will bring him to me as soon as I am well again? Place your hand on my heart and swear it to me.'

I could feel her every rib and her heart fluttering like a trapped bird beneath my fingers. 'I promise,' I said.

'I will trust you this time, but if you are lying I will never trust you again. Bring me food!'

As I hurried to the kitchen, I could not help but feel smug. Taita, the crafty, had got his own way yet again.

I mixed a bowl of warm milk and honey. We would have to begin slowly, for she had driven herself to the very edge of starvation. She vomited up the contents of the first bowl, but was able to keep down the second. If I had delayed my return by another day, it might have been too late.

 SPREAD BY the chattering slave girls, the news of my miraculous return from the grave swept through the island like the smallpox.

Before nightfall Pharaoh sent Aton to fetch me to an audience. Even my old friend Aton was strained and reserved in my presence. He leaped away nimbly when I tried to touch him, as though my hand might pass through his flesh like a puff of smoke. As he led me through the palace, slaves and nobles alike scurried out of my path, and inquisitive faces watched me from every window and dark corner as we passed.

Pharaoh greeted me with a curious mixture of respect and nervousness, most alien to a king and a god.

'Where have you been, Taita?' he asked, as though he did not really want to hear the answer.

I prostrated myself at his feet. 'Divine Pharaoh, as you yourself are part of the godhead, I understand that you ask that question to test me. You know that my lips are sealed. It would be sacrilege for me to speak of these mysteries, even to you. Please convey to the other deities who are your peers, and particularly to Anubis, the god of the cemeteries, that I have been true to the charge laid upon me. That I have kept the oath of silence imposed upon me. Tell them that I have passed the test that you set me.'

His expression glazed as he considered this, and he fidgeted nervously. I could see him forming question after question, and then discarding each of them in turn. I had left him no opening to exploit.

In the end he blurted out lamely, 'Indeed, Taita, you have passed the test I set you. Welcome back. You have been missed.' But I could see that all his suspicions were confirmed, and he treated me with that respect due to one who had solved the ultimate mystery.

I crawled closer to him and dropped my voice to a whisper. 'Great Egypt, you know the reason I have been sent back?'

He looked mystified, but nodded uncertainly. I came to my feet and glanced around suspiciously, as though I expected to be overlooked by supernatural forces. I made the sign against evil before I went on, 'The Lady Lostris. Her illness was caused by the direct influence of—' I could not say the name, but made the horn sign with two fingers, the sign of the dark god, Seth.

His expression changed from confusion to dread, and he shivered involuntarily and drew closer to me, as if for protection, as I went on, 'Before I was taken away, my mistress was already carrying in her womb the treasure of the House of Mamose when the Dark One intervened. Due to her illness, the son she was bearing you has been aborted from her womb.'

Pharaoh looked distraught. 'So that is the reason that she miscarried,' he began, and then broke off.

I picked up my cue smoothly. 'Never fear, Great Egypt, I have been sent back by forces greater than those of the Dark One to save her, so that the destiny that I foresaw in the Mazes of Ammon-Ra may run its allotted course. There will be another son to replace the one that was lost. Your dynasty will still be secured.'

'You must not leave the side of the Lady Lostris until she is well again.' His voice shook with emotion. 'If you save her and she bears me another son, you may ask from me whatever you wish, but if she dies—' he stopped as he considered what threat might impress one who had already returned from beyond, and in the end let it trail away.

'With your permission, Your Majesty, I shall go to her this instant.'

'This instant!' he agreed. 'Go! Go!'

MY MISTRESS'S recovery was so swift that I began to suspect that I had unwittingly invoked some force beyond my own comprehension, and I felt a superstitious awe at my own powers.

Her flesh filled out and firmed almost as I watched. Those pitiful empty sacs of skin swelled into plump, round breasts once again, sweet enough to make the stone image of the god Hapi which stood at the doorway to her chamber burn with envy. Fresh young blood suffused the chalk of her skin until it glowed once more, and her laughter tinkled like the fountains of our water-garden.

Very soon it was impossible to keep her to her bed. Within three weeks of my return to Elephantine, she was playing games of toss with her handmaidens, dancing about the garden and leaping high to reach the inflated bladder above the heads of the others, until, fearful that she might overtax her returning strength, I confiscated the ball and ordered her back to her chamber. She would obey me only after we had struck another bargain, and I had agreed to sing with her, or teach her the most arcane formulas of the bao board which would allow her to enjoy her first victory over Aton, who was an addict of the game.

Aton came almost every evening to enquire about my mistress's health on behalf of the king, and afterwards to play the board-game with us. Aton seemed to have decided at last that I was not a dangerous ghost, and although he treated me with a new respect, our old friendship survived my demise.

Each morning my Lady Lostris made me repeat my promise to her. Then she would reach for her mirror and study her reflection without the faintest trace of vanity, assessing every facet of her beauty to determine if it was ready yet to be looked upon by Lord Tanus.

'My hair looks like straw, and there is another pimple coming

277

up on my chin,' she lamented. 'Make me beautiful again, Taita. For Tanus' sake make me beautiful.'

'You have done the damage to yourself, and then you call for Taita to make it better,' I grumbled, and she laughed and threw her arms around my neck.

'That's what you are here for, you old scallywag. To look after me.'

Each evening when I mixed a tonic for her and brought the steaming bowl to her as she prepared for sleep, she would make me repeat my promise to her. 'Swear you will bring Tanus to me, just as soon as I am ready to receive him.'

I tried to ignore the difficulties and the dangers that this promise would bring upon us all. 'I swear it to you,' I repeated dutifully, and she lay back against the ivory headrest and went to sleep with a smile upon her face. I would worry about fulfilling my promise when the time came.

 FROM ATON, Pharaoh had a full report of Lostris' recovery and came in person to visit her. He brought her a new necklace of gold and lapis lazuli in the form of an eagle and sat until evening, playing word-games and setting riddles with her. When he was ready to leave, he called me to walk with him as far as his chambers.

'The change in her is extraordinary. It is a miracle, Taita. When can I take her to bed again? Already she seems well enough to bear my son and heir.'

'Not yet, Great Egypt,' I assured him vehemently. 'The slightest exertion on the part of my mistress might trigger a relapse.'

He no longer questioned my word, for now I spoke with all the authority of the once dead, although his previous awe of me had worn a little thin with familiarity.

The slave girls also were becoming accustomed to my resurrection, and were able to look at my face without having to make the sign. Indeed, my return from the underworld was no longer the most popular fare of the palace gossips. They had something

278

else to keep them busy. This was the advent of Akh-Horus into the lives and consciousness of every person living in the land along the great river.

The first time I heard the name Akh-Horus whispered in the palace corridors, I did not immediately place it. The garden of Tiamat beside the Red Sea seemed so remote from the little world of Elephantine, and I had forgotten the name that Hui had bestowed on Tanus. When, however, I heard the accounts of the extraordinary deeds ascribed to this demi-god, I realized who they were speaking about.

In a fever of excitement, I ran all the way back to the harem and found my mistress in the garden, besieged by a dozen visitors, noble ladies and royal wives, for she had so far recovered from her illness as to resume once more her role as court favourite.

I was so wrought up that I forgot my place as a mere slave, and to be rid of them I was quite rude to the royal ladies. They flounced out of the garden squawking like a gaggle of offended geese, and my mistress rounded on me. 'That was unlike you. What on earth has come over you, Taita?'

'Tanus!' I said the name like an incantation, and she forgot all her indignation and seized both my hands.

'You have news of Tanus! Tell me! Quickly, before I die of impatience.'

'News? Yes, I have news of him. What news! What extraordinary news. What unbelievable news!'

She dropped my hands and picked up her formidable silver fan. 'Stop your nonsense this instant,' she threatened me with it. 'I'll not put up with your teasing. Tell me, or I swear you'll have more lumps on your head than a Nubian has fleas.'

'Come! Let's go where nobody can hear us.' I led her down to the jetty and handed her into our little skiff. Out in the middle of the river we were safe from the flapping ears that lurked behind each corner of the palace walls.

'There is a fresh, clean wind blowing through the land,' I told her. 'They call this wind Akh-Horus.'

'The brother of Horus,' she breathed it with reverence. 'Is this what they call Tanus now?'

'None of them know it is Tanus. They think he is a god.'

279

'He is a god,' she insisted. 'To me, he is a god.'

'That is how they see it also. If he were not a god, how then would he know where the Shrikes are skulking, how else would he march unerringly to their strongholds, how would he know instinctively where they are waiting to waylay the incoming caravans, and to surprise them in their own ambuscades?'

'Has he accomplished all these things?' she demanded in wonder.

'These deeds and a hundred others, if you can believe the wild rumours that are flying about the palace. They say that every thief and bandit in the land runs in terror of his life, that the clans of the Shrikes are being shattered one by one. They say that Akh-Horus sprouted wings, like those of an eagle, and flew up the inaccessible cliffs of Gebel-Umm-Bahari to appear miraculously in the midst of the clan of Basti the Cruel. With his own hands, he hurled five hundred of the bandits from the top of the cliffs—'

'Tell me more!' She clapped her hands, almost capsizing the skiff in her enthusiasm.

'They say that at every crossroads and beside every caravan route he has built tall monuments to his passing.'

'Monuments? What monuments are these?'

'Piles of human skulls, high pyramids of skulls. The heads of the bandits he has slain, as a warning to others.'

My mistress shuddered with delicious horror, but her face still shone. 'Has he killed so many?' she demanded.

'Some say he has slain five thousand, and some say fifty thousand. There are even some who say one hundred thousand, but I think those must be exaggerating a little.'

'Tell me more! More!'

'They say he has already captured at least six of the robber barons—'

'And chopped off their heads!' she anticipated me with ghoulish relish.

'No, they say that he has not killed them, but transformed them into baboons. They say he keeps them in a cage for his amusement.'

'Is all of this possible?' she giggled.

'For a god, anything is possible.'

'He is my god. Oh, Taita, when will you let me see him?'

'Soon,' I promised. 'Your beauty burns up brighter every day. Soon it will be fully restored.'

'In the meantime you must gather every story and every rumour of Akh-Horus and bring them to me.'

She sent me to the shipping wharf every day to question the crews of the barges coming down from the north for news of Akh-Horus.

'They are saying now that nobody has ever seen the face of Akh-Horus, for he wears a helmet with a visor that covers all but his eyes. They say also that in the heat of battle the head of Akh-Horus bursts into flame, a flame that blinds his enemies,' I reported to her after one such visit.

'In the sunlight I have seen Tanus' hair seem to burn with a heavenly light,' my mistress confirmed.

On another morning I could tell her, 'They say that he can multiply his earthly body like the images in a mirror, that he can be in many different places at one time, for on the same day he can be seen in Qena and Kom-Ombo, a hundred miles apart.'

'Is that possible?' she asked, with awe.

'Some say this is not true. They say that he can cover these great distances only because he never sleeps. They say that in the night hours he gallops through the darkness on the back of a lion, and in the day he soars through the sky on the back of an enormous white eagle to fall upon his enemies when they least expect it.'

'That could be true.' She nodded seriously. 'I do not believe about the mirror images, but the lion and the eagle might be true. Tanus could do something like that. I believe it.'

'I think it more likely that everybody in Egypt is eager to set eyes upon Akh-Horus, and that the desire is father to the act. They see him behind every bush. As to the speed of his travels, well, I have marched with the guards and I can vouch for—' She would not allow me to finish, but interrupted primly.

'There is no romance in your soul, Taita. You would doubt that the clouds are the fleece of Osiris' flocks, and that the sun is the face of Ra, simply because you cannot reach up and touch

them. I, for my part, believe Tanus is capable of all these things.'
Which assertion put an end to the argument, and I hung my
head in submission.

 IN THE afternoons the two of us resumed our old
practice of strolling through the streets and the market-
places. As before her illness, my mistress was welcomed
by an adoring populace, and she stopped to speak with
all of them, no matter their station or their calling.
From priests to prostitutes, none was immune to her
loveliness and her unfeigned charm.

Always she was able to turn the conversation to Akh-Horus,
and the people were as eager as she was to discuss the new god.
By this time he had been promoted in the popular imagination
from demi-god to a full member of the pantheon. The citizens of
Elephantine had already begun a subscription for the building of
a temple to Akh-Horus, to which my mistress had made a most
generous donation.

A site for the temple had been chosen on the bank of the river
opposite the temple of Horus, his brother, and Pharaoh had made
the formal declaration of his intention to dedicate the building
in person. Pharaoh had every reason to be grateful. There was a
new spirit of confidence abroad. As the caravan routes were made
secure, so the volume of trade between the Upper Kingdom and
the rest of the world blossomed.

Where before one caravan had arrived from the East, now four
made a safe crossing of the desert, and as many set out on the
return journey. To supply the caravan masters, pack-donkeys
were needed in their thousands, and the farmers and breeders
drove them into the cities, grinning at the expectation of the
high prices they would receive.

Because it was now safe to work the fields furthest from the
protection of the city walls, crops were planted where for decades
only weeds had grown, and the farmers, who had been reduced
to beggars, began to prosper again. The oxen drew the sledges
piled high with produce along the roads that were now protected

by the legions of Akh-Horus, and the markets were filled with fresh produce.

Some of the profits of the merchants and the land-owners from these ventures were spent in the building of new villas in the countryside, where it was once more deemed safe to take their families to live. Artisans and craftsmen, who had walked the streets of Thebes and Elephantine seeking employment for their skills, were suddenly in demand, and used their wages to buy not only the necessities of life but luxuries for themselves and their families. The markets were thronged.

The volume of traffic up and down the Nile swelled dramatically, so that more craft were needed, and the new keels were laid down in every shipyard. The captains and crews of the river boats and the shipyard workers spent their new wealth in the taverns and pleasure-houses, so that the prostitutes and the courtesans clamoured for fine clothes and baubles, and the tailors and the jewellers thrived and built new homes, while their wives prowled the markets with gold and silver in their purses, looking for everything from new slaves to cooking-pots.

Egypt was coming to life again, after being strangled for all these years by the depredations of Akh-Seth and the Shrikes.

As a result of all this, the state revenues burgeoned, and Pharaoh's tax-collectors circled above it all with as much relish as the vultures above the corpses of the bandits that Akh-Horus and his legions were strewing across the countryside. Of course, Pharaoh was grateful.

So were my mistress and I. At my suggestion, the two of us invested in a share of a trading expedition that was setting out eastwards into Syria. When the expedition returned six months later, we found that we had made a profit of fifty times our original investment. My mistress bought herself a string of pearls and five new female slaves to make my life miserable. Prudent as always, I used my share to acquire five plots of prime land on the east bank of the river, and one of the law scribes drew up the deeds and had them registered in the temple books.

THEN CAME the day that I had been dreading. One morning my mistress studied her reflection in the mirror with even more attention than usual, and declared that she was ready at last. In all fairness, I had grudgingly to agree that she had never looked more lovely. It was as though all she had suffered recently had tempered her to a new resilience. The last traces of girlishness, uncertainty, and puppy fat had evaporated from her features, and she had become a woman, mature and composed.

'I trusted you, Taita. Now prove to me that I was not silly to do so. Bring Tanus to me.'

When Tanus and I had parted at Safaga, we had been unable to agree on any sure method of exchanging messages.

'I will be on the march every day, and who can tell where this campaign will lead me. Do not let the Lady Lostris worry if she does not hear from me. Tell her I will send a message when my task is completed. But tell her that I will be there when the fruits of our love are ripe upon the tree, and are ready for plucking.'

Thus it was that we had heard nothing of him other than the wild rumours of the wharves and bazaars.

Once again it seemed that the gods had intervened to save me, this time from the wrath of my Lady Lostris. There was a fresh rumour in the market-place that day. A caravan coming down the northern road had encountered a recently erected pyramid of human heads at the roadside not two miles beyond the city walls. The heads were so fresh that they were stinking only a little and had not yet been cleaned of flesh by the crows and vultures.

'This means only one thing,' the gossips told each other. 'This means that Akh-Horus is in the nome of Assoun, probably within sight of the walls of Elephantine. He has fallen upon the remnants of the clan of Akheku, who have been skulking in the desert since their baron had his head hacked off at Gallala. Akh-Horus has slaughtered the last of the bandits, and piled their heads at the roadside. Thanks be to the new god, the south has been cleared of the dreaded Shrikes!'

This was news indeed, the best I had heard in weeks, and I was in a fever to take it to my mistress. I pushed my way through the throng of sailors and merchants and fishermen on the wharf to find a boatman to take me back to the island.

Somebody tugged at my arm, and I shrugged the hand away irritably. Despite the new prosperity sweeping the land, or perhaps because of it, the beggars were more demanding than ever. This one was not so easily put off, and I turned back to him, angrily raising my staff to drive him off.

'Do not strike an old friend! I have a message for you from one of the gods,' the beggar whined, and I stayed the blow and gaped at him.

'Hui!' My heart soared as I recognized the sly grin of the erstwhile robber. 'What are you doing here?' I did not wait for a reply to my fatuous question, but went on swiftly, 'Follow me at a distance.'

I led him to one of the pleasure-houses in a narrow alley beyond the harbour that provided rooms to couples, of the same or of mixed gender. They rented the rooms for a short period measured by a water-clock set at the door, and charged a large copper ring for this service. I paid this exorbitant fee and the moment we were alone, I seized Hui by his ragged cloak.

'What news of your master?' I demanded, and he chuckled with infuriating insolence.

'My throat is so dry I can hardly speak.' Already he had adopted all the swagger and insolent panache of a trooper of the Blues. How quickly a monkey learns new tricks! I shouted for the porter to bring up a pot of beer. Hui drank like a thirsty donkey, then lowered the pot and belched happily.

'The god Akh-Horus sends greetings, to you and to another whose name cannot be mentioned. He bids me tell you that the task is completed and that all the birds are in the cage. He reminds you that it lacks only a few months to the next festival of Osiris and it is time to write a new script for the passion play for the amusement of the king.'

'Where is he? How long will it take for you to return to him?' I demanded eagerly.

'I can be with him before Ammon-Ra, the sun god, plunges beyond the western hills,' Hui declared, and I glanced through the window at the sun which was halfway down the sky. Tanus was lying up very close to the city, and I rejoiced anew. How I longed to feel his rough embrace, and hear that great booming laugh of his!

Grinning to myself in anticipation, I paced up and down the filthy floor of the room while I decided on the message that I would give Hui to take back to him.

 IT WAS almost dark when I stepped ashore on our little jetty and hurried up the steps. One of the slave girls was weeping at the gate, and rubbing her swollen ear.

'She struck me,' the girl whimpered, and I saw that her dignity had suffered more than her ear.

'Do not refer to the Lady Lostris as "she",' I scolded her. 'Anyway, what have you to complain of? Slaves are there to be struck.'

None the less, it was unusual for my mistress to lift a hand to anyone in her household. She must indeed be in a fine mood, I thought, and slowed my pace. Proceeding warily now, I arrived just as another of the girls fled weeping from the chamber. My mistress appeared in the doorway behind her, flushed with anger. 'You have turned my hair into a hay-stack—'

She saw me then and broke off her tirade. She rounded on me with such gusto that I knew that I was the true object of her ire.

'Where have you been?' she demanded. 'I sent you to the harbour before noon. How dare you leave me waiting so long?' She advanced upon me with such an expression that I backed off nervously.

'He is here,' I told her hastily, and then dropped my voice so that none of the slave girls could hear me. 'Tanus is here,' I whispered, 'the day after tomorrow I will make good my promise to you.'

Her mood swung in a full circle and she leaped up to throw her arms around my neck, then she went off to find her offended girls and to comfort them.

AS PART of his annual tribute the vassal king of the Amorites had sent Pharaoh a pair of trained hunting cheetahs from his kingdom across the Red Sea. The king was eager to run these magnificent creatures against the herds of gazelle that abounded in the desert dunes of the west bank. The entire court, including my mistress, had been commanded to attend the course.

We sailed across to the west bank in a fleet of small river craft, white sails and bright-coloured pennants fluttering. There was laughter and the music of lute and sistrum to accompany us. The annual flooding of the great river would begin within days, and this expectation, together with the prosperous new climate of the land, enhanced the carnival mood of the court.

My mistress was in a gayer mood than any of them, and she called merry greetings to her friends in the other boats as our felucca cut through the green summer waters at such a rate as to deck our bows with a lacy white garland of foam and leave a shining wake behind us.

It seemed that I was the only one who was not happy and carefree. The wind had a harsh, abrasive edge to it, and was blowing from the wrong quarter. I kept glancing anxiously at the western sky. It was cloudless and bright, but there was a brassy sheen to the heavens that was unnatural. It was almost as though another sun was dawning from the opposite direction to the one we knew so well.

I put aside my misgivings and tried to enter into the spirit of the outing. I failed in this, for I had more than the weather to worry about. If one part of my plan went awry, my life would be in danger, and perhaps other lives more valuable than mine would be at risk.

I must have shown all this on my face, for my mistress nudged me with her pretty painted toe and told me, 'So glum, Taita? Everyone who looks at you will know that you are up to something. Smile! I command you to smile.'

When we landed on the west bank, there was an army of slaves waiting for us there. Grooms holding splendid white riding donkeys from the royal stables, all caparisoned with silk. Pack-donkeys laden with tents and rugs and baskets of food and wine, and all the other provisions for a royal picnic. There was a regiment of slaves in attendance, some to hold sun-shades above the ladies, others to wait upon the noble guests. There were clowns and acrobats and musicians to entertain them, and a hundred huntsmen to provide the sport.

The cheetah cage was loaded on a sledge drawn by a team of white oxen, and the court gathered around the vehicle to admire these rare beasts. They did not occur naturally in our land, for they were creatures of the open grassy savannah, and there was none of this type of terrain along the river. They were the first that I had ever seen, and my curiosity was so aroused that for a while I forgot my other worries and went up as close to the cage as I could push through the crowd without jostling or treading on the toes of some irascible nobleman.

They were the most beautiful cats that I could imagine, taller and leaner than our leopards, with long, clean limbs and concave bellies. Their sinuous tails seemed to give expression to their mood. Their golden hides were starred with rosettes of deepest black, while from the inner corner of each of their eyes, a line of black was painted down the cheek like a runnel of tears. This, with their regal bearing, gave them a tragic and romantic air that I found enchanting. I longed to own one of these creatures, and I decided on the moment to put the thought into the mind of my mistress. Pharaoh had never refused one of her whims.

Too soon for my liking, the barque carrying the king across the river arrived on the west bank, and with the rest of the court we hurried to the landing to greet him.

Pharaoh was dressed in light hunting garb and for once seemed relaxed and happy. He stopped beside my mistress and while she made a ritual obeisance, he enquired graciously about her health. I was filled with dread that he might decide to keep her by his side throughout the day, which would have upset all my arrangements. However, the hunting cheetah caught his attention and he passed by without giving my mistress any order to follow.

We lost ourselves in the throng and made our way to where a donkey was being held for my Lady Lostris. While I helped her to mount, I spoke quietly to the groom. When he told me what I wanted to hear, I slipped a ring of silver into his hand, and it disappeared, as though by magic.

With one slave leading her and another holding a sun-shade over her, my mistress and I followed the king and the sledge out into the desert. With frequent stops for refreshment, it took us half the morning to reach the Valley of the Gazelles. On the way we passed at a distance the ancient cemetery of Tras which dated from the time of the very first pharaohs. Some of the wise men said that the tombs had been carved from the cliff of black rock three thousand years ago, although how they reached this conclusion I could not tell. Without making it obvious, I studied the entrances of the tombs keenly as we passed. However, from so far off I could make out no trace of recent human presence around them, and I was unreasonably disappointed. I kept glancing back, as we went on.

The Valley of the Gazelles was one of the royal hunting preserves, protected by the decrees of a long line of pharaohs. A company of royal gamekeepers was permanently stationed in the hills above the valley to enforce the king's proclamation reserving all the creatures in it to himself. The penalty for hunting here without the royal authority was death by strangulation.

The nobles dismounted on the crest of one of these hills overlooking the broad brown valley. With despatch the tents were set up to give them shade, and jars of sherbet and beer were broached to slake the thirst of their journey.

I made certain that my mistress and I secured a good vantage-point from which to watch the hunt, but one from which we could also withdraw discreetly without attracting undue attention to ourselves. In the distance I could make out the herds of gazelle through the wavering watery mirage on the floor of the valley. I pointed them out to my mistress.

'What do they find to eat down there?' my Lady Lostris asked. 'There is not a trace of green. They must eat stones, for there are enough of those.'

'Many of those are not stones at all, but living plants,' I told her. When she laughed in disbelief, I searched the rocky ground and plucked a handful of those miraculous plants.

'They are stones,' she insisted, until she held one in her hand and crushed it. The thick juice trickled over her fingers, and she marvelled at the cunning of whatever god had devised this deception. 'This is what they live on? It does not seem possible.'

We could not continue this conversation, because the hunt was beginning. Two of the royal huntsmen opened the cage and the hunting cheetahs leaped down to earth. I expected them to attempt to escape, but they were tame as temple cats and rubbed themselves affectionately against the legs of their handlers. The cats uttered a strange twittering sound, more like a bird than a savage predator.

Along the far side of the brown, scorched valley bottom I could make out the line of beaters, their forms tiny and distorted by distance and mirage. They were moving slowly in our direction, and the herds of antelope were beginning to drift ahead of them.

While the king and his huntsmen, with the cheetahs on leash, moved down the slope towards the valley bottom, we and the rest of the court remained on the crest. The courtiers were already placing wagers with one another, and I was as eager as any of them to watch the outcome of the hunt, but my mistress had her mind on other matters.

'When can we go?' she whispered. 'When can we escape into the desert?'

'Once the hunt begins, all their eyes will be upon it. That will be our opportunity.' Even as I spoke, the wind that had blown us across the river and cooled us on the march suddenly dropped. It was as though a coppersmith had opened the door of his forge. The air became almost too hot to breathe.

Once again I looked to the western horizon. The sky above it had turned a sulphurous yellow. Even as I watched, the stain seemed to spread across the heavens. It made me uneasy. However, I was the only one in the crowd who seemed to notice this strange phenomenon.

Although the hunting party was now at the bottom of the hill, it was still close enough for me to observe the great cats. They had seen the herds of gazelle which were being driven slowly towards them. This had transformed them from affectionate pets into the savage hunters they truly were. Their heads were up, intent and alert, ears pricked forward, leaning against the leash. Their concave bellies were sucked in, and every muscle was taut as a bowstring drawn to full stretch.

My mistress tugged at my skirt, and whispered imperatively, 'Let us be gone, Taita,' and reluctantly I began to edge away towards a clump of rocks that would cover our retreat and screen us from the rest of the company. The bribe of silver to the groom had procured for us a donkey that was now tethered out of sight amongst the rocks. As soon as we reached it, I checked that it carried what I had ordered, the water-skin and the leather bag of provisions. I found that they were all in order.

I could not restrain myself, and I pleaded with my mistress, 'Just one moment more.' Before she could forbid it, I scrambled to the top of the rocky outcrop and peeped down into the valley below.

The nearest antelope were crossing a few hundred paces in front of where Pharaoh held the pair of cheetahs on the leash. I was just in time to watch him slip them and send them away. They started out at an easy lope, heads up, as if they were studying the herds of daintily trotting antelope to select their prey. Suddenly the herds became aware of their rapid approach, and they burst into full flight. Like a flock of swallows they skimmed away across the dusty plain.

The cats stretched out their long bodies, reaching far ahead with their forepaws and then whipping their hindquarters through, doubling their lean torsos before stretching out again. Swiftly they built up to the top of their speed, and I had never seen an animal so swift. Compared to them, the herds of gazelle seemed suddenly to have run into swampy ground and to have had their flight impeded. With effortless elegance, the two cats overhauled the herd, and ran past one or two stragglers before they caught up with the victims of their choice.

The panic-stricken antelopes tried to dodge the deadly rush. They leaped high and changed direction in mid-air, twisting and doubling back the moment their dainty hooves touched the scorched earth. The cats followed each of the convolutions with graceful ease, and the end was inevitable. Each of them bore one of the gazelle to earth in a sliding, tumbling cloud of dust, and then crouched over it, jaws clamped across the windpipe to strangle it while the gazelle's back legs kicked out convulsively, and then at last stiffened into the rigor of death.

I found myself shaken and breathless with the excitement of it all. Then my mistress's voice roused me. 'Taita! Come down immediately. They will see you perched up there.' And I slid down to rejoin her.

Although I was still wrought up, I boosted her into the saddle and led the donkey down into the dead ground where we were out of sight of the company on the hilltop behind us. My mistress could not sustain her irritation with me for very long, and when I slyly mentioned Tanus' name again she forgot it entirely, and urged her mount on towards the rendez-vous.

Only after I had placed another ridge behind us and was certain that we were well clear of the Valley of the Gazelles, did I head back directly towards the cemetery of Tras. In the still, hot air, the sound of our donkey's hooves clinked and crackled on the stones as though it were passing over a bed of broken glass. Soon I felt the sweat break out upon my skin, for the air was close and heavy with a feeling of thunder. Long before we reached the tombs, I told my mistress, 'The air is dry as old bones. You should drink a little water—'

'Keep on! There will be plenty of time to drink your fill later.'

'I was thinking only of you, mistress,' I protested.

'We must not be late. Every moment you waste will give me that much less with Tanus.' She was right, of course, for we would have little enough time before we were missed by the others. My mistress was so popular that many would be looking to enjoy her company once the hunt was over and they were returning to the river.

As we drew closer to the cliffs, so her eagerness increased until she could no longer abide the pace of her mount. She leaped off its back and ran ahead to the next rise. 'There it is! That is where he will be waiting for me,' she cried, and pointed ahead.

As she danced on the skyline, the wind came at us like a ravening wolf, howling amongst the hills and canyons. It caught my mistress's hair and spread it like a flag, snapping and tangling it around her head. It lifted her skirts high above her slim brown thighs, and she laughed and pirouetted, flirting with the wind as though it were her lover. I did not share her delight.

I turned and looked back and saw the storm coming out of the Sahara. It towered into the sullen yellow heavens, dun and awful, billowing upon itself like surf breaking on a coral reef. The wind-blown sand scoured my legs and I broke into a run, dragging the donkey behind me on its lead. The wind thrusting into my back almost knocked me off my feet, but I caught my mistress.

'We must be quick,' I shouted above the wind. 'We must reach the shelter of the tombs before it hits us.'

High clouds of sand blew across the sun, dimming it until I could look directly at it with my naked eye. All the world was washed with that sombre shade of ochre, and the sun was a dull ball of orange. Flying sand raked the exposed skin of our limbs and the backs of our necks, until I wound my shawl around my mistress's head to protect her, and led her forward by the hand.

Sheets of driven sand engulfed us, blotting out our surroundings, so that I feared I had lost direction, until abruptly a hole opened in the curtains of sand, and I saw the dark mouth of one of the tombs appear ahead of us. Dragging my mistress with one hand and our donkey with the other, I staggered into the shelter of the cave. The entrance-shaft was carved from the solid rock. It led us deep into the hillside, and then made a sharp turn before entering the burial chamber where once the ancient mummy had been laid to rest. Centuries before, the grave-robbers had disposed of the embalmed body and all its treasures. Now all that remained were the faded frescoes upon the stone walls, images of gods and monsters that were ghostly in the gloom.

My mistress sank down against the rock wall, but her first thoughts were for her love. 'Tanus will never find us now,' she cried in despair, and I who had led her to safety was hurt by her ingratitude. I unsaddled our donkey and heaped the load in a corner of the tomb. Then I drew a cup of water from the skin and made her drink.

'What will happen to the others, the king and all our friends?' she asked, between gulps from the cup. It was her nature to think of the welfare of others, even in her own predicament.

'They have the huntsmen to care for them,' I told her. 'They are good men and know the desert.' But not well enough to have anticipated the storm, I thought grimly. Although I sought to reassure her, I knew it would go hard with the women and children out there.

'And Tanus?' she asked. 'What will become of him?'

'Tanus especially will know what to do. He is like one of the Bedouin. You can be sure he will have seen the storm coming.'

'Will we ever get back to the river? Will they ever find us here?' At last she thought of her own safety.

'We will be safe here. We have water enough for many days. When the storm blows itself out, we will find our way back to the river.' Thinking of the precious water, I carried the bulging skin further into the tomb, where the donkey would not trample it. By now it was almost completely dark, and I fumbled with the lamp that the slave had provided from the pack, and blew upon the smouldering wick. It flared and lit the tomb with a cheery yellow light.

While I was still busy with the lamp and my back was turned to the entrance, my mistress screamed. It was a sound so high and filled with such mortal terror that I was struck with equal dread, and the courses of my blood ran thick and slow as honey, although my heart raced like the hooves of the flying gazelle. I spun about and reached for my dagger, but when I saw the monster whose bulk filled the doorway, I froze without touching the weapon on my belt. I knew instinctively that my puny blade would avail us not at all against whatever this creature might be.

In the feeble light of the lamp the form was indistinct and distorted. I saw that it had a human shape, but it was too large to be a man, and the grotesque head convinced me that this was indeed that dreadful crocodile-headed monster from the underworld that devours the hearts of those who are found wanting on the scales of Thoth, the monster depicted on the walls of the tomb. The head gleamed with reptilian scales, and the beak was that of an eagle or a gigantic turtle. The eyes were deep and fathomless pits that stared at us implacably. Great wings sprouted from its shoulders. Half-furled, they flapped about the towering body like those of a falcon at bate. I expected the creature to launch itself on those wings and to rend my mistress with brazen talons. She must have dreaded this as much as I, for she screamed again as she crouched at the monster's feet.

Then suddenly I realized that the creature was not winged, but that the folds of a long woollen cape, such as the Bedouin wear, were flogging on the wind. While we were still frozen by this horrible presence, it raised both hands and lifted off the gilded war helmet with the visor fashioned like the head of an eagle. Then it shook its head and a mass of red-gold curls tumbled down on to the broad shoulders.

'From the top of the cliff I saw you coming through the storm,' it said in those dear familiar tones.

My mistress screamed again, this time with wildly ringing joy. 'Tanus!'

She flew to him, and he gathered her up as though she were a child and lifted her so high that her head brushed the rock roof. Then he brought her down and folded her to his chest. From the cradle of his arms, she reached up with her mouth for his, and it seemed that they might devour each other with the strength of their need.

I stood forgotten in the shadows of the tomb. Although I had conspired and risked so much to bring them together, I cannot bring myself to write down here the feelings that assailed me as I was made reluctant witness to their rapture. I believe that jealousy is the most ignoble of all our emotions, and yet I loved the Lady Lostris as well as Tanus did, and not with the love of a father or of a brother, either. I was a eunuch, but what I felt for her was the love of a natural man, hopeless of course, but all the more bitter because of that. I could not stay and watch them and I began to slink from the tomb like a whipped puppy, but Tanus saw me leaving and broke that kiss which was threatening to destroy my soul.

'Taita, don't leave me alone with the wife of the king. Stay with us to protect me from this terrible temptation. Our honour is in jeopardy. I cannot trust myself, you must stay and see that I bring no shame to the wife of Pharaoh.'

'Go,' cried my Lady Lostris from his arms. 'Leave us alone. I'll listen to no talk of shame or honour now. Our love has been too long denied. I cannot wait for the prophecy of the Mazes to run its course. Leave us alone now, gentle Taita.'

I fled from the chamber as though my life was in danger. I might have run out into the storm and perished there. That way I would have found surcease, but I was too much of a coward, and I let the wind drive me back. I stumbled to a corner of the shaft where the wind could no longer harry me, and I sank to the stone floor. I pulled my shawl over my head to stop my eyes and my ears, but although the storm roared along the cliff, it could not drown the sounds from the burial chamber.

For two days the storm blew with unabated ferocity. I slept for part of that time, forcing myself to seek oblivion, but whenever I awoke, I could hear them, and the sounds of their love tortured me. Strange that I had never known such distress when my mistress was with the king – but then on the other hand not so strange, for the old man had meant nothing to her.

This was another world of torment for me. The cries, the groans, the whispers tore at my heart. The rhythmic sobs of a young woman that were not those of pain threatened to destroy me. Her wild scream of final rapture was more agonizing to me than the cut of the gelding-knife.

At last the wind abated and died away, moaning at the foot of the cliffs. The light strengthened and I realized that it was the third day of my incarceration in the tomb. I roused myself and called to them, not daring to enter the inner chamber for fear of what I might discover. For a while there was no reply, and then my mistress spoke in a husky, bemused voice that echoed eerily down the shaft. 'Taita, is that you? I thought that I had died in the storm and been carried to the western fields of paradise.'

ONCE THE storm had dropped, we had little time remaining. The royal huntsmen would already be searching for us. The storm had given us the best possible excuse for our absence. I was sure that the survivors of the hunting party would be scattered across these terrible hills. But the search-party must not discover us in the company of Tanus.

On the other hand, Tanus and I had barely spoken during these last days, and there was much to discuss. Hastily we made our plans, standing in the entrance to the shaft.

My mistress was quiet and composed as I had seldom seen her before. No longer the irrepressible chatterbox, she stood beside Tanus, watching his face with a new serenity. She reminded me of a priestess serving before the image of her god. Her eyes never left his face, and occasionally she reached out to touch him, as if to reassure herself that it was truly he.

When she did this, Tanus broke off whatever he was saying and gave all his attention to those dark green eyes. I had to call him back to the business we still had not completed. In the presence of such manifest adoration, my own feelings were base and mean. I forced myself to rejoice for them.

It took longer to finish our business than I deemed wise, but at last I embraced Tanus in farewell and urged the donkey out into the sunlight that was filtered by the fine yellow dust that still filled the air. My mistress lingered, and I waited for her in the valley below.

Looking back, I saw them emerge from the cave at last. They stood gazing at each other for a long moment without touching, and then Tanus turned and strode away. My mistress watched until he was gone from her sight, then she came down to where I waited. She walked like a woman in a dream.

I helped her to mount, and while I adjusted the saddle girth, she reached down and took my hand. 'Thank you,' she said simply.

'I do not deserve your gratitude,' I demurred.

'I am the happiest creature in all the world. Everything that you told me of love is true. Please rejoice for me, even though—'

she did not finish, and suddenly I realized that she had read my innermost feelings. Even in her own great joy, she grieved that she had caused me pain. I think I loved her more in that moment than I had ever done before.

I turned away and took up the reins, and led her back towards the Nile.

ONE OF the royal huntsmen spied us from a far hilltop, and hailed us heartily.

'We have been searching for you at the king's command,' he told us, as he hurried down to join us.

'Was the king saved?' I asked.

'He is safe in the palace on Elephantine Island, and he has commanded that the Lady Lostris be brought to him directly she is found.'

As we set foot on the palace jetty, Aton was there, puffing out his painted cheeks with relief and fussing over my mistress. 'They have found the bodies of twenty-three unfortunates who perished in the storm,' he told us with ghoulish relish. 'All were certain that you would be found dead also. However, I prayed at the temple of Hapi for your safe return.' He looked pleased with himself, and I was annoyed that he tried to claim the credit for her survival for himself. He allowed us only time enough to wash hastily and anoint our dry skin with perfumed oil, before he whisked us away to the audience with the king.

Pharaoh was truly moved to have my mistress returned to him. I am sure he had come to love her as much as any of the others, and not merely for the promise of immortality that he saw in her. A tear tangled in his eyelash and smeared the paint on his cheek as she knelt before him.

'I thought you were lost,' he told her, and would have embraced her, had etiquette permitted it. 'Instead I find you prettier and livelier than ever.' Which was true, for love had gilded her with its special magic.

'Taita saved me,' she told Pharaoh. 'He guided me to a shelter and protected me through all those terrible days. Without him I would have perished, like those other poor souls.'

'Is this true, Taita?' Pharaoh demanded of me directly, and I assumed my modest expression, and murmured, 'I am but a humble instrument of the gods.'

He smiled at me, for I knew he had become fond of me also. 'You have rendered us many services, oh humble instrument. But this is the most valuable of them all. Approach!' he commanded, and I knelt before him.

Aton stood beside him, holding a small cedar-wood box. He lifted the lid and proffered it to the king. From the case Pharaoh lifted out a gold chain. It was of the purest unalloyed gold, and bore the marks of the royal jewellers to attest its weight of twenty deben.

The king held the chain over my head and intoned, 'I bestow upon you the Gold of Praise.' He lowered it on to my shoulders, and the oppressive weight was a delight to me. This decoration was the highest mark of royal favour, usually reserved for generals and ambassadors, or for high officials such as Lord Intef. I doubted that ever in the history of this very Egypt had the gold chain been placed around the neck of a lowly slave.

That was not the end of the gifts and awards that were to be bestowed upon me, for my mistress was not to be outdone. That evening while I was attending her bath, she suddenly dismissed her slaves and, standing naked before me, she told me, 'You may help me to dress, Taita.' She allowed me this privilege when she was especially well pleased with me. She knew just how much I enjoyed having her to myself in these intimate circumstances.

Her loveliness was covered only by the glossy tresses of her sable hair. It seemed that those days she had spent with Tanus had filled her with a new quality of beauty. It emanated from deep within her. A lamp placed inside an alabaster jar will shine through the translucent sides; in the same way, the Lady Lostris seemed to glow.

'I never dreamed that such a poor vessel as this body of mine could contain such joy.' She stroked her own flanks as she said it and looked down at herself, inviting me to do the same. 'All that you promised me came to pass while I was with Tanus. Pharaoh has bestowed the Gold of Praise upon you, it is fitting that I also show my appreciation to you. I want you to share my happiness in some way.'

'Serving you is all the reward I could wish for.'

'Help me to dress,' she ordered, and lifted her hands above her head. Her breasts changed shape as she moved. Over the years I had watched them grow from tiny immature figs into these round, creamy pomegranates, more beautiful than jewels or marble sculptures. I held the diaphanous nightdress over her, and then let it float down over her body. It covered her, but did not obscure her loveliness, in the same way that the morning mist decks the waters of the Nile in the dawn.

'I have commanded a banquet, and sent invitations to the royal ladies.'

'Very well, my lady. I shall see to it.'

'No, no, Taita. The banquet is in your honour. You will sit beside me as my guest.'

This was as shocking as any of the wild schemes she had thought up recently. 'It is not fitting, mistress. You will offend against custom.'

'I am the wife of Pharaoh. I set the customs. During the banquet I will have a gift for you, and I will present it to you in the sight of all.'

'Will you tell me what this gift is?' I asked, with some trepidation. I was never sure of what mischief she would dream up next.

'Certainly I will tell you what it is.' She smiled mysteriously. 'It is a secret, that's what it is.'

 EVEN THOUGH I was the guest of honour, I could not leave the arrangements for the banquet to cooks and giggling slave girls. After all, the reputation of my mistress as a hostess was at stake. I was at the market before dawn to procure the finest, freshest produce from the fields and the river.

I promised Aton that he would be invited, and he opened the king's wine cellar and let me make my selection. I hired and rehearsed the best musicians and acrobats in the city. I sent out the slaves to gather hyacinth and lily and lotus from the banks of the river to augment the masses of blooms that already decorated our garden. I had the weavers plait tiny arks of reeds on which I floated coloured glass lamps and set them adrift on the ponds of our water-garden. I set out leather cushions and garlands of flowers for each guest, and jars of perfumed oil to cool them in the sultry night and drive away the mosquitoes.

At nightfall the royal ladies began to arrive in all their frippery and high fashion. Some of them had even shaved their heads and replaced their natural hair with elaborate wigs woven from the hair which the wives of the poor were forced to sell, in order to feed their brats. This was a fashion I abhorred and I vowed to do all in my power to prevent my mistress from succumbing to such folly. Her lustrous tresses were amongst my chief delights, but when it comes to fashion, even the most sensible woman is not to be trusted.

When, at the insistence of my mistress, I seated myself on the cushion beside her, rather than taking my usual position behind her, I could see that many of our guests were scandalized by such indecorous behaviour, and they whispered to each other behind their fans. I was just as uncomfortable as they were, and to cover my embarrassment, I signalled the slaves to keep the wine cups filled, the musicians to play, and the dancers to dance.

The wine was robust, the music rousing, and the dancers were all male. They gave ample proof of their gender, for I had ordered them to perform in a state of nature. The ladies were so enchanted by this display that they soon forgot their decent outrage, and did justice to the wine. I had no doubt that many of the male dancers would not leave the harem before dawn. Some of the royal ladies had voracious appetites, and many had not been visited by the king in years.

In this convivial atmosphere my mistress rose to her feet and called for the attention of her guests. Then she commended me to them in terms so extravagant that even I blushed. She went on to relate amusing and touching episodes from the lifetime we had spent together. The wine seemed to have softened the attitude of the women towards me, and they laughed and applauded. A few of them even wept a little with wine and sentiment.

At last my mistress commanded me to kneel before her, and as I did so, there was a murmur of comment. I had chosen to wear a simple kilt of the finest linen, and the slave girls had dressed my hair in the fashion that best suited me. Apart from the Gold of Praise around my throat, I wore no other ornament. In the midst of such ostentation, my simple style was striking. With regular swimming and exercise I had kept the athletic body which had first attracted Lord Intef to me. In those years I was in my prime.

I heard one of the senior wives murmur to her neighbour, 'What a pity he has lost his jewels. He would make such a diverting toy.' This evening I could ignore the words that in other circumstances would have caused me intense pain.

My mistress was looking very pleased with herself. She had succeeded in keeping me ignorant of the nature of her gift. Usually she was not so adroit as to be able to outwit me. She looked down on my bowed head and spoke slowly and clearly, wringing the utmost enjoyment from the moment.

'Taita the slave. For all the years of my life you have been a shield over me. You have been my mentor and my tutor. You have taught me to read and to write. You have made clear to me the mysteries of the stars and the arcane arts. You have taught me to sing and to dance. You have shown me how to find happiness and contentment in many things. I am grateful.'

The royal ladies were once more beginning to become restive. They had never before heard a slave praised in such effusive terms.

'On the day of the *khamsin* you did me a service that I must reward. Pharaoh has bestowed the Gold of Praise upon you. I have my own gift for you.'

From under her robe she took a roll of papyrus secured with a coloured thread. 'You knelt before me as a slave. Now rise to your feet as a free man.' She held up the papyrus. 'This is your deed of manumission, prepared by the scribes of the court. From this day forward, you are a free man.'

I lifted my head for the first time and stared at her in disbelief. She pressed the roll of papyrus into my numbed fingers, and smiled down at me fondly.

'You did not expect this, did you? You are so surprised that you have no words for me. Say something to me, Taita. Tell me how grateful you are for this boon.'

Every word she spoke wounded me like a poisoned dart. My tongue was a rock in my mouth as I contemplated a life without her. As a freed man, I would be excluded from her presence for ever. I would never again prepare her food, nor attend her bath. I would never spread the covers over her as she prepared for sleep, nor would I rouse her in the dawn and be at her side when first she opened those lovely dark green eyes to each new day. I would never again sing with her, or hold her cup, or help her to dress and have the pleasure of gazing upon all her loveliness.

I was stricken, and I stared at her hopelessly, as one whose life had reached its end.

'Be happy, Taita,' she ordered me. 'Be happy in this new freedom I give you.'

'I will never be happy again,' I blurted. 'You have cast me off. How can I ever be happy again?'

Her smile faded away, and she stared at me in perturbation. 'I offer you the most precious gift that it is in my power to give you. I offer you your freedom.'

I shook my head. 'You inflict the most dire punishment upon me. You are driving me away from you. I will never know happiness again.'

'It is not a punishment, Taita. It was meant as a reward. Please, don't you understand?'

'The only reward I desire is to remain at your side for the rest of my life.' I felt the tears welling up from deep inside me, and I tried to hold them back. 'Please, mistress, I beg of you, don't send me away from you. If you have any feeling towards me, allow me to stay with you.'

'Do not weep,' she commanded. 'For if you do, then I will weep with you, in front of all my guests.' I truly believe that she had not, until that moment, contemplated the consequences of

303

this misplaced piece of generosity that she had dreamed up. The tears broke over my lids and streamed down my cheeks.

'Stop it! This is not what I wanted.' Her own tears kept mine good company. 'I only thought to honour you, as the king has honoured you.'

I held up the roll of papyrus. 'Please let me tear this piece of foolery to shreds. Take me back into your service. Give me leave to stand behind you, where I belong.'

'Stop it, Taita! You are breaking my heart.' Loudly she snuffled up her tears, but I was merciless.

'The only gift I want from you is the right to serve you for all the days of my life. Please, mistress, rescind this deed. Give me your permission to tear it.'

She nodded vigorously, blubbering as she used to do when she was a little girl who had fallen and grazed her knees. I ripped the sheet of papyrus once and then again. Not satisfied with this destruction, I held the fragments to the lamp flame and let them burn to crispy black curls.

'Promise me that you will never try to drive me away again. Swear that you will never again try to thrust my freedom upon me.'

She nodded through her tears, but I would not accept that. 'Say it,' I insisted. 'Say it aloud for all to hear.'

'I promise to keep you as my slave, never to sell you, nor to set you free,' she whispered huskily through the tears, and then a beam of mischief shone out of those tragic dark green eyes. 'Unless, of course, you annoy me inordinately, then I will summon the law scribes immediately.' She put out a hand to lift me to my feet. 'Get up, you silly man, and attend to your duties. I swear my cup is empty.'

I resumed my proper position behind her, and refilled the cup. The tipsy company thought it all a bit of fun that we had arranged for their amusement, and they clapped and whistled and threw flower petals at us to show their appreciation. I could see that most of them were relieved that we had not truly flouted decorum, and that a slave was still a slave.

My mistress lifted the wine cup to her lips, but before she drank, she smiled at me over the rim. Though her eyes were still wet with tears, that smile lifted my spirits and restored my happiness. I felt as close to her then as ever I had in all the years.

 THE MORNING after the banquet and my hour of freedom, we woke to find that during the night the river had swollen with the commencement of the annual flood. We had no warning of it until the joyous cries of the watchmen down at the port aroused us. Still heavy with wine, I left my bed and ran down to the riverside. Both banks were already lined with the populace of the city. They greeted the waters with prayers and songs and waving palm-fronds.

The low waters had been the bright green of the verdigris that grows on bars of copper. The waters of the inundation had flushed it all away, and now the river had swollen to an ominous grey. During the night it had crept halfway up the stone pylons of the harbour, and soon it would press against the earthworks of the embankment. Then it would force its way into the mouths of the irrigation canals that had been cracked and dry for so many months. From there it would swirl out and flood the fields, drowning the huts of the peasants, and washing away the boundary markers between the fields.

The surveying and replacement of the boundaries after each flood was the responsibility of the Guardian of the Waters. Lord Intef had multiplied his fortune by favouring the claims of the rich and the generous when the time came round each year to reset the marker stones.

From upstream echoed the distant rumble of the cataract. The rising flood overwhelmed the natural barrages of granite that were placed in its path, and, as it roared through the gorges, the spray rose into the hard blue sky, a silver column that could be seen from every quarter of the nome of Assoun. When the fine mist drifted across the island, it was cool and refreshing on our upturned faces. We delighted in this blessing, for it was the only rain we ever knew in our valley.

Even as we watched, the beaches around our island were eaten up by the flood. Soon our jetty would be submerged, and the river would lap at the gates of our garden. Where it would stop was a question that could only be calculated by a study of the levels of the Nilometer. On those levels hung prosperity or famine for the whole land and every person in it.

I hurried back to find my mistress and to prepare for the ceremony of the waters, in which I would play a prominent role. We dressed in our finest and I placed my new gold chain around my neck. Then, with the rest of our household and the ladies of the harem, we joined the spontaneous procession to the temple of Hapi.

Pharaoh and all the great lords of Egypt led us. The priests, plump with rich living, were waiting for us on the temple steps. Their heads were shaven, their pates shining with oil, and their eyes glittering with avarice, for the king would sacrifice lavishly today.

Before the king the statue of the god was carried from the sanctuary, and decked with flowers and fine crimson linen. Then the statue was drenched in oils and perfume while we sang psalms of praise and thanks to the god for sending down the flood.

Far to the south, in a land that no civilized man had ever visited, the god Hapi sat on top of his mountain and from two pitchers of infinite capacity he poured the holy waters into his Nile. The water from each pitcher was of a different colour and taste; one was bright green and sweet, the other grey and heavy with the silt which flooded our fields each season and charged them with new life and fertility.

While we sang, the king made sacrifice of corn and meats and wine and silver and gold. Then he called out his wise men, his engineers and his mathematicians, and bade them enter the Nilometer to begin their observations and their calculations.

In the time that I had belonged to Lord Intef, I had been nominated as one of the keepers of the water. I was the only slave in that illustrious company, but I consoled myself by the fact that very few others wore the Gold of Praise, and that they treated me with respect. They had worked with me before, and they knew my worth. I had helped to design the Nilometers that measured the flow of the river, and I had supervised the building of them. It was I who had worked out the complex formula to determine the projected height and the volume of each flood from the observations.

Our way lit by flickering torches of pitch-dipped rushes, I followed the high priest into the mouth of the Nilometer, a dark opening in the rear wall of the sanctuary. We descended the incline shaft, the stone steps slippery with slime and the effusions of the river. From under our feet, one of the deadly black water cobras slithered away, and with a furious hiss plunged into the dark water that had already risen halfway up the shaft.

We gathered on the last exposed step and by the light of the torches studied the marks that my masons had chiselled in the walls of the shaft. Each of the symbols had values, both magical and empirical, allotted to it.

We made the first and most crucial reading together with extreme care. Over the following five days we would take it in turns to watch and record the rising waters, and time the readings with the flow of a water-clock. From samples of the water, we would estimate the amount of silt it bore, and all these factors would influence our final conclusions.

When the five days of observation were completed, we embarked on a further three days of calculations. These covered many scrolls of papyrus. Finally, we were ready to present our findings to the king. On that day Pharaoh returned to the temple in royal state, accompanied by his nobles and half the population of Elephantine to receive the estimates.

As the high priest read them aloud, the king began to smile. We had forecast an inundation of almost perfect proportions. It would not be too low, to leave the fields exposed and baking in the sun, depriving them of the rich black layer of silt so vital to their fertility. Nor would it be so high as to wash away the canals and earthworks, and to drown the villages and cities along the banks. This season would bring forth bountiful harvests and fat herds.

Pharaoh smiled, not so much for the good fortune of his subjects, but for the bounty that his tax-collectors would gather in. The annual taxes were computed on the value of the flood, and this year there would be vast new treasures added to the store-rooms of his funerary temple. To close the ceremony of the blessing of the water in the temple of Hapi, Pharaoh announced the date of the biennial pilgrimage to Thebes to participate in the festival of Osiris. It did not seem possible that two years had passed since my mistress had played the part of the goddess in the last passion of Osiris.

I had as little sleep that night as when I had kept vigil in the shaft of the Nilometer, for my mistress was too excited to seek her own couch. She made me sit up with her until dawn, singing and laughing and repeating those stories of Tanus to which she never tired of listening.

In eight days the royal flotilla would sail northwards on the rising flood of the Nile. When we arrived, Tanus, Lord Harrab would be waiting for us in Thebes. My mistress was delirious with happiness.

THE FLOTILLA that assembled in the harbour roads of Elephantine was so numerous that it seemed to cover the water from bank to bank. My mistress remarked jokingly that a man might cross the Nile without wetting his feet by strolling over the bridge of hulls. With pennants and flags flying from every masthead, the fleet made a gallant show.

We and the rest of the court had already embarked on the vessels that had been allotted to us, and from the deck we cheered the king as he descended the marble steps from the palace and went aboard the great state barge. The moment he was safely embarked, a hundred horns sounded the signal to set sail. As one, the fleet squared away and pointed their bows into the north. With the rush of the river and the banks of oars driving us, we bore away.

There had been a different spirit abroad in the land since Akh-Horus had destroyed the Shrikes. The inhabitants of every village we passed came down to the water's edge to greet their king. Pharaoh sat high on the poop, wearing the cumbersome double crown, so that all might have a clear view of him. They waved palm-fronds and shouted, 'May all the gods smile on Pharaoh!'

The river brought down to them not only their king, but also the promise of its own benevolence, and they were happy.

Twice during the days that followed, Pharaoh and all his train went ashore to inspect the monuments that Akh-Horus had raised to his passing at the crossroads of the caravan routes. The local peasants had preserved these gruesome piles of skulls as sacred relics of the new god. They had polished each skull until it shone like ivory, and bound the pyramids with building clay so that they would stand through the years. Then they had built shrines over them and appointed priests to serve these holy places.

At both these shrines my mistress left a gold ring as an offering, joyously accepted by the self-appointed guardians. It was to no avail that I protested this extravagance. My mistress often lacked the proper respect for the wealth that I was so painstakingly amassing on her behalf. Without my restraining hand, she would probably have given it all away to the grasping priesthood and the insatiable poor, smiling as she did so.

On the tenth night after leaving Elephantine, the royal entourage camped on a pleasant promontory above a bend in the river. The entertainment that evening was to include one of the most famous story-tellers in the land, and usually my mistress loved a good story above most other pleasures. Both she and I had been looking forward to this occasion and discussing it avidly since leaving the palace. It was therefore to my surprise and bitter disappointment that the Lady Lostris declared herself too fatigued and out of sorts to attend the story-teller. Although she urged me to go, and take the rest of our household with me, I could not leave her alone when she was unwell. I gave her a hot draught and I slept on the floor at the end of her bed, so that I could be near if she needed me during the night.

I was truly worried in the morning when I tried to wake her. Usually she would spring from her bed with a smile of anticipation, ready to seize and devour the new day, a glutton for the joy of living. However, this morning she pulled the covers back over her head and mumbled, 'Leave me to sleep a little longer. I feel as heavy and dull as an old woman.'

'The king has decreed an early start. We must be aboard before the sun rises. I will bring you a hot infusion that will cheer you.' I poured boiling water over a bowl of herbs that I had picked with my own hands during the most propitious phase of the last moon.

'Do stop fussing,' she grumped at me, but I would not let her sleep again. I prodded her awake and made her drink the tonic. She pulled a face. 'I swear you are trying to poison me,' she complained, and then, without warning and before I could do anything to prevent it, she vomited copiously.

Afterwards she seemed as shocked as I was. We both stared at the steaming puddle beside her bed in consternation.

'What is wrong with me, Taita?' she whispered. 'Nothing like this has ever happened to me before.'

Only then did the meaning of it all dawn on me.

'The *khamsin*!' I cried. 'The cemetery of Tras! Tanus!'

She stared at me blankly for a moment, and then her smile lit the gloom of the tent like a lamp. 'I am making a baby!' she cried.

'Not so loud, mistress,' I pleaded.

'Tanus' baby! I am carrying Tanus' son.' It could not be the king's infant, for I had successfully kept him from her bed since her starvation sickness and her miscarriage.

'Oh, Taita,' she purred, as she lifted her nightdress and inspected her flat, firm belly with awe. 'Just think of it! A little imp just like Tanus growing inside of me.' She palpated her stomach hopefully. 'I knew that such delights as I discovered in the tomb of Tras could not pass unremarked by the gods. They have given me a memory that will last all my lifetime.'

'You race ahead,' I warned her. 'It may be only a colic. I must make the tests before we can be sure.'

'I need no test. I know it in my heart and in the secret depths of my body.'

'We will still do the tests,' I told her wryly, and went to fetch the pot. She perched upon it to provide me with the first water of her day, and I divided this into two equal parts.

The first portion of her urine I mixed with an equal part of Nile water. Then I filled two jars with black earth and in each of

310

them planted five seeds of dhurra corn. I watered one jar with pure Nile water, and the other with the mixture that my mistress had provided. This was the first test.

Then I hunted amongst the reeds in the lagoon near the camp and captured ten frogs. These were not the lively green and yellow variety with leaping back legs, but slimy, black creatures. Their heads are not separated from their sluggish, fat bodies by a neck, and their eyes sit on top of the flat skull, so that the children call them sky-gazers.

I placed five of each of the sky-gazers in two separate jars of river water. To the one I added my mistress's intimate emission and I left the other unadulterated. The following morning, in the privacy of my mistress's cabin on board the galley, we removed the cloth with which I had covered the jars and inspected the contents.

The corn watered by the Lady Lostris had thrown tiny green shoots, while the other seeds were still inert. The five sky-gazers who had not received my mistress's blessing were barren, but the other more fortunate five had each laid long silvery strings which were speckled with black eggs.

'I told you so!' my mistress chirruped smugly, before I could give my official diagnosis. 'Oh, thanks to all the gods! No more beautiful thing has happened to me in all my life.'

'I will speak to Aton immediately. You will share the king's couch this very night,' I told her grimly, and she stared at me in bewilderment.

'Even Pharaoh who believes most things I tell him, will not believe that you were impregnated by the seeds blown in on the *khamsin* wind. We must have a foster-father for this little bastard of ours.' Already I considered the infant ours, and not hers alone. Though I tried to conceal it behind my levity, I was every bit as delighted with her fecundity as she was.

'Don't you ever call him a bastard again,' she flared at me. 'He will be a prince.'

'He will be a prince only if I can find a royal sire for him. Prepare yourself. I am going to see the king.'

311

'LAST NIGHT I had a dream, Great Egypt,' I told Pharaoh. 'It was so amazing that to confirm it I worked the Mazes of Ammon-Ra.'

Pharaoh leaned forward eagerly, for he had come to believe in my dreams and the Mazes as much as any of my other patients.

'This time it is unequivocal, Majesty. In my dream the goddess Isis appeared and promised to counter the baleful influence of her brother Seth, who so cruelly deprived you of your first son when he struck down the Lady Lostris with the wasting disease. Take my mistress to your bed on the first day of the festival of Osiris, and you will be blessed with another son. That is the promise of the goddess.'

'Tonight is the eve of the festival.' The king looked delighted. 'In truth, Taita, I have been ready to perform this pleasant duty all these past months, had you only allowed me to do so. But you have not told me what you saw in the Mazes of Ammon-Ra.' Again he leaned forward eagerly, and I was ready for him.

'It was the vision as before, only this time it was stronger and more vivid. The same endless forest of trees growing along the banks of the river, each tree crowned and imperial. Your dynasty reaching into the ages, strong and unbroken.'

Pharaoh sighed with satisfaction. 'Send the child to me.'

When I returned to the tent, my mistress was waiting for me. She had prepared herself with good grace and humour.

'I shall close my eyes and imagine that I am back in the tomb of Tras with Tanus,' she confided, and then giggled saucily. 'Although to imagine the king as Tanus is to imagine that the tail of the mouse has become the trunk of the elephant.'

Aton came to fetch her to the king's tent soon after the king had eaten his dinner. She went with a calm expression and a firm step, dreaming perhaps of her little prince, and of his true father who waited for us in Thebes.

BELOVED THEBES, beautiful Thebes of the hundred gates — how we rejoiced as we saw it appear ahead of us, decorating the broad sweep of the river-bank with its temples and gleaming walls.

My mistress sang out with excitement as each of the familiar landmarks revealed itself to us. Then, as the royal barge put in to the wharf below the palace of the grand vizier, the joy of home-coming went out of both of us, and we fell silent. The Lady Lostris groped for my hand like a little girl frightened by tales of hob-goblins, for we had seen her father.

Lord Intef with his sons, Menset and Sobek, those two thumbless heroes, stood at the head of the great concourse of the nobles and the city fathers of Thebes that waited upon the quay to greet the king. Lord Intef was as handsome and suave as I had imagined him in my nightmares, and I felt my spirits quail.

'You must be vigilant now,' the Lady Lostris whispered to me. 'They will seek to have you out of their way. Remember the cobra.'

Not far behind the grand vizier stood Rasfer. During our absence he had obviously received high promotion. He now wore the head-dress of a Commander of Ten Thousand and carried the golden whip of rank. There had been no improvement in his facial muscles. One side of his face still sagged hideously and saliva dribbled from the corner of his mouth. At that moment he recognized me, and grinned at me with half his face across the narrow strip of water. He lifted his golden whip in ironic greeting.

'I promise you, my lady, that my hand will be upon my dagger and I will eat nothing but fruit that I have peeled with my own hands while Rasfer and I are in Thebes together,' I murmured, as I smiled at him and returned his salute with a cheery wave.

'You are to accept no strange gifts,' my mistress insisted, 'and you will sleep at the foot of my bed, where I can protect you at night. During the day you will stay at my side, and not go wandering off on your own.'

'I will not find that irksome,' I assured her, and over the following days I kept my promise to her and remained under her immediate protection, for I was certain that Lord Intef would not jeopardize his connection to the throne by putting his daughter in danger.

Naturally, we were often in the company of the grand vizier, for it was his duty to escort the king through all the ceremonies of the festival. During this time, Lord Intef played the role of loving and considerate father to the Lady Lostris, and he treated her with all the deference and consideration due to a royal wife. Each morning he sent her gifts, gold and jewels and exquisite little carvings of scarabs and godlets in ivory and precious woods. Despite my mistress's orders, I did not return these. I did not wish to warn the enemy, and besides, the gifts were valuable. I sold them discreetly and invested the proceeds in stores of corn held for us in the granaries of trustworthy merchants in the city, men who were my friends.

In view of the expected harvest, the price of corn was the lowest it had been for ten years. There was only one direction it could go, and that was up, although we might have to wait a while for our profits. The merchants gave me receipts in the name of my mistress which I deposited in the archives of the law courts. I kept only a fifth part to myself, which I felt was a very moderate commission.

This gave me some secret pleasure whenever I caught Lord Intef watching me with those pale leopard's eyes. That look left me in no doubt that his feelings towards me had not moderated. I remembered his patience and his persistence when dealing with an enemy. He waited at the centre of his web like a beautiful spider, and his eyes glittered as he watched me. I remembered the bowl of poisoned milk and the cobra, and despite all my precautions, I was uneasy.

Meanwhile the festival rolled on with all the ceremony and tradition, as it had for centuries past. However, this season it was not Tanus' Blues but another squadron that hunted the river-cows in the lagoon of Hapi, while another company of actors played out the passion in the temple of Osiris. Because Pharaoh's decree was observed and the version of the play was mine, the words were as powerful and moving. However, this new Isis was not as lovely as my mistress had portrayed her, nor was Horus as noble or striking as Lord Tanus. On the other hand, Seth was winsome and lovable in comparison to the way that Rasfer had played him.

The day after the passion, Pharaoh crossed the river to inspect his temple, and on this occasion he kept me close at hand throughout the day. On numerous occasions he openly consulted me on aspects of the works. Of course I wore my golden chain whenever it was proper to do so. None of this was missed by Lord Intef, and I could see him musing on the favour the king showed to me. I hoped that this might further serve to protect me from the grand vizier's vengeance.

Since I had left Thebes, another architect had been placed in charge of the temple project. It was perhaps unfair that Pharaoh should expect this unfortunate to be able to maintain the high standards that I had set, or to push the work forward at the same pace.

'By the blessed mother of Horus, I wish you were still in charge here, Taita,' Pharaoh muttered. 'If she would part with you, I would buy you from your mistress, and keep you here in the City of the Dead permanently to supervise the work. The cost seems to have doubled since this other idiot took over from you.'

'He is a naïve young man,' I agreed. 'The masons and the contractors will steal his testicles from him and he will not notice that they are missing.'

'It is my balls that they are stealing,' the king scowled. 'I want you to go over the bill of quantities with him and show him where we are being robbed.'

I was of course flattered by his regard, and there was nothing spiteful in my pointing out to Pharaoh the lapses of taste that the new architect had perpetrated when he redesigned the pediment to my temple façade, or the shoddy craftsmanship that those rogues in the guild of masons had been able to slip past him. The pediment was permeated with the decadent Syrian style that was all the rage in the Lower Kingdom, where the common tastes of the low-born red pretender were corrupting the classical traditions of Egyptian art.

As for the workmanship, I demonstrated to the king how it was possible to slip a fragment of papyrus between the joints of the stone blocks that made up the side-wall of the mortuary temple. Pharaoh ordered both the pediment and the temple wall to be torn down, and he fined the guild of masons five hundred deben of gold to be paid into the royal store-rooms.

Pharaoh spent the rest of that day and the whole of the next reviewing the treasures in the store-rooms of the funerary temple. Here at least he could find very little to complain of. In the history of the world never had such wealth been assembled in one place at one time. Even I, who love fine things, was soon jaded by the abundance of it, and my eyes were pained by the dazzle of gold.

The king insisted that the Lady Lostris remain at his side all this time. I think that his infatuation with her was slowly turning into real love, or as close a facsimile of it as he was capable of. The consequence of his affection for her was that when we returned across the river to Thebes, my mistress was exhausted, and I feared for the child she was carrying. It was too soon to tell the king of her condition and to suggest that he showed her more consideration. It was less than a week since she had returned to his couch, and such an early diagnosis of pregnancy even from me must arouse his suspicion. To him she was still a healthy and robust young woman, and he treated her that way.

 THE FESTIVAL ended, as it had for centuries past, with the assembly of the people in the temple of Osiris to hear the proclamation from the throne.

On the raised stone dais in front of the sanctuary of Osiris, Pharaoh was seated on his tall throne so that all the congregation could have a clear view of him. He wore the double crown and carried the crook and the flail.

This time there was an alteration to the usual layout of the temple, for I had made a suggestion to the king which he had been gracious enough to adopt. Against three walls of the inner temple he had ordered the erection of timber scaffolding. This rose in tiers halfway up the massive stone walls, and provided seating for thousands of the notables of Thebes from which they had a privileged and uninterrupted view of the proceedings. I had suggested that these stands be decorated with coloured bunting and palm-fronds, to disguise their ugliness. It was the first time that these structures were built in our land. Thereafter, they were to become commonplace, and they were built at most public functions, along the routes of royal processions and around the fields of athletic games. To this day they are known as Taita stands.

There had been much bitter competition for seats upon these stands, but as their designer, I had been able to procure the very best for my mistress and myself. We were directly opposite the throne and a little above the height of the king's head, so we had a fine view of the whole of the inner courtyard. I had provided a leather cushion stuffed with lamb's-wool for the Lady Lostris and a basket of fruits and cakes, together with jars of sherbet and beer, to sustain us during the interminable ceremony.

All around us were assembled the noblest in the land, lords and ladies decked out in high fashion. The generals and admirals carrying their golden whips and proudly flaunting the honours and standards of their regiments, the guild masters and the rich merchants, the priests and the ambassadors from the vassal states of the empire, they were all here.

In front of the king extended the courts of the temple, one opening into another like the boxes in a children's puzzle-game, but such was the layout of the massive stone walls that the gates were all perfectly aligned. A worshipper standing in the Avenue of Sacred Rams outside the pylons of the main gate could look through the inner gates and clearly see the king on his high throne almost four hundred paces away.

All the courts of the temple were packed with the multitudes of the common people, and the overflow spilled out into the sacred avenue and the gardens beyond the temple walls. Though I had lived almost my entire life in Thebes, I had never seen such a gathering. It was not possible to count their numbers, but I estimated that there must have been two hundred thousand assembled that day. From them rose such a hubbub of sound that I felt myself but a single bee in the vast humming hive.

Around the throne was gathered a small group of the highest dignitaries, their heads at the level of Pharaoh's feet. Of course one of these was the high priest of Osiris. During the past year

317

the old abbot had left this transitory world of ours and set off on his journey through the underworld to the western fields of the eternal paradise. This new abbot was a younger, firmer man. I knew that he would not be so easily manipulated by Lord Intef. In fact, he had collaborated with me in certain unusual arrangements for today's ceremony that I had put in hand while supervising the erection of the Taita stands.

However, the most impressive figure in the group, rivalling Pharaoh himself, was the grand vizier. Lord Intef drew all eyes. He was tall and stately in bearing, handsome as a legend. With the heavy chains of the Gold of Praise lying weightily upon his chest and shoulders, he was like a figure from the myth of the pantheon. Close behind him loomed the hideous shape of Rasfer.

Lord Intef opened the ceremony in the traditional manner by stepping into the clear space before the throne and beginning the address of welcome to the king from the twin cities of Thebes. As he spoke, I glanced sideways at my mistress, and even though I shared her loathing, I was shocked by the expression of anger and hatred that she made no attempt to conceal, and that she directed openly at her own father. I wanted to warn her to make it less obvious to all about her, but I knew that in doing so, I might merely draw further attention to her burning antagonism.

The grand vizier spoke at length, listing his own accomplishments and the loyal service he had rendered Pharaoh in the year past. The crowd murmured and rustled with boredom and discomfort. The heat was rising from so many bodies, and the rays of the sun beating down into the crowded courts were trapped within the temple walls. I saw more than one woman in the press swoon and collapse.

When at last Lord Intef finished speaking, the high priest stepped into his place. While the sun made its noon overhead, he reported to the king on the ecclesiastical affairs of Thebes. As he spoke, the heat and the stench increased; perfume and fragrant oils could no longer disguise the odour of hot, unwashed bodies and running sweat. There was no escape from the crowd to attend urgent bodily functions. Men and women simply squatted where they stood. The temple began to stink like a sty or a public latrine. I handed my mistress a silk kerchief drenched in perfume which she dabbed to her nose.

There was a sigh of relief when at last the high priest ended his address with a blessing on the king in the name of the god Osiris, and, with a deep bow, retreated to his place behind the grand vizier. For the first time since it had begun to assemble before dawn that morning, the crowd fell completely silent. The boredom and discomfort was forgotten, and they craned forward eagerly to hear Pharaoh speak.

The king rose to his feet. I wondered at the old man's fortitude, for he had sat all this time like a statue. He spread his arms in benediction, and at that moment the hallowed chalice of custom and tradition was shattered by an event that plunged the entire congregation – priests, nobles and commoners – into consternation. I was one of the few in the crowd who was not surprised by what followed, for I had done more than my share to arrange it all.

The great burnished copper doors to the sanctuary swung open. There seemed to be no human agency to the movement, it was as though the doors opened of their own accord.

A gasp, a sigh of expelled breath passed like a wind through temple courts, and rustled the densely packed ranks as though they were the leaves of a tamarind tree. Then suddenly a woman screamed, and immediately a groan of superstitious horror shook them all. Some fell to their knees, some lifted their hands above their heads in terror, others covered their faces with their shawls so that they should not be struck blind by looking on sights that were not for mortal eyes.

A god strode out through the sanctuary doors, a tall and terrifying god, whose cloak swirled about his shoulders as he moved. His helmet was crowned with a plume of egret's feathers, and his features were grotesque and metallic, half-eagle and half-man, with a hooked beak and dark slits for eyes.

'Akh-Horus!' screamed a woman, and she collapsed in a dead faint upon the stone flags.

'Akh-Horus!' the cry was taken up. 'It is the god!' Row after row, they fell upon their knees in the attitude of reverence.

Those on the high tiers of stands knelt and many of them made the sign to avert misfortune. Even the group of nobles around the throne went down. In all the temple only two persons remained on their feet. Pharaoh posed on the steps of his throne like a painted statue; and the grand vizier of Thebes stood tall and arrogant.

Akh-Horus stopped in front of the king and looked up at him through those slitted eyes in the bronze mask, and even then Pharaoh never flinched. The king's cheeks were painted dead white, so I could not tell whether he blanched, but there was a glitter in his eyes that may have been either religious ecstasy, or terror.

'Who are you?' Pharaoh challenged. 'Are you ghost or man? Why do you disturb our solemn proceedings?' His voice was strong and clear. I could detect no tremor in it, and my admiration for him was enhanced. Weak and aging and gullible perhaps, but still the old man had his full share of courage. He could face up to man or god and stand his ground like a warrior.

Akh-Horus answered him in a voice that had commanded regiments in the desperate din of battle, a voice that echoed amongst the stone pillars. 'Great Pharaoh, I am a man, not a ghost. I am your man. I come before you in response to your command. I come before you to account to you for the duty that you laid upon me in this place on this very day of Osiris two years ago.'

He lifted the helmet from his head, and the fiery curls tumbled down. The congregation recognized him instantly. A shout went up that seemed to rock the foundations of the temple.

'Lord Tanus! Tanus! Tanus!'

It seemed to me that my mistress screamed the loudest of them all, fairly deafening me, who sat so close beside her.

'Tanus! Akh-Horus! Akh-Horus!' The two names mingled and crashed against the temple walls like storm-driven surf.

'He has risen from his tomb! He has become a god amongst us!'

It did not abate until suddenly Tanus drew the sword from his scabbard and held it aloft in an unmistakable command for silence. This was obeyed, and in the silence he spoke again.

'Great Egypt, do I have your permission to speak?'

I think by now the king could no longer rely on his powers of speech, for he made a gesture with crook and flail, and then his legs seemed to give way beneath him and he dropped back on his throne.

Tanus addressed him in ringing tones that carried to the outer court. 'Two years ago you charged me with the destruction of those viperous nests of murderers and robbers who were threatening the life of the state. You placed in my trust the royal hawk seal.'

From under his cloak, Tanus drew out the blue statuette and placed it on the steps of the throne. Then he stepped back and spoke again.

'In order better to carry out the king's orders, I pretended my own death and caused the mummy of a stranger to be sealed in my tomb.'

'*Bak-Her!*' shouted a single voice, and they took up the cry until Tanus once more commanded silence.

'I led a thousand brave men of the Blues into the deserts and the wild places and sought out the Shrikes in their secret fortresses. There we slew them in their hundreds and piled their severed heads at the roadside.'

'*Bak-Her!*' they screamed. 'It is true. Akh-Horus has done all these things.' Once again Tanus silenced them.

'I broke the power of the barons. I slaughtered their followers without mercy. In all this very Egypt of ours there remains only one who still calls himself a Shrike.'

Now at last they were silent, gobbling up every word he said, fascinated and intent. Even Pharaoh could not hold his impatience in check. 'Speak, Lord Tanus, whom men now know as Akh-Horus. Name this man. Give me his name so that he may come to know the wrath of Pharaoh.'

'He hides behind the name of Akh-Seth,' Tanus roared, 'His deeds of infamy rank with those of his brother, the dark god.'

'Give me his true name,' Pharaoh commanded, rising once more to his feet in his agitation. 'Name this last of all the Shrikes!'

Tanus drew out the moment. He looked around the temple

321

slowly and deliberately. When our eyes met, I nodded so slightly that only he saw the movement, but his gaze passed on without a pause and he looked towards the open doors of the sanctuary.

The attention of all the congregation was so fixed upon Lord Tanus that they did not at first see the file of armed men that issued swiftly and silently from the sanctuary. Although they wore full armour and carried their war shields, I recognized most of them under the helmets. There were Remrem and Astes and fifty other warriors of the Blues. Swiftly, they formed up around the throne like a royal bodyguard, but, without making it obvious, Remrem and Astes moved up behind Lord Intef. As soon as they were in position, Tanus spoke again.

'I will name this Akh-Seth for you, Divine Pharaoh. He stands unashamedly in the shadow of your throne.' Tanus pointed with his sword. 'There he is, wearing the Gold of Praise about his traitor's throat. There he stands, Pharaoh's sole companion who has turned your kingdom into a playground for murderers and bandits. That is Akh-Seth, governor of the nome of Thebes, grand vizier of the Upper Kingdom.'

An awful hush fell upon the temple. There must have been ten thousand or more in the congregation who had suffered grievously at Lord Intef's hands and who had every reason to hate him, but not a voice spoke out in jubilation or in triumph against him. All knew just how terrible was his wrath, and just how certain his retribution. I could smell the stink of their fear in the air, thick as the incense smoke. Every one of them understood that even Tanus' reputation and his mighty deeds were not sufficient for his unproven accusation to prevail against such a person as Lord Intef. To show joy or open agreement at this stage would be mortal folly.

In that hush Lord Intef laughed. It was a sound full of disdain, and with a dismissive gesture he turned his back upon Tanus and spoke directly to the king. 'The desert sun has burned his brain. The poor lad has gone mad. There is not a single word of truth in all his ravings. I should be angry, but instead I am saddened that a warrior of reputation has fallen so low.' He held out both hands to Pharaoh, a dignified and loyal gesture. 'All my life I have served Pharaoh and my people. My honour is so invulnerable that I see no need to defend myself against these wild rantings. Without fear I place my trust in the wisdom and justice of the divine king. I let my deeds and my love of Pharaoh speak, in place of my tongue.'

I saw the confusion and indecision on the king's painted face. His lips trembled and his brow was furrowed, for he was not blessed with a swift and incisive mind. After a moment he opened his mouth to speak, but before he could utter any fateful or irredeemable judgement, Tanus lifted his sword again and pointed beyond the throne to the open doors of the sanctuary.

Through the doors came another procession of men so unusual that Pharaoh gaped at them with his mouth still open. Kratas led, with his visor raised and a sword in his right hand. Those who followed him wore only loin-cloths, and their heads and feet were bare. Their arms were bound behind their backs, and they shuffled like slaves on their way to the auction block.

I was watching Lord Intef's face, and I saw the shock assail him and force him to flinch, as though he had received a blow in the face. He had recognized the captives, but he had obviously believed that they were long dead, and their skulls grinning at the roadside. He darted a sideways glance at the small sacristy door in the wall that was almost hidden by the hanging linen bunting. It was his only escape from the crowded inner court, but Remrem moved one pace to his right and blocked his path to the doorway. Lord Intef looked back at the throne and lifted his chin in a confident and defiant gesture.

The six bound captives lined up before the throne and then, at a quiet order from Kratas, dropped to their knees and bowed their heads.

'Who are these creatures?' Pharaoh demanded, and Tanus stood over the first of them, seized his bound wrists and hauled him to his feet. The captive's skin was studded with the old healed scars of the smallpox and his blind eye reflected the light like a silver coin.

'The divine Pharaoh asks who you are,' Tanus said softly. 'Reply to the question.'

323

'Great Egypt, I am Shufti,' he said. 'I was once a baron of the Shrikes before Akh-Horus scattered and slew my clan at the city of Gallala.'

'Tell the king who was your overlord,' Tanus insisted.

'Akh-Seth was my overlord,' Shufti replied. 'I swore a blood-oath of allegiance to Akh-Seth, and I paid a bounty of one-quarter of all my plunder to him. In return Akh-Seth gave me immunity from the forces of law, and provided me with information on my intended victims.'

'Point out to the king the man you know as Akh-Seth,' Tanus ordered, and Shufti shuffled forward until he faced Lord Intef. He filled his mouth with spittle and spat it on to the grand vizier's gorgeous uniform. 'This is Akh-Seth,' he cried. 'And may the worms feast on his guts!'

Kratas dragged Shufti to one side and Tanus lifted the next captive to his feet. 'Tell the king who you are,' he ordered.

'I am Akheku, and I was a baron of the Shrikes, but all my men are killed.'

'Who was your overlord? To whom did you pay your bounty?' Tanus demanded.

'Lord Intef was my overlord. I paid my bounty into the coffers of the grand vizier.'

Lord Intef stood proud and aloof, showing no emotion as these accusations were hurled at him. He offered no defence as, one after the other, the barons were dragged before him and each made the same declaration.

'Lord Intef was my overlord. Lord Intef is Akh-Seth.'

The silence of the multitudes in the temple was as oppressive as the heat. They watched in horror, or in silent hatred, or in confusion and disbelief. However, not one of them dared yet to speak out against Lord Intef, or to show emotion until Pharaoh had first spoken.

The last of the barons was brought forward to confront the grand vizier. He was a tall, lean man with stringy muscles and sun-blasted skin. There was Bedouin blood in his veins, for his eyes were black and his nose beaked. His beard was thick and curling, and his expression arrogant.

'My name is Basti.' He spoke more clearly than any of the

others. 'Men call me Basti the Cruel, though I know not the reason why.' He grinned with a raffish hangman's humour. 'I was a baron of the Shrikes until Akh-Horus destroyed my clan. Lord Intef was my overlord.'

This time he was not dragged away as the others had been. Tanus spoke to him again. 'Tell the king. Did you know Pianki, Lord Harrab, who in former times was a nobleman of Thebes?'

'I knew him well. I had dealings with him.'

'What were these dealings?' Tanus asked, with death in his voice.

'I plundered his caravans. I burned his crops in the fields. I raided his mines at Sestra, and I slew the miners in such amusing fashion that no others ever came to work the copper there. I burned his villas. I sent my men into the cities to speak evil of him, so that his honesty and his loyalty to the state were tarnished. I helped others to destroy him so that in the end he drank the poisonous Datura seed from his own cup.'

I saw the hand of Pharaoh that held the royal flail shake as he listened, and one of his eyelids twitched in a manner that I had noticed before when he was sore distressed.

'Who was it that ordered these things?'

'Lord Intef commanded these things and rewarded me with a takh of pure gold.'

'What did Lord Intef hope to gain from this persecution of Lord Harrab?'

Basti grinned and shrugged. 'Lord Intef is grand vizier, while Pianki, Lord Harrab is dead. It seems to me Lord Intef achieved his purpose.'

'You acknowledge that I have offered you no clemency in return for this confession? Do you understand that death awaits you?'

'Death?' Basti laughed. 'I have never been afraid of that. It is the flour of the loaf I bake. I have fed it to countless others, so now why should I be afraid to feast on it myself?' Was he fool or brave man, I wondered, as I listened to the boast. Either way, I could find neither pity nor admiration for him in my heart. I remembered that Pianki, Lord Harrab had been a man like his son, and that is where my pity and my admiration lay.

I saw the merciless expression in the eyes of Tanus. I knew that he shared my feelings, and his grip upon the hilt of his sword tightened until his fingers turned as white as those of a drowned man.

'Take him away!' he grated. 'Let him await the king's pleasure.' I saw him compose himself with an effort, then he turned back to face the king. He went down on one knee before him.

'I have done all that you asked of me, Divine Mamose, god and ruler of *Kemit*. I wait for you to command me further.' His dignity and his grace closed up my throat so that I could not swallow. It took an effort to compose myself.

The silence in the temple persisted. I could hear my mistress's laboured breathing beside me and then I felt her take my hand and squeeze it with a strength that threatened to crack my finger-bones.

At last Pharaoh spoke, but with dismay I heard the doubt in his voice, and I sensed intuitively that he did not want any of this to be true. He had trusted Lord Intef so deeply for so long that it shook the foundations of his faith.

'Lord Intef, you have heard the accusations against you. How say you to them?'

'Divine Pharaoh, are these indeed accusations? I thought them merely the fantasies of a young man driven insane with envy and jealousy. He is the son of a convicted criminal and a traitor. Lord Tanus' motives are plain to see. He has convinced himself that the traitor Pianki might have become grand vizier in my place. In some perverse fashion, he holds me responsible for his father's downfall.'

With a wave of his hand he dismissed Tanus. It was so skilfully done that I saw the king waver. His doubts were growing stronger. For a lifetime he had implicitly trusted Lord Intef, and it was difficult for him to adjust his thinking. He wanted to believe in his innocence.

'What of the accusations of the barons?' Pharaoh asked at last. 'What reply do you make to them?'

'Barons?' Lord Intef asked. 'Must we flatter them with such a title? By their own testimony they are criminals of the basest kind – murderers, thieves, violators of women and children. Should we look for truth in them any more than we should look for honour and conscience in the beasts of the field?' Lord Intef pointed to them, and they were indeed half-naked and bound like animals. 'Let us gaze upon them, Divine Majesty. Are these not the kind of men that can be bribed or beaten into saying anything for the sake of their own skins? Would you take the word of one of these against a man who has served you faithfully all his life?'

I saw the small, involuntary nod of the king's head as he accepted the reasoning of the man he had looked upon as a friend, the man upon whom he had heaped trust and rewards.

'All you say is true. You have always served me without vice. These rogues are strangers to truth and honour. It is possible that they may have been coerced.' He vacillated, and Lord Intef sensed his advantage.

'So far I have had only words thrown at me. Surely there must be some other evidence to support such mortal charges against me? Is there one person in this very Egypt who will bring evidence against me, real evidence and not mere words? If there is, let him come forward. Then I will answer this charge. If there is no one who has this evidence, then I have nothing to answer to.'

His words troubled Pharaoh deeply, I could see that. He gazed about the hall as if seeking the evidence that Lord Intef demanded, and then he obviously reached a decision.

'Lord Tanus, what proof do you have of these things, apart from the words of murderers and criminals?'

'The beast has covered his tracks well,' Tanus admitted, 'and he has taken cover in the densest thicket where it is difficult to come at him. I have no further evidence against Lord Intef, but there may be some other who does, somebody who will be inspired by what he has heard here today. I beg you, Royal Egypt, ask your people if there is not one of them who can bring forth anything to help us here.'

'Pharaoh, this is provocation. My enemies will be emboldened to come out of the shadows where they lurk to attack me,' cried

Lord Intef in vehement protest, but Pharaoh silenced him with a brusque gesture. 'They will bear false witness against you at their peril,' he promised, and then addressed the congregation.

'My people! Citizens of Thebes! You have heard the accusations made against my trusted and well-beloved grand vizier. Is there one of you who can provide the proof that Lord Tanus lacks? Can any of you bring forward evidence against the Lord Intef? If so, I charge you to speak.'

I was standing before I realized what I had done, and my voice was so loud in my own ears that it startled me.

'I am Taita, who was once the slave of Lord Intef,' I shouted, and Pharaoh looked across at me and frowned. 'I have aught that I wish to show Your Majesty.'

'You are known to us, Taita the physician. You may approach.'

As I left my seat on the stand and went down to stand before the king, I looked across at Lord Intef and I missed my step. It was as though I had walked into a stone wall, so tangible was his hatred.

'Divine Egypt, this thing is a slave.' Lord Intef's voice was cold and tight. 'The word of a slave against a lord of the Theban circle, and a high officer of the state – what mockery is this?'

I was still so conditioned to respond to his voice and to succumb to his word, that my resolve wavered. Then I felt Tanus' hand on my arm. It was only a brief touch, but it manned and sustained me. However, Lord Intef had noticed the gesture, and he pointed it out to the king.

'See how this slave is in the thrall of my accuser. Here is another one of Lord Tanus' trained monkeys.' Lord Intef's voice was once more smooth as warm honey. 'His insolence is unbounded. There are penalties laid down in the law codes—'

Pharaoh silenced him with a gesture of his flail. 'You presume on our good opinion of you, Lord Intef. The codes of law are mine to interpret or amend. In them there are penalties laid down for the high-born as well as the common man. You would be well advised to remember that.'

Lord Intef bowed in submission and remained silent, but suddenly his face was haggard and drawn as he realized his predicament.

Now the king looked down at me. 'These are unusual circumstances, such as allow of unprecedented remedy. However, Taita the slave, let me warn you that if your words should prove frivolous, should they lack proof or substance, the strangling-rope awaits you.'

That threat and the poisonous bane of Lord Intef's gaze upon me made me stutter. 'While I was the slave of the grand vizier, I was his messenger and his emissary to the barons. I know all these men.' I pointed to the captives that Kratas held near to the throne. 'It was I who carried Lord Intef's commands to them.'

'Lies! More words, lacking proof,' Lord Intef called out, but now the edge of desperation was in his voice. 'Where is the proof?'

'Silence!' the king thundered with sudden ferocity. 'We will hear the testimony of Taita the slave.' He was looking directly at me, and I drew breath to continue.

'It was I who carried the command of Lord Intef to Basti the Cruel. The command was to destroy the estate and the fortune of Pianki, Lord Harrab. At that time I was the confidant of Intef, I knew that he desired the position of grand vizier to himself. All these things that Lord Intef commanded were accomplished. Lord Harrab was destroyed, and he was deprived of Pharaoh's favour and love, so that he drank the Datura cup. I, Taita, attest all these things.'

'It is so.' Basti the Cruel lifted his bound arms to the throne. 'All that Taita says is the truth.'

'Bak-Her!' shouted the barons. 'It is the truth. Taita speaks the truth.'

'Still these are only words,' the king mused. 'Lord Intef has demanded proof. I, your Pharaoh, demand proof.'

'For half my lifetime I was the scribe and the treasurer of the grand vizier. I kept the record of his fortune. I noted his profits and his expenses on my scrolls. I gathered in the bounty that the barons of the Shrikes paid to Lord Intef, and I disposed of all this wealth.'

'Can you show me these scrolls, Taita?' Pharaoh's expression shone like the full moon at the mention of treasure. Now I had his avid attention.

'No, Majesty, I cannot do so. The scrolls remained always in the possession of Lord Intef.'

Pharaoh made no effort to conceal his chagrin, his face hardened towards me, but I went on doggedly, 'I cannot show you the scrolls, but perhaps I can lead you to the treasure that the grand vizier has stolen from you, and from the people of your realm. It was I who built his secret treasuries for him, and hid within them the bounty that I gathered from the barons. It was in these store-rooms that I placed the wealth that Pharaoh's tax-collectors never saw.'

The king's excitement rekindled, hot as the coals on the coppersmith's forge. He leaned forward intently. Although every eye in the temple was fastened upon me, and the nobles were crowding forward the better to hear each word, I was watching Lord Intef without seeming to look in his direction. The burnished copper doors of the sanctuary were tall mirrors in which his reflection was magnified. Every nuance of his expression and every movement he made, however slight, was clear to me.

I had taken a fatal risk in assuming that his treasure still remained in the secret places where I had stored it for him. He might have moved it at any time during the past two years. Yet moving such quantities of treasure would have been a major work and the risk of doing so as great as letting it rest where it lay. He would have been forced to take others into his trust, and that was not easy for Lord Intef to do. He was by nature a suspicious man. Added to which was the fact that, until recently, he had believed me dead, and my secret with me.

I calculated that my chances were evenly balanced, and I risked my life on it. Now I held my breath as I watched Lord Intef's reflection in the copper doors. Then my heart raced and my spirits soared on the wings of eagles. I saw from the pain and panic in his expression that the arrow I had fired at him had struck the mark. I had won. The treasure was where I had left it. I knew that I could lead Pharaoh to the plunder and the loot that Lord Intef had gathered up over his lifetime.

But he was not yet defeated. I was rash to believe it would be so easily accomplished. I saw him make a gesture with his right hand that puzzled me, and while I dallied, it was almost too late.

In my triumph, I had forgotten Rasfer. The signal that Lord Intef gave him was a flick of the right hand, but Rasfer responded like a trained boar-hound to the huntsman's command to attack. He launched himself at me with such sudden ferocity that he took all of us by complete surprise. He had only ten paces to cover to reach me, and his sword rasped from its scabbard as he came.

There were two of Kratas' men standing between us, but their backs were turned to him, and Rasfer barged into them and knocked them off their feet, so that one of them sprawled across the stone flags in front of Tanus and blocked his path when he tried to spring to my aid. I was on my own, defenceless, and Rasfer threw up his sword with both hands to cleave through my skull to my breast-bone. I lifted my hands to ward off the blow, but my legs were frozen with shock and terror, and I could not move or duck away from the hissing blade.

I never saw Tanus throw his sword. I had eyes for nothing but the face of Rasfer, but suddenly the sword was in the air. Terror had so enhanced my senses that time seemed to pass as slowly as spilled oil dribbling from the jar. I watched Tanus' sword turning end over end, spinning slowly on its axis, flashing at each revolution like a sheet of summer lightning, but it had not completed a full turn when it struck, and it was the hilt and not the point that crashed into Rasfer's head. It did not kill him, but it snapped his head over, whipping his neck like the branch of a willow in the wind, so that his eyes rolled back blindly in their sockets.

Rasfer never completed the blow he aimed at me. His legs collapsed under him and he fell in a pile at my feet. His sword flew from his nerveless fingers, spinning high in the air, and then fell back. It pegged into the side of Pharaoh's throne, and quivered there. The king stared at it in shocked disbelief. The razor edge had touched his arm, and split the skin. As we all watched, a line of ruby droplets oozed from the shallow wound, and dripped on to Pharaoh's cloud-white linen kilt.

Tanus broke the horrified silence. 'Great Egypt, you saw who gave the signal for this beast to attack. You know who was to blame for endangering your royal person.' He leaped over the downed guardsman and seized Lord Intef by the arm, twisting it until he fell to his knees and cried out with pain.

'I did not want to believe this of you.' Pharaoh's expression was sorrowful as he looked down on his grand vizier. 'I have trusted you all my life, and you have spat upon me.'

'Great Egypt, hear me!' Lord Intef begged on his knees, but Pharaoh turned his face away from him.

'I have listened to you long enough.' Then he nodded to Tanus. 'Have your men guard him well, but show him courtesy, for his guilt is not yet fully proven.'

Finally Pharaoh addressed the congregation. 'These are strange and unprecedented events. I adjourn these proceedings to consider fully the evidence that Taita the slave will present to me. The population of Thebes will assemble once again to hear my judgement in this same place at noon tomorrow. I have spoken.'

WE ENTERED through the main doorway to the audience hall of the grand vizier's palace. Pharaoh paused at the threshold. Although the wound from Rasfer's sword was slight, I had bandaged it with linen and placed his arm in a sling.

Pharaoh surveyed the hall slowly. At the far end of the long room stood the grand vizier's throne. Carved from a solid block of alabaster, it was hardly less imposing than Pharaoh's own in the throne room at Elephantine. The high walls were plastered with smooth clay and on this background were painted some of the most impressive frescoes that I had ever designed. They transformed the huge room into a blazing garden of delights. I had painted them while I was Lord Intef's slave, and even though they were my own creations, they still gave me a deep thrill of pleasure when I looked upon them.

I have no doubt that these works alone, without consideration of any other of my achievements, would support my claim to the title of the most significant artist in the history of our land. It was sad that I who had created them was now to demolish them. It detracted from the triumph of this tumultuous day.

I led Pharaoh down the hall. For once we had dispensed with all protocol, and Pharaoh was as eager as a child. He followed me so closely that he almost trod upon my heels, and his royal train fell in as eagerly behind him.

I led them to the throne wall and we stopped below the huge mural depicting the sun god, Ammon-Ra, on his daily journey across the heavens. Even in his excitement, I could see the reverent expression in the king's eyes as he looked up at the painting.

Behind us, the great hall was half-filled with the king's train, the courtiers and the warriors and the noble lords, to say nothing of the royal wives and concubines who would rather have given up all their rouges and paint-boxes of cosmetics than miss such an exciting moment as I had promised them. Naturally, my mistress was in the forefront. Tanus marched only a pace behind the king. He and his Blues had taken over the duties of the royal bodyguard.

The king turned back to Tanus now. 'Have your men bring forward the Lord Intef!'

Treating him with elaborate and icy courtesy, Kratas led Intef to face the wall, but he interposed himself between the prisoner and the king and stood with his naked blade at the ready.

'Taita, you may proceed,' the king told me, and I measured the wall, stepping out exactly thirty paces from the furthest corner and marking the distance with the lump of chalk that I had brought with me for the purpose.

'Behind this wall lie the private quarters of the grand vizier,' I explained to the king. 'Certain alterations were made when last the palace was renovated. Lord Intef likes to have his wealth close at hand.'

'Sometimes you are garrulous, Taita.' Pharaoh was less than captivated by my lecture on the palace architecture. 'Get on with it, fellow. I am aflame to see what is hidden here.'

'Let the masons approach!' I called out, and a small band of these sturdy rogues in their leather aprons came down the aisle and dropped their leather tool-bags at the foot of the throne wall.

I had summoned them across the river from their work on Pharaoh's tomb. The white stone-dust in their hair gave them an air of age and wisdom that few of them deserved.

I borrowed a wooden set-square from their foreman, and with it marked out an oblong shape on the clay-plastered wall. Then I stepped back and addressed the master mason. 'Gently now! Damage the frescoes as little as you can. They are great works of art.'

With their wooden mallets and their chisels of flint, they fell upon the wall, and they paid little heed to my strictures. Paint and plaster flew in clouds as slabs of the outer wall were stripped away and thumped to the marble floor. The dust offended the ladies and they covered their mouths and noses with their shawls.

Gradually from under the layer of plaster emerged the outline of the stone blocks. Then Pharaoh exclaimed aloud and, ignoring the flying dust, he drew closer, and peered at the design that appeared from beneath the plaster skin. The regular courses of stone blocks were marred by an oblong of alien-coloured stone that followed almost exactly the outline I had chalked upon the outer layer of plaster.

'There is a hidden door in there,' he cried. 'Open it immediately!'

Under the king's urging, the masons attacked the sealed doorway with a will, and once they had removed the keystone, the other blocks came out readily. A dark opening was revealed, and Pharaoh, who had by now taken charge of the work, called excitedly for torches to be lit.

'The entire space behind this wall is a secret compartment,' I told Pharaoh, while we waited for the torches to be brought to us. 'I had it constructed on Lord Intef's orders.'

When the torches were brought, Tanus took one of them and lit the king's way into the gaping secret door. The king stepped through, and I was the next to enter after him and Tanus.

It was so long since I had last been in there that I looked around me with as much interest as the others. Nothing had changed in all that time. The chests and casks of cedar and acacia wood were stacked exactly as I had left them. I pointed out to the king those cases to which he should first devote his attention, and he ordered, 'Have them carried out into the audience hall.'

'You will need strong men to carry them,' I remarked drily. 'They are rather heavy.'

It took three of the biggest men of the Blues to lift each case and they staggered out through the jagged opening in the wall with them.

'I have never seen these boxes before,' Lord Intef protested, as the first of them was carried out and laid on the dais of the grand vizier's throne. 'I had no knowledge of a secret chamber behind the wall. It must have been built by my predecessor, and the cases placed there at his command.'

'Your Majesty, observe the seal on this lid.' I pointed it out to him and the king peered at the clay tablet.

'Whose seal is this?' he demanded.

'Observe the ring on the left forefinger of the grand vizier, Majesty,' I murmured. 'May I respectfully suggest that Pharaoh match it to the seal on this chest?'

'Lord Intef, hand me your ring if you please,' the king asked with exaggerated courtesy, and the grand vizier hid his left hand behind his back.

'Great Egypt, the ring has been on my finger for twenty years. My flesh has grown around it and it cannot now be removed.'

'Lord Tanus.' The king turned to him. 'Take your sword. Remove Lord Intef's finger and bring it to me with the ring upon it.' Tanus smiled cruelly as he stepped forward to obey, half-drawing his blade.

'Perhaps I am mistaken,' Lord Intef admitted with alacrity. 'Let me see if I cannot free it.' The ring slipped readily enough from his finger, and Tanus went down on one knee to hand it to the king.

Pharaoh bent studiously over the chest and made the comparison of ring to seal. When he straightened up again his face was dark with anger.

'It is a perfect match. This seal was struck from your ring, Lord Intef.' But the grand vizier made no reply to the accusation. He stood with his arms folded and his expression stony.

'Break the seal. Open the chest!' Pharaoh ordered, and Tanus cut away the clay tablet and prised up the lid with his sword.

The king cried out involuntarily as the lid fell away and the contents were revealed, 'By all the gods!' And his courtiers crowded forward without ceremony to gaze into the chest, exclaiming and jostling each other for a better view.

'Gold!' The king scooped both hands full with the glittering yellow rings, and then let them cascade back between his fingers. He kept a single ring in his hand and held it close to his face to study the mint marks upon it. 'Two deben weight of fine gold. How much will this case contain, and how many cases are there in the secret store-room?' His question was rhetorical, and he was not expecting an answer, but I gave him a reply nevertheless.

'This case contains—' I read the manifest that I had inscribed on the lid so many years before. 'It contains one takh and three hundred deben of pure gold. As to how many cases of gold, if my memory serves me well, there should be fifty-three of gold and twenty-three of silver in this store. However, I have forgotten exactly how many chests of jewellery we hid here.'

'Is there no one I can trust? You, Lord Intef, I treated as my brother. There was no kindness that you did not receive from my hands, and this is how you have repaid me.'

 AT MIDNIGHT the chancellor and the chief inspector of the royal taxes came to the king's chamber where I was changing the dressing on his injured arm. They presented their final tally of the amount of the treasure and Pharaoh read it with awe. Once again, his emotions warred with each other, outrage vying with euphoria at this staggering windfall.

'The rogue was richer than his own king. There is no punishment harsh enough for such evil. He has cheated and robbed me and my tax-collectors.'

'As well as murdering and plundering Lord Harrab and tens of thousands of your subjects,' I reminded him, as I secured the bandage on his arm. It was perhaps impudent of me. However, he was by now so deep in my debt that I could risk it.

'That too,' he agreed readily enough, my sarcasm wasted upon him. 'His guilt is deep as the sea and high as the heaven. I will have to devise a suitable punishment. The strangler's rope is too kind for Lord Intef.'

'Majesty, as your physician, I must insist that you rest now. It has been a day that has taxed even your great strength and endurance.'

'Where is Intef? I cannot rest until I am assured that he is well taken care of.'

'He is under guard in his own quarters, Majesty. A senior captain and a detachment of the Blues have that duty.' I hesitated delicately. 'Rasfer is also under guard.'

'Rasfer, that ugly drooling animal of his? The one who tried to kill you in the temple of Osiris? Did he survive the crack that Lord Tanus gave him?'

'He is well if not happy, Pharaoh,' I assured him. 'Did Your Majesty know that Rasfer is the one who, so long ago, used the gelding-knife upon me?' I saw the beam of pity in the king's eye, as I blurted it out.

'I will deal with him as I deal with his master,' Pharaoh promised. 'He will suffer the same punishment as Lord Intef. Will that satisfy you, Taita?'

'Your Majesty is just and omniscient.' I backed out of his presence and went to find my mistress.

She was waiting for me and, although it was after midnight and I was exhausted, she would not let me sleep. She was far too overwrought, and she insisted that for the rest of the night I sit beside her bed and listen to her chatter about Tanus and other topics of lesser importance.

DESPITE THE dearth of sleep, I was bright and clear-headed when I took my place in the temple of Osiris the following morning.

If anything, the congregation was even larger than it had been the day before. There was not a soul in Thebes who had not heard of the downfall of the grand vizier, and who was not eager to witness his ultimate humiliation. Even those of his underlings, who had most prospered under his corrupt administration, now turned upon him, like a pack of hyena who devour their leader when he is sick and wounded.

The barons of the Shrikes were led before the throne in their rags and bonds, but when Lord Intef entered the temple, he wore fine linen and silver sandals. His hair was freshly curled, his face painted, and the chains of the Gold of Praise hung around his neck.

The barons knelt before the king, but even when one of the guards pricked him with the sword, Lord Intef refused to bend the knee, and the king made a gesture for the guard to desist.

'Let him stand!' the king ordered. 'He will lie in his tomb long enough.' Then Pharaoh rose and stood before us in all his grandeur and his rage. This once he seemed a true king, as the first of his dynasty had been, a man of might and force. I, who had come to know him and his weaknesses so well, found that I was overcome with a sense of awe.

'Lord Intef, you are accused of treason and murder, of brigandage and piracy, and of a hundred other crimes no less deserving of punishment. I have heard the supported testimony of fifty of my subjects from all walks and stations of life, from lords and freemen and slaves. I have seen the contents of your secret treasury wherein you hid your stolen wealth from the royal tax-collectors. I have seen your personal seal upon the treasure chests. By all these matters your guilt is proven a thousand times over. I, Mamose the eighth of that name, Pharaoh and ruler of this very Egypt, hereby find you guilty of all the crimes of which you are accused, and deserving of neither royal clemency nor mercy.'

'Long live Pharaoh!' shouted Tanus, and the salute was taken up and repeated ten times by the people of Thebes. 'May he live for ever!'

When silence fell, Pharaoh spoke again. 'Lord Intef, you wear the Gold of Praise. The sight of that decoration on the breast of a traitor offends me.' He looked across at Tanus. 'Centurion, remove the gold from the prisoner.'

Tanus lifted the chains from Lord Intef's neck and carried them to the king. Pharaoh took the gold in his two hands, but when Tanus started to withdraw, he stayed him with a word.

'The name Lord Harrab was tarnished with the slur of treason. Your father was hounded to a traitor's death. You have proven your father's innocence. I rescind all sentences passed against Pianki, Lord Harrab, and posthumously restore to him all his honours and titles that were stripped from him. Those honours and titles descend to you, his son.'

'*Bak-Her!*' shouted the congregation. 'May Pharaoh live for ever! Hail, Tanus, Lord Harrab!'

'In addition to those titles which now come down to you as your inheritance, I bestow upon you new distinction. You have carried out my charge to you. You have destroyed the Shrikes and delivered their overlord to justice. In recognition of this service to the crown, I bestow upon you the Gold of Valour. Kneel, Lord Harrab, and receive the king's favour.'

'*Bak-Her!*' they cried, as Pharaoh placed the jangling gold chains, that had so recently belonged to Lord Intef, but to which he had now added the star pendant of the warrior's decoration, about Tanus' neck. 'Hail, Lord Harrab!'

As Tanus withdrew, Pharaoh turned his attention back to the prisoners. 'Lord Intef, you are deprived of your title as a lord of the Theban circle. Your name and rank will be erased from all the public monuments, and from your tomb that you have prepared in the Valley of the Nobles. Your estates and all your possessions, including your illicit treasure, are forfeited to the crown, except only those estates that once belonged to Pianki, Lord Harrab, and which by fell means have come into your possession. These are now returned in their entirety to his heir, my goodly Tanus, Lord Harrab.'

'*Bak-Her!* Pharaoh is wise! May he live for ever!' the people cheered wildly, and beside me my mistress was weeping unashamedly, but then so were half the royal women. Very few of them could resist that heroic figure whose golden hair seemed to dim the chains upon his breast.

Now the king took me by surprise. He looked directly at where I sat beside my mistress. 'There is one other who has done the crown loyal service, the one who revealed the whereabouts of the stolen treasure. Let the slave, Taita, stand forth.'

I went down to stand before the throne, and the king's voice was gentle. 'You have suffered unspeakable harm at the hands of the traitor Intef and his henchman Rasfer. You have been forced by them to commit nefarious deeds and capital crimes against the state, by conniving with bandits and robbers and by concealing your master's treasure from the royal tax-collectors. However, these were not crimes of your own inspiration. As a slave, you were forced to the will of your master. Therefore I absolve you from all guilt and liability. I find you innocent of any crime, and I reward you for your service to us with a bounty of two takhs of fine gold to be paid out of the treasure confiscated from the traitor, Intef.'

A murmur of astonishment greeted this announcement, and I gasped aloud. It was a staggering amount. A fortune to match those of all but the wealthiest lords in the land, enough to buy great tracts of the most fertile land along the river, and to furnish magnificent villas upon that land, to buy three hundred strong slaves to work the land, enough to fit out a fleet of trading vessels and send them to the ends of the earth to bring back more treasure. It was a sum large enough to boggle even my imagination, but the king had not finished.

'As a slave, this bounty will be paid not to you, but to your mistress, the Lady Lostris, who is a junior wife of Pharaoh.' I should have guessed that Pharaoh would keep it in the family.

I, who for a fleeting moment had been one of the richest men in Egypt, bowed to the king and returned to my place beside my mistress. She squeezed my hand to console me, but in truth I was not unhappy. Our destinies were so entwined that I was a part of her, and I knew that we would never again want for any material

340

thing. I was already planning how I would invest my mistress's fortune for her.

At last the king was ready to pass sentence on the line of prisoners, though he looked only at Intef as he spoke.

'Your crimes are unparalleled. No punishment before meted out is harsh enough to fit your case. This then is the sentence I pass upon you. At dawn on the day after the end of the festival of Osiris, you will be marched through the streets of Thebes, bound and naked. While you still live you will be nailed by your feet to the main gate of the city, with your heads hanging downwards. You will be left there until your bones are picked clean by the crows. Then your bones will be taken down and ground to powder and cast into Mother Nile.'

Even Intef paled and swayed on his feet as he listened to the sentence. By dispersing their earthly bodies so that they could never be embalmed and preserved, Pharaoh was condemning the prisoners to oblivion. For an Egyptian there could be no harsher punishment. They were being denied for all eternity the fields of paradise.

 WHEN MY mistress expressed her determination to attend the executions and to watch her father being nailed upside-down to the main gate, I do not think that she truly realized the horror of what she would witness. I was equally determined that she should not be there to see it. There had never been a sadistic streak in her. I believe that her decision was influenced by the fact that most of the other royal women were going to enjoy the diverting spectacle, and that Tanus would be in command of the execution. She would never pass up an opportunity to gaze at him, even from a distance.

In the end I persuaded her only by employing the most poignant argument in my arsenal. 'My lady, such cruel sights as these will certainly affect your unborn son. Surely you do not wish to blight his young unformed mind.'

'That is not possible,' she faltered for the first time in our argument. 'My son could know nothing of it.'

'He will see through your eyes, and the screams of his dying grandfather will pass through the walls of your stomach and enter his tiny ears.' It was an evocative choice of words, and they had the effect I was striving for.

She thought about it at length, and then sighed. 'Very well then, but I shall expect you to bring me back a full description of it all. You are not to miss a single detail. Especially I will want to know what the other royal wives were wearing.' Then she grinned at me wickedly to prove that she had not been totally gulled by my arguments. 'You can whisper it all to me, so the child sleeping in my belly cannot overhear us.'

At dawn on the day of the execution the gardens of the palace were still shrouded in darkness when I left the harem. I hurried through the water-gardens, and the stars were reflected in the black surfaces of the ponds. As I approached the wing of the palace where Lord Intef was being held in his own quarters, I saw the blaze of torches and lamps lighting the windows, and heard the frantic yelling of orders and invective from within.

I knew instantly that something was seriously amiss, and I broke into a run. I was almost speared by the guard at the door to Lord Intef's private quarters, but he recognized me at the last moment before he skewered me, and lifted his weapon and let me pass.

Tanus was in the centre of the ante-chamber. He was roaring like a black-maned lion in a trap, and aiming blows with his clenched fists at whoever came within range. Even though he had always had a stormy temper, I had never before seen him so incapacitated by rage. He seemed to have lost the power of reason or of articulate speech. His men, those mighty heroes of the Blues, cowered away from him, and the rest of the palace wing was in an uproar.

I went straight up to him, ducked under another wild punch, and shouted in his face, 'Tanus! It is I! Control yourself! In the name of all the gods, are you mad?'

He almost struck me, and I saw him wrestle with his emotions and at last take control of them.

'See what you can do for them.' He pointed at the bodies that were scattered about the ante-chamber as though a battle had raged through it.

With horror I recognized that one of them was Khetkhet, a senior captain of the regiment and a man I respected. He was curled in the corner clutching his stomach, with such agony etched on his rigid features that I hoped never to see again. I touched his cheek and the skin was cold and dead.

I shook my head, 'He is past all help that I can give him.' I lifted his eyelid with my thumb and gazed into his dead eye, then I leaned forward and smelled his mouth. The faint musty odour of mushrooms on it was dreadfully familiar.

'Poison.' I stood up. 'The others will be the same.' There were five of them curled on the tiles.

'How?' asked Tanus, in a tone of forced calm, and I picked up one of the bowls piled on the low table from which they had obviously eaten their dinner, and I sniffed it. The smell of mushrooms was stronger.

'Ask the cooks,' I suggested. Then, in a sudden access of anger, I hurled the bowl against the wall. The crumpled bodies reminded me of my pets who had died the same death, and Khetkhet had been my friend.

I took a deep breath to calm myself before I asked, 'No doubt your prisoner has escaped?' Tanus did not reply, but led me through into the grand vizier's bedchamber. Immediately I saw the painted panel that had been removed from the far wall of the empty room, and the opening behind it.

'Did you know that there was a secret passage?' Tanus demanded coldly, and I shook my head.

'I thought I knew all his secrets, but I was wrong.' My voice was resigned. I think that in my heart I had known all along that we would never bring Intef to justice. He was a favourite of the dark gods and enjoyed their protection.

'Has Rasfer escaped with him?' I asked, and Tanus shook his head.

'I have him locked in the arsenal with the barons. But Intef's two sons, Menset and Sobek, have disappeared. Almost certainly they were the ones who arranged this murder of my men, and

343

their father's escape.' Tanus had full control of that wild temper of his once more, but his anger was still there beneath it. 'You know Intef so well, Taita. What will he do? Where will he go? How can I catch him?'

'One thing I know, he will have made plans against such a day as this. I know he has treasure stored for him in the Lower Kingdom, with merchants and lawyers there. He has even had commerce with the false pharaoh. I think that he sold military information to him and his generals. He would receive a friendly welcome in the north.'

'I have already sent five fast galleys to the north, with orders to search all vessels that they overtake,' Tanus told me.

'He has friends across the Red Sea,' I said. 'And he has sent treasure to merchants in Gaza on the shores of the northern sea, to be held for him. He has had dealings with the Bedouin. Many of them are in his pay. They would help him to cross the desert.'

'By Horus, he is like a rat with a dozen escape-routes to his hole,' swore Tanus. 'How can I cover all of them?'

'You cannot,' I said. 'And now Pharaoh is waiting to witness the executions. You will have to report this to him.'

'The king will be angry, and with good reason. By allowing Intef to escape, I have failed in my duty.'

But Tanus was wrong. Pharaoh accepted the news of Intef's escape with remarkable equanimity. I cannot fathom the reason for this, except perhaps that the vast quantity of treasure he had acquired so unexpectedly had mellowed him. Deep in his heart he may still have cherished some sneaking affection for his grand vizier. On the other hand, Pharaoh was a kindly man, and may not have truly relished the prospect of watching Lord Intef being nailed to the city gates.

It is true he showed some passing annoyance, and spoke of justice being cheated, but all the time we were in his presence, he was surreptitiously studying the manifest of the treasure. Even when Tanus admitted his responsibility for the prisoner's escape, Pharaoh brushed it aside.

'The fault lies with the captain of the guard, and he has already been sufficiently punished from the poison bowl that Intef provided for him. You have sent galleys and troops in pursuit of the fugitive. You have done all that can be expected of you, Lord Harrab. It remains only for you to carry out my sentence on these other criminals.'

'Is Pharaoh ready to witness the execution?' Tanus asked, and Pharaoh looked about him for an excuse to remain with his manifests and tax-collectors' reports.

'I have much to do here, Lord Tanus. Proceed without me. Report to me when the sentences have been carried out.'

 SO GREAT was the public interest in the executions that the city fathers had erected a Taita stand in front of the main gates. They charged a silver ring for a seat upon it. There was no lack of customers, and the stand was packed to capacity. The crowds who could not find a seat upon it overflowed out into the fields beyond the walls. Many of them had brought beer and wine to make a celebration of it, and to toast the barons on their way. Very few of them had not suffered from the ravages of the Shrikes, and many of them had lost husbands or brothers or sons to them.

Stark naked and bound together, as Pharaoh had ordered, the condemned men were led through the streets of Karnak. The crowd lined their way and hurled dung and filth at them as they passed, screaming insults and shaking their fists. The children danced ahead of the procession singing bits of doggerel made up on the spur of the moment;

> Nails in my tooties, bare bum to the sky,
> I am a baron, and that's how I die.

Obedient to my mistress's wishes, I had taken up a place on the stand to watch the sentence carried out. In truth I had no eyes for the clothing and jewellery of the women of fashion around me when the prisoners were at last led through the open gates. I looked instead at Rasfer and I tried to revive and inflate my hatred for him. I forced myself to recite every cruel and wicked act that he had ever committed against me, to relive the agony of the lash and the knife that he had inflicted upon me.

Yet there he stood with his white belly sagging almost to his knees, with excrement in his hair and filth streaking his face and running down his grotesque body. It was difficult to hate him as much as he deserved.

He saw me on the stand and he grinned up at me. The paralysed muscles on one side of his face made it only half a grin, a sardonic grimace, and he called, 'Thank you for coming to wish me godspeed, eunuch. Perhaps we will meet again in the fields of paradise, where I hope to have the pleasure of cutting off your balls once again.'

That taunt should have made it easier for me to hate him, but somehow it failed, although I called back to him, 'You are going no further than the mud in the river bottom, old friend. The next catfish that I roast on the spit I will call Rasfer.'

He was the first prisoner to be lifted on to the wooden gate. It took three men on the parapet of the wall, straining on the rope, while at the same time, four more shoved from below. They held him there as one of the regimental armourers climbed the ladder beside him with a stone-headed mallet in his fist.

There were no more jokes from Rasfer when the first of the thick copper nails was driven through the flesh and bones of his huge, calloused feet. He roared and swore and twisted in the grip of the men who held him, and the crowd cheered and laughed and urged on the sweating armourer.

It was only when the nails had been driven home and the hammerman had climbed down to admire his handiwork that the flaws in this novel form of punishment became evident. Rasfer howled and roared, swinging upside-down, with the blood trickling slowly down his legs. The hang of his pendulous paunch was reversed, and the huge hairy bunch of his genitalia flapped against his belly-button. As he twisted and struggled, the nails slowly ripped through the web of flesh between his toes, until finally they tore entirely free. Rasfer fell back to earth and flopped around like a beached fish. The spectators loved the show, and howled with mirth at his antics.

Encouraged by the spectators, his executioners lifted him back on to the gate, and the armourer with his hammer climbed back up the ladder to drive in more nails. In order to pin Rasfer more securely and to prevent him struggling, Tanus ordered his hands as well as his feet to be nailed to the gate.

This time it was more successful. Rasfer hung head down, his limbs spread like some monstrous star-fish. He was no longer bellowing, for the mass of intestines in his belly were sagging down and pressing on his lungs. He struggled for every breath he drew, and had none over for shouting.

One at a time, the other condemned men were lifted on to the gate and nailed there, and the crowd hooted and applauded. Only Basti the Cruel made no sound and gave them poor sport.

As the day wore on, the sun beat down upon the crucified victims, and the heat grew steadily stronger. By noon the prisoners were so weak with pain and thirst and loss of blood that they hung as quietly as the carcasses on butchers' hooks. The spectators began to lose interest and drifted away. Some of the barons lasted longer than the others. Basti went on breathing all that day. Only as the sun was setting did he take one deep shuddering breath and finally hang inert.

Rasfer was the toughest of them all. Long after Basti was gone, he hung on. His face was filled with dark blood so it swelled to twice its normal size. His tongue protruded from between his lips, like a thick slice of purple liver. Once in a while he would utter a deep groan and his eyes would flutter open. Every time this happened, I shared his agony. The last of my hatred for him had long ago shrivelled and died, and I was racked with pity, as I would have been for any other tortured animal.

The crowd had long ago dispersed, and I sat alone on the empty stand. Not attempting to hide his disgust at such a brutal duty thrust upon him by the royal command, Tanus had stood to his post until sunset. Then finally he had handed over the death watch to one of his captains, and strode back into the city, leaving us to our vigil.

There were only the ten guards below the gate, myself on the stand and a few beggars lying like bundles of rags at the foot of the wall. The torches on either side of the gate guttered and flickered in the night breeze off the river, casting an eerie light over the macabre scene.

Rasfer groaned again, and I could stand it no longer. I took a

347

jar of beer from my basket and climbed down to speak to the captain. We knew each other from the desert, and he laughed and shook his head at my request. 'You are a soft-hearted fool, Taita. The bastard is so far-gone, he is not worth worrying about,' he told me. 'But I will look the other way for a while. Be quick about it.'

I went to the gate, and Rasfer's head was on a level with my own. I called his name softly, and his eyes fluttered open. I had no way of telling how much he understood, but I whispered, 'I have a little beer to wet your tongue.'

He made a soft gulping sound in his throat. His eyes were looking at me. If he still had feeling, I knew his thirst must be a torment of hell. I dribbled a few drops from the jar over his tongue, careful not to let any of it run back into his nose. He made a weak and futile effort to swallow. It would have been impossible, even if he had been stronger; the liquid ran out of the corners of his mouth and down his cheeks into the dung-caked hair.

He closed his eyes, and that was the moment I was waiting for. I slipped my dagger out of the folds of my shawl. Carefully I placed the point behind his ear, and then with a sharp move-ment drove it in to the hilt. His back arched in the final spasm, and then he relaxed into death. I drew out the blade. There was very little blood, and I hid the dagger in my shawl and turned away.

'May dreams of paradise waft you through the night, Taita,' the captain of the guard called after me, but I had lost my voice and could not reply. I never thought that I would weep for Rasfer, and maybe I never did so. Perhaps I wept only for myself.

AT PHARAOH'S command the return of the court to Elephantine was initially delayed for a month. The king had his new treasure to dispose of and was in buoyant mood. In all the time I had known him, I had never seen him so happy and contented. I was pleased for him. By this time I held the old man in real and warm affection. Some nights I sat up late with him and his scribes, going over the accounts of the royal treasury, which now emitted a decidedly rosy glow.

At other times, I was summoned by Pharaoh to consultations on the alterations to the mortuary temple and the royal tomb that he was now better able to afford. I calculated that at least half of the recently revealed treasure would go into the tomb with Pharaoh. He selected all the finest jewellery from Intef's hoard and sent almost fifteen takhs of bullion to the goldsmiths in his temple, to be turned into funerary objects.

Nevertheless, he found time to send for Tanus to advise him on military matters. He had now recognized Tanus as one of the foremost generals in his army.

I was present at some of these meetings. The threat from the false pharaoh in the Lower Kingdom was ever-present and preyed on all our minds. Such was Tanus' favour with the king that he was able to make the most of these fears and to persuade Pharaoh to divert a small part of Intef's treasure to the building of five new squadrons of war galleys, and to re-equipping all the guards regiments with new weapons and sandals – although he was unable to persuade the king to make up the arrears in pay for the army. Many of the regiments had not been paid for the last half-year. Morale in the army was much boosted by these reinforcements, and every soldier knew whom to thank for them. They roared like lions and raised their clenched right fists in salute, when Tanus inspected their massed formations.

Most times when Tanus was summoned to the royal audience, my mistress found some excuse to be present. Although she had the good sense to keep in the background on these occasions, she and Tanus directed such looks at each other that I feared they might scorch the false beard of the Pharaoh. Fortunately nobody but myself seemed to notice these flashing messages of passion.

Whenever my mistress knew that I was to see Tanus in private, she burdened me with long and ardent messages for him. On my return I carried his replies which matched hers in length and fire. Fortunately these outpourings were highly repetitive, and memorizing them was not a great hardship.

My Lady Lostris never tired of urging me to find some subterfuge by which she and Tanus might be alone together once more. I admit that I feared enough for my own skin and for the safety of my mistress and our unborn child, not to devote all my energies and ingenuity to satisfying this request of hers. Once when I did tentatively approach Tanus with my mistress's invitation to a meeting, he sighed and refused it with many protestations of love for her.

'That interlude in the tombs of Tras was sheer madness, Taita. I never intended to compromise the Lady Lostris' honour, but for the *khamsin*, it would never have happened. We cannot take that risk again. Tell her that I love her more than life itself. Tell her our time will come, for the Mazes of Ammon-Ra have promised it to us. Tell her I will wait for her through all the days of my life.'

On receiving this loving message, my mistress stamped her foot, called her true love a stubborn fool who cared nothing for her, broke a cup and two bowls of coloured glass, hurled a jewelled mirror which had been a gift from the king into the river, and finally threw herself on the bed where she wept until suppertime.

APART FROM his military duties, which included supervising the building of the new fleet of galleys, Tanus, these days, was much occupied with the reorganization of his father's estates that he had at last inherited.

On these matters he consulted me almost daily. Not surprisingly, the estates had never been preyed upon by the Shrikes while they belonged to Lord Intef, and accordingly they were all prosperous and in good repair. Thus Tanus had become overnight one of the most wealthy men in the Upper Kingdom.

Although I tried my best to dissuade him, he spent much of this private fortune in making up the arrears in pay to his men and in re-equipping his beloved Blues. Of course his men loved him all the more for this generosity.

Not content with these profligate expenditures, Tanus sent out his captains, Kratas and Remrem and Astes, to gather up all the crippled and blinded veterans of the river wars who now existed by begging in the streets of Thebes. Tanus installed this riff-raff in one of the large country villas that formed part of his inheritance, and although slops and kitchen refuse would have been too good for them, he fed them on meat and corn-cakes and beer. The common soldiers cheered Tanus in the streets and drank his health in the taverns.

When I told my mistress of Tanus' mad extravagances, she was so encouraged by them that she immediately spent hundreds of deben of the gold that I had earned for her, in buying and equipping a dozen buildings which she turned into hospitals and hostels for the poor people of Thebes. I had already earmarked this gold for investment in the corn market, and though I wrung my hands and pleaded with her, she could not be moved.

Needless to say, it was the long-suffering slave Taita who was responsible for the day-to-day management of this latest folly of his mistress, although she visited her charity homes every day. Thus it was possible for any loafer and drunkard in the twin cities to scrounge a free meal and a comfortable bed from us. If that was not enough, they could have their bowl of soup served to them by my mistress's own fair hand, and their running sores and purging bowels treated by one of the most eminent physicians in this very Egypt.

I was able to find a few young unemployed scribes and disenchanted priests who loved people more than gods or money. My mistress took them into her employ. I led this little band on nocturnal hunts through the back alleys and slum quarters of the city. Nightly we gathered up the street orphans. They were a filthy, verminous bunch of little savages, and very few of them came with us willingly. We had to pursue and catch them like wild cats. I received many lusty bites and scratches in the process of bathing their filth-encrusted little bodies and shaving their

351

hair that was so thick with lice and nits that it was impossible to drag a comb through it.

We housed them in one of my mistress's new hostels. Here the priests began the tedious process of taming them, while the scribes started on the long road of their education. Most of our captives escaped within the first few days, and returned to the gutters where they belonged. However, some of them stayed on in the hostel. Their slow transformation from animals to human beings delighted my mistress and gave me more pleasure than I had suspected could ever come from such an unlikely source.

All my protests against the manner in which my mistress was wasting our substance were in vain, and I vowed that if I were to be embalmed and laid in my tomb before my allotted time, the blame would surely rest entirely with these two young idiots whom I had taken under my wing, and who rewarded me by consistently ignoring my best advice.

Needless to say, it was my mistress and not me whom the widows and the cripples blessed and presented with their pitiful little gifts of wilting wild flowers, cheap beads and tattered scraps of papyrus containing poorly written texts from the *Book of the Dead*. As she walked abroad, the common people held up their brats for her blessing and tried to touch the hem of her skirt as though it were some religious talisman. She kissed the grubby babies, a practice which I warned her would endanger her health, and she scattered copper pieces to the loafers with as much care as a tree drops its autumn leaves.

'This is my city,' she told me. 'I love it and I love every person in it. Oh, Taita, I dread the return to Elephantine. I hate to leave my beautiful Thebes.'

'Is it the city you hate to leave?' I asked. 'Or is it a certain uncouth soldier who lives here?' She slapped me, but lightly.

'Is there nothing you hold sacred, not even love that is pure and true? For all your scrolls and grand language, you are at heart a barbarian.'

THUS THE days passed swiftly for all of us, until one morning I consulted my calendar and discovered that over two months had passed since my Lady Lostris had resumed her marital duties on Pharaoh's couch. Although she still showed no evidence of her condition, it was time to apprise the king of his great good fortune, his approaching paternity.

When I told my mistress what I intended, only one matter engaged her consideration. She made me promise that before I discussed it with the king, I must first tell Tanus that he was the true father of the child she was carrying. I set out to fulfil my promise that very afternoon. I found Tanus at the shipyards on the west bank of the river, where he was swearing at the shipwrights and threatening to throw them into the river to feed the crocodiles. He forgot his anger when he saw me, and took me on board the galley that they had launched that morning. Proudly, he showed me the new pump to remove water from the bilges, if the ship should ever be damaged in battle. He seemed to have forgotten that I had designed the equipment for him, and I had to remind him tactfully.

'Next you will want me to pay you for your ideas, you old rogue. I swear you are as stingy as any Syrian trader.' He clapped me on the back, and led me to the far end of the deck where none of the sailors could overhear us. He dropped his voice.

'How goes it with your mistress? I dreamed about her again last night. Tell me, is she well? How are those little orphans of hers? What a loving heart she has, what beauty! All of Thebes adores her. I hear her name spoken wherever I go, and the sound of it is as sharp as a spear thrust in my chest.'

'There will soon be two of her for you to love,' I told him, and he stared at me with his mouth agape like a man suddenly bereft of his senses. 'It was much more than just the *khamsin* that struck that night in the tombs of Tras.'

He seized me in a hug so powerful that I could not breathe. 'What is this riddle? Speak plainly, or I shall throw you into the river. What are you saying, you old scallywag? Don't juggle words with me!'

'The Lady Lostris is carrying your child. She sent me to tell

353

you so that you should be the first to know it, even before the king,' I gasped. 'Now set me free before I am permanently damaged.' He released me so suddenly, that I almost fell overboard.

'My child! My son!' he cried. It was amazing how both of them had made that immediate assumption of the poor little mite's gender. 'This is a miracle. This is a direct gift from Horus.' It was clear to Tanus in that moment that no other man in the history of the world had ever fathered an infant.

'My son!' he shook his head in wonder. He was grinning like an idiot. 'My woman and my son! I must go to them this very moment.' He set off down the deck, and I had to run to catch him. It took all my powers of persuasion to prevent him from storming the palace and bursting into the royal harem. In the end, I led him to the nearest riverside tavern to wet the baby's head. Fortunately a gang of off-duty Blues was already drinking there. I ordered and paid for a butt of the tavern's best wine and left them to it. There were men from some of the other regiments in the tavern, so there would probably be a riot later, for Tanus was in a rumbustious mood and the Blues never needed much encouragement to fight.

I went directly from the tavern to the palace, and Pharaoh was delighted to see me. 'I was about to send for you, Taita. I have decided that we have been too niggardly with the entrance-gates to my temple. I want something grander—'

'Pharaoh!' I cried. 'Great and Divine Egypt! I have wonderful tidings. The goddess Isis has kept her promise to you. Your dynasty will be eternal. The prophecy of the Mazes of Ammon-Ra will be fulfilled. The moon of my mistress has been trodden under the hooves of the mighty bull of Egypt! The Lady Lostris is bearing your son!'

For once all thought of funerals and temple-building was driven from Pharaoh's mind, and, like Tanus, his very first instinct was to go to her. Led by the king, we rushed through the palace corridors, a solid stream of nobles and courtiers turbulent as the Nile in spate, and my mistress was waiting for us in the garden of the harem. With the natural wiles of the female, she had composed the setting perfectly to show off her loveliness to full effect. She was seated on a low bench with flower-beds around her and the broad river behind her. For a moment I thought the king might throw himself to his knees in front of her, but even the prospect of immortality could not cause him to forget his dignity to that extent.

Instead, he showered her with congratulations and compliments and earnest enquiries after her health. All the while his fascinated gaze was fastened on her belly from which the miracle would in the fullness of time emerge. Finally he asked her, 'My dear child, is there anything that you lack for your happiness? Is there anything I can do to make you more comfortable during this trying time in your life?'

I was filled once more with admiration for my mistress. She would have made a great general or corn trader, for her sense of timing was impeccable. 'Your Majesty, Thebes is the city of my birth. I cannot be truly happy anywhere else in Egypt. I beg you in your generosity and understanding to allow your son to be born here in Thebes. Please do not make me return to Elephantine.'

I held my breath, the siting of the court was an affair of state. To remove from one city to another was a decision which affected the lives of thousands of citizens. It was not one to be made on the light whim of a child not yet sixteen years of age.

Pharaoh looked amazed at the request, and scratched his false beard. 'You want to live in Thebes? Very well, then, the court will move to Thebes!' He turned to me. 'Taita, design me a new palace.' He looked back at my mistress. 'Shall we site it there, on the west bank, my dear?' He pointed across the river.

'It is cool and pretty on the west bank,' my mistress agreed. 'I shall be very happy there.'

'On the west bank, Taita. Do not stint yourself in the design. It must be a fitting home for the son of Pharaoh. His name will be Memnon, the ruler of the dawn. We will call it the Palace of Memnon.'

With such simple ease my mistress saddled me with a mountain of labour, and accustomed the king to the first of many such demands in the name of the child in her womb. From this moment on, Pharaoh was not disposed to deny her aught that she asked for, whether it was titles of honour for those she loved or liked, alms for those she had taken under her protection, or rare and exotic dishes that were fetched for her from the ends of the empire. Like a naughty child, I think that she enjoyed testing the limits of this new power she wielded over the king.

She had never seen snow, though she had heard me speak of it from my fragmentary childhood memories of the mountainous land where I had been born. My mistress asked for some to be brought to her to cool her brow in the heat of the Nile valley. Pharaoh immediately commanded a special athletics games to be held, during which the hundred fastest runners in the Upper Kingdom were selected. They were despatched to Syria to bring back snow to my mistress in a special box of my design, which was intended to prevent it melting. This was probably the only one of all her whims that remained unsatisfied. All we received back from those far-off mountain peaks was a damp patch in the bottom of the box.

In all other things she was fully accommodated. On one occasion she was present when Tanus presented a report to the king on the order of battle of the Egyptian fleet. My mistress sat quietly in the background until Tanus had finished and taken his leave, then she remarked quietly, 'I have heard it said that Lord Tanus is the finest general we have. Don't you think it may be wise, divine husband, to promote him to Great Lion of Egypt and place him in command of the northern corps?' Once again I gasped at her effrontery, but Pharaoh nodded thoughtfully.

'That same thought had already occurred to me, my dear, even though he is still so young for high command.'

The following day, Tanus was summoned to a royal audience, from which he emerged as Great Lion of Egypt and the commander of the northern wing of the army. The ancient general who had preceded him was palmed off with a substantial pension and relegated to a sinecure in the royal household. Tanus now had three hundred galleys and almost thirty thousand men under his command. The promotion meant that he stood fourth in the army lists, with only Nembet and a couple of old dodderers above him.

'Lord Tanus is a proud man,' the Lady Lostris informed me, as if I were completely ignorant of this fact. 'If you should ever tell him that I had any hand in his promotion, I shall sell you to the first Syrian trader I come upon,' she threatened me ominously.

All this time her belly, once so smooth and shapely, was distending gradually. With all my other work I was obliged to relay daily bulletins on this progression, not only to the palace, but also to army headquarters, northern command.

 I BEGAN work on the construction of the Palace of Memnon five weeks after Pharaoh had given me the original instructions, for it had taken me that long to draw up the final plans. Both my mistress and the king agreed that my designs exceeded their expectations, and that it would be by far the most beautiful building in the land.

On the same day that the work began, a blockade runner who had succeeded in bribing his way past the fleets of the red pretender in the north docked in Thebes with a cargo of cedar wood from Byblos. The captain was an old friend of mine and he had interesting news for me.

Firstly, he told me that Lord Intef had been seen in the city of Gaza. It was said that he was travelling in state with a large bodyguard towards the East. He must therefore have succeeded in crossing the Sinai desert, or he had found a vessel to carry him through the mouth of the Nile and thence east along the coast of the great sea.

The captain had other news that at the time seemed insignificant, but which was to change the destiny of this very Egypt and of all of us who lived along the river. It seemed that a new and warlike tribe had come out of an unknown land to the east of Syria, carrying all before them. Nobody knew much about these warrior people, except that they seemed to have developed a form of warfare that had never been seen before. They could cross vast distances very swiftly, and no army could stand against them.

There were always wild rumours of new enemies about to assail this very Egypt. I had heard fifty like this one before, and thought as little of this one as I had of all the others. However, the captain was usually a reliable source, and so I mentioned his story to Tanus when next we met.

'No one can stand against this mysterious foe?' Tanus smiled. 'I would like to see them come against my lads, I'll show them what the word invincible truly means. What did you say they are called, these mighty warriors who come like the wind?'

'It seems that they call themselves the Shepherd Kings,' I replied, 'the Hyksos.' The name would not have slid over my tongue so smoothly if I understood then what it would mean to our world.

'The shepherds, hey? Well, they will not find my rascals an easy flock to herd.' He dismissed them lightly, and was much more interested in my news of Lord Intef. 'If only we could be certain of his true whereabouts, I could send a detachment of men to arrest him, and bring him back to face up to justice. Wherever I walk on the estates that once belonged to my family, I feel the spirit of my father beside me. I know he will never rest until I avenge him.'

'Would that it were so easy.' I shook my head. 'Intef is as cunning as a desert fox. I don't think we will ever see him in Egypt again.' As I said this, the dark gods must have chuckled to themselves.

 AS MY mistress's pregnancy advanced, I was able to insist that she limited her many activities. I forbade her to visit the hospitals or the orphanage, for fear of infecting herself and her unborn infant with the vermin and the diseases of the poor. During the heat of the day I made her rest under the barrazza that I had built in the water-garden for the grand vizier. When she protested at the boredom of this enforced inactivity, Pharaoh sent his musicians to the garden to entertain her, and I was persuaded to leave my work on the Palace of Memnon to keep her company, to tell her stories and to discuss Tanus' latest exploits with her.

I was very strict with her diet, and allowed her no wine or

beer. I had the palace gardeners provide fresh fruits and vegetables each day, and I carved all the fat off her meat, for I knew that it would make the child in her belly sluggish. I prepared each of her meals myself and every night when I saw her to her bedchamber, I mixed a special potion with herbs and juices that would strengthen her infant.

Of course, when she suddenly declared that she must have a stew made from the liver and kidneys of a gazelle, or a salad of larks' tongues or the roasted breast of the wild bustard, the king immediately sent a hundred of his huntsmen into the desert to procure these delicacies for her. I refrained from telling Lord Tanus of these strange cravings of my mistress, for I dreaded to learn that rather than prosecuting the war against the false pharaoh, the northern army had been sent into the desert to hunt gazelle or larks or bustard.

As the day of her confinement approached, I lay awake at night worrying. I had promised the king a prince, but he was not expecting his heir to arrive so expeditiously. Even a god can count the days from the first of the festival of Osiris. There was nothing that I could do if the child turned out to be a princess, but at least I could prepare Pharaoh for her early arrival.

Pharaoh had now conceived an interest in the subject of pregnancy and parturition, which temporarily rivalled his obsession with temples and tombs. I had to reassure him almost daily that the Lady Lostris' rather narrow hips were no obstacle to a normal birth, and that her tender age, far from being prejudicial, was highly favourable to a successful conclusion to our enterprise.

I took the opportunity to inform him of the interesting but little-known fact that many of the great athletes, warriors and sages of history had been prematurely exposed to the light of day.

'I believe, Your Majesty, that it's rather like the case of the sluggard who lies too long abed, and thus wastes his energy, while the great men are invariably early risers. I have noticed that you, Divine Pharaoh, are always about before sunrise. It would not surprise me to learn that you were also a premature birth.' I knew that he was not, but naturally he could not now contradict me. 'It would be a most propitious circumstance if this prince of yours should imitate his sire, and start early from his mother's womb.' I hoped that I had not belaboured my point, but the king seemed convinced by my eloquence.

In the end, the child cooperated most handsomely by overstaying its allotted term by almost two weeks, and I did nothing to hurry it along. The time span was so close to the normal that no tongues could wag, but Pharaoh was blessed with the premature birth that he had come to believe was so desirable.

It was no surprise to me that my mistress began her labour at a most inconvenient hour. Her waters broke in the third watch of the night. She was not in the habit of making matters too easy for me. At least this gave me the excuse of dispensing with the services of a midwife, for I had little faith in those hags with the black, dried blood crusted under their long, ragged fingernails.

Once she had begun, my Lady Lostris carried it off with her usual despatch and aplomb. I had barely time to shake myself fully awake, scrub my hands in hot wine and bless my instruments in the flame of the lamp, before she grunted and said quite cheerfully, 'You had better take another look, Taita. I think something is happening.' Although I knew it was much too soon, I humoured her. One glance was enough, and I shouted for her slave girls.

'Hurry, you lazy strumpets! Fetch the royal wives!'

'Which ones?' The first girl to answer my call tottered into the room half-naked and half-asleep.

'All of them, any of them.' No prince could inherit the double crown unless his birth had been witnessed, and it was formally attested that no exchange had taken place.

The royal women began to arrive just as the child revealed itself for the first time. My lady was seized by an overpowering convulsion, and then the crown of the head appeared. I had dreaded that it might be surmounted by a shock of red-gold curls, but what I saw was a thick dark pelt like that of one of the river otters. It was much later that the colour would change and the red would begin to sparkle in the black locks, like points of polished garnets, and then only when the sun shone upon it.

'Push!' I called to my mistress. 'Push hard!' And she responded lustily. The young bones of her pelvis, not yet tempered to

360

rigidity by the years, spread to give the infant fair passage, and the way was well oiled. The child took me unawares. It came out like a stone from a sling-shot, and the tiny, slippery body almost flew from my hands.

Before I had a good hold on it, my mistress struggled up on her elbows. Her hair was plastered to her scalp with sweat and her expression was desperate with anxiety. 'Is it a boy? Tell me! Tell me!'

The roomful of royal ladies crowding around the bed were witness to the very first act the child performed, as it entered this world of ours. From a penis as long as my little finger, the Prince Memnon, the first of that name, shot a fountain almost as high as the ceiling. I was full in the path of this warm stream, and it drenched me to the skin.

'Is it a boy?' my mistress cried again, and a dozen voices answered her together.

'A boy! Hail, Memnon, the royal prince of Egypt!'

I could not speak yet, for my eyes burned not only with royal urine, but with tears of joy and relief as his birth cry rang out, angry and hot with temper.

He waved his arms at me and kicked out so strongly that I almost lost my grip again. As my vision cleared I was able to make out the strong, lean body and the small, proud head with the thick pelt of dark hair.

 I LOST count long ago of how many infants I have birthed, but there had been nothing in my experience to prepare me for this. I felt all the love and devotion of which I was capable crystallized into that moment. I knew that something which would last a lifetime, and which would grow stronger with each passing day, had begun. I knew that my life had taken another random turn, and that nothing would ever be the same again.

As I cut the cord and bathed the child, I was filled with a sense of religious awe such as I had never known in the sanctuary of any one of Egypt's manifold gods. I feasted my eyes and my soul upon that perfect little body and upon the red and wrinkled face in which the signs of strength and stubborn courage were stamped as clearly as upon the features of his true father.

I laid him in his mother's arms, and as he found and latched on to her swollen nipple like a leopard on to the throat of a gazelle, my mistress looked up at me. I could not speak, but then there were no words that could frame what passed silently between us. We both knew. It had begun, something so wonderful that as yet neither of us could fully comprehend it.

I left her to the joy of her son and went to report to the king. I was in no hurry. I knew that the news would have been carried to him long since. The royal ladies are not renowned for their reticence. He was probably on his way to the harem at this very moment.

I dawdled in the water-garden, possessed by a dreaming sense of unreality. The dawn was breaking, and the sun god, Ammon-Ra, showed the tip of his fiery disc above the eastern hills. I whispered a prayer of thanks to him. As I stood with my eyes uplifted, a flock of the palace pigeons circled above the gardens. As they turned, the rays of the sun caught their wings and they flashed like bright jewels in the sky.

Then I saw the dark speck high above the circling flock, and even at that distance I recognized it immediately. It was a wild falcon, come out of the desert. It folded back its sharp wings and began its stoop. It had chosen the leading bird in the flock, and the dive was deadly accurate and inexorable. It struck the pigeon in a burst of feathers, like a puff of pale smoke, and the bird was dead in the air. Always a falcon will bind to its prey and drop to earth with it gripped in its talons.

This time that did not happen. The falcon killed the pigeon and then opened his talons and released it. The shattered carcass of the bird fell free, and, with a harsh scream, the falcon circled over my head. Three times it circled and three times it uttered that thrilling, warlike call. Three is one of the most potent magical numbers. From all these things I realized that this was no natural occurrence. The falcon was a messenger, or even the god Horus in his other form.

The carcass of the pigeon fell at my feet, droplets of its warm blood splattered my sandals. I knew that it was a token from the

god. A sign of his protection, and patronage for the infant prince.
I understood also that it was a charge to me. The god was
commending him to my care.

I took the dead pigeon in my hands, and lifted it to the sky.
'Joyfully I accept this trust that you have placed upon me, oh
Horus. Through all the days of my life I will be true to it.'

The falcon called again, one last wild shriek, and then it
banked away and on quick, stabbing wing-beats, flew out across
the wide Nile waters and disappeared into the wilderness, back
towards the western fields of paradise where the gods live.

I plucked a single wing-feather from the pigeon. Later I placed
it under the mattress of the prince's cot, for good luck.

 PHARAOH'S JOY and pride in his heir were
unbounded. He declared a nativity feast in his honour.
For one entire night the citizens of Upper Egypt sang
and danced in the streets, and gorged on the meat and
wine that Pharaoh provided, and they blessed the Prince
Memnon with every bowlful that went down their
gullets. The fact that he was the son of my Lady Lostris, whom
they loved, made the occasion of his birth all the more joyous.

So young and resilient was my mistress that within days, she
was well enough to appear before the full court of Egypt, bearing
her infant at her breast. Seated on the lesser throne below that
of the king, she made a picture of lovely young motherhood.
When she opened her robe and lifted out one of her milk-swollen
breasts and before the assembled court gave the infant suck, they
cheered her so loudly as to startle the infant. He spat out the
nipple and roared at them in scarlet-faced outrage, and the
nation took him to its heart.

'He is a lion,' they declared. 'His heart is pumped up with the
blood of kings and warriors.'

Once the prince had been quieted again, and his mouth
stopped up with the nipple, Pharaoh rose to address us, his
subjects.

'I acknowledge this child to be my issue and the direct line of
my blood and succession. He is my first-born son, and shall be

Pharaoh after me. To you noble lords and ladies, to all my subjects, I commend the Prince Memnon.'

The cheers went on and on, for no one amongst them wanted to be the first to fall silent and bring his loyalty into question.

During all of this I stood with other servants and slaves of the royal household in one of the upper galleries which overlooked the hall. By craning my head, I was able to pick out the tall figure of Lord Tanus. He was standing in the third rank below the throne with Nembet and the other military commanders. Although he cheered with the rest of them, I could read the expression on his broad, open face that he strove to disguise. His son was claimed by another and it was beyond his power to prevent it. Even I, who knew and understood him so well, could only guess at what agony he was suffering.

When at last the king ordered silence and he had their attention once more, he continued, 'I commend to you also the mother of the prince, the Lady Lostris. Know all men that she sits now closest to my throne. From this day forward she is elevated to the rank of chief consort and the senior wife of Pharaoh. From henceforth, in name she will become Queen Lostris, while in precedence and preferment she ranks after the king and his prince alone. Furthermore, until the prince has reached the age of his majority, Queen Lostris shall act as my regent and, when I am unable to do so, she will stand at the head of the nation in my stead.'

I do not think there was a soul in all the Upper Kingdom who did not love my mistress, except perhaps some of the royal wives who had been unable to provide the king with a male heir, and who now found themselves outranked by her and superseded in the order of precedence. All the rest showed their love in the acclaim with which they greeted this pronouncement.

To end the ceremony of the naming of Pharaoh's heir, the royal family left the hall. In the main courtyard of the palace, Pharaoh mounted the sledge of state, and with Queen Lostris seated at his side and the prince in her arms, they were drawn by the span of white bullocks down the Avenue of Rams to the temple of Osiris to make sacrifice to the god. Both sides of the sacred avenue were lined a hundred deep by the citizens of

Thebes. With a mighty voice they demonstrated their devotion to the king and their love for the queen and her new-born prince.

That night, as I waited on her and the child, she whispered to me, 'Oh, Taita, did you see Tanus in the crowd? What a day of mixed joy and sorrow this has been. I could have wept for my love. He was so tall and brave, and he had to watch and listen when his son was taken from him. I wanted to jump to my feet in all that throng and cry out, "This is the son of Tanus, Lord Harrab, and I love them both."'

'I am pleased for the sake of all of us, Your Majesty, that for once you were able to restrain that wayward tongue of yours.'

She giggled. 'It is so strange to have you call me that – Your Majesty – it makes me feel like an impostor.' She transferred the prince from one breast to the other, and at the movement he released from both ends of his tiny body a double blast of air which in volume and resonance was truly imperial.

'It is apparent that he was conceived in a wind-storm,' I remarked drily, and she giggled again and then immediately afterwards sighed dolefully.

'My darling Tanus will never share these intimate moments with us. Do you realize that he has not yet held Memnon in his arms, and it is possible he never will? I think I am about to cry again.'

'Restrain yourself, mistress. If you weep, it might sour your milk.' A warning which was untrue but effective in bending her to my will. She sniffed back her tears.

'Is there no way that we can let Tanus enjoy our baby as we do?'

I thought about it for a while and then made a suggestion which caused her to cry out with pleasure. As if to endorse what I had said, the prince broke resounding wind once more.

The very next day when Pharaoh came to visit his son, the queen put my suggestion into effect. 'Dear and divine husband, have you given thought to selecting official tutors for Prince Memnon?'

Pharaoh laughed indulgently. 'He is still only an infant. Should he not first learn to walk and talk, before he is instructed in other skills?'

'I think his tutors should be appointed now, so they can grow to know him, and he them.'

'Very well.' The king smiled, and took the child on to his knee. 'Who do you suggest?'

'For his schooling we need one of our great scholars. Some person who understands all the sciences and mysteries.'

The king's eyes twinkled. 'I cannot think of one who answers that description,' and he grinned at me. The child had altered Pharaoh's disposition; since Memnon's birth, he had become almost jovial, and for a moment I expected him to wink at me. However, his new, congenial attitude to life did not extend quite that far.

The queen continued, unruffled by this exchange, 'Then we need a soldier well versed in the warlike arts, and the exercise of arms to train him as a warrior. He should, I think, be young and of good breeding. Trustworthy, of course, and loyal to the crown.'

'Who do you suggest for that position, my dear? Very few of my soldiers answer to all those virtues.' I do not think there was any guile or malice in Pharaoh's question, but nevertheless my mistress was no fool. She inclined her head gracefully and said, 'The king is wise, and knows who, from all his generals, best suits that role.'

At the very next assize the king announced the prince's tutors. The slave and physician, Taita, was to be responsible for Memnon's schooling and deportment. This surprised very few, but there was a buzz of comment when the king went on, 'For his training in arms and in military tactics and strategy, the Great Lion of Egypt, Lord Harrab, shall henceforth be responsible.' Accordingly it became the duty of Lord Harrab, when he was not on campaign, to wait upon the prince at the beginning of each week.

While my mistress waited for her quarters in the new palace that I was building across the river to be completed, she had moved from the harem into a wing of the grand vizier's palace that overlooked the water-garden I had built for her father. This was in accordance with her new status as the senior wife and consort. The weekly audience that Prince Memnon held for his official tutors took place under the barrazza, with Queen Lostris in attendance. Very often there was a score of other officials or courtiers present, and occasionally Pharaoh himself arrived with all his train, so we were under considerable constraint.

However, once in a while there were just the four of us present. On the very first occasion that we had such privacy, Queen Lostris placed the prince in his father's arms for the first time and I was witness to the incoherent joy with which Tanus looked down into the face of his son. Memnon rose to the occasion by puking down the front of his father's uniform, but even then Tanus would not relinquish him.

From then onwards we reserved any special event in the child's life for when Tanus was with us. Tanus fed him his first spoonful of gruel, and the prince was so startled by this unaccustomed fare that he screwed up his face and spat the offending mess down his chin. Then he howled loudly for his mother's milk to wash the taste from his mouth. Queen Lostris took him on her lap and while Tanus watched fascinated, she gave him the breast. Suddenly Tanus reached across and tweaked the nipple from the tiny mouth. This amused everybody but the prince and me. Memnon was outraged at this cavalier treatment and made that fact known, while I was shocked. I imagined the king arriving unexpectedly to find the Great Lion of Egypt with a right royal handful which he seemed in no hurry to relinquish.

When I quite rightly protested, my mistress told me, 'Don't be such a prim old woman, Taita. We are only having a little innocent fun.'

'Fun, yes. However, there is some doubt as to the innocence of it,' I muttered, for I had seen both their faces light up at the intimate touch, and sensed their mutual passion like thunder in the air. I knew that they could not restrain themselves for much longer, and that even Tanus' sense of duty and honour must in the end succumb to so great a love as theirs.

That very evening I visited the temple of Horus and made a generous sacrifice. Then I prayed and asked the god, 'May the prophecy of the Mazes be not too long delayed, for they cannot help themselves. It will mean death and disgrace to all of us.'

Sometimes it is best for men not to attempt to interfere with destiny. Our prayers can be answered in ways which we do not expect and do not welcome.

 I WAS physician to the prince, but in truth he had little need of my medical skills. He was blessed with his father's rude and abundant health, and precocious strength. His appetite and digestion were exemplary. Anything placed in his mouth was devoured with leonine voracity, and promptly re-emerged from his nether end in the desired shape and consistency.

He slept without interruption and woke bellowing for food. If I showed him a finger, he would watch it move from side to side with those huge dark eyes, and the moment it came within range, he would seize it and attempt to haul himself into a sitting position. In this he succeeded sooner than any other child that I had attended. He raised himself and crawled at the age when others had only begun to sit up. He took his first tottering step when others would only begin to crawl.

Tanus was present on that remarkable day. He had been on campaign for the past two months, for the forces of the red usurper had captured Asyut. That city was the pivot on which our northern defences turned, and Pharaoh had ordered Tanus down-river with all his fleet to retake the city.

Much later I heard from Kratas just how terrible had been the fighting, but in the end Tanus breached the walls and was at the head of his beloved Blues when they broke in. They drove the pretender from the city and back beyond his own borders with bloody losses.

Tanus sailed back to Thebes and the gratitude of the kingdom. Pharaoh laid another chain upon his shoulders, the Gold of Valour, and made up the back-pay of all the troops who had helped him achieve this victory.

Tanus came almost directly from the king to the barrazza in the water-garden where we were waiting for him. While I stood guard at the gateway, Tanus and my mistress embraced with all the fire that had burned up so brightly while they had been apart.

At last I had to separate them, for that embrace could lead in only one direction.

'Lord Tanus,' I called sharply, 'Prince Memnon grows impatient.' Reluctantly they drew apart, and Tanus went to where the infant sprawled naked on a robe of jackal skins that I had spread for him in the shade. Tanus went down on one knee before him.

'Greetings, Your Royal Highness. I bring you tidings of the triumph of our arms—' Tanus mocked him lovingly, and Memnon gave a happy shout as he recognized his father, and then the sparkling gold chain caught his eye. With a mighty heave he hoisted himself to his feet. He took four lurching steps, seized the chain and clung to it with both hands.

All of us applauded this feat, and, supporting himself by the chain, Memnon beamed about him, accepting this praise as his due.

'By the wings of Horus, he has as sharp an eye as you do for the yellow metal, Taita,' Tanus laughed.

'It is not the gold that draws him, but the winning of it,' my mistress declared. 'One day he too will wear the Gold of Valour upon his chest.'

'Never doubt it!' Tanus swung the boy high, and Memnon shrieked with pleasure and kicked his legs to urge Tanus to further rough play.

Thus, for Tanus and me, the child's advances seemed to mark the change of seasons, just as surely as did the rise and fall of the river. On the other hand my mistress's life revolved around those hours spent alone with the child and the man. Each interval between Tanus' visits seemed too long for my mistress to support, each visit too short for her to bear.

THE INUNDATION of that summer was as benevolent as any that we had forecast at the ceremony of the
waters in Elephantine. When the flood receded, the
fields glistened under their new coat of black mud. In
their turn, they were soon obliterated by the dense
green stands of corn and fruit. By the time the prince
took his first upright step the granaries of Egypt were brimming,
and the larders of even the poorest of her subjects were filled. On
the west bank the Palace of Memnon was taking shape, and the
war in the north was running in our favour. The gods smiled on
Pharaoh and all his realm.

The only discontent in all this was that the two lovers,
though close enough to touch, were cleaved apart by a gulf
wider than the valley in which we lived. Each of them on
separate but numerous occasions taxed me with the prophecy of
the Mazes of Ammon-Ra, as though I were personally responsible
for the fulfilment of the dream visions. It was in vain to protest
that I was merely the mirror in which the future was reflected,
and not the one who moved the stones on the bao board of
destiny.

The old year died, and the river began to rise once more,
completing the endless cycle. This was the fourth flood that the
Mazes had foretold. I, as much as any of them, expected my
vision of the Mazes to be fulfilled before the end of the season.
When this did not happen, both my mistress and Tanus taxed
me severely.

'When will I be free to go to Tanus?' Queen Lostris sighed.
'You must do something, Taita.'

'It is not me, but the gods, whom you must question. I can
pray to them, but that is all I can do.'

Then another year passed without any change in our circumstances, and even Tanus was bitter. 'So much faith I have placed
in you that I have based my future happiness on your word. I
swear to you, Taita, that if you do not do something soon—' He
broke off and stared at me. The threat was all the more forceful
for not being spoken.

Yet another year drifted past, and even I began to lose faith in
my own prophecy. I came to believe that the gods had changed

their minds, or that what I had seen was my own wishful fantasy.

In the end Prince Memnon was almost five years old and his mother twenty-one, when the messenger came flying wild-eyed from the north, in one of our scouting galleys.

'The Delta has fallen. The red pretender is dead. The Lower Kingdom is in flames. The cities of Memphis and Avaris are destroyed. The temples are burned to the ground and the images of the gods thrown down,' he shouted to the king, and Pharaoh replied, 'It is not possible. I long to believe this despatch, but I cannot. How could this thing come to pass without our knowledge? The usurper was possessed of great force, for more than fifteen years we have been unable to overthrow him. How has this been accomplished in a day, and by whom?'

The messenger was shaking with fear and exhaustion, for his journey had been onerous, and he knew how the bearers of disastrous tidings were treated in Thebes.

'The red pretender was destroyed with his sword still in the scabbard. His forces were scattered before the war trumpets could sound the alarm.'

'How was this accomplished?'

'Divine Egypt, I know not. They say that a new and terrible enemy has come out of the East, swift as the wind, and no nation can stand before his wrath. Though they have never seen him, our army is in full retreat from the northern borders. Even the bravest will not stay to face him.'

'Who is this enemy?' Pharaoh demanded, and for the first time we heard the fear in his voice.

'They call him the Shepherd King. The Hyksos.'

Tanus and I had jested with that name. We would never do so again.

PHARAOH CALLED his war council into secret conclave. It was only long afterwards that I learned from Kratas all that transpired in those deliberations. Tanus, of course, would never break his oath of secrecy, not even to me or my mistress. But I was able to worm it out of Kratas, for that lovable, brawling oaf was not proof against my wiles.

Tanus had promoted Kratas to the rank of Best of Ten Thousand, and had given him the command of the Blue Crocodile Guards. The bond between them was still as solid as a granite stele. Thus, as a regimental commander, Kratas was entitled to a seat on the war council, and although at his lowly rank he was not called upon to speak, he faithfully relayed all that was said, to me and my mistress.

The council was divided between the ancients, headed by Nembet, and the new blood of which Tanus was the leader. Unfortunately the final authority lay with the old men, and they forced their archaic views upon the others.

Tanus wanted to draw our main forces back from the frontier and to set up a series of deep defences along the river. At the same time, he intended sending forward scouting and reconnaissance parties to assess and study the nature of the mysterious enemy. We had spies in all of the northern cities, but for some unknown reason no reports from them had as yet been received. Tanus wanted to gather these in and study them, before he deployed his main force to battle.

'Until we know what we are facing, we cannot devise the correct strategy to meet it,' he told the council.

Nembet and his faction countered any of Tanus' suggestions. The old admiral had never forgiven Tanus for his humiliation on the day he saved the royal barge from destruction. His opposition to Tanus was based on principle rather than on reason or logic.

'We will not yield a cubit of our sacred soil. To suggest it is cowardice. We will meet the enemy and destroy him wherever we find him. We will not dance and flirt with him like a gaggle of village maidens.'

'My lord!' roared Tanus, incensed by the suggestion of cowardice. 'Only a fool, and an old fool at that, will make a decision before he knows the facts. We have no scrap of intelligence to act upon—'

It was in vain. The seniority of the three generals above Tanus on the army lists prevailed in the end.

Tanus was ordered north immediately, to steady and rally the retreating army. He was to hold the frontier, and make his stand on the boundary stones. He was forbidden to make a strategic withdrawal to the line of hills before Asyut, which was the natural defensive line, and from which the city walls provided a second line of defence. He would have the fleet and the northern army corps under his direct command, with three hundred warships to provide the transport, and to command the river.

In the meantime, Nembet would bring in the rest of the army, even those regiments on the southern border with Cush. The black threat from the African interior must be ignored now in the face of this more pressing danger. As soon as they were assembled, Nembet would rush these reinforcements northwards to join up with Tanus. Within a month, there would be an invincible army of sixty thousand men and four hundred galleys lying before Asyut. In the meantime, Tanus must hold the frontier at all costs.

Nembet ended with a strict injunction. 'Lord Harrab is further ordered to hold all his forces on the border. He is not to indulge in raids or scouting forays to the north.'

'My Lord Nembet, these orders blindfold me, and bind my sword-arm. You are denying me the means of conducting this campaign in a prudent and efficient manner,' Tanus protested in vain. Nembet sneered with the satisfaction of having forced his authority upon his young rival, and in having gained a measure of retribution. On such petty human emotions pivots the destiny of nations.

Pharaoh himself announced his intention of taking his rightful place at the head of his army. For a thousand years the pharaoh had been present on the field whenever the decisive battles of history had been fought out. Although I had to admire the king's courage, I wished he had not chosen this moment to demonstrate it. Pharaoh Mamose was no warrior, and his presence would do little to enhance our chances of victory. There might be some bolstering of morale when the troops saw him in the van, but on balance he and his train would be a greater hindrance than assistance to Lord Tanus.

The king would not travel northwards to the battle-front alone. His entire court would attend him, including his senior wife and his son. The queen must have her retinue and Prince Memnon his tutors, and so I would be going north to Asyut and the battle-front.

Nobody knew nor understood this enemy. I felt that my mistress and the prince were being placed in unnecessary danger. On the other hand, the safety of a slave was of no account, except to the slave himself. I slept little the night before we sailed northwards on the flood of the river for Asyut and the battle-front.

 THE FARTHER north we sailed, the more numerous and troublesome were the rumours and reports coming down from the front to feed upon our contentment and confidence, like locusts upon the standing crops. Often during the voyage, Tanus came aboard our vessel, ostensibly to discuss these with me. However, on each visit he spent some time with the prince and his mother.

I have never held with the custom of women following the army into battle. In times of peace or war, they are a marvellous distraction – even a warrior of Tanus' calibre could be diverted from his main purpose. All his mind should have been on the task ahead, but when I told him so, he laughed and clapped my shoulder.

'They give me a reason to fight. Don't worry, old friend, I shall be a lion defending his cub.'

Soon we encountered the first elements of the retreating army, straggling groups of deserters who were looting the villages as they fled southwards along the banks of the river. With very little ceremony and no hesitation at all, Tanus beheaded several hundred of them and had their heads spiked on spears and planted along the bank as an example and a warning. Then he gathered up the others and regrouped them under reliable officers.

There were no further desertions and the troops stood to the colours with a new spirit.

Our flotilla came to the walled city of Asyut, overlooking the river. In defiance of his orders from Nembet, Tanus left a small strategic reserve of five thousand men here under the command of Remrem. Then we sailed on northwards to take up our positions on the border, there to await the approach of the mysterious Shepherd King.

The fleet lay at anchor across the river in its battle formations, but the vessels were under skeleton crews. The fighting men were disembarked with the main body of infantry and deployed upon the east bank of the river.

I prevailed upon Pharaoh to allow my mistress and the prince to remain on board the large and comfortable barge that had brought them here. It was cooler and healthier out on the water, and their escape would be swifter if our army met with any reverse of arms.

The king went ashore with the army, and set up his camp on the higher ground above the inundated fields. There was a deserted village here; years ago the peasants had fled from this disputed border with the false pharaoh. There were always foraging troops and bloody little skirmishes hereabouts, and the farmers had given up any attempts to work these fertile but dangerous fields. The name of the derelict village was Abnub.

The flood of the Nile had begun to subside some weeks prior to our arrival at Abnub, and although the irrigation canals were still running strongly, and the fields were morasses of black mud, the main waters had retreated back between the permanent banks of the Nile.

Within the restrictions placed upon him by Nembet, Tanus set about preparing to meet the threat. The regiments encamped in their order of battle. Astes commanded the fleet on the river, Tanus himself had the centre with his left flank anchored on the Nile, while Kratas had the right wing.

The desert stretched to the eastern horizon, dun and forbidding. No army could survive out in that burning, waterless waste. It was our right flank, secure and impregnable.

All that we knew of the Hyksos was that he had come

overland, and that he possessed no fleet of his own. Tanus expected to meet him on land, and to fight an infantry engagement. Tanus knew that he could prevent the Hyksos from crossing the river, and so he should be able to bring him to battle on the field of his own choice. Ideally, this would not have been at Abnub, but Nembet had made that decision for him.

The village of Abnub stood on a low ridge with open untended fields around it. At least it commanded a good view, and the enemy would be under our observation long before it could engage and drive in our pickets.

Tanus had thirty thousand of the finest troops in Egypt under his command. I had never seen such a large force. Indeed, I doubt that an army of this size had ever before been assembled in the valley of the Nile. Soon Nembet would arrive with another thirty thousand. Then it would be the greatest army in history.

I went with Tanus to inspect them, and the troops' morale had soared since he had taken command in person. Perhaps the presence of Pharaoh in the camp had also helped to steady them. They cheered Tanus as he strode along their massed ranks, and I felt much encouraged and relieved at the multitudes of their host, and the spirit in them.

I could not imagine an enemy powerful enough to overwhelm us. There were twelve thousand archers with polished leather helmets and padded leather breastplates that would stop an arrow, except if it were fired at very short range. There were eight thousand heavy spearmen, with long shields of hippo-skin as tough and hard as bronze. The ten thousand swordsmen in leopard-skin caps were also armed with sling-shots, the stones from which could split a skull at fifty paces.

I felt more confident with each day that passed, as I watched Tanus exercising these huge masses of armed men. Yet it worried me that we still knew so little about the Hyksos and the forces that he commanded. I pointed out to Tanus that the war council had forbidden him to send land forces forward to reconnoitre, but had said nothing of vessels being used for this purpose.

'You should have been a law scribe,' Tanus laughed, 'you can make words dance to any tune you play.' But he ordered Hui to take a single squadron of fast galleys northwards as far as Minieh, or until he encountered the enemy. This was the same Hui whom we had captured at Gallala, and who had been one of Basti's Shrikes. Under Tanus' favour, that young rogue had advanced swiftly, and now commanded a squadron of galleys.

Hui had strict orders to avoid action and to report back within four days. Dutifully, he returned on the fourth day. He had reached Minieh without seeing another ship or encountering any resistance. The villages along the river were all deserted, and the town of Minieh itself had been sacked and was in flames.

Hui had, however, captured a handful of deserters from the false pharaoh's shattered army. These were the first persons we had questioned who were actual eye-witnesses of the Hyksos invasion. However, none of them had ever stood to engage and actually fight the Shepherd King. They had all fled at his first approach. Their reports were therefore so far-fetched and garbled as to be completely incredible.

How could we believe in the existence of an army that sailed across the open desert on ships that were as swift as the wind? According to our informants, the dust-clouds that hung over this strange fleet were so tall as to obscure their numbers and to strike terror into any army that watched their advance.

'These are not men,' the prisoners reported, 'they are fiends from the underworld, and they ride on the devil winds out of the desert.'

Having questioned the prisoners carefully, and finding that even hot coals on their heads could not make them alter their stories, Tanus ordered their summary execution. He did not want these wild tales circulating and spreading despondency amongst our forces who had only recently regained their courage.

ON THE tenth day of waiting at Abnub, we received word that Nembet was at last on his way with reinforcements, and that he expected to reach Asyut within the next two weeks. The effect on the men was marvellous to behold. They were transformed at a stroke from sparrows to eagles. Tanus issued an extra ration of beer and meat to celebrate the news, and the cooking-fires were a field of stars upon the plain before Abnub. The luscious odour of burning mutton fat filled the night, and the sound of laughter and singing only died away in the final watches.

I had left my mistress on board the barge with her son, and had come ashore in response to a summons from Tanus. He wanted me to attend the final war council with his regimental commanders. 'You are always a well of ideas and wisdom, you old rascal. Perhaps you can tell us how to sink a fleet of ships that comes sailing over dry land?'

Our deliberations went on until after midnight, and for once I was able to contribute very little of value. It was too late to return to the ship that night, so Tanus gave me a straw mattress in the corner of his tent. I awoke before dawn, as was my habit, but Tanus was gone from his bed, and beyond the coarse linen wall of the tent, the camp was already astir. I felt guilty of indolence, and hastened out to watch the dawn breaking over the desert.

I climbed the hill behind the camp. From there I looked first towards the river. The blue smoke from the cooking-fires was smeared out across the surface, mingling with the streamers of river mist. The riding lamps on board the ships were reflected in the dark waters. It was still too dark and far to pick out the vessel upon which my mistress lay.

I turned then towards the east and saw the light bloom over the desert with the nacreous glow of pearly oyster-shells. The light hardened and the desert was soft and lovely, the hillocks and dunes shaded with mauve and soft purple. In the limpid air the horizons seemed close enough to touch with an outstretched hand.

Then I saw the cloud suspended on the horizon beneath the unblemished aquamarine sheen of the sky. It was no larger than the end of my thumb, and my gaze wandered past it and then drifted back to it. I felt no initial alarm, for I had to stare at it for a while before I realized that it was moving.

'How strange,' I murmured aloud. 'The beginning of the *khamsin*, perhaps.' But it was out of season, and there had been no charging of the air with those malevolent forces which herald the desert storms. The morning was cool and balmy.

Even as I pondered it, the distant cloud spread and grew taller. The base of the cloud was upon the earth, not suspended above it, and yet it was too swift and wide to be of any earthly origin. A flock of birds might move that fast, locusts may rise that thickly to the skies, but this was neither of these things.

The cloud was ochre-yellow, but at first I could not believe it was dust. I have watched herds of scimitar-horned oryx galloping through the dunes in their hundreds upon their annual migrations, but they had never raised a dust-cloud such as this. It might have been the smoke from a fire, but there was nothing out there in the desert to burn. It had to be dust, and yet I still could not wholly believe it. Swiftly it grew, and drew ever closer, while I stared in wonder and in awe.

Suddenly I saw reflected light twinkle at the base of the towering cloud. Instantly I was transported back to the vision of the Mazes of Ammon-Ra. This was the same scene. The first had been fantasy, but this was reality. I knew that those beams of light were shot from war armour and from blades of polished bronze. I started to my feet, and alone upon the hilltop I shouted to the wind a warning that nobody heard.

Then I heard the war trumpets sounding in the camp below me. The pickets on the heights had at last seen the approaching dust-cloud and sounded the alarm. The sound of the trumpets was a part of my vision. Their urgent warning shrilled in my ears and threatened to split my skull, it thrilled my blood and chilled my heart. I knew from my vision that on this fateful day a dynasty would fall and the locusts from the East would devour the substance of this very Egypt. I was filled with dread, and with terror for my mistress and the child that was part of the dynasty.

The camp below me was a tumult of men running to arms. Their armour glinted and their spear-heads sparkled as they

379

brandished them on high. They were bees from the overturned hive, massing and swarming in disarray. The shouts of the sergeants and the rallying cries of the captains were almost drowned by the braying horns.

I saw Pharaoh carried from his tent in the centre of a knot of armed men. They hustled him up the slope of the hill to where his throne was set amongst the rocks, overlooking the plain and the wide sweep of the river. They lifted him to the throne and placed the crook and the flail in his hands and the tall double crown upon his head. Pharaoh sat like a marble statue with an ash-white face, while below him his regiments fell into their battle formations. Tanus had trained and exercised them well, and out of the confusion of the first alarm, order swiftly emerged.

I ran down the hill to be near the king, and so rapid was the response of Lord Tanus' divisions that by the time I reached the foot of his throne, his army lay upon the plain like a coiled serpent to meet the menace of that boiling yellow dust-cloud that swept down upon it.

Kratas stood with his division on the right flank. I could recognize his tall figure on the first slope of the hill. His regimental officers were grouped around him, their plumes nodding and waving in the light morning breeze from the river. Tanus and his staff were directly below me, close enough for me to overhear their conversation. They discussed the advance of the enemy in cool, academic tones, as though this were a sandbox problem at an officers' training course.

Tanus had disposed his force in the classical formations. His heavy spearmen formed the front ranks. Their shields were interlocked and the spears' butts grounded. The bronze spear-heads sparkled in the early sunlight, and the men's demeanour was calm and grave. Drawn up behind them were the archers. Their bows were strung and ready. Behind each man stood his quiver boy with bundles of spare arrows. During the battle they would gather up the expended arrows of the enemy to replenish their own bundles. The swordsmen were in reserve, light and quick troops that could rush in to stop a breach or to exploit a weak point in the enemy formations.

The moves of any battle were like those of the bao board. There were classic openings with set defences that had been developed over the centuries. I had studied these and written three of the definitive scrolls on military tactics that were the prescribed reading of officers training in Thebes.

Now, reviewing Tanus' dispositions, I could find no fault in them, and my confidence soared. How could an enemy prevail against this mighty host of trained and battle-hardened veterans, and their brilliant young general, who had never lost a battle?

Then I looked once more beyond our ranks at that ominous, rolling yellow cloud, and my confidence wavered. This was something beyond military tradition, beyond the experience of any general in all our long, proud history. Were these mortal men that we were facing, or, as rumour suggested, were they fiends?

When I stared into the swirling clouds, they were now so close that I could make out dark shapes in the dun and gloomy veils of dust. My skin crawled with a kind of religious horror as I recognized the shiplike shapes that our prisoners had warned us of. But these were smaller and swifter than any vessel that had ever been launched on water, swifter even than any creature that had ever moved upon the surface of the earth.

It was difficult to follow one of these shapes with the eye, for they were ethereal and quick as moths in the light of a lantern. They wheeled and wove and disappeared in the moving clouds, so that when they reappeared, it was impossible to tell whether it was the same or another like it. There was no way to count their numbers, or even to guess at what followed the first ranks of their advance. Behind them, the dust-cloud extended back to the horizon from which they had come.

Although our own ranks stood firm and steady in the sunlight, I could sense the wonder and trepidation that gripped them all. The studied conversation of Tanus' officers had dried up, and they stood in silent awe and watched the enemy deploy before us.

Then I realized that the dust-cloud was no longer advancing upon us. It hung in the sky, and gradually began to settle and clear, so that I was able dimly to make out the stationary vehicles in the vanguard. But I was now so confused and alarmed that I could not tell whether there were a thousand of them or more.

We would learn later that this hiatus was always part of the Shepherd King's attack plan. I did not know it then, but during this lull they were regrouping and watering and gathering themselves for the final advance.

A terrible stillness had fallen on our ranks. It was so profound that the whisper of the breeze was loud through the rocks and the wadis of the hill on which we stood. The only movement was the flutter and swirl of our battle standards at the head of each division. I saw the Blue Crocodile banner waving in the centre of our line, and I took comfort from it.

Slowly, the dust-clouds subsided and row after row of the Hyksos' craft were revealed to us. They were still too distant to make out details, but I saw that those in the rear were much larger than those leading their army. It seemed to me that they were roofed over with sails of cloth or leather. From these I saw that men were unloading what looked like large water jars and carrying them forward. I wondered what men could consume such large quantities of water. Everything these foreigners did was a puzzle and made no sense to me.

The silence and the waiting drew out until every muscle and nerve in my body screamed out with the strain. Then suddenly there was movement again.

From the front ranks of the Hyksos formations some of these strange vehicles started towards us. A murmur went up from our ranks as we saw how fast they were moving. After that short period of rest, they seemed to have doubled their speed. The range closed and another cry went up from our host as we realized that these vehicles were each being drawn by a pair of extraordinary beasts.

They stood as tall as the wild oryx, with the same stiff, upstanding mane along the crest of their arched necks. They were not horned like the oryx, but their heads were more gracefully formed. Their eyes were large and their nostrils flared. Their legs were long and hoofed. Striding out with a peculiar daintiness, they seemed merely to brush the surface of the desert.

Even now, after all these years, I can recapture the thrill of gazing at a horse for the first time. In my mind the beauty of the hunting cheetah paled beside these marvellous beasts. At the same time we were all filled with fear of them, and I heard one of the officers near me cry out, 'Surely these monsters are killers, and eaters of human flesh! What abomination is this that is visited upon us?'

A stirring of horror ran through our formations, as we expected these beasts to fall upon us and devour us, like ravening lions. But the leading vehicle swung away and sped parallel to our front rank. It moved on spinning discs, and I stared at it in wonder. For the first few moments I was so stunned by what I was looking at that my mind refused to absorb it all. If anything, my first sight of a chariot was almost as moving as the horses that drew it. There was a long yoke-pole between the galloping pair, connected to what I later came to know as the axle. The high dashboard was gilded with gold leaf and the side-panels were cut low to allow the archer to shoot his arrows to either side.

All this I took in at a glance, and then my whole attention focused on the spinning discs on which the chariot sailed so smoothly and swiftly over the rough ground. For a thousand years we Egyptians had been the most cultured and civilized men on earth; in the sciences and the religions we had far outstripped all other nations. However, in all our learning and wisdom we had conceived nothing like this. Our sledges churned the earth on wooden runners that dissipated the strength of the oxen that dragged them, or we hauled great blocks of stone over wooden rollers without taking the next logical step.

I stared at the first wheel I had ever seen, and the simplicity and the beauty of it burst in upon me like lightning flaring in my head. I understood it instantly, and scorned myself for not having discovered it of my own accord. It was genius of the highest order, and now I realized that we stood to be destroyed by this wonderful invention in the same way as it must have annihilated the red usurper in the Lower Kingdom.

The golden chariot sped across our front, just out of bowshot. As it drew opposite us, I dragged my gaze from those miraculously spinning wheels and the fierce and terrifying creatures that drew them, and I looked at the two men in the cockpit of the chariot. One was clearly the driver. He leaned out over the dashboard and he seemed to control the galloping team by means of long plaited cords of leather attached to their heads. The taller man who stood behind him was a king. There was no doubting his imperial bearing.

I saw instantly that he was an Asian, with amber skin and a hooked, aquiline nose. His beard was black and thick, cut square across his breastplates, curled and intricately plaited with coloured ribbons. His body armour was a glittering skin of bronze fish-scales, while his crown was tall and square; the gold was embossed with images of some strange god and set with precious stones. His weapons hung on the side-panel of the chariot, close to his hands. His broad-bladed sword in its leather and gold scabbard had a handle of ivory and silver. Beside it, two leather quivers bulged with arrows, and each shaft was fletched with bright feathers. Later I would come to know how the Hyksos loved gaudy colours. The king's bow on its rack beside him was of an unusual shape that I had never seen before. It was not the simple, clean arc of our Egyptian bows; on the Hyksos bow, the upper and lower limbs recurved at the tips.

As the chariot flew down our line, the king leaned out and planted a lance in the earth. It was tipped with a crimson pennant, and the men around me growled in perturbation. 'What is he doing? What purpose does the lance serve? Is it a religious symbol, or is it a challenge?'

I gaped at the fluttering pennant, but my wits were dulled by all that I had seen, it meant nothing to me. The chariot sped on, still just out of bowshot, and the crowned Asian planted another lance, then wheeled and came back. He had seen Pharaoh on his throne and he halted below him. The horses were lathered with sweat, it foamed on their flanks like lace. Their eyes rolled ferociously and their nostrils flared so that the pink mucous lining was exposed. They nodded their heads on long, arched necks and their manes flew like the tresses of a beautiful woman in the sunlight.

The Hyksos greeted Pharaoh Mamose, Son of Ra, Divine Ruler of the Two Kingdoms, May He Live For Ever, with contempt. It was a laconic and ironic wave of a mailed hand, and he laughed. The challenge was as clear as if it had been spoken in perfect Egyptian. His mocking laughter floated across to us, and the ranks of our army growled with anger, a sound like far-off thunder in the summer air.

A small movement below me caught my attention, and I looked down just as Tanus took one step forward and flung up the great bow Lanata. He loosed an arrow and it rose in a high arcing trajectory against the milky-blue sky. The Hyksos was out of range to any other bow, but not to Lanata. The arrow reached its zenith and then dropped like a stooping falcon, full at the centre of the Asian king's chest. The watching multitude gasped with the length and power and aim of that shot. Three hundred paces it flew, and at the very last moment the Hyksos threw up his bronze shield and the arrow buried its head in the centre of the target. It was done with such contemptuous ease that we were all amazed and confounded.

Then the Hyksos seized his own strangely shaped bow from the rack beside him. With one movement he nocked an arrow, and drew and let it fly. It rose higher than Tanus had reached, and it sailed over his head. Fluting like the wing of a goose, it dropped towards me. I could not move and it might have impaled me without my attempting to avoid it, but it passed my head by an arm's-length and struck the base of Pharaoh's throne behind me. It quivered in the cedar strut like an insult, and the Hyksos king laughed again and wheeled his chariot and sped away, back across the plain, to rejoin his own host.

I knew then that we were doomed. How could we stand against these speeding chariots, and the recurved bows that so easily outranged the finest archer in our ranks? I was not alone in my dreadful expectations. As the squadrons of chariots began their final fateful evolutions out on the plain and sped towards us in waves, a moan of despair went up from the army of Egypt. I understood then how the forces of the red pretender had been scattered without a struggle, and the usurper had died with his sword still in its scabbard.

On the run, the flying chariots merged into columns four abreast and came directly at us. Only then did my mind clear, and I started down the slope at full pelt. Panting, I reached Tanus' side and shouted at him, 'The pennant lances mark the weak points in our line! Their main strike will come through us there and there!'

Somehow the Hyksos had known our battle order, and had recognized the laps in our formation. Their king had planted his pennants exactly between our divisions. The idea of a spy or a traitor occurred to me even then, but in the urgency of the moment I thrust it aside, and it was for the moment forgotten.

Tanus responded to my warning instantly, and shouted an order for our pickets to race forward and seize the pennants. I wanted him to move them, so that we could receive the enemy thrust on our strongest front, but there was no time for that. Before our pickets could reach and throw down the markers, the spear-head of flying chariots bore down upon them. Some of our men were shot down with arrows from the bouncing, swerving chariots. The aim of the enemy charioteers was uncanny.

The survivors turned and raced back, trying to regain the illusory safety of our lines. The chariots overhauled them effortlessly. The drivers controlled the galloping, plunging teams of horses with a lover's touch. They did not run their victims down directly, but swerved to pass them at the length of less than a cubit. It was only then that I noticed the knives. They were curved outwards from the spinning hub of the wheels like the fangs of some monstrous crocodile.

I saw one of our men struck squarely by the whirling blades. He seemed to dissolve in a bright cloud of blood. One of his severed arms was thrown high in the air and the bleeding chunks of his mutilated torso were dashed into the rocky earth as the chariot flew on without the least check. The phalanx of chariots was still aimed directly at the lap in our front line, and though I heard Kratas yelling orders to reinforce it, it was far too late.

The column of chariots crashed into our defensive wall of shields and spears, and tore through it as though it were as insubstantial as a drift of river mist. In one instant our formation, that had stood the assault of the finest Syrian and Hurrian warriors, was cleaved and shattered.

The horses spurned our strongest and heaviest men under their hooves. The whirling wheel-knives hacked through their armour and lopped off heads and limbs, as though they were the tenderest shoots of the vine. From the high carriages the charioteers showered arrows and javelins into our tightly packed ranks, then they tore on through the breach they had forced, passing entirely through our formations, fanning out behind us and driving at full tilt along our rear files, still hurling their missiles into our unprotected rear.

When our troops turned to face this assault on their rear, another phalanx of racing chariots crashed into them from the open plain. The first assault split our army in twain, dividing Tanus from Kratas on the right wing. Then those that followed so swiftly cut up the two halves into smaller, isolated groups. We were no longer a cohesive whole. Little bands of fifty and a hundred men stood back-to-back and fought with the courage of the doomed.

Across the plain on wings of swirling dust, the Hyksos came on endlessly. Behind the light two-wheeled chariots followed the heavy four-wheeled war carts, each carrying ten men. The sides of the carts were screened with sheep fleeces. Our arrows slapped ineffectually into the thick, soft wool, our swords could not reach the men in the high body of the carts. They shot their points down into us and broke up the confused masses of our fighting men into scattered knots of terrified survivors. When one of our captains rallied a few men to counter-attack them, the war carts wheeled away and stopped out of range. With their awful recurved bows, they broke up our gallant charges, and the moment we wavered, they came rolling back upon us.

I was intensely aware of the moment when the conflict ceased to be a battle and became nothing more than a massacre. The remains of Kratas' division out on our right flank had fired the last of their arrows. The Hyksos had picked out their captains by their plumed helmets and shot nearly every one of them down. The men were disarmed and leaderless. They broke into rout. They threw down their weapons and ran for the river. But it was not possible to outrun a Hyksos chariot.

The broken troops ran into Tanus' divison below the hillock, and tangled with it. With their panicking, struggling masses they clogged and smothered what little resistance Tanus was still capable of offering. The terror was infectious and the centre of our line broke and tried to fly, but the deadly chariots circled them, like wolves around the flock.

In all that chaos, in the bloody shambles and the tumult of defeat, only the Blues stood firm around Tanus and the Crocodile standard. They were a little island in the torrent of defeated men, even the chariots could not break them up, for, with the instinct of a great general, Tanus had gathered them and pulled them back into the one patch of rocks and gulleys where the Hyksos could not come at them. The Blues were a wall, a bulwark around the throne of Pharaoh.

Because I had been at the king's side, I was in the centre of this ring of heroes. It was difficult to keep my feet, for all around me men struggled and surged, washed back and forth by the waves of battle, like seaweed clinging to a rock in the full stream of tide and surf.

I saw Kratas fight his way through from the shattered right wing to join us. His plumed helmet attracted the Hyksos arrows and they flew around his head thickly as locusts, but he came through unscathed, and our ring opened for him. He saw me, and he laughed with huge delight. 'By Seth's steaming turds, Taita, this is more fun than building palaces for little princes, is it not?' He was never famous for his repartee, was Kratas, and I was too busy staying on my feet to bother with a reply.

He and Tanus met close to the throne. Kratas grinned at him like an idiot. 'I'd not have missed this for all Pharaoh's treasure. I want one of those Hyksos sledges for myself.' Neither was Kratas one of Egypt's greatest engineers. Even now he still believed that the chariots were some type of sledge. That was as far as his imagination reached.

Tanus tapped the side of his helmet with the flat of his sword in greeting, and although his tone was light, his expression was grim. He was a general who had just lost a battle and an army, and an empire.

'Our work here is finished for today,' he told Kratas. 'Let us see if these Hyksos monsters can swim as well as they run. Back to the river!' Then, shoulder-to-shoulder, the two of them shoved their way through the ranks towards the throne where I still stood.

I could see over their heads, over the periphery of our little defensive ring, out over the plain where our broken army was streaming away towards the river, still harried by the squadrons of chariots.

I saw the golden chariot of the Hyksos king wheel out of formation and cleave its way towards us, trampling our men under the flying hooves and chopping them up with the glittering wheel-knives. The driver brought the horses to a rearing, plunging halt before he reached the barrier of rocks which protected us. Balancing easily on the footplates, the Hyksos drew his recurved bow and aimed at me, or so it seemed. Even as I ducked, I realized that the arrow was not meant for me. It shrieked over my head and I turned to watch its flight. It struck Pharaoh high in the chest, and buried half its length in his flesh.

Pharaoh gave a hoarse cry and tottered on his high throne. There was no blood, for the shaft had plugged the wound, but the feathers were a pretty scarlet and green. Pharaoh slid sideways and collapsed forward towards me, and I opened my arms to receive him. His weight bore me to my knees, so I did not see the Hyksos king's chariot wheel away, but I heard his mocking laughter receding as he dashed back across the plain to lead the slaughter.

Tanus stooped over me as I held the king. 'How badly is he struck?' he demanded.

'He is killed,' the reply rose to my lips unthinkingly. The angle of entry and the depth of the wound could mean that only one outcome was possible, but I choked off the words before they were spoken. I knew that our men would lose heart if Great Egypt was slain. Instead I said, 'He is hard hit. But if we carry him back aboard the state barge, he may recover.'

'Bring me a shield here!' Tanus roared, and when it came we gently lifted Pharaoh on to it. There was still no blood, but I knew his chest was filling like a wine jar. Quickly, I felt for the head of the arrow, but it had not emerged from his back. The point was still buried deep within the cage of his ribs. I snapped off the protruding shaft, and covered him with his linen shawl.

'Taita,' he whispered. 'Will I see my son again?'

'Yes, Mighty Egypt, I swear it to you.'

'And my dynasty will survive?'

'Even as the Mazes of Ammon-Ra have foretold.'

'Ten strong men here!' Tanus bellowed. They crowded around the makeshift litter, and lifted the king between them.

'Form the tortoise! Close up on me, the Blues!' With interlocking shields, the Blues formed a wall around the king.

Tanus raced to the Blue Crocodile which still waved in our midst and tore it from its pole. He wound it around his waist and knotted the ends across his belly.

'If the Hyksos want this rag, they had better come and take it from me,' he shouted, and his men cheered this piece of foolish bravado.

'All together now! Back to the ships! At the double!'

The moment we left the shelter of our little rocky redoubt, the chariots came at us.

'Leave the men!' Tanus had found the key. 'Kill their beasts!' As the first chariot bore down upon us, Tanus flexed Lanata. His bowmen drew with him, and they all fired on his example.

Half our arrows flew wide, for we were running over uneven ground and the archers were winded. Others struck the bodywork of the leading chariot, and the shafts snapped or pegged into the wood. Still other arrows rattled off the bronzed plates that covered the chests of the horses.

Only one arrow flew hard and true. From the great bow Lanata it sang with the wind in its feathers, and struck the offside horse in the forehead. The creature went down like a rockslide, tangling the traces and dragging its team-mate down in a cloud of dust and kicking hooves. The charioteers were hurled from the cockpit as the carriage somersaulted, and the other chariots veered away to avoid the wreckage. A jubilant shout went up from our ranks, and our pace picked up. This was our first success in all that dreadful day, and it manned and encouraged our little band of Blues.

'On me, the Blues!' Tanus roared, and then, incredibly, he began to sing. Immediately the men around him shouted the opening chorus of the regimental battle hymn. Their voices were strained and rough with thirst and effort, and there was little tune or beauty to it, but it was a sound to lift the heart and thrill the blood. I threw back my head and sang with them, and my voice soared clear and sweet.

'Horus bless you, my little canary,' Tanus laughed at me, and we raced for the river. The chariots circled us with the first wariness to their manoeuvres that they had demonstrated all that day. They had seen the fate of their comrade. Then three of them swung across the front of our tortoise, and in vee-formation charged at us head-on.

'Shoot at the heads of the beasts!' Tanus shouted, and led them with an arrow that brought another horse crashing to its knees. The chariot overturned and was smashed to pieces on the stony ground, and the other vehicles in the formation veered away.

As our formation passed the shattered chariot, some of our men ran out to stab the squealing horses that were trapped in the wreckage. Already they hated and feared these animals with an almost superstitious dread, which was reflected in this vindictive piece of cruelty. They killed the fallen charioteers also, but without the same rancour.

With two of their chariots destroyed, the Hyksos seemed reluctant to attack our little formation again, and we were rapidly approaching the morass of muddy fields and flooded irrigation ditches that marked the river-bank. I think that at that stage I was the only one of us who realized that the wheeled enemy could not follow us into the swamp.

Although I ran beside the king's litter, I could see, through the gaps in our ranks, the dying acts of the battle that were being played out around us.

Ours was the only surviving detachment that still showed any cohesion. The rest of the Egyptian army was a formless and terrified rabble streaming across the plain. Most of them had thrown aside their weapons. When one of the chariots drove at them, they dropped to their knees and held up their hands in supplication. The Hyksos showed them no quarter. They did not even waste arrows upon them but swung in close to chop them to tatters with the spinning wheel-knives, or to lean out of the cockpit with the lance and cut them down, or to smash in their skulls with the stone-headed maces. They dragged the victim behind them, still spiked on the lance, until the barbed spear-head disengaged, and only then did they leave the crumpled corpse lying in their dust.

I had never seen such butchery. I had never read of anything like it in all the accounts of ancient battles. The Hyksos slaughtered our people in their thousands and their tens of thousands. The plain of Abnub was like a field of dhurra corn after the reapers had been through it with their scythes. Our dead were piled in drifts and windrows.

For one thousand years our armies had been invincible and our swords had triumphed across the world. Here on the field of Abnub an age had come to an end. In the midst of this carnage the Blues sang, and I with them though my eyes burned with tears of shame.

The first irrigation ditch was just ahead when another chariot formation swung out on our flank and came driving hard at us, three abreast. Our arrows fell all about them, but they came on with the horses blowing hard through gaping red mouths and with the drivers screaming encouragement at them. I saw Tanus shoot twice, but each time his arrows were deflected or were cheated by the erratic swerve and bounce of the chariots. The formation thundered into us and broke the tortoise of interlocking shields.

Two of the men carrying Pharaoh's litter were cut to shreds by the wheel-knives, and the wounded king was tumbled to the earth. I dropped to my knees beside him and covered him with my own body to protect him from the Hyksos lances, but the chariots did not linger. It was their concern never to allow themselves to become entangled or surrounded. They raced on and clear before our men could reach them with the sword. Only then did they wheel and regroup, and come back.

Tanus reached down and hauled me to my feet. 'If you get yourself killed, who will be left to compose a hero's ode to us?' he scolded me, then he shouted for men. Between them they picked up the king's litter and ran with it for the nearest ditch.

I could hear the squeal of the chariot wheels bearing down on us, but I never looked back. In ordinary circumstances I am a strong runner, but now I outdistanced the litter-bearers as though their feet were chained to the earth. I attempted to hurdle the ditch, but it was too wide for me to cross in a single leap, and I landed knee-deep in the black mud. The chariot that was following me struck the bank of the ditch and one of its wheels shattered. The body of the vehicle toppled into the ditch and almost crushed me, but I managed to throw myself aside.

Swiftly the Blues stabbed and hacked the horses and men as they lay helplessly in the mud, but I took the moment to wade back to the chariot.

The up-ended wheel was still spinning in the air. I placed my hand upon it as I studied it, and let it rotate beneath my fingers. I stood there only as long as it took me to draw three deep breaths, but at the end of that time I had learned as much about wheel construction as any Hyksos, and had the first inkling of the improvements I could make to it.

'By Seth's melodious farts, Taita, you'll have us all killed, if you start daydreaming now!' Kratas yelled at me.

I shook myself and seized one of the recurved bows from the rack on the side of the chariot body and an arrow from the quiver. I wanted to examine these at my leisure. Then I waded across the ditch with them in my hand, just as the squadron of chariots came thundering back, running parallel to the ditch and firing their arrows down amongst us.

The men carrying the king were a hundred paces ahead of me, and I was the last of our little band. Behind me the charioteers roared with frustration that they were unable to follow us, and they shot their arrows around me as I ran. One of them struck my shoulder, but the point failed to penetrate and the shaft glanced away. It left a purple bruise which I only discovered much later.

Although I had started from so far behind them, I caught up with the litter-bearers by the time we reached the main bank of the Nile. The river-bank was crowded with the survivors of the battle. Nearly all of these were weaponless and very few were unwounded. They were all driven by a single desire, to return as swiftly as possible to the ships that had brought them down-river from Thebes.

Tanus singled me out and called me to him as the litter-bearers came up. 'I place Pharaoh in your hands now, Taita. Take him on board the royal barge and do all you can to save his life.'

'When will you come aboard?' I asked him.

'My duty is here, with my men. I must save all of them that I can, and get them embarked.' He turned from me and strode away, picking out the captains and commanders from amongst his beaten rabble, and shouting his orders.

I went to the king and knelt beside the litter. He was still alive. I examined him briefly and found that he hovered on the edge of consciousness. His skin was as clammy-cold as that of a reptile, and his breathing was shallow. There was only a thin rime of blood around that arrow-shaft which had seeped up from the wound, but when I laid my ear to his chest I heard the blood bubbling in his lungs with each breath he drew, and a thin red snake of it crawled from his mouth down his chin. I knew that whatever I could do to save him, I must do quickly. I shouted for a boat to take him out to the barge.

The litter-bearers lifted him into the skiff, and I sat in the bilges beside him as we sculled out to where the great state barge lay anchored in the main flow of the current.

 THE KING'S suite crowded the ship's side to watch us approach. There was a gaggle of the royal women and all those courtiers and priests who had taken no part in the fighting. I recognized my mistress standing amongst them as we drew closer. Her face was very anxious and pale, and she held her young son by his hand.

As soon as those on board the barge looked down into our skiff and saw the king on his litter, with the blood on his face that I had been unable to wipe away, a terrible cry of alarm and mourning went up from them. The women keened and wailed, and the men howled with despair, like dogs.

Of all the women, my mistress stood closest at hand as the king was lifted up the ship's side and his litter laid on the deck. As the senior wife, hers was the duty to attend him first. The others gave her space as she stooped over him and wiped the mud and the blood from his haggard face. He recognized her, for I heard him breathe her name and ask for his son. My mistress called the prince to him, and he smiled softly and tried to raise his hand to touch the boy, but he did not have the strength, and the hand dropped back to his side.

I ordered the crew to carry Pharaoh to his quarters, and my mistress came to me quickly and asked low and urgently, 'What of Tanus? Is he safe? Oh, Taita, tell me that he is not slain by this dreadful enemy!'

'He is safe. Nothing can harm him. I have given you the vision of the Mazes. All this was foreseen. But now I must go to the king, and I will need your help. Leave Memnon with his nursemaids, and come with me.'

I was still black and crusted with river mud, and so was Pharaoh, for he had fallen in the same ditch as I had. I asked Queen Lostris and two of the other royal women to strip and bathe him and lay him on fresh white linen sheets, while I returned to the deck to bathe in buckets of river water that the sailors hauled up over the side. I never operate in filth, for I have found by experience that for some reason it affects the patient adversely and favours the accumulation of the morbid humours.

While I was thus occupied, I was watching the east bank where our broken army was huddled behind the protection of ditch and swamp. This sorry rabble had once been a proud and mighty force, and I was filled with shame and fear. Then I saw the tall figure of Tanus striding amongst them, and wherever he moved, the men stood up out of the mud, and reassembled into the semblance of military discipline. Once I even caught the sound of ragged and unconvincing cheers on the wind.

If the enemy should send their infantry through the swamps now, the slaughter and the rout would be complete. Not a man of all our mighty army would survive, for even Tanus would be able to offer little resistance. However, although I peered anxiously into the east, I could make out no sign of infantry shields in phalanx or the sparkle of advancing spear-heads at the shoulder-slope.

There was still that terrible dust-cloud hanging over the plain of Abnub, so the chariots were at work out there, but without enemy infantry falling upon him, Tanus could still salvage some little comfort out of this dreadful day. It was a lesson I was to remember, and which stood us in good stead in the years ahead. Chariots might win the battle, but only the foot-soldiers could consolidate it.

The battle out there on the river-bank was now entirely Tanus' affair, while I had another battle to fight with death in the cabin of the state barge.

 'WE ARE not entirely without hope,' I whispered to my mistress, when I returned to the king's side. 'Tanus is rallying his troops, and if any man alive is capable of saving this very Egypt from the Hyksos, he is the one.' Then I turned to the king, and for the moment all else was forgotten but my patient.

As is often my way, I murmured my thoughts aloud as I examined the wound. It was less than an hour, measured by a water-clock, since the fateful arrow had struck, and yet the flesh around the broken-off stub of the shaft was swollen and empurpled.

'The arrow must come out. If I leave the barb in there, he will be dead by tomorrow's dawn.' I had thought the king could no longer hear me, but as I spoke, he opened his eyes and looked directly into mine.

'Is there a chance that I will live?' he asked.

'There is always a chance.' I was glib and insincere. I heard it in my own voice, and the king heard it also.

'Thank you, Taita. I know you will strive for me, and I absolve you now from all blame, if you should fail.' This was generous of him, for many physicians before me have felt the strangling-rope as punishment for letting the life of a king slip through their fingers.

'The head of the arrow is deeply lodged. There will be a great deal of pain, but I will give you the powder of the Red Shepenn, the sleeping-flower, to still it.'

'Where is my senior wife, Queen Lostris?' he asked, and my mistress replied immediately, 'I am here, my lord.'

'There is aught that I would say. Summon all my ministers and my scribes, that my proclamation may be witnessed and recorded.' They crowded into the hot little cabin and stood in silence.

Then Pharaoh reached out to my mistress. 'Take my hand, and listen to my words,' he ordered, and she sank down beside him and did as she was ordered, while the king went on speaking in a soft and breathless whisper.

'If I should die, Queen Lostris will stand as regent for my son. I have learned in the time that I have known her that she is a person of strength and good sense. If she were not, I would not have laid this charge upon her.'

'Thank you, Great Egypt, for your trust,' Queen Lostris murmured low, and now Pharaoh spoke directly to her, although every person in the cabin could hear him.

'Surround yourself with wise and honest men. Instruct my son in all the virtues of kingship that you and I have discussed. You know my mind on all these matters.'

'I will, Majesty.'

'When he is old enough to take up the flail and the crook, do not attempt to withhold it from him. He is my lineage and my dynasty.'

'Willingly I shall do what you order, for he is not only the son of his father, but my son also.'

'While you rule, rule wisely and care for my people. There will be many who seek to wrest the emblems of kingship from your grasp – not only this new and cruel enemy, this Hyksos, but others who stand even closer to your throne. But you must oppose them all. Keep the double crown intact for my son.'

'Even as you say, divine Pharaoh.'

The king fell silent for a while and I thought that he had slipped over the edge into unconsciousness, but suddenly he groped for the hand of my mistress again.

'There is one last charge I have for you. My tomb and my

temple are incomplete. Now they are threatened, as is all my realm, by this terrible defeat that we have suffered. Unless my generals can stop them, these Hyksos will sweep on to Thebes.'

'Let us petition the gods that it does not come to pass,' my mistress murmured.

'I charge you most strictly that you will see me embalmed and interred with all my treasure in accordance with the strictest protocols of the *Book of the Dead*.'

My mistress was silent. I think that she realized even then just what an onerous charge this was that Pharaoh had laid upon her.

His grip upon her hand tightened until his knuckles turned white, and she winced. 'Swear this to me on your own life and hope for immortality. Swear it before my ministers of state and all my royal suite. Swear it to me in the name of Hapi, your patron god, and on the names of the blessed trinity, Osiris and Isis and Horus.'

Queen Lostris looked across at me with a piteous appeal in her eyes. I knew that once she had given it, she would honour her word at all and any cost to herself. In this, she was like her lover. She and Tanus were bound by the same code of chivalry. I knew also that those close to her must expect to pay the same price. An oath to the king now might one day return to burden us all, Prince Memnon and the slave Taita included. And yet there was no manner in which she could gainsay the king as he lay upon his death-bed. I nodded to her almost imperceptibly. Later I would examine the finer points of this oath, and like a law scribe I would mould it a little closer to reasonable interpretation.

'I swear on Hapi, and on all the gods,' Queen Lostris said, softly but clearly, and there would be a hundred times in the years ahead when I would wish she had not done so.

The king sighed with satisfaction and let her hand slip from his. 'Then I am ready for you, Taita. And for whatever fate the gods have decreed. Only let me kiss my son once more.'

While they brought our fine young prince to him, I drove the crowd of nobles from the cabin with little ceremony. Then I prepared a draught of the Red Shepenn for him and made it as strong as I dared, for I knew that pain could undo all my best efforts and destroy my patient as swiftly as a slip of my scalpel.

When he had drunk it all, I waited for the pupils of his eyes to contract to pinpoints, and for the lids to droop over them. Then I sent the prince away with his nursemaids.

 ON LEAVING Thebes I had expected to have to deal with arrow wounds, so I had brought my spoons with me. I had designed this instrument myself, although there was a quack in Gaza and another in Memphis who both claimed it was their invention. I blessed the spoons and my scalpels in the lamp flame, and then washed my hands in hot wine.

'I do not think it is wise to use one of your spoons when the head of the arrow is so deep and so near the heart,' my mistress told me as she watched my preparations. There are occasions when she speaks as though the student had outpaced the master.

'If I leave the arrow, it will certainly mortify. I will have killed him just as surely as if I had chopped his head off his shoulders. This is the only way that I will have a chance of saving him.'

For a moment we looked into each other's eyes, and we spoke without words. This was the vision of the Mazes of Ammon-Ra. Did we wish to avoid the benevolent consequences to ourselves?

'He is my husband. He is Pharaoh.' My mistress took my hand to emphasize her words. 'Save him, Taita. Save him, if you can.'

'You know that I will,' I answered.

'Do you need me to help you?' She had assisted me so very often before. I nodded my assent, and stooped over the king.

There were three ways that I might have attempted to withdraw the arrow. The first would be to pluck it out. I have heard of a surgeon in Damascus who bends down the supple branch of a tree and attaches this to the shaft. When he releases the branch, the arrow is whipped out of the living flesh by the strength of the sapling. I have never tried such brutal treatment for I am convinced that very few men would survive it.

The second method would be to push the arrow through the limb or the torso until the barbed head emerges on the far side. To achieve this, it can be driven along its original path with a mallet, like a nail through a plank. Then the barb is sawn off and the shaft drawn free. This treatment is almost as brutal as the first.

My method is the Taita spoon. I have named the spoon after myself in all modesty, for the claims of those others are spurious, and posterity needs to be informed of my genius.

Firstly, I examined the Hyksos arrow that I had salvaged along with the bow from the overturned chariot. I was surprised to find that the arrow-head was of worked flint rather than of bronze. Of course, flint is cheaper and easier to procure in quantity, but I have seldom known a general who tries to economize when setting out to seize a kingdom. This flint arrow-head spoke eloquently of the Hyksos' limited resources, and suggested a reason for his savage attack upon this very Egypt. Wars are fought for land or wealth, and it seemed that the Hyksos was short of both these commodities.

I had to hope that the arrow-head buried in Pharaoh's breast was of the same shape and design. I matched a pair of my spoons to the razor-edged piece of stone. My spoons are of various sizes, and I selected a pair that enclosed the head snugly, masking the wicked barbs with smoothly polished metal.

By this time, the drug had worked its full magic, and Pharaoh lay unconscious upon his cloud-white linen sheets, with the snapped-off arrow standing out as far as my forefinger from the skin, which was wrinkled with age and covered with the frosted curls of his body hair. I laid my ear on his chest once more and heard his breath sigh and gurgle in his lungs. Satisfied that he still lived, I greased the spoons that I had selected with mutton fat, to lubricate their entry into the wound. I laid the spoons close at hand and took up one of my keenest scalpels.

I nodded to the four strong guards that Queen Lostris had selected for me while I was busy with my preparations, and they took hold of Pharaoh's wrists and ankles and held him down firmly. Queen Lostris sat at the king's head and placed the wooden tube from my medical chest between his lips and deep back into his throat. This would keep his windpipe clear and open. It would also prevent him from biting or swallowing his own tongue, or grinding his teeth together and snapping them off, when the pain assaulted him too fiercely.

'First I have to enlarge the wound around the shaft to enable me to reach the head of the arrow,' I muttered to myself, and I pressed the point of the scalpel down along the line of the shaft. Pharaoh's whole body stiffened, but the men held him down remorselessly.

I worked swiftly, for I have learned that speed is crucial in an operation of this nature, if the patient is to survive. I opened a slit on each side of the shaft. The human skin is tough and elastic and would inhibit the entry of the spoons, so I had to get through it.

I dropped the knife and took up the pair of lubricated spoons. Using the arrow-shaft as a guide, I eased them deeper and deeper into the wound, until only the long handles still protruded.

By this time Pharaoh was writhing and twisting in the grip of his restrainers. Sweat was pouring from every pore of his skin, and running back over his shaven skull with its stubble of thin grey hair. His screams rang through the tube in his mouth, and reverberated through the hull of the barge.

I had taught myself to ignore the agonized distress of my patients, and I slid the spoons deeper into the widely distended mouth of the wound until I felt them touch the flint of the arrow-head. This was the delicate part of the operation. Using the handles like a pair of tweezers, I levered the spoons apart and worked them over the arrow-head. When I felt them close of their own accord, I hoped that I had entirely enclosed the coarse flint and masked the barbs.

I took a careful grasp of the handles of the spoons and of the reed shaft of the arrow, and pulled back on them all together. If the barbs were still free, they would have immediately snagged in Pharaoh's flesh and resisted my pull. I could have shouted aloud with relief as I felt it all begin to yield. Still, the suction of the wet and clinging flesh was considerable, and I had to use all my strength to draw the shaft.

Pharaoh's agony was dreadful to hear and behold, as the mass of reed and stone and metal was dragged through his chest. The Red Shepenn drug had long ago ceased to be of any effect, and the pain was raw and savage. I knew I was doing fearful damage, and I could feel tissue and sinew tearing.

401

My own sweat ran down into my eyes and burned and half-blinded me, but I never released my pull until suddenly the blood-smeared arrow came free in my hands and I staggered backwards across the cabin and crashed into the bulkhead. I leaned against it for a moment, exhausted with the effort. I watched the dark, half-congealed blood trickle and spurt from the wound for a long moment, before I could rally myself and stagger back to stem it.

I smeared the wound with precious myrrh and crystallized honey, and then bound it up tightly with clean linen bandages. As I worked, I recited the incantation for the binding up of wounds:

> I bind thee up, oh creature of Seth.
> I stop up thy mouth.
> Retreat before me, red tide.
> Retire before me, red flower of death.
> I banish you, oh red dog of Seth.

This was the recitation for a bleeding wound caused by blade or arrow. There are specific verses for all types of wound, from burns to those inflicted by the fangs or claws of a lion. Learning these is a large part of the training of a physician. I am never certain in my own mind as to just how efficacious these incantations are; however, I believe that I owe it to my patients to employ any possible means at my disposal for their cure.

In the event, Pharaoh seemed much easier after the binding-up, and I could leave him sleeping in the care of his women and go back on deck. I needed the cool river airs to revive me, for the operation had drained me almost as much as it had Pharaoh.

By this time it was evening, and the sun was settling wearily upon the stark western hills and throwing its last ruddy glow over the battlefield. There had been no assault by the Hyksos infantry, and Tanus was still bringing off the remains of his vanquished army from the river-bank to the galleys anchored in the stream.

I watched the boatloads of wounded and exhausted men passing our anchored barge, and I felt a deep compassion for them, as I did for all our people. This would be for ever the most dire day in our history. Then I saw that the dust-cloud of the Hyksos chariots was already beginning to move southwards towards Thebes. The clouds were incarnadined by the sunset to the colour of blood. It was for me a sign, and my compassion turned to dread.

 IT WAS dark by the time that Tanus himself came aboard the state barge. In the light of the torches he looked like one of the corpses from the battlefield. He was pale with fatigue and dust. His cloak was stiff with dried blood and mud, and there were dark, bruised shadows under his eyes. When he saw me, his first concern was to ask after Pharaoh.

'I have removed the arrow,' I told him. 'But the wound is deep and near the heart. He is very weak, but if he survives three days, then I will be able to save him.'

'What of your mistress and her son?' he always asked this, whenever we met.

'Queen Lostris is tired, for she helped me with the operation. But she is with the king now. The prince is as bonny as ever and sleeps now with his nurses.'

I saw Tanus reel on his feet, and knew that he was close to the end of even his great strength. 'You must rest now—' I began, but he shook off my hand.

'Bring lamps here,' he ordered. 'Taita, fetch your writing-brushes and ink-pots and scrolls. I must send a warning to Nembet, lest he walk into the Hyksos trap even as I did.'

So Tanus and I sat half that night on the open deck, and this was the despatch for Nembet that he dictated to me:

I greet you Lord Nembet, Great Lion of Egypt, Commander of the Ra division of the army of Pharaoh. May you live for ever!

Know you that we have encountered the enemy Hyksos at the plain of Abnub. The Hyksos in his strength and ferocity is a terrible foe, and possessed of strange, swift craft that we cannot resist.

Know you further that we have suffered a defeat and that our army is destroyed. We can no longer oppose the Hyksos.

Know you further that Pharaoh is gravely wounded and in danger of his life.

We urge you not to meet the Hyksos in an open field, for his craft are like the wind. Therefore take refuge behind walls of stone, or wait aboard your ships, to turn the enemy aside.

The Hyksos has no ships of his own, and it is by means of our ships alone that we may prevail against him.

We urge you to await our coming before committing your forces to battle.

I call the protection of Horus and all the gods down upon you.

It is Tanus, Lord Harrab, Commander of the Ptah division of the army of Pharaoh, who speaks thus.

I wrote out four copies of this message, and as I completed each, Tanus called for messengers to carry them to the Lord Nembet, Great Lion of Egypt, who was advancing from the south to reinforce us. Tanus sent two fast galleys speeding up-river, each with a fair copy of the despatches. Then he put his best runners ashore on the west bank, the opposite side of the river from the Hyksos army, and sent them off to find Nembet.

'Surely one of your scrolls will win through to Nembet. You can do no more until morning,' I reassured him. 'You must sleep now, for if you destroy yourself, then all of Egypt is destroyed with you.'

Even then he would not go to a cabin, but curled on the deck like a dog, so that he could be instantly ready for any new emergency. But I went to the cabin to be near my king and to give comfort to my mistress.

I was on deck again before the first glimmer of dawn. I arrived to hear Tanus giving orders to burn our fleet. It was not for me to question this decision, but he saw me gape incredulously at him, and when the messengers had been sent away he told me brusquely, 'I have just received the roll-call from my regimental commanders. Of the thirty thousand of my men who stood yesterday on the plain of Abnub to meet the chariots of the Hyksos, only seven thousand remain. Five thousand of those are wounded, and many will still die. Of those who are unwounded, very few are sailors. I am left with only sufficient men to work half our fleet. I must abandon the rest of our ships, but I cannot let them fall into the hands of the Hyksos.'

They used bundles of reeds to start the fires, and once they were set, they burned fiercely. It was a sad and terrible sight to watch, even for me and my mistress, who were not sailors. For Tanus it was far worse. He stood alone in the bows of the state barge, with despair and grief in every line of his face and in the set of those wide shoulders, as he watched his ships burn. For him they were living things, and beautiful.

Before all the court my mistress could not go to his side where she belonged, but she took my hand surreptitiously, and the two of us mourned for Tanus and for all Egypt as we watched those gallant craft burn like torches. The roaring pillars of flame from each vessel were sullied with black smoke, but still their ruddy light rivalled the approach of the sunrise.

At last Tanus gave the order to his hundred remaining galleys to weigh anchor, and our little fleet, laden with wounded and dying men, turned back into the south.

Behind us, the smoke from the funeral pyre of our fleet stood high into the early morning sky, while ahead of us the yellow dust-cloud stretched taller and wider along the east bank of the Nile as the chariot squadrons of the Hyksos drove deeper into the Upper Kingdom, towards helpless Thebes and all her treasures.

It seemed that the gods had turned their backs on Egypt and deserted us completely, for the wind, which usually blew so strongly from the north at this season of the year, died away completely, and then sprang up again with renewed vigour from the south. Thus we were forced to contend with both current and wind, and our ships were deeply laden with their cargoes of wounded. We were slow and heavy in the water, with the depleted crews slaving at the oars. We could not keep pace with the Hyksos army, and it drew away from us inexorably.

I was absorbed with my duties as physician to the king. However, on every other vessel in the fleet, men whom I could have saved were dying in their scores. Every time that I went on deck for a little fresh air and a short break from my vigil at the bedside of Pharaoh, I saw corpses being thrown over the side of the other galleys near us. At each splash there was a swirl of crocodiles beneath the surface. Those awful reptiles followed the fleet like vultures.

Pharaoh rallied strongly, and on the second day I was able to feed him a small bowl of broth. That evening he asked to see the prince again, and Memnon was brought to him.

Memnon was already at the age when he was as restless as a grasshopper and as noisy as a flock of starlings. Pharaoh had always been good with the boy, if inclined to over-indulgence, and Memnon delighted in his company. Already he was a beautiful boy, with clean, strong limbs and his mother's skin and great dark green eyes. His hair was curled like the pelt of a new-born black lamb, but in the sunlight, it was sparked with the flames of Tanus' ruddy mop.

Pharaoh's delight in Memnon was even more poignant than usual. The child and the promise that he had wrung from my mistress were his hope of immortality. Against my wishes he kept the child with him until after sunset. I knew that Memnon's boundless energy and his demands for attention were tiring the king, but I could not intervene until it was time for the prince's supper and he was led away by his nurses.

My mistress and I stayed on at the king's bedside, but he fell almost instantly into a death-like sleep. Even without his white make-up, he was as pale as the linen sheets on which he lay.

The next day was the third since the wounding, and therefore the most dangerous. If he could survive this day, then I knew I could save him. But when I woke in the dawn the cabin was thick with the musky stench of corruption. When I touched Pharaoh's skin, it burned my fingers like a kettle from the hearth.

I called for my mistress, and she came stumbling through from her alcove behind the curtain where she slept.

'What is it, Taita?' She got no further, for the answer was plain upon my face. She stood beside me as I unbound the wound. The binding-up is a high art of the surgeon's skills, and I had sewn the linen bandages in place. Now I snipped the threads that held them and peeled them away.

'Merciful Hapi, pray for him!' Queen Lostris gagged at the stench. The crusted black scab that corked the mouth of the wound burst open, and thick green pus poured out in a slow and viscous stream.

'Mortification!' I whispered. This was the surgeon's nightmare, this evil humour that struck upon the third day and spread through the body like winter fire in the dry papyrus beds.

'What can we do?' she asked, and I shook my head.

'He will be dead before nightfall,' I told her, but we waited beside his bed for the inevitable. As the word spread through the ship that Pharaoh was dying, so the cabin filled with priests and women and courtiers. We waited in silence.

Tanus was the last to arrive, and he stood at the back of the throng with his helmet under his arm, in the position of respect and mourning. His gaze rested not on the death-bed, but upon Queen Lostris. She kept her face averted from his, but I knew that she was aware of him in every fibre of her body.

She covered her head with an embroidered linen shawl, but above the waistband of her skirt, she was naked. Since the prince had been weaned, her breasts had lost their heavy burden of milk. She was as slim as a virgin, and childbirth had not scarred her bosom or her supple belly with silver lines of striae. Her skin was as smooth and unblemished as though it had been freshly anointed with perfumed oil.

I laid wet cloths upon Pharaoh's burning body in an attempt to cool the fever, but the heat evaporated the moisture and I was forced to change them at short intervals. Pharaoh tossed about restlessly and cried out in delirium, haunted by all the terrors and monsters of the other world, who waited to receive him.

At times he recited snatches from the Book of the Dead. From childhood the priests had taught him to memorize the book that was the key and the map through the shades to the far fields of paradise:

> The crystal path has twenty-one turnings.
> The narrow way is thin as the blade of bronze.
> The goddess who guards the second pylon
> is treacherous and her ways are devious.
> Lady of flame, whore of the universe,
> with the mouth of a lioness,
> your vagina swallows men up,
> they are lost in your milky dugs.

Gradually his voice and his movements became weaker, and a little after the sun had made its noon, he gave one last shuddering sigh and was still. I stooped over him and felt for the life-throb in his throat, but there was none, and the skin was cooling under my touch.

'Pharaoh is dead,' I said softly, and closed the lids over his staring eyes. 'May he live for ever!'

The mourning cry went up from all who were assembled there, and my mistress led the royal women in the wild ululation of grief. It was a sound that chilled me and made invisible insects crawl upon my skin, so I left the cabin as soon as I was able. Tanus followed me out on to the deck and seized my arm.

'You did all in your power to save him?' he demanded roughly. 'This was not another of your devices?'

I knew that this unkind treatment of me was an expression of his own guilt and fear, so I was gentle in my reply. 'He was slain by the Hyksos arrow. I did all that was in my power to save him. It was the destiny of the Mazes of Ammon-Ra, and there is no guilt or fault in any of us.'

He sighed and placed one strong arm around my shoulders. 'I had not foreseen any of this. I thought only of my love for the queen and for our son. I should rejoice that she is free, but I cannot. Too much is lost and destroyed. All of us are merely grains of dhurra corn in the grinding-mill of the Mazes.'

'There will be a time of happiness for all of us hereafter,' I reassured him, although I had no basis for this claim. 'But there is still a sacred duty on my mistress, and through her, on you and me also.' And I reminded him of the oath that Queen Lostris had sworn to the king, that she would preserve his earthly body and give it proper burial to allow his *Ka* to move on to the fields of paradise.

'Tell me how I can help in this,' Tanus replied simply, 'but remember that the Hyksos is sweeping through the Upper Kingdom ahead of us, and I cannot guarantee that Pharaoh's tomb will not be violated.'

'Then, if needs be, we must find another tomb for him. Our first concern must be to preserve his body. In this heat it will be decaying and crawling with maggots before the sun sets. I am not skilled in the embalmer's art, but I know of only one way in which we can keep our trust.'

Tanus sent his sailors down into the barge's hold, and they swung up one of the huge clay jars of pickled olives from our stores. Then, under my instructions, he emptied the jar and refilled it with boiling water. While the water was still hot, he mixed into it three sacks of the finest-quality sea salt. Then he filled four smaller wine jars with the same brine and set them all out on the deck to cool.

In the meantime I was working alone in the cabin. My mistress had wanted to help me. She felt that it was part of her duty to her dead husband, but I sent her away to care for the prince.

I slit open Pharaoh's corpse down his left flank from ribs to hip-bone. Through this opening I removed the contents of chest and belly, freeing them along the diaphragm with the knife. Naturally, I left his heart in place, for this is the organ of life and intelligence. I left the kidneys also, for these are the vessels of water and represent the sacred Nile. I packed the cavity with salt and then sutured it closed with cat-gut. I did not have an embalming-spoon to push up through the nostrils and remove that soft yellow mush from the gourd of the skull, so I left it in place. In any event, it was of no importance. The viscera I divided into its separate parts: liver, lungs, stomach and entrails. I washed out the stomach and intestines with brine, which was a loathsome task.

When this was done, I took the opportunity to examine the king's lungs minutely. The right lung was healthy and pink, but the left lung had been pierced by the arrow, and had collapsed like a punctured bladder. It was filled with rotten black blood and pus. I was amazed that the old man had lived so long with such an injury. I felt that I was absolved. No physician could have saved him, and there was no fault or failure in my treatment.

At last I ordered the sailors to bring in the cooled jars of brine. Tanus helped me to fold Pharaoh's body into the foetal position and we placed him in the olive vat. I made certain that he was completely immersed in the strong brine. We packed his viscera into the smaller Canopic wine jars. We sealed all the jars with pitch and wax, and lashed them securely into the reinforced compartment below decks in which the king stored his treasure. I think Pharaoh must have been content to rest thus, surrounded by gold and bars of silver.

I had done my best to help my mistress make good her vow. In Thebes I would hand the king's body over to the embalmers, if the Hyksos had not arrived there first, and if the city and its inhabitants still existed by the time we reached it.

 WHEN WE reached the walled city of Asyut, it was apparent that the Hyksos had left only a small force to invest it, and had continued southwards with their main army. Even though it was merely a detachment with less than a hundred chariots, the Hyksos besiegers were far too strong for us to attack them with our decimated army.

Tanus' main aim was to rescue Remrem and his five thousand, who were within the city walls, and then to push on up-river to join forces with Lord Nembet and his thirty thousand reinforcements. Anchored out in the main stream of the river, secure from attack by those deadly chariots, Tanus was able to signal his intentions to Remrem on the city walls.

Years before, I had helped Tanus draw up a system of signals, using two coloured flags by means of which he could spell out a message to any other within sight, across a valley, from peak to peak, or from city wall to plain and river. With the flags Tanus was able to warn Remrem to be ready for us that night. Then, under cover of darkness, twenty of our galleys raced into the beach below the city walls. At the same moment, Remrem threw open the side-gates, and, at the head of his regiment, fought his way through the Hyksos pickets. Before the enemy were able to harness their horses, Remrem and all his men were safely embarked.

Immediately, Tanus signalled the rest of the flotilla to weigh anchor. He abandoned the city of Asyut to sack and plunder, and we bore on upstream under oars. For the rest of that night, whenever we looked back over the stern, we saw the flames of the burning city lighting the northern horizon.

'Let those poor bastards forgive me,' Tanus muttered to me. 'I had no choice but to sacrifice them. My duty lies south of here in Thebes.'

He was soldier enough to make the hard choice without flinching, but man enough to grieve bitterly over it. I admired him then as much as I loved him.

 REMREM TOLD us that our signal frigates had sailed past Asyut the previous day, and that by now the despatches that I had drawn up on Tanus' behalf must be in Lord Nembet's hands.

Remrem was also able to give us some intelligence and news of the Hyksos, and his sweep to the south. Remrem had captured two Egyptian deserters and traitors who had gone over to the enemy and who had entered Asyut to spy on the defenders. Under torture they had howled like the jackals they were, and before they died, had told Remrem much about the Hyksos that was of value and interest to us.

The Hyksos king, whom we had so disastrously encountered on the plain of Abnub, was named Salitis. His tribe was of Semitic blood and originally a nomadic and pastoral people who had lived in the Zagros mountains near Lake Van. In this my first impression of these terrible Asians was confirmed. I had guessed at their Semitic origins from their features, but I wondered how

411

a pastoral people had evolved such an extraordinary vehicle as a wheeled chariot, and where they had found that marvellous animal that we Egyptians now spoke of as a horse, and feared as though it were a creature from the underworld.

In other areas it seemed that the Hyksos were a backward people. They were unable to read or write, and their government was a harsh tyranny by their single king and ruler, this bearded Salitis. We Egyptians hated him and feared him even more than we did those wild creatures that drew his chariot.

The chief god of the Hyksos was named Sutekh, the god of storms. It needed no deep religious instruction to recognize in him our own dreaded Seth. Their choice of god was fitting, and their behaviour did the god honour. No civilized people would burn and plunder and murder as they did. The fact that we torture traitors cannot be weighed in the same scale as the atrocities committed by these barbarians.

It is a truth that I have often observed, that a nation chooses its gods to suit its own nature. The Philistines worship Baal, and cast live infants into the fiery furnace that is his mouth. The black Cushite tribes worship monsters and creatures from the underworld with the most bizarre rituals. We Egyptians worship just and decent gods who are benevolent towards mankind and make no demands for human sacrifice. Then the Hyksos have Sutekh.

It seemed that Remrem's captives were not the only Egyptian traitors travelling with the enemy host. With a hot coal in his anus, one of Remrem's captives had told of some great Egyptian lord from the Upper Kingdom who sat upon King Salitis' war council. When I heard this, I remembered how I had wondered at the knowledge that the Hyksos had displayed of our order of battle upon the plain of Abnub. I had guessed then at the presence of a spy among them who knew our secrets.

If any of this was true, then we must expect that the enemy knew all our strengths and weaknesses. They must know the plans and defences of all our cities. Especially they would know of that rich treasure that Pharaoh had accumulated in his funerary temple.

'Perhaps this explains the haste with which King Salitis is

driving on towards Thebes,' I suggested to Tanus. 'We can expect them to attempt a crossing of the Nile at the first opportunity that presents itself to them.' And Tanus cursed bitterly.

'If Horus is kind, he will deliver this traitorous Egyptian lord into my hands.' He punched his fist into the palm of his other hand. 'We must prevent Salitis from crossing the river, our ships are the only advantage that we hold over him. I must exploit them to full advantage.'

He stamped about the deck, and looked up at the sky. 'When will this foul wind swing back into the north? Every hour the enemy's chariots draw farther ahead of us. Where is Nembet's fleet? We must join our forces and hold the river-line.'

 THAT AFTERNOON on the poop-deck of the royal barge the state council of Upper Egypt convened before the throne. The high priest of Osiris represented the spiritual body, Lord Merseket the chancellor stood for the temporal body of the state, and Tanus, Lord Harrab stood for the military authority.

Between them the three lords lifted Queen Lostris to the throne of this very Egypt, and placed her son upon her lap. While every man and woman on board the barge raised their voices in a loyal salute, the other ships of the fleet sailed past, and even the wounded soldiers dragged themselves to the rail to cheer the new regent and the young heir to the great throne of Egypt.

The high priest of Osiris strapped the false beard of the kingship upon my mistress's chin, and it did nothing to detract from her beauty and manifest womanhood. Lord Merseket bound the lion's tail around her waist and settled the tall red and white crown upon her brow. Finally, Tanus mounted the throne to place the crook and golden flail in her hands. Now Memnon saw the shining toys that Tanus carried towards him, and reached out to snatch them from him.

'A king indeed! He knows the crook is his by right,' Tanus applauded proudly, and the court roared their approval of this precocious behaviour.

413

I think this was the first time that any of us had laughed since that dreadful day on the field of Abnub. It seemed to me that the laughter was a catharsis, and that it marked a new beginning for all of us. Up until that moment we had been overwhelmed by the shock of defeat and the loss of Pharaoh. But now, as the great lords of Egypt went forward one at a time to kneel before the throne on which sat this lovely young woman and her royal child, a fresh spirit sprang up in all of us. We were rescued from the apathy of despair, and our will to fight and to endure was resuscitated.

Tanus was last of all of them to kneel before the throne and swear his allegiance. As she looked down upon him, Queen Lostris' adoration for him was so evident that it suffused her lovely face and shone like the sunrise from those dark green eyes. I was amazed that no other in all that throng seemed aware of it.

That evening after the sun had set, my mistress sent me to the bridge of the state barge with a message for the commander of her armies. She summoned him to a council of war in the main cabin. This time Tanus dared not refuse her, for he had very recently sworn an oath of obedience.

This extraordinary war council of which I was the only witness had barely begun, before the new regent of Egypt imperiously banished me from the cabin, and sent me to guard the door and turn away all other visitors. The last glimpse that I had of them as I drew the heavy curtain was as they fell into each other's arms. So great was their need, and so long had they been denied, that they rushed at each other like deadly enemies joining in mortal combat, rather than lovers.

The happy sounds of this engagement persisted for most of the night, and I was relieved that we were not at anchor but driving on up-river in haste to join with Lord Nembet. The clunk and swish of the oars, the boom of the drum setting the stroke and the chants of the rowers on their benches almost drowned out the tumult in the royal cabin.

When he came to the poop-deck at the change of the night-watch, Tanus had the smile and the satisfied air of a general who had just won a famous victory. My mistress followed him on deck shortly afterwards, and she glowed with a new and ethereal beauty that startled even me, who was accustomed to her loveliness. For the rest of that day she was loving and kind to all around her, and found numerous occasions to consult the commander of her army. Thus Prince Memnon and I were able to spend most of the day together, a circumstance that suited both of us very well.

With the prince's dubious assistance I had already started carving a series of wooden models. One of these was a chariot and wooden horses. Another was a wheel on an axle that I was experimenting with.

Memnon stood on tiptoe to watch the wheel spin smoothly on its miniature hub.

'A solid disc is too heavy, don't you agree, Mem? See how swiftly it loses momentum and slows down.'

'Give it to me!' he demanded, and snatched at the spinning disc. It flew from his chubby fingers, dashed to the deck and shattered into four almost equal segments.

'You are a Hyksos ruffian,' I told him sternly, which he seemed to take as a great compliment, and I went down on my knees to gather up my poor model.

The broken segments still lay in a circular pattern, and, before my hand touched them, I had a strange aberration of vision. In the eye of my mind, the solid segments of wood became spaces, while the cracks between them appeared solid.

'Sweet breath of Horus! You've done it, Mem.' I hugged him. 'A rim supported by struts from the hub! When you are Pharaoh, what other miracles will you perform for us?'

Thus did the Prince Royal, Memnon the first of that name, Ruler of the Dawn – with just a little help from his friend – conceive of the spoked wheel. Little did I dream then that one day the two of us together would ride to glory upon it.

WE CAME upon the first of the Egyptian dead before noon. He came floating down the river with his bloated belly buoying him up, and his face gazing blankly at the sky. There was a black crow perched upon his chest. It picked out his eyes and threw back its head to swallow them one at a time.

In silence we stood at the ship's rail and watched the dead man float serenely by.

'He wears the kilt of the Lion Guards,' Tanus said quietly. 'The Lions are the spear-head of Nembet's army. I pray to Horus that there will be no others following this one down the river.'

But there were. Ten more, then a hundred. More and still more, until the surface of the river from bank to bank was carpeted by floating corpses. They were thick as the leaves of the water-hyacinth which clog the irrigation canals in summer.

At last we found one who still lived. He was a captain of the Lion Guards who had been seconded to Nembet's staff. He clung to a mat of floating papyrus stems in the current. We fished him from the water and I attended to his wounds. The head of a stone mace had shattered the bones of his shoulder and he would never use that arm again.

When he had recovered sufficiently to speak, Tanus squatted beside his mattress.

'What of Lord Nembet?'

'Lord Nembet is slain, and all his staff with him,' the captain told him hoarsely.

'Did Nembet not receive my despatch warning him of the Hyksos?'

'He received it on the eve of the battle, and he laughed as he read it.'

'Laughed?' demanded Tanus. 'How could he laugh?'

'He said that the puppy was destroyed – forgive me, Lord Tanus, but that was what he called you – and now sought to cover his stupidity and cowardice with spurious messages. He said that he would fight the battle in the classic manner.'

'The arrogant old fool,' Tanus lamented. 'But tell me the rest of it.'

'Lord Nembet deployed upon the east bank, with the river at

his back. The enemy fell upon us like the wind, and drove us into the water.'

'How many of our men escaped?' Tanus asked softly.

'I believe that I am the only one of those who went ashore with Lord Nembet who survived. I saw no other left alive. The slaughter upon the river-bank was beyond my power to describe to you.'

'All our most famous regiments decimated,' Tanus mourned. 'We are left defenceless, except for our ships. What happened to Nembet's fleet? Was it anchored in midstream?'

'Lord Nembet anchored the greater part of the fleet, but he beached fifty galleys in our rear.'

'Why would he do that?' Tanus stormed. 'The safety of the ships is the first principle of our standard battle plan.'

'I do not know Lord Nembet's mind, except he may have kept them at hand to re-embark our troops expeditiously, should your warning have proved justified.'

'What then is the fate of our fleet? Nembet lost our army, but did he save the ships?' Tanus' tone was rough with anger and distress.

'Of the ships that were anchored in midstream, most are scuttled and burned by the skeleton crews. I saw the flames and the smoke even from where I lay on my papyrus float. A few of the others cut the anchor-lines and fled south towards Thebes. I shouted to the crews as they sailed past me, but so great was their terror that they would not heave-to and pick me from the water.'

'The fifty ships that lay upon the beach—' Tanus broke off and drew a deep breath before he finished the question. 'What has become of the squadron that was beached?'

'It has fallen into the hands of the Hyksos.' The captain trembled as he answered, for he dreaded Tanus' anger. 'I looked back as I drifted with the current, and I saw the enemy swarming aboard the galleys on the beach.'

Tanus stood up and strode to the bows. He stared upstream from where the corpses and the scorched and blackened planks of Nembet's fleet still drifted down upon the steady green flow of the river. I went to stand at his side, to be ready to halter his rage when it came.

'So the proud old fool has sacrificed his life, and the lives of all his men, simply to spite me. They should build a pyramid to his folly, for Egypt has never seen the like of it.'

'That is not all his folly,' I murmured, and Tanus nodded grimly.

'No, not all his folly. He has given the Hyksos the means to cross the river. Sweet milk of Isis' breast, but once they are across the Nile we are truly finished.'

Perhaps the goddess heard him call her name, for at that moment I felt the wind that had blown so long into our faces veer. Tanus felt it also. He spun on his heel and roared an order to his officers on the poop-deck.

'The wind turns fair. Make a general signal to the fleet. Set all sail. Relieve the men at the oars every hour by the water-clock. Drummers, increase the beat to flank speed. Make all haste southwards.'

The wind settled strongly into the north. Our sails filled and stiffened like the bellies of pregnant women. The drums gave the rowers the stroke, and we breasted the flow of the river as the whole battle-fleet raced southwards.

'All thanks to the goddess for this wind,' Tanus shouted. 'Divine Isis, let us be in time to catch them on the water.'

THE STATE barge was slow and ungainly. She began falling astern of the fleet. It seemed that the fates had intervened once more, for Tanus' old galley that he had loved so well, the *Breath of Horus*, was sailing close to us in the formation.

She was under a new captain now, but she was still a formidable little vessel, built for speed and attack. The sharp bronze ramming-horn protruded from her bows, just above the water line. Tanus hailed her alongside the barge and transferred his Blue Crocodile standard into her, taking over the command from her new captain.

My place was with my mistress and the prince. I am not certain how I found myself on board the *Breath of Horus*, standing on the poop beside Tanus, as we tore along upstream. Sometimes I am

418

guilty of folly almost as monumental as that recently demonstrated by Lord Nembet. I remember only that as soon as the state barge began to fall away astern, I began bitterly to regret my impetuosity. I thought of telling Tanus that I had changed my mind, and asking him to put about and drop me once more on the deck of the barge. But after one glance at his face, I decided that I would rather face the Hyksos again.

From the deck of the *Breath of Horus*, Tanus issued his orders. By flag and voice-hail, they were passed from vessel to vessel. Without slackening the pace of our advance, Tanus redeployed the fleet. He gathered up the galleys around him, as he forged his way to the head of the flotilla.

The wounded and those no longer fit to fight were transferred to the slower vessels which fell back to keep pace with the state barge. The faster galleys in the van were cleared for action. They were manned mostly by Remrem's fresh troops whom we had relieved from the siege of Asyut. They were spoiling for a chance to avenge the disgrace of Abnub. Tanus hoisted the Blue Crocodile standard at his masthead of the *Breath of Horus*, and they roared with the lust of battle. How swiftly he had been able to stiffen their spirit since that bloody defeat!

The signs of Nembet's recent catastrophe became ever more obvious with each league that we covered. The corpses and wreckage and all the flotsam of war were stranded in the papyrus beds on each side of the river. Then, at last, in the sky ahead of us we saw once again the dust of the chariots mingling with the smoke from the cooking-fires of the Hyksos camp.

'It is as I had hoped,' Tanus exulted. 'They have halted their headlong advance on Thebes, now that Nembet has presented them with the means of crossing the river. But they are not sailors, and they will have difficulty embarking their men and chariots. If Horus is kind, we will arrive in time to help them on their way.'

In extended battle order we swept around the last wide bend of the river, and we found the Hyksos before us. By one of those happy freaks of war, we had arrived precisely at the moment that they were fully committed to the crossing of the Nile.

There were the fifty captured galleys straggling across the river in the most lubberly fashion. The sails and sheets were in a tangle and every oarsman was keeping his own stroke. The paddles were splashing and crab-catching. The steering of each vessel was shaky and erratic, completely out of phase with the ships around it.

We could see that most of the Hyksos manning the decks were in full bronze armour. Clearly they had not realized just how difficult it is to swim in that state of dress. They stared at us in consternation as we bore down upon them. Now at last the roles were reversed. We were in our element, and they were flying in the wind like a torn sail.

I had a few moments to study the enemy, as we closed. The vast bulk of the Hyksos army was still upon the east bank. They had gone into bivouac, and they were so numerous that their encampment stretched away to the foothills of the desert, as far as I could see from the deck of the *Breath of Horus*.

King Salitis was sending only a small force across the river. Almost certainly they were under orders to race down the west bank and to capture the funerary temple of Pharaoh Mamose, before we were able to remove the treasure.

We bore down rapidly on the convoy of Hyksos ships, and I shouted to Tanus above the beat of the drums and the blood-thirsty cheers of our rascals, 'They have taken their horses across already. Look over there!'

Almost unprotected, except for a few armed guards, there was a huge herd of these terrible animals gathered on the west bank. I guessed there were several hundred of them; even at this distance, we could make out their long, flowing manes and tails streaming in the strong north wind. They were a disturbing sight to us. Some of the men around me shuddered and swore with loathing of them. I heard one of them mutter darkly, 'The Hyksos feed those monsters of theirs on human flesh, like tame lions or jackals. That is the reason for this slaughter. They must have food for them. We can only guess how many of our comrades are already in their bellies.'

I could not contradict him, and I even had a queasy feeling in my guts that he might be speaking the truth. I turned my attention from those beautiful but gory monsters to the galleys in the stream ahead of us.

'We have caught them taking the chariots and the men over,' I pointed out to Tanus. The decks of Nembet's captured vessels were piled high with chariots and equipment, and crowded with the Hyksos charioteers who were being ferried across. As they realized their predicament, some of the Hyksos tried to turn and run back for the east bank. They collided with the ships that followed them, and locked together, they drifted helplessly on the current.

Tanus laughed savagely to see their confusion, and shouted into the wind, 'General signal. Increase the beat to attack speed. Light the fire-arrows.'

The Hyksos had never experienced an attack with fire-arrows, and at the thought of what was coming, I laughed with Tanus, but nervously. Then suddenly I stiffened and my laughter choked off.

'Tanus!' I seized his arm. 'Look! Look at the galley dead ahead! On the poop. There is our traitor.'

For a moment Tanus did not recognize the tall, stately figure at the rail of the galley, for he wore fish-scale armour and a tall Hyksos war helmet. Then abruptly he roared with anger and outrage, 'Intef! Why did we not guess it was him?'

'I see it so clearly now. He has guided Salitis to this very Egypt. He went east and deliberately tempted the Hyksos with accounts of the treasures of Egypt.' My outrage and hatred matched those of Tanus.

Tanus threw up the bow Lanata and loosed an arrow, but the range was long and the point glanced off Lord Intef's armour. I saw his head jerk round at the shock, and he looked across the water directly at us. He singled us out, Tanus and myself, and for a moment I thought I saw fear in his eyes. Then he ducked out of sight below the gunwale of the galley.

Our leading squadron flew into the pack of confused and milling shipping. With a tearing crunch, our bronze ramming-horn struck Intef's galley amidships, and I was thrown off my feet by the impact. When I struggled up again, the oarsmen had already backed water, and with another rending screech of timbers we disengaged from the stricken ship.

At the same time, our archers were pouring a heavy rain of fire-arrows into her. The heads were bound with pitch-soaked papyrus stems that burned like comets, each leaving a trail of sparks and smoke as they flew into the sails and top hamper. The north wind fanned the flames and they leaped up the rigging with a fiendish exuberance.

The waters flooded in through the gaping hole we had ripped in her belly, and she listed over sharply. The sails caught fire and burned with startling rapidity. The heat singed my eyelashes even at that distance. The heavy mainsail, burning fiercely, fluttered down over the deck, trapping the crew and crowded charioteers beneath it. Their screams shrilled in our ears as their hair and clothing burst into flames. I remembered the plain at Abnub and felt no pity as they leaped in flames from the ship's side and were drawn under by the weight of their armour. Only a swirl of ripples and a lingering puff of steam marked where each of them had disappeared.

All down the line, the Hyksos galleys were burning and sinking. They had neither the experience nor the skill to counter our attack, and they were as helpless as we had been before the assault of their chariots. Our ships backed off and charged again, crushing in their hulls and sending torrents of flaming arrows into them.

I was watching the first galley that we had attacked, seeking another glimpse of Lord Intef. She was almost gone when suddenly he reappeared. He had thrown off his helmet and his armour, and wore only a linen breech clout. He balanced easily on the gunwale of the sinking ship, and then, as the flames reached out to embrace him, he joined his hands above his head and dived overboard.

He was a son of the Nile, at home in her waters. He knifed through the surface, and came up a minute later and fifty paces from where he had struck, with his long wet hair sleeked back, so that he looked like a swimming otter.

'There he goes!' I screamed at Tanus. 'Run the swine under.'

Instantly Tanus gave the order to turn the *Breath of Horus*, but quick as the helmsman was on the steering-oar, she was slow to come around. Meanwhile, Lord Intef slipped through the water like a fish, reaching out overarm for the east bank and the protection of his Hyksos allies.

'Swing hard!' Tanus signalled his starboard bank of oars, and they thrust the bows around. As soon as we were on line with the swimmer, Tanus gave the order to pull together, and we shot in pursuit. By now Lord Intef was far ahead and close in to the bank, where five thousand Hyksos archers waited with their long recurved bows strung and ready to give him covering fire.

'Seth piss on them!' Tanus yelled in defiance. 'We will take Intef out from under their noses.' And he drove the *Breath of Horus* directly at them, bearing down upon the lone swimming figure.

As we came within range of the shore, the Hyksos loosed a volley at us that darkened the sky, and their arrows fell in a whistling cloud around us. They dropped so thickly that the deck soon bristled with them like the quills in a goose's wing, and some of our sailors were struck and fell writhing and bleeding from their benches.

But we were already close on Intef, and he looked back over his shoulder and I saw the terror in his face as he realized he could not escape our sharp prow. I ignored the arrows and ran to the bows to scream down at him, 'I hated you from the first day we met. I hated every loathsome touch. I want to watch you die. You are evil! Evil!'

He heard me. I saw it in his eyes, and then his dark gods intervened yet again. One of the sinking Hyksos galleys drifted down upon us, spouting fire and smoke. If she had touched us we would have gone up with her in a tower of flame. Tanus was forced to put the steering-oar over, and to signal urgently for his oarsmen to back-water. The burning galley drifted between the shore and where we lay heaved-to. Lord Intef was hidden from my view, but when the burning galley was past, I saw him again. Three brawny Hyksos charioteers were dragging him from the water and up the steep bank.

He paused at the top of the bank and looked back at us, and then disappeared from sight, leaving me trembling with rage and frustration. Our men were still being struck down by the falling arrows, so Tanus gave the order, and we wheeled away and sped back to join in the destruction of those few vessels of the convoy that were still afloat.

As the last of these listed over and then rolled on to her back, the green Nile waters poured into her and quenched the flames in a hissing cloud of steam. Our archers leaned over the side and shot the few surviving Hyksos who splashed weakly on the surface.

Immediately they were all drowned, Tanus turned his attention to the west bank and to the small party of the enemy and the herd of horses that were stranded there. As our galley sped in to the shore, the Hyksos herders scattered and ran, but our men leaped ashore, sword in hand, and raced after them. The Hyksos were charioteers, and accustomed to riding into battle. Our lads were foot-soldiers and trained to run. Like a pack of hounds after a jackal, our men isolated and surrounded them. They hacked them down and left a hundred bleeding corpses scattered across the green fields of standing dhurra corn.

I had jumped ashore behind the first wave of our troops. I had serious business in mind. There was no point in making models and designing chariots without a means of driving the spoked wheels that I had seen in my imagination.

It required an enormous act of courage on my part to start towards that herd of terrible creatures that the Hyksos herders had abandoned close to the water's edge. Each step was an effort of will, for there were many hundreds of them, and they were obviously restless and alarmed by the shouting and the running of men and the clash of arms. I was certain that at any moment they would rush at me like wounded lions. I imagined them gobbling my still warm and twitching flesh, and my courage evaporated and I could go no closer. From a distance of a hundred paces, I stood staring in dreadful fascination at these savage predators, but I was poised to turn and rush back to the safety of the galley at the first sign of an attack.

This was the first opportunity that I had been given to study these animals. They were mostly of a dun colour, but with subtle shadings of bay and chestnut and roan. One or two of them were as black as Seth. They stood as tall as a man, with a full barrel-chest, and long necks that arched gracefully. Their manes were like the tresses of a beautiful woman, and their hides glowed in the sunlight, as though they had been burnished.

One of those nearest to me threw back its head and rolled its upper lip, and I recoiled as I saw the great square white teeth that lined its jaw. It kicked its hind-legs and emitted such a terrifying neighing sound that I turned and started back towards the ship with some alacrity.

Then a hoarse yell from one of our soldiers near me arrested my cowardly retreat. 'Kill the Hyksos monsters!'

'Kill the monsters!' The cry was taken up by the others.

'No!' I screamed, and my concern for my own safety was forgotten. 'No! Save the horses. We need them.'

My voice was lost in the angry war-cry of our troops, as they rushed at the herd of horses, with their shields raised and their swords still dripping with the blood of the herders. Some of the men paused to nock arrows to the bow and fire them into the herd.

'No!' I cried, as a glossy black stallion reared and screamed, with an arrow standing out of his withers.

'No! Please, no!' I cried again, as one of the sailors ran in with a light war-axe and hacked through the fetlock joint of a young mare. She was crippled by the blow and could not escape the next stroke of the axe that caught her between the ears and dropped her kicking in the dust.

'Leave them! Leave them!' I pleaded, but the arrows brought down a dozen of the animals, and the swords and axes maimed and killed a dozen more before the herd broke under the assault, and three hundred horses bolted and went galloping out in a mass across the dusty western plain towards the desert.

I shaded my eyes to watch them go, and it seemed to me that part of my heart went with them. When they had disappeared, I ran to protect and tend to those animals that were left maimed and arrowed amongst the papyrus beds. But the soldiers were ahead of me. So great was their fury that they gathered around the fallen carcasses. In a frenzy of hatred, they plunged their blades into the unresisting flesh and hacked at the broken heads.

A little to one side stood an isolated clump of papyrus reeds. Behind this, and screened from the rampaging soldiers, stood the black stallion that I had first seen hit by an arrow. He was sorely struck and staggering as he limped forward, the arrow deep in his chest. Without thought for my own safety, I ran towards him, and then stopped as he turned to face me.

Only then did I realize my danger. Here was a wounded beast that, like a lion in the same straits, must surely charge at me. The stallion and I stared at each other, and I felt fear fall away like a discarded cloak from my shoulders.

His eyes were huge and swimming with pain. Gentle eyes, beautiful eyes that made my heart swell with pity. He made a soft, fluttering sound, and limped towards me. I held out my hand and touched his muzzle and it felt like warm Arabian silk. He came directly to me, and pressed his forehead to my chest in a gesture of trust and appeal that was almost human. I knew that he was asking for my help.

Instinctively I flung my arms around his neck and embraced him. I wanted more than anything in my life at that moment to save him, but from his nostrils warm blood trickled down my chest. I knew he was hit through the lungs and that he was dying. He was far beyond any help that I could give him.

'My poor darling. What have those stupid, ignorant bastards done to you?' I whispered. Dimly in my distress and spiritual agony, I realized that my life had changed again, and that this dying creature had made that change. Somehow I seemed to sense that, in the years ahead, wherever I left my footsteps in the African earth, the hoof-prints of a horse would lie beside them. I had found another great love to fill my days.

The stallion made that fluttering sound once more and his breath was warm on my skin. Then his legs collapsed under him and he fell heavily on his side and lay gasping air into his punctured lungs. Bright red bubbles frothed from the wound in his chest. I went down beside him, and lifted that noble head into my lap and waited with him until he died. Then I stood up and went back to where the *Breath of Horus* was beached.

It was difficult to see my way, for my own hot tears blinded me. Once again I cursed myself for a soft and sentimental fool, but that never did much to help me brace myself. I was always so vulnerable to suffering in another creature, human or otherwise, especially in one that was noble and beautiful.

'Damn you, Taita! Where have you been?' Tanus railed at me as I scrambled aboard. 'There is a battle raging. The whole army cannot wait around while you have another of your famous daydreams.' Yet for all his bluster, he had not deserted me.

TANUS WOULD not even hear me out, but cut brusquely across my request for leave to follow the herd of runaway horses out into the desert, and for men to go with me.

'I want no truck with those foul and unholy creatures!' he shouted at me. 'I only regret that my men let them escape and that they did not slaughter the lot of them. Let us hope that the lions and the jackals make good that default.' I realized then that he hated them as much as did the most ignorant lout in his regiments.

'Were you there on the plain of Abnub?' I do not usually indulge in loud argument, but his intransigence infuriated me. 'Or was that some other dull-witted oaf standing beside me? Did you not see the future charge at you on hooves and wheels and chop your men to jackal-food? Do you not understand that without chariot and horse, you and this Egypt we know are finished?'

This amicable discussion was taking place on the poop-deck of the *Breath of Horus*. Tanus' officers were silent and stiff with shock to hear a slave address a Great Lion of Egypt and the commander of all her armies as a dull-witted oaf. However, I was past all restraint and I rushed on.

'The gods have given you this wonderful gift. Three hundred horses placed in your hands! I will build you the chariots to go with them. Are you so blind that you cannot see it?'

'I have my ships!' Tanus roared back at me. 'I don't need these foul man-eating beasts. They are an abomination in the face of decent men and all benevolent gods. They are creatures of Seth and Sutekh, and I want no part of them.'

427

Too late I realized that I had pushed Tanus into a position from which he could not retreat. He was a clever and intelligent man, until his pride hamstrung his reason. I moderated my tone and made my voice mellifluous.

'Tanus, please listen to me. I have held the head of one of these animals in my hands. They are strong, but strangely gentle. Their eyes shine with the intelligence of a faithful dog. They do not eat meat—'

'How could you tell that from one brief touch?' he sneered at me, still proud and affronted.

'The teeth,' I answered. 'They do not possess the fangs or claws of a carnivore. Pigs are the only hoofed creatures that eat flesh, and these are no pigs.'

I saw him waver at last, and I pressed my advantage. 'If that is not enough, look then at the stores that the Hyksos have brought across the river. Do they need that mountain of fodder to feed a pride of meat-eating lions?'

'Meat or fodder, I will not argue further. You have heard my decision. We will let those cursed horses perish in the wilderness. That is my decision, and it is final.' He stamped away, but I muttered under my breath, 'Final, is it? We will see about that.'

There have been very few occasions when I have not been able to have my own way with my mistress, and hers was now the highest authority in this very Egypt. I went to her that very evening, as soon as the royal barge came once more under the protection of the war galleys.

Without the knowledge of her commander and lover, I showed her the tiny working model of a chariot with the miniature carved horses in the traces, which I had crafted for her. Queen Lostris was enchanted by it. Naturally she had never seen the squadrons of war chariots in full flight, and had not conceived for them the same hatred as had the bulk of her army. Having captured her full attention with the model chariot, I then described the death of the stallion in such harrowing detail that both of us were reduced to tears. She can resist my tears as little as I am able to resist hers.

'You must go immediately and rescue these marvellous animals from the desert. When you have them, I order you to build a squadron of chariots for my armies,' she cried.

If Tanus had spoken to her before I had the chance to persuade her, I doubt that she would have given that order, and the history of our world would have been very different. As it was, Tanus was furious with my deception, and we came as close to a permanent rift in our relationship as we ever had in all the years.

It was fortunate that I had been summarily ordered ashore by Queen Lostris, and was able to escape the full force of his wrath. I had only a few hours in which to gather around me a few helpers, and the chief of these was the most unlikely of them all.

I had never taken to Hui, the Shrike whom we had captured at Gallala and who had commanded one of the galleys which Tanus had scuttled at Abnub. He was now a captain without a ship, and a man looking for a reason to go on. He sought me out as soon as rumour of my mission spread through the fleet.

'What do you know about horses?' he challenged me, which was a question I was not prepared to answer at that moment.

'Obviously not as much as you do?' I made it a cautious question.

'I was once a syce,' he boasted, in his usual endearing fashion.

'And what creature is that?'

'A groom, one who cares for horses,' he replied, and I stared at him in amazement.

'Where did you ever see a horse before that bloody day at Abnub?' I demanded.

'As an infant my parents were killed, and I was captured by a tribe of barbarians who roamed the plains far to the east, a year's travel beyond the Euphrates river. My captors were people of the horse and, as a child, I lived each day with those animals. Mare's milk was my food and I slept beneath the horses' bellies for shelter in the night, for a slave was not allowed into the tents of the tribe. When I escaped from slavery, it was upon the back of my favourite stallion. He carried me fast and far. But he died long before we reached the Euphrates.'

Thus Hui was with me when a galley set down my small party of reluctant horse-catchers upon the west bank. Sixteen men were all that I could recruit, and most of them were the dregs and riff-raff of the army. Tanus had seen to it that none of his best men would join me. He could not countermand the word of the regent of all Egypt, but he made it as difficult as he could for me to carry out her orders.

At Hui's suggestion, I had equipped my men with light linen ropes and bags of crushed dhurra corn. All of them, except Hui and myself, were terrified to the point of incontinence by the mere thought of the creatures that we had set out to follow. When I woke in the morning after our first night's camp, I found that every single one of these stalwarts had disappeared, and I never saw them again.

'We will have to turn back,' I despaired. 'There is nothing we can do alone. Lord Tanus will be pleased. This was exactly what he knew would happen.'

'You are not alone,' Hui pointed out cheerfully. 'You have me.' This was the first time that my feelings began to warm towards the young swaggerer. We divided the load of ropes and the leather bags of crushed corn, and we went on.

By this time the tracks of the horses were three days old, but they had stayed together in a single herd and so had beaten a road that was easy to follow. Hui assured me that the herd instinct was strong amongst them, and that with such lush grazing along the river-bank, they would not have wandered far. He was certain they would not have gone out into the desert, as I had feared that they might.

'Why would they do that? There is no food or water for them out there.' And in the end Hui proved right.

With the coming of the Hyksos, the peasants had deserted their farms and gone into the shelter of the walled towns. The fields were untended and the corn half-grown. We found the herd before noon the second day. It was spread out and grazing peacefully in one of the fields. Even after my experience with the wounded stallion, I was still rather nervous of these mysterious creatures.

'It will surely be a difficult and dangerous matter to capture a few of them,' I confided in Hui, seeking his reassurance and advice. At this stage, the notion of capturing all three hundred horses had not even occurred to me. I would have been satisfied with twenty, and delighted with fifty of them. I imagined that we would be forced to run each of them down and bind it with the ropes we had brought with us for that purpose.

'I have heard that you have the reputation of being a very clever slave,' Hui grinned at me, cocky and delighted by his superior understanding of the subject. 'Clearly, it is a reputation that is ill-founded.'

He showed me how to twist and braid a halter from the ropes. We made a dozen of these before he was satisfied. Then each of us armed himself with one of these and a leather sack of crushed corn, and we started towards the grazing herd. Following Hui's example, we never walked directly towards them, but strolled obliquely at a leisurely pace past the animals in the fringe of the herd.

'Slowly now,' Hui cautioned me, when they flung up their heads and studied us with that peculiarly frank and almost childlike gaze that I would come to know so well.

'Sit down.' We sank into the standing corn and remained motionless, until the horses started feeding again. Then we moved forward until they became restless once more.

'Down,' Hui ordered, and when we were crouched in the corn, he went on, 'They love the sound of a gentle voice. When I was a child, I sang to my horses to quieten them. Watch this!' He started to sing a refrain in a strange language, which I presumed was the barbaric tongue of his childhood captors.

Hui's voice was as melodious as the squawking of crows squabbling over the rotting carcass of a dead dog. The nearest horses stared at us curiously. I laid my hand on Hui's arm to quieten him. I was certain that the herd must find his efforts at song as distressing as I did.

'Let me try,' I whispered. I sang the lullaby that I had composed for my prince.

> Sleep, little Mem, who rules the dawn,
> sleep, little prince, who will rule the world,
> rest that curly head, filled with wondrous dreams,
> rest those arms, make them strong for sword and bow.

One of the mares closest to us took a few steps towards me, and when she stopped, she made that same soft fluttery sound with her lips. She was inquisitive, and I sang on softly and seductively. She had a foal at her heels, a lovely little bay-coloured creature with an appealing head and pricked-up ears.

With my special feeling for and understanding of birds and animals, I was already beginning to recognize the desirable points of breed in these new animals. I was learning swiftly and instinctively how to deal with them. I was no longer completely reliant on Hui to instruct me.

Still singing gently, I scooped up a handful of the crushed cornmeal and held it out to the mare. I could see at once that she had been hand-fed before, and that she understood my offer. She blew noisily through wide nostrils, and took another few paces towards me. Even now I can remember the thrill that almost stopped the beating of my heart when she took the last pace up to me, and delicately lowered her muzzle into my hand to taste the white meal. It powdered her whiskers as she ate, and I laughed with the joy and excitement of it. She made no effort to pull away from me as I slipped my other arm around her neck and laid my cheek softly against hers to inhale the strange, warm smell of her hide.

'The halter,' Hui reminded me softly, and I slipped it over her head, as he had shown me.

'She is yours,' Hui said.

'And I am hers,' I replied without thinking, but it was true. We had captured each other.

The rest of the herd had watched all this. As soon as the halter was on the mare, they settled down and trustingly allowed Hui and me to walk freely amongst them. They came to eat from the hand and allowed us to lift their hooves and stroke their necks and massive shoulders.

All this seemed to me at the time to be miraculous, but after only a little consideration I realized that it was quite natural. They were accustomed from birth to being handled and petted, to being fed and harnessed. They had lived always with the close and constant presence of man. The true miracle came later, when I realized that they recognized affection, and that they were able to return it in full measure.

Hui had selected and haltered one of the other mares, all the time lecturing me and displaying his learning and experience in matters equine. I was in such a euphoric mood that for once his bumptiousness did not annoy me.

'Very well,' he said at last, 'we will mount up now.' And to my utter astonishment he placed both hands on his mare's back, drew himself up and flung one leg over her, to sit astride her back. I gawked at him in disbelief, expecting the mare to react violently, to rear up and dash Hui to earth, or, at the very least, to seize his naked leg in those powerful white teeth and drag him from his perch. She did none of these things, but stood quietly and subserviently.

'Hi up, my darling!' he called to her, and dug his heels into her ribs. The mare started forward obediently, and when he urged her on again she broke into a trot and then a gallop. Hui guided her effortlessly in a manner that was not then apparent to me. Horse and rider traced out elegant patterns of movement across the field, and then circled back to where I stood.

'Come up, Taita. Try a gallop!' I could see that he was expecting me to refuse, and it was that which made me overcome my reluctance. I would not allow the little whippersnapper to have the better of me.

My first attempt at mounting up was unsuccessful, but the mare stood stoically, and Hui laughed. 'She has a great deal to teach you. You should call the poor animal Patience.' I did not see the humour of it then, but the name stuck and the mare was Patience from then onwards.

'Pull yourself higher before you swing your leg over, and be careful not to trap your balls under you when you come down,' Hui counselled, and then howled with laughter. 'And that's a piece of advice that you need not worry about. My guess is that you would love still to have a pair of those to sit on!'

All the warm feelings I was beginning to have towards Hui cooled again at that sally, and I threw myself on to the mare's back and clung with both hands around her neck, in fear of broken limbs and cracked skull.

433

'Sit up straight!' Hui began my instruction, and Patience assisted me with her sweet and forgiving nature.

I surprised myself by thinking of these creatures in human terms, but over the following days as we rode south towards Thebes, I discovered that they could be stupid or clever, suspicious or trusting, dour or mischievous, friendly or aloof, brave or timid, nervous or phlegmatic, long-suffering or impatient, surprising or predictable – in short, as close to man in temperament as any creature that walks on four legs. The more I learned about them, the more I wanted to learn. The longer I spent working with them, the more I grew to love them.

I rode ahead on Patience, her foal at heel. The herd trailed after us compliantly, all three hundred and sixteen of them. Hui brought up the rear to sweep up any stragglers. With each league we covered, I became more confident and proficient upon Patience's back, and the rapport between us became firmer. The mare became an extension of my own body, but so much swifter and stronger than my own feeble limbs. It felt so natural and right to be astride that broad and sturdy back that I was amazed that so few others were willing to share the experience with me.

Perhaps it was not only the terror that had struck them so devastatingly on the plain of Abnub, but also the words and attitude of Tanus, Lord Harrab that affected the regiments of our army. Whatever the reason, I could find no Egyptian who would mount upon the back of a horse, except Hui and, very much later, Prince Memnon. Of course, they learned to husband and breed the horse and care for him. Under my tutelage they became dexterous and dashing charioteers, but I never saw a man of them mounted on horseback, save only myself and Hui and the prince. When the chariots that I would design with their light, spoked wheels swept all before them, and made Egypt the master of this creation, Tanus never followed our example, and I never heard him express a kind sentiment towards those willing and brave animals who dragged him into battle.

Even in later years, when the horse was commonplace through all our realm, it was considered somehow indecent and obscene to mount them. When the three of us rode past astride, many of the common people spat on the ground three times and made the sign against the evil eye.

ALL THAT was in the future as I led my herd up the west bank of the river towards Thebes, and we arrived to the gratitude of my mistress, and to a gruff and unenthusiastic welcome from the commander-in-chief of the Egyptian armies.

'Just keep those evil brutes out of my sight,' Tanus told me. He still had not forgiven me for going above him to my mistress.

In fairness to him, he had more than enough excuse for his evil temper. The safety of the state and our nation were in the direst jeopardy. There had never been a time in our history when our civilization was so threatened by the barbarian.

Already Asyut was lost, and the whole east bank of the river as far as Dendera. Completely undaunted and undeterred by the naval reverse that Tanus had inflicted upon him, King Salitis with his chariots had swept on and surrounded the walled city of Thebes.

Those walls should have withstood siege for a decade, but that reckoned without the baleful presence of Lord Intef in the camp of the enemy. It transpired that while still grand vizier of the Upper Kingdom, he had secretly ordered the construction of a concealed passage beneath the city walls. Even I who knew most of his other secrets had never suspected this, and Lord Intef had murdered the workmen who had carried out this construction, so that he alone was aware of its existence. I have no idea why he should have constructed the tunnel in the first place, except that his devious mind was much given towards such devices. The palace was riddled with trap-doors and concealed corridors, like the warren of a rabbit or the lair of a desert fox.

When Lord Intef disclosed its existence to him, King Salitis sent a small party of his best men through the secret passage, and once within the walls, they stormed the unsuspecting Egyptian guards on the main gate, slaughtered them and threw the gates

435

wide. The main Hyksos horde poured into the city, and within days of the siege commencing, the city was lost and half her inhabitants massacred.

From the west bank where Tanus now had his headquarters in the half-built Palace of Memnon, we could see the burnt and blackened roofs of those buildings in the city across the river that the Hyksos had put to the torch. Each day we watched the dust-clouds of their chariots, as they raced up and down the far bank, and the glint of their spear-heads at the shoulder-slope, as they prepared for the battle that all of us knew was coming.

With his sadly depleted fleet, Tanus had thus far managed to hold the river-line, and during my absence had beaten back another attempt by the Hyksos to get across the Nile in strength. However, our defences were thinly spread, for we had to guard a great sweep of the river, while the Hyksos could make a crossing at any point they chose. We learned from our spies on the east bank that they had commandeered every single craft they could lay hands on, from barge to skiff. They had captured many of our boatmakers, and had them at work in the boatyards of Thebes. Of course, we could be sure that Lord Intef would give them pertinent advice in all these matters, for he must have been every bit as eager as the barbarian Salitis to seize Pharaoh's treasure.

The crews of our galleys stood to arms every watch of the day and night, and Tanus only slept when he could, which was not often. Neither my mistress nor I saw much of him, and when we did, he was haggard and short-tempered.

Every night saw the arrival on the west bank of many hundreds of refugees. Of both sexes and all ages, they crossed the Nile in an odd assortment of rafts and small craft. Many of the stronger ones even swam the wide stretch of water. All of them were desperate to escape the Hyksos terror. They brought us horror-stories of rapine and plunder, but also detailed and up-to-date news of Hyksos movements.

Of course we welcomed these people, they were countrymen and relatives, but their numbers strained our resources. Our main granaries had all been in Thebes, and most of the herds of cattle and sheep had fallen into the hands of the enemy. Queen Lostris gave me the responsibility of gathering up all the supplies of grain and the herds on the west bank. I drew up lists and rosters for rationing our supplies of meat and grain. Fortunately, the date palms were in full bearing, and the supply of fish from the river was inexhaustible. The Hyksos could never starve us out.

My mistress had also appointed me Master of the Royal Horse. There was no intense competition for this appointment, particularly as no pay or privileges were attached to it. I made Hui my deputy, and he managed, by means of bribes, threats and blackmail, to recruit a hundred grooms to help him care for our little herd. Later we would train them as our first chariot-drivers.

It was no hardship for me to make time every day to visit our makeshift stables in the necropolis. The mare Patience always came running to greet me, and I carried corn-cakes for her and her foal. Often I was able to sneak Prince Memnon away from his mother and his nurses and carry him into the stables on my shoulders. He squealed with excitement as soon as he saw the horses.

I held the prince on my lap as Patience and I galloped along the river-bank, and he made clucking noises and rocked his little backside, imitating the way in which I urged Patience to a harder gallop. I made certain that the route we followed on these rides would never cross Tanus' path. He had still not forgiven me, and if he had seen his son on the back of a cursed horse, I knew that I would have been in physical danger.

I also spent a great deal of my time in the armoury workshop of Pharaoh's funerary temple, where I had the assistance of some of the finest craftsmen in the world to help me build my first chariot. It was here, while working on the design of these vehicles, that I conceived devices that were to become our first line of defence against the Hyksos chariots. These were simply long wooden staves sharpened at both ends, and with the points fire-hardened. Each of our infantrymen would carry ten of these in a bundle upon his back. At the approach of a squadron of cavalry, the staves were planted in the earth at an angle, with the points at the level of the horses' chests. Our men took up their positions behind this barrier of wicked spears, and fired their arrows over them.

When I demonstrated these to Tanus, he threw his arm around

my shoulders for the first time since our quarrel over the horses, and said, 'Well, at least you have not turned senile on me yet,' and I knew that I had been at least partially forgiven.

The ground that I had gained with him here was almost completely lost over the affair of the Taita chariot.

My workmen and I at last completed the first chariot. The dashboard and sides were of split bamboo, woven into basket-work. The axle was of acacia wood. The hubs were of hand-forged bronze, greased with mutton fat, and the spoked wheels were bound with bronze rims. It was so light that two charioteers could lift it between them, and carry it over broken ground where the horses could not pull it. Even I realized that it was a masterpiece, and the workmen called it the Taita chariot. I did not object to the name.

Hui and I harnessed up two of our best horses, Patience and Blade, and took the Taita chariot for its first gallop. It took us some time to learn how to control the rig, but we learned swiftly, and the horses were bred to this and showed us the way. In the end, we were flying across the ground, and hurtling through tight turns at full gallop.

When we drove back into the stables, flushed with excitement and jubilant with our achievement, both of us were convinced that our chariot was swifter and handier than any that the Hyksos could send against us. We tested and modified this creation of mine for ten full days, working by lamplight in the armoury until the late watches of every night, before I was satisfied that I could show it to Tanus.

Tanus came to the stables with surly reluctance, and balked at climbing up into the cockpit of the chariot behind me.

'I trust this contraption of yours as much as I trust those cursed brutes who tow it,' he grumbled, but I was persuasive, and at last he stepped up gingerly on to the footplate and we were off.

At first I kept the horses to an easy trot, until I felt him relaxing and, despite himself, beginning to enjoy the exhilarating ride. Then I pushed them into a canter. 'See the speed of it. You can be upon the enemy before he knows you are there,' I exulted.

Tanus laughed for the first time, and I was encouraged. 'With your ships you rule the river. With this chariot you rule the land.

Between the two, you rule the world. Nothing can stand against you.' I was careful not to disparage his beloved ships, or to make unfavourable comparisons.

'Is this your best speed?' he shouted in the wind and the pounding of hooves. 'With a fair wind, *Breath of Horus* is faster than this.' Which was a lie and a challenge.

'Hold on to the sides and take a deep breath,' I warned him. 'I am going to take you up where the eagles fly,' and I let Patience and Blade go.

No man has ever travelled faster. The wind seared our eyes, and the tears pouring from them were blown back into our hair.

'Sweet breath of Isis!' Tanus shouted with excitement. 'This is—' I never knew what he thought this was. Tanus never finished his sentence, for at that instant our off-wheel hit a rock and the rim exploded.

The chariot capsized and somersaulted, and both Tanus and I were thrown high and clear. I struck the hard earth with a force that should have crippled me, but I was so concerned with how Tanus would be affected by this little mishap, and how my dreams and plans would be dashed, that I felt no pain.

I bounded to my feet and saw Tanus crawl to his bleeding knees twenty paces beyond me. He was coated heavily with dust and seemed to have lost the skin from one half of his face. He tried to maintain his dignity as he pushed himself upright and staggered back to the wrecked chariot, but he was limping heavily.

He stood for a long minute gazing down at the shattered ruins of my creation, and then abruptly he let out a roar like a wounded bull, and launched such a mighty kick at it that it flipped over again, as though it were a child's toy. He turned on his heel without even a glance in my direction and limped away. I did not see him again for a week, and when we did meet, neither of us mentioned the chariot.

I think that might have been the end of the matter, and we would never have assembled our first chariot squadron, if it had not been for the fact that the stubbornness of my mistress's pride surpassed even that of her lover. She had given me the original order, and would not now retract it. When Tanus tried to inveigle her into doing so, he merely made my position stronger. Hui and I rebuilt the chariot within three days, and another identical to it.

By the time the embalmers in the funerary chapel had completed the ritual seventy days of royal mummification, we had our first squadron of fifty chariots, and had trained drivers for them.

SINCE WE had returned to the Palace of Memnon from our defeat at the battle of Abnub, my mistress had been occupied with the business of state thrust upon her by the regency. Long hours were spent with her ministers and advisers.

It was now that the initial training which I had given her in the Palace of Elephantine was to bear fruit. I had taught her to pick her way unerringly through the labyrinth of power and influence. She was just twenty-one years of age, but she was a queen, and ruled like one.

Very occasionally she encountered a problem which particularly vexed or perplexed her. Then she sent for me. I would drop my work in the armoury or the stables or in the small scribery that she had set aside for me just down the corridor from her audience chamber, and I would rush to her side.

On occasion I spent days sitting below her throne and steering her through some troublesome decisions. Once again, my ability to read the lips of men without hearing their words stood us in good stead. Some nobleman at the back of the audience never realized, as he plotted or schemed with his neighbour, that I was relaying his exact words to my mistress. She swiftly acquired a reputation of sagacity and prescience. Neither of us enjoyed much rest during these dark and worrisome days.

Even though our days were full, our nights were long. Those interminable councils of war and of state lasted well past midnight. No sooner was one crisis averted, than another loomed before us. Each day the Hyksos threatened us more directly, and Tanus' hold on the river-line weakened.

Slowly, a sense of doom and despair permeated all of us. Men smiled little and never laughed out loud. Even the play of the children was muted and subdued. We had only to look across the river, and the enemy was there, gathering himself, growing stronger each day.

After seventy days, the mummification of Pharaoh was completed. My early efforts in preserving the king's body had been highly successful, and the grand master of the guild of embalmers had commended me in the presence of my mistress. He had found no evidence of decay when he removed the king's corpse from the olive jar, and even his liver, which is the part most subject to mortification, was well preserved.

Once the king had been laid out on the diorite slab in his mortuary chapel, the grand master had inserted the spoon up his nostril and scooped out the curdled contents of his skull which the pickle had hardened to the consistency of cheese. Then, still in the foetal position, the king was placed in the bath of natron salt with only his head left uncovered by the harsh fluid. When he was removed from the bath thirty days later, all the fatty tissue had dissolved, and the outer layers of the skin had peeled off, except for that of the head.

They laid him upon the mottled stone slab once again and straightened him into an extended position. He was wiped and dried, and his empty stomach was filled with linen pads soaked in resins and wax and then sutured closed. Meanwhile, his internal organs were desiccated and placed in their milk-coloured alabaster Canopic jars, which were then sealed.

For the remaining forty days, the body of the king was allowed to dry out thoroughly. The doors of the chapel had been aligned with the direction of the warm, dry prevailing winds, so that they blew over the funeral slab. By the end of the ritual period of seventy days, Pharaoh's body was as dry as a stick of firewood.

His nails, which had been removed before he was soaked in the natron bath, were replaced and fixed in position on his fingers and toes with fine threads of gold wire. The first layer of pure white linen bandages was wound into place around his body, leaving his head and neck exposed. The binding was meticulous and intricate, with the bandages crossing and criss-crossing each other in elaborate patterns. Under the bindings were laid charms and amulets of gold and precious stones. The bandages were then soaked with lacquer and resins that dried to a stony hardness.

Now it was time for the ceremony of Opening-the-Mouth, which traditionally was performed by the dead pharaoh's next of kin. Memnon was too young to take this part, so his regent was called in his stead.

My mistress and I went to the chapel together in the gloom of dawn, and we were witnesses as the linen sheet that covered the king was drawn aside. Pharaoh's head was miraculously preserved. His eyes were closed and his expression was serene. The embalmers had rouged and painted his face, and he looked better in death than he had in life.

While the high priest of Ammon-Ra and the grand master of the guild of embalmers prepared the instruments for the ceremony, we sang the Incantation against Dying for the Second Time.

> He is the reflection and not the mirror.
> He is the music and not the lyre.
> He is the stone and not the chisel that forms it.
> He will live for ever.
> He will not die a second time.

Then the high priest handed my mistress the golden spoon and led her by the hand to the funeral slab.

Queen Lostris stooped over the body of Pharaoh and laid the spoon of life upon his painted lips.

> I open thy lips that thou mayest speak once more,
> I open thy nostrils that thou mayest breathe.

She intoned the words and then touched his eyelids with the spoon.

> I open thy eyes that thou mayest behold once more the glory
> of this world, and the nether-world of the gods where you
> shall dwell from this day forward.

She touched the spoon to his bandaged chest.

> I quicken your heart, so that you may live for ever.
> You shall not die a second time.
> You shall live for ever!

Then we waited while the embalmers bound up Pharaoh's head in the neat swathes of bandages and painted them with resin. They moulded the resin-wet bandages to the shape of his face beneath them. Finally, they placed over his blind bandaged face the first of the four funeral masks.

This was the same funeral mask that we had watched being fashioned from pure gold. While he was still alive, Pharaoh had posed for the sculptor, so the mask was amazingly lifelike. The eyes of shining rock-crystal and obsidian seemed to gaze upon me with all the humanity that the man beneath the mask had once possessed. The cobra head of the *uraeus* rose from the noble brow, regal and mystical.

Then the wrapped mummy was placed in the golden inner coffin, which was sealed, and this went into the second golden coffin with another death-mask embossed upon the lid. Half the treasure recovered from Lord Intef's hoard had gone to make up that enormous weight of precious metal and jewels.

There were seven coffins in all, including the massive stone sarcophagus standing upon the golden sledge, which waited ready to carry Pharaoh along the causeway to his tomb in the gaunt hills. But my mistress refused to give her sanction for this to happen.

'I have given my sacred vow. I cannot place my husband in a tomb that may be plundered by the Hyksos barbarians. Pharaoh will lie here until I am able to make good my promise to him. I will find a secure tomb in which he may lie through eternity. I have given my word that no one will disturb his rest.'

THE WISDOM of Queen Lostris' decision to delay the entombment was proved three nights later. The Hyksos made a determined effort to cross the river, and Tanus barely succeeded in turning them back. They made the attempt on an unguarded stretch of the river two miles north of Esna. They swam their horses across in a mass, and then followed with an armada of small boats which they had carried overland from Thebes in order to conceal their intentions from us.

They actually succeeded in making a beachhead on the west bank before Tanus could rush his galleys to the spot, but he arrived before they could unload their chariots and harness the horses to them. Tanus destroyed their boats with the chariots still on board, and he then had almost three thousand Hyksos stranded on our side of the river. Their horses scattered and bolted away into the night when Tanus' troops made their first charge.

Without their chariots the Hyksos were on even terms with our troops, but they had no means of escape and they fought with grim determination. In numbers they were almost evenly matched, for Tanus had managed to bring up only one full regiment. The rest of his army was thinly spread along the west bank. The fighting was bloody and ferocious, confused by the darkness which was lit only by the burning vessels that Tanus had fired on the beach.

It was only by the wildest coincidence, or by another nudge from the gods, that Hui and I had brought our little squadron of fifty chariots and fledgling charioteers to Esna on training manoeuvres. In truth, we had driven these twenty miles from Thebes principally to escape from Tanus' disapproval and interference.

We were encamped in the sacred grove of tamarind trees beside the temple of Horus at Esna. I was exhausted after a long day of galloping and manoeuvring at high speed. On return to our encampment, Hui had produced a jar of remarkably palatable wine, and I had been somewhat intemperate in my sampling of it. I was dead asleep when Hui staggered into my tent and shook me awake.

'There are fires burning on the bank of the river downstream,' he told me, 'and when the wind shifts, you can hear the sound of cheering, and a little while ago I thought I heard many voices singing the battle hymn of the Blues. I think there is a fight going on down there.'

I was as unsteady on my feet as he was, and reckless with wine, as I shouted for him to rouse the camp and harness the horses. We were all still novices, and it was almost dawn by the time we had caught the horses and put them in the traces. In the chilly drift of the river mist and the gloomy shiver of dawn, we trotted along the north road in column of route, two chariots abreast. I was driving the lead chariot, while Hui had command of the rear-guard. Our fifty chariots had been reduced to thirty by the previous day's exercises, for I had not yet succeeded in perfecting my spoked wheels. They had an alarming tendency to fly to pieces when driven at speed, and almost half my force was out of action.

The passage of the wind over my bare chest made me shiver again, and counteracted the bravado of the wine. I was beginning to hope that Hui had been mistaken, when suddenly from far ahead there came that unmistakable chorus of shouting and cheering, and the clank and clash of bronze on bronze that could mean only one thing. Once you have heard them, the sounds of battle are not readily forgotten or mistaken. The rough farmer's track we were following along the river-bank took a turn to the left. As we came through it, the field lay open before us.

The sun was just above the horizon, and it had turned the surface of the river into a shimmering sheet of beaten copper that was painful to the eye. The ships of Tanus' squadron lay just off-shore, crowding in close to, in an attempt to bring the archers on the decks in range of the Hyksos, and to cut off any retreat across the river.

The stranded Hyksos regiment was making a stand in the centre of a field of knee-high green corn. They had formed a circle, facing outwards, shoulder to shoulder, with their shields locked together and their spears thrust forward. As we came into view, they had just repulsed another attempt by Tanus' troops to break their circle. The Egyptian regiment was pulling back to

445

regroup, leaving their dead and wounded scattered around the periphery of the enemy circle.

I am no soldier, although I have written scrolls on the conduct of war. I had accepted the rank of Commander of the Royal Horse, thrust upon me by my mistress, with the deepest reluctance. I had intended simply to perfect my chariot, train the first squadron, and then hand it over to Hui or some other person more suited to the warlike professions.

I was cold and still half-drunk as I heard my voice giving the order to deploy in arrow-head formation. It was the evolution that we had practised the previous day, and the chariots that followed mine flared out on either side with reasonable proficiency. I was acutely aware of the sound of hooves in the soft earth and the creak of the chariot harness, the squeal of the wheels turning on their metal-lined hubs, and the rattle of javelins as my charioteers drew their darts from the quivers. I looked left and right, reviewing our little squadron drawn up in the shape of an arrow-head with my chariot at the apex. It was a formation I had copied from the Hyksos. I drew a deep breath.

'Squadron will advance!' I screamed, and my voice shrilled with fear. 'At the gallop, forward!'

I had only to lift my left hand that held the traces, and Patience and Blade bounded forward. I was almost thrown over backwards, but I grabbed at the dashboard with my free hand, and we went straight at the Hyksos circle.

Beneath me the chariot leaped and jolted over the lumpy ploughed earth, and I looked over the plunging hindquarters of my horses and saw the wall of Hyksos shields, glittering and impenetrable in the early sunlight, drawing closer with every stride we took.

On either side of me, men were howling and cheering to hide their terror, and I howled with them, like a pariah dog at full moon. The horses were snorting and neighing, and suddenly Patience lifted the long plume of her tail and began to fart in rhythm and in time to her own stride. This struck me as immoderately funny. My howls of terror turned to screams of laughter. The helmet that I had borrowed from Hui was too large for me. It bounced off my head and the wind flung my hair out behind me.

Patience and Blade were the fastest pair in the squadron, and our chariot pulled ahead of the rest of the formation. I tried to slow our charge by hauling back on the traces, but Patience would have none of it. Her glee was evident, she was as excited as any of us, and she straightened her neck and ran away with me.

We tore through the retiring lines of Egyptian infantry coming back from the failed assault on the Hyksos circle, and they scattered out of our path and gawked at us in astonishment.

'Come on!' I howled with laughter. 'We will show you the way!' They turned and followed us back towards the enemy at the run. Behind me, I heard the trumpeters sounding the charge, and the braying horns seemed to spur our horses. Out on my right I saw Tanus' battle standard waving, and recognized his crested helmet standing taller than the other men around him.

'What do you think of my cursed brutes now?' I yelled at him, as we tore past, and Patience farted again, bringing on fresh gales of my nervous laughter.

The chariot on my left was running almost level with me, and then its near-side wheel burst under the strain and it went flying end over end, throwing the charioteers, and bringing the horses down screaming. The rest of us tore on without a check.

The first rank of the enemy was now so close that I could see their eyes staring at me over the top edge of their shields. Their arrows hissed around my ears. I could make out clearly the figures of beasts and demons embossed on their tall metal helmets, see the beads of sweat glittering in their plaited and beribboned beards, hear their chanted war-cry – and then we were into them.

My horses leaped together into the barrier of shields and it shattered before the weight and fury of our charge. I saw a man tossed head-high, and heard his bones crackle like kindling in the fire. On the footplate behind me, my javelineer was making deadly practice. I had chosen him as the best from amongst all my recruits, and he proved my choice now, as he stood firm and hurled his darts down into the enemy.

In succession the following chariots tore into the gap we had opened, and we hardly checked as we raced through, breaking out through the far side of the Hyksos circle, then wheeling in pods of three and coming back at them.

Tanus seized the moment and threw his infantry into the breach that we had torn open. The Hyksos formation broke up into knots of struggling men. These in turn disintegrated, and the Hyksos panicked and ran for the river. The moment they came within range, the archers on the decks of our galleys sent clouds of arrows over them.

Ahead of me there was an isolated pocket of Hyksos warriors still fighting back-to-back, and holding off our men. I swerved the chariot and drove at them in full gallop. Before I reached them, my right wheel burst asunder, the light carapace of the chariot flipped over, and I soared free and then, with a gut-tearing lurch, fell back to earth. My head struck first, and my eyes filled with stars and meteors of bright light. Then there was only darkness.

I woke again under the awning on the deck of Tanus' flag-ship. I found myself lying on a sheepskin mattress, with Tanus leaning over me. As soon as he saw that I was conscious, he masked the expression of concern and worry that had twisted his features.

'You crazy old fool.' He forced a grin at me. 'What, in the name of Horus, were you laughing about?'

I tried to sit up, but my head ached abominably and I groaned, then clutched his arm as it all came back to me.

'Tanus, the enemy horses that swam across last night – I must have them.'

'Don't worry that battered head of yours. I have already sent Hui to gather them up,' he assured me. 'If I am to have five hundred of those contraptions of yours for my new chariot division, I will need a thousand of those cursed brutes to pull them. However, those new-fangled wheels of yours are more dangerous than a regiment of Hyksos. I will not ride with you again until you do something about them.'

For a moment it did not penetrate my aching skull, then I realized that it had happened. Tanus had quashed his pride, and given in to me. My orphan chariot squadron was at last to be part of the standing army, and he would give me the men and gold to build five hundred more. He would even ride with me again, if only I could fix my wheels.

But what truly filled me with joy was that he had forgiven me at last, and we were friends once more.

 THE SUCCESS of my chariots at Esna, and the feeling of confidence that it instilled in us all, were short-lived. Secretly, I had expected and dreaded what would happen next. It was the enemy's logical move, and both Salitis and Lord Intef should have made it much earlier.

We knew that when he swept through the Lower Kingdom, Salitis had captured most of the fleet of the red pretender intact. Those ships were lying abandoned in the docks of Memphis and Tanis in the Delta. However, there must be droves of renegade Egyptians from the usurper's navy available to Salitis, and even if that were not the case, it would certainly be possible to recruit enough mercenary Syrian sailors in Gaza and Joppa, and the other ports along the eastern coast of the great sea, to man several hundred of these galleys and transports.

I had realized that this must happen, but I had refrained from warning either Tanus or my mistress of the likelihood, for I did not wish to add to the feeling of gloom, and heighten the despondency of our people. I had searched my heart for a counter to this move when Salitis and Intef made it, but there was none that I could think of. Therefore, since I could do nothing to allay these fears, I thought it best to keep them to myself.

When it finally happened, and our spies on the east side of the river opposite Asyut warned us of the approach of this fleet from the Delta, Tanus rushed his own ships northwards to meet them. His fleet was superior in every way to the one which Salitis and Intef had assembled, but the battle they fought lasted for almost a week before Tanus destroyed or drove them back into the Delta.

However, Salitis had brought his transports up behind the

449

screen of fighting galleys, and while the river battle still raged, he was able to embark almost two full regiments of horse and chariot, and ferry them intact to our side of the river, without our galleys being able to reach them.

These regiments comprised nearly three hundred of Salitis' fast war chariots, his elite divisions which he led himself. At last he had turned our flank. There was nothing to stop him now, as his chariots came bowling southwards along our side of the river. All our galleys could do was to try to keep pace with the dust-cloud he threw up, as he raced for the funerary temple of Mamose and all its treasures.

QUEEN LOSTRIS called her war council when the news of the Hyksos crossing reached us in the Palace of Memnon. She addressed her first question to Tanus.

'Now that he is across the river, can you check the barbarian?'

'I can slow him down, perhaps,' he replied frankly. 'We have learned a great deal about him. We can wait for him behind walls of stone, or behind barriers of the sharp staves that Taita has equipped us with. But Salitis need not give battle. His chariots are so fast that he can swing around our positions as he did at Asyut. No, I cannot stop him.'

Queen Lostris looked at me. 'Taita, what about your chariots? Can they not give battle to the Hyksos?'

'Your Majesty, I have forty chariots that I can send in to meet him. He has three hundred. My chariots are swifter than those of Salitis, but my men cannot match his in skill and training. There is also the matter of the wheels. I have not perfected them. Salitis will overwhelm and destroy us very easily. If I am given the time and the material, I can build new and better chariots with wheels that do not burst, but I cannot replace the horses. We dare not risk the horses. They are our only hope for eventual victory.'

While we thus debated, another messenger arrived, this time from the south. He had fled to us on the current and the wind, so his news was only a day old. Tanus ordered him into the council chamber, and the messenger fell to his knees before Queen Lostris.

'Speak, fellow,' Tanus invited him. 'What do you have to tell us?'

The messenger stuttered in fear of his life, 'Divine Majesty, while our fleet was busy at Asyut, the barbarian made another crossing at Esna. They swam the horses over as they did before, but this time there were none of our galleys ready to turn back their boats. Two Hyksos regiments are across. Their horses are in the traces and they are coming on a cloud of dust, swiftly as the flight of the swallow. They will be here in three days.'

None of us spoke until Tanus had sent the man away with orders that he be fed and cared for. The messenger, who had expected to be killed, kissed Queen Lostris' sandals.

When we were alone, Tanus said softly, 'Salitis has four regiments across the river. Six hundred chariots. It is over.'

'No!' my mistress's voice shook with the force of her denial. 'The gods cannot desert this very Egypt now. Our civilization cannot perish. We have too much to give to the world.'

'I can fight on, of course,' Tanus agreed. 'But in the end it will all be the same. We cannot prevail against their chariots.'

My mistress turned back to me. 'Taita, I have not asked you before, because I know how dearly it costs you. But I must ask you now before I make the final decision. I ask you to work the Mazes of Ammon-Ra for me. I must know what the gods require of us.'

I bowed my head in acquiescence, and whispered, 'I will fetch my chest.'

 THE SITE that I chose for the divination was the inner sanctuary of the shrine to Horus in the half-completed Palace of Memnon. The shrine had not yet been dedicated to the god, and his image had not yet been set up, but I was certain that Horus had already cast his benevolent influence over the building.

My mistress sat before me with Tanus at her side, and watched in fascination as I drank the witches' potion to open the eyes of

451

my soul, my *Ka*, the little bird-like creature that lives in the heart of every one of us, and which is our alter ego.

I laid the ivory Mazes before them and asked both Queen Lostris and Tanus to stroke and handle them, to endow them with their spirit and the spirit of the nation that they represented, this very Egypt. As I watched them divide the stacks of ivory counters, I felt the drug in my blood grow stronger, and the beat of my heart slowed as the little death crept over me.

I took up the two remaining Mazes from the last stack, and I held them to my breast. They began to grow hot against my skin, and my instinct was to draw back from the darkness that I felt coming over me. Instead, I surrendered to it and let it carry me away.

I heard my mistress's voice, as though from a great distance. 'What will become of the double crown? How can we resist the barbarian?'

The visions began to form before my eyes, and I was carried up into the days that were still to come, and I saw events that had not yet come to pass.

The morning sunlight was streaming through the aperture in the roof and striking the altar of Horus, when at last I returned from the far journey of the Mazes. I was shaken and nauseated with the effect of the hallucinatory drug, giddy and trembling with the memories of the strange sights that I had seen.

My mistress and Tanus had stayed with me during the long night. Their anxious faces were the first things that I saw on my return, but they were still so distorted and wavering that I thought they were part of the vision.

'Taita, are you all right? Speak to us. Tell us what you saw.' My mistress was concerned. She could not hide the guilt she felt at having forced me to enter the Mazes of Ammon-Ra once more.

'There was a serpent.' My voice still echoed strangely in my own ears, as though I stood apart. 'A great green serpent that crawled through the desert.'

I saw the puzzled expression on their faces, but I had not yet considered the meaning of it all myself, so I could give them no guidance.

'I am thirsty,' I whispered. 'My throat is dry and my tongue like a stone covered with moss.'

Tanus fetched a jar of wine and poured it into the bowl for me, and I drank greedily.

'Tell us of the serpent,' my mistress demanded, as soon as I lowered the bowl.

'There was no end to its sinuous body, and it shimmered green in the sunlight. It crawled through a strange land, in which lived tall naked men and strange and wonderful beasts.'

'Could you see the head or the tail of the serpent?' my mistress asked, and I shook my head.

'Where were you? Where did you stand?' she insisted. I had forgotten how keenly she enjoyed my visions, and what pleasure she took in interpreting them.

'I was riding upon the back of the serpent,' I answered. 'But I was not alone.'

'Who was with you?'

'You were at my side, mistress, and Memnon with you. Tanus was on my other hand, and the serpent carried us all.'

'The Nile! The serpent was the river,' she cried triumphantly. 'You foresaw a voyage that we were making upon the river.'

'Which way?' Tanus demanded. He was as rapt as she was. 'Which way did the river run?'

I made an effort to recall every detail. 'I saw the sun rise on my left hand.'

'South!' he cried.

'Into Africa,' said my mistress.

'At last I saw the heads of the serpent ahead of us. The body of the serpent was bifurcated, and on each branch was a head.'

'Does the Nile have two branches?' my mistress wondered aloud. 'Or is there some deeper meaning to the vision?'

'Let us hear the rest of what Taita has to tell us,' Tanus stopped her speculation. 'Continue, old friend.'

'Then I saw the goddess,' I went on. 'She sat upon a high mountain. Both the heads of the serpent worshipped her.'

My mistress could not restrain herself. 'Which of the goddesses did you see? Oh, tell me quickly who it was.'

'She had the bearded head of a man but the breasts and the

453

pudenda of a woman. From her vagina she spurted out two great streams of water into the open mouths of the double-headed serpent.'

'It is the goddess Hapi, the river god,' Queen Lostris whispered. 'She generates the river within herself, and pours it out to flow through the world.'

'What else did the vision show you?' Tanus demanded.

'The goddess smiled at us, and her face shone with love and benevolence. She spoke in a voice that was the sound of the wind and the sea. The sound of thunder on the peaks of far-away mountains.'

'What did she say to us?' Queen Lostris asked in awe.

'She said, "Let my child come to me. I will make her strong so that she will prevail and my people will not perish in the face of the barbarian."' I repeated the words that still beat like a drum in my head.

'I am the child of the river goddess,' said my mistress simply. 'At birth I was dedicated to her. Now she summons me, and I must go to the place where she dwells at the end of the Nile.'

'This is the same voyage that Taita and I contemplated once before,' Tanus mused. 'And now the goddess commands it. We cannot refuse her.'

'Yes, we must go, but we will come back,' my mistress vowed. 'This is my land, this very Egypt. This is my city, this beautiful Thebes of the hundred gates. I cannot leave them for ever. I will return to Thebes. This I swear and I call upon the goddess Hapi to witness my oath. We shall return!'

 THE DECISION to fly to the south, up above the cataracts into the wild and unexplored land beyond, was one that Tanus and I had made once before. The first time had been to escape the wrath and vengeance of Pharaoh. Now we were flying from an even more merciless foe. It was almost as though the gods were determined that we should undertake this voyage, and that they would not be denied.

There was little time for us to make our preparations for such a fateful departure. The Hyksos were coming down on us from two directions, and our pickets reported that their cohorts would be in view from the roof of the Palace of Memnon within three days at the very latest.

Tanus placed Kratas in charge of half his available force and sent him to meet King Salitis who was driving hard from Asyut in the north and was likely to be the first column to reach the necropolis and the palace. Kratas had orders to fight a running battle. Using the staves and defending every fortified position, he was to delay Salitis as long as was possible, without risking being cut off or overwhelmed. When he could hold them no longer, he was to evacuate his men on to the galleys.

Tanus himself took the other half of our army and moved south to fight another delaying battle against the Hyksos division coming at us from Esna.

While they were thus engaged, my mistress was to embark our people and all their possessions aboard the remaining ships of our fleet. My mistress delegated this duty to Lord Merkeset, but of course she made me his assistant. Lord Merkeset was not only well into his dotage, but had recently taken to himself a sixteen-year-old wife. He was not, therefore, of much use either to himself or to me. The entire planning and execution of the evacuation fell squarely on my shoulders.

However, before I could turn my mind to this, I had to take care of my horses. Even at this early stage I realized with stark clarity that they were the key to our survival as a nation and a civilized people. With those animals that we had captured at Esna, we now had several thousand in our herd. I split this herd into four parts so that they could more readily find grazing on the march. Further, the smaller herds would throw up less dust, and it would be easier for them to avoid the Hyksos scouts.

I sent Hui and my charioteers and grooms south with these herds towards Elephantine, with orders to avoid the river-bank down which the Hyksos chariots were advancing and to keep inland, closer to the edge of the desert.

Once the horses were despatched, I could turn my attention to the humans. I realized that we were limited by the number of ships available as to how many of our people were able to accompany us on the long voyage. I was certain that almost every Egyptian wanted to be part of the exodus. The cruelty and ferocity of the Hyksos were evident in every city they burned and in every atrocity that they inflicted on our people. All the unknown dangers of the African wilderness were preferable to these bloodthirsty monsters who were racing down upon us in their chariots.

In the end I calculated that we could accommodate only twelve thousand souls aboard the escaping fleet, and I reported this to my mistress.

'We will have to be ruthless in those we select and those we leave behind,' I told her, but she would not listen to my advice.

'These are my people. I would give up my own place rather than leave one of them to the Hyksos.'

'But, Majesty, what about the old and the decrepit? The sick and the very young?'

'Every citizen will be given the choice of coming with us. I will not leave a greybeard or a beggar, a day-old infant or a leper. They are my people, and if they cannot go, then Prince Memnon and I will stay with them.' Of course, she mentioned the prince to make doubly certain of her victory over me.

The ships would be gunwale-deep under this great weight of humanity, but I had no choice. Still, I had some satisfaction in first embarking all the most useful and creative citizens. I chose men from every trade and profession, masons and weavers, coppersmiths and potters, tanners and sailmakers, scribes and artists, shipbuilders and carpenters, all of them leaders in their particular discipline. These I saw safely on board the waiting transports. It gave me a particular pleasure to allocate the most uncomfortable berths in the most squalid vessels to the priesthood and the law scribes, those blood-sucking fleas on the healthy body of the state.

When all of these were boarded, I allowed the rabble to come swarming on to the wharf below the temple.

As a result of my mistress's intransigence, I had to be careful in choosing what cargo we would load. There would be no room for idle fripperies. I gathered up the weapons and tools and the raw materials that we would need to build up another civilization in the unknown lands. For the rest of the cargo I tried in every way to reduce weight and bulk. For instance, rather than grain and fruits, I loaded the seeds of every desirable plant in clay jars sealed with pitch and wax.

Every deben-weight of cargo that we loaded in our holds meant that something else must be left behind. Our voyage might last ten years or a lifetime. The road would be hard. We knew that the great cataracts lay ahead of us. We dared not burden ourselves with anything but the most essential, but then there remained my mistress's promise to Pharaoh. There was barely room for the living – how much space could we afford to give over to the dead?

'I gave my vow to the king as he lay dying,' my mistress insisted. 'I cannot leave him here.'

'Your Majesty, I will find a secure hiding-place for the king's body, an unmarked grave in the hills where no man will find him. When we return to Thebes, we will exhume him, and give him the royal burial that you promised him.'

'If I break my vow, the gods will desert us and our voyage will be doomed. The body of the king must go with us.'

One glance at her expression warned me that there would be no profit in further argument. We opened the massive granite sarcophagus and lifted out the six inner coffins. Even these were so bulky that it would have needed a galley to carry them alone.

I made a decision without consulting Queen Lostris. I had the workmen remove only the two innermost golden coffins. These we covered with a thick linen canvas shroud which we stitched over them as protection. The size and weight were thus reduced to acceptable proportions, and we stowed these two canvas-covered coffins in the hold of the *Breath of Horus*.

The bulk of Pharaoh's treasure, all the gold and silver and the precious stones, was packed into cedar-wood boxes. I ordered the goldsmiths to strip the bullion from the discarded coffins and from the wooden frame of the great funeral sledge, and melt it down into bars. I was secretly delighted to be the instrument of destruction of that tasteless monstrosity. The treasure chests and the bars of bullion were carried down to the wharf and loaded on board the waiting ships. I distributed these so that every ship carried at least one chest or a stack of bullion bars. In this way, the risk that the entire treasure could be lost at a single stroke of misfortune was greatly reduced.

There was much of the funerary treasure that we could not take with us, all the furniture and the statuary, the ceremonial armour and the boxes of *ushabti* statues, and of course the ungainly framework of the hearse from which I had stripped the gold. Rather than have it fall into the hands of the Hyksos, we piled all of this in the temple courtyard, and I personally hurled a burning torch on top of the mountain of treasure, and watched it burn to ashes.

All this was done in dreadful haste, and before the last ship was loaded the lookouts on the roof of the palace shouted the warning that the dust-clouds of the Hyksos chariots were in sight. Within the hour, our exhausted and battle-weary troops who, under command of Tanus and Kratas, had been fighting the long grim rear-guard action, began to pull back into the necropolis, and to embark on the waiting galleys.

I met Tanus as he came up on to the causeway at the head of a squad of the guards. So far, by dint of courage and sacrifice, he and his men had managed to win a few extra days for us to complete the evacuation. They could do no more, and the enemy was driving them in.

When I waved and called his name, Tanus saw me and shouted over the heads of the crowd, 'Queen Lostris and the prince? Have they gone aboard the *Breath of Horus?*'

I forced my way through the throng to his side. 'My mistress will not leave until all her people are on board the ships. She ordered me to take you to her as soon as you arrived. She is waiting for you in her quarters in the palace.'

He looked at me aghast. 'The enemy are pressing us hard. Queen Lostris and the prince are more precious than all this rabble. Why did you not force her?'

I laughed. 'She is not an easy lady to force. You should know that as well as I do. She will leave none of her people to the Hyksos.'

'Seth blast that woman's pride! She will get all of us killed.' But his harsh words were belied by the expression of pride and admiration on his dusty, sweat-streaked face, and he grinned at me. 'Well, if she will not come on her own, we shall have to go and fetch her.'

We pushed our way through the long lines of passengers, laden with bundles of their possessions and carrying their infants, that were streaming down to the dock to go aboard the ships. As we hurried along the causeway, Tanus pointed over the battlements at the ominous clouds of dust bearing down upon us from both directions.

'They are moving faster than I had believed possible. They have not even halted to water their horses. Unless we speed up the embarkation, they will catch us with half our people still ashore,' he said grimly, and pointed down on to the wharf below us.

The wharf was wide enough to allow only two vessels to come alongside at one time. The masses of refugees clogged the causeway and congested the entrance gates to the dock. Their weeping and lamentation added to the confusion, and at that moment someone at the rear of the column screamed, 'The Hyksos are here! Run! Save yourselves! The Hyksos are here!'

The panic spread through the crowd and it surged forward mindlessly. Women were crushed against the stone gates, and children were trampled under foot. All order and control were breaking down, decent and dignified citizens and disciplined soldiers were being reduced to a desperate mob struggling for survival.

I had to use the sharpened stave I carried to force a way through them, as Tanus and I fought our way back towards the palace. At last we broke out of the crowd and ran to the palace gates.

The halls and corridors were empty and deserted except for a few looters who were picking through the empty rooms. They ran when they saw Tanus. He was a dreadful sight, gaunt and dusty and battle-worn, with a ruddy stubble of beard covering his jaw. Ahead of me, he burst into the private quarters of the queen, and we found her chamber unguarded and the door standing wide. We rushed through it.

My mistress sat alone on the terrace under the spreading vine, with Prince Memnon on her lap. She was pointing out to him the fleet of ships on the Nile below the terrace, and the two of them were enthusing over the spectacle.

'Look at the pretty ships.'

Queen Lostris stood up smiling when she saw us, and Memnon slid off her lap and ran to Tanus.

Tanus swung him up on to his shoulder, and then embraced my mistress with his free hand.

'Where are your slaves? Where are Aton and Lord Merkeset?' Tanus demanded.

'I sent them to the ships.'

'Taita says that you refused to go yourself. He is very angry with you, and rightly so.'

'Forgive me, dear Taita.' Her smile could light my life, or break my heart.

'Rather beg the forgiveness of King Salitis,' I suggested stiffly. 'He will be here soon enough.' I seized her arm. 'Now that this rude soldier of yours has at last arrived, can we please go to the ships?'

We hurried from the terrace and back through the palace corridors. We were entirely alone, even the looters and the thieves had disappeared like rats into their holes. The only one of us who was completely unconcerned was Prince Memnon. For him it was another jolly game. Sitting astride Tanus' shoulders, he dug in his heels and shouted, 'Hi up!' as he had learned from me when we were riding Patience.

We raced across the palace gardens to the stone staircase that led up on to the causeway. That was the shortest way to the temple dock. As we hurried along the causeway, I realized that circumstances had changed drastically in the time that had passed since we had left to fetch my mistress and the prince from the palace. Ahead of us the causeway was deserted, the last of the refugees had gone on board the ships in the dock. Beyond the stone battlements I could see their masts moving slowly down the canal towards the open river.

With a hollow feeling in the pit of my stomach, I realized that we were the last persons left ashore, and that we still had half a mile to cover before we reached the empty dock. All of us stopped together, and watched the last galleys sail away.

'I told the captain to wait,' I groaned, 'but with the Hyksos so close, their only concern is with their own safety.'

'What can we do now?' my mistress breathed, and even Memnon's happy cries dried up.

'If we can reach the river-bank, surely Remrem or Kratas will see us and send in a skiff to pick us up?' I suggested, and Tanus agreed immediately.

'This way! Follow me!' he cried. 'Taita, see to your mistress.'

I took her arm to help her along, but she was as strong and agile as a shepherd boy and ran easily at my side. Then suddenly I heard the horses, and the squeal of chariot wheels. The sounds were unmistakable and terrifyingly near at hand.

Our own horses had left three days ago, and must be well on their way to Elephantine by this time. Our own chariots were dismantled and loaded in the holds of the departing fleet. The chariots I heard now were still out of sight below the wall of the causeway, but we knew to whom they belonged.

'The Hyksos!' I said softly, and we stopped in a tight little group. 'It must be one of their advance scouting parties.'

'It sounds like only two or three of their chariots,' Tanus agreed, 'but that is enough. We are cut off.'

'It seems that we have left it a little late,' said my mistress with a calmness that I knew was feigned, and she looked at Tanus and myself with complete trust. 'What do you suggest now?'

Her effrontery flabbergasted me. Her obstinacy was entirely responsible for our predicament. If she had followed my urging we would all of us have been on the *Breath of Horus* and making our way up-river to Elephantine by this time.

Tanus held up his hand for silence, and we stood and listened to the sounds of the enemy chariots driving along the pathway at the foot of the wall. The closer they came, the more certain it became that this was only a small advance party.

Suddenly the sounds of turning wheels stopped, and we heard the horses blowing and stamping, then men's voices speaking a harsh and guttural tongue. They were just below us, and Tanus made another urgent signal for silence. Prince Memnon was not accustomed to restraint, nor to keeping the peace against his inclinations. He also had heard and recognized the sounds.

'Horses!' he shouted in his usual high and ringing tones. 'I want to see the horses.'

There was an instant outcry. Hyksos voices shouted orders, and weapons rattled in their scabbards. Then heavy footfalls pounded upon the stone staircase as a party of the enemy came dashing up on to the causeway.

Their tall helmets appeared above the stone balustrade just ahead of us, and then the rest of them came into view. There were five of them in a body and they rushed up at us with drawn swords, big men with fish-scale shirts of mail and brightly coloured ribbons in their beards. But one of them was taller than the rest. I did not recognize him at first, for he had grown a beard and decorated it with ribbons in the Hyksos fashion, and the visor of his helmet hid half his face. Then he shouted in that voice that I would never forget, 'So it's you, young Harrab! I killed the old dog, and now I will kill his puppy!'

I should have known that Lord Intef would be the very first of them to come sniffing like a hungry hyena after Pharaoh's treasure. He must have raced ahead of the main Hyksos division to be the first into the funerary temple. Despite his boast, he did not rush to meet Tanus, but waved the band of Hyksos chari- oteers forward to do the job for him.

Tanus swept Prince Memnon from his shoulders and tossed him to me as though he were a doll.

'Run!' he ordered. 'I will buy you a little time here.' He rushed the Hyksos while they were still bunched on the staircase and had no room to wield their swords. He killed the first one cleanly, with that thrust through the throat which he always performed so skilfully.

'Don't stand there gawking,' he shouted over his shoulder. 'Run!'

I was not gawking, but with the child clutched to my chest, I knew how futile was his command. Burdened as I was, I would never reach the river-bank.

I stepped to the parapet of the causeway and glanced over.

There were two Hyksos chariots parked directly below me, with the horses blowing and stamping in the traces. Only one man had been left to hold them, while his companions rushed up the staircase. He stood at the heads of the two teams and his whole attention was fixed on his charges. He had not seen me on the causeway above his head.

Still clutching Memnon, I threw my legs over the parapet and pushed myself outwards. The prince shrieked with alarm as we dropped. From the top of the causeway to where the Hyksos charioteer stood was four times the height of a tall man. I might easily have broken a leg in the fall, except that I landed neatly on the unsuspecting Hyksos' head. The impact broke his neck; clearly I heard the vertebrae snap, and he crumpled under us, breaking our fall.

I scrambled to my feet, with Memnon howling in outrage at this rough treatment, but there was more of it to follow. I dropped him into the cockpit of the nearest chariot and looked up at my mistress. She was peeping over the parapet high above me.

'Jump!' I shouted. 'I will catch you!' She never even hesitated, but flung herself over the edge so promptly that I was not yet braced to receive her. She came hurtling down on top of me, with her short skirts blowing up and exposing those long sleek thighs. She hit me squarely and knocked the wind out of my lungs. We went down together in a heap.

I scrambled up wheezing for breath, and dragged her to her feet. I shoved her roughly over the footplate of the chariot and shouted at her, 'See to Memnon!' She grabbed him just as he tried to escape from the cockpit of the chariot. He was still howling with anger and fright. I had to scramble over the top of them to reach the reins and take control of the horses.

'Hang on tight!' The pair of horses responded instantly to my hands, and I wheeled the whole rig smartly under the wall. One wheel bounced over the body of the man that I had killed with my fall.

'Tanus!' I screamed. 'This way!'

High above us he jumped up on to the parapet, and balanced there easily, exchanging parry and thrust with the group of charioteers who bayed around him, like hounds around a treed leopard.

'Jump, Tanus, jump!' I yelled, and he stepped out over the edge of the stone wall and let himself drop. With his cloak billowing around his head and shoulders, he landed astride the back of the off-side horse. His sword jerked out of his hand and clattered on the hard earth, and Tanus threw both arms around the animal's neck.

'Hi up!' I called to the pair, and whipped the end of the reins around their hindquarters. They surged forward into a full gallop. I steered them across the pathway and into the open fields that led down to the riverbank. I could see the sails of our fleet out there in midstream, and I could even recognize the pennant of the *Breath of Horus* flying amongst the forest of masts. We had half a mile to go to reach the bank, and I glanced over my shoulder.

Lord Intef and his men had rushed down the staircase. Even as I watched, they were climbing up into the other chariot. I cursed myself that I had not disabled it. It would have taken only a moment to cut the traces and chase away the horses, but I had been in a panic to get my mistress and the prince away.

Now Lord Intef was coming after us. His chariot had not covered a hundred paces before I realized that it was faster than the one I was driving. Tanus' weight on the back of the off-side horse was hampering its gallop; he was a heavy man and he still clung to its neck with both arms. He seemed frozen with terror. I think that this was the first time that I had ever seen him truly afraid. I have seen him stand firm and shoot down a charging lion with his bow, but the horse terrified him.

I tried to ignore the following chariot, and I looked ahead and concentrated all my newly acquired skill on piloting us over the open cultivated fields and through the maze of irrigation canals and ditches to the bank of the Nile. The Hyksos chariot was heavy and unwieldy, compared to my Taita vehicle. The solid wooden wheels with their glinting and turning knives around the rims bit deeply into the clay loam of the ploughed lands, and all that bronze armour and ornamentation on the dashboard and side-frames weighed us down. The horses must have been driven hard before I took control of them. They were lathered with sweat and white froth dripped from their muzzles.

We had not covered half the distance to the river-bank when I heard the shouts of the Hyksos charioteer closing with us, and the pounding of hooves. I glanced back to see them not three lengths behind. The driver was lashing the horses with a whip of knotted leather tails and yelling at them in that coarse and ugly language. Beside him, Lord Intef was leaning out eagerly over the dashboard. His ribboned beard was streaming back on either side of his jaw, and his handsome features were lit by the rapture of the hunter.

He shouted at me, and his voice carried over the sounds of the two labouring teams of horses. 'Taita, my old darling, do you still love me? I want you to prove it once more before you die.' And he laughed. 'You are going to kneel in front of me and die with your mouth full.' My skin prickled with insects' feet of horror at the image his words conjured up.

There was an irrigation ditch ahead of us, and I swerved to run alongside it, for the sides were deep and sheer. The Hyksos chariot followed us round, gaining on us with every stride.

'And you, my lovely daughter, I will give you to the Hyksos soldiers to play with. They will teach you a few tricks that Harrab forgot to show you. I don't need you, now that I have your brat.' Queen Lostris clutched the prince closer to her chest and her face was pale and set.

I understood Lord Intef's design immediately. A child of the royal blood of Egypt, even as a satrap of the Hyksos, would command the loyalty of all our people. Prince Memnon was the puppet through which King Salitis and Lord Intef intended to rule the two kingdoms. It was an ancient and effective device of the conqueror. I pushed my horses to their utmost, but they were tiring and slowing, and Lord Intef closed with us so swiftly that he no longer needed to shout to make himself heard.

'Lord Harrab, this is a pleasure long delayed. What shall we do with you, I wonder? First, you and I will watch the soldiers entertain my daughter—' I tried to stop my ears to his filth, but his voice was insidious.

I was still gazing ahead, concentrating on the rough and

dangerous ground, but from the corner of my eye I saw the heads of the Hyksos pair draw level with our vehicle. Their manes flowed back, and their eyes were wild as they tore up beside us at full gallop.

I looked back at them. The burly Hyksos archer on the footplate behind Intef nocked an arrow to his short recurved bow. The range was so short that even from the bouncing and leaping platform, he could not miss hitting one of us.

Tanus was out of the fight. He had dropped his sword. He was still clinging to the neck of the horse on the side furthest from the overtaking chariot. I had only my little dagger, and Queen Lostris was down on her knees trying to shield the prince with her own body.

It was only then that I realized the mistake that the Hyksos driver had made. He had pushed his team of horses into the gap between us and the deep irrigation ditch. He had left himself no room to manoeuvre.

The archer lifted his bow and drew the fletchings of the arrow to his lips. He aimed at me. I was looking into his eyes over the barbed flint of the arrow-head. His brows were black and dense and bushy, his eyes as dark and implacable as those of a lizard. The Hyksos horses were running level with the hub of my near-side wheel, and I gathered my reins and swerved towards them. The flashing bronze knives that stood out of my wheel-rims buzzed softly as they spun towards the legs of the horses.

The Hyksos driver shouted with consternation as he realized his error. His horses were trapped between the ditch and those cruel knives. The blades were less than a hand-span from the knees of the big bay stallion running nearest to me.

At that same instant, the Hyksos archer loosed his arrow, but my sudden swerve had beaten him also. The arrow seemed to fly quite slowly towards my head, but this was an illusion produced by my terror. In reality it flashed like a beam of sunlight over my shoulder, the flint edge touched my ear, and a drop of blood dripped from the grazed skin on to my chest.

The other driver had tried to counter my swerve by turning away from me, but now his far wheel was running along the lip of the irrigation ditch. It was crumbling away beneath the bronze-bound rim, and the chariot lurched and teetered on the edge.

I gathered my horses and swung them again, turning into the other chariot. My wheel-blades hacked into the legs of the nearest horse, and the poor beast squealed with agony. I saw pieces of skin and hair fly into the air above the sideboard of my chariot, and I steeled myself to the whinnying cry of the horse, and turned hard into him again. This time blood and bone chips flew in a mush from the broken legs, and the horse went down, kicking and squealing, pulling his team-mate down with him. The Hyksos chariot went over the edge of the ditch. I saw the two passengers in the cockpit thrown clear, but the driver was carried over and crushed beneath the capsized truck and the heavy, spinning wheels.

Our own chariot was now tearing along dangerously close to the edge of the ditch, but I managed to gather the horses and bring them back in hand.

'Whoa!' I slowed them, and turned to look back. A cloud of dust hung over the ditch where the Hyksos chariot had disappeared. I brought my team down to a trot. The river-bank was two hundred paces ahead, and nothing stood in our way to safety.

I turned for one last look behind me. The Hyksos archer, who had fired his arrow at me, lay in a crumpled and broken heap where he had been thrown. Lord Intef lay a little further from the edge of the ditch. I truly believe I might have left him there if he had not stirred, but at that moment he sat up and then pushed himself unsteadily to his feet.

Suddenly all my hatred of him came back to me with such force and clarity that my mind seethed with it. It was as though a vein had burst behind my eyes, for my vision darkened, and was glazed over with the reddish sheen of blood. A savage, incoherent cry burst from my throat, and I wheeled the horses in a tight circle until we were headed back towards the causeway.

Lord Intef stood directly in my path. He had lost his helmet and his weapons in the fall, and he seemed half-dazed, for he swayed upon his feet. I whipped the horses up into a gallop once more, and the heavy wheels rumbled forward. I aimed the chariot directly at him. His beard was dishevelled and the ribbons in it sullied with dust. His eyes also were dull and bemused, but as I drove the horses down on him, suddenly they cleared and his head came up.

'No!' he shouted, and began to back away, throwing out his hands towards me as if to fend off the massive carriage and the running horses. I aimed directly for him, but at the last moment, his dark gods defended him one last time. As I was right upon him, he threw himself to one side. I had seen him staggering and I had supposed that he was weak and helpless. Instead, he was as quick and nimble as a jackal pursued by the hounds. The chariot was heavy and unwieldy, and I could not turn it swiftly enough to follow his side-step and dodge.

I missed him and went on by. I wrestled with the reins, but the horses carried me on a hundred paces before I could get them under control and swing the heavy vehicle round again. By the time we came around, Intef was running for the shelter of the ditch. If he reached it, he would be safe – I realized that. I swore bitterly as I drove the team after him.

It was then that his gods finally abandoned him. He had almost reached the ditch, but he was looking back over his shoulder at me, and he was not watching his footing. He ran into a patch of clay clods, hard as rocks, and his ankle turned under him. He fell heavily but rolled back on to his feet like an acrobat. He tried to run again, but the pain in his broken ankle brought him up. He hobbled a pace or two and then tried to hop forward towards the ditch on one leg.

'You are mine at last!' I screamed at him, and he spun around to face me, balanced on one leg as I drove the chariot down on him. His face was pale, but those leopard eyes blazed up at me with all the bitterness and hatred of his cruel and twisted soul.

'He is my father!' my mistress cried at my side, holding the prince's face to her bosom so that he would not see it. 'Leave him, Taita. He is of my blood.'

I had never disobeyed her in my life, this was the first time. I made no move to check the horses, but gazed into Lord Intef's eyes, for once without fear.

At the very end, he almost cheated me again. He flung himself sideways, and such were his agility and his strength that he twisted himself clear of the truck and the wheels of the chariot, but he could not quite avoid the wheel-knives. One of the spinning blades hooked in the fish-scale links of his coat of mail. The point of the knife tore through the armour and hooked in the flesh of his belly. The knife was spinning and his entrails snagged and wrapped around it, so that his guts were drawn out of him, as though he was one of those big blue perch from the river being disembowelled by a fishwife on the market block.

He was towed along behind us by the slippery ropes of his own entrails, but he fell slowly behind as more coils and tangles of his gut were torn from his open stomach cavity. He clutched at them with both hands, as they were stripped out of him, but they slid through his fingers like some grotesque umbilical cord that bound him to the turning wheel of the chariot.

His screams were a sound that I wish never to hear again as long as I live. The echoes of them still sometimes haunt my nightmares, so that in the end he inflicted his last cruelty upon me. I have never been able to forget him, as I would so dearly have wished.

When at last the gruesome rope by which he was being dragged across the black earth snapped, he was left lying in the centre of the field. At last those cries of his were stilled, and he lay without movement.

I pulled up the horses and Tanus slid down off the back of his mount and came back to the chariot. He lifted my mistress and the prince down and held them close to his chest. My mistress was weeping.

'Oh, it was so terrible! Whatever he did to us, he was still my father.'

'It's all right now,' Tanus hugged her. 'It's all over now.'

Prince Memnon was peering back over his mother's shoulder at the sprawling figure of his grandfather with all the fascination that children have with the macabre. Suddenly he piped up in that ringing treble, 'He was a nasty man.'

'Yes,' I agreed softly, 'he was a very nasty man.'

'Is the nasty man dead now?'

'Yes, Mem, he is dead. Now we can all sleep better at nights.'

I had to drive the horses hard along the river-bank to catch up with our departing flotilla, but at last I drew level with Kratas' galley, and he recognized us in the unfamiliar vehicle. Even across that wide stretch of water, his astonishment was apparent. Later he told me that he had believed we were safely aboard one of the leading ships of the flotilla.

I turned the horses loose before I left the chariot. Then we waded out into the water to reach the small boat which Kratas sent in to pick us up.

THE HYKSOS would not let us go that easily. Day after day, their chariots pursued our flotilla down both banks of the Nile as we fled southwards.

Whenever we looked back over the stern of the *Breath of Horus*, we saw the dust of the enemy columns following us. Very often the dust was mingled with the darker clouds of smoke that rose from the towns and villages on the river-banks which the Hyksos burned as they sacked them. As we passed each of the Egyptian towns, a flock of small craft sailed out to join our fleet, so that our armada increased in numbers with each day that passed.

There were times, when the wind was unfavourable, that the columns of chariots overhauled us. Then we saw their cohorts gleaming on the banks on either side of us, and heard their harsh but futile jeers and challenges ring out across the water. However, eternal Mother Nile gave us her protection, as she had over the centuries, and they could not reach us out on the stream. Then the wind would veer back into the north and we drew ahead of them once more, and the dust-clouds fell back on to the northern horizon.

'Their horses cannot keep up this chase much longer,' I told Tanus on the morning of the twelfth day.

'Don't be too smug about it. Salitis has the lure of the treasure of Pharaoh Mamose and the legitimate heir to the double crown,' Tanus replied simply. 'Gold and power have a marvellous way of stiffening a man's resolve. We have not seen the last of the barbarian yet.'

The next morning the wind had changed again, and the chariots slowly gained upon us once more, and overtook the leading ships of our flotilla just as we approached the Gates of Hapi, the first of the granite walls that constricted the river below Elephantine. Between them the Nile narrowed to less than four hundred paces across from bank to bank, and the black granite cliffs rose almost sheer on each side. The flow of the current was full against us as it swirled through the Gates of Hapi, so that our speed bled off and Tanus ordered fresh men to the rowing-benches.

'I think you are right, Taita. This is where they will be waiting,' he told me grimly, and then almost immediately afterwards he pointed ahead. 'There they are.'

Leading the fleet, the *Breath of Horus* was just entering the gates, so we had to throw our heads back to look up the cliff-faces. The figures of the Hyksos archers high up on the rocky ledges were foreshortened by the angle, so that they appeared as grotesque dwarfs.

'From that height they could shoot their arrows clear across from bank to bank,' Tanus muttered. 'We will be in easy range for most of this day. It will be hard on all of us, but more especially on the women and the children.'

It was even worse than Tanus expected. The first arrow, fired at our galley from the cliffs above us, left a trail of smoke against the blue vault of the sky as it arced down and struck the water only a cubit ahead of our bows.

'Fire-arrows,' Tanus nodded. 'You were right once again, Taita. The barbarian does learn quickly.'

'It's easy enough to teach an ape new tricks.' I hated the Hyksos as much as any man in the fleet.

'Now let us see if your bellows can pump water into a ship as well as they pump it out,' Tanus said.

I had anticipated this attack with fire and so, for the last four days, I had been working on those galleys that Tanus had fitted with the water-pumps which I had designed for him. Now, as each of our vessels came up, Tanus ordered the captain to lower his sails, and we pumped water over the decks and soaked the rigging. Leather buckets were filled and placed ready upon the decks, and then one of the galleys escorted the ship into the granite-lined gut of the river and the rain of Hyksos fire-arrows.

It took two full days to get the flotilla through, for the cliffs blanketed the wind. It was hot and still in the gap, and each ship had to be rowed all the way against the current. The arrows fell upon us in pretty, sparking parabolas, rapping into the masts and the decks. Each of them started its own blaze that had to be quenched by the bucket chains or by the leather hoses of the pumps on the escort galley. There was no way for us to retaliate against this attack, for the archers were high up on the cliff-faces. They were well out of range of our own less powerful bows. When Remrem led a shore party to dislodge them from their perches, they were able to fire down on his men and drive them back into the boats with heavy losses.

Those vessels that won through were all scarred with black scorched patches. Many others were less fortunate. The flames aboard them had beaten the buckets and the pumps and engulfed them. They had to be cut free and left to drift down on the current, causing pandemonium amongst the rest of the fleet coming up into the gap. In most cases we managed to take the crew and passengers off before the flames were out of hand, but with some we were too late. The screams of the women and the children in the heart of the flames were enough to stop the blood in my heart. I am left for ever with an image from that dreadful day of a young woman leaping from the deck of a burning barge with her long hair wreathed in flames, like a wedding garland.

We lost over fifty ships in the Gates of Hapi. There were mourning banners flying on every ship as we sailed on towards Elephantine, but at least the Hyksos seemed to have exhausted themselves and their horses in this long chase southwards. The dust-clouds no longer besmirched our northern horizon, and we had a respite in which to mourn our dead and repair our vessels.

However, none of us believed that they had given up entirely. In the end, the lure of Pharaoh's treasure must prove too much to resist.

CONFINED AS we were to the deck of the galley, Prince Memnon and I spent much time together sitting under the awning on the poop-deck. There he listened avidly to my stories, or watched me design and whittle the first model of a new bow for our army, based on the Hyksos recurved type. He had by now learned the old trick of asking questions to keep my attention focused upon him.

'What are you doing now, Tata?'

'I am making a new bow.'

'Yes, but why?'

'All right, I will tell you. Our own single-curve bows, apart from lacking the same power and carry, are too long to be used from the chariot.' He listened gravely. Even when he was an infant I had tried never to indulge in baby-talk with him, and I always addressed him as an equal. If sometimes he did not understand, at least he was happy with the sound of my voice.

'I am now totally convinced that our future lies with the horse and chariot, I am sure that Your Royal Highness agrees with me.' I looked up at him. 'You love horses too, don't you, Mem?'

He understood that well enough. 'I love horses, especially Patience and Blade,' he nodded vehemently.

I had already filled three scrolls with my musings and diagrams of how I conceived these military assets could be used to best advantage. I wished that I was able to discuss these in detail with Tanus, but the Great Lion of Egypt's interest in matters equine was grudging and superficial.

'Build the cursed things if you must, but don't keep chattering about them,' Tanus told me.

The prince was a much more receptive audience, and while I worked, we conducted these long discussions, which were only much later to bear their full harvest. As a companion, Memnon's first choice was always Tanus, but I was not far behind in his affections, and we spent long, happy hours in each other's company.

From the very first he was an exceptionally precocious and intelligent child, and under my influence he developed his gifts more swiftly than any other I had ever instructed. Even my mistress at the same age had not been as quick to learn.

473

I had made Memnon a toy bow of the design I was studying, and he mastered it almost immediately and could soon shoot one of his tiny arrows the full length of the galley's deck, much to the agitation of the slave girls and nursemaids who were usually his targets. None of them dared bend over when the prince was armed with his bow, he seldom missed an inviting pair of feminine buttocks at under twenty paces.

After his bow, his favourite toy was the miniature chariot and horse that I had carved for him. I had even made the tiny figure of a charioteer to stand in the cockpit, and reins for him to drive the pair. The prince promptly named the mannikin Mem, and the horses were christened Patience and Blade. He crawled tirelessly up and down the deck, pushing the chariot in front of him, making appropriate horsey noises and uttering cries of 'Hi up!' and 'Whoa!'

For such a small boy he was always aware of his surroundings. Those sparkling dark eyes missed very little of what was happening around him. It was no surprise to me when he was the first of any of the crew of the *Breath of Horus* to spot the strange figure far ahead of us on the right bank of the river.

'Horses!' he shrieked, and then moments later, 'Look, look! It is Hui!'

I rushed up to where he stood in the bows, and my heart soared as I realized that he was right. It was Hui astride Blade coming down the river-bank to meet us at a full gallop.

'Hui has got the horses through to Elephantine. I forgive him all his other sins and stupidities. Hui has saved my horses.'

'I am very proud of Hui,' said the prince gravely, imitating my words and intonation so exactly that my mistress and all those around us burst out laughing.

WE WERE given a respite once we reached Elephantine. There had been no sign of the pursuing chariots for so many days that a new optimism spread through the fleet and the city. Men started speaking of abandoning the flight to the south, and of remaining here below the cataracts to build up a new army with which to oppose the invader.

I never allowed my mistress to be seduced by this spirit of confidence which was rooted in such shallow soil. I convinced her that my vision of the Mazes had shown us the true path and that our destiny still lay to the south. In the meantime, I continued my preparations for the voyage unabated. I think that by this time, it was the adventure itself that had cast its spell over me, even more than the necessity of running from the Hyksos.

I wanted to see what lay beyond the cataracts, and in the nights after a full day's work in the docks, I sat up into the late watches in the palace library, reading the accounts of men who had taken that first step into the unknown before us.

They wrote that the river had no end, that it ran on to the very ends of the earth. They wrote that after the first cataract, there was another more formidable, one that no man or ship could ever surmount. They said that to voyage from the first cataract to the next was a full year of travel, and still the river ran on.

I wanted to see it. More than anything in my life I wanted to see where this great river, that was our life, began.

When at last I fell asleep in the lamplight over the scrolls, I saw again in my dream the vision of the welcoming goddess seated on a mountain-top, with the twin spouts of water gushing from her great vagina. Although I had slept but little, I awoke with the dawn, refreshed and excited, and I rushed back to the docks to continue the preparations for the journey.

I was fortunate in that most of the ropes for our shipping were woven and braided in the sail-yards here in Elephantine. Thus I had the pick of the finest linen cables at my disposal. Some of these were as thick as my finger, and others as thick as my thigh. With them I filled every available space in the holds of the ships not already crammed with stores. I knew just how desperately we would need these, when we came to the cataracts.

It was not surprising that here in Elephantine those of our company with faint hearts and weak resolve made themselves known. The rigours of the flight from Thebes had convinced many of these that the compassion and mercy of the Hyksos were preferable to a continuation of the voyage into the burning southern deserts where even more savage men and beasts awaited them.

When Tanus heard that there were so many thousands of these citizens anxious to desert from the fleet, he roared, 'Damned traitors and renegades! I know what to do with them.' And he expressed his intention of turning his legions upon them, and driving them back on board the ships.

At first he had my mistress's support in this. Her motives were very different from his. She was concerned only with the welfare of her subjects, and her vow that she would leave none of them to the Hyksos terror.

I had to spend half the night arguing with both of them before I could convince them that we were better off without reluctant passengers. In the end, Queen Lostris issued a decree that any person who wished to remain in Elephantine might do so, but she added a neat little touch of her own to the proclamation. This was read aloud in every street of the city, and upon the docks where our ships lay.

I, Queen Lostris, regent of this very Egypt, mother of Prince Memnon, the heir to the double crown of the two kingdoms, now deliver to the people of this land my solemn promise.

I make oath before the gods and call upon them to witness it. I swear to you that on the majority of the prince, I shall return with him to this city of Elephantine, here to elevate him to the throne of Egypt and place the double crown upon his brow that he may cast out the oppressor and rule over you with justice and in mercy all the days of his life.

It is I, Queen Lostris, regent of this very Egypt, who speaks thus.

This act and declaration increased one hundredfold the love and the loyalty that the common people felt towards my mistress and the prince. I doubt that in all our history there had ever been a ruler so cherished as was she.

When the lists were drawn up of those who would come with us beyond the cataracts, I was not surprised to see that it comprised most of those whose loyalty and skills we most valued. Those who wished to stay in Elephantine were the ones we were happiest to lose, including most of the priesthood.

However, time would prove that those who remained behind us in Elephantine were of great value to us also. During the long years of the exodus they kept alive the flame in the hearts of the people, the memory of Prince Memnon and the promise of Queen Lostris to return to them.

Gradually, through all the long, bitter years of the Hyksos tyranny, the legend of the return of the prince spread through the two kingdoms. In the end, all the people of Egypt, from the first cataract to the seven mouths of the Nile in the great Delta, believed that he would come back, and they prayed for that day.

HUI HAD my horses waiting for me on the fields of the west bank, below the orange dunes hard by the river. The prince and I visited them every day, and although he was growing heavier, Memnon rode upon my shoulder to have a better view over the herd.

By now Memnon knew all his favourites by name, and Patience and Blade came to eat corn-cakes from his hand when he called them. The first time he rode upon her back without my hand to steady him, Patience was as gentle with him as she was with her own foal, and the prince shouted out loud with the thrill of cantering alone around the field.

Hui had learned a great deal about the management of the herds on the march, and using this knowledge, we planned in detail for their welfare on the next stage of the journey. I also explained to Hui the role that I wished the horses to play in the passage of the cataracts, and set him and the charioteers and grooms to work plaiting and splicing harness.

At the very first opportunity, Tanus and I went up-river to scout the cataract. The water was so low that all the islands were exposed. The channels between them were so shallow that in places it was possible for a man to wade through without the water covering his head.

The cataracts extended for many miles, a vast confusion of shining, water-worn granite boulders and serpentine streams that wriggled and twisted their way between them. Even I was daunted and discouraged by the task that lay ahead of us, while Tanus was his usual brutally straightforward self.

'You won't be able to push a skiff through here without ripping the belly out of it. What will you do with a heavily laden galley? Carry it through on the back of one of your cursed horses?' he laughed, but without the least trace of humour.

We started back to Elephantine, but before I reached the city, I had made up my mind that the only way forward was to abandon the ships and go on overland. The hardships that this course would bring down upon us were difficult to imagine. However, I reckoned that we might be able to rebuild the flotilla on the river-banks above the cataracts.

When we returned to the palace on Elephantine Island, Tanus and I went directly to the audience chamber to report to Queen Lostris. She listened to everything that we told her, and then shook her head.

'I do not believe that the goddess has deserted us so soon,' and she led us and all her court to the temple of Hapi on the south tip of the island.

She made a generous sacrifice to the goddess, and we prayed all that night and asked for the guidance of Hapi. I do not believe that the favour of the gods can be bought by cutting the throats of a few goats and placing bunches of grapes upon the stone altar, nevertheless, I prayed with all the fervour of the high priest, although by dawn my buttocks ached hideously from the long vigil on the stone benches.

As soon as the rays of the rising sun struck through the doors of the sanctuary and illuminated the altar, my mistress sent me down the shaft of the Nilometer. I had not reached the bottom step before I found myself ankle-deep in water.

Hapi had listened to our prayers. Although it was weeks early, the Nile had begun to rise.

 THE VERY day after the waters began to rise, one of our fast scouting galleys that Tanus had left to watch the movements of the Hyksos cohorts came speeding up-river on the wings of the north wind. The Hyksos were on the march again. They would be in Elephantine within the week.

Lord Tanus left immediately with his main force to prepare for the defence of the cataracts, leaving Lord Merkeset and myself to see to the embarkation of our people. I was able to prise Lord Merkeset off the belly of his young wife just long enough for him to sign the orders which I had prepared for him so meticulously. This time we were able to avoid the chaos and panic that had overtaken us at Thebes, and the fleet prepared to sail for the tail of the cataracts in good order.

Fifty thousand Egyptians lined both banks of the river, weeping and singing psalms to Hapi and waving palm-fronds in farewell as we sailed away. Queen Lostris stood in the bows of the *Breath of Horus* with the little prince at her side, and both of them waved to the crowds on the bank as they passed slowly up-river. At twenty-one years of age, my mistress was at the zenith of her beauty. Those who gazed upon her were struck with an almost religious awe. That beauty was echoed in the face of the child at her side, who held the crook and the flail of Egypt in his small, determined hands.

'We will return,' my mistress called to them, and the prince echoed her, 'We will return. Wait for us. We will return.'

The legend that would sustain our blighted and oppressed land through its darkest times was born that day on the banks of the mother river.

WHEN WE reached the tail of the cataract the following noon, the rock-studded gorge had been transformed into a smooth green chute of rushing waters. In places it tumbled and growled in white water and froth, but it had not yet unleashed its full and terrible power.

This was the moment in the life-cycle of the river most favourable to our enterprise. The waters were high enough to allow our ships through without grounding in the shallows, but the flood was not yet so wild and headstrong as to hurl them back and dash them to driftwood on the granite steps of the cataract.

Tanus himself managed the ships, while Hui and I, under the nominal command of Lord Merkeset, managed the shore party. I placed the jovial old man, with a large jar of the very best wine on his one hand and his pretty little sixteen-year-old wife on the other, under a thatched shelter on the high ground above the gorge. I ignored the garbled and contradictory orders that the noble lord sent down to me from time to time over the ensuing days, and we got on with the business of the transit of the first cataract.

The heaviest linen lines were laid out upon the bank, and our horses were harnessed in teams of ten. We found out quickly enough that we were able to bring forward ten teams at a time – one hundred horses – and couple them to the main ropes. Any greater numbers were unmanageable.

In addition to the horses, we had almost two thousand men upon the secondary ropes and the guide-lines. Horses and men were changed every hour so that the teams were always fresh. At every dangerous turn and twist of the river, we stationed other parties upon the bank, and on the exposed granite islands. These were all armed with long poles to fend the hulls off the rocks as they were dragged through.

Our men had been born on the river-banks and understood their boats and the moods of the Nile better than they did their own wives'. Tanus and I arranged a system of horn signals between the ships and the shore party that functioned more smoothly even than I had hoped.

On board the vessels, the sailors were also armed with poles to punt themselves forward and to fend off the bows. They sang the ancient river shanties as they worked, and the *Breath of Horus* was the first to make the attempt. The sound of song and the cries of the horse-handlers mingled with the muted thunder of the Nile waters as we hauled her forward and she thrust her bows into the first chute of smoothly racing waters.

The green waters piled up against her bows, but their thrust was unable to overcome our determination and the strength of two thousand men and one hundred straining horses. We dragged the *Breath of Horus* up the first rapid, and we cheered when she glided into the deep green pool at the head.

But there were six miles still to go. We changed the men and horses and dragged her bows into the next tumbling, swirling stretch of broken water in which the rocks stood like the heads of gigantic hippopotami ready to rip out her frail timbers with fangs of granite. There were six miles of these hellish rapids to negotiate, with death and disaster swirling around every rock. But the ropes held, and the men and the horses plodded on and upwards in relays.

My mistress walked along the bank beside the teams of sweating men. She looked as fresh and cool as a flower, even in the baking sunlight, and her laughter and banter gave them fresh purpose. She sang the working songs with them, and I joined with her in the chorus. We made up fresh words as we went along. The men laughed at the saucy couplets and hauled on the ropes with renewed strength.

Prince Memnon rode on the back of Blade, in the leading team of horses. Hui had tied a rope around the horse's chest behind the front legs to give him a hand-hold, because Memnon's legs were still too short to afford him a firm grip, and stuck out at an undignified angle on each side of Blade's broad back. The prince waved back proudly at his father on the poop-deck of the galley.

When at last we broke out into the deep, unruffled flow of the main river above the rapids, the working chant of the boatmen turned to a hymn of praise to Hapi, who had seen us through.

Once my mistress had gone back on board the galley, she called for the master mason. She ordered him to cut an obelisk from the granite massif that hemmed in the gorge. While we laboured to bring the rest of the fleet through the gorge, the masons worked with fire and chisel to lift a long, slender column of mottled stone from the mother lode. When they had freed it from the matrix, they chiselled the words that my mistress dictated to them, using the pharaonic hieroglyphics in which her name and that of the prince were enclosed in the royal cartouche.

 AS WE proceeded with the transit of the cataract, we became more expert with each pace we gained against the river.

It had taken us a full day to bring the *Breath of Horus* up the rapids. Within the following week we were making the transit in half that time, and we had five or six vessels in the gorge simultaneously. It was almost a royal procession with one galley coming up behind the other, stem to stern. Ten thousand men and nearly a thousand horses were in the traces at any one time.

There were over a hundred vessels moored along the bank in the quiet, deep green reach of the Nile above the rapids, when the Hyksos fell upon us once more.

King Salitis had been delayed by his sack and plunder of the city of Elephantine, and he had not realized immediately that we had continued on up-river with the great bulk of Pharaoh's treasure in the holds of our galleys. Everything that he knew about the river, all that his spies and Lord Intef had been able to tell him, had convinced him that the cataracts were a barrier that could not be navigated. He had wasted all that time in the city of Elephantine before setting after us again.

He had ransacked the city and the palace on the island; he had paid informers and tortured captives in an attempt to learn what had become of the treasure and the prince. The citizens of Elephantine had served their prince well. They had held out against the Hyksos in order to give our flotilla a chance to complete the transit.

Of course, it could not last indefinitely, and at last some poor soul broke under the torture of the tyrant. King Salitis harnessed up his horses yet again and came storming after us into the gorge of the cataract.

However, Tanus was well prepared to meet him. Under his command, Kratas and Remrem and Astes had made their dispositions with care. Every single man who could be spared from the work of hauling the ships through the gorge was sent back to help defend it.

The terrain was our greatest ally. The gorge was steep and rocky. The path along the bank was narrow and twisted with the broken ground crowding down upon it. At every turn of the river there rose high bluffs and cave-riddled cliffs, each of them a natural fortress for us to exploit.

In the confines of the gorge the chariots were unable to manoeuvre. They were unable to leave the river and make a detour around the gorge through the open desert. There was neither water nor fodder for their horses out there in the sandy wastes, and the going was soft and treacherous. Their heavy chariots would have bogged down and been lost in the trackless desert, before they could reach the river again. There was no alternative for them, they were forced to come at us in single file along the narrow river-bank.

On the other hand, Kratas had been given ample grace in which to improve the natural defences of the ground by building stone walls in the most readily defensible places. He positioned his archers in the cliffs above these obstacles, and set up man-made rock-slides on the high ground overlooking the pathway.

As the Hyksos vanguard came up the gorge, they were met with a downpour of arrows from stone-walled redoubts on the high ground above them. Then, when they dismounted from their chariots and went forward to clear the stone barriers that had been placed across the track, Kratas yelled the order and the wedges were knocked from under the rock-slides balanced on the lip of the precipice.

The landslides came tumbling and rolling down upon the Hyksos, sweeping men and horses and chariots off the bank into the surging green waters of the Nile. Standing on the top of the cliff with Kratas, I watched their heads go bobbing and spinning through the cascades, and heard their faint and desperate cries echoing from the cliffs, before the weight of their armour pulled them below the surface and the river overwhelmed them.

King Salitis was tenacious. He sent still more of his legions forward to clear the pathway, and others to climb up the cliffs and dislodge our troops from the heights. The Hyksos' losses in men and horses were frightful, while we were almost unscathed. When they laboured up the cliffs in their heavy bronze armour, we rained our arrows down upon them. Then, before they could reach our positions, Kratas ordered our men to fall back to the next prepared strongpoint.

There could be only one outcome to this one-sided encounter. Before he had fought his way halfway up the gorge, King Salitis was forced to abandon the pursuit.

Tanus and my mistress were with us on the cliff-tops when the Hyksos began their retreat back down the gorge. They left the path strewn with the wreckage of their chariots and cluttered with abandoned equipment and the detritus of their defeat.

'Sound the trumpets!' Tanus gave the order, and the gorge echoed to the mocking fanfare that he sent after the retreating Hyksos legions. The last chariot in that sorry cavalcade was the gilded and embossed vehicle of the king himself. Even from our perch on top of the precipice, we could recognize the tall and savage figure of Salitis, with his high bronze helmet and his black beard flowing back over his shoulders. He raised his bow, that he held in his right hand, and shook it at us. His face was contorted with frustration and rage.

We watched him out of sight. Then Tanus sent our scouts after them to follow them back to Elephantine, in case this was a ruse, a false withdrawal. In my heart I knew that Salitis would not come after us again. Hapi had fulfilled her promise, and offered us her protection once more.

Then we turned, and followed the pathway made by the wild goats along the precipice, back to where the flotilla was moored.

THE MASONS had finished work on the obelisk. It was a shaft of solid granite three times the height of a man. I had marked out the proportions and the shape of it upon the mother rock before the masons had made their first cut. Because of this, the lines of the monument were so elegant and pleasing that it appeared to be much taller, once it was set on the summit of the bluff above the last wild stretch of the cataract, overlooking the scene of our triumph.

All our people gathered below it, as Queen Lostris dedicated the stone to the goddess of the river. She read aloud the inscription that the masons had engraved upon the polished stone.

> I, Queen Lostris, Regent of Egypt and widow of Pharaoh Mamose, the eighth of that name, mother of the Crown Prince Memnon, who shall rule the two kingdoms after me, have ordained the raising of this monument.
>
> This is the mark and covenant of my vow to the people of this very Egypt, that I shall return to them from the wilderness whence I have been driven by the barbarian.
>
> This stone was placed here in the first year of my rule, the nine-hundredth year after the building of the great pyramid of Pharaoh Cheops.
>
> Let this stone stand immovable as the pyramid until I make good my promise to return.

Then, in sight of all the people, she placed the Gold of Valour upon the shoulders of Tanus and Kratas and Remrem and Astes, all those heroes who had made possible the transit of the cataract.

Then, last of all, she called me to her, and as I knelt at her feet, she whispered so I alone might hear, 'How could I forget you, my dear and faithful Taita? We could never have come this far without your help,' she touched my cheek lightly, 'and I know how dearly you love these pretty baubles.' And she placed around my neck the heavy Gold of Praise. I weighed it later at thirty deben, five deben heavier than the chain that Pharaoh had bestowed upon me.

On the way back down the side of the gorge, I walked beside my mistress to hold the sun-shade of ostrich feathers over her head, and she smiled at me more than once. Each smile was more precious to me than the heavy chain upon my shoulders.

The following morning we went back on board the *Breath of Horus* and turned our bows once more towards the south. The long voyage had begun.

 WE FOUND that the river had changed its mien and character. It was no longer the broad and serene presence that had comforted and sustained us all our lives. This was a sterner, wilder being. There was little gentleness and compassion in its spirit. It was narrower and deeper. The land on each side of it was steeper and more rugged, and the gorges and nullahs were crudely gouged from the harsh earth. The brooding and darkling cliffs frowned down upon us with furrowed brows.

In some places the bottom lands along the banks narrowed down so that the horses and cattle and sheep had to pass in single file along the crude track that the wild goats had trodden between the cliffs and the water. In other places the track disappeared completely, as the bluffs and the cliffs pushed boldly into the flood of the Nile. Then there was no way forward for our herds. Hui was forced to drive them into the river and swim them across the green expanse of water to the far bank, where the cliffs had retreated and left the way open for them to pass.

As the weeks wore on, we saw little sign of any human presence. Once, our scouts found the worm-eaten hull of a crude dugout canoe washed up on a sand-bank, and upon the bottom land an abandoned cluster of huts. The sagging roofs were thatched with reeds and the sides were open. There were the remains of fish-smoking racks and the ashes of the fires, but that was all. Not a shard of pottery or a bead to hint at who these people might be.

We were anxious to make our first contact with the tribes of

Cush, for we needed slaves. Our entire civilization was based on the keeping of slaves, and we had been able to bring very few of them with us from Egypt. Tanus sent his scouts far ahead of the fleet, so that we might have good warning of the first human habitations in ample time to organize our slave-catchers. I found no irony in the fact that I, a slave myself, spent so much of my time and thought in planning the taking of other slaves.

All wealth can be counted in four commodities, land and gold and slaves and ivory. We believed that the land that lay ahead of us was rich in all of these. If we were to grow strong enough to return and drive the Hyksos from our very Egypt, then we must discover this wealth in the unexplored land to which we were sailing.

Queen Lostris sent out her gold-finders into the hills along the river as we passed. They climbed up through the gorges and the dry nullahs, scratching and digging in every likely spot, chipping fragments off the exposed reefs of quartz and schist, crushing these to powder, and washing away the dross in a shallow clay dish, hoping always to see the gleaming precious tail remaining in the bottom of the dish.

The royal huntsmen went out with them to search for game with which to feed our multitudes. They searched also for the first sign of those great grey beasts who carry the precious teeth of ivory in their monstrous heads. I made vigorous enquiry through the fleet for any man who had ever seen one of these elephant alive, or even dead. Though their teeth were a commonplace throughout the civilized world, there was not a single man who could help me in my enquiries. I felt a strange and unaccountable excitement at the thought of our first encounter with these fabulous beasts.

There was a host of other creatures inhabiting this wild land, some of them familiar to us and many that were strange and new.

Wherever reeds grew upon the river-bank, we found herds of hippopotami lying like rounded granite boulders in the shallows. After long and erudite theological debate, it was still uncertain whether these beasts above the cataract belonged to the goddess, as did those below, or whether they were royal game belonging to the crown. The priests of Hapi were strongly of one persuasion,

487

and the rest of us, with an appetite for the rich fat and tender flesh of these animals, were of the opposite opinion.

It was entirely by coincidence that at this point the goddess Hapi chose to appear to me in one of my celebrated dreams. I saw her rise from the green waters, smiling beneficently, and place in my mistress's hand a tiny hippopotamus no bigger than a wild partridge. As soon as I awoke, I lost no time in relaying the substance of this weird and thrilling dream to the regent. By now my dreams and divination were accepted by my mistress, and therefore by the rest of our company, as the manifest will and law of the gods.

That evening we all feasted on luscious river-cow steaks grilled on the open coals on the sand-bank against which the ships had moored. My reputation and popularity, which were already high throughout the fleet, were much enhanced by this dream. The priests of Hapi alone were not carried along by the general warmth of feeling towards me.

The river teemed with fish. Below the cataract, our people had fished the river for a thousand years and longer. These waters were untouched by man or his nets. We drew from the river shining blue perch heavier than the fattest man in our company, and there were huge catfish, with barbellate whiskers as long as my arm, that were too strong and weighty to be captured in the nets. With a flick of their great tails they ripped the linen threads as though they were the fragile webs of spiders. Our men hunted them in the shallows with spears, as though they were river-cows. One of these giants could feed fifty men with rich yellow flesh that dripped fat into the cooking-fires.

In the cliffs above the river hung the nests of eagles and vultures. From below they appeared like masses of driftwood, and the droppings of the huge birds painted the rocks beneath them with streaks of shining white. The birds floated above us on wide pinions, circling and swaying on the heated air that rose from the black rocks of the gorge.

From the heights, flocks of wild goats watched us pass with regal and disdainful mien. Tanus went out to hunt them on their airy crags, but it was many weeks before he succeeded in bringing back one of these trophies. They had the eyesight of vultures and the agility of the blue-headed rock lizards that could run effortlessly up a vertical wall of granite.

One of these old rams stood as tall as a man's shoulder. His beard flowed from his chin and throat to sweep the rock on which he posed. His horns curled upon themselves from mighty crenellated bases. When Tanus finally brought him down, it was with an arrow shot across a gorge a hundred paces deep, from peak to pinnacle of these rugged hills. The goat dropped into the gulf and twisted over and over in the air before it hit the rocks below.

Because of my passionate interest in all wild things, after he had skinned out and butchered the carcass, Tanus carried the head and the horns home for me. It took all his vast strength to bring down such a burden from those murderous crags. I cleaned and bleached the skull and set it up on the bows of our galley as a figurehead, as we sailed on into the unknown.

THE MONTHS passed, and below our keels the river began to dwindle away as the inundation abated. As we passed the sheer headlands, we could see the height of the river measured upon the cliff where all the previous inundations had left their watermarks.

At night Memnon and I sat up on deck as late as his mother would allow us, and together we studied the stars that illuminated the firmament of the sky with a milky radiance. I taught him the name and the nature of each of these fiery points of light and how they affected the destiny of every man born under them. By watching the heavenly bodies, I was able to determine that the river was no longer taking us directly into the south, but that we were veering towards the west. These observations stirred up another heated controversy amongst the scholars and the wise men of our company.

'The river is taking us directly to the western fields of paradise,' suggested the priests of Osiris and Ammon-Ra. 'It is a ruse of Seth. He wishes to confuse and confound us,' argued the priests of Hapi, who up until now had exerted undue influence over our councils. Queen Lostris was a child of their goddess, and it had been generally accepted by most of us that Hapi was the patron of our expedition. The priests were angry to see their position weakened by this wayward perambulation of the river. 'Soon the river will turn south once more,' they promised. It always appals me to watch how unscrupulous men manipulate the wishes of the gods to coincide with their own.

Before the matter could be resolved, we came to the second cataract.

This was as far as any civilized man had ever ventured, and not one of them had reached further. When we scouted and surveyed the cataract, the reason for this was abundantly evident. These rapids were more extensive and formidable than those we had already negotiated.

Over a vast area, the stream of the Nile was split by several massive islands and hundreds of smaller ones. It was low-water now, and at most places the bed of the river was exposed. A maze of rock-strewn canals and branches extended for miles ahead of us. We were awed by the grandeur and menace of it.

'How do we know that there is not another cataract, and then another, guarding the river?' those who were easily discouraged asked each other. 'We will expend our strength and in the end find ourselves trapped between the rapids without the strength to advance or retreat. We should turn back now, before it is too late,' they agreed amongst themselves.

'We will go on,' decreed my mistress. 'Those who wish to turn back now, are free to do so. However, there will be no vessels to carry them nor horses to draw them. They will return on their own, and I am certain the Hyksos will bid them a hearty welcome.'

There were none who accepted her magnanimous offer. Instead, they went ashore on the fertile islands that choked the course of the river.

The spray from the rapids during the flood, and the water filtering up through the soil during low ebb, had transformed these islands into verdant forests, in stark contrast to the dry and terrible deserts on either bank. Springing from seeds brought down by the waters from the ends of the earth, tall trees, of a kind that none of us had ever seen before, grew on the silt that Mother Nile had piled up on the granite foundation of the islands.

We could not attempt a transit of these rapids until the Nile brought down her next inundation and gave us sufficient depth of water for our galleys. That was still many months away.

Our farmers went ashore and cleared land to plant the seeds that we had brought with us. Within days the seed had sprouted, and in the hot sunlight the plants seemed to grow taller under our eyes. Within a few short months the dhurra corn was ready to be harvested, and we were gorging on the sweet fruits and vegetables that we had missed so much since leaving Egypt. The muttering amongst our people died away.

In fact these islands were so attractive, and the soil so fertile, that some of our people began to talk about settling here permanently. A delegation from the priests of Ammon-Ra went to the queen and asked for her permission to erect a temple to the god on one of the islands. My mistress replied, 'We are travellers here. In the end we will return to Egypt. That is my vow and promise to all my people. We will build no temples or other permanent habitation. Until we return to Egypt we will live as the Bedouin, in tents and huts.'

 I NOW had at my disposal the timber from those trees we had felled upon the islands. I was able to experiment with these and to explore their various properties.

There was an acacia whose wood was resilient and strong. It made the finest spokes for my chariot wheels of any material which I had so far tested. I put my carpenters and weavers to work on reassembling the chariots that we had brought with us, and building new ones from the woods and bamboos that grew on the islands.

The flat bottom lands were several miles wide on the left bank below the cataract. Soon our squadrons of chariots were training and exercising upon these smooth and open plains once more. The spokes of the wheels still broke under hard driving, but not as frequently as they once had. I was able to entice Tanus back on to the footplate; however, he would not ride with any driver but myself.

At the same time, I was able to complete the first successful recurved bow upon which I had been working since we had left Elephantine. It was made from the same composite materials as was Lanata, wood and ivory and horn. However, the shape was different. When it was unstrung, the upper and lower limbs were curved out and away from the archer. It was only when the weapon was strung that they were forced back into the familiar bow shape, but the tension in the stock and the string was multiplied out of all proportion to the much shorter length of the bow.

At my gentle insistence, Tanus finally agreed to shoot the bow at a series of targets that I had erected upon the east bank. After he had shot twenty arrows he said little, but I could see that he was astonished by the range and accuracy of it. I knew my Tanus so well. He was a conservative and a reactionary to the marrow of his bones. Lanata was his first love, both the woman and the bow. I knew it would be a wrench for him to acknowledge a new love, so I did not pester him for an opinion, but let him come to it in his own time.

It was then that our scouts came in to report a migration of oryx from out of the desert. We had seen several small herds of these magnificent animals since we had passed the first cataract. Usually they were grazing upon the river-bank, but they fled back into the desert as our ships sailed towards them. What our scouts reported now was a massive movement of these animals such as took place only very occasionally. I had witnessed it just once before. With the freak occurrence of a thunderstorm in the desert fastnesses once in twenty years or so, the flush of green grass that sprang from the wet earth would attract the scattered herds of oryx from hundreds of miles around.

As they moved towards the fresh grazing grounds, the herds amalgamated into one massive movement of animals across the desert. This was happening now, and it offered us the chance of a change of diet and the opportunity to run our chariots in earnest.

For the first time, Tanus showed a real interest in my chariots, now that there was game to pursue with them. As he took his place on the footplate of my vehicle, I noticed that it was the new recurved bow that he hung on the rack, and not his faithful old Lanata. I said not a word, but shook up the horses and headed them towards the gap in the hills that offered us a route out of the narrow valley of the Nile and gave access to the open desert.

We were fifty chariots in the squadron, followed by a dozen heavy carts with solid wheels that carried sufficient fodder and water for five days. We trotted in column of route, two vehicles abreast, and with three lengths between the files. This had already become our standard travelling formation.

To keep down the weight, we were stripped to loin-cloths, and all our men were in superb physical condition from long months of work on the rowing-benches of the galleys. Their muscled torsos were all freshly oiled and gleamed in the sunlight, like the bodies of young gods. Each chariot carried its brightly coloured recognition pennant on a long, whippy bamboo rod. We made a brave show as we came up the goat track through the hills. When I looked back down the column, even I, who never was a soldier, was affected by the spectacle.

I did not clearly recognize the truth then, but the Hyksos and the exodus had forced a new military spirit upon the nation. We had been a race of scholars and traders and priests, but now, with the determination of Queen Lostris to expel the tyrant, and led by Lord Tanus, we were fast becoming a warlike people.

As we led the column over the crest of the hills, and the open desert lay ahead of us, a small figure stepped out from behind the last pile of rocks where it had been lying in ambush.

'Whoa!' I reined down the horses. 'What are you doing out here so far from the ships?'

I had not seen the prince since the previous evening, and had believed that he was safe with his nursemaids. To come across him here on the edge of the desert was a shock, and my tone was outraged. At that time he was not quite six years of age, but he had his toy bow over his shoulder and a determined expression on his face that mirrored that of his father, when Tanus was in one of his most intractable moods.

'I am coming on the hunt with you,' said Memnon.

'No, you are not,' I contradicted him. 'I am sending you back to your mother this very instant. She will know how to deal with small boys who sneak out of the camp without telling their tutors where they are going.'

'I am the crown prince of Egypt,' declared Memnon, but his lip trembled despite this weighty declaration. 'No man durst forbid me. It is my right and my sacred duty to lead my people in time of need.'

We had now moved on to dangerous ground. The prince knew his rights and his responsibilities. It was I who had taught them to him. However, in all truth, I had not expected him to exercise them so soon. He had made it an affair of royal protocol, and it was difficult, even impossible, to argue with him. Desperately I sought for an escape.

'Why did you not ask me before?' I was merely bidding for time.

'Because you would have gone to my mother,' he said with simple honesty, 'and she would have supported you, as she always does.'

'I can still go to the queen,' I threatened, but he looked back into the valley where the ships were small as toys, and he grinned at me. We both knew that I could not order the entire squadron to drive all that way back.

'Please let me come with you, Tata,' he changed his tune. The little devil was attacking me on all fronts. I found it impossible to resist him when he exerted all his charm. Then I was struck with inspiration. 'Lord Harrab is the commander of this expedition. You must ask him.'

The relationship between these two was a strange one. Only three of us – the two parents and myself – were aware of Memnon's true paternity. The prince himself thought of Tanus as his tutor and the commander of his armies. Although he had come to love Tanus, he still held him in considerable awe. Tanus was not the type of man that a small boy, even a prince, would trifle with.

The two of them looked at each other now. I could see

Memnon was pondering his best plan of attack, while I could feel Tanus trembling with the effort of holding back his laughter.

'Lord Harrab,' Memnon had decided on the formal approach, 'I wish to come with you. I think it will be a very useful lesson for me. After all, one day I will have to lead the army.' I had taught him logic and dialectic. He was a student to be proud of.

'Prince Memnon, are you giving me an order?' Tanus managed to cover his amusement with a horrific scowl, and I saw tears begin to well up in the prince's eyes.

He shook his head miserably. 'No, my lord.' He was a small boy once more. 'But I would very much like to come hunting with you, please.'

'The queen will have me strangled,' said Tanus, 'but hop up here in front of me, you little ruffian.'

The prince loved Tanus to call him a ruffian. It was a term that he usually reserved for the men of his old Blues regiment, and it made Memnon feel that he was one of them. He let out a yelp of glee and almost tripped over his own feet in his haste to obey. Tanus reached down and caught his arm. He swung him up and placed him securely between us on the footplate.

'Hi up!' Memnon shouted to Patience and Blade, and we drove out into the open desert, but not before I had sent a messenger back to the fleet with a message for the queen to tell her that the prince was safe. No lioness could be as fierce as my mistress in the care of its cub.

When we struck the migration road, it was a broad swathe of churned sand many hundreds of yards wide. The hooves of the oryx are broad and splayed to cover the soft desert sands. They leave a distinctive track, the shape of a Hyksos spear-head. Many thousands of the huge antelope had passed this way.

'When?' Tanus asked, and I dismounted to examine the trail. I took Memnon down with me, for I never missed an opportunity to instruct him. I showed him how the night breeze had eroded the spoor, and how small insects and lizards had superimposed their own tracks over those of the herd.

'They passed here yesterday evening at sunset,' I gave my

opinion, and had it endorsed by the prince. 'But they are travelling slowly. With luck we can catch them before noon.'

We waited for the wagons to come up. We watered the horses, and then went on, following the broad trodden road through the dunes.

Soon we found the carcasses of the weaker animals that had succumbed. They were the very young and the oldest, and now the crows and the vultures squawked and squabbled over their remains, while the little red jackals slunk around the fringes, hoping for a mouthful.

We followed the broad road until at last we saw the thin filtering of dust upon the southern horizon, and we quickened our pace. When we topped a line of rugged hills whose crests danced in the heat-mirage, we saw the herds spread out below us. We had reached the area where the thunderstorm had broken weeks before. As far ahead as we could see, the desert had been transformed into a garden of flowers.

The last rains might have fallen here a hundred years ago. It seemed impossible, but the seeds of that harvest had lain sleeping all that time. They had been burned and desiccated by sun and desert wind, while they waited for the rains to come once again. For any who doubted the existence of the gods, this miracle was proof. For any man who doubted that life was eternal, this held out the promise of immortality. If the flowers could survive thus, then surely the soul of man, which is infinitely more wonderful and valuable, must also live for ever.

The landscape below us was painted with shades of soft greens, the contours and the outlines of the hills were picked out with sweeps of darker green. This formed a background to the wonderful rainbow of colour that lit the earth. The flowers grew in banks and drifts. The blooms of each variety seemed to seek the company of their own kind, as do the herds of antelope and the flocks of birds. The orange-coloured daisies grew in pools and lakes together, those with white petals frosted entire hillsides. There were fields of blue gladiolus, scarlet lilies and yellow ericas.

Even the wiry brush plants in the gorges and nullahs, that had seemed seared and dried as mummies of men dead a thousand years, were now decked in fresh robes of green, with wreaths of yellow blooms crowning their ancient blasted heads. Lovely as it now was, I knew that it was ephemeral. Another month and the desert would triumph again. The flowers would wither on the stem, and the grass would turn to dust and blow away on the furnace blasts of the winds. Nothing would remain of this splendour except the seeds, tiny as grains of sand, waiting out the years with a monumental patience.

'Such beauty should be shared with the one you love,' Tanus breathed in awe. 'Would that the queen were with me now!'

That Tanus had been so moved by it proved the glory of the spectacle. He was a soldier and a hunter, but for once he gave no thought to the quarry, but gazed upon the spectacle with a religious awe.

It was a shout from Kratas in one of the following chariots that roused us from this reverie of beauty. 'By Seth's stinking breath, there must be ten thousand of them down there.'

The oryx were spread out to the green silhouette of the farther hills. Some of the old bulls were solitary, keeping all others away, but the rest of them were in herds of ten or a hundred, and some of the herds were beyond count. They were merely huge tawny stains, like cloud shadow upon the plains. It seemed to me that every oryx in all of Africa was gathered here.

We watered the horses again before the hunt began. This gave me a chance to go forward and to gaze down upon this great concourse of living things. Of course, I took Memnon with me, but when I tried to lead him by the hand he disentangled his fingers from my grip. 'Don't hold my hand in front of the men, Tata,' he told me solemnly. 'They will think I am still a baby.'

As we stood on the sky-line, the nearest animals raised their heads and regarded us with mild curiosity. It occurred to me that they had probably never before seen a human being, and that they detected no danger in our presence.

The oryx is a magnificent creature, standing as tall as a horse, with the same full, flowing, dark tail that sweeps the ground. Its face is painted with intricate whorls and slashes of black upon a pale, sand-coloured mask. A stiff, dark mane runs down the neck, enhancing the horse-like appearance, but its horns are like those of no other animal created by the gods. They are slim and straight and tipped like the dagger on my belt. Almost as long as the animal that bears them is tall, they are formidable weapons. Whereas all other antelope are meek and inoffensive, preferring flight to aggression, the oryx will defend itself even against the attack of the lion.

I told Memnon of their courage and their powers of endurance, and explained how they could live their entire lives without drinking water from pool or river. 'They take their water from the dew, and from the desert roots and tubers which they dig out of the earth with their hooves.'

He listened avidly, for he had inherited the love of the chase in his father's blood, and I had taught him to revere all wild things.

'The true huntsman understands and respects the birds and the animals that he hunts,' I told him, and he nodded seriously.

'I want to be a true huntsman and a soldier, just like Lord Tanus.'

'A man is not born with such gifts. He must learn them, in the same way that you must learn to be a great and just ruler.'

I felt a pang of regret when Tanus called to me that the horses were watered, and I looked back to see the charioteers mounting up. I would have preferred to spend the rest of that day with my prince watching the royal show upon the plains below me. I went back reluctantly to take up the reins and to drive our chariot back to the head of the column.

On the footplates of the other chariots, the archers had their bows strung, and the fever of the hunt gripped every man. They were like hounds on a short leash with the scent in their nostrils.

'Ho, Lord Tanus!' Kratas shouted across to us. 'A wager on the outcome?'

Before Tanus could reply, I murmured, 'Take one for me. The old braggart has never shot from the back of a flying chariot.'

'Clean kills only,' Tanus called back to him. 'Any animal with another man's arrow in it, not to count.' Every archer marked the shaft of his arrow with his own motif, so that he might claim it later. Tanus' mark was the Wadjet, the wounded Eye of Horus. 'One gold deben for each oryx with your arrow in it.'

'Make it two,' I suggested. 'One for me.' I am not a gambling man, but this was not a gamble. Tanus had his new recurved bow, and I was the best charioteer in the whole of our army.

We were still novices, but I had studied the Hyksos' use of the chariot. Every evolution that their squadrons had performed on that terrible day on the plain of Abnub was graven on my memory. To me this was not merely a hunt for meat and sport, but practice and training for the much greater game of war. We had to learn to run our formations to the very best advantage and to control them in the full flight and confusion of battle, while circumstances changed with every movement of the enemy, and every chance and hazard of war.

As we trotted down on to the plain, I gave the first signal, and the column split into three files. Smoothly we opened up like the petals of a lily. The flankers curled out like the horns of a bull to surround the quarry, while my column in the centre deployed into line abreast, with three chariot lengths between our wheel-hubs. We were the chest of the bull. The horns would hold the enemy while we came up and crushed him in our savage embrace.

Ahead of us, the scattered herds of gazelle threw up their heads and gazed at us with the first stirring of alarm. They began to drift away, gathering up their fellows as they passed, small herds combining into larger, the way that a single boulder rolling down the slope will bring down the landslide. Soon the entire plain was alive with moving oryx. They cantered with a peculiar rocking motion, and dust rose in a pale mist and hung over their swaying backs. Their long, dark tails swished from side to side.

I held my own squadron down to a walk. I did not want to tire the horses too soon with a long, stern chase. I was watching the denser, taller dust-clouds thrown up by the two flanking columns circling swiftly out on each side of the herd.

At last they came together far ahead, and the ring was closed. The herds of oryx slowed down as they found their escape-route blocked. They began to mill in confusion as those in the lead turned back and ran into the ranks that followed.

Obedient to my orders, once the flanking columns had completed the encircling movement, they also slowed to an easy walk, and turned in towards the centre of the circle. We had the huge herd of oryx in our fist, and slowly we closed our grip upon them. Most of the bewildered animals came to a halt, uncertain in which direction to run. Every way they gazed, they saw the lines of chariots bearing down upon them.

Closer we came, at a steady walk, and our horses were still fresh and eager to run. They had sensed the excitement, and threw their heads, fighting with the traces, snorting and rolling their eyes until the whites showed. The oryx herd began to move again, but in no definite direction. They milled upon themselves, making uncertain dashes in one direction before coming up short and then swinging around and rushing back again.

I was pleased with the control and discipline of our squadrons. They held their formations rigidly, without bunching up and leaving gaps in the ranks. The signals that I gave were repeated down the line and acted upon instantly. We were at last becoming an army. Soon we would be able to meet any foe on favourable terms, even the Hyksos veterans who had spent their entire lives on the footplate of a chariot.

I reached behind me and took Prince Memnon by the arm. I drew him forward and placed him against the dashboard. I wedged him there with my own body, and he gripped the front panel. Now Tanus had both hands free to shoot his bow, and the prince was safe.

'Let me take the reins, Tata. I will drive,' Memnon pleaded. I had let him drive before, so he meant it seriously, though he was barely tall enough to see over the dashboard. I dared not laugh at him, for he took himself very seriously.

'Next time, Mem. This time just watch and learn.'

At last we were less than a hundred paces from the nearest oryx, the pressure was too great for them to tolerate. Led by one scarred old cow, a hundred of them charged straight at our line in a mass. At my signal we shortened our line until we were running hub to hub, a solid wall of horses and men, and the trumpeters sounded the charge. I lashed my team into a full gallop and we raced headlong to meet them.

Tanus was firing past my right shoulder. I could watch each of his arrows fly out across the closing gap. This was the first time he had shot from a running chariot, and his first three arrows flew wide of the mark, as the chariot careered into the herd of

500

racing oryx. But he was a master archer, and he adjusted his aim swiftly. His next arrow took the old cow, who was still leading the charge, full in the chest. It must have split her heart, for she went down, nose into the sand, and rolled over her own head. The animals following her swerved out on either side of her, offering Tanus broadside targets. It was fascinating to watch his next two arrows curl away and fall behind the racing oryx.

The temptation is always to shoot directly at a running target, and not at the place in the empty air ahead of it, where it will be when the arrow reaches it. This calculation of forward aim is further complicated by the movement of the chariot in relation to the target. I was trying to give him the easiest shot by turning the chariot with the run of the game. All the same, I was not surprised when two more of Tanus' arrows missed behind the target.

Then, like the master of the bow that he is, he adjusted his aim, and the following arrow plunged feathers-deep into the chest of the next oryx. He killed three more with three arrows, while all around us the hunt disintegrated into the wild confusion of battle, and dust obscured all but the closest glimpses of running chariots and racing animals.

I was driving close behind a pair of oryx, overhauling them slowly, when the flying hooves of one of them threw up a chip of sharp flint the size of the last joint of my thumb. Before he could duck, it struck Memnon on the forehead, and when he looked up at me I saw the blood trickling from the shallow cut above his eye.

'You are hurt, Mem,' I cried, and started to rein down the horses.

'It is nothing,' he told me, and used the corner of his shawl to mop the blood. 'Don't stop, Tata! Keep after them. Kratas will beat us, if you don't.'

So I drove on into the dust, and beside me Tanus' bow sang its awful song, and the prince yipped and yelped with excitement like a puppy the first time that it chases a rabbit.

Some of the oryx broke free of our lines and escaped into the open desert, while others were turned back into the trap. Men shouted with excitement and triumph, horses whinnied, and the oryx snorted and bellowed as the arrows slapped into them and brought them crashing down in a tangle of flying hooves and scimitar horns. All around us was the thunder of hooves and wheels, and we were immersed in the yellow fog of dust.

There is a limit to how long even the finest and most willing team of horses can be driven at full gallop. When finally I reined Patience and Blade down to a walk, the dust had caked like mud in the sweat that lathered their flanks, and they hung their heads with exhaustion.

Slowly, the dust-clouds that had obscured the field drifted aside and dissipated. The field was a terrible sight.

Our squadron was scattered over the entire plain. I counted five chariots whose wheels had shattered during the chase, and the up-ended vehicles looked like the broken toys of a petulant giant. The injured men lay on the sandy earth beside their shattered chariots, with their comrades kneeling over them as they tended their wounds.

Even those chariots that had survived undamaged were halted. The horses were blown and exhausted. Their flanks heaved as they strained for breath, and the white froth dripped from their muzzles. Each one of them was soaked with sweat, as though it had swum across the river.

The game was scattered upon the field in the same disorder and lack of purpose or design. Many of the great beasts were dead, and their carcasses lay stretched out on their sides. Many others were crippled and maimed. Some stood with their heads hanging. Others limped away through the dunes with slow and halting gait. Each arrow-shaft left a dark stain of wet blood upon the pale, roan-coloured hide.

This was the pitiful end to every hunt, when the heat and excitement have cooled and the wounded game has to be gathered up and put out of its misery.

Near us I saw one old bull oryx sitting on his paralysed haunches with his front legs stiff in front of him. The arrow that had crippled him stood out so high from his back that I knew that the point had severed his spine. I took the second bow from the rack on the side-panel of our chariot, and I jumped down from the footplate to the ground. As I walked towards the crippled bull, he swung his head to watch me. Then he made one last courageous effort, and dragged his crippled back legs as he came at me. He slashed those long black horns at me, but his eyes swam with the tears of mortal agony. I was forced to drive two arrows deep into the cavity of his chest before he gave one last groan and rolled over on to his side, kicked once convulsively, and was still.

When I climbed back into the chariot, I glanced at the prince's face. His eyes were wet with tears and his blood-smeared face was crumpled into an expression of pity for the oryx. He turned his face away from me, so that I could not see his tears, but I was proud of them. He who lacks compassion for the game he pursues is no true huntsman.

I took his curly head in my hands and turned his face back to me. Gently, I cleaned the wound on his forehead and bandaged it with a strip of linen.

We camped that night upon the plain of flowers, and their sweet perfume scented the darkness, and overlaid the smell of fresh-spilled blood.

There was no moon, but the stars filled the entire sky. The hills were bathed in their silver luminosity. We sat late at the camp-fires and feasted on the livers and hearts of oryx roasted on the coals. To begin with, the prince sat between Tanus and me at the fireside, but the officers and men vied for his attention. He had stolen all their hearts, and at their invitation he moved easily from one group to the next. They mended their language and banter to fit his ears, and the prince was at ease in their company.

They made a great fuss of his bandaged head. 'Now you are a real soldier,' they told him, 'just like one of us.' And they showed him their own scars.

'You did the right thing by allowing him to come with us,' I told Tanus, as we both watched him proudly. 'This is the best training any young cadet can ever have.'

'The men love him already,' Tanus agreed. 'There are two things that a general needs. One is luck and the other is the devotion of his troops.'

'Memnon must be allowed to go out with every expedition, just as long as it is not too dangerous,' I decided, and Tanus chuckled.

'I leave you to convince his mother of that. There are some things that are beyond my powers of persuasion.'

On the other side of the camp-fire, Kratas was teaching Memnon the expurgated version of the lyrics of the regimental marching songs. The prince had a sweet, clear voice, and the men clapped the time, and came in on the chorus. They protested loudly and rudely when at last I tried to send Memnon to the bed I had prepared for him under the body of the chariot, and even Tanus supported them.

'Let the boy stay with us a little longer,' he ordered, and it was well after midnight when at last I was able to roll the prince in my sheepskin rug.

'Tata, will I ever be able to shoot the way that Lord Tanus does?' he asked sleepily.

'You will be one of the great generals of our very Egypt, and one day I will carve an account of your victories on obelisks of stone, so that all the world will know of them.'

He thought about that for a while and then sighed. 'When will you make me a real bow, not just a baby's toy?'

'As soon as you can draw it,' I promised.

'Thank you, Tata. I should like that.' And he went to sleep as suddenly as I would blow out the flame of a lamp.

 WE RETURNED in triumph to the fleet, the wagons loaded with the salted and sun-dried meat of the oryx herd. I had expected my mistress to tax me severely for having abducted the prince. I had prepared my defence and was determined to place the blame squarely on the broader shoulders of Lord Harrab.

However, her censure was milder than I had anticipated. She told Memnon that he was a wicked child for having caused her worry, and then hugged him until he was in danger of suffocation. When she turned to me, I launched into a long explanation of Tanus' role in the affair, and the valuable training and experience that the prince had received, but she seemed to have dismissed the entire episode.

'When did you and I last go fishing together?' she asked. 'Fetch your fishing-spears, Taita. We will take one of the skiffs. Just the two of us on the river, the way we used to be in the old days.'

I knew that we would do little fishing. She wanted me alone on the water where we could not be overheard. Whatever was troubling her was of serious importance.

I paddled downstream on the shrunken and slow green waters until the bend of the river and the high rocky bluff hid us from the fleet. All my attempts at conversation had failed, so I put aside my paddle and took up my lute. I strummed and sang the tunes she loved best, and waited for her to speak.

At last she looked up at me, and her eyes were filled with a strange mixture of joy and worry.

'Taita, I think I am going to have another baby.'

I can think of no reason why this statement should have surprised me so. After all, every night since we had left Elephantine, she and the commander of her army had been locked in secret conclave, while I kept guard at the door of her cabin. Nevertheless, I was so alarmed that my hand froze on the lute strings and the song died in my throat. It was some moments before I could regain my voice.

'My lady, did you use the infusion of herbs that I prepared for you?' I asked diffidently.

'At times I did, but at others I forgot.' She smiled shyly. 'Lord Tanus can be a very impatient man. Besides which, it is so unromantic to fiddle with pots and jars, when there are better and more urgent things waiting to be done.'

'Things like making babies who have no royal father to claim them.'

'It is rather serious, isn't it, Taita?'

I struck a chord on the lute while I framed a reply. 'Rather serious? Oh, I think that is the wrong word. If you give birth to a bastard, or if you take a husband, then you will be obliged to relinquish the regency. That is the custom and the law. Lord Merkeset would be the next in line as regent, but there will be covert warfare amongst all the nobility for the position. Without your protection as regent, the prince would be in great danger. We would be torn by internecine strife—' I broke off, and shuddered at the prospect of it.

'Tanus could become regent in my stead, and then I could marry him,' she suggested brightly.

'Don't think I have not thought of that before,' I told her sombrely. 'It would be the solution to all our difficulties. But then there is Tanus.'

'If I ask him, he will do it gladly, I am sure of that,' she smiled with relief, 'and I will be his wife. We need no longer play these shams and subterfuges to be alone together.'

'I wish it were that easy. But Tanus will never agree. He cannot—'

'What is this silliness?' The first sparks of anger lit her eyes, and I hurried on.

'That night at Thebes, the night that Pharaoh sent men to arrest Tanus on charges of sedition, we tried to force Tanus to declare for the crown. Kratas and all his officers swore their support, and that of all the army. They wanted to march on the palace and place Tanus on the throne.'

'Why did Tanus not agree to them? He would have been a fine king, and it would have saved all of us so much heartache.'

'Tanus spurned their offer. He declared that he was not a traitor, and that he would never mount the throne of Egypt.'

'That was long ago. Things have all changed,' she cried with exasperation.

'No, they have not changed. Tanus swore an oath that day, and he called on the god Horus to witness it. He swore that he would never take the crown.'

'But it no longer counts. He can go back on that oath.'

'Would you go back on an oath that you had sworn in the sight of the god Horus?' I demanded, and she looked away and hung her head.

'Would you?' I insisted, and she shook her head reluctantly.

'No,' she whispered, 'I could not.'

'The same code of honour binds Tanus. You cannot call upon him to do what you dare not do yourself,' I explained gently. 'Of

506

course, we can put it to him, but you and I both know what his reply must surely be.'

'There must be something that you can do?' She looked at me with that blind trust that angered me. Whenever she had run herself into the deepest danger, she simply turned to me and said, 'There must be something that you can do?'

'There is something, but you will not agree to it, any more than Tanus will agree to wear the crown.'

'If you care anything for me, you will not even suggest it.' She understood me immediately, and recoiled from me as though I had struck her. 'I would rather die myself than kill this miracle of love that Tanus has placed in my womb. The child is him and me and our love. I could never murder all of that.'

'Then, Your Majesty, there is nothing more that I can suggest to you.'

She smiled at me with such sublime trust and confidence that it took my breath away. 'I know you will think of something, my darling Taita. You always do.'

And so I had a dream.

 I RELATED my dream before a full session of the council of state called by the regent of this very Egypt.

Queen Lostris and Prince Memnon were seated upon the throne high on the poop-deck of the *Breath of Horus*. The galley was moored to the west bank of the Nile. The members of the council were seated upon the beach below her.

Lord Merkeset and the nobility represented the secular arm of the state. The high priests of Ammon-Ra and Osiris and Hapi represented the sacred arm. Lord Harrab and fifty of his senior officers stood for the military.

I stood upon the open deck below the throne and faced this distinguished gathering. I had taken even greater pains than usual with my appearance. My make-up was subtle and cunning. My hair was dressed with fragrant oils, and coiled in the fashion that I had made popular. I wore the two chains of the Gold of

Praise around my neck, and my chest and arms were shaped and hardened by chariot-driving. I must have presented an extraordinary figure of beauty to them, for many of them gaped at me, and I saw the lust in the eyes of those whose inclinations ran in that direction.

'Your Majesties,' I made the low salutation to the pair upon the throne, and Prince Memnon grinned at me cheekily. His head was still bandaged, although it was no longer necessary. He was so proud of his war wound that I had let him keep it on. I frowned at him, and he adjusted his expression to be more in keeping with the occasion.

'Your Majesties, last night I dreamed a strange and wonderful dream which I feel it is my duty to relate. I beg your leave to speak.'

Queen Lostris replied graciously, 'Every person in this company is aware of the sacred gift that you have. The prince and I know that you are able to see into the future, and to divine the will and the wishes of the gods through dreams and visions. I command you now to speak of these mysteries.'

I bowed again and turned to face the council.

'Last night I slept at the door to the royal cabin, as is my duty. Queen Lostris lay alone upon her couch, and the prince slept in his alcove beyond her bed.'

Even Lord Merkeset leaned forward and held his cupped hand behind his good ear, the other being stone-deaf. They all loved a good story and a fruity prophecy.

'In the third watch of the night I awoke, and there was a strange light glowing throughout the ship. I felt a cold wind blowing upon my cheek although every door and porthole was closed.'

My audience stirred with interest. I had struck the right ghostly tone.

'Then I heard footsteps echoing through the hull, slow and majestic footsteps, such as never were made by mortal man.' I paused dramatically. 'These weird and eerie sounds came from the hold of the galley.' I paused again for them to absorb this.

'Yes, my lords, from the hold where the gold coffin of Pharaoh Mamose, the eighth of that name, lies awaiting burial.'

Some of my audience shuddered with awe, while others made the sign against evil.

'These footsteps drew closer to where I lay at the queen's door. The heavenly glow of light grew stronger, and while I trembled, a figure appeared before me. It was the shape of a man, but it was not human, for it glowed like the full moon and its face was a divine reincarnation of the king as I had known him, yet altered and filled with all the terrible divinity of his godhead.'

They were rapt and silent. Not a man stirred. I searched their faces for any sign of incredulity, but I found none.

Then suddenly a child's voice broke the silence, as the prince cried out high and clear, '*Bak-Her*! It was my father. *Bak-Her*! It was Pharaoh!'

They took up the cry, '*Bak-Her*! It was Pharaoh. May he live for ever!'

I waited for the silence, and when it returned I let it draw out to the point where they were almost overwhelmed by the suspense.

'Pharaoh came towards me, and I could not move. He passed me and entered the cabin of Her Gracious Majesty, Queen Lostris. Though I could neither move nor utter a sound, I saw all that came to pass. While the queen still slept, the divine pharaoh mounted upon her in all his splendour, and he took his husbandly pleasure with her. Their bodies were joined as man and woman.'

There was still no sign of disbelief on any face. I waited for the full effect of my words and then I went on, 'Pharaoh rose from the bosom of the sleeping queen, and he looked upon me and he spoke thus.'

I am able to mimic the sound of other men's voices so faithfully that others believe they hear the one I am imitating. I spoke now in the voice of Pharaoh Mamose.

'I have endowed the queen with my godhead. She has become one with me and the gods. I have impregnated her with my divine seed. She who has known no man but me, will bear a child of my royal blood. This will be a sign to all men that she enjoys my protection, and that I will watch over her still.'

I bowed once more to the royal pair upon the throne. 'Then

the king passed back through the ship, and entered once more his golden coffin where he now rests. That was all my vision.'

'May Pharaoh live for ever!' shouted Lord Tanus, as I had coached him, and the cry was taken up.

'Hail, Queen Lostris! May she live for ever! Hail, the divine child she bears! May all her children live for ever!'

That night when I prepared to retire, my mistress called me to her, and she whispered, 'Your vision was so vivid and you told it so well that I shall not be able to sleep lest Pharaoh come again. Guard the door well.'

'I dare say there may be one bold and importunate enough to disturb your royal slumber, but I doubt that it will be Pharaoh Mamose. If some rascal does come to take advantage of your kind and loving nature, what should I do?'

'Sleep soundly, dear Taita, and stop your ears.' Her cheeks glowed pink in the lamplight as she blushed.

Once again my premonition of future events was proved accurate. That night there came a secret visitor to my mistress's cabin, and it was not the ghost of Pharaoh. I did what Queen Lostris had ordered. I stopped my ears.

 THE NILE flooded once again, reminding us that another year had passed. We had reaped the corn that we had planted upon the islands, and we gathered in our herds. We broke down the chariots and packed them on the open decks of the galleys. We rolled up the tents and stowed them in the holds. Finally, when all was ready for our departure, we laid out the ropes upon the bank and put every able-bodied man and horse into the traces.

It took us almost a month of heart-breaking labour to make the transit of this fearsome cataract. We lost sixteen men drowned, and five galleys broken and chewed to splinters by the fangs of black rock. But at last we were through, and we set sail upon the smooth flow of the river above the rapids.

As the weeks turned to months, the Nile described a slow and majestic bend beneath our keels. Since leaving Elephantine, I had charted the course of the river. I had used the sun and the stars to give me direction, but I had come upon a great difficulty in measuring the distance that we travelled. At first I had ordered one of the slaves to walk along the bank and count every pace he took, but I knew that this method was so inaccurate that it would set all my calculations to nought.

The solution came to me one morning while we were out on chariot manoeuvres. I watched my right-hand wheel turning, and realized that each revolution of the rim made an exact measure of the ground that it had covered. Thereafter a chariot followed the bank of the river. One wheel had a flag on the rim, and a reliable man sat on the footplate and made a mark on a scroll for each time the flag came around.

Each evening I calculated the direction and distance we had travelled during the day, and marked it up on my chart. Slowly, the design and shape of the river made itself clear to me. I saw that we had made a vast loop out into the west, but that now the river had turned back into the south, as the priests of Hapi had predicted.

I showed my findings to Tanus and the queen. Many nights we sat late in the royal cabin, discussing the course of the river and how it would affect our plans to return to Egypt. It seemed that every mile along the river that we travelled, far from dimming my mistress's determination, served but to enhance the force of the vow she had made to return.

'We will build no temple nor palace of stone in the wilderness,' she ordered. 'We will set up no monument or obelisk. Our sojourn here is transitory. We will build no cities, but will live in our ships, or under tents and huts made of grass and reeds. We are a caravan on a journey that in the end will take us back to the city of my birth, beautiful Thebes of a hundred gates.'

In private she counselled me, 'Keep your charts well, Taita. I trust you to find the easy way home for us.'

So our river caravan journeyed onwards, and the desert on either hand changed its face with every mile, and yet in the end was unchanged.

We who sailed upon the river had become a close-knit community, almost an itinerant city without walls or permanent structure. Life burgeoned and faded. Our numbers increased, for most of those who had come with us from Elephantine were in the full bloom of life, and the women were fruitful. Young couples married upon the river-bank, and broke the jar of Nile water between them. Children were born, and we watched them grow.

Some of our old people died, and there were accidents and dangers that took toll of the younger ones. We embalmed them and dug tombs for them in the wild hills and left them to their slumber, and went onwards.

We observed the festivals and prayed to our gods. We feasted and fasted in the correct season, and danced and sang and studied the sciences. I held lessons for the older children upon the deck of the galley, and Memnon was the prize of all my students.

Before the year had run out, and while the course of the river still ran southwards, we came upon the third cataract that bestrode the course of the Nile. Once again we went ashore and cleared the land and planted our crops, while we waited for the Nile to rise and help us through.

 IT WAS here at the third great cataract that another joy came to fill my life to overflowing.

In a linen tent upon the bank of the river, I attended my mistress in her labour, and brought forth into this world the Princess Tehuti, the acknowledged daughter of the long-dead Pharaoh Mamose.

In my eyes Tehuti was beautiful as only a miracle might be. Whenever I had the opportunity, I sat beside her cot and examined her tiny feet and hands with wonder and awe. When she was hungry and waited for her mother's nipple, I would sometimes place my little finger in her mouth for the pleasure of feeling her chewing on it with her bald gums.

The river rose at last and allowed us to make the transit of the third cataract. We sailed onwards, and almost imperceptibly the river turned back into the east, describing a vast loop beneath our keels.

Before the year was out it was necessary for me to dream another of my famous dreams, for my mistress had once more suffered a virgin pregnancy that could only be explained by supernatural means. The ghost of the dead pharaoh had been on the prowl again.

My mistress was huge with child when we reached the fourth great cataract of the river. This chute of tumbling waters and rocks like the teeth of crocodiles was even more formidable than those that had come before, and there was much despondency in our company. When they thought that no one could overhear them they complained to each other, 'We are beset by these infernal rock barriers. The gods have placed them across the river to prevent us going onwards.'

I read their lips as they huddled together on the bank of the river. None of them realized that I was able to understand what they said without hearing their words.

'We will be trapped behind these terrible rapids, and we will never be able to return down-river. We should turn back now, before it is too late.'

Even at the councils of state, I saw the words on the lips of some of the great lords of Egypt who sat at the back of the gathering and spoke to each other in muted tones. 'If we go on, we shall all die in this desert, and our souls will wander eternally through it without rest.'

There was an element amongst the young nobility that was both arrogant and headstrong. They were fostering discontent, and hatching insurrection. I knew that we had to act swiftly and with resolution, when I saw the Lord Aqer say to one of his henchmen, 'We are in the hands of this woman, this little harlot of a dead king, when what we really need is a strong man to lead us. There must be some way we can rid ourselves of her.'

Firstly, with the help of my old friend Aton, I ferreted out the names of all the malcontents and potential traitors. It did not surprise me that at the head of this list was this same Lord Aqer, the eldest son of Lord Merkeset, on whose lips I had read those traitorous sentiments. Aqer was an angry young man with inflated ideas of his own worth and importance. I suspected that he had the gall to see a vision of himself seated upon the throne of the two kingdoms with the double crown upon his head.

When I explained to Tanus and my mistress what I thought

must be done, they called a full and solemn state council on the river-bank.

Queen Lostris opened the conclave. 'I know very well how you pine for your own land, and how you weary of this long voyage. I share with you every dream of Thebes.'

I saw Aqer exchange meaningful glances with his cronies, and had my suspicions strengthened.

'However, citizens of Egypt, nothing is as bad as it seems. Hapi has watched over our expedition, as he promised. We are much closer to Thebes than any one of you can imagine. When we return to our beloved city, we will not have to retrace our same weary footsteps. We will not have to face once again the dangers and the hardships of those hellish cataracts that block the course of the river.'

There was a stirring through her audience, and whispers of doubt and disbelief. Aqer laughed, not loud enough to cross the borders of respect and propriety, nevertheless my mistress singled him out. 'I see, Lord Aqer, that you question my word?'

'By no means, Your Majesty. I curse such a disloyal thought.' Aqer made a hasty retreat. He was not yet strong enough, nor sure enough of his support, to force a confrontation. I had caught him out before he was prepared.

'My slave, Taita, has plotted the course of the river that we have covered in these last years,' Queen Lostris went on. 'You have all seen the chariot with the flagged wheel that has measured the ground, and Taita has studied the heavenly bodies to find the direction of our journey. I order him now to arise before the council and reveal to us his calculations.'

Prince Memnon had helped me to trace copies of my chart on to twenty new scrolls. At nine years of age, the prince was already a fine pen-man. I passed these out to all the senior nobles, so that they might follow my lecture more clearly. I drew their attention to the almost circular course that we had followed since we had left Elephantine.

Their astonishment was evident. Only the priests had some prior knowledge of what had occurred, they also studied the stars and had some expertise in navigation. But even they were taken aback by the extent of the river's loop. This was not surprising, since the copies of the map that I showed them were not entirely accurate. I had taken certain liberties with the facts for the benefit of Aqer and his faction, and made the distance across the bight seem shorter than my calculations suggested was the case.

'My lords, as you can see by these charts, since we left the second cataract we have travelled very nearly a thousand miles, but we stand now not much more than a few hundred miles from the point of our departure.'

Kratas rose to his feet to ask a question that I had placed in his mouth before the meeting began. 'Does this mean that it should be possible to take this short cut across the desert and reach the second cataract in the same time as it takes to travel from Thebes to the Red Sea and return? I have made that journey several times.'

I turned to him. 'I was your companion on that same journey. Ten days in each direction it took us, and we did not have horses then. The crossing of this narrow strip of desert would be no more onerous. It means that from here one could be back in the city of Elephantine within a few short months, and it would be necessary to transit only the first cataract at Assoun.'

There was a buzz of comment and amazement. The maps were passed from hand to hand and scrutinized avidly. The entire mood of the assembly changed, as I watched. There was a pathetic eagerness amongst all of them to accept my theory. This unexpected proximity to home and the land they knew cheered all of them.

Only Aqer and his friends were out of countenance. He had been deprived of the top dice in the game he was playing. As I had hoped he would do, he rose angrily to his feet now to put the next question to me.

'How accurate are this slave's scribblings?' His tone was offensive and his expression haughty. 'It is a simple matter to make a few pen-strokes on a scroll, but when those are turned into miles of sand and rock, it is another matter entirely. How will this slave prove that these wild theories of his are fact?'

'My lord Aqer has come to the very heart of the matter,' my mistress intervened pleasantly, 'and, in so doing, has proven his astute grasp of the problem that faces us. I intend to send an expedition of good men to cross the neck of the desert and to open up our return route to the north, the road home to beautiful Thebes.'

I saw Aqer's expression change suddenly as he caught the slant of the queen's speech and realized the trap that had been set for him. He sat down again hurriedly, and tried to appear remote and disinterested. However, my mistress continued remorselessly, 'I was undecided as to who was best suited to lead this expedition, but now Lord Aqer has, by his perception and understanding, proposed himself for this vital task. Is that not the case, my lord?' she asked sweetly, and then went on smoothly before he could refuse.

'We are grateful to you, Lord Aqer. You are to have whatever men and equipment you require. I command that you make your departure before the next full moon. The moon will make it easier for you to travel during the night, and so avoid the heat of the day. I will send with you men who are able to navigate by the stars. You could win through to the second cataract and be back here before the end of the month, and, if you succeed, I will place the Gold of Praise upon your shoulders.'

Lord Aqer stared at her with open mouth, and he was still sitting rigid with shock on his stool after all his companions had dispersed. I fully expected him to find some excuse to back out of the task that we had tricked him into, but in the end he surprised me by coming to me to ask for my advice and help in arranging the scouting party. It seemed that I might have misjudged him, and that now he had been given some worthwhile mission, there was a chance that he would change from a trouble-maker to a useful member of the company.

I selected some of our best men and horses for him and gave him five of our most sturdy carts, which could carry water-skins that, if used sparingly, would last them for thirty days. By the time the full moon came around, Aqer was quite cheerful and optimistic, and I felt guilty about having minimized the distance and the hazards of the journey.

When the expedition set out, I went a short way into the desert with them to point them on the right road, and then I stood alone and watched them merge into the silvery moonlit wastes, aimed at that set of stars we call the Lute which marks the northern horizon.

I thought of Aqer every day over the weeks that followed while we lay below the fourth cataract, and I hoped that the map I had given him was not as inaccurate as I feared it was. At least the immediate threat of a rebellion had disappeared with him into the north.

While we waited, we planted our crops on the cleared islands and the river-banks. However, the lie of the land was steeper than at the other sites lower down the river. It was more difficult to raise the water to irrigate our crops, and I could see that the quantity and the quality of the harvest must suffer in consequence.

Naturally, we had set up the traditional shadoofs on their long, counter-balanced arms to lift the water from the river. These were worked by a slave who swung the clay pot at the end of the arm into the water and then lifted and spilled it into the irrigation ditch on the bank. It was a slow and back-breaking task. When the bank was high, as it was here, it was also an extremely wasteful method of collecting water.

Each evening Memnon and I drove our chariot along the river-bank, and I was troubled by the paucity of the harvest that we watched growing there. We had many thousands of mouths to feed, and cornmeal was still the staple of our diet. I foresaw a time of famine, unless we were able to bring more water to the fields.

I do not know what made me think of the wheel for this purpose, except that the science of the wheel had by this time become an obsession and a passion in my life. I was still plagued by the problem of the bursting of the wheels of our chariots. My dreams were filled with turning and spinning and shattering wheels, wheels with bronze knives on the rim or with flags to measure the distance run. Large wheels and small, the images haunted me and troubled my sleep.

I had heard from one of the priests of Hapi that some varieties of timber can be made harder and more resilient by soaking them in water for a long period, so I was driven to experiment with this idea. As we were lowering one of the chariot wheels into the

517

river for this purpose, the current playing on the rim began to turn the wheel on its hub. I watched this idly, but as the wheel sank lower in the water, the movement ceased, and I thought no more about it.

Some days later, one of the small boats crossing between the islands capsized, and the two men in it were swept into the rapids and drowned. Memnon and I watched this tragedy from the bank, and we were both distressed by it. I took the opportunity to warn the prince once more of the danger and the power of the river.

'It is so strong that it will even turn the wheel of a chariot.'

'I don't believe you, Tata. You are saying that to frighten me. You know how I love to swim in the river.'

So I arranged an exhibition for him, and we were both duly impressed by the wheel turning, seemingly of its own accord, when it was dipped into the running water.

'It would go faster, Tata, if it had paddles fixed around the rim,' Memnon gave his opinion at last, and I stared at him in wonder. He was a little over ten years old at the time, and yet he saw all things with a fresh and enquiring eye.

By the time the full moon came around again, we had built a wheel driven by the river which lifted the water in a series of small baked-clay jars and spilled it into a canal lined with clay tiles at the top of the high Nile bank. Even with her big belly, my mistress came ashore to watch this wondrous contraption. She was delighted by it.

'You are so clever with the things you do with water, Taita,' she told me. 'Do you remember the water-stool you built for me at Elephantine?'

'I could make another for you now, if only you would allow us to live in a decent home like civilized people.'

Tanus was similarly impressed with the water-wheel, though of course he would not show it. Instead, he grinned at me.

'Very clever, but when will it burst like one of your famous chariot wheels?' he demanded, and Kratas and those other military oafs thought that was hugely funny. Thereafter, whenever a chariot wheel broke, they said that it had 'gone Tata', the pet name that the prince called me.

Despite this levity, the fields of dhurra soon grew dense and green in the loamy soil on the high banks, and the ears of golden corn drooped heavily in the bright Nile sunlight. This was not the only harvest that we gathered in at the fourth cataract. Queen Lostris gave birth to another little royal princess. If anything, the infant was more exquisite than her elder sister.

It was passing strange that Princess Bekatha was born with a cap of golden-red curls. Her divine and ghostly father, Pharaoh Mamose, had been of swarthy cast, and her mother's hair was dark as the wing of the black eagle. No one could think of any reason for this aberrant coloration, but all agreed how pretty it was.

Princess Bekatha was two months old when the Nile began to rise once more, and we made our preparation for the transit of the fourth cataract. By now we were experienced in what had become an annual labour, and we had learned every trick and artifice to beat the rapacious river.

 WE HAD not yet begun the transit, when there was tremendous excitement in the encampment. I heard the shouting and the cheering from the far bank of the river where Prince Memnon and I were inspecting the horses and making certain that all was ready for the ascent of the cataract.

We hurried back to the boats and crossed to the east bank, to find the camp in an uproar. We pushed our way through the crowds who were all waving palm-fronds and singing the songs of welcome and honour. At the centre of all this we found a small caravan of battered wagons and skeletal horses, and a band of lean, travel-hardened veterans, burned black by the sun and tempered by the desert.

'Seth damn you and that map of yours, Taita,' Lord Aqer shouted at me from the leading wagon. 'I don't know which of you lies worst. It was almost twice as far as you promised us.'

'Did you truly reach the north side of the river loop?' I shouted back at him, hopping with excitement and trying to fight my way through the crowd.

'There and back!' he laughed, mightily pleased with his accomplishment. 'We camped at the second cataract and dined on fresh fish from the Nile. The road back to Thebes is open.'

My mistress ordered a feast to welcome back the travellers, and Lord Aqer was the man of the day. At the height of the celebration, Queen Lostris placed the Gold of Praise around his neck, and promoted him to the rank of Best of Ten Thousand. My gorge rose to see the fellow preen and strut. As if that was not enough, she gave him command of the fourth division of chariots, and issued him a warrant that would entitle him to one hundred feddan of prime land on the river-bank when we returned to Thebes.

I thought all this a little excessive, especially the gift of so much land which must come out of my mistress's own estate. After all, Aqer had been on the brink of mutiny, and though his achievement had been laudable, it was I who had proposed and planned the expedition. In the circumstances, it seemed to me that another gold chain for the poor slave Taita might not have been out of place.

Nevertheless, I had to applaud my mistress's cunning and statesmanship. She had transformed Lord Aqer, who had been potentially one of her most dangerous enemies, into an ardent and loyal adherent who would prove his value to her many times in the years ahead. She had a way with all men, and was gaining in statecraft each day.

The taming of Lord Aqer and the discovery of the route across the bight had secured our rear, and we could go on above the fourth cataract with high spirits and brave heart.

 WE HAD not travelled more than a month before we realized how our fortunes had changed and how the goddess had made good her promise.

It was clearer each day that we had come through the worst. The desert was behind us at last, and the broad, smooth flow of the river turned into the south once more and carried us into a land such as none of us had seen before.

It was here that for the first time many of our company witnessed the miracle of rain. Although of course I had seen it in the Lower Kingdom, they had never seen water fall from the sky. The rain beat down into our upturned and astonished faces, while the thunder rolled across the heavens and the lightning blinded us with its white fire.

These copious and regular rains engendered a new and exciting landscape, the like of which we could only wonder at. On either bank of the Nile, as far as we could see from the deck of the leading galley, stretched a broad savannah grassland. This magnificent plain, rich with grazing for our horses, set no boundaries to the range of our chariots. We could drive out at will, with no dunes or rocky hills to block our progress.

This was not the only blessing that the goddess had bestowed. There were trees. In the narrow valley that was our home, there might once have been forests, no man could tell. But they had fallen centuries before to the appetite and axes of man. Wood was to us Egyptians a rare and treasured commodity. Each stick of it had to be carried in by ship or on the back of beasts of burden, from far and foreign lands.

Now, wherever we looked, we saw great trees. They grew, not in the same dense forests that we had found on the islands in the cataracts, but in lofty groves with broad grassy spaces between the majestic trunks. There was timber enough upon these plains to rebuild all the fleets of all the nations on all the seas of the worlds. More than that, there was enough to rebuild the cities of all the civilized world, and to roof and furnish every room in them. After that there would still be enough left over to burn as fuel over the centuries to come. We who all our lives had cooked our food on bricks made from the dung of our animals, stared around us in wonder.

This was not the only treasure that we found for our taking in this legendary land of Cush that we had reached at last.

I saw them first in the distance and thought that they were monuments of grey granite. They stood upon the yellow grass plains and in the shade beneath the spreading branches of the acacia groves. Then, as we watched in perplexity, these great rocks began to move.

'Elephants!' I had never seen one before, but they could be nothing else. The cry was taken up by those on the deck around me.

'Elephants! Ivory!' These were riches that Pharaoh Mamose, with all his funerary treasure, could not have dreamed of. Wherever we looked, the vast herds stood.

'There are thousands of them.' Tanus gazed around him, the passion of the huntsman beginning to dawn in his eyes. 'Just look at them, Taita. There is no end to their numbers.'

The plains were thronged with living creatures, not only the herds of elephant. There were antelopes and gazelle, some of which we knew, and others that we had never seen or heard of before. We would come to know all of them well in the future, and find names for their abundant and diverse species.

Oryx mingled with herds of purple waterbuck whose horns curved like the bow that I had built for Tanus. There were spotted giraffe with necks that reached to the top branches of the acacia trees. The horns that grew from the snouts of the rhinoceros were as tall as a man and as sharp as his spear. The buffalo wallowed in the mud at the river's edge. They were huge bovine beasts, black as Seth's beard, and every bit as ugly. We would soon learn the malevolence behind that melancholy stare with which they regarded our passing, and the menace of those drooping black horns.

'Unload the chariots from the holds,' Tanus roared with impatience. 'Put the horses into the traces. The hunt is on!'

If I had known the danger that we were riding into, I would never have allowed Prince Memnon to mount the footplate behind me as we drove out on our first elephant hunt. To us who knew no better, they appeared such docile brutes, slow and clumsy and stupid. Surely they would be easy game.

Tanus was bristling with impatience to go out against this new quarry, and he would not wait for all four divisions of our chariots to be reassembled. As soon as the first division of fifty vehicles was ready, he gave the order to mount up. We shouted challenges to the other drivers, and made our wagers on the outcome of the hunt as the long columns of chariots rolled out through the groves along the river-bank.

'Let me drive, Tata,' the prince demanded. 'You know I drive as well as you do.' Although he was a natural horseman with gentle hands and an instinctive way with his team, and he practised the art almost every day, the prince's boast was unfounded. He certainly was not as good a charioteer as I was, no man in the army could make that claim, certainly not a scamp of eleven years.

'Watch me and learn,' I told him sternly, and when Memnon turned to Tanus, he supported me for once.

'Taita is right. This is something none of us has done before. Keep your mouth closed and your eyes open, boy.'

Ahead of us a small herd of these strange grey beasts were feasting on the seed-pods that had fallen from the top branches of the trees. I studied them with avid curiosity as we approached at a trot. Their ears were enormous, and they fanned them out and turned to face us. They lifted their trunks high, and I guessed that they were taking up our scent. Had they ever smelled a man or a horse before, I wondered.

There were small calves with them, and the mothers gathered them into the centre of the herd and stood guard over them. I was touched to see this maternal concern, and I had the first inkling then that these animals were not as slow and stupid as they appeared to be. 'These are all females,' I called over my shoulder to Tanus on the footplate. 'They have young at heel, and their ivory is small and of little value.'

'You are right.' Tanus pointed over my shoulder. 'But look beyond them. Those two must surely be bulls. See how tall they stand and how massive is their girth. Look how their tusks shine in the sun.'

I gave the signal to the chariots that followed us, and we veered away from the breeding herd of cows and calves. We ran on, still in column, through the acacia grove towards those two great bulls. As we drove forward, we were forced to swerve around the branches that had been torn from the trees, and to dodge the trunks of giant acacia that had been uprooted. As yet we knew nothing of the unbelievable strength of these creatures, and I called back to Tanus, 'There must have been a great storm through this forest to wreak such destruction.' It did not even occur to me then that the elephant herds were responsible; they seemed so mild and defenceless.

The two old bulls we had selected had sensed our approach and turned to face us. It was only then that I realized the true size of them. When they spread their ears they seemed to block out the sky, like a dark grey thunder-cloud.

'Just look at that ivory!' Tanus shouted. He was unperturbed, and concerned only with the trophy of the chase, but the horses were nervous and skittish. They had picked up the scent of this strange quarry, and they threw their heads up and crabbed in the traces. It was hard to control them and keep them running straight.

'That one on the right is the biggest,' squeaked Memnon. 'We should take him first.' The pup was every bit as keen as his sire.

'You heard the royal command,' Tanus laughed. 'We will take the one on the right. Let Kratas have the other, it's good enough for him.'

So I raised my fist and gave the hand-command that split the column into two files. Kratas wheeled away on our left with twenty-five chariots following him in line astern, while we ran on straight at the huge grey beast that confronted us with the yellow shafts of ivory, thick as the columns of the temple of Horus, standing out from his vast grey head.

'Go hard at him!' Tanus shouted. 'Take him before he turns to run.'

'Hi up!' I called to Patience and Blade, and they opened up into a gallop. We both expected the huge animal to run from us as soon as he realized that we menaced him. No other game we had ever hunted had stood to receive our first charge. Even the lion runs from the hunter until he is wounded or cornered. How could these obese animals behave differently?

'His head is so big, it will make a fine target,' Tanus exulted, as he nocked an arrow. 'I will kill him with a single shaft, before he can escape. Run in close under that long, ridiculous nose of his.'

Behind us the rest of our column was strung out in single file. Our plan was to come in and split on each side of the bull, firing our arrows into him as we passed, then wheeling around and coming back in classic chariot tactics.

We were right on the bull now, but still he stood his ground. Perhaps these animals were every bit as dull-witted as they looked. This would be an easy kill, and I sensed Tanus' disappointment at the prospect of such poor sport.

'Come on you old fool!' he shouted contemptuously. 'Don't just stand there. Defend yourself!'

It was as though the bull heard and understood the challenge. He threw up his trunk and loosed a blast of sound that stunned and deafened us. The horses shied wildly, so that I was thrown against the dashboard with a force that bruised my ribs. For a moment I lost control of the team, and we swerved away.

Then the bull squealed again, and he ran.

'By Horus, look at him come!' Tanus roared with astonishment, for the beast was not running from us, but directly at us, in a furious charge. He was swifter than any horse, and nimble as an angry leopard set upon by the hounds. He kicked up bursts of dust with each long flying stride, and was on us before I could get the horses under control again.

I looked up at him, for he towered directly over us, reaching out with his trunk to pluck us from the cockpit of the chariot, and I could not believe the size of him, nor the fury in those eyes. They were not the eyes of an animal, but those of an intelligent and alert human being. This was no porcine sloth, but a courageous and terrible adversary that we had challenged in our arrogance and ignorance.

Tanus got off a single arrow. It struck the bull in the centre of his forehead, and I expected to see him collapse as the bronze point pierced the brain. We did not know then that the brain of the elephant is not situated where you would expect it to be, but is far back in the mountainous skull and protected by a mass of spongy bone that no arrow can penetrate.

The bull did not even check or swerve. He merely reached up with his trunk and gripped the shaft of the arrow with the tip, as a man might do with his hand. He pulled the shaft from his own flesh and threw it aside and came on after us, reaching out towards us with the blood-smeared trunk.

Hui in the second chariot of our line saved us, for we were defenceless against the old bull's fury. Hui came in from the side, lashing his horses and yelling like a demon. His archer from the footplate behind him fired an arrow into the bull's cheek a hand's-span below the eye, and that pulled his attention from us.

The elephant wheeled to chase after Hui, but he was at full gallop and raced clean away. The next chariot in line was not so fortunate. The driver lacked Hui's skill, and his turn away was inept. The bull lifted his trunk high and then swung it down like an executioner's axe.

He struck the near-side horse across the back, just behind the withers, and broke its spine so cleanly that I heard the vertebrae shatter like a brittle potsherd. The maimed horse went down and dragged its team-mate down with it. The chariot rolled over and the men were hurled from it. The elephant placed one forefoot on the body of the fallen charioteer and, with its trunk, plucked off his head and tossed it aloft like a child's ball. It spun in the air spraying a bright feather of pink blood from the severed neck.

Then the next chariot in line tore in, distracting the bull from his victim.

I pulled up my horses at the edge of the grove, and we stared back aghast at the carnage of our shattered squadron. There were broken chariots scattered across the field, for Kratas out on the left had fared no better than we had.

The two great bull elephants bristled with arrow-shafts, and the blood streamed down their bodies, leaving wet streaks on their dusty grey hide. However, the wounds had not weakened them, but seemed only to have aggravated their fury. They rampaged through the grove, smashing up the capsized chariots, stamping the carcasses of the horses under those massive padded feet, throwing the bodies of screaming men high in the air and trampling them as they fell back to earth.

Kratas raced up alongside us, and shouted across at us, 'By the itching crabs in Seth's crotch, this is hot work! We have lost eight chariots in the first charge.'

'Better sport than you expected, Captain Kratas,' Prince Memnon yelled back at him. He would have done better to keep his opinion to himself, for up until that moment we had forgotten about the boy in the confusion. Now, however, both Tanus and I rounded on him together.

'As for you, my lad, you have had enough sport for one day,' I told him firmly.

'It's back to the fleet with you, and that right swiftly,' agreed Tanus, and at that moment an empty chariot cantered by. I do not know what had happened to the crew, they had probably been thrown from the cockpit or been plucked out of it bodily by one of the infuriated beasts.

'Catch those horses!' Tanus ordered, and when the empty chariot was brought back to us, he told the prince, 'Out you get. Take that chariot back to the beach and wait there for our return.'

'My Lord Tanus,' Prince Memnon drew himself to his full height, reaching as high as his father's shoulder, 'I protest—'

'None of your royal airs with me, young man. Go back and protest to your mother, if you must.' He lifted the prince with one hand and dropped him into the vacant cockpit of the other vehicle.

'Lord Tanus, it is my right—' Memnon made one last despairing attempt to remain in the hunt.

'And it is my right to wrap the scabbard of my sword around your royal backside, if you are still here when I look around again,' said Tanus, and turned his back on him. Both of us put the boy out of our minds.

'Gathering ivory is not quite as easy as picking up mushrooms,' I remarked. 'We will have to think up a better plan than this.'

'You cannot kill these creatures by shooting them in the head,' Tanus growled. 'We will go in again and try an arrow through the ribs. If they have no brain in their skull, then surely they have lungs and a heart.'

I gathered up the reins, and lifted the heads of the team, but I could feel that Patience and Blade were as nervous as I was at the prospect of returning to the field. None of us had enjoyed our first taste of elephant hunting.

'I'll go at him head-on,' I told Tanus, 'and then turn out to give you a broadside shot into his ribs.'

I put the horses into a trot, and then gradually pushed up their

speed as we entered the acacia grove. Dead ahead of us our bull
rampaged over the ground that was littered with the wreckage of
overturned chariots and the bodies of dead men and broken
horses. He saw us coming and let out another of those terrible
squeals that chilled my blood, and the horses flicked their ears
and shied again. I gathered them up with the reins and drove
them on.

The bull charged to meet us, like a landslide of rock down a
steep hillside. He was a terrible sight in his rage and his agony,
but I held my team steady, not yet pushing them to the top of
their speed. Then, as we came together, I lashed them up and
yelled them into a full, mad gallop. At the same moment I swung
out hard left, opening the bull's flank.

At a range of less than twenty paces, Tanus fired three arrows
in quick succession into his chest. All of them went in behind
the shoulder, finding the gaps between the ribs, and burying
themselves full-length in the seared grey skin.

The bull squealed again, but this time in mortal agony. Though
he reached out for us, we raced clear of the stretch of his trunk. I
looked back and saw him standing in our dust, but when he
bellowed again, the blood spurted from the end of his trunk, like
steam from a kettle.

'The lungs,' I shouted. 'Good work, Tanus. You have hit him
through the lungs.'

'We have found the trick of it now,' Tanus exulted. 'Take us
back. I will give him another one through the heart.'

I wheeled about and the horses were still strong and willing.

'Come on, my beauties,' I called to them. 'One more time. Hi
up!'

Though he was mortally struck, the old bull was still far from
death. I would learn just how tenacious of life these magnificent
beasts were, but now he charged to meet us once again with a
courage and splendour that filled me with reverence. Even in the
heat of the hunt and terror for my own safety, I felt shame at the
torture we were inflicting on him.

Perhaps it was because of this that I let the horses go in very
close. Out of respect for him, I wanted to match his courage with

528

my own. When it was almost too late, I swung my horses out of the charge, meaning to pass him just out of reach of that wicked trunk.

Just then the off-side wheel of the chariot burst under us. There was that giddy moment as I somersaulted through the air like an acrobat, but this was not the first time I had been thrown, and I had learned to fall like a cat. I rode the shock and let myself roll twice. The earth was soft and the grass as thick as a mattress. I came up on my feet unhurt and with my wits still all about me. I saw at a glance that Tanus had not come through as well as I had. He was sprawled flat out and unmoving.

The horses were up, but anchored by the dead weight of the broken chariot. The bull elephant attacked them. Blade was nearest to him and he broke my darling mare's back with a single blow of the trunk. Blade went down on her knees screaming, and Patience was still linked to her. The bull thrust one thick tusk through Blade's chest and jerked his head up, lifting the kicking and struggling animal high in the air.

I should have run then, while the bull was so distracted, but Patience was still unhurt. I could not leave her. The elephant was turned half-away from me, his own ears, spread like a ship's sail, blanketed me from his view, and he did not see me run in. I snatched Tanus' sword from the scabbard on the rack of the capsized chariot, and darted to Patience's side.

Although the great bull was dragging her along by the leather harness that attached her to Blade, and although the blood from the other horse splashed over her neck and shoulders, she was still unhurt. Of course, she was wild with terror, squealing and kicking out with both back legs, so that she almost cracked my skull as I darted up behind her. I ducked as her hooves flew past my head and grazed my cheek.

I hacked at the rawhide tackle that pinned her to the drive-shaft of the chariot. The sword was sharp enough to shave the hair from my head, and the leather split under that bright edge. Three hard strokes, and Patience was free to run. I snatched at her mane to pull myself up on to her back, but she was so terror-struck that she bounded away before I could find a grip. Her shoulder crashed into me and sent me spinning away. I was thrown heavily to the ground, under the side of the wrecked chariot.

I struggled up to see Patience dashing off through the grove; she ran with a free and light stride, so I knew she was unhurt. I looked for Tanus next. He lay ten paces away from the chariot, face down against the earth, and I thought he was dead, but at that moment he raised his head and looked around at me with a bewildered and groggy expression. I knew that any sudden movement might draw the bull elephant's attention to him, and I willed him to lie still. I dared not utter a sound, for the enraged animal was still standing over me.

I looked up at the bull. Poor Blade was impaled upon his tusk, and the rawhide traces were entangled with his trunk. The bull started to move off, dragging the battered chariot with him. He was attempting to dislodge the weight of Blade's dangling carcass from his tusk. The point of the tusk had ripped open the horse's belly, and the stink of the stomach contents mingled with the reek of blood and the elephant's peculiar rank and gamey odour. Stronger than all that, the stench of the sweat of my own fear filled my nostrils.

I made sure that the bull's head was still turned away from me, before I pushed myself up and ran doubled-over to where Tanus lay. 'Up! Get up!' I croaked in a hoarse whisper, and I tried to lift him to his feet, but he was a heavy man and still only half-conscious. Desperately I looked back at the bull. He was moving away from us, still dragging the whole tangle of broken equipment and the dead horse with him.

I draped Tanus' arm around my neck and put my shoulder into his armpit. With all my strength I managed to lever him to his feet, and he hung against me unsteadily. I swayed under his weight. 'Brace up!' I whispered urgently. 'The bull will spot us at any moment.'

I tried to drag Tanus along with me, but he took only one pace before he gave a groan and fell back against me. 'My leg,' he grunted. 'Can't move. Knee gone. Twisted the cursed thing.'

The full realization of our predicament struck me then, as it had not before. My old sin of cowardice overwhelmed me once more, and the strength went out of my own legs.

'Get out of it, you old fool,' Tanus grated in my ear. 'Leave me. Run for it!'

The elephant lifted his head and shook it in the same way that a dog shakes the water from its ears after it has swum back to the shore. Those vast leathery ears slapped and rattled against his own shoulders, and Blade's crushed carcass slid off the tusk and was hurled aside as if it were no heavier than a dead rabbit. The strength of the elephant bull was past all belief. If he could toss the weight of horse and chariot so easily, what might he do with my own frail body?

'Run, for the love of Horus, run, you fool!' Tanus urged me, and tried to push me away, but some strange obstinacy prevented me from leaving him, and I hung on to his shoulder. Afraid as I was, I could not leave him.

The bull had heard the sound of Tanus' voice and he swung around with those ears flaring wide open like the mainsail of a fighting galley. He stared full at us, and we were less than fifty paces from him.

I did not know then, as I would learn later, that the eyesight of the elephant is so poor that he is almost blind. He relies almost entirely on his hearing and his sense of smell. Only movement attracts him, and if we had stood still he would not have seen us.

'He has seen us,' I gasped, and I dragged Tanus with me, forcing him to hop on his good leg beside me. The bull saw the movement and he squealed. I shall never forget that sound. It deafened and stunned me, sending us both reeling so that we staggered together and almost fell.

Then the bull charged straight at us.

He came with long, driving strides, and his ears flapped about his head. Arrows bristled from the great weathered forehead, and blood streamed down his face like tears. Each time he squealed, the lung blood spurted in a cloud from his trunk. As tall as a cliff, and as black as death, he came at us in full charge. I could see every seam and crease in the folded skin around his eyes. The lashes of his eyes were thick as those of a beautiful girl, but such

531

a glare of rage shone through them that my heart turned to a stone in my chest, and weighed down my legs so I could not move.

The passage of time seemed to slow down, and I was overcome with a sense of dreamlike unreality. I stood and watched death bear down upon us with a slow and stately deliberation, and could make no move to avoid it.

'Tata!' A child's voice rang in my head, and I knew that it was a delusion of my terror. 'Tata, I am coming!'

In total disbelief I swung my head away from the vision of death before me. Across the open ground of the grove a chariot was tearing towards us at full gallop. The horses were stretched out and their heads were going like the hammers on a copper-smith's anvil. Their ears were laid back, and their nostrils flared wide open, pink and wet. I could see no driver at the reins.

'Get ready, Tata!' Only then did I see the neat little head, barely showing above the dashboard. The reins were gripped in two small fists, the knuckles white with tension.

'Mem,' I cried, 'go back! Turn back!'

The wind blew his hair out in a cloud behind his head, and the sunlight struck ruby sparks from the thick dark curls. He came on without a pause or check.

'I'll thrash the little ruffian for disobeying me,' growled Tanus, as he teetered on one leg. We had both of us forgotten our own danger.

'Whoa!' Memnon cried, and brought the team down from a full gallop. He wheeled the carriage into such a sharp turn that the inside wheel stopped dead and swivelled on its rim. He had cut in front of the two of us, shielding us for an instant from the charging bull, and as the chariot spun about there was a moment when it was standing still. It was beautifully done.

I heaved my shoulder up under Tanus' armpit and threw him sprawling on the footplate. The very next instant I hurled myself headlong on top of him. As I landed, Memnon gave the horses their heads, and we bounded forward so sharply that I was almost jerked backwards off the platform, but I grabbed at the side-panel and steadied myself.

'Go, Mem,' I screamed, 'for all you're worth!'

'Hi-up!' Memnon screamed. 'Yah hah!' The chariot careered away with the frightened horses driven to full flight by the enraged squeals of the charging bull close behind.

All three of us stared back over the tail-board. The head of the bull hung over us, seeming to fill all my vision. The trunk reached out for us, so close that each time the bull squealed, the bloody cloud sprayed over us and speckled our upturned faces, so that we looked like the victims of some horrible plague.

We could not draw clear of his rush, and he was unable to overtake us. Matched in speed, we went racing through the glade with the great bloody head hanging over us as we cowered on the floorboards of the bouncing chariot. It needed only one small mistake from our driver to send us into a hole or rip our wheels off against a stump of a fallen tree, and the bull would have been upon us in an instant. But the prince handled the traces like a veteran, picking his route through the grove with a cool hand and practised eye. He sent the chariot careening through the turns on one wheel, within an ace of capsizing, holding off the bull's mad charge. He never faltered once, and then suddenly it was all over.

One of the arrows buried in the bull's chest had worked itself in deeper and sliced open the heart. The elephant opened his mouth wide, and a flood of bright blood shot up his throat and he died in his tracks. His legs went out from under him and he came down with a crash that jarred the earth under us, and lay upon his side with one long curved tusk thrust up in the air as if in a last defiant and regal gesture.

Memnon pulled in the horses, and Tanus and I stumbled down out of the carriage and stood together staring back at that mountainous carcass. Tanus clung to the side of the chariot to favour his damaged leg, and slowly turned back to look at the boy who did not know he was his father.

'By Horus, I have known some brave men in my time, but none of them better than you, lad,' he said simply, and then he lifted Memnon in his arms and hugged him to his chest.

I did not see much more of it, for those everlasting and tedious tears of mine blotted out my vision. Even though I knew myself for a sentimental fool, I could not staunch them. I had waited too long to see this happen, to watch the father embrace his son.

I only managed to regain control of my errant emotions when I heard the faint sound of distant cheers. What none of us had realized was that the chase had taken place in full view of the fleet. The *Breath of Horus* lay close in against the bank of the Nile, and I could see the slim figure of the queen upon the high poop. Even at this distance her face looked pale and her expression set.

 THE GOLD of Valour is the warrior's prize, higher in honour and in esteem than the Gold of Praise. It is only ever worn by heroes.

We gathered on the deck of the galley, those closest to the queen and the commanders of all the divisions of her army. Stacked against the mast, the tusks of the elephants were on display like the spoils of war, and the officers wore all their regimental finery. The standard-bearers stood to attention behind the throne, and the trumpeters blew a fanfare as the prince knelt before the queen.

'My beloved subjects!' the queen spoke out clearly. 'Noble officers of my council, generals and officers of my army, I commend to you the crown prince, Memnon, who has found favour in my sight and in the sight of you all.' She smiled down on the eleven-year-old boy who was being treated like a victorious general.

'For his courageous conduct in the field, I command that he be received into the regiment of the Blue Crocodile Guards, with the rank of subaltern of the second class, and I bestow upon him the Gold of Valour, that he may wear it with pride and distinction.'

The chain had been especially forged by the royal goldsmiths to fit the neck of a boy of Memnon's age, but with my own hands I had sculpted the tiny golden elephant that was suspended from the chain. It was perfect in every detail, a miniature masterpiece with garnet chips for eyes and real ivory tusks. It looked well as it hung against the smooth, unblemished skin of the prince's chest.

I felt my tears coming on again as the men cheered my beautiful prince, but I fought them back with an effort. I was not the only one who was wallowing in sentiment like a wart-hog in a mud bath; even Kratas and Remrem and Astes, for all their hardbitten and cavalier attitudes which they usually cultivated so assiduously, were grinning like idiots, and I swear I saw more than one pair of wet eyes in their ranks. In the same way as his parents, the boy had a way with the affections and loyalties of men. Every officer of the Blues came forward at the end to salute the prince and embrace him gravely as a comrade-in-arms.

That evening, as we drove together along the bank of the Nile in the sunset, Memnon suddenly reined in the horses and turned to me. 'I have been called to my regiment. I am a soldier at last, so you must make me my own bow now, Tata.'

'I will make you the finest bow that any archer has ever drawn,' I promised.

He considered me gravely for a while, and then he sighed, 'Thank you, Tata. I think this is the happiest day of all my life.' The way he said it made eleven years seem like hoary old age.

The next day after the fleet had moored for the night, I went to look for the prince and found him alone upon the bank in a spot that was hidden from casual observation. He had not seen me, so I could observe him for a while.

He was stark naked. Despite my warnings about currents and crocodiles, it was obvious that he had been swimming in the river, for his hair was sopping wet upon his shoulders. However, I was puzzled by his behaviour, for he had selected two large round stones from the beach and was holding one of these in each hand, raising and lowering them in some strange ritual.

'Tata, you are spying on me,' he said suddenly, without turning his head. 'Do you want something from me?'

'I want to know what you are doing with those stones. Are you worshipping some strange new Cushite god?'

'I am making my arms strong so that I can draw my new bow. I want it to have a full draw-weight. You are not to fob me off with another toy, Tata, do you hear?'

THERE WAS one more cataract across the river, the fifth and what would later prove to be the penultimate that we would encounter upon our voyage. However, this was not the same barrier to our progress that the other four had been. With the change in the surrounding terrain, we were no longer restricted to the course of the river.

While we waited for the Nile to rise again, we planted our crops as usual, but we were able to send out our chariots to range far and wide across the savannah. My mistress despatched expeditions southwards to pursue the elephant herds and bring back the ivory.

Those vast herds of the magnificent grey beasts that had greeted us so trustingly when first we had sailed into Cush, were now flown and scattered. We had hunted them ruthlessly wherever we found them, but these sage creatures learned their lesson well and right swiftly.

When we arrived at the fifth cataract, we found the herds grazing in the groves on either bank. The elephant were in their thousands, and Tanus ordered the chariots into action immediately. We had refined our tactics of hunting them and we had learned how to avoid the losses that those first two bulls had inflicted upon us. At the fifth cataract, on the very first day, we killed one hundred and seven elephant, for the loss of only three chariots.

The following day there was not a single elephant in sight from the decks of the ships. Although the chariots pursued the herds, following the roads they had left through the forest as they fled, it was five days before they caught up with them again.

Very often now the hunting expeditions returned to our encampment below the cataract after being out for many weeks on end without having found a single elephant or gathered a single tusk. What had seemed to us at first to be an endless supply of ivory had proved an illusion. As the prince had remarked on that very first day, elephant-hunting was not as simple as it first seemed.

However, those chariots ranging southwards did not return

entirely empty-handed. They had found something even more valuable to us than ivory. They had found men.

I had not left the encampment for several months for I had been involved in the eternal experimentation with my chariot wheels. It was at this period that I at last found the solutions to the problem which had plagued me from the very beginning, and which had been such a source of amusement and ridicule to Tanus and his military cronies – the occasional failure of some of my designs.

In the end, it was not a single answer, but a combination of factors, beginning with the material from which the spokes of the wheels were made. I now had an almost unlimited selection of various types of wood to work with, and the horn of oryx and rhinoceros which we hunted close to our settlement, and which, unlike the elephant herds, did not move away after being harassed.

I found that soaking the red heartwood of the giraffe acacia rendered it so hard that it would turn the edge of the sharpest bronze axe-head. I compounded this wood with layers of horn and bound it all up together with bronze wire, very much in the same fashion as I had done with the bowstock of Lanata. The result was that at last I had a wheel that could be driven to the utmost over any type of terrain without collapsing. When Hui and I had completed the first ten chariots with these new wheels, I challenged Kratas and Remrem, who were the most notoriously heavy-handed and destructive drivers in all the army, to try to smash them up. The wager that we agreed on was ten deben of gold a side.

This was a game much to the liking of those two overgrown children, and they entered into the spirit of it with boyish gusto. For weeks thereafter, their raucous cries and the sound of pounding hooves rang through the groves on the banks of the Nile. By the time their limit was up, Hui came to me complaining bitterly that they had worn out twenty teams of horses. However, it was some consolation to him that we had won the wager. Our new wheels had stood the most stringent test.

'If you had given us a few days more,' Kratas groused as he

handed over his gold with a marked lack of sporting grace, 'I know I would have managed another Tata.' And he treated us to a pantomime which he thought amusing and which was supposed to suggest a shattering wheel and a somersaulting driver.

'You are a gifted clown, brave Kratas, but I have your gold.' I jingled it under his nose. 'All you have is a tired old jest that has gone sour on you.'

It was then that the scouting expedition, led by Lord Aqer, that had gone out to find elephant, came back with the news that instead they had found human habitation further to the south.

We had expected to come across the tribes as soon as we passed the first cataract. For centuries the land of Cush had produced slaves. These had been captured by their own people, probably in tribal warfare, and carried down with other commodities of trade – ivory and ostrich feathers and rhinoceros horn and gold dust – to the outposts of our empire. Queen Lostris' saucy black handmaidens were natives of this land and had come to her from the slave-markets in Elephantine.

I still cannot explain why we had not found people before this. Perhaps they had been driven back by wars and slave raids, in the same way as we had scattered the elephant herds. They may have been wiped out by famine or plague, it was impossible to say. Up until now we had found scant evidence of human presence.

However, now that we had finally caught up with them, the excitement was an epidemic in our company. We needed slaves more even than we needed ivory or gold. Our whole civilization and way of life was based upon the system of slave ownership, a system that was condoned by the gods and sanctified by ancient usage. We had been able to bring very few of our own slaves with us from Egypt, and now it was imperative for our survival and growth as a nation that we capture more to replace those we had been forced to abandon.

Tanus ordered a full-scale expeditionary force to be sent out immediately. He would lead it himself, for we were uncertain what we would find up-river. Apart from those taken as prisoners of war, we Egyptians had always purchased our slaves from foreign traders, and this was the first time in centuries, as far as I knew, that we were forced to resort to catching our own. It was sport as new to us as elephant-hunting, but at least this time we did not expect our quarry to be either docile or dull-witted.

Tanus would still not ride with any other driver than me, and even Kratas' and Remrem's unsuccessful efforts to destroy them had not yet convinced him of the virtue of my new chariots. We led the column, but the second chariot in line was driven by the youngest subaltern of the Blues, the crown prince, Memnon.

I had chosen the two very best charioteers to act as crew for Memnon. His own weight was so light that the chariot could carry an extra man, and the prince's strength had not developed sufficiently for him to be able to lift his end of the chariot when it was necessary to dismount and carry it over the obstacles that could not be driven over. He needed that extra man to help him.

The first villages we came across were on the river-bank, three days' travel above the cataract. They were groups of miserable grass shelters too rudimentary to be called huts. Tanus sent scouts forward to reconnoitre, and then in the dawn we surrounded them with a single swift rush.

The people that stumbled out of these crude shelters were too dazed and shocked to offer any resistance, or even attempt to run from us. They clung together and chattered and gaped at the ring of chariots and shields that we had thrown around them.

'A fine catch!' Tanus was delighted as we looked them over. The men were tall and lean, with long, slim limbs. They towered over most of the men in our ranks; even Tanus seemed short in comparison as we walked amongst them, sorting them into groups as a farmer might apportion his herds.

'There are some really good specimens,' he enthused. 'Look at that beauty.' He had picked out a young man of exceptional physique. 'He would fetch ten rings of gold on the slave-market at Elephantine on any day.'

Their women were strong and healthy. Their backs were straight and their teeth were white and even. Every mature female carried an infant on her hip and led another by the hand.

Yet they were the most primitive peoples I had ever encountered. Neither men nor women wore a shred of clothing, and they left their pudenda shamelessly bared, though the younger girls wore a single string of beads made from the shells of ostrich eggs around their waist. I could see at once that the mature women had all been circumcised in the most brutal fashion. Later I learned that either a flint knife or a sliver of bamboo was used for this operation. Their vaginas were scarred and deformed into open pits, and then infibulated with slivers of bone or ivory. The younger girls had not yet suffered this mutilation, and I determined that this custom would be outlawed in the future. I was certain that I could rely on the support of my mistress in this.

Their skins were so dark that their naked bodies appeared purple in the early sunlight, the colour of an over-ripe black grape. Some of them had smeared themselves with a paste of ashes and white clay, on which they had daubed crude patterns with their fingertips. They had dressed their hair with a mixture of ox-blood and clay into a tall, shiny helmet which exaggerated their already impressive height.

One thing that struck me immediately was that there were no old people among them. I learned later that it was their custom to break the legs of the elderly with their war clubs and leave them on the bank of the river as a sacrifice to the crocodiles. They believed that the crocodiles were reincarnations of their dead ancestors, and that by feeding them, the victim became a part of this process.

They had forged no metal artefacts. Their weapons were wooden clubs and sharpened sticks. The potter's art had eluded them and their vessels were the gourds of wild plants. They planted no crops, but lived on the fish they caught in basket-traps, and on the herds of stunted long-horned cattle which were their most prized possessions. They bled them from a vein in the neck and mixed the blood with milk warm from the udder, and drank the curdled mess with the utmost relish.

When I studied them over the months that followed, I found that they could neither read nor write. Their only musical instrument was a drum hollowed from a tree-trunk, and their songs were the grunting and braying of wild animals. Their dances were flagrant parodies of the sexual act in which ranks of naked men and women approached each other, stamping and grinding their hips until they met. When this happened, the imitation was transformed into reality, and the most licentious debaucheries were enacted.

When Prince Memnon questioned me as to what right we had to capture these people and take possession of them like cattle, I told him, 'They are savages, and we are civilized people. As a father has a duty to his son, it is our duty to lift them from their brutish state, and to show them the true gods. Their part of the bargain is that they repay us with their labour.' Memnon was a bright lad, and after I had explained it to him he never again questioned the logic or the morality of it.

At my suggestion, my mistress had allowed two of her black handmaidens to accompany the expedition. My personal relationship with these little hussies had not been entirely untroubled, but now they rendered invaluable service. Both these girls had childhood memories of the time before their capture, and they retained a rudimentary knowledge of the language of these tribes of Cush. This was just sufficient for us to begin the process of taming our captives. As a musician, I have an ear tuned to the sounds of the human voice; added to this, I have also a natural linguistic ability. Within a very few weeks I was able to speak the language of the Shilluk, which was what these people were called.

Their language was as primitive as their customs and their way of life. Their entire vocabulary did not exceed five hundred words, which I recorded on my scrolls and taught to the slave-masters and to the army instructors whom Tanus appointed over the fresh-caught slaves. For among these people Tanus had found his infantry regiments to complement the chariot divisions.

This first raid gave us no real warning of the true warlike nature of the Shilluk. It had all gone too easily, and we were unprepared for what followed when we swept down on the next straggle of villages. By this time the Shilluk had been alerted, and they were ready to meet us.

They had driven away their cattle herds and hidden their women and children. Naked and armed only with wooden clubs, they came in their hordes against our chariots and recurved bows and swords, with a courage and tenacity that surpassed belief.

'By the putrid wax in Seth's ear-hole,' Kratas swore with delight after we had driven back another charge, 'every one of these black devils is a soldier born.'

'Trained and armed with bronze, these Shilluk will stand out against any other foot-soldiers in the world,' Tanus agreed. 'Leave the bows on the racks. I want as many of them as we can catch alive.'

In the end, Tanus ran them to exhaustion with the chariots, and only when they fell to their knees with even their extraordinary stamina and reckless courage totally expended, could the slave-masters put the ropes on them.

Tanus selected the best of them for his infantry regiments, and he learned their language as readily as I did. The Shilluk soon looked upon him as a god to replace their crocodiles, and Tanus came to love them almost as much as I loved my horses. In the end it was no longer necessary to catch the Shilluk like animals. These marvellously tall and willowy spearmen came out of their hiding-places in the reeds and bushy gulleys of their own accord, to seek Tanus out and to beg to be allowed to join his regiments.

Tanus armed them with long bronze-tipped spears and shields made from elephant hide, and he uniformed them in kilts of wild-cat tails and head-dresses of ostrich feathers. His sergeants drilled them in all the classic evolutions of war, and we learned swiftly to integrate these tactics with those of the chariots.

Not all the Shilluk were selected for the army. The others proved to be indefatigable oarsmen on the rowing-benches of the galleys, and dedicated herdsmen and grooms, for they were born to tend their herds.

We very soon learned that their hereditary enemies were the tribes that lived further to the south, the Dinka and the Mandari. These other tribes were even more primitive, and lacked the fighting instincts of our Shilluk. Nothing pleased Tanus' new Shilluk regiments better than to be sent south with their Egyptian officers and supported by the chariots against their ancient foes. They rounded up the Dinka and Mandari in their thousands. We used them for the heavy unskilled work. None of them came in willingly, as some of our Shilluk had done.

ONCE WE had brought the fleet up through the fifth cataract, the entire land of Cush lay open to us. With our Shilluk now to guide us, the fleet sailed on up-river, while our chariot divisions ranged widely along each bank, and returned with more ivory and fresh levies of slaves.

Soon we reached a wide river-course that joined the main flow of the Nile from the east. The flow of this river was restricted to a sullen trickle down its shrunken pools. However, the Shilluk assured us that in its season this river, which we named the Atbara, would become a raging torrent, and its waters would augment the annual flood of the Nile. Queen Lostris despatched an expedition of gold-seekers, with Shilluk guides, to follow the Atbara as far as they were able. The fleet sailed on southwards, hunting and slave-raiding along the way.

I worried to see it, and tried to prevent it, but so often these days Prince Memnon's chariot was at the head of one of these flying columns. Naturally, he was supported by good men, I could at least see to that, but there was constant hazard and danger out there in the African bush, and he was still only a boy.

I felt he should spend more time with me and his scrolls studying on the deck of the *Breath of Horus*, rather than disporting himself with the likes of Kratas and Remrem. Those two hooligans had as little concern for the prince's safety as they had for their own. They egged him on with wagers and challenges and extravagant praise for his more daring feats. He was soon as much of a dare-devil as any of them, and when he returned from these forays, he took great pleasure in horrifying me with accounts of his escapades.

When I protested to Tanus, he merely laughed. 'If he is to wear the double crown one day, he must learn to spurn danger and lead men.' My mistress agreed with Tanus in the training of Memnon. I had to content myself with making the most of what time I still had to be alone with my prince.

At least I had my two little princesses. They were a wonderful consolation. Tehuti and Bakatha grew more enchanting each day, and I was their slave in more than name alone. Because of our peculiar circumstances I was closer to them than their true father could be. The first word that Bakatha ever said was 'Tata', and Tehuti refused to sleep unless I first told her a story. She pined when I was obliged to leave the fleet on other business. I think that this was the most happy period of my life. I felt that I was at the centre of my family, and solid in the affections of all of them.

The fortunes of our nation were almost as bright as my own. Soon one of our gold-seekers returned from the expedition up the Atbara river. He knelt before Queen Lostris and laid a small leather bag at her feet. Then, at her bidding, he opened the neck of the bag and poured from it a stream of gleaming pebbles. Some of these were as small as grains of sand, and others as large as the end of my thumb. All of them shone with that peculiar radiance that cannot be mistaken.

The goldsmiths were summoned and they worked with their furnaces and clay crucibles, and finally declared these nuggets to be veritable gold of an extraordinary purity. Tanus and I rode back up the Atbara to the site where this gold had been discovered. I helped to plan the methods that were used to mine the gravel-beds in the water-course of the river in which the gold had been trapped.

We used thousands of Mandari and Dinka slaves to scoop out basketloads of gravel and carry these up to the sluices that the masons had carved out of the granite slopes in the hills above the river.

To take back to my mistress I sketched pictures of the long lines of naked black slaves, their wet skins gleaming in the sunlight, toiling up the hillside, each with a heavy basket balanced on his head. When we left the miners hard at work and went back to rejoin the fleet, we carried with us five hundred deben of newly smelted gold rings.

WE ENCOUNTERED yet another cataract on our voyage southwards. This was the sixth and final set of rapids, but this transit proved swifter and easier than any of the others. Our chariots and wagons were able to detour around the rapids, and so at last we reached the mystical confluence of two mighty rivers that between them became the Nile we knew and loved so well.

'This is the place that Taita saw in his vision of the Mazes of Ammon-Ra. Here Hapi lets her waters flow and mingle. This is the sacred site of the goddess,' Queen Lostris declared. 'We have completed our voyage. It is at this place that the goddess will strengthen us for the return to Egypt. I name it Qebui, the Place of the North Wind, for it is that wind which blew us here.'

'It is a propitious place. Already the goddess has shown her favour by providing us with slaves and gold,' the great lords of the state council agreed. 'We should voyage no further.'

'It remains only to find a site for the tomb of my husband, Pharaoh Mamose,' Queen Lostris decreed. 'Once the tomb is built and Pharaoh sealed in it, then my vow will have been fulfilled and it will be time to return in triumph to our very Egypt. Only once that has been done can we go up against the Hyksos tyrant and drive him from our mother-land.'

I think that I was one of the very few of all our company who was not happy and relieved by this decision. The others were consumed by home-sickness and weary of the long years of travel. I, on the other hand, had been stricken by a malady even more pernicious, that of wanderlust. I wanted to see what lay beyond the next bend of the river and over the crest of the next hill. I wanted to go on and on, to the very end of the world. Therefore I was delighted when my mistress chose me as the one to seek out the site of the royal tomb, and ordered Prince Memnon to escort me on this expedition with his squadron of chariots. Not only would I be able to indulge this new appetite of mine for travel, but I would once more have the undiluted pleasure of the prince's company.

At fourteen years of age, Prince Memnon was placed in command of the expedition. This was not exceptional. There have been pharaohs in our history who commanded great armies

545

in battle when they were no older. The prince took his responsibilities on this his first independent command most seriously. The chariots were made ready, and Memnon inspected each horse and vehicle personally. We had two spare teams of horses for each chariot, so that these could be changed and rested regularly.

Then the two of us deliberated at great length and in even greater detail as to which direction we should follow in our search for the ideal site for the king's tomb. This should be in some rugged and uninhabited area not readily accessible to grave-robbers. There must be a cliff into which the tomb with all the subsidiary passages could be cut.

There was no area that we had come upon since we had entered the land of Cush that satisfied these requirements. We reviewed what we knew of the land behind us and tried to divine what lay ahead. Where we stood now at Qebui, the meeting-point of the two rivers, was the loveliest place we had visited on all the long voyage.

It seemed that all the birds of the air had gathered here, from tiny jewelled kingfishers to stately blue cranes, from whistling flocks of duck that darkened the sun in their multitudes to plovers and lapwings that scurried along the water's edge, pausing only to ask the plaintive question, 'Pee-wit? Pee-wit?' In the silvery acacia groves and out on the open savannah, the herds of antelope grazed in their countless millions. It was almost as though this seat of the goddess was sacred to all degrees of life. The waters below the juncture of the rivers roiled with shoals of fish, while in the sky above the white-headed fish eagles turned slow circles against the startling blue of the African sky and uttered their weird, yelping chant.

Each of these twin rivers expressed a different character and mood, just as two infants sprung from the same womb can vary in every detail of body and mind. The right-hand branch was slow and yellow, greater in volume than the other, but not so assertive. The eastern branch was a murky grey-blue, an angry, overbearing flood that shoved its twin aside when they met, refusing to mingle its waters, crowding the other against the bank and retaining its own turbid character for many miles downstream before sullenly allowing itself to be absorbed by the gentler yellow stream.

'Which river must we follow, Tata?' Memnon demanded, and I sent for the Shilluk guides.

'The yellow river comes out of a vast and pestilent swamp that has no end. No man can enter there. It is a place of crocodiles and hippopotamus and stinging insects. It is a place of fever where a man might lose his way and wander for ever,' the Shilluk told us.

'What of the other river?' we asked.

'The dark river comes out of the sky, down cliffs of stone that rise up into the clouds. No man can climb the dreadful gorges.'

'We will follow the dark left-hand fork,' the prince decided. 'In those rocky places we will find a resting-place for my father.'

So we journeyed into the east until we saw the mountains rise on the horizon. They formed a blue rampart so tall and formidable as to surpass anything that we had ever seen or believed possible. Beside these great mountains, the hills we had known in the Nile valley were like the scratching of little birds in the sand-banks of the river. Each day as we journeyed towards them they climbed higher into the heavens and dwarfed all the world below.

'No man can go up there,' Memnon marvelled. 'That must be the abode of the gods.'

We watched the lightning play upon the mountains, flickering and flaring inside the tumbling banks of cloud that blanketed the peaks from our view. We listened to the thunder growling like a hunting lion amongst the gorges and the sheer valleys, and we were awestruck.

We ventured no further than the foothills of this terrible range, and then the cliffs and gorges barred our way and turned our chariots back. In these foothills we found a hidden valley with vertical sides of stone. For twenty days the prince and I explored this wild place, until at last we stood before a black cliff-face and Memnon spoke quietly. 'This is where my father's earthly body will rest for all eternity.' He stared up at the sheer stone with a dreamy and mystical expression. 'It is as though I can hear his voice speaking in my head. He will be happy here.'

So I surveyed this place and marked out the cliff, driving

bronze pegs into the cracks in the rock, setting out the direction and the angle of the entrance passage for the masons who would come to begin this work. When this was done, we extricated ourselves from the maze of valleys and snarling gorges, and returned down the Nile to the meeting-place of the rivers, where our fleet lay.

WE WERE camped on the great plains only a few days' travel from Qebui when I was awakened in the night by the eerie grunting cries and the sound of a moving mass of animals that seemed to come from the darkness all around us.

Memnon ordered the trumpeter to blow the call to arms, and we stood to, within the circle of chariots. We threw wood on the watch-fires and stared out into the night. In the flicker of the flames we saw a dark flood, like the spate of the Nile, streaming past us. The eerie honking cries and the snorting sounds were almost deafening, and the press of animals in this throng was so heavy that they bumped into the outer ring of chariots, and some of the vehicles were thrown over on their sides. It was not possible to rest in this uproar, and we stood to arms all the rest of that night. The flood of living creatures never abated in all that time.

When dawn lit the scene, we were presented with the most extraordinary spectacle. In every direction as far as the eye could see, the plains were covered with a carpet of moving animals. They were all travelling in the same direction, trudging onwards with a strange fatalistic determination, heads hanging, shrouded in the dust of their own passage, uttering those weird, mournful cries. Every so often, some section of this endless herd took fright, for no reason, and tossed up their heels. They cavorted and snorted and chased each other in aimless circles, like whirlpools in the surface of a smoothly flowing river. Then they would settle back into the same plodding gait and follow the swarms ahead of them into the hazy distance.

We stood and stared in amazement. Every animal in this vast concourse was of the same species, and each individual was identical in every respect to the next. They were all of a dark purplish hue, with a shaggy-maned dewlap and horns shaped like the crescent moon. Their heads were misshapen, with ugly bulbous noses, while their bodies sloped back from high shoulders to spindly hindquarters.

When at last we harnessed the chariots and resumed our own journey, we passed through this living sea of animals like a fleet of galleys. They opened to allow us passage, streaming by on either hand so close that we could reach out and touch them. They were completely unafraid, and stared at us with dull, incurious eyes.

When it was time for the midday meal, Memnon strung his bow and killed five of these antelope with as many arrows. We skinned and butchered the carcasses as their fellows streamed by us at arm's-length. Despite the animals' strange appearance, their flesh, when grilled on the coals of an open fire, was as good to eat as any wild game I had tasted.

'This is another gift from the gods,' Memnon declared. 'As soon as we rejoin the main army, we will send out an expedition to follow these herds. We will be able to smoke enough meat to feed all our armies and our slaves from now until these beasts come again next year.'

From our Shilluk guides we learned that this incredible migration was an annual occurrence as the herds moved from one grazing-ground to another, several hundred miles apart. The Shilluk called these beasts gnu, in imitation of their strange honking cry. 'This will be a never-ending supply, one that is replenished each year,' I informed the prince.

None of us was then able to foresee the catastrophic events which would flow from this visitation of the ungainly gnu. I might have been warned by the manner in which they threw up their heads and snorted without reason, or by the discharge of mucus from the nostrils of some of these beasts, that I noticed as they streamed past us. However, I gave little thought to this behaviour, and judged them to be mild and harmless creatures who could bring us nothing but great benefit.

As soon as we reached the twin rivers, we reported the migration of gnu to Queen Lostris, and she agreed with Prince

Memnon's suggestion. Assisted by Kratas and Remrem, she put him in command of a column of two hundred chariots, supported by wagons and several thousand Shilluk. She ordered him to slaughter as many gnu as could be cut up and smoked for army rations.

I did not accompany the expedition, for the role of butcher's assistant was not to my fancy. However, we could soon see the smoke from the fires, on which the meat was curing, darkening the horizon, and before many more days had passed, the wagons started to return, each one loaded high with blackened slabs of cured meat.

Exactly twenty days from our first encounter with the gnu herds, I was sitting under a shady tree on the bank of the Nile, playing bao with my old and dear friend Aton. As a small indulgence to myself and out of deference to Aton, I had opened one of the precious jars of three-palm quality wine that remained from the stock which I had brought from Egypt. Aton and I played and haggled as old friends do, and sipped the wine with deep appreciation.

We had no means of knowing that catastrophe was rushing down upon us to overwhelm us all. On the contrary, I had every reason to be pleased with myself. The previous day I had completed the drawings and plans for the building of Pharaoh's tomb, in which I had incorporated several features to deter and frustrate the depredations of any grave-robber. Queen Lostris had approved these plans and appointed one of the master masons as the overseer. She told me that I might requisition all the slaves and equipment that I needed. My mistress was determined that she would not stint in making good her vow to her dead husband. She would build him the finest tomb that my genius could design.

I had just won the third successive board of bao from Aton and was pouring another jar of the truly excellent wine, when I heard the beat of hooves and looked up to see a horseman coming at full gallop from the direction of the chariot lines. When he was still at a distance I recognized Hui. Very few others rode astride, and certainly not at such a headlong pace. As he raced towards where we sat, I saw the expression on his face, and it alarmed me so that I stood up abruptly enough to spill the wine and upset the bao board.

'Taita!' he screamed at me from a hundred yards. 'The horses! Sweet Isis have mercy on us! The horses!'

He reined down his mount, and I swung up behind him and seized him around the waist. 'Don't waste time talking,' I shouted in his ear. 'Ride, fellow, ride!'

I went to Patience first. Half the herd was down, but she was my first love. The mare lay upon her side with her chest heaving. She was old now, with grey hairs frosting her muzzle. I had not used her in the traces since the day that Blade had been killed by the elephant bull. Although she no longer pulled a chariot, she was the finest brood mare in all our herds. Her foals all inherited her great heart and vivid intelligence. She had just weaned a beautiful little colt who stood near her now, watching her anxiously.

I knelt beside her. 'What is it, my brave darling?' I asked softly, and she recognized my voice, and opened her eyes.

The lids were gummed with mucus. I was appalled by her condition. Her neck and throat were swollen to almost twice their normal girth. A vile-smelling stream of yellow pus streamed from her mouth and nostrils. The fever was burning her up, so that I could feel the heat radiate from her, as though from a camp-fire.

She tried to rise when I stroked her neck, but she was too weak. She fell back, and her breath gurgled and wheezed in her throat. The thick, creamy pus bubbled out of her nostrils, and I could hear that she was drowning in it. Her throat was closing, so that she had to battle for each breath.

She was watching me with an almost human expression of trust and appeal. I was overcome with a sense of helplessness. This affliction was beyond my previous experience. I slipped the snowy-white linen shawl from my shoulder and used it to mop the streaming pus from her nostrils. It was a pathetically inadequate attempt, for as fast as I wiped it away, fresh trickles of the stinking stuff poured from her.

'Taita!' Hui called to me. 'Every one of our animals has been stricken by this pestilence.' Grateful for the distraction, I left Patience and went through the rest of the herd. Half of them were down already, and those still upright were mostly staggering or beginning to drool the thick yellow pus from their mouths.

'What must we do?' Hui and all the charioteers appealed to me. I was burdened with their trust. They expected me alone to avert this terrible disaster, and I knew that it was beyond my powers. I knew of no remedy, and could not think of even the most drastic and unlikely treatment.

I stumbled back to where Patience lay, and wiped away the latest flood of stinking discharge from her muzzle. I could see that she was sinking away swiftly. Each breath she drew now was a terrible struggle. My grief weakened me, and I knew that in my helplessness I would soon melt into tears and be of no further use to any of them, neither horses nor men.

Somebody knelt beside me, and I looked up to see that it was one of the Shilluk grooms, a willing and likely fellow whom I had befriended and who now looked upon me as his master. 'It is the sickness of the gnu,' he told me in his simple language. 'Many will die.'

I stared at him, as what he said began to make sense in my muddled mind. I remembered the snorting, drooling herds of slate-coloured animals darkening the plains with their numbers, and how we had thought it a gift of the benevolent gods.

'This sickness kills our cattle when the gnu come. Those that live through it are safe. They are never sick again.'

'What can we do to save them, Habani?' I demanded, but he shook his head.

'There is nothing to be done.'

I was holding Patience's head in my arms when she died. The breath choked away in her throat and she shuddered and her legs stiffened and then relaxed. I let out a low moan of grief and was on the very edge of the abyss of despair, when I looked up and through my tears saw that Patience's colt was down, with the yellow slime bubbling up from his throat.

In that moment my despair was replaced with a burning anger. 'No!' I shouted. 'I will not let you die also.'

I ran to the foal's side and shouted to Habani to bring leather buckets of hot water. With a linen cloth I bathed the colt's throat in an attempt to reduce the swelling, but it had no effect. The pus still poured from his nostrils, and the hot skin of his neck stretched out as the flesh ballooned like a bladder filling with air.

'He is dying.' Habani shook his head. 'Many will die.'

'I will not let it happen,' I swore grimly, and sent Hui to the galley to fetch my medicine chest.

By the time he returned, it was almost too late. The colt was in extremis. His breath was choking out of him and I could feel his strength draining away under my frantic hands. I felt for the ridged rings of his windpipe at the juncture of his throat and his chest. With one shallow cut through the skin I exposed the white sinewy pipe, and then I pressed the point of my scalpel into it and pierced the tough sheath. Immediately air hissed through the aperture and I saw the colt's chest swell as his lungs inflated. He began to breathe again to a steady and even rhythm, but I saw almost immediately that the puncture-wound in his throat was closing again with blood and mucus.

In frantic haste I hacked a length of bamboo from the framework of the nearest chariot, and I cut a hollow tube from the end of it and pushed this into the wound. The bamboo tube held the wound open and the colt relaxed his struggles as the air sucked and blew unimpeded through it.

'Hui!' I yelled for him. 'I will show you how to save them.'

Before night fell, I had trained a hundred or more of the charioteers and grooms to perform this crude but effective surgery, and we worked on through the night by the wavering, uncertain light of the oil lamps.

There were over thirteen thousand horses in the royal herds by this time. We could not save them all, although we tried. We worked on, with the blood from the severed throats caking black up to our elbows. When exhaustion overcame us, we fell on a bale of hay and slept for an hour and then staggered up and went back to work.

Some of the horses were not as badly affected by this pestilence, which I had named the Yellow Strangler. They seemed to have an in-born resistance to its ravages. The discharge from their nostrils was no more copious than I had seen in the gnu herds, and many of these remained on their feet and threw off the disease within days.

Many others died before we were able to open the windpipe, and even some of those, on which we had successfully operated, died later from mortification and complication of the wound which we had inflicted. Of course, many of our horses were out on expeditions into the plains and beyond my help. Prince Memnon lost two out of every three of his steeds and had to abandon his chariots and return to the Qebui rivers on foot.

In the end we lost over half our horses, seven thousand dead, and those that survived were so weakened and cast down that it was many months before they were strong and fit enough to pull a chariot. Patience's colt survived and replaced his old dam in my affections. He took the right-hand trace in my chariot, and was so strong and reliable that I called him Rock.

'How has this pestilence affected our hopes of a swift return to Egypt?' my mistress asked me.

'It has set us back many years,' I told her, and saw the pain in her eyes. 'We lost most of our best-trained old horses, those like Patience. We will have to breed up the royal herds all over again, and train young horses to take their places in the traces of the chariots.'

I waited for the annual migration of the gnu the following year with dread, but when it came and their multitudes once more darkened the plains, Habani was proved correct. Only a few of our horses developed the symptoms of the Yellow Strangler, and these in a mild form that set them back for only a few weeks before they were strong enough to work again.

What struck me as strange was that the foals born in the period after the first infection of the Yellow Strangler, those who had never been exposed to the actual disease, were as immune as their dams who had contracted a full dose. It was as though the immunity had been transferred to them in the milk that they sucked from their mother's udder. I was certain that we would never again have to experience the full force of the plague.

MY MAJOR duty now, laid upon me by my mistress, was the construction of Pharaoh's tomb in the mountains. I was obliged to spend much of my time in that wild and forbidding place, and I became fascinated by those mountains and all their moods.

Like a beautiful woman, the mountains were unpredictable, sometimes remote and hidden in dense moving veils of clouds that were shot through with lightning and riven with thunder. At other times they were lovely and seductive, beckoning to me, challenging me to discover all their secrets and experience all their dangerous delights.

Although I had eight thousand slaves to prosecute the task, and the unstinted assistance of all our finest craftsmen and artists, the work on the tomb went slowly. I knew it would take many years to complete the elaborate mausoleum which my mistress insisted we must build, and to decorate it in a fashion fit for the Lord of the Two Kingdoms. In truth there was no point in hurrying the work, for it would take as long to rebuild the royal horse herds and train the Shilluk infantry regiments until they were a match for the Hyksos squadrons against which they would one day be matched.

When I was not up in the mountains working at the tomb, I spent my time at Qebui, where there were myriad different tasks and pleasures awaiting me. These ranged from the education of my two little princesses to devising new military tactics with Lord Tanus and the prince.

By this time it was clear that, whereas Memnon would one day command all the chariot divisions, Tanus had never outgrown his first distrust of the horse. He was a sailor and an infantryman to the bone, and as he grew older, he was ever more conservative and traditional in his use of his new Shilluk regiments.

The prince was growing into a dashing and innovative charioteer. Each day he came to me with a dozen new ideas, some of them far-fetched, but others quite brilliant. We tried them all, even the ones that I knew were impossible. He was sixteen years old when Queen Lostris promoted him to the rank of Best of Ten Thousand.

Now that Tanus rode with me so seldom, I slowly took over

the role of Memnon's principal driver. We developed a rapport which became almost instinctive, and which extended to our favourite team of horses, Rock and Chain. When we were on the march, Memnon still liked to drive, and I stood on the footplate behind him. However, as soon as we engaged in action, he would toss me the reins and seize his bow or his javelins from the rack. I would take the chariot into the fray and steer it through the evolutions we had dreamed up together.

As Memnon matured and his strength increased, we began to win some of the prizes at the games and the military tattoos that were a feature of our lives at Qebui. First, we triumphed in the flat races where our team of Rock and Chain could display its paces to the full; then we began to win the shooting and javelin contests. Soon we were known as the chariot that had to be beaten before anyone could claim the champion's ribbon from Queen Lostris.

I remember the cheers as our chariot flew through the final gate of the course, myself at the traces and Memnon on the footplate hurling a javelin right and left into the two straw-filled dummies as we passed, then the mad dash down the straight, with the prince howling like a demon and the long wind-blown plait of his hair standing out behind his head, like the tail of a charging lion.

Soon there were other encounters in which the prince began to distinguish himself, and those without any assistance from me. Whenever he strode past the young girls, with the Gold of Valour gleaming on his chest and the champion's ribbon knotted into his plait, they giggled and blushed and slanted their eyes in his direction. Once I entered his tent in haste with some important news for him, only to come up short as I found my prince well mounted and oblivious to all but the tender young body and the pretty face beneath him. I withdrew silently, a little saddened that the age of his innocence was past.

Of all these pleasures, none for me could compare with those precious hours that I was still able to spend with my mistress. In this her thirty-third year she was in the very high summer of her beauty. Her allure was enhanced by her sophistication and her poise. She had become a queen indeed, and a woman without peer.

All her people loved her, but none of them as much as I did. Not even Tanus was able to surpass me in my devotion to her. It was my pride that she still needed me so much, and relied upon me and my judgement and my advice so trustingly. Notwithstanding the other blessings that I had to adorn my existence, she would ever be the one great love of my life.

 I SHOULD have been contented and replete, but there is a restlessness in my nature that was exacerbated by this new wanderlust that had come to plague me. Whenever I paused from my labours at Pharaoh's tomb, and looked up at them, the mountains beckoned me. I began to make short excursions into their lonely gorges, often alone but sometimes with Hui or some other companion.

Hui was with me when I first saw the herds of wild ibex high above us in the lofty crags of the mountain. They were of a species we had never seen before. They stood twice as tall as the wild goats that we knew from the Nile valley, and some of the old billy-goats carried such a mass of curling horn that they seemed as monstrous as some fabulous beast.

It was Hui who carried reports of these huge ibex back to the twin rivers where the fleet lay at Qebui, and within the month, Lord Tanus arrived at the valley of the king's tomb, with his bow over his shoulder and Prince Memnon at his side. The prince was fast becoming as ardent a huntsman as his father, and was every bit as eager for the chase. As for myself, I welcomed the chance to explore those fascinating highlands in such company.

We had meant to venture only as far as the first line of peaks, but when we climbed to their crest, we were presented with a vista that was breathtaking. We saw other mountains against the sky that were shaped like flat-topped anvils, and were the tawny colour of lions. They dwarfed the peaks on which we stood and lured us onwards.

The Nile climbed in concert with us up through precipitous

valleys and dark gorges that churned its waters to gleaming white. We could not always follow its course, but in places were forced to climb above it and follow giddy goat-tracks across the face of a frowning mountain.

Then, when we had been lured deep into its maw, the mountain loosed its full fury upon us.

We were one hundred men in our company, with ten pack-horses to carry our provisions. We were camped in the depths of one of these fathomless gorges, with the fresh trophies of Tanus' and Memnon's latest hunt laid out upon the rocky floor for our appraisal and admiration. These were two goat's heads, the largest we had seen in all our travels, so heavy in horn that it took two slaves to lift one of them. Suddenly it began to rain.

In our Egyptian valley it may rain once in twenty years. None of us had ever imagined anything even remotely like the rain that fell upon us now.

First, dense black clouds roofed over the narrow strip of sky that showed between the cliffs that walled us in, so that we were plunged from sunny noon into deep twilight. A cold wind raced down the valley and chilled our bodies and our spirits. We huddled together in dismay.

Then lightning lanced from the sombre belly of the clouds and shattered the rocks around us, filling the air with the smell of sulphur and sparks struck from flint. Thunder burst upon us, magnified as it rolled from cliff to cliff, and the earth jumped and trembled beneath our feet.

Then the rain fell. It did not come down upon us in the form of drops. It was as though we stood under one of the cataracts of the Nile when the river was in full flood. There was no longer air to breathe, water filled our mouths and our nostrils so that we felt that we were drowning. The rain was so thick that we could see only the blurred outline of the man who stood an arm's-length away. It battered us so that we were thrown down and cringed beneath the nearest rock for shelter. Still it assaulted all the senses and stung our exposed skin like a swarm of angry hornets.

It was cold. I had never known such cold, and we were covered only with our thin linen shawls. The cold sucked the force out of my limbs, and we shivered until our teeth clattered together in our mouths, and we could not still them even though we bit down with all the strength of our jaws.

Then, above the sound of the falling rain, I heard a new sound. It was the sound of water which had become a ravening monster. Down the narrow valley where we lay swept a wall of grey water. It stretched from cliff to cliff, and carried everything before it.

I was caught up in it and tumbled end over end. I felt life being beaten out of me as I was thrown against the rocks, and icy water filled my throat. Darkness overwhelmed me, and I thought that I was dead.

I have a vague recollection of hands dragging me from the flood, and then I was wafted away to some dark and distant shore. The voice of my prince called me back. Before I could open my eyes I smelled wood-smoke, and felt the warmth of the flames on one side of my body.

'Tata, wake up! Speak to me.' The voice was insistent, and I opened my eyes. Memnon's face floated before me, and he smiled at me. Then he called over his shoulder, 'He is awake, Lord Tanus.'

I found that we were in a rock cave and that outside, the night had fallen. Tanus came across from the smoky fire of damp wood and squatted beside the prince.

'How are you, old friend? I don't think you have broken any bones.'

I struggled into a sitting position, and gingerly tested every part of my body before I replied, 'My head is cracked through, and every limb aches. Apart from that, I am cold and hungry.'

'You will live then,' Tanus chuckled, 'though a while ago I doubted any of us would. We have to get out of these cursed mountains before something worse happens. It was madness ever to venture into a place where the rivers come out of the sky.'

'What about the others?' I asked.

Tanus shook his head. 'They are all drowned. You were the only one that we were able to drag from the flood.'

'What about the horses?'

'Gone,' he grunted. 'All gone.'

'Food?'

'Nothing,' Tanus replied. 'Even my bow is lost in the river. I have only the sword at my side and the clothes on my body.'

AT DAWN we left our rock shelter and started back down that treacherous valley. At the foot of the gorge we found the bodies of some of our men and the horses strewn upon the rocks where they had been stranded when the flood receded.

We scavenged amongst the rocks and scree, and we managed to recover some of our stores and equipment. To my great joy I found my medicine chest still intact, though flooded with water. I laid out the contents on a rock, and while they dried, I fashioned a sling from a leather harness to carry the chest upon my back.

In the meantime, Memnon had cut strips of meat from the carcass of one of the horses and grilled them over another fire of driftwood. When we had eaten our fill, we saved the rest of the meat, and set out on the return.

The journey slowly descended into nightmare as we scaled steep rocky slopes and dropped into the gorges beyond. There seemed to be no end to this terrible wilderness, and our bruised feet in open sandals protested each step. At night we shivered miserably around a smoky little fire of driftwood.

By the second day we all knew that we had lost the way, and that we were wandering aimlessly. I was certain that we were doomed to die in these terrible mountains. Then we heard the river and, as we topped the next saddle between peaks, we found the infant Nile winding through the depths of the gorge below us. That was not all. On the banks of the river we saw a collection of coloured tents, and amongst them moved the shapes of men.

'Civilized men,' I said immediately, 'for those tents must be of woven cloth.'

'And those are horses,' Memnon agreed eagerly, pointing out the animals tethered on the lines beyond the encampment.

'There!' Tanus pointed. 'That was the flash of sunlight off a sword-blade or a spear-head. They are metal-workers.'

'We must find out who these people are.' I was fascinated by what tribe could live in such an inhospitable land.

'We will get our throats cut,' Tanus growled. 'What makes you believe these mountaineers are not as savage as the land in which they live?' Only later would we come to know these people as Ethiopians.

'Those are magnificent horses,' Memnon whispered. 'Our own are not so tall, or so sturdy. We must go down and study them.' The prince was a horseman above all else.

'Lord Tanus is right.' His warning had aroused my usual prudent nature, and I was ready to counsel caution. 'These might be dangerous savages, with but the trappings of civilized men.'

We sat upon the shoulder of the mountain and debated for a while longer, but in the end curiosity got the better of all three of us and we crept down through one of the ravines to spy upon these strangers.

As we drew closer, we saw that they were tall, well-built people, probably more robust in stature than we Egyptians are. Their hair was thick and dark and curled profusely. The men were bearded, and we are clean-shaven. They wore full-length robes, probably woven of wool, and brightly coloured. We go bare-chested and our kilts are usually pure white in colour. They wore soft leather boots, as opposed to our sandals, and a bright cloth wound around their heads.

The women we saw working amongst the tents were unveiled and cheerful. They sang and called to each other in a language I had never heard before, but their voices were melodious as they drew water, or squatted over the cooking-fires, or ground corn on the millstones.

One group of men was playing a board-game that, from where I hid, looked very much like bao. They were wagering and arguing over the play of the stones. At one stage, two of them leapt to their feet and drew curved daggers from their belts. They confronted each other snarling and hissing, like a pair of angry tom-cats.

At that stage a third man, who had been sitting alone, rose to his feet and stretched, like a lazy leopard. He sauntered across and, with his sword, knocked up the daggers. Immediately the two protagonists subsided and slunk away.

The peace-maker was clearly the chief of the party. He was a tall man, with the wiry frame of a mountain goat. He was goat-like in other ways. His beard was as long and thick as that of an ibex ram, and his features were coarse and goaty; he had a heavy, hooked nose and a wide mouth with a cruel slant to it. I thought that he probably stank like one of the old rams that Tanus had shot from the cliff-face.

Suddenly I felt Tanus grip my arm, and he whispered in my ear, 'Look at that!'

This chieftain wore the richest apparel of any of them. His robe was striped in scarlet and blue and his earrings were stones that glowed like the full moon. But I could not see what had excited Tanus.

'His sword,' Tanus hissed. 'Look at his sword.'

I studied it for the first time. It was longer than one of our weapons and the pommel was obviously of pure gold filigree-work, of a delicacy that I had never seen before. The hand-guard was studded with precious stones. It was a masterpiece that clearly had occupied some master craftsman his lifetime.

This was not what had captured Tanus' attention, however. It was the blade. As long as the chief's own arm, it was made of a metal that was neither yellow bronze nor red copper. In colour it was a strange silvery glittering blue, like the living scales of a Nile perch taken fresh from the river. It was inlaid with gold, as if to highlight its unique value.

'What is it?' Tanus breathed. 'What metal is that?'

'I do not know.'

The chief resumed his seat in front of his tent, but now he laid the sword across his lap, and, with a phallus-shaped piece of volcanic rock, began lovingly to stroke the edge of the blade. The metal emitted a ringing thrill of sound to each touch of the stone. No bronze ever resounded like that. It was the purr of a resting lion.

'I want it,' Tanus whispered. 'I will never rest until I have that sword.'

I gave him a startled glance, for I had never heard such a tone in his voice. I saw that he meant what he said. He was a man struck with a sudden overpowering passion.

'We cannot remain here longer,' I told him softly. 'We will be discovered.' I took his arm, but he resisted. He was staring at the weapon.

'Let us go to look at their horses,' I insisted, and at last he allowed me to draw him away. I led Memnon by the other hand. At a safe distance we circled the camp, and crept back towards the horse-lines.

When I saw the horses close up, I was struck with a passion as fierce as Tanus had conceived for the blue sword. These were a different breed from our Hyksos horses. They were taller and more elegantly proportioned. Their heads were noble and their nostrils wider. I knew those nostrils were the mark of stamina and good wind. Their eyes were situated further forward in the skull and were more prominent than those of our animals. They were great soft eyes, shining with intelligence.

'They are beautiful,' whispered Memnon at my side. 'Look at the way they hold their heads and arch their necks.'

Tanus longed for the sword, we coveted the horses with a passion that equalled his.

'Just one stallion like that to put to our mares,' I pleaded to any god who was listening. 'I would exchange my hope of eternal life for a single one.'

One of the foreign grooms glanced in our direction, then said something to the fellow beside him and began to walk in our direction. This time I had no need to insist, and all three of us ducked down behind the boulder that sheltered us and crawled away. We found a secure hiding-place further down-river, amongst a tumbled heap of boulders, and immediately launched into one of those discussions in which all spoke together and none listened.

'I will go in and offer him a thousand deben of gold,' Tanus swore, 'I must have that sword.'

'He would kill you first. Did you not see him stroke it as though it was his first-born son?'

'Those horses!' marvelled Memnon. 'I never dreamed of such beauty. Horus must have beasts like that to draw his chariot.'

'Did you see those two fly at each other?' I cautioned. 'They are savage men, and bloodthirsty. They would rip out your guts before you opened your mouth to utter a word. Besides, what do you have to offer in return? They will see we are destitute beggars.'

'We could steal three of their stallions tonight and ride them down on to the plain,' Memnon suggested, and though the idea had appeal, I told him sternly, 'You are the crown prince of Egypt, not a common thief.'

He grinned at me. 'For one of those horses, I would cut throats like the worst footpad in Thebes.'

As we debated thus, we were suddenly aware of the sound of voices approaching along the river-bank from the direction of the foreign camp. We looked about for better concealment and hid away.

The voices drew closer. A party of women came into view and they stopped below us at the water's edge. There were three older women, and a girl. The women wore robes of a drab hue, and cloths of black around their hair. I thought that they were servants or nursemaids. It did not occur to me then that they were gaolers, for they treated the girl with unusual deference.

The girl was tall and slim, so that when she walked, she moved like a papyrus stem in the Nile breeze. She wore a short robe of rich wool, striped in yellow and sky blue, which left her knees bared. Though she wore short boots of soft stitched leather, I could see that her legs were lithe and smooth.

The women stopped below our hiding-place, and one of the older women began to disrobe the girl. The other two filled the clay jars that they had carried down on their heads with water from the Nile. The river was still swollen with flood-water. No one could safely enter that icy torrent. It was clear that they intended bathing the girl from the jars.

One of the women lifted the girl's robe over her head and she stood naked at the water's edge. I heard Memnon gasp. I looked

564

at him and saw that he had forgotten entirely about stealing horses.

While two of the women poured the water from the jars over the girl, the third woman wiped her down with a folded cloth. The girl held her hands above her head and circled slowly to allow them to wet every part of her body. She laughed and squealed at the cold, and I saw tiny goose-bumps rise around her nipples, which were the rich ruby of polished garnets, mounted like jewels on the peak of each smooth, round breast.

Her hair was a dark bush of tight curls, her skin was the colour of the heart-wood of the acacia, when it has been buffed and oiled to a high patina. It was a rich, ruddy brown, that glowed in the high sunlight of the mountains.

Her features were delicate, her nose narrow and chiselled. Her lips were soft and full, but without any thickness. Her eyes were large and dark, slanted above high cheek-bones. Her lashes were so thick that they tangled together. She was beautiful. I have only known one other woman who was more so.

Suddenly she said something to the women with her. They stood aside, and she left them and climbed on those long naked legs towards us. But before she reached our hiding-place, she stepped behind a boulder that shielded her from her companions, but left her full in our view. She glanced around quickly, but did not see us. The cold water must have affected her, for she squatted quickly and her own water tinkled on the rock beneath her.

Memnon groaned softly. It was instinctive, not intentional, a sound of longing so intense as to have become agony. The girl sprang to her feet and stared directly at him. Memnon was standing a little to one side of Tanus and me. While we were concealed, he was full in her view.

The two of them stared at each other. The girl was trembling, her dark eyes enormous. I expected her to run or scream. Instead, she looked back over her shoulder in a conspiratorial gesture, as if to make certain that the women had not followed her. Then she turned back to Memnon and, in a soft sweet voice, asked a question, at the same time holding out her hand to him in a gesture of appeal.

'I do not understand,' Memnon whispered, and spread his own hands in a gesture of incomprehension.

The girl stepped up to him and repeated the question impatiently, and when Memnon shook his head, she seized his hand and shook it. In her agitation, her voice rose as she demanded something of him.

'Masara!' One of her attendants had heard her. 'Masara!' It was obviously the girl's name, for she made a gesture of silence and caution to Memnon and turned to go back.

However, the three women had all started up the slope after Masara. They were chattering with alarm and agitation, and they came round the side of the boulder in a pack and stopped when they saw Memnon.

For a moment nobody moved, and then all three women screamed in unison. The naked girl seemed poised to run to Memnon's side, but as she started forward, two of the women seized her; all four of them were screaming now, as the girl struggled to be free.

'Time to go home,' Tanus jerked my arm, and I was after him in a bound.

From the direction of the camp came the shouts of many men aroused by the screams of the women. When I paused to look back, I saw them coming over the ridge in a body. I saw also that Memnon had not followed us, but had leaped forward to the girl's assistance.

They were all big women and held the girl hard, redoubling their screams. Although Masara was trying desperately to pull free, Memnon could not get her away from them.

'Tanus!' I yelled. 'Memnon is in trouble.'

We turned back and between us grabbed him and hauled him away. He came reluctantly. 'I will come back for you,' he shouted to the girl, looking back over his shoulder as we ran with him between us. 'Be brave. I will come back for you.'

When somebody tells me nowadays that there is no such thing as love at first sight, I smile quietly to myself and think of the day that Memnon first saw Masara.

We had lost time in the struggle to get Memnon away, and our pursuers were already pressing us hard as we took to one of the goat-tracks and ran for the crest of the slope. An arrow flitted past Memnon's shoulder and clattered against the rocks beside the path. It spurred us to greater speed.

We were in single file along the narrow path. Memnon led us and Tanus followed him. I was last in the file, and, burdened by the heavy medicine chest on my back, I began to fall further behind. Another arrow passed over our heads, and then the third struck the pack on my back with a force that made me stagger. But the chest stopped the arrow that would otherwise have transfixed my body.

'Come on, Taita,' Tanus shouted back at me. 'Throw off that cursed box of yours, or they will have you.'

He and Memnon were fifty paces ahead of me and drawing away, but I could not discard my precious chest. At that moment the next arrow struck, and this time I was not so fortunate. It hit me in the leg, in the fleshy part of the thigh, and I went tumbling across the path and fell hard.

I rolled into a sitting position and looked with horror at the reed shaft of the arrow that protruded from my leg. Then I looked back at our pursuers. The bearded chieftain in the striped robe led them, and he had outdistanced his own men by a hundred paces. He was coming up the track in a series of great elastic bounds, covering the ground as swiftly as one of the ibex rams that he resembled in so many other ways.

'Taita!' Tanus called back at me. 'Are you all right?' He had paused on the brow of the slope, and was looking back anxiously. Memnon had crossed over and was out of sight.

'I am arrowed!' I yelled back. 'Go on and leave me. I cannot follow.'

Without a moment's hesitation, Tanus turned back, and came leaping down towards where I lay. The Ethiopian chieftain saw him coming and bellowed a challenge. He drew the glittering blue sword and brandished it as he came on up the hillside.

Tanus reached the spot where I sat, and tried to lift me to my feet. 'It's no use. I am hard hit. Save yourself,' I told him, but the Ethiopian was almost upon us. Tanus dropped my arm, and drew his own sword.

The two of them came together, going for each other in a

murderous rush. I was not in any doubt as to the outcome of this duel, for Tanus was the strongest and most skilled swordsman in all Egypt. When he killed the Ethiopian, we would all be doomed, for we could expect no mercy from his henchmen.

The Ethiopian swung first with a full-blooded overhand cut at Tanus' head. It was an imprudent stroke to aim at a swordsman of his opponent's calibre. I knew that Tanus' response would be a parry in the line of the head and a natural riposte, with all the momentum of his shoulder behind it, that would drive the point through the chieftain's beard and into his throat. It was one of Tanus' favourite strokes.

The two blades met, but there was no ringing clash. The blue blade hacked clean through Tanus' yellow bronze, as though it were a wand of green willow. Tanus was left with the hilt in his hand and a finger's-length remaining from that once long and deadly bronze blade.

Tanus was stunned by the ease with which the Ethiopian had disarmed him, and he was slow to defend himself from the next stroke that followed like a thunderbolt. He leaped backwards just in time, but the blue point opened a long, shallow cut across the bulging muscles of his naked chest, and the blood came swiftly.

'Run, Tanus!' I screamed. 'Or he will kill us both.'

The Ethiopian went for him again, but I was lying in the middle of the narrow path. He was forced to leap over me to get at Tanus. I seized him around the knees with both arms, and brought him down on top of me in a snarling, thrashing heap.

The Ethiopian was trying to drive the point of the blue sword into my belly, as I lay under him, and I twisted so violently aside that both of us rolled off the path and began to slide away down the steep slope of loose scree. As we rolled more swiftly, gathering momentum, I had one last glimpse of Tanus peering down over the edge of the path, and I screamed in a despairing wail, 'Run! Take care of Memnon!'

The shale and loose scree were as treacherous as swamp quicksands, and gave no anchor or purchase. The Ethiopian and I were flung apart, but both of us were carried to the edge of the torrent. I was battered and hammered to the edge of consciousness, and lay there groaning until rough hands dragged me to my feet, and blows and harsh curses rained upon my head.

The chieftain stopped them from killing me and throwing my body into the river. He was covered with dust, as I was, and his robe was torn and filthy from the fall, but the blue sword was still gripped in his right fist and he snarled at his men. They began to drag me away towards the encampment, but I looked around me desperately and saw my medicine chest amongst the rocks. The leather harness had snapped, and it had come off my back.

'Bring that,' I ordered my captors with as much force and dignity as I could muster, and pointed to the chest. They laughed at my insolence, but the chieftain sent one of his men to retrieve it.

Two men were obliged to support me, for the shaft in my thigh was beginning to cause me crippling pain. Every pace back to the camp was agony, and when they reached it, they threw me roughly to the ground in the open space in the centre of the ring of tents.

Then they argued long and fiercely. It was obvious that they were puzzling over my origins and my motives, and trying to decide what they should do with me. Every once in a while, one of them would stand over me and kick me in the ribs, while he shouted questions at me. I lay as quietly as I could, so as not to provoke further violence.

There was a distraction when the party that had pursued Tanus and Memnon returned empty-handed. There was more shouting and armwaving as bitter recriminations and insults were exchanged. I was cheered by the thought that the two of them had got clean away.

After a while my captors remembered me, and they came back to vent their frustration on me with more kicks and blows. In the end their chieftain called them off, and ordered them not to torment me further. After that, most of them lost interest in me and wandered away. I was left lying on the bare ground, covered with dirt and bruises, with the arrow still lodged in my flesh.

The Ethiopian chieftain resumed his seat in front of the largest tent, which was clearly his own, and while he stropped the edge of his sword, he regarded me with a steady but inscrutable expression. Occasionally he exchanged a few low words with one of his men, but it seemed that my immediate danger was past.

I judged my moment carefully, and then addressed him directly. I pointed to my medicine chest, which had been thrown against one of the tents, and I made my voice mild and placatory. 'I need my chest. I must tend this wound.'

Although the chieftain did not understand the words, he understood my gestures. He ordered one of his men to bring the chest across to him. He made them set it down in front of him and opened the lid. He unpacked the chest methodically, examining each separate item. Anything that particularly caught his attention he held up, and asked a question to which I tried to give an answer with signs.

He seemed satisfied that, apart from my scalpels, the chest contained no dangerous weapon. I am not sure if he realized at this stage that these were medical items. However, with signs I showed him what I needed to do, pointing to my leg and making a pantomime of pulling the arrow. He stood over me with the sword in his hand, and made it clear that he would lop off my head at the first sign of treachery, but he allowed me to use my instruments.

The arrow had entered at an angle and position which made it awkward for me to reach. In addition to this, the pain that I inflicted upon myself, as I used the Taita spoons to trap and mask the barbs that were buried deep in my flesh, brought me more than once to the point of fainting away.

I was panting and drenched in sheets of sweat when at last I was ready to draw the arrow-head. By this time I had an audience of half the men in camp. They had returned to crowd around me and watch my surgery with garrulous interest.

I took a firm hold on the handles of the spoons, placed a wooden wedge between my teeth and bit down on it hard, and drew the clamped arrow-head out of the wound. There were shouts of wonder and amazement from my audience. Obviously none of them had ever seen a barb drawn with such ease and with so little damage to the victim. They were impressed even further when they watched the skill and dexterity with which I laid on the linen bandages.

In any nation and in any culture, even the most primitive, the healer and the physician have a special place of honour and esteem. I had demonstrated my credentials in the most convincing manner, and my status in the Ethiopian camp was drastically altered.

At the orders of the chief, I was carried to one of the tents and laid on a straw mattress. My medicine chest was placed at the head of my bed, and one of the women brought me a meal of corn-bread and chicken stew and thick sour milk.

In the morning, when the tents were struck, I was placed in a pole-litter behind one of the horses in the long caravan, and pulled along the rough and precipitous tracks. To my dismay, I saw from the angle of the sun that we were headed back into the fastness of the mountains, and I feared that I was lost to my own people, probably for all time. The fact that I was a physician had probably saved my life, but it had also placed such value on me that I would never be turned free. I knew that I was now a slave in more than name alone.

DESPITE THE jolting of the litter, my leg began to heal cleanly. This further impressed my captors, and soon they were bringing to me any member of the band who was sick or injured.

I cured a ringworm and lanced a whitlow under a thumbnail. I sewed together a man who had won too much gambling with his quick-tempered friends. These Ethiopians had a penchant for settling arguments with the dagger. When one of the horses threw its rider down a gulley, I set his broken arm. It knitted straight, and my reputation was enhanced. The Ethiopian chieftain looked at me with a new respect, and I was offered the food-bowl after he had made his selection of the choice cuts, before any of the other men were allowed to eat.

When my leg had healed sufficiently for me to walk again, I was given the run of the camp. However, I was not allowed out of sight. An armed man followed me and stood over me, even when I was on the most private and intimate business amongst the rocks.

I was kept away from Masara and only saw her from afar at the start of each day's journey, and again when we camped for the night. During the long day's ride through the mountains we were separated; I rode near the head of the caravan, while she was brought along at the rear. She was always accompanied by her female gaolers, and usually surrounded by armed guards.

Whenever we did catch sight of each other, Masara cast the most desperate and appealing looks at me, as though I would be able to help her in some way. It was obvious that she was a prisoner of rank and of importance. She was such a lovely young woman that I often found myself thinking of her during the day, and trying to fathom the reason for her captivity. I decided she was either an unwilling bride, being taken to meet her future husband, or that she was a pawn in some political intrigue.

Without a knowledge of the language I could not hope to understand what was taking place, or to learn anything about these Ethiopians. I set out to learn the Geez tongue.

I have the ear of a musician, and I played my tricks upon them. I listened attentively to all the chatter around me, and picked up the cadence and the rhythm of their speech. Very early on, I was able to deduce that the chieftain's name was Arkoun. One morning before the caravan set out, Arkoun was giving orders for the day's march to his assembled band. I waited until he had delivered a long and heated harangue, and then I repeated it in precisely the same tone and cadence.

They listened to me in stunned silence, and then burst into uproar. They roared with laughter and beat each other on the back, tears of mirth streamed down their cheeks, for they had a direct and uncomplicated sense of humour. I had not the least idea what I had said, but it was obvious that I had got it exactly right.

They shouted excerpts from my speech at each other, and wagged their heads, mimicking Arkoun's pompous manner. It took a long time for order to be restored, but at last Arkoun strutted up to me and shouted an accusatory question at me. I

572

did not understand a word of it, but I shouted the same question back at him, word for exact word.

This time there was pandemonium. The joke of it was too rich to be borne. Grown men clung to each other for support, they screamed and wiped their streaming eyes. One of them fell into the fire and singed his beard.

Even though the joke was on him, Arkoun laughed along with them and patted me on the back. From then onwards, every man and woman in the camp was my teacher. I had only to point at any object and the Geez word for it was shouted at me. When I began to string those words into sentences, they corrected me eagerly, and were inordinately proud of my progress.

It took me some time to fathom the grammar. The verbs were declined in a manner which had no relationship to Egyptian, and the gender and plurals of the nouns were strange. However, within ten days I was speaking intelligible Geez, and had even built up a good selection of choice curses and invective.

While I learned the language and treated their ailments, I studied their mores and manners. I learned that they were inveterate gamblers, and that the board-game that they played endlessly was a passion. They called it dom, but it was a simplified and rudimentary form of bao. The number of cups in the board and the quantity of stones brought into play varied from bao. However, all the objects and the principles were similar.

Arkoun himself was the dom champion of the band, but as I studied his play, I saw that he had no inkling of the classic rule of seven stones. Nor did he understand the protocol of the four bulls. Without a thorough knowledge of these, no bao player could aspire to even the lowly third grade of masters. I debated with myself the risk that I would run in humiliating such a vain and overbearing tyrant as Arkoun, but in the end I decided that it was the only way to gain ascendancy over him.

The next time he sat in front of his tent and set up the board, smirking and twirling his moustaches as he waited for a challenger to step forward, I elbowed aside the first aspirant and settled myself cross-legged opposite Arkoun.

'I have no silver to wager,' I told him in my still rudimentary Geez. 'I play for love of the stones.'

He nodded gravely. As an addict of the board, he understood that sentiment. The news that I was taking the board against Arkoun ran through the camp, and they all came laughing and jostling to watch.

When I allowed Arkoun to lay three stones in the east castle they nudged each other and chuckled with disappointment that the game would be so swiftly lost. One more stone in the east, and the board was his. They did not understand the significance of the four bulls that I had banked in the south. When I loosed my bulls, they strode invincibly across the board, splitting his unsupported stones and isolating the east castle. He was powerless to prevent it. Four moves and the board was mine. I had not even been called upon to demonstrate the rule of seven stones.

For some moments they all sat in shocked silence. I do not think that Arkoun realized the extent of his defeat for a while. Then, when it sank in upon him, he stood up and drew the terrible blue sword. I thought that I had miscalculated, and that he was about to lop my head, or at least an arm.

He lifted the sword high and then swung it down with a shout of fury. With a dozen strokes he hacked the board to kindling and scattered the stones about the camp. Then he strode out into the rocks, tearing his beard and shouting my death threats to the towering cliffs, that hurled them onwards down the valleys in a series of diminishing echoes.

It was three days before Arkoun set up the board again, and gestured to me to take my seat opposite him. The poor fellow had no inkling of what lay in store for him.

EACH DAY my command of the Geez language increased, and I was at last able to glean some understanding of my captor and the reason for this long journey through the canyons and gorges.

I had underrated Arkoun. He was not a chieftain but a king. His full name was Arkoun Gannouchi Maryam, Negusa Naghast, King of Kings and ruler of the Ethiopic state of Aksum. It was only later that I learned that in this land any mountain brigand with a hundred horses and fifty wives was likely to set himself up as a king, and that at any one time there might be as many as twenty Kings of Kings on the rampage for land and loot.

Arkoun's nearest neighbour was one Prester Beni-Jon, also claiming to be King of Kings and ruler of the Ethiopic state of Aksum. There appeared to be a certain amount of ill-feeling and rivalry between these two monarchs. They had already fought a number of inconclusive battles.

Masara was the favourite daughter of Prester Beni-Jon. She had been kidnapped by one of the other robber chieftains, one of those who had not yet crowned himself, nor taken the obligatory title of King of Kings. In a straightforward trading arrangement, Masara had been sold to Arkoun for a horse-load of silver bars. Arkoun intended using her to gain political ground from her doting father. It seemed that hostage-taking and ransom were very much a part of Ethiopian statesmanship.

Not trusting any of his own men with such a valuable commodity, Arkoun had gone himself to take possession of Princess Masara. Our caravan was carrying her back to Arkoun's stronghold. I gathered this and other information from the gossipy women slaves who brought me my meals, or in casual conversation over the dom board. By the time we reached Amba Kamara, the mountain fortress of King Arkoun Gannouchi Maryam, I was an expert on the complicated and shifting politics of the various Ethiopic states of Aksum, and the numerous claimants to the throne of the empire.

I was aware of an increasing excitement running through our caravan as we approached our journey's end, and at last we climbed the narrow winding pathway, no more than just another goat-track, to the summit of yet another amba. These ambas were the massifs that made up the mountain ranges of central Ethiopia. Each of them was a flat-topped mountain with sheer sides that plunged like a wall into the valley that divided it from the next mountain.

It was easy to see, when I stood at the top of the precipice, how the land was fragmented into so many tiny kingdoms and principalities. Each amba was a natural and impregnable fortress. The man on top of it was invincible, and might call himself a king without fear of being challenged.

Arkoun rode up beside me and pointed to the mountains on the southern sky-line. 'That is the hiding-place of that horse-thief and scoundrel, Prester Beni-Jon. He is a man of unsurpassed treachery.' He hawked in his throat and spat over the edge of the cliff in the direction of his rival.

I had come to know Arkoun as a man of not inconsiderable cruelty and treachery himself. If he conceded Prester Beni-Jon as his master in these fields, Masara's father must be a formidable man indeed.

We crossed the tableland of the Amba Kamara, passing through a few villages of stone-walled hovels, and fields of sorghum and dhurra corn. The peasants in the fields were all tall, bushy-haired ruffians, armed with swords and round copper shields. They appeared as fierce and warlike as any of the men in our caravan.

At the far end of the amba, the path led us to the most extraordinary natural stronghold that I had ever seen. From the main table of the mountain a buttress had eroded until it stood alone, a sheer pinnacle of rock with precipitous sides, separated from the table by an awe-inspiring abyss.

This gulf was bridged by a narrow causeway, a natural arch of stone, that joined it to the tableland. It was so narrow that two horses could not pass each other on the pathway, so narrow that once a horse started out across the bridge, it could not turn round and return, until it had reached the other side.

The drop under the causeway was a thousand feet, straight into the river gorge below. It was so unnerving to the horses that the riders were forced to dismount, blindfold them, and lead them over. When I was halfway across, I found myself trembling with vertigo, and I dared not peer over the edge of the pathway into the void. It required all my self-control to keep walking, and not to throw myself flat and cling to the rocks beneath my feet.

Perched on top of this pinnacle of rock was an ungainly, lopsided castle of stone blocks and reed thatch. The open windows were covered with curtains of rawhide, and the raw sewage and odious refuse running from the fortress stained and littered the cliff beneath it.

Festooning the walls and battlements like pennants and decorations celebrating some macabre festival, were the corpses of men and women. Some had hung there so long that their bones had been picked white by the flocks of crows that circled above the abyss or roosted squawking upon the roofs. Other victims were still alive, and I watched their feeble last movements with horror as they hung by their heels. However, most of them were already dead and in various stages of decomposition. The smell of rotting human carcasses was so thick that even the wind that whined eternally around the cliffs could not disperse it.

King Arkoun called the crows his chickens. Sometimes he fed them on the walls, and at other times he threw their food from the causeway into the gorge. The dwindling wail of another unfortunate victim falling away into the depths was a feature of our life on the pinnacle of Adbar Seged, the House of the Wind Song.

These executions and the daily floggings and chopping-off of hands or feet, or the pulling-out of tongues with red-hot tongs were King Arkoun's principal diversions when he was not playing dom, or planning a raid on one of the other neighbouring king of kings. Very often Arkoun wielded the axe or the tongs in person, and his roars of laughter were as loud as the screams of his victims.

As soon as our caravan had crossed the causeway and pulled into the central courtyard of Adbar Seged, Masara was whisked away by her female gaolers into the labyrinth of stone passageways, and I was led to my new quarters which abutted those of Arkoun.

I was allotted a single stone cell. It was dark and draughty. The open fireplace blackened the walls with soot and gave out little heat. Though I wore the woollen robes of the land, I was never warm in Adbar Seged. How I longed for the sunlight on the Nile and the bright oasis of my very Egypt! I sat on those wind-swept battlements and pined for my family, for Memnon and Tanus, for my little princesses, but most of all for my mistress. Sometimes I woke in the night with the tears chilling my face, and I had to cover my head with my sheepskin blanket, so that Arkoun would not hear my sobs through the thick stone wall.

Often I pleaded with him to release me.

'But why do you want to leave me, Taita?'

'I want to go back to my family.'

'I am your family now,' he laughed. 'I am your father.'

I made a wager with him. If I won a hundred successive boards of dom from him, he agreed that he would let me go and give me an escort back down the Nile to the great plains. When I won the hundredth game, he chuckled and shook his head at my naïvety.

'Did I say a hundred? I think not. Surely it was a thousand?' He turned to his henchmen. 'Was the bargain a thousand?'

'A thousand!' they chanted. 'It was a thousand!'

They all thought it a grand joke. When in a pique I refused to play another board with Arkoun, he hung me naked from the walls of the citadel by my heels until I squealed for him to set up the board.

When Arkoun saw me naked, he laughed and prodded me. 'You may have a way with the dom board, but it seems you have lost your own stones, Egyptian.' This was the first time since my capture that my physical mutilation had been revealed. Once again, men called me 'eunuch', much to my shame and mortification.

However, in the end the consequences were beneficial. If I had been a man entire, they would never have let me go to Masara.

 THEY CAME for me in the night and led me shivering through the passages to Masara's cell. The room was lit by a dim oil lamp and smelled of vomit. The girl was curled on a straw mattress in the centre of the floor, with her vomit puddled on the stone floor beside her. She was in terrible pain, groaning and weeping and holding her stomach.

I set to work immediately, and examined her carefully. I was afraid that I would find her stomach as hard as a stone, the symptom of the swelling and bursting of the gut that would drench her insides with the contents of her intestines. There was no remedy for this condition. Not even I, with all my skills, could save her, if this was her affliction.

To my great relief I found her stomach warm and soft. There was no fever in her blood. I continued my examination, and though she groaned and screamed with agony when I touched her, I could not find any cause for her condition. I was puzzled and I sat back to think about it. Then I realized that although her face was contorted with agony, she was watching me with a candid gaze.

'This is worse than I feared.' I turned to her two female attendants and spoke in Geez. 'If I am to save her, I must have my chest. Fetch it immediately.'

They scrambled for the door, and I lowered my head to hers and whispered, 'You are a clever girl and a good actress. Did you tickle your throat with a feather?'

She smiled up at me and whispered back, 'I could think of no other way to meet you. When the women told me that you had learned to speak Geez, I knew that we could help each other.'

'I hope that is possible.'

'I have been so lonely. Even to speak to a friend will be a joy to me.' Her trust was so spontaneous that I was touched. 'Perhaps between us we will find a way to escape from this dreadful place.'

At that moment we heard the women returning, their voices echoing along the outside passage. Masara seized my hand.

'You are my friend, aren't you? You will come to me again?'

'I am and I will.'

'Quickly, tell me before you must go. What was his name?'

'Who?'

'The one who was with you on that first day beside the river. The one who looks like a young god.'

'His name is Memnon.'

'Memnon!' She repeated it with a peculiar reverence. 'It is a beautiful name. It suits him.'

The women burst into the room, and Masara clutched her healthy little belly and groaned as though she were at the point of death. While I clucked and shook my head with worry for the benefit of her women, I mixed a tonic of herbs that would do her some good, and told them that I would return in the morning.

In the morning Masara's condition had improved, and I was able to spend a little longer with her. Only one of the women was present, and she soon became bored and wandered away to the far side of the room. Masara and I exchanged a few quiet words.

'Memnon said something to me. I could not understand. What was it he said?'

'He said, "I will come back for you. Be brave. I will come back for you."'

'He could not mean that. He does not know me. He had met me only fleetingly.' She shook her head, and tears filled her eyes. 'Do you think he meant it, Taita?' There was a haunting plea in her tone that moved me, and I could not allow her to suffer more than she had already.

'He is crown prince of Egypt, and a man of honour. Memnon would not have said it unless he meant every word.'

That was all we could say then, but I came back the next day. The very first thing she asked of me was, 'Tell me again what Memnon said to me,' and I had to repeat his promise.

I told Arkoun that Masara was improving in health, but that she must be allowed out each day to walk on the battlements. 'Otherwise I cannot answer for her health.'

He thought about that for a day. However, Masara was a valuable asset for which he had paid a horse-load of silver bars, and at last he gave his permission.

Our daily exercise periods slowly extended, as the guards became accustomed to seeing us together. In the end Masara and I were able to spend most mornings in each other's company, strolling around the walls of Adbar Seged and talking endlessly.

Masara wanted to know everything that I had to tell about Memnon, and I racked my memory for anecdotes about him to entertain her. She had favourite stories which I was obliged to repeat until she knew them by heart, and she corrected me when I erred in the retelling. She particularly enjoyed the account of how he had rescued Tanus and me from the wounded bull elephant, and how he had received the Gold of Valour for his deed.

'Tell me about his mother the queen,' she demanded, and then, 'Tell me about Egypt. Tell me about your gods. Tell me about when Memnon was a baby.' Always her questions returned to him, and I was glad to appease her demands, for I longed for my family. Speaking about them made them seem closer to me.

One morning she came to me distraught. 'Last night I had a dreadful dream. I dreamed that Memnon came back to me, but I could not understand what he said to me. You must teach me to speak Egyptian, Taita. We will start today, this very minute!'

She was desperate to learn and she was a clever little thing. It went very quickly. Soon we were talking only Egyptian between ourselves, and it was useful to be able to speak privately in front of her guards.

When we were not talking about Memnon, we were discussing our plans to escape. Of course, I had been thinking of this ever since our arrival at Adbar Seged, but it helped to have her thoughts on the same subject to compare with my own.

'Even if you escape from this fortress, you will never pass through the mountains without help,' she warned me. 'The paths are like a skein of twisted wool. You will never unravel them. Every clan is at war with the next. They trust no strangers, and they will cut your throat as a spy.'

'What must we do, then?' I asked.

'If you are able to get away, you must go to my father. He will protect you and guide you back to your own people. You will tell Memnon where I am, and he will come to save me.' She said this with such shining confidence that I could not meet her eyes.

I realized then that Masara had built up an image of Memnon in her mind that was not based on reality. She was in love with a god, not a stripling as young and untried as she was herself. I was responsible for this, with my clever stories about the prince. I could not wound her now and shatter her hope by telling her how forlorn all these imaginings truly were.

'If I go to Prester Beni-Jon, your father, he will think I am one of Arkoun's spies. He will have my head.' I tried to extricate myself from the responsibilities she had laid upon me.

581

'I will tell you what to say to him. Things that only he and I know. That will prove to him that you come from me.'

She had blocked me there, so I tried a different escape. 'How would I find my way to your father's fortress? You have told me that the path is a tangled skein.'

'I will explain the way to you. Because you are so clever you will remember everything I tell you.'

By this time, naturally, I loved her almost as much as I loved my own little princesses. I would take any risk to shield her from hurt. She reminded me so strongly of my mistress at the same age that I could deny her nothing.

'Very well. Tell it to me.' And so we began to plan our escape. It was a game for me, which I played mostly to keep her hopes alive and her spirits buoyant. I had no serious expectation of finding a way off this pinnacle of rock.

We discussed ways of making a rope to lower ourselves down the cliff, although every time I looked over the causeway from the terrace outside her cell, I shuddered at that gaping void of space. She began to collect scraps of wool and cloth which she hid under her mattress. From these she planned to plait a rope. I could not tell her that a rope long enough and strong enough to support our weight and take us down to the floor of the valley would fill her cell to the ceiling.

For two long years we languished on the height of Adbar Seged, and we never were able to devise a plan of escape, but Masara never lost faith. Every day she asked me, 'What did Memnon say to me? Tell me again what he promised.'

'He said, "I will come back for you. Be brave."'

'Yes. I am brave, am I not, Taita?'

'You are the bravest girl I know.'

'Tell me what you will say to my father when you meet him.'

I repeated her instructions, and then she would reveal to me her latest plan of escape.

'I will catch the little sparrows that I feed on the terrace. You will write a letter to my father to tell him where I am. We will tie it to the sparrow's leg, and it will fly to him.'

'It is more likely to fly to Arkoun, who will have us both thrashed, and we will not be allowed to see each other again.'

In the end I escaped from Adbar Seged by riding out on a fine horse. Arkoun was going out on another raid against King Prester Beni-Jon. I was commanded to accompany him, in the capacity of personal physician and dom player.

As I walked my blindfolded horse across the causeway, I looked back and saw Masara standing on her terrace looking down at me. She was a lovely, lonely figure. She called to me in Egyptian. I could just make out her words above the sough of the wind.

'Tell him I am waiting for him. Tell him I have been brave.' And then softly, so I was not certain that I had heard the words right, 'Tell him I love him.'

The wind turned the tears upon my cheeks as cold as ice, as I rode away across Amba Kamara.

 THE NIGHT before the battle, Arkoun kept me sitting late in his tent. While he gave his last orders to his commanders, he stropped the edge of the blue sword. Once in a while he would shave a few hairs off his wrist with the steely, glittering blade to test the edge, and nod with satisfaction.

At last he rubbed down the blade with clarified mutton fat. This strange, silver-blue metal had to be kept well greased, otherwise a red powder would form upon it, almost as though it was bleeding.

The blue sword had come to exert the same fascination on me as it had on Tanus. Occasionally, when he was in a specially benevolent mood, Arkoun would allow me to handle it. The weight of the metal was surprising, and the sharpness of the edge was incredible. I imagined what havoc it could wreak in the hands of a swordsman like Tanus. I knew that if we ever met again, Tanus would want every detail of it, and so I questioned Arkoun, who never tired of boasting about it.

He told me that the sword had been forged in the heart of a volcano by one of the pagan gods of Ethiopia. Arkoun's great-grandfather had won it from the god in a game of dom that had lasted for twenty days and twenty nights. I found all this quite plausible, except the part of the legend about winning the weapon in a dom game. If Arkoun's great-grandfather had played dom at the same standard as Arkoun, then it must have been a very stupid god who lost the sword to him.

Arkoun asked my opinion of his battle plan for the next day. He had learned that I was a student of military tactics. I told him his plan was brilliant. These Ethiopians had as much grasp of military tactics as they had of the play of the dom stones. Of course, the terrain would not allow full use of the horses, and they had no chariots. Nevertheless, their battles were fought in a haphazard and desultory manner.

Arkoun's grand strategy for the morrow would be to split his forces into four raiding parties. They would hide among the rocks and rush out, seize a few hostages, slit a few throats, and then run for it.

'You are one of the great generals of history,' I told Arkoun, 'I would like to write a scroll to extol your genius.' He liked the idea, and promised to provide me with whatever materials I required for the project, as soon as we returned to Adbar Seged.

It seemed that King Prester Beni-Jon was a commander of equal panache and vision. We met his forces the following day in a wide valley with steep sides. The battlefield had been mutually agreed upon some months in advance, and Prester Beni-Jon had taken up his position at the head of the valley before we arrived. He came forward to shout insults and challenges at Arkoun from a safe distance.

Prester Beni-Jon was a stick of a man, thin as a staff, with a long white beard and silver locks down to his waist. I could not make out his features over that distance, but the women had told me that as a young man he had been the most handsome swain in Ethiopia and that he had two hundred wives. Some women had killed themselves for love of him. It seemed clear to me that his talents might be more gainfully employed in the harem than on the battlefield.

Once Prester Beni-Jon had had his say, Arkoun went forward and replied at length. His insults were flowery and poetic, they rolled off the cliffs and echoed down the gorge. I committed some of his pithier remarks to memory, for they were worth recording.

When Arkoun subsided at last, I expected that battle would be joined, but I was mistaken. There were several other warriors on both sides who wished to speak. I fell asleep against a rock in the warm sun, smiling to myself as I imagined what sport Tanus and a company of his Blues would enjoy against these Ethiopian champions of rhetoric.

It was afternoon when I woke and started up at the clash of arms. Arkoun had loosed his first assault. One of his detachments raced forward against Prester Beni-Jon's positions, beating their swords against their copper shields. Within a remarkably short space of time they returned with great alacrity to their starting-point, without having inflicted or suffered casualties.

Further insults were exchanged, and then it was Prester Beni-Jon's turn to attack. He charged and retired with equal verve and similar results. So the day passed, insult for insult, charge for charge. At nightfall both armies retired. We camped at the foot of the valley and Arkoun sent for me.

'What a battle!' he greeted me triumphantly, as I entered his tent. 'It will be many months before Prester Beni-Jon will dare take the field again.'

'There will be no battle on the morrow?' I asked.

'Tomorrow we will return to Adbar Seged,' he told me, 'and you will write a full account of my victory in your scrolls. I expect that after this salutary defeat Prester Beni-Jon will soon sue for peace.'

Seven of our men had been wounded in this ferocious encounter, all by arrows fired at extreme range. I drew the barbs and dressed and bandaged the wounds. The following day I saw the wounded loaded on to the litters and walked beside them, as we started back.

One of the men had received a stomach wound and was in much pain. I knew he would be dead from gangrene within the week, but I did my best to ease his suffering and to cushion the bouncing of the litter over the rougher sections of the track.

Late that afternoon we came to a ford in the river, one that we had crossed on our way to give battle to Prester Beni-Jon. I had recognized this ford from the description that Masara had given me of the countryside and the route to her father's stronghold. The river was one of the numerous tributaries of the

Nile that descended from the mountains. There had been rain over the preceding days, and the level of the ford was high.

I began the crossing, wading beside the litter of my patient with the stomach wound. He was already delirious. Halfway across the ford I realized that we had under-estimated the height and strength of the water. The flood caught the side of the litter and swung it sideways. It twisted the horse around, dragging the poor animal into deeper water where its hooves lost purchase on the gravel bottom.

I was hanging on to the harness, and the next moment the horse and I were both swimming. We were washed away downstream in the icy green flood. The wounded man was tumbled out of the litter, and when I tried to reach him, I lost my hold on the horse's harness. We were swept apart.

The wounded man's head disappeared below the surface, but by this time I was swimming for my own life. I rolled on to my back and pointed my feet downstream. This way I was able to fend off the rocks with my feet, as the current hurled me against them. For a short while some of Arkoun's men ran along the bank beside me, but soon the river swept me through a bend and they could not find a way around the base of the cliff. The horse and I were alone in the river.

Below the bend, the speed of the current slackened, and I was able to swim back to the horse and throw one arm over its neck. For the moment I was safe. For the first time I thought of escape, and realized that the gods had made an opportunity for me. I muttered a prayer of thanks, and used a handful of the horse's mane to steer it on down the middle of the river.

We had come downstream several miles and it was dark before I steered my horse into the bank. We clambered ashore on a sand-bar. I judged that I was safe from pursuit and recapture until morning. None of Arkoun's men would venture down the gorge in darkness. However, I was so chilled that my whole body shivered in uncontrollable spasms.

I led the horse to a sheltered place out of the wind, and then pressed my body to his flank. His wet hide steamed in the moonlight. Gradually the warmth of the animal permeated me, and my shivering subsided. Once I was half-warmed, I was able to gather up driftwood from the sand-bank. Using the Shilluk method, I managed with much difficulty to start a fire. I spread my robes out to dry, and crouched over the fire for the rest of that night.

As soon as it was light enough to see the path, I dressed myself and mounted the horse. I headed away from the river, for I knew that Arkoun's men would concentrate their search along the banks.

Two days later, following the directions that Masara had given me, I reached one of the fortified hilltop villages in the domain of Prester Beni-Jon. The headman of the village expressed the intention of cutting my throat immediately and taking my horse. I made full use of all my persuasive gifts, and eventually he agreed to keep the horse but lead me to the fortress of Prester Beni-Jon.

 THE GUIDES who were escorting me to King Prester Beni-Jon spoke of him in warm and affectionate terms. The villages that we passed along the way were cleaner and more prosperous than those of Arkoun. The herds of kine were fatter, the crops well cultivated and the people better fed. The horses I saw were magnificent. Their beauty brought tears to my eyes.

When at last we came in sight of the castle high on another amba, it was in a better state of repair than that of Arkoun, and no grisly trophies decorated the walls.

From close at hand, King Prester Beni-Jon was indeed an extemely handsome man. His silver hair and beard endowed him with a singular air of dignity. His complexion was fair and his eyes dark and intelligent. At first he was highly sceptical of my story, but gradually his manner changed towards me, as I recited the intimate knowledge with which Masara had armed me.

He was deeply affected by the messages of love and duty that I brought to him from his daughter, and he questioned me eagerly as to her health and welfare. Then his servants led me to quarters that, by Ethiopian standards, were sumptuous, and I was provided with fresh woollen robes to replace my rags.

After I had eaten and rested, the servants led me back to the dank and smoky cell that was Prester Beni-Jon's audience chamber.

'Your Majesty, Masara has been a prisoner of Arkoun these past two years,' I pointed out to him immediately. 'She is a young and tender girl. She pines away in his stinking dungeons.' I embroidered the facts a trifle, to bring home to him the urgency of her plight.

'I have tried to assemble the ransom that Arkoun demands for my daughter,' Prester Beni-Jon excused himself. 'But I would have to melt down every plate and bowl in Aksum to put together such a hoard of silver as would satisfy his greed. In addition, he demands great tracts of my land and scores of my principal villages. To relinquish these to him would weaken my realm and condemn tens of thousands of my subjects to his tyranny.'

'I could lead your army to his stronghold of Adbar Seged. You could lay siege to the castle and force him to hand over Masara to you.'

Prester Beni-Jon looked startled by this proposal. I do not think such a course of action had occurred to him. It was not the Ethiopian way of waging war.

'I know Adbar Seged very well, but it is impregnable,' he answered me primly. 'Arkoun has a mighty army at his back. We have fought many fierce battles against him. My men are lions, but we have never been able to defeat him.' I had seen the lions of Prester Beni-Jon in battle, and I saw that his estimate of the situation was correct. The army he commanded could never hope to storm Adbar Seged and free Masara by force of arms.

The following day I returned with another proposal. 'Great Emperor of Aksum, King of Kings, as you well know, I am of the Egyptian nation. Queen Lostris, the regent of Egypt, lies with her armies at the confluence of the two rivers, where the Nile meets its twin.'

He nodded. 'This I know. These Egyptians have entered my territory without my leave. They are digging mines in my valleys. Soon I will fall upon them and annihilate them.'

It was my turn to be startled. Prester Beni-Jon was aware of the work on Pharaoh's tomb, and our people there were in danger of attack. Accordingly, I modified the suggestion that I was about to put to him.

'My people are skilled in the art of siege and war,' I explained. 'I have influence with Queen Lostris. If you send me safely back to her side, I will prevail on her to extend you her friendship. Her troops will storm the fortress of Adbar Seged and free your daughter.'

Although Prester Beni-Jon tried to disguise the fact, I saw that my suggestion appealed to him. 'What would your queen require in return for her friendship?' he asked carefully.

We haggled for five days, but in the end the bargain was struck. 'You will allow Queen Lostris to continue the mining work in your valley, and you will declare those valleys a prohibited area. Your own people will be forbidden to enter there on pain of death,' I told him. This was for my mistress. It would secure the tomb of Pharaoh from desecration.

'I agree,' said Prester Beni-Jon.

'You will deliver to Queen Lostris two thousand horses that I will choose from your herds.' This was for me.

'One thousand,' said the king.

'Two thousand.' I was firm.

'I agree,' said Prester Beni-Jon.

'Once she is free, the Princess Masara shall be allowed to marry any man she chooses. You will not forbid it.' That was for Memnon and the girl.

'It is against our custom,' he sighed. 'But I agree.'

'When we capture them, Arkoun and the stronghold of Adbar Seged will be handed over to you.' He looked more cheerful and nodded vigorously.

'Finally, we Egyptians shall be allowed to keep all the spoils of war that we capture from Arkoun, including the legendary blue sword.' That was for Tanus.

'I agree,' said Prester Beni-Jon, and I could see that he thought that he had made a bargain.

He gave me an escort of fifty men, and I set out the following day on the return to Qebui, riding a fine stallion that was the king's parting gift to me.

WE WERE still five days' ride from Qebui, when I saw the swift dust-cloud ahead of us, racing towards us across the plain. Then I saw the chariots dancing through the heat-mirage. As they approached, the columns deployed into attack formation at the gallop. It was beautiful to watch. The dressing was perfect, and the spacing between each vehicle so exact that they looked like a string of beads. I wondered who commanded them.

I shaded my eyes as they drew closer, and my heart leaped as I recognized the horses of the leading chariot. They were Rock and Chain, my own darlings. However, I did not immediately recognize the charioteer behind them. It was almost three years since last I had laid eyes on Memnon. The difference in age between seventeen and twenty is the difference between the boy and the man.

I had taken to riding with saddle-cloth and stirrups, in the Ethiopian manner, and so now I stood high in the stirrups and waved. I saw the chariot swerve, as Memnon recognized me and whipped up the team to full charge.

'Mem!' I howled. 'Mem!' and his answering shout came back to me on the wind.

'Tata! By the sweet milk of Isis, it's you!'

He pulled up the horses, sprang from the footplate and dragged me from my horse. First he hugged me, then he held me at arm's-length and we studied each other avidly.

'You are pale and thin, Tata. The bones are sticking out of you. Are those grey hairs I see here?' He tugged at my temples.

He was taller than I was now, lean in the waist and broad in the shoulder. His skin was tanned and oiled to the colour of burnished amber, and cords of muscle stood out in his throat when he laughed. He wore wrist-guards of gold and the Gold of Valour on his bared chest. Although it seemed impossible, he was more handsome than when I had last seen him. He reminded me of a leopard, supple and sleek.

He lifted me bodily and set me on the footplate of the chariot. 'Take up the traces,' he ordered. 'I want to see if you have lost any of your old skill.'

'Which way?' I asked.

'West, to Qebui, of course,' he ordered. 'My mother will be angry if I do not bring you directly to her.'

That night we sat at a camp-fire together, away from the other officers, so that we could talk in private. We sat in silence for a while, looking up at the silver blaze of stars, and then Memnon said, 'When I thought I had lost you, it was as though I had lost a part of myself. You are woven into my very first memory of life.'

I, who deal in words, could find no words to answer him. We were silent again, and then at last he laid a hand on my shoulder.

'Did you ever see the girl again?' he asked, and though his tone was casual, his grip upon my shoulder was not.

'Which girl?' I asked, to tease him.

'The girl at the river, on the day we were parted.'

'Was there a girl?' I frowned, as I tried to remember. 'What did she look like?'

'Her face was a dark lily, and her skin was the colour of wild honey. They called her Masara, and the memory of her still troubles my sleep.'

'Her name is Masara Beni-Jon,' I told him, 'and I have spent two years imprisoned with her in the fortress of Adbar Seged. There I learned to love her, for her nature is even sweeter than her face.'

He seized me with both hands now and shook me without mercy. 'Tell me about her, Tata! Tell me everything. Leave nothing out.'

So we sat the rest of that night beside the fire and we talked about the girl. I told him how she had learned to speak Egyptian for his sake. I told him how his promise to her had sustained her through the dark, lonely days, and in the end I told him the message that she had sent to him, the message she had called out to me from the battlements of Adbar Seged as I rode away and left her.

'Tell him I was brave. Tell him I love him.'

He was silent for a long while, staring into the flames, and then he said softly, 'How can she love me? She does not know me.'

'Do you know her any better than she knows you?' I asked, and he shook his head.

'Do you love her?'

'Yes,' he answered simply.

'Then she loves you in the same way.'

'I made her a promise. Will you help me make good my promise to her, Tata?'

I HAVE never in my life known such joy as was mine on my return to Qebui when I went aboard the *Breath of Horus*.

Memnon had sent a messenger ahead to warn them of my return, and they were all waiting for me.

'By the stinking crust between Seth's toes!' Kratas shouted. 'I thought we had got rid of you at last, you old rogue.' And he crushed me to his chest until I thought my ribs were all staved in.

Tanus seized my shoulders and stared into my eyes for a moment before he grinned, 'But for you, that hairy Ethiop would have had me. He got the better bargain when he took you instead. Thank you, old friend.' I saw how Tanus had aged. Like me, there was grey in his hair now, and his face was weather-beaten, beginning to erode like a granite cliff.

My little princesses were no longer little, but they were still adorable. They were shy towards me, for their memory of me had faded. They stared at me with big eyes as I made my obeisance. The colour of Bekatha's hair had darkened to copper. I looked forward to rekindling her affection.

Tehuti recognized me at last. 'Tata!' she said. 'Did you bring me a present?'

'Yes, Your Highness,' I replied, 'I have brought you my heart.'

My mistress smiled at me as I walked towards her along the deck. She wore the light *nemes* crown and the golden head of the cobra on her brow. When she smiled, I saw that she had lost her first tooth, and the gap marred her smile. She had thickened around the waist, and the heavy affairs of state had furrowed her brow and etched crow's feet at the corners of her eyes. To me, however, she was still the most lovely woman in the world.

592

She stood up from the throne as I knelt before her. This was the highest mark of her favour. She laid her hand on my bowed head, and it was a caress.

'You have been away from us too long, Taita,' she said, so softly that only I could hear her. 'Tonight you will sleep at the foot of my bed once more.'

That night, when she had drunk the bowl of herb broth that I had prepared for her, and I had covered her with a fur blanket, she murmured softly as she closed her eyes, 'Can I trust you not to kiss me when I am asleep?'

'No, Your Majesty,' I replied, and stooped over her. She smiled as my lips touched hers.

'Never leave us again for so long, Taita,' she said.

 MEMNON AND I had planned our tactics meticulously, and we executed them with the same precision as one of our chariot manoeuvres.

Tanus was easy to convince. His defeat by Arkoun still rankled. In his presence Memnon and I discussed the ease with which the blue sword had sheered his bronze blade, and how Arkoun would certainly have killed him, if I had not intervened. Tanus bristled with humiliation.

Then Memnon questioned me on the magical origins and properties of the legendary weapon. Tanus forgot his pique and joined in with avid questions of his own.

'This Prester Beni-Jon has declared the blue sword a prize of war. Whoever can seize it, may hold it,' I told them.

'If we went against Arkoun, we would not be able to use chariots in those valleys,' Memnon mused. 'It would have to be the infantry. How do you think your Shilluk would fare against the Ethiops, Lord Tanus?' Memnon still addressed Tanus formally. Obviously he had not learned in my absence that Tanus was his real father.

By the time we had finished with him, Tanus was as hot for the venture as either of us. He was totally in league with us as we started our campaign on Queen Lostris.

From the very beginning my mistress had understood, as Tanus never had, just how vital the horses and chariots would be, if ever we were to fulfil the dream of the return to our very Egypt. I displayed the stallion that Prester Beni-Jon had given me, and pointed out to my mistress his finer points of breed.

'Look at his nostrils, Majesty. See the depth of his chest, and the balance of muscle to bone. The Hyksos have nothing to match these Ethiopian horses.'

Then I reminded her of her promise to the dead pharaoh, and told her, 'Prester Beni-Jon will cede the valley of the tomb to you. His warriors will guard it against the grave-robbers. He will place a taboo upon the valley, and these Ethiops are superstitious people. They will respect the prohibition even long after we have returned to Thebes.'

I warned Memnon not to mention to Queen Lostris his amorous interest in an expedition against Arkoun. It would do our cause no good. Every mother is also a lover; she seldom takes any pleasure in seeing her son led away by another younger woman.

No woman, not even a queen, could resist the combined charm and cunning of the three of us, Tanus and Memnon and myself. Queen Lostris gave her consent to our expeditionary force marching on Adbar Seged.

WE LEFT the wagons and the chariots at the valley of Pharaoh's tomb, and struck out into the mountains. Prester Beni-Jon had sent a company of guides to meet us. They were a hundred of his best and most reliable men.

Tanus had selected a full division of his wild and bloodthirsty Shilluk, and promised them all the cattle they could capture. Each of these black pagans carried a cloak of thick jackal fur rolled upon his back, for we remembered the cold wind of the mountain passes.

For support we had three companies of Egyptian archers, led by Lord Kratas. That old ruffian had joined the company of nobles during my sojourn in Adbar Seged. He was spoiling for a real fight. He and every one of his men were armed with the new compound recurved bows that could outdrive the Ethiopian long-bows by two hundred paces.

Memnon had selected a small band of the finest swordsmen and rough fighters that we had. Remrem was one of these, of course, as were Lord Aqer and Astes. I was part of this special detachment, not for my warlike skills, but simply because I was the only one who had ever entered the fortress of Adbar Seged.

Hui wanted to come with us and offered me every bribe at his disposal. In the end I gave in to him, mainly because I needed an expert to help me select the horses that Prester Beni-Jon had promised me.

I impressed on both Tanus and the prince how vital it was to move swiftly, not only for reasons of surprise, but also because the rains must soon break upon the mountains. During my days in Adbar Seged I had studied the patterns of the weather and the seasons. If the rains caught us in the valleys, they would prove a more dangerous enemy than any Ethiop army.

We made the approach march to Amba Kamara in less than a month. Our column wound through the passes like a long, deadly cobra. The bronze spear-heads of the Shilluk glittered in the high sunlight like the scales of the serpent. We met no person to oppose us. The villages we passed through were deserted. The inhabitants had fled and taken their herds and their women with them. Although each day the clouds gathered black and sullen on the mountain peaks, and at night the thunder muttered at us, the rains held off and the fords of the rivers were low.

Twenty-five days after setting out, we stood in the valley below the massif of Amba Kamara, and looked up the winding track to the heights looming over us.

On my previous journeys up and down the mountain I had studied the defences that Arkoun had erected along the pathway. These comprised rockfalls and stone-walled redoubts. I pointed these out to Tanus, and we could make out the bushy, unhel-meted heads of the defenders showing above the walls of the strongpoints.

'The weakness of a rockfall is that you can only let it come down once, and my Shilluk are quick enough on their feet to dodge a charging buffalo,' Tanus said thoughtfully.

He sent them up the path in small parties, and when the defenders knocked out the wedges from under the rockfall and sent it rolling down on the track, those long-legged black spearmen ran out to the side with the agility of mountain goats. Once the slide of boulders had rumbled past them, they turned straight up the almost sheer mountainside. Bounding from rock to rock, and howling in such a horrible fashion that they started the hair on the nape of my neck, they drove the defenders up the mountain and over the crest.

They were held up only by Arkoun's archers hidden behind the walls of the stone redoubts. When this happened, Kratas led his archers up the mountain. With their superior bow-range, the Egyptians were able to stand back and shoot massed volleys, almost straight into the sky.

It was fascinating to watch a swarm of arrows climb into the air like a flock of black birds and then drop down on to the redoubt so steeply that the stone wall afforded the men behind it no protection. We heard their screams and then saw them break and scurry away up the slope. Immediately the Shilluk were after them, baying like a pack of hunting dogs. Even from the bottom of the valley I could hear their battle cry, '*Kajan! Kajan!* Kill! Kill!'

Though my legs were hard and my wind strong with so much marching, I had difficulty keeping up with Memnon and the rest of our small group. The years were beginning to take their toll.

We were all wearing long woollen Ethiopic robes, and we carried the traditional round shields of our enemies. However, we had not yet placed the horse-hair wigs on our heads. It would have been extremely unwise to resemble the Ethiopian too closely while the Shilluk were in their present mood.

When at last I came out on the flat tableland of the amba, I saw at a glance that Tanus was rallying and regrouping his infantry. The one fault of the Shilluk as fighting men is that once they have wet their spears with blood, they go berserk, and it is almost impossible to control them. Tanus was roaring like a bull elephant and laying about him with his golden whip of rank. Once more in hand, the Shilluk formed ranks and moved forward against the first village where the Ethiopians were waiting behind the stone walls. As the wave of tall black figures, topped by a foam of white ostrich-feather head-dresses, washed towards them, they loosed a shower of arrows from their long bows. But the Shilluk had their tall shields up.

As the Shilluk charge burst upon them, some of the Ethiopians rushed forward, brandishing their swords. They were not lacking in courage, but this type of warfare was new to them. They had never been forced to meet a charge that was carried through to the death.

I stayed long enough to see them heavily engaged, and then I called to Memnon and his band, 'The wigs!' Each of them pulled one of the wigs of black horse-hair over his scalp. I had made these with my own hands, and styled them on the Ethiopian model of beauty, full and floccose. Clad in the long striped robes and with the wigs on our heads, we could pass as a mob of Arkoun's clansmen.

'This way! Follow me!' I cried, and let out an ululating Ethiopic war cry. They yodelled and howled behind me, as we skirted the village where the fight was still raging, and ran in a disorderly bunch through the cornfields.

We had to reach the fortress and be at Masara's side to protect her when Arkoun finally realized that he had lost the day. I knew that he would not hestitate to kill her as soon as she was no longer of value to him. I thought that he would probably take the blue sword to her or throw her from the causeway into the gorge. Those were his favourite means of despatching his victims.

As we made our way across the amba, we found the entire tableland in turmoil. Bands of bushy-headed warriors milled about in confusion. Women dragged their children by the arm, their possessions piled on their heads, wailing with terror as they ran about like frightened chickens who smell the fox. Herds of goats bleated, and cattle lowed and churned the dust. The herd-boys had fled. Nobody paid us the least attention as we trotted through the fields and kept clear of the villages.

We followed the general movement towards Adbar Seged at

the far end of the table, and as we neared the causeway the crowds thickened and congealed until we were obliged to force our way through them. There were guards at the head of the causeway. They were turning the fugitives back with drawn swords and clubs. Women were screaming and pleading for shelter in the fortress, holding up their babies for mercy's sake. Some of them were knocked down in the press and were trampled under the feet of those coming on from behind.

'Form the tortoise.' Memnon gave the order quietly, and our small band closed up and locked the edges of our Ethiopian shields. We cut through the crowd like a shark through a shoal of sardines. Some of the weaker ones at the front were pushed forward and forced over the edge of the precipice. Their screams added to the panic. When we reached the head of the causeway, the guards there tried to stop us, but they were themselves so crowded by the mob that they could not swing their weapons, and were in danger of being overwhelmed and thrown over the cliff.

'We are under King Arkoun's direct orders. Stand aside!' I shouted at them in Geez.

'The password?' the captain of the guard yelled at me, as he struggled to stay on his feet. The crowd surged back and forward in panic. 'You must give the password.' He poked his sword at me, but Memnon struck the blade aside.

During my imprisonment I had heard the password repeated a thousand times, for my cell had been above the main gate. It might have been changed since then, and I was ready to have the captain killed, as I yelled the old password at him: 'The mountain is high!'

'Go across!' He stood aside, and we struggled out of the throng, kicking and shoving back those who tried to follow us. We ran out on to the bridge. So urgent was the need to reach Masara that I barely noticed the drop on either hand, and without a qualm I led them across the gaping void.

'Where is King Arkoun?' I shouted at the guards who blocked the gateway. When they hesitated, I told them, 'The mountain is high! I have urgent despatches for the king. Stand aside! Let us pass!' We barged through the open gate before they could decide to oppose us, and, with twelve good men at my back, I raced for the outer staircase that led to the upper terrace.

There were two armed men at the door to Masara's chamber, and I rejoiced to see them. I had worried that the girl might have been moved to another part of the fort, but the presence of the guards assured me that she had not.

'Who are you?' one of them shouted, and drew his sword. 'By what authority—' He did not finish the challenge. I stepped aside and allowed Memnon and Remrem to brush past me. They flew at the guards and cut them down before they could defend themselves.

The door to Masara's chamber was barred from within, and when we hurled our combined weight against it, there came a chorus of feminine screams and wails from the other side. At the third attempt the door gave way and I was propelled through the opening into the room beyond. It was in deep gloom, and I could barely make out the huddle of women in the far corner.

'Masara!' I called her name, as I plucked the wig from my head, and let my own hair fall around my shoulders. She recognized me by it.

'Taita!' She bit the wrist of the woman who tried to hold her, and ran to me. She flung both arms around my neck, and then she looked over my shoulder and her grip slackened, her dark eyes opened wide and the colour flooded her cheeks.

Memnon had pulled off his wig. Without it, he was strikingly and unmistakably a prince. I stepped aside and left Masara standing alone. The two of them stared at each other. Neither of them moved or spoke for what seemed like an eternity, but was a moment only. Then Masara said softly and shyly in Egyptian, 'You came. You kept your promise. I knew that you would.'

I think that this was the only time that I ever saw Memnon at a loss. He could only nod his head, and then I witnessed an amazing phenomenon. Blood flooded up his neck and suffused his face, so that even in the gloom of the chamber it glowed. The Crown Prince of Egypt, son of Pharaoh, commander of the first division of chariots, Best of Ten Thousand, holder of the Gold of Valour, stood there blushing and as tongue-tied as a peasant clod.

Behind me one of the women squawked like a startled hen, and before I could put out a hand to hold her, she had ducked under my arm and darted down the inner staircase. Her screams reverberated up the stair-well. 'Guards! The enemy has broken into the east wing. Come quickly!' and almost immediately there was a rush of booted feet on the staircase.

On the instant, Memnon was transformed from the blushing young lover to a hard-faced guardsman. 'Take care of her, Tata. Let no harm come to her,' he told me grimly, and stepped past me to the head of the stairs.

He killed the first man coming up with that classic thrust to the throat that Tanus had taught him. Then he placed his foot in the centre of his chest. As he jerked his blade free, he kicked the dead man backwards down the stair-well. The falling corpse tumbled into the other men coming up from below, and swept the stairs clean.

Memnon looked at me. 'Do you think we can reach the gate before they close it?'

'We must,' I answered. 'Our best route is back down the outer staircase.'

'Remrem, lead us. Tata and the princess in the centre. I will bring up the rear-guard,' he said crisply, and stabbed the next man coming up the stairs in the eye.

The Ethiopian dropped his weapon and clutched his face with both hands. Memnon stabbed him again through the chest and pushed him backwards down the stairs, clearing them a second time. 'Follow Remrem,' he shouted at me. 'Don't stand there. After him as fast as you can.'

I grabbed Masara's arm, but there was no need to pull her along. She came with me readily, so quick and agile that she was leading me.

The sunlight struck us as we ran out on to the terrace. After the dark room it dazzled me. I blinked to clear my vision, and then I looked across the causeway to the edge of the tableland on the far side of the gulf. Tanus' Shilluks were there. I saw their feathers dancing and their shields held high.

'*Kajan*! Kill! Kill!' they sang, and their spear-heads were dulled with fresh blood. The panic-stricken peasants scattered before them, and they reached the head of the causeway.

There were two or three hundred of Arkoun's soldiers there. They had the abyss at their backs, and necessity made heroes of every one of them. Now they had truly become lions. Although a score of them were driven back over the edge, and plunged to their death in the valley far below, the survivors hurled back the first charge of the Shilluk.

I saw Tanus then, exactly where I expected him to be, holding the centre. His helmet shone like a beacon in the dark sea of Shilluk warriors. I saw him throw back his head and begin to sing.

The savage Shilluk words carried over the gulf to where I stood on the terrace of the fortress. The men around him took up the chorus, and they surged forward, still singing. This time nothing could stand before them. They stabbed and hacked their way through the defenders, and Tanus was the first man on to the causeway. He ran lightly for such a big man, and he was still singing. His Shilluk followed him on to the stone arch, but it was so narrow that they were forced into single file.

Tanus was halfway across, when the song died on his lips, and he stopped.

From the gateway of Adbar Seged, below where I stood, another man stepped out on to the causeway to confront Tanus. I was looking down and so could not see his face, but there was no mistaking the weapon in his right hand. The blue sword caught the sunlight and flashed like a sheet of summer lightning.

'Arkoun!' Tanus bellowed. 'I have been looking for you.'

Arkoun could not understand the words, but the sense of them was unmistakable. He laughed into the wind, and his beard blew out like smoke around his goaty face.

'I know you!' He swung the silver-blue blade around his head, and it hissed and whined in the air. 'This time I will kill you.' He started forward, out along the narrow arch of stone, running with long, lithe strides straight at Tanus.

Tanus altered his grip on the handle of his bronze shield, and tucked his head in behind it. He now knew the power in that glittering blade, and I saw that he did not intend meeting it with his own softer bronze. Arkoun had also learned discretion from their last brief encounter. From the way he carried the blue sword, I guessed that he would not attempt another rash overhand stroke.

As they came together, Arkoun gathered himself. I saw his shoulders brace and his weight swing forward. He used the impetus of his charge to send the straight thrust at Tanus' head. Tanus lifted the shield and caught the blue blade in the centre of the heavy bronze target. It would have snapped a sword of inferior metal, but the blue sword sheared through it as if it were goatskin. Half its silver length was buried in the yellow bronze.

Then I realized Tanus' intention. He twisted the shield at an angle so that the blade was trapped. Arkoun struggled to withdraw his weapon, he wrestled and heaved, throwing his full weight backwards, but Tanus had the blue sword in a vice of bronze.

Arkoun gathered all his strength and pulled back again. This time Tanus did not resist him. He leaped forward in the direction that Arkoun was heaving, and this unexpected move threw Arkoun off-balance.

Arkoun staggered away, tripped and teetered on the brink of the chasm. In order to keep his balance, he was forced to relinquish his grip on the hilt of the blue sword, and to leave it still embedded in the shield.

He windmilled his arms as he swayed out over the drop. Then Tanus shifted his ground, put his shoulder behind the shield and barged forward. The shield crashed into Arkoun's chest, and the pommel of the blue sword caught him in the pit of his belly with all Tanus' weight and strength behind it.

Arkoun was thrown backwards, out into empty space. He turned a slow somersault in the air and then went straight down, with his robe ballooning around him, and his beard streaming like a chariot pennant in the wind of his fall.

From where I stood, I watched him make the same last journey on which he had sent so many other unfortunate souls. From the causeway until he struck the rocks a thousand feet below, he screamed all the way down, on a high, receding note that was cut off abruptly at the end.

Tanus stood alone in the middle of the causeway. He still held the shield on high with the sword buried in the metal.

Slowly the tumult and the fighting died away. The Ethiopians had seen their king vanquished and cast down. The heart went out of them. They threw down their weapons and grovelled for mercy. The Egyptian officers were able to save some of them from the blood-crazed Shilluk, and these were dragged away to where the slave-masters waited to bind them.

I had no eyes for any of this, for I was watching Tanus out there on the bridge. He began to walk towards the gateway of the fortress, and the men cheered him and raised their weapons in salute.

'There is plenty of fight in the old bull yet,' Memnon laughed in admiration, but I did not laugh with him. I felt the chill premonition of some awful tragedy, like the air stirred by the beat of vultures' wings as they settle to their gruesome feast.

'Tanus,' I whispered. He walked with a slow and hampered gait. He lowered the shield as he came down the bridge of stone, and only then did I see the stain spreading on his breastplate.

I thrust Masara into Memnon's arms and ran down the outer staircase. The Ethiopian guards at the gate tried to surrender their weapons to me, but I pushed my way past them and ran out on to the causeway.

Tanus saw me running towards him and he smiled at me, but the smile was lop-sided. He stopped walking and slowly his legs buckled beneath him, and he sat down heavily in the middle of the bridge. I dropped on my knees beside him, and saw the rent in the crocodile-skin of his breastplate. Blood oozed from it, and I knew that the blue sword had bitten deeper than I had believed possible. Arkoun had driven the point through the bronze shield, on through the tough leather breastplate, and into Tanus' chest.

Carefully I untied the straps that held his armour, and lifted away the breastplate. Tanus and I both looked down at the wound. It was a penetrating slit the exact width of the blade, like a tiny mouth with wet red lips. Every breath that Tanus drew frothed through that horrid opening in a rash of pink bubbles. It was a lung wound, but I could not bring myself to say it. No man can survive a sword-cut through one of his lungs.

'You are wounded.' It was an asinine remark, and I could not look at his face as I said it.

'No, old friend, I am not wounded,' he replied softly. 'I am killed.'

TANUS' SHILLUK made a litter with their spears, and covered it with a rug of sheepskin. They lifted him and carried him, gently and slowly, into the fortress of Adbar Seged.

We laid him on the bed of King Arkoun, and then I sent them all away. When they were gone, I placed the blue sword upon the bed beside him. He smiled and laid his hand on the gold and jewelled hilt. 'I have paid a high price for this treasure,' he murmured. 'I would have liked to wield it just once upon the battlefield.'

I could offer him no hope or comfort. He was an old soldier, and he had seen too many lung wounds. I could not hope to deceive him as to the final outcome. I bound up the wound with a pad of wool and a linen bandage. While I worked, I recited the incantation to quell the bleeding, 'Retreat from me, creature of Seth—'

But he was sinking away from me. Each breath he drew was an effort, and I could hear the blood stirring in his lungs like a hidden creature in the deep swamps.

I mixed a draught of the sleeping-flower, but he would not drink it. 'I will live every minute of my life,' he told me. 'Even the very last one.'

'What else is there that I can do for you?'

'You have done so much already,' he said. 'But there is no end to the demands that we all make upon you.'

I shook my head, 'There is no end to what I would give.'

'These last things then I ask of you. Firstly, you will never tell Memnon that I am his sire. He must always believe that the blood of the pharaohs runs in his veins. He will need every strength to meet the destiny that awaits him.'

'He would be as proud to share your blood as that of any king.'

'Swear to me you will not tell him.'

'I swear it,' I replied, and he lay a while gathering his strength. 'There is one other boon.'

'I grant it before you name it,' I said.

'Take care of my woman who was never my wife. Shield and succour her as you have done all these years past.'

'You know I will.'

'Yes, I know you will, for you have always loved her as much as I have. Take care of Lostris and of our children. I give them all into your hands.'

He closed his eyes, and I thought that the end was close, but his strength surpassed that of other men. After a while he opened them again.

'I wish to see the prince,' he said.

'He waits for you on the terrace,' I answered, and went to the curtained doorway.

Memnon stood at the far end of the terrace. Masara was with him, and the two of them stood close together but not touching. Their expressions were grave and their voices muted. They both looked up as I called.

Memnon came immediately, leaving the girl standing alone. He went directly to Tanus' bed and stood looking down at him. Tanus smiled up at him, but the smile was unsteady. I knew what effort it had cost him.

'Your Highness, I have taught you all I know of war, but I cannot teach you about life. Each man must learn that for himself. There is nothing else I have to tell you before I start out on this new journey, except to thank you for the gift of knowing and serving you.'

'You were ever more than a tutor to me,' Memnon answered softly. 'You were the father I never knew.'

Tanus closed his eyes, and his expression twisted.

Memnon stooped and took his arm in a firm grip, 'Pain is just another enemy to be met and overcome. You taught me that,

Lord Tanus.' The prince thought it was the wound that had affected him, but I knew that it was the pain of the word 'father'.

Tanus opened his eyes. 'Thank you, Your Highness. It is good to have you to help me through this last agony.'

'Call me friend, rather than highness.' Memnon sank on one knee beside the bed, and he did not release the grip on Tanus' arm.

'I have a gift for you, friend.' The congealing blood in Tanus' lungs blurred his voice. He groped for the handle of the blue sword that still lay on the mattress beside him, but he did not have the strength to lift it.

He took Memnon's hand from his arm and placed it upon the jewelled hilt. 'This is yours now,' he whispered.

'I will think of you whenever I draw it from its scabbard. I will call your name whenever I wield it on the battlefield.' Memnon took up the weapon.

'You do me great honour.'

Memnon stood up, and with the sword in his right hand took the classic opening stance in the centre of the room. He touched the blade to his lips, saluting the man lying on the bed.

'This is the way you taught me to do it.'

Then he began the exercise of arms, in which Tanus had drilled him when he was still a child. He performed the twelve parries, and then the cuts and the lunges with an unhurried perfection. The silver blade circled and swooped like a glittering eagle. It fluted and whined through the air, and lit the gloom of the chamber with darting beams of light.

Memnon ended it with the straight thrust, aimed at the throat of an imaginary enemy. Then he placed the point between his feet and rested both hands upon the pommel.

'You have learned well,' Tanus nodded. 'There is nothing more that I can teach you. It is not too soon for me to go.'

'I will wait with you,' Memnon said.

'No.' Tanus made a weary gesture. 'Your destiny waits for you beyond the walls of this dreary room. You must go forward to meet it without looking back. Taita will stay with me. Take the girl with you. Go to Queen Lostris and prepare her for the news of my death.'

'Go in peace, Lord Tanus.' Memnon would not degrade that solemn moment with futile argument. He crossed to the bed and kissed his father on the lips. Then he turned and, without a backward glance, he strode from the room with the blue sword in his hand.

'Go on to glory, my son,' Tanus whispered, and turned to face the stone wall. I sat at the foot of his bed and looked at the dirty stone floor. I did not want to watch a man like Tanus weep.

I WOKE in the night to the sound of drums, those crude wooden drums of the Shilluk, beating out there in the darkness. The doleful sound of the Shilluk's voices chanting their savage dirge made me shudder with dread.

The lamp had burned low, and was guttering beside the bed. It threw grotesque shadows on the ceiling, like the beating and fluttering of the wings of vultures. I crossed slowly and reluctantly to where Tanus lay. I knew that the Shilluk were not mistaken – they have a way of sensing these things.

Tanus lay as I had last seen him, with his face to the wall, but when I touched his shoulder I felt the chill in his flesh. That indomitable spirit had gone on.

I sat beside him for the remainder of that night and I lamented and mourned for him, as his Shilluk were doing.

In the dawn I sent for the embalmers.

I would not let those crude butchers eviscerate my friend. I made the incision in his left flank. It was not a long, ugly slash, such as the undertakers are wont to perform, but the work of a surgeon.

Through it I drew his viscera. When I held Tanus' great heart in my hands, I trembled. It was as though I could still feel all his strength and power beat in this casket of flesh. I replaced it with reverence and love in the cage of his ribs, and I closed the gash in his side and the wound in his chest, that the blue sword had made, with all the skill at my command.

I took up the bronze spoon, and pressed it up his nostril until I felt it touch the thin wall of bone at the end of the passage. This flimsy partition I pierced with one hard thrust, and scooped out the soft matter from the cavity of his skull. Only then was I content to deliver him over to the embalmers.

Even though there was no more for me to do, I waited with Tanus through the forty long days of the mummification in the cold and gloomy castle of Adbar Seged. Looking back upon it now, I realize that this was weakness. I could not bear the burden of my mistress's grief when first she heard the news of Tanus' death. I had allowed Memnon to assume the duty that was rightfully mine. I hid with the dead, when I should have been with the living who needed me more. I have ever been a coward.

There was no coffin to hold Tanus' mummified body. I would make him one when at last we reached the fleet at Qebui. I had the Ethiopian women weave a long basket for him. The mesh of the weave was so fine that it resembled linen. It would hold water like a pot of fired clay.

 WE CARRIED him down from the mountains. His Shilluk easily bore the weight of his desiccated body. They fought each other for the honour. Sometimes they sang their wild songs of mourning as we wound our way through the gorges and over the windswept passes. At other times they sang the fighting songs that Tanus had taught them.

I walked beside his bier all that weary way. The rains broke on the peaks and drenched us. They flooded the fords so that we had to swim ropes across. In my tent at night, Tanus' reed coffin stood beside my own cot. I spoke aloud to him in the darkness, as if he could hear and answer me, just as we had done in the old days.

At last we descended through the last pass, and the great plains lay before us. As we approached Qebui, my mistress came to meet our sad caravan. She rode on the footplate of the chariot behind Prince Memnon.

As they came towards us through the grassland, I ordered the Shilluk bearers to lay Tanus' reed coffin under the spreading branches of a giant giraffe acacia. My mistress dismounted from the chariot and went to the coffin. She placed one hand upon it, and bowed her head in silence.

I was shocked to see what ravages sorrow had wrought upon her. There were streaks of grey in her hair, and her eyes were dulled. The sparkle and the zest had gone out of them. I realized that the days of her youth and her great beauty were gone for ever. She was a lonely and tragic figure. Her bereavement was so evident, that no person who looked upon her now could doubt that she was a widow.

I went to her side to warn her. 'Mistress, you must not make your grief clear for all to see. They must never know that he was more than just your friend and the general of your armies. For the sake of his memory and the honour that he held so dear, hold back your tears.'

'I have no tears left,' she answered me quietly. 'My grief is all cried out. Only you and I will ever know the truth.'

We placed Tanus' humble reed coffin in the hold of the *Breath of Horus*, beside the magnificent gold coffin of Pharoah. I stayed at the side of my mistress, as I had promised Tanus I would, until the worst agonies of her mourning had subsided into the dull eternal pain that would never leave her again. Then, at her orders, I returned to the valley of the tomb to supervise the completion of Pharaoh's sepulchre.

Obedient to my mistress, I also selected a site further down the valley for the tomb of Tanus. Though I did my very best with the material and craftsmen available to me, Tanus' resting-place would be the hut of a peasant compared to the funerary palace of Pharaoh Mamose.

An army of craftsmen had laboured all these years to complete the magnificent murals that decorated the passages and the subterranean chambers of the king's tomb. The store-rooms of the tomb were crammed with all the treasure that we had carried with us from Thebes.

Tanus' tomb had been built in haste. He had accumulated no treasure in his lifetime of service to the state and the crown. I painted scenes upon the walls that depicted the events of his earthly existence, his hunting of mighty beasts and his battles with the red pretender and the Hyksos, and the last assault on the fortress of Adbar Seged. However, I dared not show his nobler accomplishments, his love for my mistress and his steadfast friendship to me. The love of a queen is treason, the friendship of a slave is degrading.

When at last it was completed, I stood alone in Tanus' modest tomb, where he would spend all eternity, and I was suddenly consumed by anger that this was all I could do for him. In my eyes he was more a man than any pharaoh who had ever worn the double crown. That crown could have been his, it should have been his, but he had spurned it. To me he was more a king than ever Pharaoh had been.

It was then that the thought first dawned upon me. It was so outrageous that I thrust it from me. Even to contemplate it seriously was a terrible treason, and offence in the eyes of men and the gods.

However, over the weeks that followed, the thought kept creeping back into my mind. I owed Tanus so much, and Pharaoh so little. Even if I was damned to perdition, it would be a fair price to pay. Tanus had given me more than that over my lifetime.

I could not accomplish it alone. I needed help, but who was there to turn to? I could not enlist either Queen Lostris or the prince. My mistress was bound by the oath she had sworn to Pharaoh, and Memnon did not know which of the two men was his natural father. I could not tell him without breaking my oath to Tanus.

In the end there was one person only who had loved Tanus almost as much as I had, who feared neither god nor man, and who had the brute physical strength I lacked.

'By Seth's unwiped backside!' Lord Kratas roared with laughter when I revealed my plan to him. 'No one else but you could have dreamed up such a scheme. You are the biggest rogue alive, Taita, but I love you for giving me this last chance to honour Tanus.'

The two of us planned it carefully. I even went to the lengths of sending the guards at the entrance to the hold of the *Breath of Horus* a jug of wine heavily laced with the powder of the sleeping-flower.

When Kratas and I at last entered the hold of the ship where the two coffins lay, my resolve wavered. I sensed that the *Ka* of Pharaoh Mamose watched me from the shadows and that his baleful spirit would follow me all the days of my life, seeking vengeance for this sacrilege.

Big, bluff Kratas had no such qualms, and he set to work with such a will that several times during the course of the night, I had to caution him against the noise he was making as we opened the golden lids to the royal coffin and lifted out the mummy of the king.

Tanus was a bigger man than Pharaoh, but fortunately the coffin-makers had left us some space, and Tanus' body had shrunk during the embalming. Even so, we were obliged to unwind several layers of his wrappings before he fitted snugly into the great golden cask.

I mumbled an apology to Pharaoh Mamose as we lifted him into the humble wooden coffin, painted on the outside with a likeness of the Great Lion of Egypt. There was room to spare, and before we sealed the lid we packed this with the linen bandages that we had unwrapped from Tanus.

AFTER THE rains had passed and the cool season of the year returned, my mistress ordered the funeral procession to leave Qebui and set out for the valley of the tomb.

The first division of chariots, headed by Prince Memnon, led us. Behind followed fifty carts loaded with the funerary treasure of Pharaoh Mamose. The royal widow, Queen Lostris, rode on the wagon that carried the golden coffin. I rejoiced to see her take this last journey in the company of the one man she had loved, even though she thought it was another. I saw her glance back more than once towards the end of the long caravan that crept dolefully across the plains, five miles from its head to its tail.

The wagon at the rear of the column that carried the lighter wooden coffin was followed by a regiment of Shilluk. Their magnificent voices carried clearly to us at the head of the column as they sang the last farewell. I knew that Tanus would hear them and know for whom the song was sung.

WHEN WE at last reached the valley of the tomb, the golden coffin was placed beneath a tabernacle outside the entrance to the royal mausoleum. The linen roof of the tent was illuminated with texts and illustrations from the *Book of the Dead*.

There were to be two separate funerals. The first was the lesser, that of the Great Lion of Egypt. The second would be the grander and more elaborate royal funeral.

So it was that three days after our arrival at the valley, the wooden coffin was placed in the tomb that I had prepared for Tanus, and the tomb was consecrated by the priests of Horus, who was Tanus' patron, and then sealed.

During this ritual, my mistress was able to restrain her grief and to show nothing more than the decent sorrow of a queen towards a faithful servant, although I knew that inside her something was dying that would never be reborn.

All that night the valley resounded to the chant of the Shilluk regiment as they mourned for the man who had now become one of their gods. To this day they still shout his name in battle.

Ten days after the first funeral, the golden coffin was placed on its wooden sledge and dragged into the vast royal tomb. It required the efforts of three hundred slaves to manoeuvre the coffin through the passageways. I had designed the tomb so precisely that there was only the breadth of a hand between the sides and the lid of the coffin and the stone walls and roof.

To thwart all future grave-robbers and any others who would desecrate the royal tomb, I had built a labyrinth of tunnels beneath the mountain. From the entrance in the cliff-face, a wide passage led directly to an impressive burial vault that was decorated with marvellous murals. In the centre of this room stood an empty granite sarcophagus, with the lid removed and cast dramatically aside. The first grave-robber to enter here would believe that he was too late and that some other had plundered the tomb before him.

In fact, there was another tunnel leading off at right-angles from the entrance passage. The mouth of this was disguised as a store-room for the funerary treasure. The coffin had to be turned and eased into this secondary passage. From there it entered a maze of false passages and dummy burial vaults, each more serpentine and devious than the last.

In all there were four burial chambers, but three of these would remain forever empty. There were three hidden doors and two vertical shafts. The coffin had to be lifted up one of these, and lowered down the other.

It took fifteen days for the coffin to be inched through this maze, and installed at last in its final resting-place. The roof and walls of this tomb were painted with all the skill and genius with which the gods have gifted me. There was not a space the size of my thumbnail that was not blazing with colour and movement.

Five store-rooms led off from the chamber. Into these were packed that treasure which Pharaoh Mamose had accumulated over his lifetime, and which had come close to beggaring our very Egypt. I had argued with my mistress that, instead of being buried in the earth, this treasure should be used to pay for the army and the struggle that lay ahead of us in our efforts to expel the Hyksos tyrant and to liberate our people and our land.

'The treasure belongs to Pharaoh,' she had replied. 'We have built up another treasure of gold and slaves and ivory here in Cush. That will suffice. Let the divine Mamose have what is his – I have given him my oath on it.'

Thus on the fifteenth day, the golden coffin was placed within the stone sarcophagus that had been hewn out of the native rock. With a system of ropes and levers, the heavy lid was lifted over it and lowered into place.

The royal family and the priests and the nobles entered the tomb to perform the last rites.

My mistress and the prince stood at the head of the sarcophagus, and the priests droned on with their incantations and their readings from the *Book of the Dead*. The sooty smoke from the lamps and the breathing of the throng of people in the confined space soured the air, so it was soon difficult to breathe.

In the dim yellow light I saw my mistress turn pale and the

perspiration bead on her forehead. I worked my way through the tightly packed ranks, and I reached her side just as she swayed and collapsed. I was able to catch her before she struck her head on the granite edge of the sarcophagus.

We carried her out of the tomb on a litter. In the fresh mountain air she recovered swiftly, but still I confined her to her bed in her tent for the rest of that day.

That night as I prepared her tonic of herbs, she lay quietly and thoughtfully, and after she had drunk the infusion she whispered to me, 'I had the most extraordinary sensation. As I stood in Pharaoh's tomb, I felt suddenly that Tanus was very close to me. I felt his hand touch my face and his voice murmur in my ear. That was when I fainted away.'

'He will always be close to you,' I told her.

'I believe that,' she said simply.

I can see now, though I could not see it then, that her decline began on the day that we laid Tanus in his grave. She had lost the joy of living and the will to go on.

I WENT back into the royal tomb the next day with the masons and the corps of slave labourers to seal the doorways and the shafts, and to arm the devices that would guard the burial chamber.

As we retreated through the maze of pasageways, we blocked the secret doorways with cunningly laid stone and plaster, and painted murals over them. We sealed the mouths of the vertical shafts so that they appeared to be smooth floor and roof.

I set rockfalls that would be triggered by a footstep on a loose paving slab, and I packed the vertical shafts with balks of timber. As these decayed over the centuries and the fungus devoured them, they would emit noxious vapours that would suffocate any intruder who succeeded in finding his way through the secret doorways.

But before we did all this, I went to the actual burial chamber to take leave of Tanus. I carried with me a long bundle wrapped in a linen sheet. When I stood for the last time beside the royal sarcophagus, I sent all the workmen away. I would be the very last to leave the tomb, and after me the entrance would be sealed.

When I was alone I opened the bundle I carried. From it I took the long bow, Lanata. Tanus had named it after my mistress and I had made it for him. It was a last gift from the two of us. I placed it upon the sealed stone lid of his coffin.

There was one other item in my bundle. It was the wooden *ushabti* figure that I had carved. I placed it at the foot of the sarcophagus. While I carved it, I had set up three copper mirrors so that I could study my own features from every angle and reproduce them faithfully. The doll was a miniature Taita.

Upon the base I had inscribed the words: 'My name is Taita. I am a physician and a poet. I am an architect and a philosopher. I am your friend. I will answer for you.'

As I left the tomb, I paused at the entrance and looked back for the last time.

'Farewell, old friend,' I said. 'I am richer for having known you. Wait for us on the other side.'

IT TOOK me many months to complete the work on the royal tomb. As we retreated through the labyrinth, I personally inspected every sealed doorway and every secret device that we left behind us.

I was alone, for my mistress and the prince had gone up into the mountains to the fortress of Prester Beni-Jon. They had gone with all the court to prepare for the wedding of Memnon and Masara. Hui had accompanied them to select the horses from the Ethiopian herds that were part of our payment for the storming of Adbar Seged, and the recovery of Masara.

When at last my work in the tomb was completed and my workmen had sealed the outer entrance in the cliff-face, I also set off into the mountains, over those cold and windy passes. I was anxious not to miss the wedding feast, but I had left it late. The completion of the tomb had taken longer than I had planned. I travelled as hard as the horses could stand.

I reached Prester Beni-Jon's palace five days before the wed-

615

ding, and I went directly to that part of the fortress where my mistress and her suite were lodged.

'I have not smiled since last I saw you, Taita,' she greeted me. 'Sing for me. Tell me your stories. Make me laugh.'

It was not an easy task she set me, for the melancholy had entered deeply into her soul, and the truth was that I was not myself cheerful or light-hearted. I sensed that more than sorrow alone was affecting her. Soon we abandoned our attempts at merriment, and fell to discussing affairs of state.

It might have been a love match, and a meeting of twin souls blessed by the gods as far as the two lovers were concerned, but for the rest of us, the joining of Memnon and Masara was a royal wedding and a contract between nations. There were agreements and treaties to negotiate, dowries to be decided, trade agreements to draw up between the King of Kings and ruler of Aksum, and the regent of Egypt and the wearer of the double crown of the two kingdoms.

As I had predicted, my mistress had been at first less than enchanted by the prospect of her only son marrying a woman of a different race.

'In all things they are different, Taita. The gods they worship, the language they speak, the colour of their skins – oh! I wish he had chosen a girl of our own people.'

'He will,' I reassured her. 'He will marry fifty, perhaps a hundred Egyptians. He will also marry Libyans and Hurrians and Hyksos. All the races and nations he conquers in the years to come will provide him with wives, Cushites and Hittites and Assyrians—'

'Stop your teasing, Taita.' She stamped her foot with something of her old fire. 'You know full well what I mean. Those others will all be marriages of state. This, his first, is a marriage of two hearts.'

What she said was true. The promise of love that Memnon and Masara had exchanged in those fleeting moments beside the river was now blossoming.

I was especially privileged to be close to them in these heady days. They both acknowledged and were grateful for my part in bringing them together. I was for both of them a friend of long standing, somebody that they trusted without question.

I did not share my mistress's misgivings. Though they were different in every way that she had listed, their hearts were turned from the same mould. They both possessed a sense of dedication, a fierceness of the spirit, a touch of the ruthlessness and the cruelty that a ruler must have. They were a matched pair, he the tiercel and she the falcon. I knew that she would not distract him from his destiny, but rather that she would encourage and incite him to greater endeavour. I was content with my efforts as a matchmaker.

One bright mountain day, watched by twenty thousand men and women of Ethiopia and of Egypt who crowded the slopes of the hills around them, Memnon and Masara stood together on the river-bank and broke the jar of water that the high priest of Osiris had scooped from the infant Nile.

The bride and the groom led our caravan down from the mountains, laden with the dowry of a princess and the treaties and the protocols of kinship sealed between our two nations.

Hui and his grooms drove a herd of five thousand horses behind us. Some of these were in payment for our mercenary services, and the rest made up Masara's dowry. However, before we reached the junction of the two rivers at Qebui, we saw the dark stain on the plains ahead as though a cloud had cast its shadow over the savannah – but the sun shone out of a cloudless sky.

The gnu herds had returned on their annual migration.

Within weeks of this contact with the gnu, the Yellow Strangler disease fell upon our herd of Ethiopian horses, and it swept through them like a flash-flood in one of the valleys of the high mountains.

Naturally, Hui and I had been expecting the plague to strike when the gnu returned, and we had made our preparations. We had trained every groom and charioteer to perform the tracheotomy, and to treat the wound with hot pitch to prevent mortification until the animal had a chance to recover from the Strangler.

For many weeks none of us enjoyed much sleep, but in the

617

end, fewer than two thousand of our new horses died of the disease, and before the next flooding of the Nile, those that survived were strong enough to begin training in the chariot traces.

 WHEN THE floods came, the priests sacrificed on the banks of the river, each to his own god, and they consulted the auguries for the year ahead. Some consulted the entrails of the sacrificial sheep, others watched the flight of the wild birds, still others stared into vessels filled with water from the Nile. They divined in their separate ways.

Queen Lostris sacrificed to Hapi. Although I attended the service with her and joined in the liturgy and the responses of the congregation, my heart was elsewhere. I am a Horus man, and so are Lord Kratas and Prince Memnon. We made a sacrifice of gold and ivory to our god and prayed for guidance.

It is not usual for the gods to agree with each other, any more than it is for men to do so. However, this year was different from any other that I had known. With the exception of the gods Anubis and Thoth and the goddess Nut, the heavenly host spoke with one voice. Those three, Anubis and Thoth and Nut, are all lesser deities. Their counsel could be safely discounted. All the great gods, Ammon-Ra and Osiris and Horus and Hapi and Isis and two hundred others, both great and small, gave the same counsel: 'The time has come for the return to the holy black earth of *Kemit*.'

Lord Kratas, who is a pagan at heart and a cynic by nature, suggested that the entire priesthood had conspired to place these words in the mouths of their patron gods. Although I expressed shocked indignation at this blasphemy, I was secretly inclined to agree with Kratas' opinion.

The priests are soft and luxurious men, and for almost two decades we had lived the hard lives of wanderers and warriors in the wild land of Cush. I think they hungered for fair Thebes even more than did my mistress. Perhaps it was not gods, but men who had given this advice to return northwards.

Queen Lostris summoned the high council of state, and when she made the proclamation that endorsed the dictates of the gods, the nobles and the priests stood and cheered her to a man. I cheered as loud and as long as any of them, and that night my dreams were filled with visions of Thebes, and images of those far-off days when Tanus and Lostris and I had been young and happy.

SINCE THE death of Tanus, there had been no supreme commander of our armies, and the war council met in secret conclave. Of course, I was excluded from this assembly, but my mistress repeated to me every word that was spoken.

After long argument and debate, the command was offered to Kratas. He stood before them, grizzled and scarred like an old lion, and he laughed that great laugh of his and he said, 'I am a soldier. I follow. I do not lead. Give me the command of the Shilluk, and I will follow one man to the borders of death and beyond.' He drew his sword then and pointed with it at the prince. 'That is the man I will follow. Hail, Memnon! May he live for ever.'

'May he live for ever!' they shouted, and my mistress smiled. She and I had arranged exactly this outcome.

At the age of twenty-two years Prince Memnon was elevated to the rank of Great Lion of Egypt and commander of all her armies. Immediately he began to plan the Return.

Though my rank was only that of Master of the Royal Horse, I was on Prince Memnon's staff. Often he appealed to me to solve the logistical problems that we encountered. During the day I drove his chariot with the blue pennant fluttering over our heads as he reviewed the regiments, and led them in exercises of war.

Many nights the three of us, the prince and Kratas and I, sat up late over a jar of wine as we discussed the Return. On those nights Princess Masara waited upon us, filling the cups with her own graceful brown hand. Then she sat on a sheep-skin cushion at Memnon's feet and listened to every word. When our eyes met, she smiled at me.

Our main concern was to avoid the hazardous and onerous transit of all the cataracts on the way down-river. These could only be navigated in flood season, and would thus limit the periods in which we could travel.

I proposed that we build another fleet of barges below the fifth cataract; with these we could transport our army down to the departure-point for the desert crossing of the great bight. When we regained the river above the first cataract, we would rebuild another squadron of fast fighting galleys and barges to carry us down to Elephantine.

I was sure that if we timed it correctly, and if we could shoot the rapids and surprise the Hyksos fleet anchored in the roads of Elephantine, we would be able to deal the enemy a painful blow and capture the galleys we needed to augment our force of fighting ships. Once we had secured a foothold, we would then be able to bring down our infantry and our chariots through the gorge of the first cataract, and engage the Hyksos on the flood-plains of Egypt.

We began the first stage of the Return the following flood season. At Qebui, which had been our capital seat for so many years, we left only a garrison force. Qebui would become merely a trading outpost of the empire. The riches of Cush and Ethiopia would flow northwards to Thebes through this entrepôt.

When the main fleet sailed back into the north, Hui and I, with five hundred grooms and a squadron of chariots, remained behind to await the return of the gnu migration. They came as suddenly as they always did, a vast black stain spreading over the golden savannah grasslands. We went out to meet them in the chariots.

It was a simple matter to capture these ungainly brutes. We ran them down with the chariots, and dropped a noose of rope over their ugly heads as we ran alongside them. The gnu lacked the speed and the spirit of our horses. They fought the ropes only briefly and then resigned themselves to capture. Within ten days, we had penned over six thousand of them in the stockades on the bank of the Nile which we had built for this purpose.

It was here in the stockades that their lack of stamina and strength was most apparent. Without cause or reason, they died in their hundreds. We treated them kindly and gently. We fed them and watered them as we would our horses. It was as though their wild wandering spirits would not be fettered, and they pined away.

In the end we lost over half of those that we had captured, and many more died on the long voyage to the north.

 TWO FULL years after Queen Lostris had commanded the Return, our people assembled on the east bank of the Nile above the fourth cataract. Before us lay the desert road across the great bight of the river.

For the whole of the previous year the caravans of wagons had set out from here. Each of them had been laden with clay jars filled to the brim with Nile water, and sealed with wooden plugs and hot pitch. Every ten miles along the dusty road we had set up watering stations. At each of these, thirty thousand water jars had been buried to prevent them cracking and bursting in the rays of that furious sun.

We were nearly fifty thousand souls and as many animals, including my dwindling herd of captured gnu. The water-carts set out from the river each evening. Their task was unending.

We waited on the river-bank for the rise of the new moon to light our way across the wilderness. Although we had planned our departure for this the coolest season of the year, still the heat and the sun would be deadly to both man and beast. We would travel only at night.

Two days before we were due to begin the crossing, my mistress said, 'Taita, when did you and I last spend a day together fishing on the river? Make ready your fish-spears and a skiff.'

I knew that she had something of deep import that she wished to discuss with me. We drifted down on those green waters until I could moor the skiff to a willow tree on the far bank, where we were out of earshot of the inquisitive.

First we spoke of the imminent departure along the desert road, and the prospects of the return to Thebes.

'When will I see her shining walls again, Taita?' my mistress sighed, and I could only tell her that I did not know.

'If the gods are kind, we might be in Elephantine by this time next season when the Nile flood carries our ships down the first cataract. After that, our fortunes will ebb and flow like the river, with the hazards and fortunes of war.'

However, this was not what she had brought me out on to the river to discuss, and now her eyes swam with tears as she asked, 'How long has Tanus been gone from us, Taita?'

My voice choked as I answered, 'He set out on his journey to the fields of paradise over three years ago, mistress.'

'So it is longer than that by many months that I last lay in his arms,' she mused, and I nodded. I was uncertain in which direction her questions were leading us.

'I have dreamed of him almost every night since then, Taita. Is it possible that he might have returned to leave his seed in my womb while I still slept?'

'All things in heaven are possible,' I replied carefully. 'We told the people that was how Tehuti and Bekatha were conceived. However, in all truth and seriousness, I have never heard of it happening before.'

We were both silent for a while, and she trailed her hand in the water and then lifted it to watch the drops fall from her fingertips. Then she spoke again without looking at me. 'I think I am to have another child,' she whispered, 'My red moon has waned and withered away.'

'Mistress,' I answered her quietly, and with tact, 'you are approaching that time of your life when the rivers of your womb will begin to dry up.' Our Egyptian women are like desert flowers that bloom early but fade as swiftly.

She shook her head. 'No, Taita. It is not that. I feel the infant growing within me.'

I stared at her silently. Once again I felt the wings of tragedy brush lightly past me, stirring the air and raising the hair upon my forearms.

'You do not have to ask me if I have known another man.' This time she looked directly into my eyes as she spoke. 'You know that I have not.'

'This I know full well. Yet I cannot believe that you have been impregnated by a ghost, no matter how beloved and welcome that ghost might be. Perhaps your desire for another child has fathered your imagination.'

'Feel my womb, Taita,' she commanded. 'This is a living thing within me. Each day it grows.'

'I will do so tonight, in the privacy of your cabin. Not here upon the river where prying eyes might discover us.'

 MY MISTRESS lay naked upon the linen sheets, and I studied first her face and then her body. When I looked upon her with the eyes of a man, she was still lovely to me, but as a physician I could see clearly how the years and the hardships of this life in the wilderness had wrought their cruel change. Her hair was more silver than sable now, and bereavement and the cares of the regency had chiselled their grim message on her brow. She was growing old.

Her body was the vessel which had given life to three other lives. But her breasts were empty now, there was none of the milk of a new pregnancy swelling them. She was thin. I should have noticed that before. It was an unnatural thinness, almost an emaciation. Yet her belly protruded like a pale ivory ball out of proportion to those slim arms and legs.

I laid my hands lightly upon her belly, upon the silvery streaks where the skin had once stretched to accommodate a joyful burden. I felt the thing within her and I knew at once that this was not life beneath my fingers. This was death.

I could not find words. I turned away from her and went out on to the deck and I looked up at the night stars. They were cold and very far away. Like the gods, they did not care. There was no profit in appealing to them, gods or stars.

I knew this thing that was growing within my mistress. I had felt it in the bodies of other women. When they died, I had opened the dead womb and seen the thing that had killed them. It was horrible and deformed, bearing no resemblance to anything human or even animal. It was a shapeless ball of red and angry flesh. It was a thing of Seth.

It was a long time before I could gather the courage to return to the cabin.

My mistress had covered herself with a robe. She sat in the centre of the bed and looked at me with those huge, dark green eyes that had never aged. She looked like the little girl I once had known.

'Mistress, why did you not tell me about the pain?' I asked gently.

'How do you know about the pain?' she whispered back. 'I tried to hide it from you.'

 OUR CARAVAN set out into the desert, travelling by moonlight across the silver sands. Sometimes my mistress walked at my side, and the two princesses frolicked along with us, laughing and excited by the adventure. At other times, when the pain was bad, my mistress rode in the wagon that I had equipped for her comfort. Then I sat beside her and held her hand until the powder of the sleeping-flower worked its magic and gave her surcease.

Every night we travelled just as far as the next watering-station along the road that was now well beaten by the thousands of vehicles that had preceded us. During the long days we lay beneath the awning of the wagon and drowsed in the sweltering heat.

We had been thirty days and nights upon the road when in the dawn we saw a remarkable sight. A disembodied sail upon the desert, moving gently southwards over the sands. It was not until we had journeyed on for many more miles that we saw how we had been deceived. The hull of the galley had been hidden from us by the bank of the Nile, and below the dunes the river ran on eternally. We had crossed the loop.

Prince Memnon and all his staff were there to greet us. Already the squadron of new galleys had almost completed fitting out. It was the sail of one of these that we had first descried as we approached the river again. Every plank and mast had been cut and sawn on the great plains of Cush, and transported across the loop of the river. All the chariots were assembled. Hui had herded all the horses across the desert, and the wagons had carried their fodder with them. Even my gnu were waiting in their stockades upon the river-bank.

Although the wagon caravans carrying the women and the children still followed, the main body of our nation had been brought across. It had been an undertaking that almost defied belief, a labour of godlike proportions. Only men like Kratas and Remrem and Memnon could have accomplished it in so short a time.

Now only the first cataract still stood between us and the sacred earth of our very Egypt.

We went on northwards again. My mistress sailed in the new barge that had been built for her and the princesses. There was a large and airy cabin for her, and I had equipped it with every luxury that was available to us. The hangings were of embroidered Ethiopian wool, and the furniture was of dark acacia wood inlaid with ivory and the gold of Cush. I decorated the bulkheads with paintings of flowers and birds and other pretty things.

As always, I slept at the foot of my mistress's bed. Three nights after we sailed, I woke in the night. She was weeping silently. Although she had stifled her sobs with a pillow, the shaking of her shoulders had awakened me. I went to her immediately.

'The pain has come again?' I asked.

'I did not mean to wake you, but it is like a sword in my belly.'

I mixed her a draught of the sleeping-flower, stronger than I had ever given to her before. The pain was beginning to triumph over the flower.

She drank it and lay quietly for a while. Then she said, 'Can you not cut this thing out of my body, Taita?'

'No, mistress. I cannot.'

'Then hold me, Taita. Hold me the way you used to do when I was a little girl.'

I went into her bed, and I took her in my arms. I cradled her, and she was as thin and light as a child. I rocked her tenderly, and after a while she slept.

THE FLEET reached the head of the first cataract above Elephantine, and we moored against the bank in the quiet flow of the river before the Nile felt the urging of the cascades and plunged into the gorge.

We waited for the rest of the army to be ferried down to us, all the horses and the chariots and Lord Kratas' pagan Shilluk regiments. We waited also for the Nile to rise and open the cataract for us to pass down into Egypt.

While we waited, we sent spies down through the gorge. They were dressed as peasants and priests and merchants with goods to trade. I went down with Kratas into the gorge to map and mark the passage. Now, at low water, every hazard was exposed. We painted channel-markers on the rocks above the high-water line, so that even when the flood covered them, we would still know where those obstacles lurked.

We were many weeks at this labour, and when we returned to where the fleet was moored, the army was assembled there. We sent out scouting parties to find a route for the chariots and the horses through the rock desert down into Egypt. We could not risk such a precious cargo to the wild waters of the cataract.

Our spies began to return from Elephantine. They came in secretly and singly, usually in the night. They brought us the very first news of our mother-land that we had heard in all the years of exile.

King Salitis still reigned, but he was old now, and his beard had turned silver-white. His two sons were the mighty men of the Hyksos legions. Prince Beon commanded the infantry and Prince Apachan commanded the chariots.

The might of the Hyksos exceeded all our estimates. Our spies reported that Apachan disposed of twelve thousand chariots. We had brought down only four thousand from Cush. Beon had forty thousand archers and infantry. Even with Kratas' Shilluk, we could muster only fifteen thousand. We were heavily outnumbered.

There was cheering news also. The great bulk of the Hyksos force was held in the Delta, and Salitis had made his capital at the city of Memphis. It would take months for him to move his forces south to Elephantine and Thebes. He would not be able to bring his chariots up-river until the floods abated and the land dried. There was only a single squadron of chariots guarding the city of Elephantine, one hundred chariots to oppose our entry. They were of the old solid-wheel type. It seemed that the Hyksos had not yet perfected the spoked wheel.

Prince Memnon laid out his battle plan for us. We would pass through the cataract on the flood, and seize Elephantine. Then, while Salitis moved southwards to oppose us, we would march on Thebes, raising the populace in insurrection as we went.

We could expect Salitis to give battle with his full army on the flood-plains before Thebes, once the Nile waters had subsided. By then we could hope that the disparity in the numbers of the two armies would be redressed in part by the Egyptian troops that would rally to our standard.

We learned from our spies that the Hyksos did not suspect the presence of our army of liberation so close to their border, and that we could expect to gain the element of surprise with our first assault. We learned also that Salitis had adopted our Egyptian way of life. These days he lived in our palaces and worshipped our gods. Even his old Sutekh had changed his name to Seth, and was, very appropriately, still his principal god.

Although all his senior officers were Hyksos, many of Salitis' captains and sergeants had been recruited from amongst the Egyptians, and half the common soldiers were of our own nation. Most of these would have been infants or not yet born at the time of our exodus. We wondered where their loyalties would lie, when Prince Memnon led our army down into Egypt.

All was in readiness now. The scouts had marked a road through the desert of the west bank, and the water wagons had laid down stores of fodder and water jars along the length of it, enough to see our chariots through to the fertile plains of our very Egypt. Our galleys were rigged and manned for battle. When the Nile flooded, we would sail, but in the meantime there was one last ritual to complete.

We climbed the bluff above the river to where the obelisk that my mistress had raised over two decades before, still stood, a tall and elegant finger of stone pointing into the cloudless blue of the African sky.

My mistress was too weak to climb the rugged pathway to the summit. Ten slaves carried her up in a sedan-chair, and set her down below the tall monument. She walked painfully slowly to the foot of the pillar on the arm of Prince Memnon, and gazed up at the inscription carved in the granite. Our whole nation watched her, all those souls who had found their way back to this point from which we had set out so long ago.

My mistress read the inscription aloud. Her voice was soft, but still so musical that it carried clearly to where I stood behind the great lords and the generals.

'I, Queen Lostris, Regent of Egypt and widow of Pharaoh Mamose, the eighth of that name, mother of the Crown Prince Memnon, who shall rule the two kingdoms after me, have ordained the raising of this monument . . .'

When she had finished the reading, she turned to face her people and spread her arms.

'I have done that which was required of me,' she said, and her voice regained some of its old power. 'I have led you back to the border of your land. My task is completed and I relinquish the regency.' She paused, and for a moment her eyes met mine over the heads of the nobles. I nodded slightly to encourage her, and she went on.

'Citizens of Egypt, it is fitting that you have a true Pharaoh to lead you the last steps of the way home. I give to you the divine Pharaoh Tamose, who once was the Crown Prince Memnon. May he live for ever!'

'May he live for ever!' the nation roared in one voice. 'May he live for ever!'

Pharaoh Tamose stepped forward to face his people. 'May he live for ever!' they shouted the third time, and our new pharaoh drew the blue sword from its jewelled scabbard and saluted them with it.

In the silence that followed, his voice rang and echoed from the gaunt red crags of the hills.

'I take up this sacred trust. I swear on my hope of eternal life to serve my people and my land all my days. I shall not flinch from this duty, and I call upon all the gods to witness my oath.'

THE FLOOD came. The waters rose up the rocks that guarded the entrance to the gorge, and the colour changed from green to grey. The cataract began to growl like a beast in its lair and the spray-cloud rose into the sky and stood as high as the hills that flanked the Nile.

I went aboard the leading galley with Lord Kratas and Pharaoh. We dropped our mooring and shoved off into the stream. The rowers on the benches were stripped to their breech-clouts, their faces turned up to watch Kratas as he stood high in the stern, gripping the steering-oar in his bear-like fists.

In the bows two teams of sailors under the king stood ready with heavy oars to fend off. I stood beside Kratas, with the map of the rapids spread on the deck in front of me, ready to call the twists and turns of the channel to him as we came to them. I did not really need the map, for I had memorized every line drawn upon it. In addition to which, I had stationed reliable men on the sides of the gorge and on the islands in the main stream ahead of us. They would use signal flags to show us the way through.

As the current quickened beneath our keel, I cast one last glance backwards and saw the rest of the squadron fall into line astern behind us, ready to follow us down the cataract. Then I looked forward again, and felt the fist of fear tighten on my bowels so that I was forced to squeeze my buttocks together. Ahead of us the gorge smoked like the mouth of a furnace.

Our speed built up with deceptive stealth. The rowers touched the surface lightly with the blades of the oars, just enough to keep our bows pointed downstream. We floated so lightly and so smoothly that we seemed to be drifting. It was only when I looked at the banks, and saw them streaming past us, that I realized how fast we were running. The rock portals of the gorge flew to meet us. None the less, it was only when I noticed the grin on Kratas' craggy face that I realized the true danger of what we were attempting. Kratas only grinned like that when he saw death crook a bony finger at him.

'Come on, you rogues!' he shouted at his crew. 'This day I'll make your mothers proud of you, or I'll find work for the embalmers.'

The river was split by three islands, and the channel narrowed.

'Bear to port, and steer for the blue cross,' I tried to sound casual, but at that moment I felt the deck tip beneath my feet, and I clutched at the rail.

We flew down a chute of grey water, and our bows swung giddily. I thought that we were already out of control, and waited for the crunch of rock and for the deck to burst open beneath my feet. Then I saw the bows steady, and the blue cross painted on the wall of rock was dead ahead.

'Hard to starboard as we come up to the flag!' my voice squeaked, but I picked out the man on the centre island flagging us into the turn, and Kratas put the steering-oar over and yelled at the benches, 'All back right, pull together left!' The deck canted sharply as we spun into the turn.

The wall of rock flashed past us, and we were going at the speed of a galloping horse. One more turn and the first rapids lay ahead. Black rock stood across our path, and the waters piled upon it. The water took on the shape of the rocks beneath it. It bulged and stood in tall static waves. It opened into smooth green gulleys. It curled upon itself and exploded into veils of white through which the rock snarled at us with black fangs. My stomach clenched as we leaped over the edge and dropped down the slope. At the bottom we wallowed and spun, like a stalk of dry grass in a whirlwind.

'Pull left!' Kratas bellowed. 'Pull till your balls bounce!' We steadied and aimed for the next gap in the rock, and the white water dashed over the deck and into my eyes. It hissed alongside, running in tandem with us, and the waves stood taller than our poop-deck.

'By Seth's tattered and festering foreskin, I've not had so much sport since I tupped my first ewe!' Kratas laughed, and the rock sprang at us like a charging bull elephant.

We touched once, and the rock rasped along our belly. The deck shuddered beneath our feet, and I was too afraid to scream. Then Memnon's team poled us free and we raced on down.

Behind us I heard the shattering crash as one of the other

galleys struck hard. I dared not look round as I judged our next turn, but soon there were wreckage and the heads of drowning men bobbing and swirling in the torrent on both sides of us. They screamed to us as they were borne away and dashed upon the spurs of rock, but we could offer them no succour. Death pressed hard upon our heels and we ran on with the stench of it in our nostrils.

In that hour I lived a hundred lives, and died in every one of them. But at last we were hurled from the bottom of the cataract into the main body of the river. Of the twenty-three galleys that had entered the gorge, eighteen followed us out. The others had been smashed to flotsam, and the corpses of their drowned crew washed down beside us in the grey Nile flood.

There was not time for us to celebrate our deliverance. Dead ahead lay the Island of Elephantine, and on both banks of the river stood the well-remembered walls and buildings of the city.

'Archers, string your bows!' King Tamose called from the bows. 'Hoist the blue pennant! Drummer, increase the beat to attack speed!'

Our tiny squadron flew into the mass of shipping that clogged the roads of Elephantine. Most of it was made up of trade barges and transports. We passed these by, and went for the Hyksos galleys. The Hyksos had manned their fighting ships with Egyptian sailors, for nobody knew the river better. Only their officers were Hyksos. Most of them were ashore, carousing in the pleasure-palaces of the docks.

Our spies had told us which was the flag of the southern admiral, a swallowtail of scarlet and gold so long that the end of it dipped in the water. We steered for the ship that flew her, and Memnon boarded her over the side with twenty men at his back.

'Freedom from the Hyksos tyrant!' they roared. 'Stand up for this very Egypt!'

The crew gaped at them. They had been taken completely by surprise, and most of them were unarmed. Their weapons were locked away below decks, for the Hyksos officers trusted them not at all.

The other galleys of our squadron had each picked out one of the enemy fighting-ships and boarded it as swiftly. On all of them the reaction of the crew was the same. After the first surprise they shouted the question, 'Who are you?'

And the reply was, 'Egyptian! The army of the true Pharaoh Tamose. Join with us, countrymen! Cast out the tyrant!'

They turned on their Hyksos officers and cut them down before we could reach them. Then they embraced our men, roaring out a welcome.

'For Egypt!' they cheered. 'For Tamose! For Egypt and Tamose!'

The cheering jumped from ship to ship. Men danced upon the rails and swarmed up the masts to tear down the Hyksos banners. They broke open the arms stores and passed out bows and swords.

Then they poured ashore. They dragged the Hyksos from the taverns and hacked them to bloody shreds, so that the gutters discharged a scarlet flood into the harbour waters. They ran through the streets to the barracks of the garrison, and fell upon the guard.

'For Egypt and Tamose!' they chanted.

Some of the Hyksos officers rallied their men, and held out for a while in pockets surrounded by the rabble. Then Kratas and Memnon came ashore with their veterans, and within two hours the city was ours.

Most of the Hyksos chariots were abandoned in their lines, but half a squadron was escaping through the east gate and galloping away over the causeway that crossed the inundated fields to the dry ground beyond.

I had left the ship and hurried through the back alleys, that I knew so well, to the north tower on the city walls. From there I knew I would have the best view over the city and the surrounding countryside. Bitterly, I watched the escaping detachment of chariots. Every one that got away now would have to be fought later, and I wanted those horses. I was about to turn away and watch what was happening in the city below me, when I saw a little finger of dust rising from the foot of the harsh southern hills.

I shaded my eyes and stared at it. I felt the quickening of excitement. The dust was coming towards us swiftly, I could make out the dark shapes beneath it.

'By Horus, it's Remrem!' I whispered with delight. The old warrior had brought the first division of chariots through the bad ground of the hills quicker than I would have believed possible. It was only two days since we had parted.

I watched with professional pride as the first division opened from columns of four into line abreast. Hui and I had trained them well. It was perfectly done, and Remrem had the Hyksos in enfilade. Half their vehicles were still on the causeway. It seemed to me that the enemy commander was not even aware of the massed squadrons bearing down upon his exposed flank. I think he must still have been looking back over his shoulder. At the very last moment he tried to swing into line abreast to meet Remrem's charge, but it was far too late. He would have done better to have turned tail and run for it.

Remrem's chariots poured over him in a wave, and he was washed away like debris in the stream of the Nile. I watched until I was certain that Remrem had captured most of the Hyksos horses, and only then did I sigh with relief and turn to look down into the city.

The populace had gone wild with the joy of liberation. They were dancing through the streets, waving any piece of blue cloth that came to hand. Blue was the colour of Pharaoh Tamose. The women tied blue ribbons in their hair, and the men wound blue sashes around their waists and tied on blue arm-bands.

There was still some isolated fighting, but gradually the surviving Hyksos were cut down or dragged from the buildings they were trying to defend. One of the barracks with several hundred men still inside it was put to the torch. I heard the screams of the men as they burned, and soon the aroma of scorched flesh drifted up to me. It smelled like roasting pork.

Of course there was looting, and some of our upstanding citizens broke into the taverns and the wine shops and carried the jars out into the street. When one of the jars broke, they went down on all fours and guzzled the wine out of the gutter like hogs.

I saw three men chase a girl down the alley below where I stood. When they caught her they threw her down and ripped her skirt away. Two of them pinned her limbs and held her spread-eagled while the third man mounted her. I did not watch the rest of it.

As soon as Memnon and Kratas had stamped out the last pockets of Hyksos resistance, they set about restoring order to the city. Squads of disciplined troops trotted through the streets, using the shafts of their war spears as clubs to beat sense into the drunken and delirious mob.

Memnon ordered a handful of those taken in the act of rape and looting to be strangled on the spot, and their corpses were hung by the heels from the city gates. By nightfall the city was quiet, and decent men and women could once more safely walk her streets.

Memnon set up his headquarters in Pharaoh Mamose's palace, which had once been our home on Elephantine Island. The moment I stepped ashore I hurried to our old quarters in the harem.

They were still luxuriously appointed and had escaped the looters. Whoever had occupied them had treated my murals with the respect they warranted. The water-garden was a profusion of lovely plants, and the ponds were filled with fish and lotus. The Egyptian gardener told me that the Hyksos garrison commander who had lived here had admired our Egyptian ways, and had tried to ape them. I was thankful for that.

Within days I had restored the rooms and garden to a state in which they were once more fit to receive my mistress. Then I went to Memnon to ask permission to bring the queen home.

Pharaoh was distracted by the burden of taking firm hold of his kingdom. There were ten thousand matters that demanded his attention, but he put them aside for the moment and embraced me.

'It all goes well, Tata.'

'A happy return, Your Majesty,' I replied, 'but there is still so much to do.'

'It is my royal command that when you and I are alone like this, you continue to call me Mem.' He smiled at me, 'But you are right, there is much to do, and little time left to us before Salitis and all his host marches up from the Delta to oppose us.

We have won the first little skirmish. The great battles lie ahead of us.'

'There is one duty that will give me great pleasure, Mem. I have prepared quarters for the queen mother. May I go up-river and bring her home to Elephantine? She has waited too long already to set foot on Egyptian soil.'

'Leave at once, Tata,' he commanded, 'and bring Queen Masara down with you.'

The river was too high and the desert road too rough. One hundred slaves carried the litters of the two queens along the banks of the Nile, through the gorge and down into our green valley.

It was not pure coincidence that the first building we came to as we crossed the border was a small temple. I had planned our route to bring us here.

'What shrine is this, Taita?' my mistress drew aside the curtain of her litter to ask.

'It is the temple of the god Akh-Horus, mistress. Do you wish to pray here?'

'Thank you,' she whispered. She knew what I had done. I helped her down from the litter, and she leaned heavily upon me as we entered the cool gloom of the stone building.

We prayed together, and I felt certain that Tanus was listening to the voices of the two people in all the world who had loved him most. Before we went on, my mistress ordered me to hand over all the gold that we had with us to the priests, and promised to send more for the upkeep and the beautification of the temple.

By the time we reached the Palace of Elephantine, she was exhausted. Each day the thing in her womb grew larger as it fed upon her wasting body. I laid her on a couch under the barrazza in the water-garden, and she closed her eyes and rested for a while. Then she opened them again and smiled at me softly. 'We were happy here once, but will I ever see Thebes again before I die?' I could not answer her. It was idle to make promises to her that were not mine to keep.

'If I die before that, will you promise to take me back and build me a tomb in the hills from where I can look across and see my beautiful city?'

'That I promise you with all my heart,' I replied.

 IN THE days that followed, Aton and I resuscitated our old spider's web of spies and informers across the Upper Kingdom. Many of those who had once worked for us were long dead, but there were also many who were not. With the bait of gold and patriotism, they recruited other younger spies in every village and city.

Soon we had spies in the palace of the Hyksos satrap in Thebes, and others as far north as the Delta of the Lower Kingdom. Through them we learned which Hyksos regiments were billeted in each town, and which of them were on the march. We learned their strength, and the names and foibles of their commanders. We had an exact count of the numbers of their ships and their chariots, and as the flood-waters of the Nile receded, we were able to follow the southward movement of this huge mass of men and fighting machines, as King Salitis marched on Thebes.

I smuggled secret messages in the name of Pharaoh Tamose to those Egyptians in the regiments of the enemy, urging them to revolt. They started to trickle in through our lines, bringing more valuable intelligence with them. Soon the trickle of deserters from the Hyksos armies became a flood. Two full regiments of archers came marching in under arms, with the blue banner waving over them, and chanting, 'Egypt and Tamose!'

The crews of a hundred fighting galleys mutinied and slew their Hyksos officers. When they came sailing up-river to join us, they drove before them a fleet of barges that they had captured in the port of Thebes. These were laden with grain and oil and salt and flax and timber, all the sinews of war.

By this time, all our own forces were down through the cataract and deployed around the city, except only the small herd of tame gnu. These I had left until the very last. From my lookout in the north tower, I could see the horse-lines extending for miles along both banks, and the smoke from the cooking-fires of the regimental encampments turned the air blue.

Each day we were growing stronger, and the whole of Egypt was in a ferment of excitement and anticipation. The heady aroma of freedom perfumed each breath we drew. *Kemit* was a nation in the process of rebirth. They sang the patriotic anthems in the streets and the taverns, and the harlots and the wine merchants grew fat.

Aton and I, poring over our maps and secret despatches, saw a different picture emerging. We saw the Hyksos giant shaking itself awake, and stretching out a mailed fist towards us. From Memphis and every city and town in the Delta, King Salitis' regiments were on the march. Every road was crowded with his chariots, and the river ran with his shipping. All of this was moving south upon Thebes.

I waited until I knew that Lord Apachan, the commander of the Hyksos chariots, had reached Thebes and was encamped outside the city walls with all his vehicles and all his horses. Then I went before the war council of Pharaoh Tamose.

'Your Majesty, I have come to report that the enemy now have one hundred and twenty thousand horses and twelve thousand chariots massed at Thebes. Within two months, the Nile will have subsided to the level that will enable Apachan to begin his final advance.'

Even Kratas looked grave. 'We have known worse odds—' he began, but the king cut him short.

'I can tell by his face that the Master of the Royal Horse has more to tell us. Am I right, Taita?'

'Pharaoh is always right,' I agreed. 'I beg your permission to bring down my gnu from above the cataract.'

Kratas laughed. 'By Seth's bald head, Taita, do you intend riding out against the Hyksos on one of those clownish brutes of yours?' I laughed with him politely. His sense of humour has the same subtlety as that of the savage Shilluk he commands.

The next morning Hui and I set off up-river to bring down the gnu. By this time there were only three hundred of these sorry creatures left alive out of the original six thousand, but they were quite tame and could be fed from the hand. We herded them down at a gentle pace, so as not to weaken them further.

The horses that Remrem had captured in that first brief battle with the escaping Hyksos chariots had on my orders been kept separated from our own horses that we had brought down with us from Cush. Hui and I moved the gnu into the same pasture with them, and after the first uneasiness between the two species, they were all feeding peaceably together. That night we penned gnu and Hyksos horses in the same stockade. I left Hui to watch over them and returned to the palace on Elephantine Island.

I will admit now to a great deal of uncertainty and worry over the days that followed. I had invested so much faith in the success of this ruse, which, after all, depended on a natural event that I did not fully understand. If it failed, we would be faced with the full fury of an enemy that outnumbered us by at least four to one.

I had worked late with Aton and had fallen asleep over my scrolls in the palace library, when I was shaken awake by uncouth hands, and Hui was shouting in my ear. 'Come on, you lazy old rascal! Wake up! I have something for you.'

He had horses waiting at the landing. We hurried to them as soon as the ferry put us ashore, and mounted up. We galloped all the way along the river-bank in the moonlight, and rode into the horse-lines with our mounts in a lather. The grooms had lamps lit and were working in the stockade by their feeble yellow light.

Seven of the Hyksos horses were down already with the thick yellow pus pouring from their mouths and nostrils. The grooms were cutting into their windpipes and placing the hollow reeds to save them from choking and suffocating.

'It worked!' Hui shouted, and seized me in a coarse embrace and danced me in a circle. 'The Yellow Strangler! It worked! It worked!'

'I thought of it, didn't I?' I told him with all the dignity that his antics allowed me. 'Of course it worked.'

The barges had been moored against the bank these weeks past, ready for this day. We loaded the horses immediately, all of those who could still stand upright. The gnu we left in the stockade. Their presence would be too difficult to explain where we were going.

With one of the captured Hyksos galleys towing each of the barges, we rowed out into the current and turned northwards. With fifty oars a side and the wind and current behind us, we made good speed as we hurried down to Thebes to deliver our gift to Lord Apachan.

 AS SOON as we passed Kom-Ombo we lowered the blue flag, and hoisted captured Hyksos banners. Most of the crew of the galleys that were towing the barges had been born under Hyksos rule, some of them were of mixed parentage and spoke the foreign language with colloquial fluency.

Two nights north of Kom-Ombo, we were hailed by a Hyksos galley. They laid alongside and sent a boarding party over to inspect our cargo.

'Horses for the chariots of Lord Apachan,' our captain told them. His father was Hyksos but his mother was an Egyptian noblewoman. His deportment was natural and his credentials convincing. After a cursory inspection they passed us through. We were stopped and boarded twice more before we reached Thebes, but each time our captain was able to deceive the Hyksos officers who came aboard.

My chief concern by this time was the state of the horses. Despite our best efforts, they were beginning to die, and half of those still alive were in a pitiful condition. We threw the carcasses overboard, and ran on northwards at our best speed.

My original plan had been to sell the horses to the Hyksos quartermasters in the port of Thebes, but no man who knew horseflesh would look at this pitiful herd. Hui and I decided upon another course.

We timed the last leg of our voyage to arrive at Thebes as the sun was setting. My heart ached as I recognized all the familiar landmarks. The walls of the citadel glowed pinkly in the last rays of the sun. Those three elegant towers that I had built for Lord

Intef still pointed to the sky, they were aptly named the Fingers of Horus.

The Palace of Memnon on the west bank, which I had left uncompleted, had been rebuilt by the Hyksos. Even I had to admit that the Asiatic influence was pleasing. In this light the spires and watch-towers were endowed with a mysterious and exotic quality. I wished that my mistress was there to share this moment of homecoming with me. We had both longed for it over half her lifetime.

In the fading light we were still able to make out the vast concourse of men and horses and chariots and wagons that lay outside the city walls. Although I had received accurate reports, it had not been possible to visualize such multitudes. My spirits quailed as I looked upon them, and remembered the gallant little army I had left at Elephantine.

We would need every favour of the gods, and more than a little good fortune to triumph against such a host. As the last light faded into night, the fires of the Hyksos bloomed and twinkled upon the plain, like a field of stars. There was no end to them – they stretched away to the limit of the eye.

As we sailed closer, we smelled them. There is a peculiar odour that a standing army exudes. It is a blend of many smells, of dung-fires and of cooking food, the sweet smell of new-cut hay and the ammoniacal smell of the horses, and the stench of human sewage in open pits, of leather and pitch and horse-sweat and woodshavings and sour beer. Most of all it is the smell of men, tens of thousands of men, living close to each other in tents and huts and hovels.

We sailed on, and the sounds floated across the star-lit waters to our silent ship; the snort and the whinny of horses, the sound of the coppersmiths' hammers on the anvil beating out spear-heads and blades, the challenges of the sentries, and the voices of men singing and arguing and laughing.

I stood beside the captain on the deck of the leading galley and guided him in towards the east bank. I remembered the wharf of the timber merchants outside the city walls. If it still stood, it would be the best point at which to disembark our herd.

I picked out the entrance to the dock, and we pushed in under oars. The wharf was exactly as I remembered it. As we came alongside, the harbour-master came fussing on board, demanding our papers and our licence to trade.

I fawned upon him, bowing and grinning obsequiously. 'Excellency, there has been a terrible accident. My licences were blown from my hand by the wind, a trick of Seth, no doubt.'

He blew himself up like an angry bullfrog, and then subsided again as I pressed a heavy gold ring into his fat paw. He tested the metal between his teeth, and went away smiling.

I sent one of the grooms ashore to douse the torches that illuminated the wharf. I did not want curious eyes to see the condition of the horses that we brought ashore. Some of our animals were too weak to rise, others staggered and wheezed, they drooled the stinking mucus from mouth and nostrils. We were forced to place head-halters on them and coax them out of the barge on to the wharf. In the end there were only a hundred horses strong enough to walk.

We led them down the wagon-track to the high ground where our spies had told us the main horse-lines were laid out. Our spies had also provided us with the password of the Hyksos first division of chariots, and the linguists among us replied to the challenges of the sentries.

We walked our horses the entire length of the enemy encampment. As we went, we began to turn our stricken animals loose, leaving a few of them to wander through the lines of every one of the Hyksos' twenty chariot divisions. We moved so casually and naturally that no alarm was raised, we even chatted and joked with the enemy grooms and horse-handlers we met along the way.

As the first streaks of dawn showed in the eastern sky, we trudged back to the timber wharf on which we had disembarked. Only one of the galleys had waited to take us off, the rest of the flotilla had cast off and turned back southwards as soon as they had discharged their cargo of diseased horses.

We went aboard the remaining ship, and although Hui and the other grooms threw themselves exhausted upon the deck, I stood at the stern-rail and watched the walls of my beautiful Thebes, washed by the pure early light, sink from view behind us.

Ten days later, we sailed into the port of Elephantine, and after I had reported to Pharaoh Tamose, I hurried to the water-garden in the harem. My mistress lay in the shade of the barrazza. She was pale and so thin that I could not keep my hands from trembling as I stretched out to her in obeisance. She wept when she saw me.

'I missed you, Taita. There is so little time left for us to be together.'

THE NILE began to shrink back into her bed. The fields emerged from under the inundation, glistening black under a thick new coat of rich mud. The roads began to dry out, opening the way northwards. Soon it would be time for the plough, and the time for war.

Aton and I waited anxiously, perusing every report from our spies in the north. It came at last, the intelligence for which we had waited and prayed. The news was carried by a fast felucca, flying to us on the wings of the north wind. It docked in the third watch of the night, but the messenger found Aton and me still working by lamplight in his cell.

I hurried with the dirty scrap of papyrus to the royal apartments. The guards had orders to let me pass at any hour, but Queen Masara met me at the curtained doorway to the king's bedchamber.

'I will not let you wake him now, Taita. The king is exhausted. This is his first night's uninterrupted sleep in a month.'

'Your Majesty, I must see him. I am under his direct orders—'

While we still argued, a deep young voice called to me from beyond the curtain, 'Is that you, Tata?' The curtain was thrown aside and the king stood before us in all his naked splendour. He was a man as few others I have ever known, lean and hard as the blade of the blue sword, majestic in all his manly parts, so that I was all the more conscious of my own disability when I looked upon him.

'What is it, Tata?'

'Despatches from the north. From the camp of the Hyksos. A terrible pestilence is sweeping through the lines of the Hyksos. Half their horses are stricken, and thousands of others fall prey to the disease with each new day.'

'You are a magician, Tata. How could we have ever mocked you and your gnu!' He gripped my shoulders and stared into my eyes. 'Are you ready to ride to glory with me?'

'I am ready, Pharaoh.'

'Then put Rock and Chain into the traces, and fly the blue pennant over my chariot. We are going home to Thebes.'

 SO WE stood at last before the city of a hundred gates with four divisions of chariots and thirty thousand foot. King Salitis' host lay before us, but beyond his multitudes the Fingers of Horus beckoned to us, and the walls of Thebes shone with a pearly radiance in the dawn light.

The Hyksos army deployed ponderously in front of us, like the uncoiling of some gigantic python, column after column, rank upon rank. Their spear-heads glittered and the golden helmets of the officers blazed in the early sunlight.

'Where is Apachan and his chariots?' the king demanded, and I stared at the Finger of Horus that stood nearest the river. I had to strain my eyesight to make out the tiny coloured scraps that waved from the top of the tower.

'Apachan has five divisions in the centre, and he holds six more in reserve. They are hidden beyond the city wall.'

I read the flag signals of the spy I had posted in the tallest of the three towers. I knew that from there he had a falcon's view across the battlefield.

'That is only eleven divisions, Tata,' the king fumed. 'We know he has twenty. Where are the others?'

'The Yellow Strangler,' I answered him. 'He has fielded every horse that can still stand.'

'By Horus, I hope you are right. I hope that Apachan is not planning a pretty little surprise for us.' He touched my shoulder.

'The dice are in the cup, Tata. It is too late to change them now. We must play this coup with what the gods have given us. Drive out in review.'

I took up the reins and wheeled the chariot out in front of our army. The king was showing himself to his troops. His presence would give them heart, and stiffen their spines. I took the horses down the long ranks at a tight hand-trot. Rock and Chain were brushed until their coats shone like polished copper in the sunlight. The carriage of the royal chariot was dressed in a thin skin of gold-leaf. This was the only concession I had made, in my quest for lightness.

The gold was beaten thinner than a papyrus sheet, and it added less than a hundred deben to the overall weight of our vehicle, yet it made a dazzling display. Friend or enemy who looked upon it could not doubt that this was Pharaoh's chariot, and take heart or be struck by awe in the thick of battle. On its long, whippy bamboo rod the blue pennant nodded and streamed in the breeze high above our heads, and the men cheered us as we drove down their ranks.

On the day we had left Qebui to begin the Return, I had made a vow not to cut my hair until I had made sacrifice in the temple of Horus in the centre of Thebes. Now my hair reached to my waist, and to hide the streaks of grey in it, I had dyed it with henna imported from those lands beyond the Indus river. It was a ruddy gold mane that set off my beauty to perfection. I wore a simple starched kilt of the whitest linen, and the Gold of Praise upon my naked chest. I did not wish in any way to detract from the glory of my young pharaoh, so I wore no make-up and no other ornament.

We passed in front of the massed regiments of the Shilluk spearmen in the centre. Those magnificent bloodthirsty pagans were the rock that anchored our line. They cheered us as we rode by, '*Kajan!* Tanus! *Kajan!* Tamose!' Their ostrich feathers seethed white as the foam of the river in the cataracts as they raised their spears in salute. I saw Lord Kratas there in the midst of them, and he shouted at me. His words were lost in the roar of ten thousand voices, but I read his lips: 'You and I will get puking drunk tonight in Thebes, you old hooligan.'

The Shilluk were stacked in depth, file upon file and regiment upon regiment. Kratas had exercised them ceaselessly in the tactics that I had helped him evolve to deal with chariots. Apart from their long spears, each of them carried a bundle of javelins, and a sling of wood and leather to launch these with added power. They had set the sharpened wooden staves into the earth to form a palisade in front of their line. The Hyksos chariots had to break through that spiny barrier to reach them.

The Egyptian archers were drawn up behind them, ready to move forward through their ranks or retreat again, as the vagaries of the battle called for each differing tactic. They raised their recurved bows on high and cheered Pharaoh. 'Tamose! Egypt and Tamose!'

Pharaoh wore the blue war crown, with the golden circlet of the *uraeus* around his brow, the heads of the vulture and the cobra of the two kingdoms entwined, their jewelled eyes glittering. He returned their salute with the bare blade of the blue sword held high.

We wheeled around our own left flank, and before we started back, Memnon stopped me with a hand on my shoulder. For a short while we looked back over the field. The Hyksos were moving forward already. Their front line was twice the length of our own.

'From your own treatise, Tata,' he quoted, '"A circumspect defence until the enemy is committed, and then the rapid and audacious attack."'

'You have remembered the lesson well, sire.'

'It is certain we will be outflanked, and Apachan will probably throw in his first five chariot divisions at the start.'

'I agree with you, Mem.'

'But we know what we have to do, don't we, Tata?' He tapped my shoulder and we started back to where our own chariots were holding in the rear.

Remrem headed the first division, Astes had the second, and Lord Aqer the third. Newly promoted to the rank of Best of Ten Thousand, Captain Hui commanded the fourth division. Two regiments of Shilluk guarded our baggage and the spare horses.

'Look at that old hunting dog,' Memnon nodded at Remrem.

'He is chafing to be away. By Horus, I'll teach him a little patience before this day is done.'

We heard the horns sounding in the centre.

'It begins now.' Memnon pointed to the front, and we saw the Hyksos chariots looming through the dust-clouds. 'Yes, Apachan has turned loose his chariots.'

He looked back at our divisions, and Remrem raised his sword high. 'The first is ready, Majesty,' he called eagerly, but Memnon ignored him and signalled to Lord Aqer. The third division came forward in column of fours behind us, and Pharaoh led them out.

The Hyksos chariots lumbered forward, heavy and majestic, aimed at the centre of our line. Memnon cut across in front of them, interposing our thin column between their hordes and the infantry. Then, at his signal, we wheeled into line abreast and we flew straight at them. It seemed suicidal, as futile as charging one of our frail wooden galleys at the rocks of the cataract.

As we came together, our archers fired head-on into the Hyksos, aiming for the horses. Gaps opened in their line as the animals were brought down by our arrows, then at the last possible moment our own line dissolved like wind-driven smoke. Our drivers used their superior speed and manoeuvrability. Instead of coming into collision with the Hyksos line and being crushed beneath the juggernaut, we swerved into the gaps and raced through them. Not all our chariots escaped, and some were broken and overturned, but Lord Aqer led four out of every five of them through.

We emerged in the rear of the Hyksos charge and spun around in a full-locked turn, re-forming the line at the gallop and again using our speed to overhaul the Hyksos, coming into them from the rear, firing our arrows into them at shortening range.

The Hyksos chariots were designed to give protection to the crew from the front, and their archers were stationed on the footplate to fire their arrows forward. Confusion spread down their line as they tried to meet our attack from the rear. Hard-pressed, some of the drivers attempted to turn back to confront us, and they collided with the chariots alongside. Those fearsome wheel-scythes cut into the legs of the neighbouring horses, and brought them down in a screaming, whinnying tangle.

The confusion spread among them just as the first volley of arrows from the Egyptian archers rose up over the massed ranks of Shilluk and dropped among the Hyksos. Immediately this happened, Memnon gave the order, and we wheeled away and let them run down on that palisade of sharpened staves. Half their horses were maimed or killed by those fierce points. Those who broke through were met by the Shilluk and a cloud of javelins. Struck by stake and arrow and javelin, their horses panicked, kicking and rearing in the traces.

Those chariots that were still under control hurled themselves into the Shilluk phalanx. They met no resistance. The black ranks opened before them, allowing the horses to run through, but then they closed up behind them.

Every one of those tall, willowy black devils was an athlete and an acrobat. They leaped up on to the footplate of the racing chariots from behind, and they stabbed and hacked at the crew with dagger and spear. They swallowed that first charge of chariots the same way a jellyfish engulfs a swift silver sardine in its myriad arms and amorphous body.

The Hyksos spearmen were moving forward to follow up and exploit the chariot charge, but now they were exposed. Loose horses and the surviving chariots tore back into their massed ranks, and forced them to open up and let them through. For the moment they were stranded in disorder in the middle of the field, and Memnon skilfully seized the opportunity.

Lord Aqer's horses were blown, and Memnon led them back into reserve. He and I changed teams. It was but a moment's work for the grooms to loosen the tack that coupled Rock and Chain, and to lead in a fresh team from the horses being held in reserve. We had six thousand fresh horses ready in the rear. I wondered how many Hyksos horses had escaped the Strangler, how many fresh teams they were holding.

As we wheeled back into line, Remrem called to us desperately, 'Your Majesty! The first! Let my first division go!'

Pharaoh ignored him and signalled to Astes. The second moved forward behind us and formed up at the trot.

The Hyksos infantry was still tangled in the middle of the field. They had extended to overlap our shorter line, but had lost their dressing. The line was crumpled and twisted. With a general's eye, Memnon picked out the weakest point, a salient in their left flank.

'The second division will advance. Trot-march! Forward! Pods of eight, charge!'

We tore into the salient in the line, eight chariots abreast. Pod after pod, we crashed into them and ripped them open. Their left flank buckled, while their right still pressed forward. We had them canted across the field, their centre was shearing, and Memnon re-formed the third division at the gallop, and set them up to tear open the enemy centre.

At the moment before we were committed to the charge, I glanced across at the city. Dust had almost obscured the range, but I glimpsed the two white flags on the summit of the Finger of Horus. It was the warning signal from my lookout posted there, and I swivelled round and looked back at the eastern fort of the city.

'Sire!' I cried, and pointed back. The king followed my arm, and saw the first squadron of Hyksos chariots trot out from concealment behind the curve of the wall. The others followed, like a column of black warrior ants on the march.

'Apachan is throwing in his reserves to save his infantry,' Memnon shouted, above the din of battle. 'A moment more, and he would have had us in enfilade. Well done, Tata.'

We had to let the infantry escape, as we wheeled into line to face Apachan's chariots. We charged at each other across a field littered with smashed and overturned chariots, loose arrows and javelins, dead and wounded horses and dying men. As we came together, I stood taller on the footplate and peered ahead. There was something unusual about the run of the enemy chariots, and then it dawned upon me.

'Sire,' I cried, 'look at the horses! They are running sick animals.' The chests of the leading teams were painted with a glistening coat of yellow mucus that streamed from their gaping mouths. Even as I watched, one of the horses coming towards us staggered and fell headlong, bringing its team-mate down with it.

'Sweet Isis, you are right. Their horses are finished before they have begun,' Memnon answered. He saw instantly what he had to do. It was the measure of his superb control that he was able to deflect a charge of his chariots once it was fully launched. At this very last moment he declined the head-on engagement.

We opened like a flower before their charge, peeling away on either side of them, turning and running back for our own lines, drawing them on, straining their sick and gasping horses to their utmost.

We ran before them in a tight, compact formation. Their own line began to waver and fall apart as the weaker horses broke down. Some of them fell as though struck in the head by an arrow. Others merely slowed and stopped, standing with their heads hanging, mucus pouring from their mouths in shiny golden ropes.

Lord Aqer's own horses were almost blown by now. They had driven two furious charges without a rest. Still pursued by the remnants of Apachan's division, Memnon led them back to where Hui's fourth division was drawn up alongside Remrem and his first.

'Pharaoh! The first is ready. Let me go! In the name of all the gods, let me go!' Remrem howled with frustration.

Memnon hardly glanced in his direction. I turned my chariot in alongside that of Hui. A team of grooms slipped our sweat-soaked horses from the traces and led in a fresh pair. While Lord Aqer's exhausted division streamed back past us, we faced the oncoming Hyksos.

'Are you ready, Captain Hui?' Memnon called to him, and Hui raised his bow in salute.

'For Egypt and Tamose!' he shouted.

'Then forward march. Charge!' Memnon laughed, and our horses jumped against the traces and we shot forward.

There were six full divisions of Apachan's chariots scattered across the field in front of us. Half of them were broken down, with the horses fallen or drooping in the traces, suffocated and dying from the Yellow Strangler. Most of the others were reduced to a walk, the horses staggering and wheezing. However, the remaining chariots came on in good order.

We went out to meet them face to face. In the centre of their charge rode a tall chariot, its coachwork clad in shining bronze.

On the footplate stood a man so tall that he towered above his driver. He wore the high golden helmet of Hyksos royalty, and his dark beard was plaited with coloured ribbons that fluttered in the wind like pretty butterflies hovering over a flowering shrub.

'Apachan!' Memnon challenged him. 'You are a dead man.'

Apachan heard him, and he picked out our golden chariot. He swerved to meet us, and Memnon tapped my shoulder.

'Lay me alongside the bearded hog. It's time for the sword, at last.'

Apachan loosed two arrows at us as we closed. Memnon caught one on his shield. I ducked under the other, but I never lost my concentration. I was watching those terrible spinning scythes on the hubs of Apachan's wheels. They could hack my horses' legs out from under them.

Behind me I heard the gravelly rasp as Memnon drew the blue sword from its scabbard on the side panel, and from the corner of my eye I caught the steely flash of the blade as he went on guard.

I swung my horses' heads over, feinting to the right to confuse the Hyksos driver, but the instant we started to turn away, I changed direction again. I avoided his scythes and passed him close, then I turned in sharply behind him. With my free hand I snatched up the grappling-hook and tossed it over the side-panel of the other chariot. Now we were locked together, but I had achieved the advantage, for we lay across his stern.

Apachan swivelled around, and aimed a sword-cut at me, but I fell to my knees under it, and Memnon gathered up the blow on his shield, then swung the blue sword. A shard of bronze curled from the edge of Apachan's weapon, sliced away by the steel, and he shouted in angry disbelief, and flung up his copper shield at the next blow.

Apachan was a superb swordsman, but no match for my king and the blue sword. Memnon mangled his shield to strips, and then swung hard at his bronze blade, as Apachan tried to defend his head. The blue blade sheared the bronze cleanly, and Apachan was left with only the hilt in his fist.

He opened his mouth wide and bellowed at us. The teeth in the back of his jaw were black and rotten, and his spittle blew into my face in a cloud. Memnon used that classic straight thrust to end it. He drove the point of the blue blade through Apachan's open mouth, deeply into the back of his throat. His angry bellow was drowned out by the torrent of bright blood that burst through his hairy lips.

I cut the rope of the grappling-hook, and let the Hyksos chariot run free. The horses were out of control and they slewed away and ran down the line of locked and battling chariots. Apachan clutched at the dashboard, holding himself erect even though he was dying, and the blood spurted from his mouth and cascaded down his breastplate.

It was a sight that struck dismay into the hearts of his charioteers. They tried to disengage their sick and staggering horses, but we ran hub-to-hub with them and hurled our javelins into them. We followed them all the way back, until we came within range of their archers, and flocks of arrows fell around us and forced us to break off.

'It is not over yet,' I warned Memnon, as we walked our tired horses back. 'You have broken Apachan's chariots, but you still have to deal with Beon's infantry.'

'Take me to Kratas,' Pharaoh ordered.

I stopped our chariot in front of the massed regiments of Shilluk, and Memnon called across to Kratas, 'What heart, my Lord?'

'I fear, sire, that my fellows will fall asleep if you cannot find a little work for us to do.'

'Then let us hear a tune from them as you take them forward to seek employment.'

The Shilluk began their advance. They moved with a curious shuffling gait, and every third pace they stamped in unison with a force that made the ground jump beneath their horny bare feet. They sang in those deep, melodious African voices, a sound like a swarm of angry black bees, and they drummed their spears upon their rawhide shields.

The Hyksos were disciplined and brave, they could not have conquered half the world if they had not been so. We had smashed up their chariots, but they stood to meet Kratas' advance behind a wall of bronze shields.

The two armies came together like fighting temple bulls. The black and the white bulls locked horns and fought it out breast-to-breast and spear-to-spear.

While the two armies of foot-soldiers mauled each other, Pharaoh held back his chariots, using them with skill and daring only when there was an opening or a weakness in the enemy positions. When a pocket of the Hyksos infantry was isolated on the left, he sent in Aqer's division, and annihilated them with two swift charges. When Lord Beon tried to send reinforcements forward to assist his beleaguered front, Pharaoh despatched Astes with five hundred chariots to frustrate him.

The Hyksos rallied every one of their remaining chariots, and every one of their horses that could still stand, and threw them against our right. Memnon sent Hui and Astes out to meet them, and to break up their attack. He left Remrem cursing and pleading and stamping up and down beside his chariot, and ignored his pleas.

Pharaoh and I circled the fighting in the golden chariot, watching each shift and change in the conflict. He pushed in his reserves in exactly those places where they were most needed, and with the timing and anticipation that can never be taught or learned. It was as though the pulse and the tempo of the battle beat in his heart, and he sensed it in his blood.

Always I looked for Kratas in the thick of it. Many times I lost him, and I dreaded that he was down, but then his helmet showed again with the ostrich-feather plume cut away, and the bronze splattered with his own blood and the blood of other men.

It was there in the centre where Kratas fought that the Hyksos ranks began to give. It was like the first trickle through the earth wall of a dam, their line bulged and stretched to the breaking-point. Their rear ranks began to fall in upon themselves under the relentless pressure.

'By the love of Horus and the compassion of all the gods, Tata, this is the moment of our victory.' Memnon saw it even before I did.

We galloped across to where Remrem still waited, and Pharaoh hailed him, 'Are you ready, my Lord Remrem?'

'I have been ready since dawn, sire, but I am no lord.'

'Would you argue with your king, sir? You are a lord now. The enemy centre is breaking. Take your chariots and chase them back to Memphis!'

'May you live for ever, Pharaoh!' Lord Remrem roared, and he sprang to the footplate. He led out the first. Their horses were fresh and strong, and their fighting spirit was chafed raw and angry with long restraint.

They crashed into the Hyksos right flank. They cut through them with barely a check, and swung round and went into the enemy centre from the rear. It was the perfect moment when the battle teetered, and the Hyksos centre broke. Within the time it takes to draw and hold a long breath, they were in rout.

They streamed back towards the city gates, but even Kratas' Shilluk were too far-gone to follow them. They stood knee-deep in the piles of dead and dying men, they rested on their spears and let the Hyksos go. This was when the genius of Memnon was made apparent. He had kept the first in hand for this moment. They took up the chase, and I saw Remrem's sword rise and fall to a terrible rhythm as he drove them on.

The first of the fleeing enemy reached the city gates, but they found them slammed closed in their faces. My spies and agents had done their work well. The populace of Thebes was in revolt, and the city was ours. They barred the gates to the broken Hyksos legions.

Remrem pursued the Hyksos until night fell and his horses were exhausted. He drove them back thirty miles, and every yard of the north road was littered with their discarded weapons and the bodies of the slain.

I DROVE Pharaoh's golden chariot up to the main gate of the city, and he stood tall on the footplate and shouted to the sentinels on the parapet above us. 'Open the gates! Let me pass through!'

'Who is it that demands entry to Thebes?' they called down.

'I am Tamose, ruler of the two kingdoms.'

'Hail Pharaoh! May you live for ever!'

The gates swung open, and Memnon touched my shoulder. 'Drive through, Tata.'

I turned to face him. 'Forgive me, Majesty. I have taken oath that I will not enter the city, except at the side of my mistress, Queen Lostris. I must pass the reins to you.'

'Dismount,' he ordered me gently. 'Go! Fetch your mistress and make good your oath.'

He took the reins from my hand, and I climbed down into the dusty roadway. I watched him drive the golden chariot through the gateway, and the sound of cheering was like the thunder of waters in the cataracts at high flood. The people of Thebes greeted their king.

I stood at the roadside as our depleted and battered army followed Pharaoh into the city. I realized what a bitter price we had paid for our victory. We would not be fit to pursue the Hyksos until we had rebuilt our army. By this time King Salitis would be strong again, and his horses recovered from the Yellow Strangler. We had won the first battle, but I knew that many more lay ahead of us before the tyrant could be cast out of this very Egypt.

I looked for Kratas as the Shilluk regiments marched past, but he was not there.

Hui had a chariot and fresh horses for me. 'I will ride with you, Taita,' he offered, but I shook my head.

'I will travel faster alone,' I told him. 'Go into the city and enjoy your triumph. A thousand pretty maids are waiting to welcome you home.'

Before I took the south road, I drove first to the battlefield. The jackals and the hyena were already at the feast that we had set for them, their growls and howls blended with the groans of the dying. The dead were piled like the flotsam on the river-bank when the flood-waters recede.

I drove the chariot through to where I had last seen Kratas, but this was the most gruesome corner of that awful field. The corpses were piled high as my chariot wheels. I saw his helmet lying in the dust that blood had turned to thick mud. I dismounted and took it up. The crest was gone and the helm was all dented and battered in by heavy blows.

I threw the helmet aside and began to search for Kratas' body. I saw his leg protruding like the branch of a giant acacia from beneath a pile of bodies. They were Shilluk and Hyksos lying together in the truce of death. I dragged them aside and found Kratas on his back. He was drenched in clotted black blood, his hair was matted with it and his face was a black, crusted mask.

I knelt beside him, and I whispered softly, 'Must they all die? Every one I truly love, must they all die?' I leaned forward and kissed his bloody lips.

He sat up and stared at me. Then he grinned that wide boyish grin of his. 'By the plug of dried snot in Seth's left nostril, that was a real fight,' he greeted me.

'Kratas!' I stared at him with delight. 'You will truly live for ever.'

'Never doubt it for a moment, my lad. But right now I need a noggin.'

I ran to the chariot and fetched the wine flask. He held it at arm's-length and let the red wine squirt down his throat without swallowing. When the flask was empty he threw it aside and belched.

'That will do well enough for a start,' he winked at me. 'Now point me towards the nearest tavern, you old reprobate.'

FASTER THAN any ship could sail against the current, I carried the news to Elephantine. I was one man in the chariot, and the horses ran lightly. I changed the teams at every relay station along the south road, and galloped on without a check. The grooms handed me a flask or a crust of corn-bread and cheese as they changed the horses, and I never slept or even rested.

During the night, the stars and the moon revealed the path to me, and Horus guided my weary hands upon the traces, for though I ached in every limb and I reeled on the footplate with fatigue, I met with no mishap.

At each relay station and in each village along the way, I shouted the joyous news. 'A victory! A mighty victory! Pharaoh has triumphed at Thebes. The Hyksos is cast down.'

'Praise to all the gods!' they cheered me. 'Egypt and Tamose.'

I galloped on, and they still speak of my ride to this day along the south road. They tell of the gaunt rider with wild bloodshot eyes, his robe thick with dust and the stains of dried blood, his long hair blowing in the wind, the harbinger of victory, bringing the news to Elephantine of the battle that set Egypt on the road to freedom.

I drove from Thebes to Elephantine in two days and two nights, and when I reached the palace, I barely had the strength left to stagger into the water-garden where my mistress lay, and throw myself down beside her couch.

'Mistress,' I croaked through cracked lips and a throat that was parched with dust, 'Pharaoh has won a mighty victory. I have come to take you home.'

WE SAILED down-river to Thebes. The princesses were with me to keep their mother company and to cheer her. They sat with her on the open deck and sang to her. They rhymed and riddled and laughed, but there were tones of sadness in their laughter and deep concern in their eyes as they watched over my mistress.

Queen Lostris was as frail as a wounded bird. There was no weight to her bones and her flesh was as translucent as mother-of-pearl. I could lift and carry her as easily as I had done when she was ten years of age. The powder of the sleeping-flower was no longer able to still the pain that gnawed into her belly like some terrible clawed crab.

I carried her to the bows of the galley when at last the walls of Thebes opened to our view around the last bend in the river. With an arm around her thin shoulders I supported her, as we delighted together in all those long-remembered scenes, and lived again a thousand joyous memories of our youth.

But the effort tired her. When we docked below the Palace of Memnon, half the populace of Thebes was waiting to welcome her. Pharaoh Tamose stood at the head of this vast throng.

When the litter-bearers carried her ashore, they cheered her. Although most of them had never laid eyes upon her, the legend of the compassionate queen had persisted during her long exile. Mothers lifted up their infants for her blessing, and they reached out to touch her hand as it trailed from the edge of the litter.

'Pray to Hapi for us,' they pleaded. 'Pray for us, Mother of Egypt.'

Pharaoh Tamose walked beside her litter like the son of a commoner, and Tehuti and Bekatha followed close behind. Both the princesses smiled brightly, though the tears jewelled their eyelids.

Aton had prepared quarters for the queen. At the door I sent them all away, even the king. I laid her on the couch beneath the vine arbour on the terrace. From there she could look across the river to the shining walls of her beloved Thebes.

When darkness fell, I carried her to her bedchamber. As she lay upon the linen sheets, she looked up at me. 'Taita,' she murmured, 'one last time, will you work the Mazes of Ammon-Ra for me?'

'Mistress, I can refuse you nothing.' I bowed my head and went to fetch my medicine chest.

I sat beside her bed, cross-legged upon the stone slabs, and she watched me prepare the herbs. I crushed them in the alabaster pestle and mortar, and heated the water in the copper kettle.

I raised the steaming cup and saluted her with it.

'Thank you,' she whispered, and I drained the cup. I closed

my eyes and waited for the familiar but dreaded slide over the edge of reality, into the world of dreams and visions.

When I returned, the lamps were guttering and smoking in their brackets, and the palace was silent. There was no sound from the river or from the sleeping city on the far bank, only the sweet trill of a nightingale in the gardens, and the light breath of my mistress as she lay upon her silken pillow.

I thought she was sleeping. But the moment I lifted my trembling hand to wipe the cold and nauseous sweat from my face, she opened her eyes. 'Poor Taita, was it so bad?'

It had been worse than ever before. My head ached and my vision swam. I knew that I would never work the Mazes again. This was the last time, and I had done it for her alone.

'I saw the vulture and the cobra stand on either side of the river, divided by the waters. I saw the waters rise and fall one hundred seasons. I saw one hundred sheaves of corn, and one hundred birds fly over the river. Below them, I saw the dust of battle and the flash of swords. I saw the smoke of burning cities mingle with the dust.

'At last I saw the cobra and the vulture come together in congress. I saw them mating and entwined on a sheet of pure blue silk. There were blue banners on the city walls and banners of blue flew on the temple pylons.

'I saw the blue pennants on the chariots that drove out across the world. I saw monuments so tall and mighty that they would stand for ten thousand years. I saw the peoples of fifty different nations bow down before them.'

I sighed and pressed my fingers into my temples to still the throbbing in my skull, and then I said, 'That was all my vision.'

Neither of us spoke or moved for a long while thereafter, then my mistress said quietly, 'One hundred seasons must pass before the two kingdoms are united, one hundred years of war and striving before the Hyksos are at last driven from the sacred soil of this very Egypt. It will be hard and bitter for my people to bear.'

'But they will be united under the blue banner, and the kings of your line will conquer the world. All the nations of the world will pay homage to them,' I interpreted the rest of my vision for her.

'With this I am content.' She sighed and fell asleep.

I did not sleep, for I knew that she still needed me near her.

She woke again in that hour before dawn which is the darkest of the night. She cried out, 'The pain! Sweet Isis, the pain!'

I mixed the Red Shepenn for her. After a while she said, 'The pain has passed, but I am cold. Hold me, Taita, warm me with your body.'

I took her in my arms and held her while she slept.

She awoke once more as the first timid rays of dawn crept in through the doorway from the terrace.

'I have loved only two men in my life,' she murmured, 'and you were one of those. Perhaps in the next life, the gods will treat our love more kindly.'

There was no reply I could give. She closed her eyes for the last time. She stole away quietly and left me. Her last breath was no louder than the one before, but I felt the chill in her lips when I kissed them.

'Goodbye, my mistress,' I whispered. 'Farewell, my heart.'

I HAVE written these scrolls during the seventy days and nights of the royal embalming. They are my last tribute to my mistress.

Before the undertakers took her away from me, I made the incision in her left flank, as I had done for Tanus. I opened her womb and took from it that terrible incubus that had killed her. It was a thing of flesh and blood, but it was not human. When I cast it into the fire, I cursed it, and I cursed the foul god Seth who had placed it in her.

I have prepared ten alabaster jars to hold these scrolls. I will leave them with her. I am painting all the murals of her tomb with my own hand. They are the finest I have ever created. Each stroke of my brush is an expression of my love.

I wish that I could rest with her in this tomb, for I am sick and weary with grief. But I still have my two princesses and my king to care for.

They need me.

AUTHOR'S NOTE

On 5 January 1988, Doctor Duraid ibn al Simma of the Egyptian Department of Antiquities opened and entered a tomb on the west bank of the Nile in the Valley of the Nobles. The reason why this tomb had not been previously excavated was that in the ninth century AD an Islamic mosque had been built over the site. It was only after long and delicate negotiations with the religious authorities that the excavation was permitted.

Immediately upon entering the passage that led to the burial chamber, Dr Al Simma was greeted by a marvellous display of murals which covered all the walls and the ceilings. They were the most elaborate and vivacious that he had ever encountered in a lifetime spent studying the monuments.

He told me that he knew at once that he had made a significant find, for from amongst the hieroglyphics on the walls stood out the royal cartouche of an Egyptian queen who had not been previously recorded.

His excitement and anticipation increased as he approached the burial chamber, only to be dashed as he saw that the seals upon the doorway had been damaged, and the entrance had been forced. In ancient times, the tomb had been robbed and stripped of its sarcophagus and all its treasures.

Nevertheless, Dr Al Simma was able to date the tomb with reasonable accuracy to that dark night of strife and disaster that overwhelmed Egypt in about 1780 BC. For the next century the Two Kingdoms were in a state of flux. We have little record of the events of this period, but from the chaos eventually rose a line of princes and pharaohs that finally expelled the Hyksos invader, and lifted Egypt into its period of greatest glory. It gives me pleasure to think that the blood of Lostris and Tanus and Memnon ran strongly in their veins.

It was almost a year after the tomb was first opened, while Dr

Al Simma's assistants were copying and photographing the decorations of the walls, that a section of the plaster fell away to reveal a hidden niche in which stood ten sealed alabaster vases.

When Dr Al Simma asked me to assist in the transcription of the scrolls contained in the vases, I was both honoured and filled with trepidation. I was not, of course, qualified to work on the original scrolls, which were written in the hieratic script. This work was done at Cairo Museum by a team of international Egyptologists.

Dr Al Simma asked me to rewrite this original transcription in a style that would make it more accessible to the modern reader. With this end in view I have included some anachronisms in the text. For instance I have, in places, used such comparatively modern measures of distance and weight as miles and ounces. I have also indulged myself with words such as 'djinn' and 'houri' and 'hooligan' which Taita never employed, but which, I feel certain, he would have used if they had formed part of his vocabulary.

Very soon after beginning work on the texts all my reservations began to evaporate as I became totally involved in the times and character of the ancient author. Despite all his bombast and vainglory, I developed an affinity and affection for the slave Taita that reached back over the millennia.

I am left with a realization of how little the emotions and aspirations of man have changed in all that time, and a lingering excitement that to this day somewhere in the Abyssinian mountains near the source of the Blue Nile the mummy of Tanus still lies in the unviolated tomb of Pharaoh Mamose.

W.S.

GOLD MINE

This book is for Danielle

– 1 –

It began in the time when the world was young, in the time before man, in the time before life itself had evolved upon this planet.

The crust of the earth was still thin and soft, distorted and riven by the enormous pressures from within.

What is now the flat, compacted shield of the African continent, stable and unchanging, was a series of alps. It was range upon range of mountains, thrown up and tumbled down by the movements of the magma at great depth. These were mountains such as man has never seen, so massive as to dwarf the Himalayas, mountains of steaming rock from whose clefts and gaping wounds the molten magma trickled.

It came up from the earth's centre along the fissures and weak places in the crust, bubbling and boiling, yet cooling steadily as it neared the surface so that the least volatile minerals were deposited deeper down, but those with a lower melting point were carried to the surface.

At one point in the measureless passage of time, another series of these fissures opened upon one of the nameless mountain ranges, but from them gushed rivers of molten gold. Some natural freak of temperature and chemical change had resulted in a crude but effective process of refinement during the journey to the earth's surface. The gold was in high concentration in the matrix, and it cooled and solidified at the surface.

If the mountains of that time were so massive as to challenge the imagination of man, then the storms of wind and rain that blew around them were of equal magnitude.

It was a hellish landscape in which the gold field was conceived, cruel mountains reaching stark and sheer in the clouds. Cloud banks dark with the sulphurous gases of the belching earth, so thick that the rays of the sun never penetrated them.

The atmosphere was laden with all the moisture that was to become the seas, so heavy with it that it rained in one perpetual wind-lashed storm upon the hot rock of the cooling earth, then the moisture rose in steam to condense and fall again.

As the years passed by their millions, so the wind and the rain whittled away at the nameless mountain range with its coating of gold-rich ore, grinding it loose and carrying it down in freshets and rivers and rushes of mud and rock into the valley between this range and the next.

Now as the country rock cooled, so the waters lay longer upon the earth before evaporating, and they accumulated in this valley to form a lake the size of an inland sea.

Into this lake poured the storm waters from the golden mountains, carrying with them tiny particles of the yellow metal which settled with other sand and quartz gravel upon the lake bed, to be compacted into a solid sheet.

In time all the gold was scoured from the mountains, transported and laid down upon the lake beds.

Then, as happened every ten million years or so, the earth entered another period of intense seismic activity. The earth shuddered and heaved as earthquake after mammoth earthquake convulsed it.

One fearsome paroxysm cracked the bed of the lake from end to end draining it and fracturing the sedimentary beds, scattering fragments haphazardly so that great sheets of rock many miles across tilted and reared on end.

Again and again the earthquakes gripped and shook the

earth. The mountains tottered and collapsed, filling the valley where the lake had stood, burying some of the sheets of gold-rich rock, pulverizing others.

That cycle of seismic activity passed, and the ages wheeled on in their majesty. The floods and the great droughts came and receded. The miraculous spark of life was struck and burned up brightly, through the time of the monstrous reptiles, on through countless twists and turns of evolution until near the middle of the Pleistocene age a man-ape – Australopithecus – picked up the thigh bone of a buffalo from beside an outcrop of rock to use it as a weapon, a tool.

Australopithecus stood at the centre of a flat, sun-seared plateau that reached five hundred miles in each direction to the sea, for the mountains and the lake beds had long ago been flattened and buried.

Eight hundred thousand years later, one of the Australopithecus' distant but direct line stood at the same spot with a tool in his hand. The man's name was Harrison and the tool was more sophisticated than that of his ancestor, it was a prospector's pick of wood and metal.

Harrison stooped and chipped at the outcrop of rock that protruded from the dry brown African earth. He freed a piece of the stone and straightened with it in his hand.

He held it to catch the sun and grunted with disgust. It was a most uninteresting piece of stone, conglomerate, marbled black and grey. Without hope he held it to his mouth and licked it, wetting the surface before again holding it to the sun, an old prospectors' trick to highlight the metal in the ore.

His eyes narrowed in surprise as the tiny golden flecks in the rock sparkled back at him.

History remembers only his name, not his age nor his antecedents, not the colour of his eyes nor how he died, for within a month he had sold his claim for £10 and disappeared – in search, perhaps, of a really big strike.

3

He might have done better to retain his title to those claims.

In the eighty years since then an estimated five hundred million ounces of fine gold have been recovered from the fields of the Transvaal and Orange Free State. This is a fraction of that which remains, and which in time will be taken from the earth. For the men who mine the South African fields are the most patiently persistent, inventive and pig-headed of all Vulcan's brood.

This mass of precious metal is the foundation on which the prosperity of a vigorous young nation of eighteen million souls is based.

Yet the earth yields her treasure reluctantly – men must coax and wrest it from her.

– 2 –

Even with the electric fan blowing up a gale from the corner it was stinking hot in Rod Ironsides' office.

He reached for the silver Thermos of iced water at the edge of his desk, and arrested the movement as the jug began to dance before his finger tips touched it. The metal bottle skittered across the polished wooden surface; the desk itself shuddered, rustling the papers upon it. The walls of the room shook, so that the windows rattled in their frames. Four seconds the tremor lasted, and then it was still again.

'Christ!' said Rod, and snatched up one of the three telephones on his desk.

'This is the Underground Manager. Get me the rock mechanic's lab, honey, and snap it up, please.'

He drummed his fingers on the desk impatiently as he waited to be connected. The interleading door of his office opened and Dimitri put his head around the jamb.

'You feel that one, Rod? That was a bad one.'

'I felt it.' Then the telephone spoke into his ear.

'Dr Wessels here.'

'Peter, it's Rod. Did you read that one?'

'I haven't got a fix on it yet – can you hold on a minute?'

'I'll wait.' Rod curbed his impatience. He knew that Peter Wessels was the only person who could read the mass of complicated electronic equipment that filled the instrument room of the rock mechanic's laboratory. The laboratory was a joint research project by four of the major gold-mining companies; between them they had put up a quarter of a million Rand to finance an authoritative investigation of rock and seismic activity under stress. They had selected the Sonder Ditch Gold Mining Company's lease area as the site for the laboratory. Now Peter Wessels had his microphones sited thousands of feet down in the earth, and his tape recorders and stylus graphs ready to pinpoint any underground disturbance.

Another minute ticked by, and Rod swivelled his chair and stared out of the plate glass window at the monstrous head gear of No. 1 shaft, tall as a ten-storey building.

'Come on, Peter, come on, boy,' he muttered to himself. 'I've got twelve thousand of my boys down there.'

With the telephone still pressed to his ear, he glanced at his watch.

'Two-thirty,' he muttered. 'The worst possible time. They'll still be in the stopes.'

He heard the receiver picked up on the other end, and Peter Wessels' voice was almost apologetic.

'Rod?'

'Yes.'

'I'm sorry, Rod, you've had a force seven pressure burst at 9,500 feet in sector Sugar seven Charlie two.'

'Christ!' said Rod and slammed down the receiver. He was up from his desk in one movement, his face set and angry.

'Dimitri,' he snapped at his assistant still in the doorway.

'We won't wait for them to call us, it's a top sequence emergency. That was a force seven bump, with its source plumb in the middle of our eastern longwall at 95 level.'

'Sweet Mary Mother,' said Dimitri, and darted back into his own office. He bent his glossy black head of curls over the telephone and Rod heard him start his top sequence calls.

'Mine hospital ... emergency team ... Chief Ventilation Officer ... General Manager's office.'

Rod turned away, as the outer door of his office opened and Jimmy Paterson, his electrical engineer, came in.

'I felt it, Rod. How's it look?'

'Bad,' said Rod, then there were the other line managers crowding into his office talking quietly, lighting cigarettes, coughing and shuffling their feet, but all of them watching the white telephone on Rod's desk. The minutes crawled by like crippled insects.

'Dimitri,' Rod called out to break the tension. 'Have you got a cage held at the shaft head?'

'They're holding the Mary Anne for us.'

'I've got five men checking the high tension cable on 95 level,' said Jimmy Paterson, and they ignored him. They were watching the white phone.

'Have you located the boss yet, Dimitri?' Rod asked again; he was pacing in front of his desk. It was only when he stood close to other men that you saw how tall he was.

'He's underground, Rod. He went down at twelve-thirty.'

'Put in an all-stations call for him to contact me here.'

'I've done that already.'

The white phone rang.

Only once, a shrill note that ripped along Rod's nerve ends. Then he had the receiver up to his ear.

'Underground Manager,' he said. There was a long silence and he could hear the man breathing on the other end.

'Speak, man, what is it?'

'The whole bloody thing has come down,' said the voice.
It was husky, rough with fear and dust.

'Where are you speaking from?' Rod asked.

'They're still in there,' said the voice. 'They're screaming
in there. Under the rock. They're screaming.'

'What is your station?' Rod made his voice cold, hard,
trying to reach the man through his shock.

'The whole stope fell in on them. The whole bloody
thing.'

'God damn you! You stupid bastard!' Rod bellowed into
the phone. 'Give me your station!'

There was stunned silence for a moment. Then the
man's voice came back, steadier now, angry from the insult.

'95 level main haulage. Section 43. Eastern longwall.'

'We're coming.' Rod hung up, picked up his yellow
fibreglass hard helmet and lamp from the desk.

'43 section. The hanging wall has come down,' he said
to Dimitri.

'Fatals?' the little Greek asked.

'For sure. They've got squealers under the rock.'

Rod clapped on his hat.

'Take over on surface, Dimitri.'

– 3 –

R od was still buttoning the front of his white overalls
as he reached the shaft head. Automatically he
read the sign above the entrance:

STAY ALERT.   STAY ALIVE.
WITH YOUR CO-OPERATION THIS MINE HAS WORKED
16 FATALITY-FREE DAYS.

'We'll have to change the number again,' Rod thought
with grim humour.

The Mary Anne was waiting. Into its heavily wired confines were crowded the first aid team and emergency squad. The Mary Anne was the small cage used for lowering and hoisting personnel, there were two much larger cages that could carry one 120 men at one trip, while the Mary Anne could handle only forty. But that was sufficient for now.

'Let's go,' said Rod as he stepped into the cage, and the onsetter slammed the steel roller doors closed. The bell rang once, twice, and the floor dropped away from under him as the Mary Anne started down. Rod's belly came up to press against his ribs. They went down in one long continuous rush in the darkness. The cage jarring and racketing, the air changing in smell and taste, becoming chemical and processed, the heat building up rapidly.

Rod stood hunch-shouldered, leaning against the metal screen of the cage. The head room was a mere six foot three, and with his helmet on Rod stood taller than that. So today we get another butcher's bill, he thought angrily.

He was always angry when the earth took its payment in mangled flesh and snapping bones. All the ingenuity of man and the experience gained in sixty years of deep mining on the Witwatersrand were used in trying to keep the price in blood as low as possible. But when you go down into the ultra-deep levels below 8,000 feet and from those depths you remove a quarter of a million tons of rock each month, mining on an inclined sheet of reef that leaves a vast low-roofed chamber thousands of feet across, then you must pay, for the stress builds up in the rock as the focal points of pressure change until the moment when it reaches breaking point and she bumps. That is when men die.

Rod's knees flexed under him as the cage braked and then yoyoed to a halt at the brightly lit station on 66 level.

Here they must trans-ship to the sub-main shaft. The door rattled up and Rod left the cage, striding out down the main haulage the size of a railway tunnel; concreted and whitewashed, brightly lit by the bulbs that lined the roof, it curved gently away.

The emergency team followed Rod. Not running, but walking with the suppressed nervous energy of men going into danger. Rod led them towards the sub-main shaft.

There is a limit to the depth which you can sink a shaft into the earth and then equip it to carry men suspended on a steel cable in a tiny wire cage. The limit is about 7,000 feet.

At this depth you must start again, blast out a new headgear chamber from the living rock and below it sink your new shaft, the sub-main.

The sub-main Mary Anne was waiting for them, and Rod led them into it. They stood shoulder to shoulder, and the door rattled shut and again the stomach-swooping rush down into darkness.

Down, down, down.

Rod switched on his head lamp. Now there were tiny motes in the air – air that had been sterilely clean before.

Dust! One of the deadly enemies of the miner. Dust from the burst. As yet the ventilation system had been unable to clear it.

Endlessly they fell in darkness and now it was very hot, the humidity building up so the faces about him, both black and white, were shiny with sweat in the light of his head lamp.

The dust was thicker now, someone coughed. The brightly lit stations flashed past them – 76, 77, 78 – down, down. The dust was a fine mist now. 85, 86, 87. No one had spoken since entering the cage. 93, 94, 95. The deceleration and stop.

The door rattled up. They were 9,500 feet below the surface of the earth.

'Come on,' said Rod.

9

There were men cluttering the lobby of 95 station, a hundred and fifty, perhaps two hundred of them. Still filthy from their work in the stopes, clothing sodden with sweat, they were laughing and chattering with the abandon of men freshly released from frightful danger.

In a clear space in the centre of the lobby lay five stretchers, on two of them the bright red blankets were pulled up to cover the faces of the men upon them. The faces of the other three men looked as though they had been dusted with flour.

'Two' – grunted Rod – 'so far.'

The station was a shambles, with men milling aimlessly; each minute more of them came back down the haulages as they were pulled out of the undamaged stopes, which were now suspect.

Quickly Rod looked about him, recognizing the face of one of his mine captains.

'McGee,' he shouted. 'Take over here. Get them sitting down in lines ready to load. We'll start hauling the shift out immediately. Get onto the hoist room, tell them I want the stretcher cases out first.'

He paused long enough to watch McGee take control. He glanced at his watch. Two fifty-six. He realized with astonishment that only twenty-six minutes had passed since he felt the pressure burst in his office.

McGee had the station under a semblance of control. He was shouting into the hoist room telephone, on Rod's authority demanding priority to clear 95 station.

'Right,' said Rod. 'Come on.' And he led into the haulage.

The dust was thick. He coughed. The hanging wall was lower here. As he trudged on once more, Rod pondered the unfortunate choice of mining terminology that had named the roof of an excavation 'the hanging wall'. It made one think of a gallows, or at the best it emphasized the fact that there were millions of tons of rock *hanging* overhead.

The haulage branched, and unerringly Rod took the right fork. In his head he carried an accurate three-dimensional map of the entire 176 miles of tunnels that comprised the Sonder Ditch's workings. The haulage came to a T-junction and the arms were lower and narrower. Right to 42 section, left to 43 section. The dust was so thick that visibility was down to ten feet. The dust hung in the air, sinking almost imperceptibly.

'Ventilations knocked out here,' he called over his shoulder. 'Van den Bergh!'

'Yes, sir.' The leader of the emergency squad came up behind him.

'I want air in this drive. Get it on. Use canvas piping if you have to.'

'Right.'

'Then I want pressure on the water hoses to lay this dust.'

'Right.'

Rod turned into the drive. Here the foot wall – the floor – was rough and the going slower. They came upon a line of steel trolleys filled with gold reef abandoned in the centre of the drive.

'Get these the hell out of the way,' ordered Rod, and went on.

Fifty paces and he stopped abruptly. He felt the hair on his forearms stand on end. He could never accustom himself to the sound, no matter how often he heard it.

In the deliberately callous slang of the miner they called them 'squealers'. It was the sound of a grown man, with his legs crushed under hundreds of tons of rock, perhaps his spine broken, dust suffocating him, his mind unhinged by

11

the mortal horror of the situation in which he was trapped, calling for help, calling to his God, calling for his wife, his children, or his mother.

Rod started forward again, with the sound of it becoming louder, a terrifying sound, hardly human, sobbing and babbling into silence, only to start again with a blood-chilling scream.

Suddenly there were men ahead of Rod in the tunnel, dark shapes looming in the dust mist, their head lamps throwing shafts of yellow light, grotesque, distorted.

'Who is that?' Rod called, and they recognized his voice.

'Thank God. Thank God you've come, Mr Ironsides.'

'Who is that?'

'Barnard.' The 43 section shift boss.

'What's the damage?'

'The whole hanging wall of the stope came down.'

'How many men in the stope?'

'Forty-two.'

'How many still in?'

'So far we've got out sixteen unhurt, twelve slightly hurt, three stretcher cases and two dead 'uns.'

The squealer started again, but his voice was much weaker.

'Him?' asked Rod.

'He's got twenty ton of rock lying across his pelvis. I've hit him with two shots of morphine, but it won't stop him.'

'Can you get into the stope?'

'Yes, there is a crawling hole.' Barnard flashed his lamp over the pile of fractured blue quartzite that jammed the drive like a collapsed garden wall. On it was an aperture big enough for a fox terrier to run through. Reflected light showed from the hole, and faintly from within came the grating sounds of movement over loose rock and the muffled voices of men.

'How many men have you got working in there, Barnard?'

'I – ' Barnard hesitated, 'I think about ten or twelve.'

And Rod grabbed a handful of his overall front and jerked him almost off his feet.

'You think!' In the head lamps Rod's face was white with fury. 'You've put men in there without recording their numbers? You've put twelve of my boys against the wall to try and save nine?' With a heave Rod lifted the shift boss off his feet and swung him against the side wall of the drive, pinning him there.

'You bastard, you know that most of those nine are chopped already. You know that stope is a bloody killing ground, and you send in *twelve* more to get the chop *and* you don't record their numbers. How the hell would we ever know who to look for if the hanging fell again?' He let the shift boss free, and stood back. 'Get them out of here, clear that stope.'

'But, Mr Ironsides, the General Manager is in there, Mr Lemmer is in there. He was doing an inspection in the stope.'

For a moment Rod was taken aback, then he snarled. 'I don't give a good damn if the State President is in there, clear the stope. We'll start again and this time we'll do it properly.'

Within minutes the rescuers had been recalled, they came squirming out of the aperture, white with dust like maggots wriggling from rotten cheese.

'Right,' said Rod, 'I'll risk four men at a time.'

Quickly he picked four of the floury figures, among them an enormous man on whose right shoulder was the brass badge of a boss boy.

'Big King – you here?' Rod spoke in Fanikalo, the lingua franca of the mines which enabled men from a dozen ethnic groups to communicate.

'I am here,' answered Big King.

'You looking for more awards?' A month before, Big King had been lowered on a rope 200 feet down a vertical orepass to retrieve the body of a white miner. The bravery award by the company had been 100 rand.

'Who speaks of awards when the earth has eaten the flesh of men?' Big King rebuked Rod softly. 'But today is children's play only. Is the Nkosi coming into the stope?' It was a challenge.

Rod's place was not in the stope. He was the organizer, the co-ordinator. Yet, he could not ignore the challenge, no Bantu would believe that he had not stood back in fear and sent other men in to die.

'Yes,' said Rod, 'I'm coming into the stope.'

He led them in. The hole was only just big enough to admit the bulk of Rod's body. He found himself in a chamber the size of an average room, but the roof was only three and a half feet high. He played his lamp quickly across the hanging wall, and it was wicked. The rock was cracked and ugly, 'a bunch of grapes' was the term.

'Very pretty,' he said, and dropped the beam of his lamp.

The squealer was within an arm's length of Rod. His body from the waist up protruded from under a piece of rock the size of a Cadillac. Someone had wrapped a red blanket around his upper body. He was quiet now, lying still. But as the beam of Rod's lamp fell upon him, he lifted his head. His eyes were crazed, unseeing, his face running with the sweat of terror and insanity. His mouth snapped open, wide and pink in the shiny blackness of his face. He began to scream, but suddenly the sound was drowned by a great red-black gout of blood that came gushing up his throat, and spurted from his mouth.

As Rod watched in horror, the Bantu posed like that, his head thrown back, his mouth gaping as though he were a gargoyle, the life blood pouring from him. Then slowly the head sagged forward, and flopped face downwards. Rod crawled to him, lifted his head and pillowed it on the red blanket.

14

There was blood on his hands and he wiped it on the front of his overalls.

'Three,' he said, 'so far.' And leaving the dying man he crawled on towards the broken face of the fall.

Big King crawled up beside him with two pinch bars. He handed one to Rod.

Within an hour it had become a contest, a trial of strength between two men. Behind them the other three men were shoring up and passing back the rock that Rod and Big King loosened from the face. Rod knew he was being childish, he should have been back in the main haulage, not only directing the rescue, but also making all the other decisions and alternative arrangements that were needed now. The company paid him for his brains and his experience, not for his muscle.

'The hell with it,' he thought. 'Even if we miss the blast this evening, I'm staying here.' He glanced at Big King, and reached forward to get his hands onto a bigger piece of rock in the jam. He strained, using his arms first, then bringing the power of his whole body into it – the rock was solid. Big King placed huge black hands on the rock, and they pulled together. In a rush of smaller rock it came away, and they shoved it back between them, grinning at each other.

At seven o'clock Rod and Big King withdrew from the stope to rest and eat sandwiches, and drink Thermos coffee while Rod spoke to Dimitri over the field telephone that had been laid up to the face.

'We've pulled shift on both shafts, Rod, the workings are clear to blast. Except for your lot, there are fifty-eight men in your 43 section.' Dimitri's voice was reedy over the field telephone.

'Hold on.' Rod revolved the situation in his mind. He worked it out slower than usual, for he was tired, emotionally and physically drained. If he stopped the blast on both shafts for fear of bringing down more rock in 43

15

section, it would cost the Company a day's production, 10,000 tons of gold reef worth sixteen rand a ton, the formidable sum of R160,000 or £80,000 or $200,000 whichever way you looked at it.

It was highly probable that every man in the stope was already dead, and the original pressure burst had de-stressed the rock above and around the 95 level, so there was little danger of further bumps.

And yet there might be someone alive in there, someone lying pinned in the womb-warm darkness of the stope with a bunch of loose grapes hanging over his unprotected body. When they hit all the blast buttons on the Sonder Ditch Mine, they fired eighteen tons of Dynagel. The kick was considerable, it would bring down those grapes.

'Dimitri,' Rod made his decision, 'burn all longwalls on No. 2 shaft at seven-thirty exactly.' No. 2 shaft was three miles away. That would save the Company R80,000. 'Then at precisely five-minute intervals burn south, north and west longwalls here on No. 1 shaft.' Spreading the blast would reduce the disturbance, and that put another R60,000 in the shareholders' pockets. The total monetary loss inflicted by the disaster was around R20,000. Not too bad really, Rod thought sardonically, blood was cheap. You could buy it at three rand a pint from the Central Blood Transfusion Service.

'All right,' he stood up, and flexed his aching shoulders. 'I'm pulling everybody back into the safety of the shaft pillar while we blast.'

5

After the successive earth tremors of the blast, Rod put them back into the stope, and at nine o'clock they uncovered the bodies of two machine boys crushed against the metal of their own rock drill. Ten feet further on they found the white miner; his body was unmarked, but his head was flattened.

At eleven o'clock they found two more machine boys. Rod was in the haulage when they dragged them out through the small opening. Neither of them were recognizable as human, they looked more like lumps of raw meat that had been rubbed in dirt.

A little after midnight Rod and Big King went into the stope again to take over from the team at the face, and twenty minutes later they holed through the wall of loose rock into another chamber that had been miraculously left standing.

The air in here was steamy with heat. Rod recoiled instinctively from the filthy moist gush of it against his face. Then he forced himself to crawl forward and peer into the opening.

Ten feet away lay Frank Lemmer, the General Manager of the Sonder Ditch Mine. He lay on his back. His helmet had been knocked from his head, and a deep gash split the skin above his eye. Blood from the gash had run back into his silver hair and clotted black. He opened his eyes and blinked owlishly in the dazzle of Rod's lamp. Quickly Rod averted the beam.

'Mr Lemmer,' he said.

'What the bloody hell are you doing with the rescue team?' growled Frank Lemmer. 'It's not your job. Haven't you learned a single goddamned thing in twenty years of mining?'

'Are you all right, sir?'

'Get a doctor in here,' replied Frank Lemmer. 'You're going to have to cut me loose from this lot.'

Rod wriggled up to where he lay, and then he saw what Frank Lemmer meant. From the elbow his arm was pinned under a solid slab of rock. Rod ran his hands over the slab, feeling it. Only explosive would shift the rock. As always Frank Lemmer was right.

Rod wriggled out of the opening and called over his shoulder.

'Get the telephone up here.'

After a few minutes delay he had the receiver, and was through to the station at 95 level which had been set up as an advance aid post and rest station for the rescuers.

'This is Ironsides, get me Doctor Stander.'

'Hold on.'

Then moments later, 'Hello, Rod, it's Dan.'

'Dan, we've found the old man.'

'How is he, conscious?'

'Yes, but he's pinned – you'll have to cut.'

'Are you sure?' Dan Stander asked.

'Of course I'm bloody well sure,' snapped Rod.

'Whoa, boy!' admonished Dan.

'Sorry.'

'Okay, where's he caught?'

'Arm. You'll have to cut above the elbow.'

'Charming!' said Dan.

'I'll wait here for you.'

'Right. I'll be up in five minutes.'

6

'It's funny, you see them chopped time and again, but you know it will never happen to you.' Frank Lemmer's voice was steady and even. The arm must be numb, Rod thought as he lay beside him in the stope.

Frank Lemmer rolled his head towards Rod. 'Why don't you go farming, boy?'

'You know why,' said Rod.

'Yes.' Lemmer smiled a little, just a twitching of the lips. With his free hand he wiped his mouth. 'You know, I had just three months more before I went on pension. I nearly made it. You'll end like this, boy, in the dirt with your bones crunched up.'

'It's not the end,' said Rod.

'Isn't it?' asked Frank Lemmer, and this time he chuckled. 'Isn't it?'

'What's the joke?' asked Dan Stander, poking his head into the tiny chamber.

'Christ, it took you long enough to get here,' growled Frank Lemmer.

'Give me a hand, Rod.' Dan passed his bag through, then as he crawled forward he spoke to Frank Lemmer.

'Union Steel closed at 98 cents tonight. I told you to buy.'

'Over-priced, over-capitalized,' snorted Frank Lemmer. Dan lay on his side in the dirt and laid out his instruments, and they argued stocks and shares. When Dan had the syringe full of pentathol and was swabbing Frank Lemmer's stringy old arm, Lemmer rolled his head towards Rod again.

'We made a good dig here, Rodney, you and I. I wish they'd give it to you now, but they won't. You're still too young. But whoever they put in my place, you keep an eye on him, you know the ground – don't let him balls it up.'

And the needle went in.

Dan cut through the arm in four and a half minutes, and twenty-seven minutes later Frank Lemmer died of shock and exposure in the Mary Anne on his way to the surface.

– 7 –

Once he had paid Patti's alimony there was not too much of Rod's salary left for extravagances, but one of these was the big cream Maserati. Although it was a 1967 model, and had done nearly 30,000 miles when he bought it, yet the instalments still took a healthy bite out of his monthly pay cheque.

On mornings like this he reckoned the expense worthwhile. He came twisting down from the Kraalkop ridge, and when the national road flattened and straightened for the final run into Johannesburg he let the Maserati go. The car seemed to flatten against the ground like a running lion, and the exhaust note changed subtly, becoming deeper, more urgent.

Ordinarily, it was an hour's run from the Sonder Ditch Mine into the city of Johannesburg, but Rod could clip twenty minutes off that time.

It was Saturday morning, and Rod's mood was light and expectant.

Since the divorce Rod had lived a Jekyll and Hyde existence. Five days of the week he was the company man in top-line management, but on the last two days of the week he went into Johannesburg with his golf clubs in the boot of the Maserati, the keys to his luxury Hillbrow apartment in his pocket, and a chuckle on his lips.

Today the anticipation was keener than ever for, in addition to the twenty-two-year-old blonde model who was prepared to devote her evening to entertaining Rodney Ironsides, there was the mysterious summons from Dr Manfred Steyner to answer.

The summons had been delivered by a nameless female caller describing herself as 'Dr Steyner's Secretary'. It had come the day after Frank Lemmer's funeral, and was for Saturday at 11 a.m.

Rod had never met Manfred Steyner, but he had, of course, heard of him. Anyone who worked for any of the fifty or sixty companies that comprised the Central Rand Consolidated Group must have heard of Manfred Steyner, and the Sonder Ditch Gold Company was just one of the Group.

Manfred Steyner had a bachelor's degree in Economics from Berlin University, and a Doctor's degree in Business Administration from Cornell. He had joined CRC a mere twelve years previously at the age of thirty, and now he was the front runner. Hurry Hirschfeld could not live for ever, although he gave indications of doing so, and when he went down to make a takeover bid on Hades, the word was that Manfred Steyner would succeed him as Chairman of CRC.

Chairmanship of CRC was an enviable position, the incumbent automatically became one of the five most powerful men in Africa, and that included heads of state.

The betting favoured Dr Steyner for a number of good reasons. He had a brain that had earned him the nickname of 'The Computer'; no one had yet been able to detect in him the slightest evidence of a human weakness, and more than this he had taken the trouble ten years previously to catch Hurry Hirschfeld's only granddaughter as she emerged from Cape Town University and marry her.

Dr Steyner was in a strong position, and Rod was intrigued with the prospect of meeting him.

The Maserati was registering 125 miles an hour as he went under the over-pass of the Kloof Gold Mining Company property.

'Johannesburg, here I come!' Rod laughed aloud.

It was ten minutes before eleven o'clock when Rod

found the brass plaque reading 'Dr M. K. Steyner' in a secluded lane of the lush Johannesburg suburb of Sandown. The house was not visible from the road, and Rod let the Maserati roll gently in through the tall white gates, with their imitation Cape Dutch gables.

The gates, he decided, were a display of shocking taste but the gardens beyond them were paradise. Rod knew rock, but flowers were his weak suit. He recognized the massed banks of red and yellow against the green lawns as cannas, but after that he had no names for the blazing beauty spread about him.

'Wow!' he muttered in awe. 'Someone has done a hell of a lot of work around here.'

Around a curve in the macadamized drive lay the house. It also was Cape Dutch and Rod forgave Dr Steyner his gates.

'Wow!' he said again, and involuntarily braked the Maserati to a standstill.

Cape Dutch is one of the most difficult styles to copy effectively, where one line in a hundred out of place could spoil the effect; this particular example worked perfectly. It gave the feel of timelessness, of solidarity, and mixed it subtly with a grace and finesse of line. He guessed that the shutters and beams were genuine yellow wood and the windows hand-leaded.

Rod looked at it, and felt envy prickle and burn within him. He loved fine things, like his Maserati, but this was another concept in material possessions. He was jealous of the man that owned it, knowing that his own entire year's income would not be sufficient for a down payment on the land alone.

'So I've got my flat,' he grinned ruefully, and coasted down to park in front of the line of garages.

It was not clear which was the correct entrance to use, and he chose at random from a number of paved paths that all led in the general direction of the house.

Around a bend in this path he came on another spectacle. Though smaller it had, if anything, a more profound effect on Rod than the house had. It was a feminine posterior of equal grace and finesse of line, clad in Helanka stretch ski-pants, and protruding from a large and exotic bush.

Rod was captivated. He stood and watched as the bush shook and rustled, and the bottom wriggled and heaved.

Suddenly, in ladylike tones there issued from the bush a most unladylike oath and the bottom shot backwards and its owner straightened up with her forefinger in her mouth, sucking noisily.

'It bit me!' she mumbled around the finger. 'Damned stinkbug bit me!'

'Well, you shouldn't tease them,' said Rod.

And she spun round to face him. The first thing Rod noticed were her eyes, they were enormous, completely out of proportion to the rest of her face.

'I wasn't—' she started, and then stopped. The finger came out of her mouth. Instinctively one hand went to her hair, and the other began straightening her blouse and brushing off bits of vegetation that were clinging to her.

'Who are you?' she asked, and those huge eyes swept over him. This was fairly standard reaction for any woman between the ages of sixteen and sixty viewing Rodney Ironsides for the first time, and Rodney accepted it gracefully.

'My name is Rodney Ironsides. I've an appointment to see Dr Steyner.'

'Oh.' She was hurriedly tucking her shirt-tails into her slacks. 'My husband will be in his study.'

He had known who she was. He had seen her photographs fifty times in the Group newspaper; but in them she was usually in full-length evening dress and diamonds, not in a blouse with a tear in one sleeve nor pig-tails that were coming down. In the pictures her make-up was immaculate, now she had none at all and her face was flushed and dewed with perspiration.

'I must look a mess. I've been gardening,' said Theresa Steyner unnecessarily.

'Did you do this garden yourself?'

'Only a very little of the muscle work, but I planned it,' she answered. She decided he was big and ugly – no, not really ugly, but battered-looking.

'It's beautiful,' said Rod.

'Thank you.' No, not battered-looking, she changed her mind, tough-looking, and the chest hair curled out of the V of his open neck shirt.

'This is a protea, isn't it?' He indicated the bush from which she had recently emerged. He was guessing.

'Nutans,' she said; he must be in his late thirties, there was greying at his temples.

'Oh, I thought it was a protea.'

'It is. "Nutans" is its proper name. There are over two hundred different varieties of proteas,' she answered seriously. His voice didn't fit his appearance at all, she decided. He looked like a prize fighter but spoke like a lawyer, probably was one. It was usually lawyers or business consultants who came calling on Manfred.

'Is that so? It's very pretty.' Rod touched one of the blooms.

'Yes, isn't it? I've got over fifty varieties growing here.'

And suddenly they were smiling at each other. 'I'll take you up to the house,' said Theresa Steyner.

'**M**r Ironsides is here, Manfred.'

'Thank you.' He sat at the stinkwood desk in a room that smelled of wax polish. He made no effort to rise from his seat.

'Would you like a cup of coffee?' Theresa asked from the doorway. 'Or tea?'

'No, thank you,' answered Manfred Steyner without consulting Rod who stood beside her.

'I'll leave you to it, then,' she said.

'Thank you, Theresa.' And she turned away. Rod went on standing where he was, he was studying this man of whom he had heard so much.

Manfred Steyner appeared younger than his forty-two years. His hair was light brown, almost blond, and brushed straight back. He wore spectacles with heavy black frames, and his face was smooth and silky-looking, soft as a girl's with no beard shadow on his chin. His hands that lay on the polished desk top were hairless, smooth, so that Rod wondered if he had used a depilatory on them.

'Come in,' he said, and Rod moved to the desk. Steyner wore a white silk shirt in which the ironing creases still showed, the cloth was snowy white and over it he wore a Royal Johannesburg Golf Club tie, with onyx cuff links. Suddenly Rod realized that neither shirt nor tie had ever been worn before; that much was true of what he had heard then. Steyner ordered his shirts hand-made by the gross and wore each once only.

'Sit down, Ironsides.' Steyner slurred his vowels slightly, just a trace of a Teutonic accent.

'Dr Steyner,' said Rod softly, 'you have a choice. You may call me Rodney or Mr Ironsides.'

There was no change in Steyner's voice nor expression.

'I would like to go over your background, please, Mr

Ironsides, as a preliminary to our discussion. You have no objection?'

'No, Dr Steyner.'

'You were born October 16th, 1931, at Butterworth in the Transkei. Your father was a native trader, your mother died January 1939. Your father was commissioned Captain in the Durban Light Infantry and died of wounds on the Po River in Italy during the winter of 1944. You were raised by your maternal uncle in East London. Matriculating from Queen's College, Grahamstown, in 1947, you were unsuccessful in obtaining a Chamber of Mines scholarship to Witwatersrand University for a B.Sc. (Mining Engineering) degree. You enrolled in the GMTS (Government Mining Training School) and obtained your blasting ticket during 1949. At which time you joined the Blyvooruitzicht Gold Mining Company Ltd as a learner miner.'

Dr Steyner stood up from his desk and crossing to the panelled wall he pressed a concealed switch and a portion of the panelling slid back to reveal a wash basin and towel rack. As he went on talking he began very meticulously to soap and wash his hands.

'In the same year you were promoted to miner and in 1952 to shift boss, 1954 to mine captain. You successfully completed the examination for the Mine Manager's ticket in 1959, and in 1962 you came to us as an Assistant Underground Manager, and in 1968 you achieved your present position as Underground Manager.'

Dr Steyner began drying his hands on a snowy white towel.

'You've memorized my company record pretty thoroughly,' Rod admitted.

Dr Steyner crumpled the towel and dropped it into a bin below the wash basin. He pressed the button and the panelling slid closed, then he came back to the desk stepping precisely over the glossy polished wooden floor,

26

and Rod realized that he was a small man, not more than five and a half feet tall, about the same height as his wife.

'This is something of an achievement,' Steyner went on. 'The next youngest Underground Manager in the entire Group is forty-six years of age, whereas you are not yet thirty-nine.'

Rod inclined his head in acknowledgement.

'Now,' said Dr Steyner as he reseated himself and laid his freshly washed hands on the desk top. 'I would like briefly to touch on your private life – you have no objections?'

Again Rod inclined his head.

'The reason that your application for the Chamber of Mines scholarship was refused, despite your straight A matriculation, was the recommendation of your headmaster to the selection board in effect that you were of unstable and violent disposition.'

'How the hell did you know that?' ejaculated Rod.

'I have access to the board's records. It seems that once you had received your matric you immediately assaulted your former headmaster.'

'I beat the hell out of the bastard,' Rod agreed happily.

'An expensive indulgence, Mr Ironsides. It cost you a university degree.'

And Rod was silent.

'To continue: In 1959 you married Patricia Anne Harvey. Of the union was born a girl child in the same year, to be precise, seven and a half months after the wedding.'

Rod squirmed slightly in his chair, and Dr Steyner went on quietly.

'This marriage terminated in divorce in 1964. Your wife is suing you on the grounds of adultery, and receiving custody of the child, alimony and maintenance in the sum of R450.000 monthly.'

27

'What's all this about?' demanded Rod.

'I am attempting to establish an accurate picture of your present circumstances. It is necessary, I assure you.' Dr Steyner removed his spectacles and began polishing the lens on a clean white handkerchief. There were the marks of the frames on the bridge of his nose.

'Go on, then.' Despite himself, Rod was fascinated to learn just how much Steyner knew about him.

'In 1968 there was a paternity suit brought against you by a Miss Diane Johnson and judgement for R150.00 per month.'

Rod blinked and was silent.

'I should mention two further actions against you for assault, both unsuccessful on the grounds of justification or self-defence.'

'Is that all?' asked Rod sarcastically.

'Almost,' admitted Dr Steyner. 'It is only necessary to note further recurrent expenditure in the form of a monthly payment of R150.00 on a continental sports car, and a further R100.00 per month rental on the premises 596 Glen Alpine Heights, Corner Lane, Hillbrow.'

Rod was furious, he had believed that no one in CRC knew about the flat.

'Damn you! You've been prying into my affairs!'

'Yes,' agreed Dr Steyner levelly. 'I am guilty, but in good cause. If you bear with me, you'll see why.'

Suddenly Dr Steyner stood up from the desk, crossed the room to the concealed wash basin, and again began to wash his hands. As he dried them, he spoke again.

'Your monthly commitments are R850. Your salary, after deduction of tax, is less than one thousand Rand. You have no mining degree, and the chances of your taking the next step upwards to General Manager without it are remote. You are at your ceiling, Mr Ironsides. On your own ability you can go no further. In thirty years' time you will not be the youngest Underground Manager in the CRC Group, but the oldest.' Dr Steyner paused. 'That is, provided that your rather expensive tastes have not landed you in a debtors' prison, and that neither the quickness and heat of your temper, nor the matching speed and temperature of your genitalia have gotten you into really serious trouble.'

Steyner dropped the towel in the bin and returned to his seat. They sat in absolute silence, regarding each other for a full minute.

'You got me all the way up here to tell me this?' asked Rod, his whole body tense, his voice slightly husky. It needed only an ounce more of provocation to launch him across the desk at Steyner's throat.

'No.' Steyner shook his head. 'I got you up here to tell you that I will use all my influence, which I flatter myself is considerable, to secure your appointment – and I mean immediate appointment – to the position of General Manager of the Sonder Ditch Gold Mining Company Ltd.'

Rod recoiled in his chair as though Steyner had spat in his face. He stared at him aghast.

'Why?' he asked at last. 'What do you want in exchange?'

'Neither your friendship, nor your gratitude,' Dr Steyner told him. 'But your unquestioning obedience to my instructions. You will be my man – completely.'

Rod went on staring at him while his mind raced. Without Steyner's intervention he would wait at the very least ten years for this promotion, if it ever came. He wanted it, my God, how he wanted it. The achievement, the increase in income, the power that went with the job. His own mine! His own mine at the age of thirty-eight – and an additional 10,000 rand per annum.

Yet Rod was not gullible enough to believe that Manfred Steyner's price would be cheap. When the instruction came that he was to follow with unquestioning obedience, he knew it would stink like a ten-day corpse. But once he had the job he could refuse the instruction. Get the job first, then decide once he received the instruction whether to follow it or not.

'I accept,' he said.

Manfred Steyner stood up from the desk.

'You will hear from me,' he said. 'Now you may go.'

– 9 –

Rod crossed the wide-flagged stoep without seeing or hearing; vaguely he wandered down across the lawns towards his car. His mind was harrying the recent conversation, tearing it to pieces like a pack of wild dogs on a carcass. He almost bumped into Theresa Steyner before he saw her, and abruptly his mind dropped the subject of the General Managership.

Theresa had changed her clothing, made up her face and eyes, and the pig-tails were concealed under a lime-coloured silk scarf, all this in the half hour since their last meeting. She was hovering over a flower bed with a flower basket on one arm, as bright and pleasing as a hummingbird.

Rod was amused and flattered, vain enough to realize that the change was in his honour, and connoisseur enough to appreciate the improvement.

'Hello.' She looked up, contriving successfully to look both surprised and artless. Her eyes were really enormous, and the make-up was designed to enhance their size.

'You are a busy little bee.' Rod ran a knowledgeable appraisal over the floral slack suit she wore, and saw the colour start in her cheeks as she felt his eyes.

'Did you have a successful meeting?'

'Very.'

'Are you a lawyer?'

'No. I work for your grandfather.'

'Doing what?'

'Mining his gold.'

'Which mine?'

'Sonder Ditch.'

'What's your position?'

'Well, if your husband is as good as his word, I'm the new General Manager.'

'You're too young,' she said.

'That's what I thought.'

'Pops will have something to say on the subject.'

'Pops?' he asked.

'My grandfather.' And Rod laughed before he could stop himself.

'What's so funny?'

'The Chairman of CRC being called "Pops".'

'I'm the only one who calls him that.'

'I bet you are.' Rod laughed again. 'In fact I'd bet you'd get away with a lot of things no one else would dare.'

Suddenly the underlying sexuality of his last remark occurred to them both and they fell silent. Theresa looked down and carefully snipped the head off a flower.

'I didn't mean it that way,' apologized Rod.

'What way, Mr Ironsides?' She looked up and enquired with mischievous innocence, and they laughed together with the awkwardness gone again.

She walked beside him to the car, making it seem a completely natural thing to do, and as he slipped behind the steering-wheel she remarked:

'Manfred and I will be coming out to the Sonder Ditch next week. Manfred is to present long service and bravery awards to some of your men.' She had already refused the invitation to accompany Manfred, she must now see to it that she was re-invited. 'I shall probably see you then.'

'I look forward to it,' said Rod, and let in the clutch.

Rod glanced in the rear view mirror. She was a remarkably provocative and attractive woman. A careless man could drown in those eyes.

'Dr Manfred Steyner has got himself a big fat problem there,' he decided. 'Our Manfred is probably so busy soaping and scrubbing his equipment, that he never gets round to using it.'

– 10 –

Through the leaded windows Dr Steyner caught a glimpse of the Maserati as it disappeared around the curve in the driveway, and he listened as the throb of the engine dwindled into silence.

He lifted the receiver of the telephone and wiped it with the white handkerchief before putting it to his ear. He dialled and while it rang he inspected the nails of his free hand minutely.

'Steyner,' he said into the mouthpiece. 'Yes – yes.' He listened.

'Yes . . . He has just left . . . Yes, it is arranged . . . No, there will be no difficulty there, I am sure.' As he spoke he was looking at the palm of his hand, he saw the tiny beads of perspiration appear on his skin and an expression of disgust tightened his lips.

'I am fully aware of the consequences. I tell you, I know.'

He closed his eyes and listened for another minute without moving as the receiver squawked and clacked, then he opened his eyes.

'It will be done in good time, I assure you. Goodbye.'

He hung up and went to wash his hands. Now, he thought, as he worked up lather, to get it past the old man.

11

He was old now, seventy-eight long hard years old. His hair and his eyebrows were creamy white. His skin was folded and creased, freckled and spotted, hanging in unexpected little pouches under his chin and eyes.

His body had dried out, so he stood gaunt and stooped like a tree that has taken a set before the prevailing winds; but there was still the underlying urgency in the way he held himself, the same urgency that had earned him the name of 'Hurry' Hirschfeld when first he bustled into the gold fields sixty years ago.

On this Monday morning he was standing before the full length windows of his penthouse office, looking down on the city of Johannesburg. Reef House stood shoulder to massive shoulder with the Schlesinger Building on the Braamfontein ridge above the city proper. From this height it seemed that Johannesburg cowered at Hurry Hirschfeld's feet, as well it should.

Long ago, even before the great depression of the 'thirties, he had ceased to measure his wealth in terms of money. He owned outright a little over a quarter of the issued share capital of Central Rand Consolidated. At the present market price of R120 per share, this was a staggering sum. In addition, through a complicated arrangement of trusts, proxy rights and interlocking directorates, he had control of a further massive block of twenty per cent of the company's voting rights.

The overhead intercom pinged softly into this room of soft fabrics and muted colours, and Hurry started slightly.

'Yes,' he said, without turning away from the window.

'Dr Steyner is here, Mr Hirschfeld,' his secretary's voice whispered, ghostly and disembodied into the luscious room.

'Send him in,' snapped Hurry. That goddamned intercom

always gave him the creeps. The whole goddamned room gave him the creeps. It was, as Hurry had said often and loudly, like a fairy brothel.

For fifty-five years he had worked in a bleak uncarpeted office with a few yellowing photographs of men and machinery on its walls. Then they had moved him in here – he glanced around the room with the distaste that five years had not lulled. What did they think he was, a bloody ladies' hairdresser?

The panelling door slid noiselessly aside and Dr Manfred Steyner stepped neatly into the room.

'Good morning, Grandfather,' he said. For ten years, even since Terry had been bird-brained enough to marry him, Manfred Steyner had called Hurry Hirschfeld that, and Hurry hated it. He remembered now that Manfred Steyner was also responsible for the design and decor of Reef House, and therefore the author of his recent irritation.

'Whatever it is you want – No!' he said, and he moved across to the air-conditioning controls. The thermostat was already set at 'high', now Hurry turned it to 'highest'. Within minutes the room would be at the correct temperature for growing orchids.

'How are you this morning, Grandfather?' Manfred seemed not to have heard, his expression was bland and neutral as he moved to the desk and laid out his papers.

'Bloody awful,' said Hurry. It was impossible to disconcert the little prig, he thought, you might as well shout insults at an efficiently functioning piece of machinery.

'I am sorry to hear that.' Manfred took out his handkerchief and touched his chin and forehead. 'I have the weekly reports.'

Hurry capitulated and went across to the desk. This was business. He sat down and read quickly. His questions were abrupt, cutting and instantly answered, but Manfred's handkerchief was busy now, swabbing and dabbing. Twice he removed his spectacles and wiped steam from the lenses.

'Can I turn the air-conditioning down a little, Grandfather?'

'You touch it and I'll kick your arse,' said Hurry without looking up.

Another five minutes and Manfred Steyner stood up suddenly.

'Excuse me, Grandfather.' And he shot across the office and disappeared into the adjoining bathroom suite. Hurry cocked his head to listen, and when he heard the taps hiss he grinned happily. The air-conditioning was the only method he had discovered of disconcerting Manfred Steyner, and for ten years he had been experimenting with various techniques.

'Don't use all the soap,' he shouted gleefully. 'You are the one always on about office expenses!'

It did not seem ludicrous to Hurry that one of the richest and most influential men in Africa should devote so much time and energy to baiting his personal assistant.

At eleven o'clock Manfred Steyner gathered his papers and began packing them carefully in his monogrammed pigskin briefcase.

'About the appointment of a new General Manager for the Sonder Ditch to replace Mr Lemmer. You will recall my memo regarding the appointment of younger men to key positions—'

'Never read the bloody thing,' lied Hurry Hirschfeld. They both knew he read everything, and remembered it.

'Well—' Manfred went on to enlarge his thesis for a minute, then ended, 'In view of this, my department, myself concurring entirely, urges the appointment of Rodney Barry Ironsides, the present Underground Manager, to the position. I hoped that you would initial the recommendation and we can put it through at Friday's meeting.'

35

Dexterously Manfred slid the yellow memo in front of Hurry Hirschfeld, unscrewed the cap of his pen and offered it to him. Hurry picked the memo up between thumb and forefinger as though it were someone's dirty handkerchief and dropped it into the waste-paper bin.

'Do you wish me to tell you in detail what you and your planning department can do?' he asked.

'Grandfather,' Manfred admonished him mildly, 'you cannot run the company as though you were a robber baron. You cannot ignore the team of highly trained men who are your advisers.'

'I've run it that way for fifty years. You show me who's going to change that.' Hurry leaned back in his chair with vast satisfaction and fished a powerful-looking cigar out of his inner pocket.

'Grandfather, that cigar! The doctor said—'

'And I said Fred Plummer gets the job as Manager of the Sonder Ditch.'

'He goes on pension next year,' protested Manfred Steyner.

'Yes,' Hurry nodded. 'But how does that alter the position?'

'He's an old dodderer,' Manfred tried again, there was a desperate edge to his voice. He had not anticipated one of the old man's whims cutting across his plans.

'He's twelve years younger than I am,' growled Hurry ominously. 'How's that make him an old dodderer?'

12

Now that the weekend was over, Rod found the apartment oppressive, and he longed to get out of it.

He shaved, standing naked before the mirror, and he caught a whiff of the reeking ashtrays and half-empty glasses in the lounge. The char would have her customary Monday-morning greeting when she came in later today. From Louis Botha Avenue the traffic noise was starting to build up and he glanced at his watch – six o'clock in the morning. A good time to examine your soul, he decided, and leaned forward to watch his own eyes in the mirror.

'You're too old for this type of living,' he told himself seriously. 'You've had four years of it now, four years since the divorce, and that's about enough. It would be nice now to go to bed with the same woman on two consecutive nights.'

He rinsed his razor, and turned on the taps in the shower cabinet.

'Might even be able to afford it, if our boy Manfred delivers the goods.' Rod had not allowed himself to believe too implicitly in Manfred Steyner's promise; but during the whole of these last two days the excitement had been there beneath the cynicism.

He stepped into the shower and soaped himself, then turned the cold tap full on. Gasping he shut it off and reached for his towel. Still drying himself, he went through and stood at the foot of the bed; as he towelled himself he examined the girl who lay among the tousled sheets.

She was tanned dark toffee brown so she appeared to be dressed in white transparent bra and panties where the skin was untouched by the sun. Her hair was a blonde-gold flurry across her face and the pillow, at odds with the jet black triangle of body hair. Her lips in sleep were fixed in a soft pink pout, and she looked disquietingly young. Rod had to make a conscious effort to remember her name, she was not the companion with whom he had begun the weekend.

'Lucille,' he said, sitting down beside her. 'Wake up. Time to roll.'

She opened her eyes.

'Good morning,' he said and kissed her gently.

'Mmm.' She blinked. 'What time is it? I don't want to get fired.'

'Six,' he told her.

'Oh, good. Plenty of time.' And she rolled over and snuggled down into the sheets.

'Like hell.' He slapped her bottom lightly. 'Move, girl, can you cook?'

'No—' She lifted her head. 'What's your name again?' she asked.

'Rod,' he told her.

'That's right – Piston Rod,' she giggled. 'What a way to die! Are you sure you aren't powered by steam?'

'How old are you?' he asked.

'Nineteen. How old are you?'

'Thirty-eight.'

'Daddy, you're vintage!' she told him vehemently.

'Yes, sometimes I feel that way.' He stood up. 'Let's go.'

'You go. I'll lock up when I leave.'

'No sale,' he said, the last one he had left in the flat had cleaned it out – groceries, liquor, glasses, towels, even the ashtrays. 'Five minutes to dress.'

Fortunately she lived on his way. She directed him to a run-down block of flats under the mine dumps at Booysens.

'I'm putting three blind sisters through school. You want to help?' she asked as he parked the Maserati.

'Sure.' He eased a five-rand note out of his wallet and handed it to her.

'Ta muchly.' And she slipped out of the red leather seat, closed the door and walked away. She did not look back

38

before she disappeared into the block, and Rod felt an unaccountable wave of loneliness wash over him. It was so intense that he sat quiescent for a full minute before he could throw it off, then he hit the gears and screeched away from the kerb.

'My little five-rand friend,' he said. 'She really cares!'

He drove fast, so that as he topped the Kraalkop ridge the shadows were still long, and the dew lay silver on the grass. He pulled the Maserati into a layby and climbed out. Leaning against the bonnet he lit a cigarette, grimacing at the taste, and looked down at the valley.

There was no natural surface indication of the immense treasure house that lay below. It was like any of the other countless grassy plains of the Transvaal. In the centre stood the town of Kitchenerville, which for half a century had rejoiced in the fact that Lord Kitchener had camped one night here in pursuit of the wily Boer: a collection of three dozen buildings which had expanded miraculously into three thousand, around a magnificent town hall and shopping complex. Dressed in public lawns and gardens, wide streets and bright new houses, all of it paid for by the mining houses whose lease areas converged on the town.

Out of the bleak veld surrounding the town their headgears stood like colossal monuments to the gold hunger of man. Around the headgears clustered the plants and workshops. There were fourteen headgears in the valley. The field was divided into five lease areas, following the original farm titles, and was mined by five separate companies. Thornfontein Gold Mining, Blaauberg Gold Mining, West Tweefontein Mining, Deep Gold Levels, and the Sonder Ditch Gold Mining Company.

It was to this last that Rod naturally directed his attention.

'You beauty,' he whispered, for in his eyes the mountainous dumps of blue rock beside the shafts were truly beautiful. The complex but carefully thought out pattern of the works

39

buildings, even the sulphur-yellow acres of the slimes dam, had a functional beauty.

'Get it for me, Manfred,' he spoke aloud. 'I want it. I want it badly.'

On the twenty-eight square miles of the Sonder Ditch's property lived 14,000 human beings, 12,000 of them were Bantu who had been recruited from all over Southern Africa. They lived in the multi-storied hostels near the shaft heads, and each day they went down through two small holes in the ground to depths that were scarcely credible, and came up again out of those same two holes. 12,000 men down, 12,000 up. That was not all: out of those two same holes came 10,000 tons of rock daily, and down them went timber and tools and piping and explosive, ton upon ton of material and equipment. It was an undertaking that must evoke pride in the men who accomplished it.

Rod glanced at his watch, 7.35 a.m. They were down already, all 12,000 of them. They had started going down at three-thirty that morning and now it was accomplished. The shift was in. The Sonder Ditch was breaking rock, and bringing the stuff out.

Rod grinned happily. His loneliness and depression of an hour ago were gone, swallowed up in the immensity of his involvement. He watched the massive wheels of the headgears spinning, stopping briefly, and then spinning again.

Each of those shafts had cost fifty million rand, the surface plant and works another fifty million. The Sonder Ditch represented an investment of 150 million rand, 220 million dollars. It was big, and it would be his.

Rod flicked away the butt of his cigarette. As he drove down the ridge, his eyes moved eastward down the valley. All mining activity ceased abruptly along an imaginary north-south line, drawn arbitarily across the open grassland.

There was no surface indication why this should be so, but the reason was deep down.

On that line ran a geological freak, a dyke, a wall of hard serpentine rock that had been named 'the Big Dipper'. It cut through the field like an axe stroke, and beyond it was bad ground. The gold reef existed in the bad ground, they knew this; but not one of the five companies had gone after it. They had prospected it tentatively and then shied away from it, for the boreholes that they sank were frightening in their inconsistency.

A big percentage of the Sonder Ditch lease area lay on the far side of the Dipper, and there was a diamond-drilling team working there now. They had already completed five holes.

Rod could remember accurately the results:-

Borehole SD No. 1.	Abandoned in water at 4,000 ft.
SD No. 2.	Abandoned in dry hole at 5,250 ft.
SD No. 3.	Intersected carbon leader reef at 6,600 ft.
Assay valve	27,323-inch penny-weights.
First deflection	6,212-inch penny-weights.
Second deflection	2,114-inch penny-weights.
SD No. 4.	Abandoned in artesian water at 3,500 ft.
SD No. 5.	Intersected carbon leader at 8,116 ft.
Assay valve	562-inch penny-weights.

And they were drilling the deflections on that one now.

The problem was to build up a picture from results like that. It looked like a mess of faulted and waterlogged ground with the gold reef fragmented and fluky, showing unbelievably high values at one spot, and then more than likely pinching out fifty feet away.

They may mine it one day, thought Rod, but I hope to hell I'm on pension by the time they do.

In the distance beyond the slimes dam he could just make out the spidery triangle of the drilling rig against the grown grass.

'Go to it, boys,' he muttered. 'Whatever you find there won't make much difference to me.'

And he went in through the imposing gates at the entrance to the mine property, halting carefully at the stop sign where the railway line crossed the road and he forked two fingers at the traffic policeman lurking behind the gates.

The traffic cop grinned and waved; he had caught Rod the previous week, so he was still one up.

Rod drove down to his office.

– 13 –

That Monday morning Allen 'Popeye' Worth was preparing to drill his first deflection on the SD No. 5. borehole. Allen was a Texan – not a typical Texan. He stood five feet four inches tall, but was as tough as the steel drill with which he worked. Thirty years before he had started learning his trade on the oilfields around Odessa and he had learned it well.

Now he could start at the surface and drill a four-inch hole down 13,000 feet through the earth's crust, keeping the hole straight all the way, an almost impossible task if you took into account the whippiness and torque in a jointed rod of steel that long.

If, as happened occasionally, the steel snapped and broke off thousands of feet down, Allen could fit a fishing tool on the end of his rig, and patiently grope for the stump, find it, grapple it and pull it out of the borehole. When he hit the reef down there, he could purposely kick his drill off the line and pierce the reef again and again to sample it over an area of hundreds of feet. This was what was meant by deflecting.

Allen was one of the best. He could command his own salary and behave like a prima donna, and his bosses would still fawn on him, for the things he could do with a diamond drill were almost magical.

Now he was assessing the angle of his first deflection. The previous day he had lowered a long brass bottle to the end of his borehole and left it overnight. The bottle was half filled with concentrated sulphuric acid, and it had etched the brass of the bottle. By measuring the angle of the etching he knew just how his drill was branching off from his original hole.

In the tiny wood and iron building beside the drilling rig he finished his measurements and stood back from the work bench, grunting with satisfaction.

From his hip pocket he drew a corncob pipe and pouch. Once he had stuffed tobacco into the pipe and lit it, it became very clear as to why his nickname was 'Popeye'. He was a dead ringer for the cartoon character, aggressive jaw, button eyes, battered maritime cap and all.

He puffed contentedly, watching through the single window of the shack as his gang went about the tedious business of lowering the drilling bit down into the earth. Then he took the pipe from his mouth and spat accurately through the window, replaced the pipe and stooped to minutely check his measurements.

His foreman driller interrupted him from the doorway.

'On bottom, and ready to turn, boss.'

'Huh!' Popeye checked his watch. 'Two hours forty to get down, you don't reckon to rupture a gut do you?'

'That's not bad,' protested the foreman.

'And it sure as hell isn't good either! Okay, okay, cut the cackle and let's get her turning.' He bounced out of the

43

shed and set off for the rig, darting quick beady little glances about him. The rig was a fifty-foot-high tower of steel girders and within it the drill rod hung down until it disappeared into the collar. The twin 200-horsepower diesel engines throbbed expectantly, waiting to provide the power, their exhausts smoking blue in the early morning sunlight. Beside the rig lay a mountainous heap of drilling rods, beyond them the 10,000-gallon puddling reservoir to provide water for the hole. Water was pumped into the hole continuously to cool and lubricate the tool as it cut into the rock.

'Stand by to turn her,' Popeye called to his gang, and they moved to their stations. Dressed in blue overalls, coloured fibreglass helmets, and leather gloves, they stood ready and tensed. This was an anxious moment for the whole team: power had to be applied with a lover's touch to the mile and a half length of rod, or it would buckle and snap.

Popeye climbed nimbly up onto the collar, and glanced about him to make sure all was in readiness. The foreman driller was at the controls, watching Popeye with complete absorption, his hands resting on the levers.

'Power up!' shouted Popeye and made the circular motion with his right hand. The diesels bellowed harshly, and Popeye reached out to lay his left hand on the drilling rod. This was how he did it, feeling the rod with his bare hand as he brought in the power, judging the tension by ear and eye and touch.

His right hand gestured and the foreman delicately let in the clutch, the rod moved under Popeye's hand, he gestured again and it revolved slowly. He could feel it was near breaking point and he cut down the power instantly, then let it in again. His right hand moved eloquently, expressively as an orchestral conductor, and the foreman followed it, the junior member of a highly skilled team.

Slowly the tension of the gang relaxed as the revolutions

of the drill built up steadily, until Popeye gave the clenched fist 'okay' and jumped down from the collar. They scattered casually to their other duties, while Popeye and the foreman strolled back to the shed, leaving the drill to grind away at a steady four hundred revolutions a minute.

'Got something for you,' said the foreman, as they entered the shed.

'What?' demanded Popeye.

'The latest *Playboy*.'

'You're kidding!' Popeye accused him delightedly, but the foreman fished the rolled magazine out of his lunch box.

'Hey, there!' Popeye snatched it from him and turned immediately to the coloured foldout.

'Isn't that something!' He whistled. 'This dolly could get a job in a stockyard beating the oxen to death with her boo-boos!'

The foreman joined the discussion of the young lady's anatomy, and so neither of them noticed the change in the sound of the drill until two minutes had passed. Then Popeye heard it through an erotic haze. He flung the magazine from him, and went through the door of the shed white-faced.

It was fifty yards from the shed to the rig, but even at that distance Popeye could see the vibration in the drilling rod. He could hear the labouring note of the diesels as they carried increased load, and he ran like a fox terrier, trying to reach the controls and shut off the engines before it happened.

He knew what it was. His drill had cut into one of the many fissures with which this badly faulted ground was criss-crossed. The puddling water from his borehole had drained away leaving the bit to run dry against dry rock. The friction head had built up, the dust from the cut was not being washed away – and in consequence the rod had jammed. It was being held tightly at one end while at the

45

other the two big diesels were straining to turn it. The whole rig was seconds away from a twist-off.

There should have been an operator at the controls to meet just such an emergency, but he was a hundred yards away, just emerging from the wood and iron latrine beyond the puddling dam. He was desperately trying to hoist his pants, clinch the buckle of his belt and run all at the same time.

'You whore's chamberpot!' roared Popeye, as he ran. 'What the hell you goofing off—'

The words choked off in his throat, for as he reached the door of the engine room there was a report like a cannon shot as the rod snapped, and immediately the diesels screamed into over-rev as they were relieved of the load. Just too late, Popeye punched the earth buttons on the magnetos, and the engines spluttered into silence.

In that silence Popeye was sobbing with exertion and frustration and anger.

'A twist-off,' he sobbed. 'A deep one. Oh no! God, no!' It might take two weeks to fish out the broken rod, pump cement into the fissure to seal it, and then start again.

He removed the cap from his head, and with all his strength hurled it on the engine room floor. He then proceeded to jump on it with both feet. This was standard procedure. Popeye jumped on his cap at least once a week, and the foreman knew that when he had finished doing that he would then assault anybody within range.

Quietly the foreman slipped behind the wheel of the Ford truck, and the rest of the gang scrambled aboard. They all bumped away down the rutted track. There was a roadhouse on the main road where they went for coffee at times like this. When the mists of rage had dispersed sufficiently from his mind for Popeye to start seeking a human sacrifice, he looked about to find the drilling area strangely still and deserted.

'Stupid bunch of yellow-bellied baboons!' he bellowed in

frustration after the retreating truck, and, as the next best thing, went into the shed to phone his Managing Director.

This gentleman sitting in the air-conditioned offices of 'Hart Drilling and Cementation' high above Rissik Street in Johannesburg was a little taken aback to learn from Popeye Worth that he, the Managing Director, was directly responsible for the twist-off of an expensive diamond drill at the Sonder Ditch No. 5 hole.

'If you used that sack of custard that passes for a brain, you'd fight shy of trying to sink holes into this bunch of knitting,' Popeye yelled into the mouthpiece. 'I'd prefer to stick my old man into a meat grinder than put a drill into this ground. It stinks, I tell you! It's really ugly down there. God help the poor son of a bitch who tries to mine it!'

He slammed down the phone and stuffed his pipe with trembling fingers. Ten minutes later his breathing had returned to normal and his hands were steady. He picked up the phone again and dialled the number of the road-house. The proprietor answered.

'José, tell my boys it's okay, they can come home now,' said Popeye.

– 14 –

For Rod Ironsides there was more excitement than usual in meeting and solving the dozen paper problems that lay on his desk to welcome him back to the office. As he worked he kept remembering that Manfred Steyner might be able to do it, might just be able to do it.

The Sonder Ditch might really belong to him soon. He dispatched the last problem and lay back in his swivel chair. His mind was clear of the last cobwebs of dissipation and, as always, he felt purged and cleansed.

If I get her, I'll make her the star performer in the whole field, he thought greedily, they'll talk about the Sonder

Ditch from Wall Street to the Bourse, and about the man who is running her. I know how to do it too. I'll cut the costs to the bone, I'll tighten her up solid. Frank Lemmer was a good man, he could get the stuff out of the ground, but he let it creep up on him. It cost him almost nine rand a ton to mill it.

Well, I'll get it out as well as he did *and* I'll get it out cheaper. An operation takes its temperament from the man at the head. Frank Lemmer would talk about costs every now and then, but he didn't mean it and we knew he didn't mean it. We have become a wasteful operation because we are on a rich reef, we have become big spenders. Well, I'm going to talk costs, and I'll skin the arse of anybody who thinks I'm joking.

Last year Hamilton at Western Holdings kept his working costs per ton milled down to just a touch over six rand. I could do the same here! I could jump our profits twelve million Rand in one year, if only they give me the job I'll shout the Sonder Ditch's name across the financial markets of the world.

The problem that Rod was pondering was the nightmare of the gold mining industry. Since the 1930s the price of gold had been fixed at $35 a fine ounce. Each year since then the cost of mining had crept up steadily. In those days they reckoned four penny-weights of gold in a ton of ore was payable value. Now around eight penny-weights was the marginal value.

So in the interim all those millions of tons of ore whose values fell between four and eight penny-weights had been placed beyond the reach of man until such time as they increased the price of gold.

There were many mines with vast reserves of goldbearing ore, millions in bullion, whose values lay just below the magical number eight. Those mines stood deserted and forlorn, rust reddening their headgears, and the corrugated iron roofs of the buildings collapsing wearily. Rising costs had shot the guts out of them, they were condemned by the single word 'UNPAY'.

The Sonder Ditch was running twenty to twenty-five penny-weights per ton. She was fat, but she could be fatter, Rod decided.

There was a knock at the door.

'Come in!' called Rod, and looked at his watch. It was nine o'clock already. Time for the Monday meeting of his mine captains.

They came in singly and in pairs, twelve of them. These were Rod's front-line men, his combat officers. They went down there each day, each to his own section, and directed the actual assault on the rock.

While they chatted idly, waiting for the meeting to begin, Rod looked them over surreptitiously and was reminded of a remark that Herman Koch of Anglo American had made to him once.

'Mining is a hard game, and it attracts a hard breed of men.'

These were men of the hard breed, physically and mentally tough, and Rod realized with a start that he was one of them. No, more than one of them. He was their leader, and with a fierce affection and pride he opened the meeting.

'Right, let's hear your gripes. Who is going to be first to break my heart?'

There are some men with a talent for controlling, and getting the very best results out of other men. Rod was one of them. It was more than his physical size, his compelling voice and hearty chuckle. It was a special magnetism, a personal charm and unerring sense of timing. Under his chairmanship the meeting would erupt, voices crackle and snap, then subside into chuckles and nods as Rod spoke.

They knew he was as tough as they were, and they respected that. They knew that when he spoke it made sense, so they listened. They knew that when he promised, he delivered, so they were placated. And they knew that when he made a decision or judgement, he acted upon it, so every man knew exactly where he stood.

If asked, any one of these mine captains would have admitted grudgingly that 'there was no bulldust in Ironsides'. This was the equivalent of a presidential citation.

'Very well then.' Rod terminated the meeting. 'You have spent a good two hours of the company's time beating your gums. Now, will you kindly haul arse, go down there and start sending the stuff out.'

– 15 –

As these men planned the week's operation, so their men were at work in the earth below them.

On 87 level, Kowalski moved like a great bear down the dimly-lit drive. He had switched off the lamp on his helmet, and he moved without sound, lightly for a man of such bulk. He heard their voices ahead of him in the dimly-lit tunnel, and he paused, listening intently. There was no sound of shovel crunching into loose rock, and Kowalski's Neanderthal features convulsed into a fearsome scowl.

'Bastards!' he muttered softly. 'They think I am in stopes, hey? They think it all right if they sit on fat black bum, no move da bloody rock, hey?'

He started forward again, a bear on cat's feet.

'They find plenty different from what they bloody think, soon!' he threatened.

He stepped round the angle of the drive and flashed his lamp. There were three men Kowalski had put on lashing, shovelling the loose stuff from the footwall into waiting cocopans. Two of them sat against the cocopan, smoking contentedly while the third regaled them with an account of a beer drink he had attended the previous Christmas.

Their shovels and sledge hammers leaned unemployed against the side wall of the drive.

All three of them froze into rigidity as the beam of Kowalski's lamp played over them.

'So!' The word burst explosively from Kowalski, and he snatched up a fourteen-pound hammer in one massive fist, reversed it and struck the butt of the handle against the foot wall. The steel head of the hammer fell off and Kowalski was left with a four-foot length of selected hickory in his hand.

'You, boss boy!' he bellowed, and his free hand shot out and fastened on the throat of the nearest Bantu. With one heave he jerked him off his feet onto his knees and began dragging him away up the drive. Even in his rage, Kowalski was making sure there were no witnesses. The other two men sat where they were, too horrified to move, while their companion's wails and cries receded into the darkness.

Then the first blow reverberated in the confined space of the drive, followed immediately by a shriek of pain.

The next blow, and another shriek.

The crack, thud, crack, thud, went on repeatedly, but the accompanying shrieks dwindled into moans and soft whimperings, then into complete silence.

Kowalski came back down the drive alone, he was sweating heavily in the lamp light, and the handle of the hammer in his hand was black and glistening with wet blood.

He threw it at their feet.

'Work!' he growled, and was gone, big and bearlike, into the shadows.

16

On 100 level, Joseph M'Kati was hosing down and sweeping the spillings from under the giant conveyor belt. Joseph had been on this job for five years, and he was a contented and happy man.

Joseph was a Shangaan approaching sixty years of age; the first frost was touching his hair. There were laughter lines around his eyes and at the corner of his mouth. He wore his helmet pushed to the back of his head, his overalls were hand-embroidered and ornamentally patched in blue and red, and he moved with a jaunty bounce and strut.

The conveyor was many hundreds of yards long. From all the levels above the shattered gold reef was scraped from the stopes and trammed back down the haulages in the cocopans. Then from the cocopans it was tipped into the mouths of the ore-passes. These were vertical shafts that dropped down to 100 level, hundreds of feet through living rock to spew the reef out onto the conveyor belt. A system of steel doors regulated the flow of rock onto the conveyor, and the moving belt carried it down to the shaft and dumped it into enormous storage bins. From there it was fed automatically into the ore cage in fifteen-ton loads and carried at four-minute intervals to the surface.

Joseph worked on happily beneath the whining conveyor. The spillings were small, but important. Gold is strange in its behaviour, it moves downwards. Carried by its own high specific gravity it works its way down through almost any other material. It would find any crack or irregularity in the floor and work its way into it. It would disappear into the solid earth itself if left long enough.

It was this behaviour of gold that accounted in some measure for Joseph M'Kati's contentment. He had worked his way to the end of the conveyor, washing and sweeping, and now he straightened, laid his bast broom aside and rubbed his kidneys with both hands, looking quickly around to make certain that there was no one else in the conveyor tunnel. Beside him was the ore storage bin into which the conveyor was emptying its load. The bin could hold many thousands of tons.

Satisfied that he was alone, Joseph dropped onto his hands and knees and crawled under the storage bin, ignoring the continuous roar of rock into the bin above him, working his way in until he reached the holes.

It had taken Joseph many months to chisel the heads off four of the rivets that held the seam in the bottom of the bin, but once he had done it, he had succeeded in constructing a simple but highly effective heavy media separator.

Free gold in the ore that was dumped into the storage bin immediately and rapidly worked its way down through the underlying rock, its journey accelerated by the vibration of the conveyor and bin as more reef was dropped. When the gold reached the floor of the bin, it sought an avenue through which to continue its downward journey, and it found Joseph's four rivet holes, beneath which he had spread a square of polythene sheet.

The gold-rich fines made four conical piles on the sheet of polythene, looking exactly like powdered black soot.

Crouched beneath the bin, Joseph carefully transferred the black powder to his tobacco pouch, replaced the polythene to catch the next filtering, stuffed the pouch into his hip pocket, and scrambled out from under the bin. Whistling a tribal planting tune Joseph picked up his broom and returned to the endless job of sweeping and hosing.

17

Johnny Delange was marking his shot holes. Lying on his side in the low stope of 27 section he was calculating by eye the angle and depth of a side cutter blast to straighten a slight bulge in his longwall.

In the Sonder Ditch they were on single blast. One daily, centrally fired, blast. Johnny was paid on *fathomage*, the cubic measure of rock broken and taken out of his stope. He must, therefore, position his shot holes to achieve the maximum disruption and blow-out from the face.

'So,' he grunted, and marked the position of the hole in red paint. 'And so.' With one bold stroke of the paint brush he set the angle on which his machine boy was to drill.

'Shaya, madoda!' Johnny clapped the shoulder of the black man beside him. 'Hit it, man.'

Machine boys were selected for stamina and physique; this one was a Greek sculpture in glistening ebony.

'Nkosi!' The machine boy grinned an acknowledgement, and with his assistant lugged his rock drill into position. The drill looked like a gargantuan version of a heavy-calibre machine gun.

The noise as the big Bantu opened the drill was shattering in the low-roofed, constricted space of the stope. The compressed air roared and fluttered into the drill, buffeting the eardrums. Johnny made the clenched-fist gesture of approval, and for a second they smiled at each other in the companionship of shared labour. Then Johnny crawled on up the stope to mark the next shot hole.

Johnny Delange was twenty-seven years old, and he was top rock breaker on the Sonder Ditch. His gang of forty-eight men were a tightly-knit team of specialists. Men fought each other for a place on 27 section, for that's where the money was. Johnny could pick and choose, so each month when the surveyors came in and measured up, Johnny Delange was way out ahead in fathomage.

Here was the remarkable position where the man at the lowest point of authority earned more than the man at the top. Johnny Delange earned more than the General Manager of the Sonder Ditch. Last year he had paid super-tax on an income of R22,000. Even a miner like Kowalski, who brutalized and bullied his gang until he was left with the dregs of the mine, would earn eight or nine thousand rand a year, about the same salary as an official of Rod Ironsides' rank.

Johnny reached the top of his longwall and painted in the last shot holes. Down the inclined floor of the stope below him all his drills were roaring, his machine boys lying or crouching behind them. He lay there on one elbow, removed his helmet and wiped his face, resting a moment.

Johnny was an extraordinary-looking young man. His long jet black hair was swept back and tied with a leather thong at the back of his head in a curlicue. His features were those of an American Indian, gaunt and bony. He had cut the sleeves out of his overalls to expose his arms – arms as muscular and sinuous as pythons, tattooed below the elbows, immensely powerful but supple. His body was the same, long and sinewy and powerful.

On his right hand he wore eight rings, two on each finger, and it was clear from the design of the rings that they were not merely ornamental. They were heavy gold rings with skull and cross-bones, wolves' heads and other irregularities worked into them, a mass of metal that formed a permanent knuckleduster. Of the big eyes in the one skull's head Rod Ironsides had once asked: 'Are those real rubies, Johnny?' And Johnny had replied seriously:

'If they aren't, then I've sure as hell been gypped out of three rand fifty, Mr Ironsides.'

Johnny Delange had been a really wild youngster, until

eight months ago. It was then he had met and married Hettie. Courtship and marriage occupying the space of one week. Now he was settling down very well. It was all of ten days since he had last fought anybody.

Lying in the stope he allowed himself five minutes to think about Hettie. She was almost as tall as he was, with a wondrously buxom body and chestnut red hair. Johnny adored her. He was not the best speech-maker in Kitchenerville when it came to expressing his affection, so he bought her things.

He bought her dresses and jewellery, he bought her a deep-freezer *and* a fifteen cubic foot Frigidaire, he bought her a Chrysler Monaco with leopard-skin upholstery and a Kenwood Chef. In fact, it was becoming difficult to enter the Delange household without tripping over at least one of Johnny's gifts to Hettie. The congestion was made more acute by the fact that living with them was Johnny's brother, Davy.

'Hell, man!' Happily Johnny shook his head. 'She's a bit of all-right, hey!'

There was an eye-level oven he had spotted in a furniture store in Kitchenerville the previous Saturday.

'She'll love that, man,' he muttered, 'and it's only four hundred rand. I'll get it for her on pay day.'

The decision made, he clapped his helmet onto his head and began crawling out of the stope. It was time now to go up to the station and collect the explosives for the day's blast.

His boss boy should have been waiting for him in the drive, and Johnny was furious to find no sign of him nor the piccaninny who was his assistant.

'Bastard!' he grunted, playing the beam of his lamp up and down the drive. 'He's been acting up like hell.'

The boss boy was a pock-marked Swazi, not a big man, but powerful for his size and highly intelligent. He was also a man of mean disposition; Johnny had never seen him smile, and for an extrovert like Johnny it was galling to work with someone so sullen and taciturn. He tolerated the Swazi because of his drive and reliability, but he was the only man in the gang that Johnny disliked.

'Bastard!' The drive was deserted, the roar of the rock drills was muted.

'Where the hell is he?' Johnny scowled impatiently. 'I'll skin him when I find him.'

Then he remembered the latrine.

'That's where he is!' Johnny set off down the drive. The latrine was a rock chamber cut into the side of the drive. A flap of canvas served as a door; beyond was a regular four-holer over sanitary buckets.

Johnny pulled the canvas aside and stepped into the cubicle. The boss boy and his assistant were there. Johnny stared in surprise, for a moment not understanding what they were doing. They were so absorbed they were unaware of Johnny's presence.

Suddenly realization dawned, and Johnny's face tightened with revulsion and disgust.

'You filthy—' Johnny snarled, and catching the boss boy by the shoulders pulled him backwards and pinned him against the wall. He lifted his heavily metalled fist and drew it back ready to hurl it into the boss boy's face.

'Strike me and you know what happens,' said the boss boy softly, his expression flat and neutral, looking steadily into Johnny's eyes. Johnny hesitated. He knew the Company rules, he knew the Government labour officers' attitude, he knew what the police would do. If he hit him, they would crucify him.

'You are a pig!' Johnny hissed at him.

'You have a wife,' said the boss boy. 'My wife is in Swaziland. Two years I have not seen her.'

Johnny lowered his fist. Twelve thousand men, and no women. It was a fact. The actuality sickened him, but he understood why it happened.

'Get dressed.' He stepped back, releasing the boss boy. 'Get dressed both of you. Come to the station. I will meet you there.'

– 18 –

For a week now, since the fall of hanging in 43 section, Big King had been out of the stopes.

Rod had ordered it that way. The excuse was that Big King's white miner had been killed in the fall and now he must await an allocation to another section. In reality Rod wanted to rest him. He had seen the strain both physical and emotional that Big King had undergone during the rescue. When together they had unearthed the miner's corpse, the man with whom Big King had worked and laughed, Rod had seen the tears roll unashamedly down Big King's cheeks as he picked up the body and held it easily against his chest.

'Hamba gahle, madoda,' Big King had muttered. 'Go in peace, man.'

Big King was a legend on the Sonder Ditch. They boasted about him; how much Bantu beer he could drink in a sitting, how much rock he could lash single-handed in a shift, how he could dance any other man off his feet. He had been awarded a total of over a thousand rand in bravery awards. Big King set the pace, others tried to equal him.

Rod had put him in charge of a transport team. For the first few days Big King had enjoyed the opportunity of showing off his strength and socializing, for the transport team moved about the workings allowing Big King to visit most of his numerous friends during a shift. But now Big King was becoming bored. He wanted to get back into the stopes.

'This,' he told his transport team contemptuously, 'is

work for old men and young women.' And with one snatch and lift he picked up a forty-four-gallon drum of dieseline and unaided placed it on the platform of the loco.

A forty-four-gallon drum of dieseline weighs a little over 800 lbs avoirdupois.

– 19 –

All this fuss for that. Davy Delange paused in his labour of tamping the Dynagel into the shot holes. He leaned forward to inspect the reef. In the face of the stope it was a black line, drawn against the blue quartz rock.

The carbon leader reef, it was called. A thin layer of carbon, never more than a few inches thick, more often half an inch. Black soot, that's what it was. Davy shook his head thoughtfully. You could not even see the gold in it.

Davy was two years older than his brother Johnny, and there was no physical or mental resemblance between the two of them. Davy's sandy hair was cropped into a conventional 'short back and sides'. He wore no personal jewellery, and his manner was quiet and reserved.

Johnny was tall and lean, Davy squat and muscular. Johnny was extravagant, Davy careful beyond the point of meanness. Their only common trait was that they were both first-class miners. If Johnny broke more rock than Davy, it was only because Davy was more careful than Johnny; he did not take the same chances, he observed all the safety procedures which Johnny frequently flouted.

Davy earned less money than Johnny, but saved every penny he could. It was for his farm. Davy was going to buy a farm one day. Already he had saved a little over R49,000 towards it. In five more years he would have enough. Then he could get himself a farm and a wife to help run it. Johnny, on the other hand, spent every penny he earned. He was usually in debt to Davy by the end of each month.

'Lend us a hundred till pay day, Davy.' Disapprovingly, Davy lent him the money. Davy disapproved of Johnny, his appearance, attire and habits.

Abandoning his microscopic inspection of the carbon leader reef, Davy resumed tamping in the explosive, working carefully and precisely on this highly dangerous procedure. The sticks of explosive were charged with detonators and ready to burn. By law, nobody but the miner-in-charge could perform this operation, but Davy did it automatically while he thought about Johnny's latest trespass. He had raised Davy's rent.

'A hundred rand a month!' Davy protested aloud. 'I've got a good mind to move out and find my own digs.'

But he knew he would do no such thing. Hettie's cooking was too good, and her presence too feminine and alluring. Davy would stay on with them.

– 20 –

'Rod.' Dan Stander's voice was serious and low. 'I've got a nasty one for you.'

'Thanks for nothing.' Rod made his own voice weary and resigned as he spoke into the telephone. 'I'm just going on my underground tour. Can't it wait?'

'No,' Dan assured him. 'Anyway, it's on your way. I'm speaking from the first-aid station at the shaft head. Come across.'

'What is it?'

'Assault. White on Bantu.'

'Christ.' Rod jerked upright in his chair. 'Bad?'

'Ugly. Worked him over with the handle of a fourteen-pound hammer. I've put in forty-seven stitches, but I am worried about a fracture of the skull.'

'Who did it?'

'Miner by the name of Kowalski.'

'Him!' Rod was breathing heavily. 'All right, Dan. Can he make a statement?'

'No. Not for a day or two.'

'I'll be there in a few minutes.'

Rod hung up the phone and crossed the office.

'Dimitri.'

'Boss?'

'Pull Kowalski out of the stopes. I want him in my office soonest. Put someone in to finish his shift.'

'Okay, Rod, what's the trouble?'

'He beat up one of his boys.'

Dimitri whistled softly, and Rod went on.

'Call personnel, get them onto the police.'

'Okay, Rod.'

'Have Kowalski here when I get back from my tour.'

Dan was waiting for him in the first-aid room.

'Take a look.' He indicated the figure on the stretcher. Rod knelt beside him, his mouth tightening into a thin pale line.

The catgut stitches lay neatly across the dark swollen gashes in the man's flesh. One ear had been torn off, and Dan had sewn it back on. There was a black gap where teeth had been behind the swollen purple lips.

'You will be all right now.' Rod spoke gently, and the Bantu's eyes swivelled towards him. 'The man who did this will be punished.'

Rod stood up. 'Let me have a written report on his injuries, Dan.'

'I'll fix it. See you for a drink at the Club after work?'

'Sure,' said Rod, but underneath he was seething with anger, and it stayed with him during the whole of his underground tour.

Rod dropped straight down to 100 level. His first duty was to get the stuff out, and he wanted to check the reserve in the ore storage bins. He came into the long brightly-lit tunnel beneath the ore passes, and paused. The loaded conveyor belt whined monotonously, speeding the broken reef towards the bins.

The tunnel was deserted, except for the lonely figure of the sweeper at the far end. It was one of the phenomena of a well-run gold mine that in a tour through the workings you encountered so few human beings. Mile after mile of haulage and drive were silent and devoid of life, and yet there were 12,000 men down here.

Rod set off towards the bins at the shaft end of the tunnel.

'Joseph,' he greeted the old sweeper with a smile.

'Nkosi.' Joseph ducked and bobbed with shy pleasure.

'All is well?' Rod asked. Joseph was one of Rod's favourites, he was always so cheerful, so uncomplaining, so patently honest and without guile. Rod always made a point of stopping to chat to him.

'It is well with me, Nkosi. Is it well with you?'

Rod's smile died suddenly, he had noticed the fine white powdering of dust on Joseph's upper lip.

'You old rogue!' he scolded him. 'How often must I tell you to hose down before you sweep? Water! You must use water!'

This was part of the ceaseless battle of the miner to keep down the dust.

'The dust will eat your lungs!'

Phthisis, the dread incurable occupational disease of the miner, caused by silica particles being drawn into the lungs and there solidifying.

Joseph grinned shamefaced, shifting from one foot to the

other. He was always embarrassed by Rod's childish obsession with dust. In Joseph's opinion this was one of the few flaws in Rod Ironsides' character. Apart from this weird delusion that dust could hurt a man, he was a good boss.

'It is much harder to sweep wet dirt than dry dirt,' Joseph explained patiently. Rod never seemed to understand this self-evident fact, Joseph had to point it out to him every time they had this particular discussion.

'Listen to me, old man, without water the dust will enter your body.' Rod was exasperated. 'The dust will kill you!'

Joseph bobbed again, grinning at Rod to placate him.

'Very well, I will use plenty water.'

To prove it he picked up the hose and began spraying the floor with enthusiasm.

'That is good!' Rod encouraged him. 'Use plenty of water.' And Rod went on down to the storage bins.

When Rod was out of sight, Joseph turned off the hose and leaned on his broom.

'The dust will kill you!' he mimicked Rod, and chuckled merrily, shaking his head in wonder at the childishness of it.

'The dust will kill you!' he repeated, and burst into delighted laughter, slapping his thigh.

He did a few shuffling dance steps, it was so funny.

The dance steps were awkward, for under his trousers, strapped to the calves of both legs, were heavy polythene bags filled with gold fines from under the bins.

– 22 –

Rod stepped out of the Mary Anne at 85 level, and paused to watch Big King loading a baulk of timber onto the loco while his transport team stood back respectfully and watched him. Turning from his task Big King saw Rod standing on the station landing and marched up to him.

'I see you,' he greeted Rod. Big King was not one to make hasty judgements, it was only after the rescue operations in 43 section that he had decided Rod was a man. He was now ready to accept him as an equal.

'I see you also, King Nkulu.' Rod returned the greeting.

'Find me work with men. I sicken of this.'

'You will be back in the stopes before the week is ended,' Rod promised.

'You are my father,' Big King thanked him and went back to the transport team.

– 23 –

Johnny Delange saw the Underground Manager coming up the haulage towards him. There was no mistaking that tall wide-shouldered silhouette, nor the man's free swinging stride.

'Whee!' Johnny whistled with relief, grateful for the premonition that had warned him to pack the fifty-pound cardboard cartons of Dynagel into the explosives locker of the railway truck, rather than, as he usually did, pile them haphazard onto the platform in defiance of safety standards.

'Stop!' Johnny commanded the boss boy and his assistant who were pushing the truck, and it trundled to a halt beside Rod.

'Morning, Johnny.'

'Hello, Mr Ironsides.'

'How's it going?'

Johnny hesitated before replying, and immediately Rod was aware of the tension between the three men. He glanced at the two Swazis, they were sullen and apprehensive.

'There's been trouble,' he thought. 'Not like Johnny, he's too clever to let tension cut down his fathomage.'

'Well—' Johnny paused again. 'Look, Mr Ironsides, get rid of this bastard for me.' He jerked his thumb at the boss boy. 'Give me someone else.'

'What's the trouble?'

'No trouble, I just can't work with him.'

Rod raised an eyebrow in disbelief, but turned to the boss boy.

'Are you happy in this section, or do you want transfer?'

'I want transfer!' growled the boss boy.

'Right.' Rod was relieved, sometimes in a case like this the Swazi would refuse transfer. 'Tomorrow you will be told your new section.'

'Nkosi!' The boss boy glanced sideways at his assistant. 'It is the wish of my friend that he transfers with me.'

So that's it, Rod thought, the ever-present spectre which we must ignore because we can find no way to lay it. Johnny had probably caught them at it.

'Your friend shall go with you,' Rod nodded, telling himself that this was not condonation, but merely practical politics. If he separated them, the boss boy would pick on someone else who might not be receptive. Then there would be more trouble, stabbings, faction fighting.

'I'll get you a replacement,' he told Johnny, and then suddenly a thought occurred to him. My God, yes! What a team they would make!

'Johnny, how would you like Big King?'

'Big King!' Johnny's gaunt bony features split into a wide smile. 'Now you're talking, boss!'

At three o'clock Rod had finished his tour and was in the cage on the way to the surface. The cage was crowded, men pressed shoulder to shoulder, the stench of sweat almost overpowering. They were hauling shift now, the day's work was over, the stopes were scraped and washed down, the shot holes drilled and charged, the fuses connected into the electrical circuit.

The men were out of the stopes now, falling back in orderly companies and battalions along the haulages to the stations. There to wait patiently for their turn to enter the cages and be whisked to the surface.

Rod was mulling over the myriad problems he had encountered during the day, and the solutions he had dreamed up. He had opened a new section in the back pages of his notebook and headed it simply 'costs'.

Already there were two entries there. Let them give me the job, he thought fervently, just let me have it one month and I'll move the world.

'Mr Ironsides.' The man beside him spoke. Rod glanced down at him recognizing him.

'Hello, Davy.' It was remarkable how dissimilar the two brothers were.

'Mr Ironsides, my boss boy has worked his ticket. He's going home at the end of the month. Can you see that I get a good man to replace him?'

'Your brother's boss boy has asked for transfer. Will you take him?'

'Ja!' Davy Delange nodded. 'I know him, he's a good boy.'

And that takes care of one more detail, thought Rod, as he stepped out of the cage into a bright summer's afternoon and tasted the fresh sweet air with pleasure. Now there are only the butt ends of the day's work to tidy up. Then I can go and fetch the drink that Dan promised me.

Dimitri met him in the passage outside the office.

'I've got Kowalski in my office.'

'Good,' said Rod grimly. He went into his own office and sat on the edge of his desk.

'Send him in,' he called through to Dimitri.

Kowalski came through the door and stopped. He stood very still, his long arms hanging slackly at his side, his belly bulging out over his belt.

'You call me,' he muttered thickly, his English hardly intelligible. It was a peasant's face, coarse-featured, dull-eyed. He had not shaved, dirt from the stopes clung in the thick black stubble of beard.

'You beat a man today?' Rod asked softly.

'He no work,' Kowalski nodded. 'I beat him. Maybe next time his brothers they work. No bloody nonsense!'

'You're fired,' said Rod. 'Pull your time and get the hell off this property.'

'You fire?' Kowalski blinked in surprise.

'There will be criminal charges pressed against you by the Company.' Rod went on. 'But in the meantime I want you off the property.'

'Police?' Kowalski growled. There was expression on his face now.

'Yes,' said Rod, 'police.'

The spade-sized hands at the end of Kowalski's arms balled slowly into massive fists.

'You call da bloody police!' He took a step towards the desk, big, menacing.

'Dimitri,' Rod called sharply, 'close the door.'

Dimitri had been listening intently, now he jumped up from his desk and closed the interleading door. He stood with his ear pressed to the panelling. For thirty seconds more there was the growl and mutter of voices, then suddenly a thud, a bellow, another thud and a shattering crash.

Dimitri winced theatrically.

'Dimitri!' Rod's voice, and he pushed the door open.

Rod sat on the edge of his desk, swinging one leg casually, he was sucking the knuckle of his right hand.

'Dimitri, tell them not to put so much polish on the floor. Our friend slipped and hit his jaw on the desk.'

Dimitri clucked sympathetically as he stood over the reclining hulk of the big Pole. Kowalski was snoring loudly through his mouth.

'Gave himself a nasty bump,' said Dimitri. 'Shame!'

– 25 –

Dr Steyner worked on quietly for the remainder of Monday morning. He favoured the use of a tape recorder, for this cut out human contact which Manfred found vaguely repellent. He disliked having to speak his thoughts to a female who sat opposite him with skirts up around her thighs, squirming her bottom and touching her hair. However, what he really could not abide was the odour. Manfred was very sensitive to smells, even his own body smell of perspiration disgusted him. Women, he found, had a peculiar cloying odour that he could detect beneath their perfume and cosmetics. It nauseated him. This was why he had insisted on separate bedrooms for Theresa and himself. Naturally he had not told her the reason, but had insisted instead that he was such a light sleeper that he could not share a room with another person.

His office was in white and ice-blue, the air clean and cold from the air-conditioning unit, his voice was crisp and impersonal, the whirr of the recorder subdued, and with the conscious portion of his mind Manfred was happily absorbed in his conjuring tricks with figures and money, past performance and future estimates, a three-dimensional structure of variables and contingencies which only a super-normal brain could visualize. But beneath it was a sense of disquiet; he was waiting, hanging in time, and the outward sign of his agitation was the way the fingers of his right hand ran up and down his thigh as he worked, a caressing narcissistic gesture.

A few minutes before noon the unlisted direct telephone on his desk rang, and the movement of his hand stilled. Only one caller could reach him here, only one caller had that number. For a few seconds he sat unmoving, delaying the moment, then deliberately he switched off the recorder and lifted the telephone.

'Dr Manfred Steyner.' He identified himself.

'You have got our man in?' the voice enquired.

'Not yet, Andrew.'

There was silence from the other end, a dangerous crackling silence.

'But there is no cause for alarm. It is nothing. A delay merely, not a setback.'

'How long?'

'Two days – at the latest by the end of the week.'

'You will be in Paris next week?'

'Yes.' Manfred was an adviser to the Government team which was to meet the French for gold price talks.

'He will meet you there. It would be best for you that your side of the bargain were completed by then. You understand?'

'I understand, Andrew.'

The discussion was ended, but Manfred interjected to prevent the caller from hanging up.

'Andrew!'

'Yes.'

'Will you ask him if—' Manfred's tone had changed almost imperceptibly, there was an obsequious edge in it. 'Ask him if I may play tonight, please, Andrew.'

'Wait.'

The minutes drifted by, and then the voice came back on the line.

'Yes, you may play. Simon will inform you of your limits.'

'Thank you. Tell him, thank you.'

Manfred made no effort to conceal his relief as he cradled the receiver. He sat beaming at the ice-blue paper on the far wall of his office, even his spectacles seemed to sparkle.

– 26 –

There were five men in the opulently furnished room. One of the men was subservient to the others, he was younger than they, attentive to their moods and wishes. Clearly he was a servant. Of the remaining four, one was just as obviously the host. He was seated at the focus of all their attention. He was fat, but not excessively so, the fat of good living not of gluttony. He was speaking, addressing himself to his three guests.

'You have expressed doubts as to the reliability of the tool I intend using in the coming venture. I have arranged a demonstration which I hope will convince you that your concern is groundless. That is the reason for the invitation that Andrew here conveyed to you this afternoon.'

The host turned to the younger man. 'Andrew, would you be good enough to go through and wait for Dr Steyner to arrive; as soon as that happens, please let Simon seat him while you come through and inform us.' He gave his orders with dignity and courtesy, a man accustomed to command.

'Now, gentlemen, while we wait may I offer you a drink?'

The conversation that sprang up between the four of them as they sipped their drinks was knowledgeable, and extraordinarily well informed. At its root was one subject:

70

wealth. Mineral wealth, industrial wealth, the harvest of the land and the sea. Oil, steel, coal, fish, wheat and – gold.

There were clues to the stature of these men in the cut and quality of the cloth they wore, the sparkle of a stone on a finger, the tone of authority in a voice, the casual unaffected use of a high name.

'He is here, sir,' Andrew interrupted them from the doorway.

'Oh! Thank you, my boy.' The host stood up. 'Would you mind stepping this way, please, gentlemen.'

He crossed the room and drew aside one of the gold and maroon drapes. Behind it was a window.

The four men clustered about the window and looked through into the room beyond. It was a gaming room of an expensive gambling establishment. There were men and women sitting about a baccarat table, and none of them so much as glanced up at the window overlooking them.

'This is a one-way glass, gentlemen,' the host explained. 'So you need not worry about being seen in such a den of iniquity.'

They chuckled politely.

'What kind of profit does this place show you?' one of them asked.

'My dear Robert!' The host feigned shock. 'You don't for a moment believe that I would be in any way associated with an illegal undertaking?'

This time they chuckled with genuine amusement.

'Ha!' exclaimed the host. 'Here he is.'

Across the gaming room Dr Manfred Steyner was being ushered to a seat at the table by a tall sallow-faced young man, who in his evening dress looked like an undertaker.

'I have asked Simon to place him so that you may watch his face as he plays.'

They were intent now, leaning forward slightly, scrutinizing the man as he arranged the plaques that Simon had stacked at his elbow.

Dr Manfred Steyner began to play. His face was completely devoid of expression, but the pallor was startling. Every few seconds the pink tip of his tongue slipped out between his lips, then disappeared again. In the intervals between each coup, there was a reptilian stillness about him, the stillness of a lizard or an iguana. Only a pulse beat steadily in his throat and his spectacles glittered like a snake's eyes.

'May I direct your attention to his right hand during the play of this coup,' the host murmured, and all their eyes flicked downwards.

Manfred's right hand lay open beside the pile of his chips, but as his card was laid before him so his fingers closed.

'*Carte.*' Soundlessly he mouthed the word, and now his hand was a fist, the knuckles whitened, the tension was so fierce that his fist trembled. Yet, still his face was neutral.

The banker flipped his card.

'*Sept!*' The croupier's mouth formed the number. He faced Manfred's card, then he swept Manfred's stake away. Manfred's hand flopped open and lay soft and hairless as a dead fish on the green baize.

'Let us leave him to his pleasures,' suggested the host and drew the curtains across the window. They returned to their chairs, and they were strangely subdued.

'Jesus,' muttered one of the guests. 'That was ugly. I felt like a peeping Tom, like watching someone, you know, pulling his pudding.'

The host glanced at him quickly, surprised at his perception.

'In effect, that is exactly what you were watching,' he told him. 'You will excuse me playing the role of lecturer, but I know a little about this man. It cost me nearly four hundred rand for an analytic report on him by one of our leading psychiatrists.'

The host paused, assuring himself of their complete attention.

'The reasons are obscure, probably arising from an event or series of events during the period in which Dr Steyner was an orphan wandering through the smoking ruins of war-torn Europe.' The host coughed, deprecating his own flight of oratory. 'Be that as it may. The results are there for all to see. Dr Manfred Kurt Steyner's intelligence quotient is a genius rating of 158. He neither smokes nor drinks. He has no hobbies, plays no sport, has never made so much as an improper remark to any woman other than his wife, and there is some doubt as to just how often or to what extent she is favoured by his attentions.' The host sipped his drink conscious of their intense interest. 'Mechanically, if that is the correct term, Dr Steyner is neither impotent nor deficient in his manhood. However, he finds all bodily contact, and especially the secretions that may arise from such contact, to be utterly loathsome. For arousal he relies on the baccarat cards, for release he might endure a brief contact with a member of the opposite sex, but more likely he would – oh, what was the expression you used, Robert?'

They absorbed this in silence.

'He is, to be precise, a compulsive gambler. He is also a compulsive loser.'

They stirred with disbelief.

'You mean he tries to lose?' demanded Robert incredulously.

'No.' The host shook his head. 'Not on the conscious level. He believes he is trying to win, but he lays bets against odds that, with his magnificent brain, he must realize are suicidal. It is a deep-seated subconscious need to lose, to be humiliated. A form of masochism.'

The host opened a black leather notebook and checked its contents.

'During the period from 1958 to 1963 Dr Steyner lost

the total sum of R227,000 at this table. In 1964 he was able to arrive at an arrangement with his sole creditor to discharge the debt plus the accumulated interest.'

You could see the faces change as they rapidly searched their memories for a set of circumstances which would fit the dates and principals. Robert reached the correct deduction first. In 1964 their host had sold his majority holdings in the North Maun Copper Co. to CRC at a price that could only be considered advantageous. Just prior to this Dr Steyner had been made head of finance and planning at CRC.

'North Maun Copper,' said Robert with admiration. That is how he had done it, the cunning old fox! He had forced Steyner to buy well above market value.

The host smiled softly, deferentially, neither confirming nor denying.

'Since 1964 to the present Dr Steyner has continued to patronize this establishment. His gambling losses for this further period amount to—' He consulted his notebook again, pretending surprise at the figure, 'to a touch over R300,000.'

They sighed and moved restlessly. Even to these men it was a very large sum of money.

'I think we can rely on him.' The host closed his notebook with a snap, and smiled around at them.

– 27 –

Theresa lay in the dark. The night was warm, the stillness spoiled only by the klonking of a frog down at the fishpond. The moonlight came in through the window, playing shadow pictures through the branches of the Pride of India tree onto the wall of her bedroom.

She threw back the single sheet, and swung her legs off the bed. She could not sleep, it was too warm, her nightdress kept binding under her armpits. She stood up and on a sudden reckless impulse she drew the nightdress off over her head and tossed it through the open door of her dressing-room, then, naked, she walked out onto the wide veranda. Into the moonlight, with the cool stone flags under her bare feet, and the warm night air moving like the touch of fairy hands on her skin.

She felt suddenly devilish and daring, she wanted to run down across the lawns and to have someone catch her doing it. She giggled, uncertain of this mood. It was so far removed from Manfred's conception of a good German Hausfrau's behaviour.

'He'd be furious,' she whispered with wicked delight, and then she heard the motor of the car.

She froze with horror, the headlights flicked through the trees as the car came up the driveway and she darted back into her room; in panic she dropped to her knees and searched for her nightgown, found it and ran to the bed as she dragged it on over her head.

She lay in the darkness and listened to the car door slam. There was silence until she heard him pass her door. His heels clacked on the yellow wood floor, he was almost running. Theresa knew the symptoms, the late night return, the suppressed urgency, and she lay rigid in her bed, waiting.

The minutes passed slowly, and then the interleading door from Manfred's suite swung open silently.

'Manfred, is that you?' She sat up and reached for the switch of the bedside lamp.

'Don't put the light on.' His voice was breathless, slurred as though he had been drinking but there was no trace of liquor on his breath as he stooped over her and kissed her. His lips were dry and tightly closed, as he slipped off his dressing-gown.

Two and a half minutes later he stood up from the bed, turning his back to Theresa as he quickly shrugged into the silk dressing-gown.

'Excuse me a minute, Theresa.' The breathlessness was gone from his voice. He went through the door of his own suite, and seconds later she heard the hiss of the shower and the tinkling splash of water.

She lay on her back and her fingernails cut into the palms of her hands. Her body was trembling with a mixture of revulsion and desire, it had been so fleeting a contact – enough to stir her, but so swift as to leave her with a feeling of having been used and sullied. She knew that the rest of the night would pass infinitely slowly, with restless burning tension, remorse and self-pity alternating with wild elation and half-crazed erotic fantasy.

'Damn him,' she screamed silently within her skull. 'Damn him! Damn him!'

She heard the shower stop, and then Manfred returned to her room. He smelt of 4711 Eau de Cologne, and he sat down carefully on the end of the bed.

'You may turn on the light, Theresa.'

It required a conscious effort for her to unclench her hand and reach out for the lamp switch. Manfred blinked behind his spectacles at the flood of light. His hair was damp and freshly combed, his cheeks shone like ripe apples.

'I hope you had an enjoyable day?' he asked, and listened seriously to her reply. Despite her tension, Theresa found herself falling under the almost hypnotic influence he wielded over her. His voice precise, almost monotonous. The glitter of his spectacles, the reptilian stillness of his body and features.

As she had so many times before, she thought of herself as a warm fluffy rabbit sitting tense and fascinated before the cobra.

'It is late,' he said at last and he stood up.

Looking down at her as she lay cuddled into the white silk sheets, he asked with as little emphasis as if he were requesting her to pass the sugar: 'Theresa, could you raise three hundred thousand rand without your grandfather knowing?'

'Three hundred thousand!' She sat up startled.

'Yes. Could you?'

'Good Lord, Manfred, that's a small fortune.' She truly saw nothing unusual in her choice of adjective. 'You know it's all in the Trust Fund, well, most of it. There is the farm and the – no, I couldn't find half of that without Pops knowing.'

'Pity,' murmured Manfred.

'Manfred, you aren't in – difficulties?'

'No. Good Lord, no. It was just a thought. Forget that I asked. Good night, Theresa, I hope you sleep well.'

Involuntarily she lifted her hands towards him in invitation.

'Good night, Manfred.'

He turned and left the room, she let her hands fall to her sides. For Theresa Steyner the long night had begun.

– 28 –

'Ladies and Gentlemen, it is customary for the General Manager to introduce the distinguished guest who presents our special service awards. Last week, in tragic circumstances, our General Manager, Mr Frank Lemmer, was killed in the Company's service, a loss which we all bitterly regret, and I am sure you all join me in sincere condolence to Mrs Eileen Lemmer.' Rod paused for the acknowledging murmur from his audience. There were 200 of them packed into the Mine Club hall. 'It falls upon me, therefore, as Acting General Manager, to introduce to you Dr Manfred Steyner who is a senior Director of Central Rand Consolidated, our parent company. He is also head of the Departments of Finance and Planning.'

Sitting beside her husband, Theresa Steyner had noticed

Manfred's irritation at Rod's mention of Frank Lemmer. It was company policy not to draw public attention to accidental death or injury inflicted on employees by the Company's operation. She liked Rod the better for his small tribute to Frank Lemmer.

Theresa was wearing sunglasses, for her eyes were swollen and red. In the dawning, after a sleepless night, she had succumbed suddenly to a fit of bitter weeping. The tears were without cause, or reason, and had left her feeling strangely lightheaded and with a brittle sense of well-being. However, her enormous eyes always showed up badly for hours after she had wept.

She sat with her legs demurely crossed, immaculate in a suit of cream shantung, a black silk scarf catching her hair and then letting it fall in a dark glossy brown cascade onto her shoulders. She leaned forward in polite attention to the speaker, one elbow on her knee, her chin cupped in her palm, one long tapered finger against her cheek. A lady with diamonds on her fingers and pearls at her throat, smiling an acknowledgement at Rod's reference to 'the lovely granddaughter of our Chairman'.

Except for the slight incongruity of the sunglasses, she was the perfect image of the young matron. Polished, poised, cosseted, secure in her unassailable virtue and duty.

However, the thoughts that were running through Theresa Steyner's head, and the flutterings and sensations that were prickling and tickling her, had they been known, would have broken up the assembly in disorder. All the formless fantasy and emotional disturbance of the previous night were now directed at one target – Rodney Ironsides. Suddenly, with a start of amusement and alarm, she was aware of a phenomenon that she had last experienced many years ago. She moved quickly, shifting her seat, for the cream shantung marked so easily with any moisture.

'Terry Steyner!' she thought, deliciously shocked at

herself, and found with relief that Rod had finished speaking and Manfred was standing up to reply. She joined in the applause enthusiastically to distract her errant fancy.

Manfred briefly mentioned the six gentlemen sitting in the front row of seats whose courage and devotion to duty they had come to honour, he then went on into an exploration of the prospects of an increase in the price of gold. In measured, carefully considered terms, he set out the advantages and benefits that would accrue to the industry, the nation and the world at large. It was an erudite and convincing dissertation, and there was a large contingent of newspaper men to record it. The press had been alerted by the public relations department of CRC to the text of Dr Steyner's speech and all the leading dailies, weeklies, financial gazettes and journals were represented.

At intervals a photographer would come to crouch below the platform and pop a flash bulb up at Dr Steyner. On the eve of the gold price talks with France this would make good copy, for Steyner was the boy genius in the South African team.

The six heroes sat uncomfortably, forlorn in their best suits, scrubbed like schoolboys at a prize-giving ceremony, staring up at the speaker, not understanding a single word of the foreign language, but maintaining expressions of grave dignity.

Rod caught Big King's eye and winked at him. Solemnly Big King's right eyelid drooped and rose in reply, and quickly Rod averted his gaze to prevent himself laughing out loud.

He looked straight into Theresa Steyner's face, taking her completely off her guard. Not even the dark glasses could conceal her thoughts, they were as clear as if she had spoken them aloud. Before she could drop her eyes to examine the hem of her skirt, Rod knew with a stomach swoop of excitement how it could be if he chose.

With a new awareness he examined her from the corner

of his eye, seeing her for the first time as an accessible woman, a highly desirable woman, but nevertheless still the granddaughter of Hurry Hirschfeld and the wife of Manfred Steyner. This made her as dangerous as a force ten pressure burst, he knew, but the desire and temptation were hard to deny, inflamed perhaps rather than dampened by the danger.

He saw that she was blushing now, her fingers picking nervously at the hem of her skirt. She was as agitated as a schoolgirl, she knew he was watching her. Rod Ironsides, who until five minutes before had been thinking of nothing but his speech, now found himself impelled into a completely new and exciting dimension.

After the awards had been made, tea had been drunk, biscuits consumed and the crowd had dispersed, Rod escorted the Steyners down across the vivid green lawns of Kikuyu grass to where the chauffeur was holding the Daimler.

'What a magnificent physique that Shangaan has, what was his name – King?' Terry was walking between the two men.

'King Nkulu. Big King, we call him.'

Rod found his speech unsteady, he had stuttered slightly. This thing between the two of them was suddenly overpowering, it hummed like a turbine, making the space between them crackle with tension. Unless he was deaf, Manfred Steyner must be aware of it.

'He is pretty special. There is nothing he can't do, and do it far and away better than his nearest rival. My God, you should see him dance.'

'Dance?' enquired Terry with interest.

'Tribal dancing, you know.'

'Of course.' Terry hoped the relief in her voice was not obvious; she had been racking her badly flustered brain for an excuse to visit the Sonder Ditch again or have Rod Ironsides come to Johannesburg. 'I have a friend who is absolutely mad keen on seeing the dances. She pesters me every time I see her.'

Quickly she selected a name from her list of friends, she must have one ready should Manfred ask.

'They dance every Saturday afternoon, bring her out any time.' Rod fielded the ball neatly.

'What about this Saturday?' Terry turned to her husband, 'Would that be all right, Manfred?'

'What's that?' Manfred looked at her vaguely, he had not been following the conversation. Manfred Steyner was a worried man, he was pondering his obligation to gain control of the management of the Sonder Ditch within two days.

'May we come out here on Saturday afternoon to watch the tribal dancing?' Terry repeated her question.

'Have you forgotten that I fly to Paris on Saturday morning, Theresa?'

'Oh, dear.' Terry bit her lip thoughtfully. 'It *had* slipped my mind. What a pity, I would have enjoyed it.'

Manfred frowned slightly, irritated.

'My dear Theresa, there is no reason why you shouldn't come out to the Sonder Ditch without me. I am sure you will be safe enough in Mr Ironsides' hands.'

His choice of words brought the colour to Terry's cheeks again.

– 29 –

After the award ceremony, Big King's first stop was the Recruiting Agency office at the entrance to the No.1 shaft hostel. There were men clustered about the counter, but they stood aside for Big King and he acknowledged the courtesy by slapping their backs indiscriminately and greeting them with:

'Kunjane, madoda. How is it, men?'

The clerk behind the counter hurried to serve him. Up at the Mine Club Big King might be a little out of his depth, but here he was treated like a reigning monarch.

In two neat bundles Big King placed the award money on the counter.

'Twenty-five rand you will send to my senior wife.' He instructed the clerk. 'And twenty-five rand you will put to my book.'

Big King was scrupulously fair. Half of all his earnings was remitted to the senior of his four wives, and half was added to the substantial sum already credited in his savings bank passbook.

The Agency was the procurer of labour for the insatiably man-hungry gold mines of the Witwatersrand and Orange Free State. Its representatives operated across the southern half of the continent. From the swamps and fever lagoons along the great Zambesi, from among the palm groves fringing the Indian Ocean, out of these simmering plains that the bushmen called 'the big dry', down from the mountains of Basutoland and the grass lands of Swaziland and Zululand they gathered the Bantu, the men themselves completing the first fifty or sixty miles of the journey on foot. Individuals meeting on a footpath to become pairs, arriving at a little general dealer's store in the bleak scrub desert to find three or four others already waiting, the arrival of the recruiting truck with a dozen men and their luggage aboard, the long bumping grinding progress through the bush. The stops at which more men scrambled aboard, until a full truck load of fifty or sixty disembarked at a railway siding in the wilderness.

Here the tiny trickle of humanity joined a stream, and at the first major centre they trans-shipped and became part of the great flood that washed towards 'Goldi'.

However, once they had reached Johannesburg and been allocated to one of the sixty major gold mines, the Agency's obligations towards its recruits were not yet discharged.

Between them the employing mine and the Agency must provide each man with employment, training, advice and comfort, maintain contact between him and his family, for very few of them could write, reassure him when he worried that his goats were sick or his wife unfaithful. They must provide a banking and savings service with a personal involvement unknown to any commercial banking institute. They had, in short, to make certain that a man taken from an environment that had not changed in a thousand years and deposited into the midst of a sophisticated and technological society would retain his health, happiness and sanity, so that at the end of his contract he would return to the place from which he had come and tell them all how wonderful it was at 'Goldi'. He would show them his hard helmet, and his new suitcase crammed with clothes, his transistor radio and the little blue book with its printed figures, inflaming them also with the desire to make the pilgrimage, and keep the flood washing towards 'Goldi'.

Big King completed his business transactions and went in through the gates of the hostel. He was going to take advantage of the fact that he had missed the shift and would be among the first at the ablutions and dining-hall.

He went down across the lawns to his block. Despite the size of an establishment that housed 6,000 men, the Company had tried to make it as attractive as possible. The result was an unusual design, halfway between a motel and an advanced penitentiary.

As a senior boss boy, Big King rated a room of his own. An ordinary labourer would share with five others.

Carefully Big King brushed down his suit and hung it in the built-in cupboard, wiped down his glossy shoes and racked them, then with a towel around his waist he set off for the ablution block and was irritated to find it already filled with new recruits up from the acclimatization centre.

Big King ran an appraising eye over their naked bodies and judged that this batch must be nearing the completion of their eight-day acclimatization. They were sleek and shiny, the muscle definition showing clearly through the skin.

You could not take a man straight out of his village, probably suffering from malnutrition, and put him down a gold mine to lash and bar and drill in a dry bulb heat of 91° Fahrenheit and 84% relative humidity, without running a serious risk of killing him with heat stroke or exhaustion.

Every recruit judged medically fit to work underground went into acclimatization. For eight days, eight hours a day, he and hundreds of others stood with only a loin cloth about his middle in a vast barn-like hall stepping up onto and down from a platform. The height of the platform was carefully matched to the man's height and body weight, the speed of his movements was regulated by a flashing panel of lights, the temperature and humidity were controlled at 91° and 84%, every ten minutes he was given water and his body temperature was registered by the half dozen trained medical assistants in charge of the room.

At the end of the eighth day he emerged as fit as an olympic athlete, and quite able to perform heavy physical labour in conditions of high temperature and humidity without discomfort or danger.

'Gwedeni!' growled Big King, and the nearest recruit, still white with soap suds, hurriedly vacated his shower with a respectful 'Keshle!' in deference to Big King's rank and standing. Big King removed his towel and stepped under the shower, revelling as always in the rush of hot water over his skin, flexing the great muscles of his arms and chest.

The messenger found him there.

'King Nkulu, I have word for thee.' The man used Shangaan, not the bastard Fanikalo.

'Speak,' Big King invited, soaping his belly and buttocks.

'The Induna bids you call at his house after you have eaten the evening meal.'

'Tell him I will attend his wishes,' said Big King and held his face up into the rush of steaming water.

Dressed in a white open-necked shirt and blue slacks, Big King sauntered down to the kitchens. Again the recruits were ahead of him, queueing with bowls in hand outside the serving hatches. Big King walked past them through the door marked 'No Admittance – Staff Only'.

The kitchens were cavernous, glistening with white porcelain tiles and stainless steel cookers and bins that could serve 18,000 hot meals a day.

When Big King entered a room, even one as large as this, no one was unaware of his presence. One of the assistant cooks snatched up a bowl not much smaller than a baby's bath, and hurried across to the nearest stainless steel bin. He opened the lid and looked expectantly at Big King. Big King nodded and the cook ladled about two litres of steaming sugar beans into the bowl, before passing on to the next bin where he again looked for and obtained Big King's approval. He added an equal quantity of mixed vegetables to the bowl, slammed down the lid and scampered across to where a second assistant waited with a spade beside yet another bin.

The spade was the same as those used for lashing gold reef underground, but the blade of this one had been polished to gleaming cleanliness. The second cook dug into the bin and came up with a spadeful of white maize porridge, cooked stiff as cake, the smell of it as saliva-making as the smell of new bread. This was the staple of Bantu diet. He deposited the spadeful in the bowl.

'I am hungry.' Big King spoke for the first time, and the second cook dug out another spadeful and added it to the bowl. They passed on to the end of the kitchens and at their approach another cook lifted the lid on a pressure cooker the size of a washing machine. From it arose a cloud of fragrant steam.

85

Apologetically the cook held out his hand and Big King produced his meat ticket. Meat was the only food that was rationed. Each man was limited to one pound of meat a day; the Company had long ago discovered to its astonishment and cost that a Bantu, offered unlimited supplies of fresh meat, was quite capable of eating his own weight of it monthly.

Having ascertained that Big King was entitled to his daily pound, the cook proceeded to ladle at least five pounds of it into the bowl.

'You are my brother,' Big King thanked him, and the little procession moved on to where yet another cook was filling a half-gallon jug of thick, gruel-like, mildly alcoholic Bantu beer from one of the multiple spiggots beneath the thousand-gallon tank.

The bowl and jug were ceremonially handed to Big King and he went out onto the covered terraces where benches and tables were set out for alfresco dining in mild weather.

While he ate, the terrace began to fill, for the shift was out of the mine now. Every man who passed his table greeted Big King, but only a few privileged persons took the liberty of seating themselves at the same table. One of them was Joseph M'Kati, the little old sweeper from 100 level.

'It has been a good week, King Nkulu.'

'You say so.' Big King was non-committal. 'I go now to a meeting with the Old One. Then we shall see.'

The Old One, the Shangaan Induna, lived in a Company house. A self-contained residence with lounge and dining-room, kitchen and bathroom. He was handsomely paid by the Company, provided with servants, food, furniture and all the other appurtenances of his rank and station.

He was the head of the Shangaan community on the Sonder Ditch. A chief of the blood, a greybeard and member of the tribal councils. In similar houses and with the same privileges and in equal style lived the Indunas of the other tribal groups that made up the labour force of the

Sonder Ditch. They were the paternal figureheads, the tribal jurists, ruling and judging within the framework of law and custom. The Company could not hope to maintain harmony and order without the assistance of these men.

'Baba!' Big King greeted his Induna from the doorway of his house, touching the forehead in respect not only for the man but also for what he represented.

'My son.' The Induna smiled his greeting. 'Come and sit by me.' He gestured for his servants to leave the room, and Big King went to squat at the feet of the old man. 'Is it true you go now to work with the mad one?' That was Johnny Delange's nickname.

They talked, the Induna questioning him on fifty matters that affected the welfare of his people. For Big King this was a comforting and nostalgic experience, for the Induna stood in the place of his father.

At last, satisfied, the Induna went on to other matters.

'There is a parcel ready tonight. Crooked Leg waits for you.'

'I shall go for it.'

'Go in peace then, my son.'

On his way through the gates of the hostel Big King stopped to chat with the guards. These men had the right to search over any person entering or leaving the hostel. Particularly they were concerned with preventing either women disguised as men or bottles of spirits entering the premises, both of which tended to have a disruptive effect on the community. As an afterthought they were also instructed to look out for stolen property entering or leaving. Big King had to ensure that none of them would ever, under any circumstances, take it into his head to search Big King.

While he stood at the gates, the last glow of the sunset faded and the lights began to come on across the valley. The clusters of red aerial warning lights atop the headgears, the massed yellow squares of the hotels, the strings of street lamps and the isolated pinpricks of the residential areas up on the ridge.

When it was truly dark, Big King left the guards and sauntered down the main road, until a bend in the road took him out of their sight. Then Big King left the road and started up the slope. He moved like a night animal, swiftly and with certainty of the path he followed.

He passed the ranch-type split-levels of the line management officials with their wide lawns and swimming-pools, pausing only once when a dog yapped nearby, then moving on again until he was into the broken rock and rank grass of the upper ridge; he crossed the skyline and started down the far side until he made out the grass-covered mound of rubble in the moonlight. He slowed and moved cautiously forward until he found the rusty barbed wire fence that guarded the entrance. He vaulted it easily and went on into the black mouth of the tunnel.

Fifty years before, a long-defunct mining company had suspected the existence of a gold reef in this area and had driven prospecting adits into the side of the ridge, exhausting its funds in the process, and finally abandoning the network of tunnels in despair.

Big King paused long enough to draw an electric torch from his pocket before going on into the tunnel, flashing the beam ahead of him. Soon the air stank of bats and their wings swished about his head. Unperturbed, Big King went on deeper and deeper into the side of the hill, taking a turning and fork in the tunnel without hesitation. At last there was a faint glow of yellow light ahead and Big King switched off his torch.

'Crooked Leg!' he called, his voice bounced and boomed along the tunnel. There was no reply.

'It is I, Big King!' he shouted again, and immediately a shadow detached itself from the sidewall and limped towards him, sheathing a wicked-looking knife as it came.

'All is ready.' The little cripple came to greet him. 'Come, I have it here.'

Crooked Leg had earned his limp and his nickname in a rockfall a dozen years ago. Now he owned and operated the concession photographic studio on the mine property, a flourishing enterprise, for dearly the Bantu love their own image on film. Not, however, as profitable as his nocturnal activities in the abandoned workings beyond the ridge.

He led Big King into a small rock chamber lit by a suspended hurricane lantern. Mingled with the bat stench was the acrid reek of sulphuric acid in high concentration.

On a wooden trestle table that occupied most of the chamber were earthenware jars, heavy glass bowls, polythene bags, and a variety of shoddy and very obviously second-hand laboratory equipment. In a clear space amongst all this clutter stood a large screw-topped bottle. The bottle was filled with a dirty yellow powder.

'Ha!' Big King exclaimed his pleasure. 'Plenty!'

'Yes. It has been a good week,' Crooked Leg agreed.

Big King picked up the bottle, marvelling once again at the unbelievable weight of it. This was not pure gold, for Crooked Leg's acid reduction methods were crude, but it was at least sixteen carats fine.

The bottle represented the week's collection of fines and concentrates by men like Joseph M'Kati from a dozen vulnerable points along the line of production; in some cases carried out from the company reduction works itself under the noses of the heavily armed guards.

All the men involved in this surreptitious milking off of the company's gold were Shangaans. There was only one man in whom was vested sufficient authority and prestige to prevent the greed and hostility which gold breeds from destroying the whole operation. That was the Shangaan Induna. There was only one man with the physical presence and necessary command of the Portuguese language to negotiate the disposal of the gold. That was Big King.

Big King placed the bottle in his pocket. The weight pulled his clothing out of shape.

'Run like a gazelle, Crooked Leg.' He turned back into the dark tunnel.

'Hunt like a leopard, King Nkulu,' chuckled the little cripple, as he disappeared into the moving shadows.

– 30 –

'A packet of Boxer tobacco,' said Big King. The eyes of José Almeida, the Portuguese owner of the mine concession store and the local roadhouse, narrowed slightly. He took down the yellow four-ounce packet from the shelves and handed it across the counter, accepted Big King's payment and counted the change into his palm.

He watched as the giant Bantu wandered down between the loaded shelves and racks of merchandise to disappear through the front door of the store into the night.

'Take charge,' he muttered in Portuguese to his plump little wife with her silky dark moustache, and she nodded in understanding, moving into José's place in front of the cash register. José went through into his storerooms and living quarters behind the store.

Big King was waiting in the shadows. When the back door opened he slipped through and José closed the door behind him. José led him through into a cubicle of an office, and from a cupboard he took down a jeweller's balance. Under Big King's watchful eye he began to weigh the gold.

José Almeida purchased the gold from the unofficial outlet of each of the five major mines on the Kitchenerville field, paying five Rands an ounce and selling again for sixteen. He justified the large profit margin he allowed himself by the fact that mere possession of unregistered gold was a criminal offence in South Africa, punishable by up to five years' imprisonment.

Almeida was a man in his middle thirties with lank black hair that he continually pushed back from his forehead, bright brown inquisitive eyes and dirty fingernails. Despite his grubby and well-worn clothing and unkempt hairstyle, he was a man of substance.

He had been able to pay in cash the 40,000 rand demanded by the Company for the monopoly concession to trade on the mine property. He had, therefore, an exclusive clientele of 12,000 well-paid Bantu, and had recovered his 40,000 during his first year of trading. He did not really need to run the risk of illicit gold buying, but gold is strange material. It infects most men who touch it with a reckless greed.

'Two hundred and sixteen ounces,' said José. His scale was set to record a twenty per cent error – in José's favour.

'One thousand and eighty rand,' agreed Big King in Portuguese, and José went to the big green safe in the corner.

– 31 –

Terry Steyner entered the 'Grape and Gable' bar of the President Hotel at 1.14 p.m. precisely, and as Hurry Hirschfeld stood to greet her he reflected that fourteen minutes was hardly late at all for a beautiful woman. Terry's grandmother would have considered herself to be early if she was only that late.

'You're late,' growled Hurry. No sense in letting her get away with it unscathed.

'And you are a big, cuddly, growly, lovable old bear,' said Terry and kissed him on the tip of his nose before he could duck. Hurry sat down quickly scowling thunderously with pleasure. He decided he didn't give a good damn if Marais and Hardy, who further down the bar were listening and trying to cover their grins, repeated the incident to the entire membership of the Rand Club.

'Good day, Mrs Steyner.' The scarlet-jacketed barman smiled his greeting. 'Can I mix you a Manhattan?'

'Don't tempt me, Thomas. I'm on a diet. I'll just have a glass of soda water.'

'Diet,' snorted Hurry. 'You're skinny enough as it is. Give her a Manhattan, Thomas, and put a cherry in it. Never was a Hirschfeld woman that looked like a boy, and you'll not be the first of them.' As an afterthought, he added: 'I've ordered your lunch also, you'll not starve yourself in my company.'

'You are a shocker, Pops,' said Terry fondly.

'Now, young lady, let's hear what you've been up to since I last saw you.'

They talked together as friends, very dear and trusted friends. The affection they felt for each other went beyond the natural duty of their blood tie. There was a kinship of the spirit as well as the flesh. They sat close, heads together, watching each other's face as they talked, completely lost in the pleasure of each other's company, the murmur of their voices interrupted by a tinkling burst of laughter or a deep chuckle.

They were so absorbed that Peter, the headwaiter, came through from the Transvaal Room to find them.

'Mr Hirschfeld, the chef is in tears.'

'Good Lord.' Hurry looked at the antique clock above the bar. 'It's almost two o'clock. Why didn't someone tell me?'

The oysters had been flown up from Mossel Bay that morning, and Terry sighed with pleasure after each of them.

'I was out at the Sonder Ditch with Manfred on Wednesday.'

'Yes, I saw the photograph in the paper.' Hurry engulfed his twelfth and final oyster.

'I must say I like your new General Manager.'

Hurry laid down his fork and a little flush of anger started in his withered old cheeks.

'You mean Fred Plummer?'

'Don't be silly, Pops, I mean Rodney Ironsides.'

'Has that cold fish of yours been briefing you?' Hurry demanded.

'Manfred?' She was genuinely puzzled by the question, Hurry could see that. 'What's he got to do with it?'

'All right, forget it.' Hurry dismissed Manfred with a shake of his head. 'Why do you like Ironsides?'

'Have you heard him speak?'

'No.'

'He's very good. I'm sure he must be a first-class mining man.'

'He is.' Hurry nodded, watchful and non-commital.

Peter whisked Terry's plate away, giving her the respite she needed to gather her resources. In the previous few seconds she had realized that Rodney Ironsides was not, as she had believed, a certainty for the job. In fact, Pops had already chosen old plum-faced Plummer for the General Managership. It took another moment for her to decide that she would use even the dirtiest in-fighting to see that Rod was not overlooked.

Peter laid plates of cold rock lobster in front of them, and when he had withdrawn Terry looked up at Hurry. She had perfected the trick of enlarging her already enormous eyes. By holding them open like this she could flood them with tears. The effect was devastating.

'Do you know, Pops, he reminds me so much of the photographs of Daddy.'

Colonel Bernard Hirschfeld, Terry's father, had burned to death in his tank at Sidi Rezegh. She saw Hurry

93

Hirschfeld's expression crack with pain, and Terry felt a sick little flutter of guilt. Had it been necessary to use such a vicious weapon to achieve her ends?

Hurry pushed at the rock lobster with his fork, his head was bowed so she could not see his face. She reached out to touch his hand.

'Pops—' she whispered, and he looked up. There was a restrained excitement in Hurry's manner.

'You know, you're bloody well right! He does look a bit like Bernie. Did I ever tell you about the time when your father and I—'

Terry felt dizzy with relief. I didn't hurt him, she told herself, he likes the idea, he really does. With a woman's instinct she had chosen the only form of persuasion that could have moved Hurry Hirschfeld from his decision.

– 32 –

Manfred Steyner fastened his safety belt and lay back in the seat of the Boeing 707, feeling slightly nauseated with relief.

Ironsides was in, and he was safe. Hurry Hirschfeld had sent for him two hours before to wish him farewell and good luck with the talks. Manfred had stood before him, trying desperately to think of some way in which he could bring up the subject naturally. Hurry saved him the trouble.

'By the way, I'm giving Ironsides the Sonder Ditch. Reckon it's about time we had some young blood in top management.'

It was as easy as that. Manfred had difficulty in persuading himself that those threats which had kept him lying awake during the past four nights were no longer of consequence. Ironsides was in. He could go to Paris and tell them. *Ironsides is in. We are ready to go.*

The note of the jets changed, and the Boeing began to roll forward. Manfred twisted his head against the neck rest and peered through the Perspex porthole. He could not distinguish Terry's figure amongst the crowd on the observation balcony of Jan Smuts Airport. They taxied past a Pan Am Boeing which cut off his view and Manfred looked straight ahead. Instantly his nostrils flared, he looked around quickly.

The passenger in the seat beside him had stripped to his shirtsleeves. He was a big beefy individual who very obviously did not use deodorant. Almost in desperation Manfred looked about. The aircraft was full, there would be little chance of changing seats and beside him the beefy individual produced a pack of cigarettes.

'You can't smoke,' cried Manfred. 'The light's on.' The combination of body odour and cigarette smoke would be unbearable.

'I'm not smoking,' said the man, 'yet.' And placed a cigarette between his lips, his lighter ready in the other hand.

Nearly two thousand miles to Nairobi, thought Manfred, with his stomach starting to heave.

– 33 –

'Terry darling, why on earth should I go all the way out to Kitchenerville to watch a lot of savages prancing around?'

'As a favour to me, Joy,' Terry pleaded into the telephone.

'It means mucking up my whole weekend. I've got rid of the kids to their grandmother, I've got a copy of *A Small Town in Germany* and I was going to have a lovely time reading and—'

'Please, Joy, you're my last hope.'

'What time will we be home?' Joy was weakening. Terry sensed her advantage and pressed forward ruthlessly.

'You might meet a lovely man out at the mine, and he'll sweep you—'

'No, thanks.' Joy had been divorced a little over a year ago, some people took longer than others to recover. 'I've had lovely men in big fat chunks.'

'Oh, Joy, you can't sit around moping for ever. Come on, I'll pick you up in half an hour.'

Joy sighed with resignation. 'Damn you, Terry Steyner.'

'Half an hour,' said Terry and hung up before she could change her mind.

'I'm playing golf. It's Saturday, and I'm playing golf,' said Doctor Daniel Stander stubbornly.

'You remember when I drove all the way to Bloemfontein to—' Rod began, and Dan interrupted quickly.

'All right, all right, I remember. You don't have to bring that up again.'

'You owe me plenty, Stander,' Rod reminded him. 'All I am asking is one of your lousy Saturday afternoons. Is that so much?'

'I can't let the boys down. It's a long-standing date.' Dan wriggled to escape.

'I've already phoned Ben. It will be a pleasure for him to take your place.'

There was a long gloomy silence, then Dan asked, 'What's this bird like?'

'She's a beautiful, rich nymphomaniac, and she owns a brewery.'

'Yeah! Yeah!' said Dan sarcastically. 'All right, I'll do it. But I hereby declare all obligations and debts to you fully discharged.'

'I'll give you a written receipt,' Rod agreed.

Dan was still sulking when the Daimler came up the drive and parked in the front of the Mine Club. He and Rod were standing at the Ladies' Bar, watching for the arrival of their guests.

Dan had just ordered his third beer.

'Here they come,' said Rod.

'Is that them?' Dan's depression lifted magically as he peered through the coloured-glass windows. The chauffeur was letting the two ladies out of the Daimler. They were both in floral slack suits and dark glasses.

'That's them.'

'Jesus!' said Dan with rare approval. 'Which one is mine?'

'The blonde.'

'Ha!' Dan grinned for the first time since their meeting. 'Why the hell are we standing here?'

'Why indeed?' asked Rod, his stomach was tied up in knots that twisted tighter as he went down the front steps toward Terry.

'Mrs Steyner. I'm so glad you could come.' With a wild lift of elation he saw it was still there, he had not imagined it, it was there in her eyes and her smile.

'Thank you, Mr Ironsides.' She was like a schoolgirl again, uncertain of herself, flustered.

'I'd like you to meet Mrs Albright. Joy, this is Rodney Ironsides.'

'Hello.' He smiled at her as he clasped her hand. 'It's gin time, I think.'

Dan was waiting at the bar for them, and Rod made the introductions.

'Joy is so excited at the chance of watching the dancing,' said Terry as they sat down on the bar stools. 'She's been looking forward to it for days.' And for an instant Joy looked stunned.

'You'll love it,' agreed Dan, moving in to take up a position at Joy's elbow. 'I wouldn't miss it for anything.'

Joy was a tall slim girl with long straight golden hair that hung to her shoulders, her eyes were cool green but her mouth when she smiled was soft and warm. She smiled now full into Dan's eyes.

'Nor would I,' she said, and with relief Rod knew he could devote all his attention to Terry Steyner. Joy Albright would be more than adequately looked after. He ordered drinks, and all four of them promptly lost further interest in tribal dancing.

At one stage Rod told Terry Steyner, 'I am going up to Johannesburg this evening. There is no point in your unfortunate chauffeur sitting around all afternoon. Let him go, and I'll take you home.'

'Good,' Terry agreed immediately. 'Would you tell him, please?'

The next time Rod looked at his watch it was half past three.

'Good Lord!' he exclaimed. 'If we don't hurry, it will be all over.' Reluctantly Joy and Dan, who had their heads close together, drew apart.

The overflow from the amphitheatre pressed about them, a merry jostling throng, all inhibitions long since evaporated in the primeval excitement of the dance, much like the crowd at a bull ring.

Rod and Dan ran interference for the girls, ploughing a path through the main gateway and down to their reserved seats in the front row. All four of them were laughing and flushed by the time they were seated, the excitement about them was infectious and the liquor had heightened their sensibilities.

An expectant hum of voices.

'The Shangaans!' And the audience craned towards the entrance from which pranced a dozen drummers, their long wooden drums hung on rawhide straps about their necks, they took up stations around the circular earthen stage.

Tap, tap. Tap, tap – from one of the drummers, and silence gripped the amphitheatre.

Tap, tap. Tap, tap. Naked, except for their brief loin cloths, stooped over the drums that they clasped between their knees, they began to lay down the rhythm of the dance. It was a broken, disturbing beat, that jerked and twitched like a severed nerve. A compelling, demanding sound, the pulse of a continent and a people.

Then came the dancers, shuffling, row upon row, head-dresses dipping and rustling, the animal tail kilts swirling, war rattles at the wrists and ankles, black muscles already oiled with the sweat of excitement, coming in slowly rank upon majestic rank, moving as though the drums were pumping life into them.

A shrill blast on a duiker horn and the ranks whirled like dry leaves in a wind, they fell again into a new pattern, and through the opening in their midst came a single gigantic figure.

'Big King!' The name blew like a sigh through the audience, and immediately the drums changed their rhythm. Faster, demanding, and the dancers hissed in their throats a sound like storm surf rushing up a stony beach.

Big King flung his arms wide, braced on legs like black marble columns, his head thrown back. He sang a single word of command, shrilling it, and in instantaneous response every right knee was brought up to the level of the chest. Half a second's pause and then 200 horny bare feet stamped down simultaneously with a crash that shook the amphitheatre to its foundations. The Shangaans began to dance, and reality was gone in the moving, charging, swirling, retreating ranks.

Once Rod tore his eyes from the spectacle. Terry Steyner was sitting forward on the bench, eyes sparkling, lips slightly parted, completely lost in the erotic turmoil and barbaric splendour of it.

Joy and Dan had a firm hold on each others' hands, their shoulders and the outside of their thighs were pressed tightly together, and Rod was stabbed by a painful thrust of envy.

Afterwards, back in the Ladies' Bar of the Club, there was very little conversation but they were all of them tensed up, restless, moved by strange undercurrents and interplays of primitive desires and social restraints.

'Well,' said Rod at last, 'if I am to get you two ladies back to Johannesburg at a decent hour—'

Dan and Joy spoke together.

'Don't worry, Rod, I'll—'

'Dan says he will—' Then they stopped and grinned at each other sheepishly.

'I take it that Dan has suddenly remembered that he has to go to Johannesburg this evening also, and he has offered to give you a lift?' asked Rod dryly, and they laughed in confirmation.

'It looks as though we are on our own, Mrs Steyner.' Rod turned to Terry.

'I'll trust you,' said Terry.

'If you do that, you're crazy,' said Dan.

Outside the Maserati, darkness was falling swiftly. The horizon blending into the black sky, isolated lights winking at them out of the surrounding veld.

Rod switched on the headlights, and the instrument panel glowed softly, turning the interior into a warm secluded place, isolating them from the world. The wind whispered, and the tyres and the engine hummed a gentle intimate refrain.

Terry Steyner sat with her legs curled up under her, cuddled into the soft maroon leather of the bucket seat.

She was staring ahead down the path of the headlights, and she seemed withdrawn and yet very close. Every few minutes Rod would take his eyes from the road and study her profile briefly. He did so again, and this time she met his gaze frankly.

'You realize what is happening?' she asked.

'Yes,' he answered as frankly.

'You know how dangerous it could be for you?'

'And you.'

'No, not me. I am invulnerable. I am a Hirschfeld – but you, it could destroy you.'

Rod shrugged.

'If we counted the consequences before every action, nobody would do anything.'

'Have you thought that I might be a spoiled little rich girl amusing myself? I might do this all the time.'

'You might,' Rod agreed. They were silent for a long while, then Terry spoke again.

'Rod?' She used his given name for the first time.

'Yes?'

'I don't, you know, I really don't.'

'I guessed that.'

'Thank you.' She opened her bag. 'I need a cigarette. I feel as though I'm standing poised on the edge of a cliff and I've got this terrible compulsion to hurl myself over the edge.'

'Light me one, Terry.'

'You need one also?'

'Badly.'

They smoked in silence again, both of them staring ahead, then Terry rolled down the window and flicked the cigarette butt away.

'You've got the job, you know.' All day she had wanted to tell him, it had been bubbling inside her. Watching his face, she saw his lips stiffen, his eyes crease into slits.

'Did you hear me?' she asked at last, and he braked the

Maserati, swinging it off onto the shoulder of the road. He pulled on the hand brake and turned to face her.

'Terry, what did you say?'

'I said, you've got the job.'

'What job?' he demanded harshly.

'Pops signed the instruction this morning. You'll receive it on Monday. You're the new General Manager of the Sonder Ditch.' She wanted to go on and say – *and I got it for you. I made Pops give it to you.*

I never will, she promised, I will never spoil it for him. He must believe he won it fairly, not as my gift.

– 34 –

It was Saturday night, the big night in Dump City.

The Blaauberg Mine was the oldest producer on the Kitchenerville field. There were sections of its property which had been worked out completely, and the old waste dumps were now abandoned and overgrown. Among the scrub and head-high weed in the valleys between these man-made hills had grown up a shanty town. Dump City, the inhabitants had named it. The buildings were made of discarded galvanized iron sheets and flattened oil drums, there was no sanitation or running water.

Remote from the main roads, the residential communities of the neighbouring mines or the town of Kitchenerville, hidden among the dumps, accessible only to a man on foot, never visited by members of the South African Constabulary, it was ideally suited to the purposes for which its 300 permanent inhabitants had chosen it.

Every one of the shacks was a shebeen, a clip joint where watered liquor was sold at inflated prices, where dagga*

* Marijuana.

was freely obtainable and where men from the surrounding mines gathered to carouse.

They came not so much for the liquor. Each of the mine hostels had a bar where a full range of liquor was on sale at club prices. Very few of them came for the dagga. There was little addiction amongst these well-fed, hard-worked and contented men. What they came for were the women.

Five mines in the area, each employing ten or twelve thousand men. Here at Dump City were 200 women, the only available women within twenty miles. It was not necessary for the young ladies of Dump City to solicit custom, even the fat, the withered, the toothless, could behave like queens.

Big King came down the path that skirted the mine dump. With him were two dozen of his fellow tribesmen, big Shangaans wearing their regalia, carrying their fighting sticks and still tensed up from the dancing. They came at a trot, Big King leading them. They were singing, not the gentle planting or courting melodies, not the work chant nor the song of welcome.

They were singing the fighting songs, those their fore-fathers had sung when they carried the spear in search of cattle and slaves. The driving inflammatory rhythm, the fiercely patriotic words wrought so mightily on the delicate susceptibilities of the average Shangaan that the Company had found it necessary to ban the singing of these songs.

Like a Scot hearing the pipes, when a Shangaan began singing these warlike chants, he was ready for violence.

The song ended as Big King led them down to the nearest shanty, and pushed aside the sacking that acted as a door. He stooped through the opening, and his comrades crowded in behind him.

A brittle electric silence fell on the large room. The air was so thick with smoke, and the light from the suspended hurricane lamps so feeble, that it was impossible to see the far wall. The room was filled with men, forty or fifty of them, the smell of humanity and bad liquor was solid. Among this press of men were half a dozen bright spots of the girls' dresses, but with their curiosity aroused by the singing more girls were coming through from the interleading doorways at the back, some of them had men with them and were still shrugging into their clothing. When they saw Big King and his warriors in full war kit, they fell silent and watchful.

At Big King's shoulder one of his Shangaans whispered:

'Basutos! They are all Basutos!' He was right, Big King saw that they were all men of that mountainous little independent state.

Big King started forward, swaggering just enough to make his leopard tail kilt swing and swirl and the heron feathers of his head-dress rustle. He reached the primitive bar counter.

'Flying Bird,' he told the crone who owned the house, and she placed a bottle of Eagle Brandy on the counter.

Big King half filled a tumbler, conscious that every eye was on him, and drained it.

Slowly he turned and surveyed the room.

'What is it,' he asked in a voice that carried to every corner, 'that sits on top of a mountain and scratches its fleas. Is it a baboon, or a Basuto?'

A roar of delight went up from his Shangaans.

'A Basuto!' they shouted, crowding forward to the bar, while a growl and a mutter went up from the rest of the room.

'What is it,' shouted a Basuto jumping to his feet, 'that has feathers on its head and crows from a dungheap? Is it a rooster, or a Shangaan?'

Without seeming to move, Big King picked up the bottle of Eagle Brandy and hurled it. With a crack it burst against the Basuto's forehead and he went over backwards taking two of his companions with him.

The old crone snatched up her cash register and ran as the room exploded into violent movement.

There was not enough space in which to use the fighting sticks, Big King realized, so he lifted a section of the bar counter off its trestles and, holding it in front of him like the blade of a bulldozer, he charged across the room, flattening all and everything before him.

The crash of breaking furniture and the yelp and squeal of men being struck down drove Big King beyond the frontiers of sanity into the red atavistic fury of the berserker.

Basuto is also one of the fighting tribes of the N'guni group. These wiry mountaineers rushed into the conflict with the same savage joy as the Shangaans, a conflict that raged and roared out of the single room to engulf the entire population of Dump City.

One of the girls, her dress ripped from her back so she was left with only a tattered pair of bloomers, had climbed on top of the remains of the bar counter from where, with her big melon breasts swinging in the lamp light, she shrilled that peculiar ululation that Bantu women used to goad their menfolk into battle frenzy. A dozen of the other girls joined in, trilling, squealing, and the sound was too much for Big King.

With the bar top held ahead of him he charged straight through the flimsy wall of the shack, bursting it open like a paper bag. The roof sagged down wearily, and Big King raged on unchecked down the narrow dirt street, striking down any man who crossed his path, scattering chickens and yelping dogs, roaring like a bull gorilla.

He turned at the end of the encampment and came back, his frustration mounting as he found the street deserted except for a few prostrate bodies; through the gaping hole in the wall he entered the shebeen once more to find that here also the fighting had died down. A few of the participants were crawling, or moaning as they lay on the carpet of broken glass.

Big King glared about him, seeking a further outlet for his wrath.

'King Nkulu!' The girl was still on the trestle table, her eyes bright with excitement, her legs trembling with it.

Big King let out another roar, and hurled the bar top from him. It clattered against the far wall and Big King started towards her.

'You are a lion!' She shrieked encouragement at him, and she took one of her big black velvety breasts in each hand and pointed them at him, squeezing them together, shaking with excitement.

'Eat me!' she screamed, as Big King swept her off the table and, lifting her high, ran with her out into the night. Carrying her into the scrub below the mine dumps, holding her easily with one arm, ripping the leopard-tail kilt from his own waist as he ran.

– 35 –

It was Saturday night in Paris also, but there were men who were still working, for there were lights burning in the upstairs rooms of one of the big embassies in the rue Royale.

The fat man who had been the host in the gambling establishment in Johannesburg was now the guest. He sat at ease in a leather club easy chair, his corpulence and the steel-grey hair at his temples giving him dignity. His face heavy, tanned, intelligent. His eyes glittery and hard as the diamond on his finger.

He was listening intently to a man of about the same age as himself who stood before a projected image on a screen that covered one wall of the room. There was that in the man's bearing and manner that marked him as a scholar, he was speaking now, addressing himself directly to the listener in the easy chair, pointing with a marker to the screen beside him.

'You see here a plan of the working of the five producing gold mines of the Kitchenerville fields in relation to each other.' He touched the screen with the marker. 'Thornfontein, Blaauberg, Tweefontein, Deep Gold Levels and Sonder Ditch.'

The man in the chair nodded. 'I have seen and studied this diagram before.'

'Good, then you will know that the Sonder Ditch property sits in the centre of the field. It has common boundaries with the other four mines and here,' he tapped the screen again, 'it is intersected by the massive serpentine dyke which they call the Big Dipper.'

Again the fat man nodded.

'It is for these reasons we have selected the Sonder Ditch as the trigger point.' The lecturer touched a button on the wall panel and the image on the screen changed.

'Now, here is something you have not seen before.'

The man in the chair crouched forward.

'What is it?'

'It is an underground map based on the borehole results of the five companies who have been exploring the ground to the east of the Big Dipper. These results have been pooled and interpreted by some of the finest brains in the fields of geology and hydrophysics. You have here a carefully considered representation of exactly what lies on the far side of the Big Dipper fault.'

The big man moved uncomfortably in his chair.

'It's a monster!'

'Yes, a monster. Lying just beyond the fault is an underground lake, no, that is not the correct word. Let us call it an underground sea, the size of, say, Lake Eyrie. The water is held in a vast sponge of porous dolomite rock.'

'My God.' For the first time the fat man had lost his

poise. 'If this is right, why don't the mining companies arrive at the same conclusion and keep well away from it?'

'Because,' the lecturer switched off the image and the overhead lights came on, 'because of their highly competitive attitude none of them has access to the findings of the others. It is only when all the results are studied that the picture becomes clear.'

'How did your government come to be in possession of *all* the results?' demanded the fat man.

'That is not important.' The lecturer was brusque, impatient of the interruption. 'We are also in possession of the findings of a certain Dr Peter Wessels who is at present head of a research team in Rock Mechanics based on the Sonder Ditch mine property. It is Company classified information and consists of a paper that Dr Peter Wessels has written on the shatter patterns and stresses of rock. His researches are directly related to the Ventersdorp quartzites which comprise the country rock of the Sonder Ditch workings.'

The lecturer picked up a pamphlet from his desk.

'I will not weary you by asking you to wade through its highly technical findings. Instead I will give it to you in capsule form. Dr Wessels arrives at the conclusion that a column of Ventersdorp quartzite 120 feet thick would shatter under a side pressure of 4,000 pounds per square inch.'

The lecturer dropped the pamphlet back on the desk.

'As you know, by law, the gold mining companies are bound to leave a barrier of solid rock 120 feet thick along their boundaries. That is all that separates one mine's working from another, just that wall of rock. You understand?'

'Of course. It is very simple.'

'Simple? Yes, it is simple! This Dr Steyner, over whom you have control, will instruct the new General Manager of the Sonder Ditch to drive a tunnel through the Big Dipper dyke. The drive will puncture the vast underground reservoir and the water will run back and flood the entire Sonder Ditch workings. Once they are flooded, the pressure delivered by a 6,000-foot head of water at the lower levels will be in excess of 4,000 pounds per square inch. That is sufficient to burst the rock walls, and flood the Thornfontein, the Blaauberg, Deep Gold Levels and Tweefontein gold mines.'

'The entire Kitchenerville gold fields would be effectively and permanently put out of production. The consequences for the economy of the Republic of South Africa would be catastrophic.'

The fat man was visibly shaken.

'Why do you want to do it?' he asked, shaking his head in awe.

'My colleague here,' the lecturer indicated a man who was sitting quietly in one corner, 'will explain that to you presently.'

'But – people!' the fat man protested. 'There will be people down there when it bursts, thousands of them.'

The lecturer smiled, raising one eyebrow. 'If I were to tell you that six thousand men would drown, would you refuse to proceed, and forfeit the million-dollar payment my government has offered you?'

The fat man looked down, embarrassed, and muttered barely audibly, 'No.'

The lecturer chuckled. 'Good! Good! However, you may salve you aching conscience by assuring yourself that we do not expect more than forty or fifty fatalities from the flooding. Naturally, those men actually working on the face will be killed. But that tremendous volume of water under immense pressure should make it a merciful death. For the rest of them, the mine can be evacuated swiftly enough to allow them excellent chances of survival. The surrounding mines will have days to evacuate before the water pressure builds up sufficiently to burst through the boundary walls.'

There was silence then in the room for nearly a minute.

'Have you any questions?'

The fat man shook his head.

'Very well, in that case I will leave it to my colleague to complete the briefing. He will explain the necessity for this operation, will arrange the terms of payment and conditions upon which you will proceed.' The lecturer gathered up the pamphlet and other papers from the desk. 'It remains only for me to wish you good luck.' He chuckled again and left the room quickly.

The little man, who up until them had remained silent, suddenly bounced out of his chair and began pacing up and down the wall-to-wall carpeting. He spoke rapidly, shooting occasional sideways glances at his audience, his bald head shining in the fluorescent lighting, wriggling his moustache like rabbit whiskers, puffing nervously at his cigarette.

'Reasons first. I'll make it short and sweet, right? The South Africans and the Frogs have got together. They're here in Paris now cooking up mischief. We know what they're up to, they're going to launch an all-out attack on my government's currency. Gold price increase, you know. Very complicated and very nasty for us, right? They might just be able to do it, South Africa is the world's biggest gold producer. With the Frogs helping her, they might just be able to force an increase.'

He stopped in front of the fat man and thrust out an accusing finger.

'Are we going to sit back and let them have a free run? No, sir! We are going to throw down our own curve ball! In three months time the Syndicate will be ready to attack. At that precise moment we will kick the chair out from under the South Africans by cutting their gold production in half. We will flood the Kitchenerville goldfields and the attack will fizzle out like a damp squib, right?'

'As simple as that?' asked the fat man.

'As simple as that!' The bald head nodded vigorously.

'Now, my next duty is to make clear to you that the agreed million dollars is *all* the reward you receive. Neither you nor your agents may indulge in any financial transactions that might, in retrospect, show that this was a planned operation, right?'

'Right.' The fat man nodded.

'You give your assurance that you will not deal in any of the shares of the companies involved?'

'You have my solemn word.' The fat man told him earnestly, and not for the first time in his life reflected how easily and painlessly a promise could be given.

With the assistance of the three men who had watched Manfred Steyner that night at the gambling club in Johannesburg, he intended launching a bear offensive on the stock exchanges of the world.

On the day that they drilled into the Big Dipper dyke he and his partners would sell millions of the shares of the five mining companies for one of the biggest financial killings in the history of money.

'We are agreed then.' The bald head bobbed. 'Now, as for this Dr Steyner, we have had a screening and personality analysis and we believe that, despite the secure hold you have on his loyalties, he would jib at giving the order to drive on the Big Dipper if he were aware of the consequences. Therefore we have prepared a second geological report,' he produced from his brief case a thick manila folder, 'incorporating those figures which he will recognize. In other words the drilling results of the CRC exploration teams, but the other figures are fictitious. This report purports to prove the existence of a fabulously rich gold reef beyond the fault.' He crossed to the fat man and handed him the folder. 'Take it. It will help you convince Dr Steyner, and he in turn to convince the new General Manager of the Sonder Ditch gold mine.'

'You have been thorough,' said the fat man.

'We try to give a satisfactory service to our customers,' said the bald man.

– 36 –

The game was five-card stud poker, and there were two big winners at the table, Manfred Steyner and the Algerian.

Manfred had timed his arrival in Paris to ensure himself an uninterrupted weekend before the rest of the delegates came in on the Monday morning flight.

He had checked in at the Hotel George Cinq on Saturday afternoon, bathed and rested for three hours until eight in the evening, then he had set out for the Club Chat Noir by taxi.

He had been playing now for five hours, and a steady succession of strong cards had pushed his winnings up to a formidable sum. It lay piled in front of him, a fruit salad of garish French bank notes. Across the table sat the Algerian, a slim dark-skinned Arab with toffee eyes and a silky black moustache. His teeth were very white against the creamy brown skin. He wore a turtle-neck shirt in pink silk, and a linen jacket of baby blue. With long brown fingers he kept smoothing and stacking his own pile of bank notes.

A girl sat on the arm of his chair, an Arab girl in a skin-tight gold trouser suit. Her hair was shiny black and hung onto her shoulders, her eyes were disconcertingly level as she watched Manfred.

'Ten thousand.' Manfred's voice was explosive, like that of a teutonic drillmaster. He was betting on his fourth card which had just been dealt to him. He and the Algerian were the remaining players in the game. The others had folded their hands and were sitting back watching with the casual interest of men no longer involved.

The Algerian's eyes narrowed slightly and the girl leaned down to whisper softly in his ear. He shook his head, annoyed, and drew on his cigarette. He had a pair of queens and a six showing and he leaned forward to study Manfred's cards.

The dealer's voice prodded. 'The bet is ten thousand francs, from four, five, seven of clubs. Possible straight flush.'

'Bet or drop,' said one of the uncommitted players. 'You're wasting time.'

The Algerian flashed him a venomous glance.

'Bet,' he said, and counted out ten thousand-franc notes into the pool.

'*Carte.*' The dealer slid a card face down in front of each of them. Quickly the Algerian lifted one corner of his card with his thumb, glanced at it and then closed the face.

Manfred sat very still, the card lying inches from his right hand. His face was pale, calm, but he was seething internally. Far from a possible straight flush, Manfred was holding four, five, seven of clubs and the eight of hearts. A six was the only card that could improve his hand and one six was already showing among the Algerian's cards. His chances were remote.

His lower belly and loins were tight and hot with excitement, his chest constricted. He drew out the sensation, wanting it to last for ever.

'Pair of queens still to bet,' murmured the dealer.

'Ten thousand.' The Algerian pushed the notes forward.

He has found another queen, thought Manfred, but he is uncertain of my flush or straight.

Manfred placed his smooth white hand over his fifth card, cupping it. He lifted it.

'Table,' said Manfred calmly, and there was a gasp and rustle from the watchers. The girl's hand tightened on the Algerian's sleeve, she stared with hatred into Manfred's face.

113

'The gentleman has made a table bet,' intoned the croupier. 'House rules. Any player may bet the entire stake he has upon the table.' He reached across and began to count the notes in front of Manfred.

Minutes later he announced the total. 'Two hundred and twelve thousand francs.' He looked across at the Algerian. 'It is now up to you to bet against the possible straight flush.'

The girl whispered urgently into the Arab's ear, but he snapped a single word at her and she recoiled. He looked about the room, as if seeking guidance, then he lifted and examined his hole cards again.

Suddenly his face hardened, and he looked steadily across at Manfred.

'Call!' he blurted, and Manfred's clenched right hand fell open upon the table.

The Arab faced his hand. Three queens. The whole room looked expectantly at Manfred.

He flicked over his last card. Two of diamonds. His hand was worthless.

With a birdlike cry of triumph the Algerian leaped from his seat and reaching across the table began raking Manfred's stake with both arms towards him.

Manfred stood up from the table, and the Arab girl grinned maliciously at him, taunting him in Arabic. He turned quickly away and almost ran down the steps that led to the cloakrooms. Twenty minutes later, feeling weak and slightly dizzy, Manfred slipped into the back seat of a Citroën taxi cab.

'George Cinq,' he told the driver. As he entered the lobby of the hotel he saw a tall figure rise from one of the leather armchairs and follow him across to the lifts. Shoulder to shoulder they stepped into the lift and as the doors slid closed the tall man spoke.

'Welcome to Paris, Dr Steyner.'

'Thank you, Andrew. I presume you have come to give me my instructions?'

'That is correct. He wishes to see you tomorrow at ten o'clock. I will call for you.'

It was Saturday night in Kitchenerville and in the men's bar of the Lord Kitchener Hotel the daily-paid men from the five gold mines were bellying up to the counter three deep.

The public dance had been in progress for three hours. At tables along the veranda the women-folk sat primly sipping their port and lemonade. Although they all were admirably ignoring the absence of the men, yet a constant and merciless vigil was kept on the door to the men's bar. Most of the wives already had the automobile keys safely in their handbags.

In the dining-hall, cleared of its furniture and sprinkled liberally with French chalk, the local four-piece band who played under the unlikely name of the 'Wind Dogs' launched without preliminaries into a lively rendition of 'Die Ou Kraal Liedjie', and from the men's bar, in various stages of inebriation, answering the call to arms came the troops.

Many of them had shed their jackets, the knots of their ties had slipped, their voices were boisterous and legs were a little unsteady as they led their women onto the dance floor and immediately showed to which school of the dance they belonged.

There was the cavalry squadron which tucked partner under one arm, very much like a lance, and charged. At the other end of the scale were those who plodded grimly around the perimeter, looking neither left nor right, speaking to no one, not even their partners. Then there were the sociables who reeled about the floor, red in the face, their movements completely unrelated to the music, shouting to their friends and attempting to pinch any feminine posterior that came within range. Their unpredictable progress interfered with the revolutions of the dedicated.

The dedicated took up their positions in the centre of the floor and twisted. A half dozen years previously the twist had swept like an Asian 'flu epidemic through the world and then faded out. Gone, forgotten, except in places like Kitchenerville. Here it had been taken and firmly entrenched into the social culture of the community.

Even in this stronghold of the twist, there was one master. 'Johnny Delange? Gott man, but he can twist, hey!' they murmured with awe.

With the sinuous erotic movements of an erect cobra, Johnny was twisting with Hettie. His shiny rayon suit caught the light and the lace ruffles of his shirt fluttered at his throat. There was a fierce grin of pleasure on his hawk features, and the jewelled buckles of his pointed Italian shoes twinkled as he danced.

A big girl with copper hair and creamy skin, Hettie was light on her feet. She had a tiny waist and a swelling regal bottom under the emerald-green skirt. She laughed as she danced, a full healthy laugh to match her body.

The two of them moved with the expertise of a couple who have danced together often. Hettie anticipated each of Johnny's movements, and he grinned his approval at her.

From the veranda Davy Delange watched them. He stood in the shadows, clutching a tankard of beer, a squat, lonely figure. When another dancing couple cut off his view of Hettie's luscious revolving buttocks he would exclaim with irritation and move restlessly.

The music ended and the dancers spilled out onto the veranda, laughing and breathless, mopping streaming faces;

girls squealing and giggling as the men led them to their seats, deposited them and then headed for the bar.

'See you.' Johnny left Hettie reluctantly, he would have liked to stay with her, but he was sensitive about what the boys would say if he spent the whole evening with his wife.

He was absorbed into the masculine crowd, to join their banter and loud laughter. He was deeply involved in a discussion of the merits of the new Ford Mustang, which he was considering buying, when Davy nudged him.

'It's Constantine!' he whispered, and Johnny looked up quickly. Constantine was a Greek immigrant, a stoper on the Blaauberg Mine. He was a big strong black-haired individual with a broken nose. Johnny had broken his nose for him about ten months previously. As a bachelor Johnny would fight him on the average of once a month, nothing serious, just a semi-friendly punch-up.

However, Constantine could not understand that nowadays Johnny was forbidden by his brand new wife from indulging in casual exchanges of fisticuffs. He had developed the erroneous theory that Johnny Delange was afraid of him.

He was coming down the bar room now, holding his glass in his massive hairy right hand with the little finger extended genteely. On his hip rested his other hand and he minced along with a simpering smile on his blue-jowled granite-textured features. Stopping in front of the mirror to pat his hair into place, he winked at his cronies and then came on down to where Johnny stood. He paused and ogled Johnny heavily, fluttering his eyelids and wriggling his hips. His colleagues from the Blaauberg Mine were weak with laughter, gurgling merrily, hanging onto each other's shoulders.

Then with a bump and grind that raised another howl of laughter Constantine disappeared into the lavatories, to emerge minutes later and blow Johnny a kiss as he went back to join his friends. They plied liquor on the Greek in appreciation of his act. Johnny's smile was a little strained as he resumed the discussion on the Mustang's virtues.

Twenty minutes and half a dozen brandies later, Constantine repeated his little act again on the way to the latrine. His repertoire was limited.

'Hold it, Johnny,' whispered Davy. 'Let's go and sit on the veranda.'

'He's asking for it. I'm telling you!' Johnny's smile had disappeared.

'Come on, Johnny, man.'

'No, hell, they'll think I'm running. I can't go now.'

'You know what Hettie will say,' Davy warned him. For a moment longer Johnny hesitated.

'The hell with what Hettie says.' Johnny bunched his right fist with its array of gold rings as he moved down to Constantine and leaned beside him on the counter.

'Herby,' he called the barman, and when he had his attention he indicated the Greek. 'Please give the lady a port and lemonade.'

And the bystanders scattered for cover. Davy shot out of the door onto the veranda to report to Hettie.

'Johnny!' he gasped. 'He's fighting again.'

'Is he!' Hettie came to her feet like a red-headed Valkyrie. But her progress to the men's bar was delayed by the crowd of spectators that jammed the doorway and all the windows. The crowd was tiptoeing and climbing onto the chairs and tables for a better view, every thud or crash of breaking furniture was greeted with a roar of delight.

Hettie had her handbag clutched in her right hand, and like a jungle explorer hacking his way through the undergrowth with a machete, she opened a path for herself to the bar room door.

At the door she paused. The conflict had reached a critical stage. Among a litter of broken glass and shattered stools, Johnny and the Greek were circling each other warily, waving and feinting, all their wits concentrated upon each other. Both of them were marked. The Greek was bleeding from his lip, a thin red ribbon of blood down his chin that dripped onto his shirt. Johnny had a shiny red swelling closing one eye. The crowd was silent, waiting.

'Johnny Delange!' Hettie's voice cracked like a Mauser rifle fired from ambush. Johnny started guiltily, dropping his hands, half turning towards her as the Greek's fist crashed into the side of his head. Johnny spun from the blow, hit the wall and slid down quietly.

With a roar of triumph Constantine rushed forward to put the boot into Johnny's prostrate form, but he pitched forward to sprawl unconscious beside Johnny. Hettie had hit him with the water bottle snatched up from one of the table tops.

'Please help me get my husband to the car,' she appealed to the men around her, suddenly helpless and little-girlish.

She sat beside Davy in the front of the Monaco, fuming with anger.

Johnny lay at ease upon the back seat. He was snoring softly.

'Don't be angry, Hettie.' Davy was driving sedately.

'I've told him, not once, a hundred times.' Hettie's voice crackled like static. 'I told him I wouldn't put up with it.'

'It wasn't his fault. The Greek started it,' Davy explained softly and placed his hand on her leg.

'You stick up for him, just because he is your brother.'

'That's not true,' Davy soothed her, stroking her leg. 'You know how I feel about you, Hettie.'

'I don't believe you.' His hand was moving higher. 'You men are all the same. You all stick together.'

Her anger was fast solidifying into a burning resentment of Johnny Delange, one in which she was willing to take a calculated revenge. She knew that Davy's hand was no longer trying to comfort her and quench her anger. Before she married Johnny Delange, Hettie had had every opportunity to learn about men, and she had been an enthusiastic and receptive pupil. She placed no special importance on an act of the flesh, dispensing her favours as casually as someone might offer a cigarette-case around.

'Why not?' she thought. 'That will fix Mr Johnny Delange! Not all the way, of course, but just enough to get my own back on him.'

'No, Hettie. It's true – I tell you.' Davy's voice was husky, as he felt her knees fall apart under his hand. He touched the silky-smooth skin above her stocking top.

The Monaco slowed to almost walking pace, and it was ten minutes more before they reached the company-owned house on the outskirts of Kitchenerville.

In the back seat Johnny groaned. Immediately Davy's hand jerked back to the steering-wheel, and Hettie sat up in the seat, straightening her skirt.

'Help me get him inside,' she said, and her voice was shaky and her cheeks flushed. She was no longer angry.

– 38 –

They were both a little tipsy. They had stopped to celebrate Rod's promotion at the Sunnyside Hotel. They had sat side by side in one of the booths, drinking quickly, excitedly, laughing together, sitting close but not touching.

Terry Steyner could not remember when she had last behaved this way. It must have been all of ten years ago, her last term at Cape Town varsity, swigging draught beer in the Pig and Whistle at Randall's Hotel and talking the most inane rubbish. All the matronly dignity that Manfred insisted she maintain was gone, she felt like a freshette on a first date with the captain of the rugby team.

'Let's get out of here,' Rod said suddenly, and she stood

up unquestioningly. He took her arm down the stairs, and the light touch of his fingers tingled on her bare skin.

In the Maserati again she experienced the feeling of isolation from reality.

'How often do you see your daughter, Rod?' she asked as he settled into the seat beside her, and he glanced at her, surprised.

'Every Sunday.'

'Tomorrow?'

'Yes.'

'How old is she?'

'Nine next birthday.'

'What do you do with her?'

Rod pressed the starter.

'How do you mean?'

'Where do you take her, what do you do together?'

'We go rowing on Zoo Lake, or eat ice cream sundaes. If it's cold or raining we sit in the apartment and we play mah-jong.' He let in the clutch, and as they pulled away he added, 'She cheats.'

'The apartment?'

'I keep a hideaway in town.'

'Where?'

'I'll show you,' said Rod quietly.

She sat on the studio couch and looked about her with interest. She had not expected the obvious care that he had taken in furnishing the apartment. It was in wheatfield gold, chocolate brown and copper. There was a glorious glowing autumn landscape on the far wall that she recognized as a Dino Paravano.

She noticed a little ruefully how Rod stage-managed the lighting for full romantic effect, and then moved automatically to the liquor cabinet.

'Where is the bathroom?' Terry asked.

'Second left, down the passage.'

She lingered in the bathroom, opening the medicine cabinet like a thief. There were three toothbrushes hanging in the slots, and below them an aerosol can of Bidex. Quickly she shut the cabinet. Feeling disturbed, not sure if it was jealousy or guilt at her own prying.

The bedroom door was open and so she could not help seeing the double bed as she went back to the lounge. She stood in front of the painting.

'I love his work,' she said.

'Not too photographic for your taste?'

'No. I love it.'

He gave her the drink and stood beside her, studying the painting. She tinkled the ice in her glass, and he turned towards her. The feeling of unreality was still holding Terry as she felt him take the glass from her hand.

She was conscious of his hands only, they were strong and very practised. They touched her shoulders, and then moved onto her back calmly. She felt a voluptuous shudder shake her whole body, and then his mouth came down over hers and the sense of unreality was complete. It was all warm and misty, and she let him take control.

She never knew how long afterwards she jerked back to complete, chilling reality. They were on the couch. She lay in his arms. The front of her slack suit was open to the waist and her bra was unhooked. His head was bowed over her and with a handful of thick springy hair she was directing his lips in their quest. His mouth was warm and sucky on her breast.

'I must be mad!' she gasped, and struggled violently from his arms. She was trembling with fright, horrified with herself. Nothing like this had ever happened to her before.

'This is madness!' Her eyes were great dark pools in her pale face, and her fingers were frantic as she buttoned her blouse. As the last button slipped into its hole, anger replaced her fright.

'How many women have you seduced on that couch, Rodney Ironsides?'

Rod stood up, reaching out a hand to reassure her.

'Don't touch me!' She stepped back. 'I want to go home!'

'I'll take you home, Terry. Just calm down. Nothing happened.'

'That's not your fault,' she blazed.

'No, it's not,' he agreed.

'If you had your way, you'd have—' she bit it off.

'Yes, I would have.' Rod nodded. 'But only if you wanted the same thing.'

She stared at him, starting to recover her temper and her control.

'I shouldn't have come up here, I know. It was asking for trouble, but please take me home now.'

– 39 –

The telephone woke Rod. He checked his wrist watch as he tottered naked and half asleep through to the lounge. Eight o'clock.

'Ironsides!' He yawned into the mouthpiece, and then came fully awake as he recognized her voice.

'Good morning, Rodney. How's your hangover?'

He had not expected to hear from her again.

'Just bearable.'

'I called to thank you for an amusing and – instructive evening.'

'Hark at the girl!' He grinned and scratched his chest. 'She changes with the wind. Last night I expected a bullet between the eyes.'

'Last night I got one big fright,' she admitted. 'It comes

as a bit of a shock to discover suddenly that you are quite capable of acting the wanton. Not all the names I called you were meant.'

'I am sorry for my contribution to your distress,' Rod said.

'Don't be, you were very impressive.' Then quickly, changing the subject, 'You are picking up your daughter today?'

'Yes.'

'I'd like to meet her.'

'That could be arranged.' Rod was cautious.

'Does she like horses?'

'She's crazy about them.'

'Would you like to take her and me out to my stud farm on the Vaal river?'

Rod hesitated. 'Is it safe? I mean, being seen together?'

'It's my reputation, I'll look after it.'

'Fine!' Rod agreed. 'We'd love to visit your farm.'

'I'll meet you at your apartment. When?'

'Half past nine!'

Patti was still in her dressing-gown and she offered Rod her cheek casually to be pecked. There were curlers in her hair and from her eyes he could tell she'd had a late night.

'Hello, you're getting thin. Melly is dressing. Do you want some coffee? Your maintenance cheque was late again this month.' And she took a swipe at the spaniel pup as it squatted on the carpet. 'Damn dog pees all over the place. *Melanie.*' She raised her voice. 'Hurry up! Your Papa is here.'

'Hello, Daddy!' Melanie's voice shrieked delightedly from the interior of the apartment.

'Hello, baby.'

'You can't come in, Daddy, I haven't got any clothes on.'

'Well hurry up! I've come a million miles to see you.'

'Not a *million*!' You couldn't fool Melanie Ironsides.

'Did you say you wanted coffee? It's no trouble, it's made already.' Pattie led him through into the sitting-room.

'Thanks.'

'How are things?' she asked as she filled a cup and gave it to him.

'They've made me General Manager of the Sonder Ditch.' He could not prevent himself, it was too good. He had to boast.

Patti looked at him, startled.

'You're joking!' she accused, and then he saw her mind beginning to work like a cash register.

He almost laughed out loud. 'No. It's true.'

'God!' She sat down limply. 'It will nearly *double* your salary.'

He looked at her dispassionately, and not for the first time felt a great wash of relief as he realized he was no longer shackled to her.

'It's usual to offer congratulations,' he prompted her.

'You don't deserve it.' She was angry now. 'You are a selfish, philandering bastard, Rodney Ironsides, you don't deserve the good things that keep happening to you.' He had cheated her. She could have been the General Manager's wife, first lady of the goldfields. Now she was a divorcée, stuck with a miserable four fifty a month. It had seemed good before, but not now.

'I hope you will have enough conscience to make a suitable adjustment for Melanie and me. We are entitled to a share.'

The door burst open and Melanie Ironsides arrived at a gallop to wrap herself around Rod's neck. She had long blonde hair and green eyes.

'I got nine out of ten for spelling!'

'You're not clever, you're a genius. Also you're beautiful.'

'Will you carry me down to the car, Daddy?'

'What's wrong? Your legs in plaster?'

'Please, please, pretty please times three.'

Patti interrupted the love feast. 'Have you got your jersey, young lady?'

And Melanie flew.

'I'll have her back before seven,' said Rod.

'You haven't answered my question.' Patti was surly. 'Do we get a share?'

'Yes, of course,' said Rod. 'The same big juicy four fifty you've had all along.'

They had been in Rod's apartment ten minutes when the doorbell announced Terry's arrival. She was in jeans and a checked shirt with her hair in a plait, and she greeted Rod self-consciously. When he introduced her to Melanie, she did not look much older than his daughter.

The two girls summed each other up solemnly. Melanie was suddenly very demure and refined, and Rod was relieved to see that Terry had the good sense not to gush over the child.

They were in the Maserati and half way to the village of Parys on the Vaal River before Melanie had completed her microscopic scrutiny of Terry.

'Can I come up front and sit on your lap?' she asked at last.

'Yes, of course.' Terry was hard put to conceal her relief and pleasure. Melanie scrambled over the seat and settled on Terry's lap.

'You are pretty,' Melanie gave her considered opinion.

'Thank you. So are you.'

'Are you Daddy's girlfriend?' Melanie demanded. Terry glanced across at Rod, then burst out laughing.

'Almost,' she gurgled, and then all three of them were laughing.

They laughed often that day. It was a day of sunshine and laughter.

Terry and Rod walked together with fingers almost touching through the green paddocks along the willow-lined bank of the Vaal. Melanie ran ahead of them shrieking with glee at the antics of the foals.

They went up to the stables where Melanie fed sugar lumps to a winner of the Cape Metropolitan Handicap and then kissed his velvety muzzle.

They swam in the pool beside the elegant whitewashed homestead, laughter mingling with the splashes, and when they drove back to Johannesburg in the evening Melanie curled in exhausted slumber on Terry's lap, her head cushioned on Terry's bosom.

Terry waited in the Maserati while Rod carried the sleeping child up to her mother, and when he returned and slipped into the driver's seat, Terry murmured, 'My car is at your apartment. You'll have to take me with you.'

Neither of them spoke until they were back in Rod's sitting-room. Then he said, 'Thank you for a wonderful day.' And he took her to his chest and kissed her.

In the darkness she lay pressed to his sleeping body, clinging to him, as though he might be taken from her. She had never felt such intensity of emotion before, it was a compound of awed wonder and gratitude. She had just been admitted to a new level of human experience she had never suspected existed.

The sheets were still damp. She felt bruised internally, aching, a slow voluptuous pulse of pain that she cherished.

Lightly she touched his body, not wanting to wake him, running her fingertips through the coarse curls that covered his chest, marvelling still at the infinity that separated this from what she had known before.

She shuddered with almost unbearable pleasure as she remembered his voice describing her body to her, making her proud of it for the first time in her life. She remembered the words he had used to tell her exactly what they were doing together, and the feel of his hands, so gentle, sure, so lovingly possessive upon her.

He was so unashamed, taking such obvious joy in her, that the reserves which the barren years of her marriage had placed in her mind were swept away and she was able to go with Rodney Ironsides beyond the storm into that tranquil state where mind and body are completely at peace.

She became aware of him awakening beside her, and she touched his face, his lips and his eyes with her fingertips.

'Thank you,' she whispered, and he seemed to understand, for he took her head and drew it gently down into the hollow of his shoulder.

'Sleep now,' he told her softly, and she closed her eyes and lay very still and quiet beside him, but she did not sleep. She would not miss one moment of this experience.

– 40 –

Rod's letter of appointment lay on his desk when he arrived at his office at seven-thirty on the Monday morning.

He sat down and lit a cigarette. Then he began to read it slowly, savouring each word.

'Duly instructed by the Board of Directors,' it began, and ended, 'it remains only to tender the congratulations of the Board, and to voice their confidence in your ability.'

Dimitri came through from his office, distracted.

'Hey! Rod! Christ what a start to the week! We've got a fault in the main high voltage cable on 90 level, and—'

'Don't come squealing to me,' Rod cut him short. 'I'm not the Underground Manager.'

Dimitri gaped at him, taken by surprise.

'What the hell, have they fired you?'

'Next best thing,' said Rod and flipped the letter across the desk. 'Look what the bastards have done to me.'

Dimitri read and then whooped, 'My God, Rod! My God!' He shot down the passage to carry the news to the other line managers. Then they were all in his office, shaking his hand. He judged most of their reactions as favourable, though occasionally he detected a false note. A twinge of envy here, one there who had recently had his ears burned by the Ironsides tongue, and an incompetent who knew his job was now in danger. The phone rang. Rod answered it, his expression changed and he cleared his office with a peremptory wave.

'Hirschfeld here.'

'Morning, Mr Hirschfeld.'

'Well, you've got your chance, Ironsides.'

'I'm grateful for it.'

'I want to see you. I'll give you today to sort yourself out. Tomorrow morning at nine o'clock, my office at Reef Buildings.'

'I'll be there.'

'Good.'

Rod hung up, and the day dissolved into a welter of activity and reorganization, constantly interrupted by a stream of well-wishers. He was still running the Underground Manager's job in addition to the General Manager's. It would be some considerable time before a new Underground Manager was transferred in from one of the other group mines. He was trying to arrange his move to the big office in the main Administrative Block up on the ridge, when he had another visitor, Frank Lemmer's secretary, Miss Lily Jordan, looking like a wardress from Ravensbruck in a severe grey flannel suit.

'Mr Ironsides, you and I have not seen eye to eye in the past.'

This was the understatement of the year. 'It is unlikely that we will in the future. Therefore, I have come to tender my resignation. I have made arrangements.'

The phone rang. Dan Stander's voice, breezy and carefree.

'Rod, I'm in love.'

'Oh Christ, no!' Rod groaned. 'Not this morning.'

'I've got to thank you for introducing me to her. She's the most wonderful—'

'Yeah, yeah!' Rod cut him short. 'Look, Dan, I'm rather busy. Some other time, all right?'

'Oh yes, I forgot. You are the new General Manager they tell me. Congratulations. You can buy me a drink at the Club. Six o'clock.'

'Right. By then I'll need one.' Rod hung up, and faced the hanging-judge expression of Miss Lily Jordan.

'Miss Jordan, in the past our interests have conflicted. In the future they will not. You are the best private secretary within a hundred miles of the Sonder Ditch. I need you, the Company needs you.'

That was the magic word. Miss Jordan had twenty-five years' service with the Company. She wavered visibly.

'Please, Miss Jordan, give me a chance.' Shamelessly Rod switched on his most engaging smile. Miss Jordan's femininity was not so completely atrophied that she could resist that smile.

'Very well, then, Mr Ironsides. I'll stay on initially until the end of the month. We'll see after that.' She stood up. 'Now, I'll get your things moved up to the new office.'

'Thank you, Miss Jordan.' With relief he let her take over, and tackled the problems that were piling up on his desk. One man, two jobs. Now he was responsible for surface operation as well as underground. The phone rang, men queued up in the passage, memos kept coming through from Dimitri's office. There was no lunch hour, and by the time she rang he was exhausted.

'Hello,' she said. 'Do I see you tonight?' Her voice was as refreshing as a wet cloth on the brow of a prizefighter between rounds.

'Terry.' He simply spoke her name in reply.

'Yes or no. If it's *no*, I intend jumping off the top of Reef Building.'

'Yes,' he said. 'Pops has summoned me to a meeting at nine tomorrow morning, so I'll be staying overnight at the apartment. I'll call you as soon as I get in.'

'Goody! Goody!' said she.

At five-thirty Dimitri stuck his head around the door.

'I'm going down to No. 1 shaft to supervise the shoot, Rod.'

'My God, what time is it?' Rod checked his watch. 'So late already.'

'It gets late early around here,' Dimitri agreed. 'I'm off.'

'Wait!' Rod stopped him. 'I'll shoot her.'

'No trouble.' Dimitri demurred. Company standard procedure laid down that each day's blast must be supervised by either the Underground Manager or his assistant.

'I'll do it,' Rod repeated. Dimitri opened his mouth to protest further, then he saw that expression on Rod's face and changed his mind quickly.

'Okay then. See you tomorrow.' And he was gone.

Rod grinned at his own sentimentality. The Sonder Ditch was his now and, by God, he was going to shoot his own first blast on her.

They were waiting for him at the steel door of the blast control room at the shaft head. It was a small concrete room like a wartime pillbox, and there were only two keys to the door. Dimitri had one, Rod the other.

The duty mine captain and the foreman electrician added their congratulations to the hundreds he had received

131

during the day, and Rod opened the door and they went into the tiny room.

'Check her out,' Rod instructed, and the mine captain began his calls to the shaft overseers at both No. 1 and No. 2 for their confirmation that the workings of the Sonder Ditch were deserted, that every human being who had gone down that morning had come out again this evening.

Meanwhile, the foreman electrician was busy at the electrical control board. He looked up at Rod.

'Ready to close the circuits, Mr Ironsides.'

'Go ahead,' Rod nodded and the man touched a switch. A green light showed up on the board.

'No. 1 north longwall closed and green.'

'Lock her in,' Rod instructed and the electrician touched another switch.

'No. 1 east longwall closed and green.'

'Lock her in.'

The green light showed that the firing circuit was intact. A red light would indicate a fault and the faulty circuit would not be locked into the blast pattern.

Circuit after circuit was readied until finally the foreman stood back from the control board.

'All green and locked in.'

Rod glanced at the mine captain.

'All levels clear, Mr Ironsides. She's ready to burn.'

'Cheesa!' said Rod, the traditional command that had come down from the days when each fuse had been individually lit by a hand-held igniter stick.

'Cheesa' was the Bantu word for 'burn'.

The mine captain crossed to the control board and opened the cage that guarded a large red button.

'Cheesa!' echoed the mine captain and hit the button with the heel of his hand.

Immediately the row of green lights on the control board was extinguished, and in its place showed a row of red lights. Every circuit had been broken by the explosions.

The ground under their feet began to tremble. Throughout the workings the shots were firing. In the stopes the head charges fired at the top of the inclines, then in succession the other shots went off behind them. Each charge taking a ten-ton bite of rock and reef out of the face.

At the end of the development drives, a more complicated pattern was shooting. First a row of *cutters* went off down the middle of the oval face. Then the *shoulder charges* at the top corners, followed by the *knee charges* at the bottom corners. A moment's respite with the dust and nitrous fumes swirling back down the drive, then a roar as the *easers* on each side shaped the hole. Another respite and then the *lifters* along the bottom picked up the heap of broken rock and threw it back from the face.

Rod could imagine it clearly. Though no human eye had ever witnessed the blast, he knew exactly what was taking place down there.

The last tremor died away.

'That's it. A full blast,' said the mine captain.

'Thank you.' Rod felt tired suddenly. He wanted that drink, even though their brief exchange that morning had warned him that Dan would probably be insufferable. He could guess the conversation would revolve around Dan's new-found love.

Then he smiled as he thought about what waited for him in Johannesburg later that night, and suddenly he wasn't all that tired.

They sat facing each other.

'Only three things worry me,' Terry told Rod.

'What are they?' Rod rubbed soap into the face flannel.

'Firstly, your legs are too long for this bath.'

Rod rearranged his limbs, and Terry shot half out of the water with a squeak.

'Rodney Ironsides, would you be good enough to take a bit more care where you put your toes!'

'Forgive me.' He leaned forward to kiss her. 'Tell me what else worries you.'

'Well, the second thing that worries me is that I'm not worried.'

'What part of Ireland did you say you were from?' Rod asked. 'County Cork?'

'I mean, it's terrible but I'm not even a little conscience-stricken. Once I believed that if it ever happened to me I would never be able to look another human being in the eyes, I'd be so ashamed.' She took the flannel from his hands and began soaping his chest and shoulders. 'But, far from being ashamed, I'd like to stand in the middle of Eloff Street at rush hour and shout "Rodney Ironsides is my lover".'

'Let's drink to that.' Rodney rinsed the soap from his hands and reached over the side of the bath to pick up the two wine glasses from the floor. He gave one to Terry and they clinked them together, the sparkling Cape burgundy glowed ruby red.

'Rodney Ironsides is my lover!' she toasted him.

'Rodney Ironsides is your lover,' he agreed and they drank.

'Now, I give *you* a toast,' he said.

'What is it?' She held her glass ready, and Rod leaned

forward and poured the red wine from the crystal glass between her breasts. It ran like blood down her white skin and he intoned solemnly:

'Bless this ship and all who sail in her!'

Terry gurgled with delight.

'To her captain. May he keep a firm hand on the rudder!'

'May her bottom never hit the reef!'

'May she be torpedoed regularly!'

'Terry Steyner, you are terrible.'

'Yes, aren't I?' And they drained their glasses.

'Now,' Rod asked, 'what is your third worry?'

'Manfred will be home on Saturday.'

They stopped laughing, Rod reached down for the burgundy bottle and refilled the glasses.

'We still have five days,' he said.

– 42 –

It had been a week of personal triumph for Manfred Steyner. His address to the conference had been the foundation of the entire talks, all discussion had revolved upon it. He had been called upon to speak at the closing banquet which General de Gaulle had attended in person, and afterwards the General had asked Manfred to take coffee and brandy with him in one of the ante-rooms. The General had been gracious, had asked questions and listened attentively to the answers. Twice he had called his finance minister's attention to Manfred's replies.

Their farewells had been cordial, with a hint of state recognition for Manfred, a decoration. In common with most Germans, Manfred had a weakness for uniforms and decorations. He imagined how a star and ribbon might look on the snowy front of his dress shirt.

There had been a wonderful press both in France and at

home. Even a bad-tempered quarter column in *Time* magazine, with a picture, de Gaulle stooping over the diminutive Manfred solicitously, one hand on his shoulder. The caption read: 'The huntsman and the hawk. To catch a dollar?'

Now standing in the tiny cloakroom in the tail of the South African Airways Boeing, Manfred was whistling softly as he stripped his shirt and vest, crumpled them into a ball and dropped them into the waste bin.

Naked to the waist, he wiped his upper body with a wet cloth and then rubbed 4711 Eau de Cologne into his skin. From the briefcase he took an electric razor. The whistling stopped as he contorted his face for the razor.

Through his mind ran page after page of the report that Andrew had delivered that morning to his hotel room. Manfred had total recall when it came to written material. Although the report was in the briefcase beside him, in his mind's eye he could review it word for word, figure for figure.

It was a stupendous piece of work. How the authors had gained access to the drilling and exploration reports of the five Kitchenerville field companies he could not even guess, for the gold mining companies' security was as tight as that of any national intelligence agency. But the figures were genuine. He had checked those purporting to be from CRC carefully. They were correct. So therefore the other four must also be genuine.

The names of the authors of the report were legend. They were the top men in the field. Their opinions were the best in Harley Street. The conclusion that they reached was completely convincing. In effect it was this:

If a haulage was driven from 66 level of the Sonder Ditch No. 1 shaft through the Big Dipper dyke, it would pass *under* the limestone water-bearing foundations, and just beyond the fault it would intersect a reef of almost unbelievable value.

It had not needed the lecture that Manfred had received

from his corpulent creditor to show him the possibilities. The man who gave the order to drive through the Big Dipper would receive the credit. He would certainly be elected to the chairmanship of the Group when that office fell vacant.

There was another possibility. A person who purchased a big packet of Sonder Ditch shares immediately before the reef was intersected would be a very rich man when he came to sell those shares later. He would be so rich that he would no longer be dependent on his wife for the means to live the kind of life he wanted, and indulge his own special tastes.

Manfred blew the hairs from his razor and returned it to his brief case. Then as he took out a fresh shirt and vest, he began to sing the words to the tune:

'Heute ist der schönste Tag
In meinem Leben.'

He would telephone Ironsides from Jan Smuts Airport as soon as he had passed through customs. Ironsides would come up to the house on Sunday morning and receive his orders.

As he knotted the silk of his tie Manfred knew that he stood at the threshold of a whole new world, the events of the next few months would lift him high above the level of ordinary men.

It was the chance for which he had worked and waited all these years.

Circumstances had changed completely since his last visit, Rod reflected, as he took the Maserati up the drive towards the Dutch gabled house.

He parked the car and switched off the ignition, sitting a while, reluctant to face the man who had sponsored his career and whom Rod in return had presented with a fine pair of horns.

'Courage, Ironsides!' he muttered and climbed out of the Maserati and went up the path across the lawns.

Terry was on the veranda in a gay print dress, with her hair loose, sprawled in a canvas chair with the Sunday papers scattered about her.

'Good morning, Mr Ironsides,' she greeted him as he came up the steps. 'My husband is in his study. You know the way, don't you?'

'Thank you, Mrs Steyner.' Rod kept his voice friendly but disinterested, then as he passed her chair he growled softly, 'I could eat you without salt.'

'Don't waste it, you gorgeous beast,' Terry murmured and ran the tip of her tongue over her lips.

Fifteen minutes later, Rod sat stony-faced and internally chilled before Manfred Steyner's desk. When at last he forced himself to speak, it felt as though the skin on his lips would tear with the effort.

'You want me to drive through the Big Dipper,' he croaked.

'More than that, Mr Ironsides. I want you to complete the drive within three months, and I want a complete security blanket on the development,' Manfred told him primly. Despite the fact that it was Sunday he was formally dressed, white shirt and dark suit. 'You will commence the drive from No. 1 shaft 66 level and make an intersect on reef at 6,600 feet with the SD No. 3 borehole 250 feet beyond the calculated extremity of the serpentine intrusion of the Big Dipper.'

'No,' Rod shook his head. 'You can't go through that. No one can take the chance. God alone knows what is on the other side, we only know that is bad ground. Stinking rotten ground.'

'How do you know that?' Manfred asked softly.

'Everybody on the Kitchenerville field knows it.'

'How?'

'Little things.' Rod found it hard to put into words. 'You get a feeling, the signs are there and when you've been in the game long enough you have a sixth sense that warns you when—'

'Nonsense,' Manfred interrupted brusquely. 'We no longer live in the days of witchcraft.'

'Not witchcraft, experience,' Rod snapped angrily. 'You've seen the drilling results from the other side of the fault?'

'Of course,' Manfred nodded. 'SD No. 3 found values of thousands of penny-weights.'

'And the other holes went dry and twisted off, or had water squirting out of them like a pissing horse!'

Manfred flushed fiercely. 'You will be good enough not to employ bar-room terminology in this house.'

Rod was taken off balance, and before he could answer Manfred went on.

'Would you put the considered opinions of,' Manfred named three men, 'before your own vague intuitions?'

'They are the best in the business,' Rod conceded reluctantly.

'Read that,' snapped Manfred. He tossed a manila folder onto the desk top, then stood up and went to wash his hands at the concealed basin.

Rod picked up the folder, opened it and was immediately engrossed. Ten minutes later, without looking up from the report, he fumbled a pack of cigarettes from his pocket.

139

'Please do not smoke!' Manfred stopped him sharply.

Three-quarters of an hour later, Rod closed the folder. During that time Manfred Steyner had sat with reptilian stillness behind his desk, with the glitter of his eyes the only signs of life.

'How the hell did you get hold of those figures and reports?' Rod asked with wonder.

'That does not concern you.' Manfred retrieved the folder from him, his first movement in forty-five minutes.

'So that's it!' muttered Rod. 'The water is in the limestone near the surface. We go in under it!' He stood up from the chair abruptly and began to pace up and down in front of Manfred's desk.

'Are you convinced?' Manfred asked, and Rod did not answer.

'I have promoted you above older and more experienced men,' said Manfred softly. 'If I tear you down again, and tell the world you were not man enough for the job, then, Rodney Ironsides, you are finished. No one else would take a chance on you again, ever!'

It was true. Rod knew it.

'However, if you were to follow my instructions and we intersected this highly enriched reef, then part of the glory would rub off on you.'

That was also true. Rod stopped pacing, he stood with shoulders hunched, in an agony of indecision. Could he trust that report beyond his own deep intuition? When he thought about that ground beyond the dyke, his skin tickled with gooseflesh. He almost had the stink of it in his nostrils. Yet he could be wrong, and the weight of the opposition was heavy. The eminent names on the report, the threats which he knew Manfred would not hesitate to put into effect.

'Will you give me a written instruction?' Rod demanded harshly.

'What effect would that have?' Manfred asked mildly.

140

'As General Manager, the decision to work certain ground or not to work it is technically yours. In the very unlikely event that you encountered trouble beyond the fault, it would be no defence to produce a written instruction from me. Just as if you murdered my wife you could not defend yourself by producing a written instruction from me to do so.'

This again was true. Rod knew he was trapped. He could refuse, and wreck his career. Or he could comply and take the consequences whatever they may be.

'No,' said Manfred, 'I will not give you a written instruction.'

'You bastard,' Rod said softly.

Manfred answered as gently. 'I warned you that you would not be able to refuse to obey me.'

And the last twinge of remorse that Rod felt for his association with Terry Steyner faded and was gone.

'You've given me three months to hit the Big Dipper. All right, Steyner. You've got it!'

Rod turned on his heel and walked out of the room.

Terry was waiting for him among the protea plants on the bottom lawn. She saw his face and dropped all pretence. She went to meet him.

'Rod, what is it?' Her hand on his arm, looking up into his eyes.

'Careful!' he warned her, and she dropped her hand and stood back.

'What is it?'

'That bloody Gestapo bastard,' Rod snarled, and then, 'I'm sorry, Terry, he's your husband.'

'What has he done?'

'I can't tell you here. When can I see you?'

'I'll find an excuse to get away later today. Wait for me at your apartment.'

Later she sat on the couch below the Paravano painting and listened while he told her about it. All of it, the report, the threat and the order to pierce the Big Dipper.

She listened but expressed neither approval nor disapproval of his decision.

Manfred turned away from the window and went back to his desk. Even at that distance there had been no doubt about his wife's gesture. The hand outstretched, the face turned up, the lips parted in anxious enquiry, and then the guilty start and withdrawal.

He sat down at his desk, and laid his hands neatly in front of him. For the first time he was thinking of Rodney Ironsides as a man and not a tool.

He thought how big he was, tall and as wide across the shoulders as a gallows. Any reprisal on Ironsides could not be physical, and it could not be immediate. It must be after the drive to the Big Dipper.

I can wait, he thought coldly, there is time for everything in this life.

– 44 –

Johnny and Davy Delange sat in the two chairs before Rod's desk. They were both awkward and uncomfortable up here in the big office with picture windows looking out over the Kitchenerville valley.

I don't blame them, Rod thought, even I am not accustomed to it yet. Wall-to-wall carpeting, air-conditioning, original paintings on the wood-panelled walls.

'I have sent for you because you two are the best rock breakers on the Sonder Ditch,' Rod began.

'Tin Ribs wants something,' thought Davy, with all the suspicion of the union man for management.

'We will now have a few words from our sponsor,' Johnny grinned to himself. 'Before we start the programme.'

Rod looked at their faces and knew exactly what they were thinking. He had been on daily pay himself once. Cut out the compliments, Ironsides – he advised himself – these are two tough cookies and they are not impressed.

'I am pulling you out of the stopes and putting you onto a special development end. You will take it in turns to work day and night shift. You will be directly responsible to me and there will be a security blanket on your activity.'

They watched him without reaction, their expressions guarded. Johnny broke the short silence.

'One end, one blast a day?' He was thinking of his pay. Calculated on the amount of rock broken, he would earn little more than basic salary with a blast on one small face daily.

'No.' Rod shook his head. 'Ultra-fast, multi-blast, and shaft sinkers' rates.'

And both the Delange brothers sat forward in their chairs.

'Multi-blast?' Davy asked. That meant that they could shoot just as soon as they were ready. A good team could blast three – maybe four times a shift.

'Ultra-fast?' Johnny demanded. That was language Johnny understood. It was a term employed only in emergency, as when driving in to rescue trapped men after a fall. It was tacit approval from management to waive standard safety procedure in favour of speed. Christ, Johnny exulted, I can shoot her four – maybe five times a shift.

'Shaft sinkers' rates?' they asked together. That was a 20 per cent bonus on stopers' rates. It was a fortune they were being offered.

Rod nodded affirmative to their questions, and waited for the reaction which he knew would follow. It came immediately.

The Delange brothers now began to look for the catch.

They sat stolidly turning the deal over in their minds, like two cautious housewives examining a tomato for blemishes because the price was too cheap.

'How long is this drive?' Johnny asked. If the drive was short, a few hundred feet, then it was worth nothing. They would hardly get into their stride before it was completed.

'Close on six thousand feet,' Rod assured him. They looked relieved.

'Where is it headed?' Davy discovered the rub.

'We are going to drive through the Big Dipper to intersect on reef at 6,000 feet.'

'Jesus!' said Johnny. 'The Big Dipper!' He was awed but unafraid. It excited him, the danger, the challenge. Had he been born earlier, Johnny Delange would have made a fine Spitfire pilot.

'The Big Dipper,' Davy murmured, his mind was racing. Nothing in this world or beyond would entice Davy Delange to drive through the Big Dipper. He had an almost religious fear of it. The name alone conjured up all sorts of hidden menace and unspeakable horror. Water. Gas. Friable ground, faults. Mud-rushes. All a miner's nightmare.

There was no question of him doing it, yet the money was too good to pass up. He could net ten or eleven thousand rand on those terms.

'All right, Mr Ironsides,' he said. 'I'll take the first night shifts. Johnny can start the day shifts.'

Davy Delange had made his decision. He would work until his drills hit the greenish-black serpentine rock of the dyke. He would then walk out of the drive and quit. He would go up to, but not beyond the dyke.

Afterwards, any of the other mines would snap him up, he had an impeccable record and he would force Johnny to follow him.

'Hey, Davy!' Johnny was delighted, he had expected Davy to turn the deal down flat.

Now he would be able to buy the Mustang for certain –

and perhaps an MGB GT for Hettie – and take a holiday to Durban over Christmas, and . . .

Rod was puzzled by Davy's easy agreement. He studied him a moment and decided that he had ferrety eyes. He's a sneaky little bastard, Rod decided, I'll have to watch him.

– 45 –

It took one shift only to prepare for the development. Rod selected the starting point. The main haulage curved away from the shaft on 66 level. 1,000 feet along this tunnel there was a chamber that had been cut out as a loco repair station but which was now out of use. Two large batwing ventilation doors were fitted to the opening of the chamber to provide privacy and behind them the chief underground surveyor set up his instruments and marked out the head of the tunnel that would fly arrow straight a mile and more through the living rock to strike through the Big Dipper into the unknown.

The area surrounding the head chamber was roped off band sign-posted with warnings.

DANGER

INDEPENDENT BLASTING

The mine captains were instructed to keep their men well away, and all loco traffic was rerouted through a secondary haulage.

On the doors of the chamber another notice was fixed.

FIERY MINE PROCEDURE IN FORCE

NO NAKED LIGHTS BEYOND THIS POINT

Owing to small deposits of coal and other organic substance in the upper stratas of rock, the Sonder Ditch was classed as a fiery mine and subject to the government legislation covering this subject. No matches, lighters or other spark-generating devices were allowed into a new development end, because the presence of methane gas was always suspected.

Colourless, odourless, tasteless, detectable only by test with a safety lamp, it was a real and terrifying danger. A nine per cent concentration in air was highly explosive. Stringent precautions were taken against accidental triggering of methane that may have oozed out of a fissure or cavity in the rock.

From the main compressed air-pipes running down the corners of the shaft were taken leads to air tanks in the haulage, ensuring that sixty pounds per square inch of pressure was available for the rock drills. Then drills, pinchbars, hammers, shovels, and the other tools were unloaded from the cage at 66 level and stored at the shaft head.

Lastly, explosive was placed in the red lockers at the head of the development, and on the evening of October 23rd 1968, thirty minutes after the main blast, Davy Delange and his gang disembarked from the cage and went to the disused loco shop.

Davy, with the surly little Swazi boss boy beside him, stood before the rock wall on which the surveyor had marked the outline of the tunnel. Behind him his gang had fallen unbidden to their labour, each man knowing exactly what was expected of him.

Already the machine boys and their assistants were lugging their ungainly tools forward.

'You! You! You! You!' Davy indicated to each of them the hole on which he was to begin and then stepped back.

'Shaya!' he commanded. 'Hit it!' And with a fluttering bellow that buffeted the eardrums the drive began.

The drilling ceased and Davy charged the holes. The

fuses hung like the tails of white mice from their holes. Each length carefully cut to ensure correct firing sequence.

'Clear the drive!' The boss boy's whistle shrilled, the tramp of heavy boots receded until silence hung heavy in the chemically cleaned air.

'Cheesa!' Davy and the boss boy, with the igniters burning like children's fireworks in their right hands, touched them to the hanging tails until the chamber was lit by the fierce blue light of the burning fuses. The shadows of the two men flickered gigantic and distorted upon the walls.

'All burning. Let's go!' And the two men walked quickly back to where the gang waited along the haulage.

The detonations sucked at their ears, and thrust against their lungs, so that afterwards the silence was stunning.

Davy checked his wristwatch. By law there was a mandatory thirty minutes' wait before anyone could go back to the face. There may be a hang-fire waiting to blow the eyes out of someone's head. Even if there were not, there was still the cloud of poisonous nitrous fumes that would destroy the hair follicles in a man's nostrils and render him still more vulnerable to the fine particles of rock dust that would seek to enter his lungs.

Davy waited those thirty minutes, by which time the ventilation had sucked away the fumes and dust.

Then, alone, he went up the haulage. With him he carried his safety lamp, its tiny blue flame burning behind the screen of fine brass wire mesh. That mesh was flash proof and insulated the flame from any methane in the air.

Standing before the raw circular wound in the rock wall, Davy tested for methane gas. Watching the blue flame for the tell-tale cap. There was no sign of it, and satisfied he extinguished the lamp.

'Boss boy!' he yelled, and the Swazi came up uncoiling the hose behind him.

'Water down!'

Only when the rock face and all the loose rubble below it were glistening and dripping with water was Davy satisfied that the dust was laid sufficiently to bring up his gang.

'Bar boys!' he yelled, and they came up, carrying the twelve-foot-long pinchbars, a tool like a giant crowbar.

'Bar down. Make safe!' And the bar boys attacked the bunches of loose rock that were flaking and crumbling from the hanging wall. Two of them manipulating one bar between them, with the steel point striking sparks from the rock. The dislodged fragments rained down, heavily at first and then less and less until the rock above their heads was solid and clean.

Only then did Davy scramble over the pile of rubble to reach the face and begin marking in the shot holes.

Behind him his gang were lashing the stuff into the waiting cocopans, and his machine boys were dragging the drills up to the face.

Davy's gang made three blasts that first night. As he rode up in the cage into a pink, sweet-smelling dawn, Davy was satisfied.

'Perhaps tonight we will get in four blasts,' he thought.

In the Company change house he showered, running the water steaming hot so his skin turned dull angry red, and he worked up a fat white lather of soap suds over his head and at his armpits and crotch.

He rubbed down with a rough thick towel and dressed quickly. Crossing the parking lot to his battered old Ford Anglia he felt happy and good-tired; hungry and ready for bed.

He drove into Kitchenerville at a steady forty miles an hour, and by this time the sun was just showing over the Kraalkop ridge. The dawn was misty rose, with long shadows against the earth, and he thought that this was how it would be in the early mornings on the farm.

On the outskirts of the town Johnny's Monaco roared past him going in the opposite direction. Johnny waved and blew the horn, shouting something that was lost in the howl of wind and motor.

'They'll catch him yet.' Davy shook his head in disapproval. 'The speed limit is forty-five along here.'

He parked the Anglia in the garage and let himself in through the kitchen door. The Bantu maid was busy over the stove.

'Three eggs,' he told her and went through to his bedroom. He shrugged off his jacket and threw it on the bed. Then he returned to the door and glanced quickly up and down the passage. It was deserted, and there was no sound besides the clatter of the maid in the kitchen.

Davy sidled into the passage. The door to Johnny's bedroom was ajar, and Davy moved quietly down to it. His heart was pounding in his throat, his breathing was stifled by his guilt and excitement.

He peered around the edge of the door and gasped aloud. This morning it was better than usual.

Hettie was a sound sleeper. Johnny always maintained it would take a shot of Dynagel to wake her. She never wore night clothes and she never rose before ten-thirty in the morning. She lay on her stomach, hugging a pillow to her chest, her hair a joyous tangle of flaming red against the green sheets. The morning was warm and her blankets had been kicked aside.

Davy stood in the passage. A nerve in his eyelid began to twitch, and under his shirt a drop of perspiration slid from his armpit down along his flank. On the bed Hettie mumbled unintelligibly in her sleep, drew her knees up and rolled slowly onto her back. One arm came up and flopped limply over her face, her eyes were covered by the crook of her elbow.

She sighed deeply. The twin mounds of her bosom were pulled out of shape by their own weight and the angle of her arm. The hair in her armpit and at the base of her belly was bright shiny red-gold. She was long and smooth and silky white, crowned and tipped with flame.

She moved her body languorously, voluptuously, and then settled once more into slumber.

'Breakfast ready, master,' the maid called from the kitchen. Davy started guiltily, then retreated down the passage.

He found with surprise that he was panting, as though he had run a long way.

– 46 –

Johnny Delange leaned against the sidewall of the haulage, his hard helmet tilted at a jaunty angle and a cigarette dangling from his lips.

Down at the face the shots began to fire. Johnny recognized each detonation, and when the last dull jar disrupted the air about them, he pushed himself away from the wall with his shoulder.

'That was the *lifters*,' he announced. 'Come on Big King!'

Not for Johnny Delange a thirty-minute waste of time. As he and Big King set off down the haulage together they were binding scarves over their noses and mouths. Ahead of them a bluey-white fog of dust and fumes filled the tunnel, and Big King had the hose going, using a fine mist spray to absorb the fumes and particles.

They pushed on up to the face, Johnny stooping over the safety lamp. Even he had a healthy respect for methane gas.

'Bar boys!' he bellowed, not waiting for Big King to finish watering down. They came up like ghosts in the fog. Hard behind them the machine boys hovered with their drills.

Taking calculated risks Johnny had his drills roaring

forty-five minutes sooner than Davy Delange would have in the same circumstances.

When he came back to the face from cutting fuses and priming his explosives, he found his lashing gang struggling with a massive slab of rock that had been blown intact from the face. Five of them were beating on it with fourteen-pound hammers in an attempt to crack it into manageable pieces. As Johnny reached them, Big King was berating them mercilessly.

'You look like a bunch of virgins grinding millet.'

The hammers clanged and struck sparks from the slab. Sweat oozed from every pore of the hammer boys' skin, greasing their bodies, flying from their heads in sparkling droplets with each blow.

'Shaya!' Big King goaded them on. 'Between you all you wouldn't crack the shell of an egg. Hit it, man! Hit it!'

One by one the men fell back exhausted, their chests heaving, gulping air through gaping mouths, blinded by their own sweat.

'All right,' Johnny intervened. The rock was holding up the whole blast. It warranted drastic measures to break it up.

'I'll pop her,' he said, and any government inspector or mine safety officer would have paled at those words.

'Stand far back and turn your faces away,' Big King instructed his gang. From the forehead of one of his men he took a pair of wire mesh goggles, designed to shield the eyes from flying splinters and rock fragments. He handed them to Johnny who placed them over his eyes.

From the canvas carrying bag he took out a stick of Dynagel. It looked like a candle wrapped in yellow greased paper.

'Give me your knife.' Big King opened a large clasp knife and handed it to Johnny.

Carefully Johnny cut a coin-shaped sliver of explosive from one end of the stick, a piece twice as thick as a penny.

He returned the remains of the stick to the bag and handed it to Big King.

'Get back,' he said and Big King moved away.

Johnny eyed the slab of rock thoughtfully and then placed the fragment of Dynagel in the centre of it. He adjusted the goggles over his eyes, and picked up one of the fourteen-pound hammers.

'Turn your eyes away,' he warned and took deliberate aim. Then with a smooth overhead two-handed swing he brought the hammer down on the Dynagel.

The explosion was painful in the confined space of the drive, and afterwards Johnny's ears hummed with it. A tiny drop of blood ran down his cheek from the scratch inflicted by a flying splinter. His wrists ached from the jolt of the hammer in his hands.

'Gwenyama!' grunted Big King in admiration. 'The man is a lion.'

The explosion had cracked the slab into three wedge-shaped segments. Johnny pushed the goggles onto his forehead and wiped the blood from his cheek with the back of his hand.

'Get it the hell out of here,' he grinned, then he turned to Big King.

'Come.' He jerked his head towards the end of the tunnel. 'Help me charge the holes.'

The two of them worked quickly, sliding the sticks of Dynagel into the shot holes and tamping them home with the charging sticks.

For anyone who was not in possession of a blasting licence, to charge up was an offence punishable by a fine of one hundred rand or two months' imprisonment, or both. Big King had no licence, but his assistance saved fifteen minutes on the operation.

Johnny and his gang blew the face five times that day, but as they rode up in the cage into the cool evening air he was not satisfied.

'Tomorrow we'll shoot her six times,' he told Big King.

'Maybe seven,' said Big King.

Hettie was waiting for him in the lounge when he got home. She flew to him and threw her arms about his neck.

'Did you bring me a present?' she asked with her lips against his ear, and Johnny laughed tantalizingly. It was very seldom that he did not have a gift for her.

'You did!' she exclaimed, and began to run her hands over his pockets.

'There!' She thrust her hand into the inside pocket of his jacket, and brought out the little white jeweller's box.

'Oh!' She opened it, and then her expression changed slightly.

'You don't like them?' Johnny asked anxiously.

'How much did they cost?' she enquired as she examined the porcelain and lacquer earrings, representing two vividly coloured parrots.

'Well,' Johnny looked shamefaced, 'you see, Hettie, it's the end of the month, you see, and well, like I'm a bit short till pay day, you see, so I couldn't—'

'How much?'

'Well, you see,' he took a breath, 'two rand fifty.'

'Oh,' said Hettie, 'they're nice.' And she promptly lost interest in them. She tossed the box carelessly onto the crowded mantelpiece and set off for the kitchen.

'Hey, Hettie,' Johnny called after her. 'How about we go across to Fochville? There's a dance there tonight. We go and twist, hey?'

Hettie turned back, her expression alive again.

'Gee, yes, man!' she enthused. 'Let's do that. I'll go and change, hey!' And she ran up the passage.

Davy came out of his bedroom, on his way to work.

'Hey, Davy.' Johnny stopped him. 'You got any money on you?'

'Are you broke again?'

'Just till pay day.'

'Hell, man, Johnny, you got a cheque for eleven hundred the beginning of the month. You spent it all?'

'Next month,' Johnny winked, 'I'm going to get a cheque for two or three thousand. Then watch me go! Come, Davy, lend me fifty. I'm taking Hettie dancing.'

– 47 –

For Rod the days flicked past like telegraph poles viewed from a speeding automobile. Each day he gained confidence in his own ability. He had never doubted that he could handle the underground operation and now he found that he had a firm grasp on the surface as well. He knew that his campaign to reduce working costs was having effect, but its full harvest would only be apparent when the quarterly reports were drafted.

Yet he lay awake in the big Manager's residence on the ridge in which he and his few sticks of furniture seemed lost and lonely, and he worried. There were always myriad nagging little problems, but there were others more serious.

This morning Lily Jordan had come through into his office.

'Mr Innes is coming up to see you at nine.'

'What's he want?' Herbert Innes was the Manager of the Sonder Ditch Reduction works.

'He wouldn't tell me,' Lily answered. The end of the month had come and gone and Lily was still with him. Rod presumed that he had been approved.

Herby Innes, burly and red-faced, sat down and drank the cup of tea that Lily provided, while he regaled Rod with a stroke by stroke account of his Sunday afternoon golf round. Rod interrupted him after he had hit a nine-iron short at the third and shanked his chip.

'Okay, Herby. What's the problem?'

'We've got a leak, Rod.'

'Bad?'

'Bad enough,' Herby grunted. To him the loss of a single ounce of gold during the process of recovery and refinement was catastrophic.

'What do you reckon?'

'Between the wash and the pour we are losing a couple hundred ounces a week.'

'Yes,' Rod agreed. 'That is bad enough.'

20,000 rand a month, 120,000 a year.

'Have you any ideas?'

'It's been going on for some time, even in Frank Lemmer's day. We have tried everything.'

Rod was a little hazy about the workings of the reduction plant, not that he would admit that, but he was. He knew that the ore was weighed and sampled when it reached the surface, from this a fairly accurate estimate of gold content was made and compared with actual recovery. Any discrepancy had to be investigated and traced.

'What is your recovery rate for the last quarter?'

'Ninety-six point seven-three.'

'That's pretty good,' Rod admitted. It was impossible to recover all the gold in the ore that was surfaced but Herby was getting most of it out. 96.73 per cent of it, to be precise. Which meant that very little of the missing 200 ounces was being lost into the dumps and the slimes dam.

'I tell you what, Herby,' Rod decided. 'I'll come down to the plant this afternoon. We'll go over it together, perhaps a fresh eye may be able to spot the trouble.'

'May do.' Herby was sceptical. 'We've tried everything else. We are pouring this afternoon. What time shall I expect you?'

'Two o'clock.'

They started at the shaft head, where the ore cage, the copie, arrived at the surface every four minutes with its cargo of rock which it dumped into a concrete shute. Each load was classified as either 'reef' or 'waste'.

The reef was dropped into the massive storage bins, while the waste was carried off on a conveyor to the wash house to be sluiced down before going to the dump. Tiny particles of gold sticking to the waste rock were gathered in this way.

Herby put his lips close to Rod's ear to make himself heard above the rumbling roar of rock rolling down the chute.

'I'm not worried about this end. It's all bulk here and very little shine.' Herby used the reduction plant slang for gold. 'The closer we get to the end, the more dangerous it is.'

Rod nodded and followed Herby down the steel ladder until they reached a door below the storage bins. They went through into a long underground tunnel very similar to the ore tunnel on 100 level.

Again there was a massive conveyor belt moving steadily along the tunnel while ore from the bins above was fed onto it. Rod and Herby walked along beside the belt until it passed under a massive electromagnet. Here they paused for a while. The magnet was extracting from the ore all those pieces of metal which had found their way into the ore passes and bins.

'How much you picking up?' Rod asked.

'Last week fourteen tons,' Herby answered, and taking Rod's arm led him through the door beside them. They were in an open yard that looked like a scrap-metal merchant's premises. A mountain of pinchbars, jumper bits, shovels, steel wire rope, snatch blocks, chains, spanners, fourteen-pound hammers, and other twisted and unrecognizable pieces of metal filled the yard. All of it was rusted, much of it unusable. It had been separated from the ore by the magnet.

Rod's mouth tightened. Here he was presented with indisputable evidence of the carelessness and it-belongs-to-the-company attitude of his men. This pile of scrap represented a waste that would total hundreds of thousands of rand annually.

'We will see about that!' he muttered.

'If one of those hammers got into my jaw mills it would smash it to pieces,' Herby told him dolefully and led him back into the conveyor tunnel.

The belt angled upwards sharply and they followed the catwalk beside it. They climbed steadily for five minutes and Herby was puffing like a steam engine. Through the holes in the honeycomb steel plate under his feet, Rod could see that they were now a few hundred feet above ground level.

The conveyor reached the head of a tall tower and dumped its load of ore into the gaping mouths of the screeners. As the rock fell down the tower to ground level again it was sorted for size, and the larger pieces diverted to the jaw crushers which chewed it into fistsize bites.

'See anything?' Herby asked, barely concealing the sarcasm.

Rod grinned at him.

They climbed down the steel ladders that seemed endless. The screeners rattling and the crushers hammering, until Rod's eardrums pleaded for mercy.

At last they reached ground level and went through into the mill room. This was a cavernous galvanized-iron shed the size of a large aircraft hangar. At least one hundred yards long and fifty feet high, it was filled with long rows of the cylindrical tube mills.

Forty of them in all, they were as thick as the boiler of a steam locomotive and about twice as long. Into one end of them was fed the ore which had been reduced in size by the jaw crushers. The tube mills revolved and the loose steel balls within them pounded the rock to powder.

If the noise before had been bad, it was hideous in the mill room. Rod and Herby made no effort to speak to each other until they had walked through into the comparative quiet of the first heavy-media separator room.

'Now,' Herby explained. 'This is where we start worrying.' He indicated the rows of pale blue six-inch piping that came through the wall from the mill room.

'In there is the powdered rock mixed with water to a smooth flowing paste. About forty per cent of the gold is free.'

'No one can get into those pipes and you've checked for any possible leak?' Rod asked. Herby nodded.

'But,' he said, 'have a look here!'

Along the far wall was a series of cages. They were made of heavy steel mesh, the perforations would not allow a man's finger through. The heavy steel doors were barred and locked. Outside each battery of cages stood a Bantu attendant in clean white overalls. They were all concentrating on the manipulation of the turncock that obviously regulated the flow of the powdered ore through the pipes.

Herby stopped at one of the cages.

'Shine!' He pointed. Beyond the heavy guard screen the grey paste of rock powder was flowing from a series of nozzles over an inclined black rubber sheet. The surface of the rubber sheet was deeply corrugated, and in each corrugation the free gold was collecting, held there by its own weight. The gold was thick as butter in a Dagwood sandwich, greasy yellow-looking in the folds of rubber.

Rod laid hold of the steel screen and shook it.

'No,' Herby laughed. 'No one will get in that way.'

'How do you clean the gold off that sheet? Does someone have access to the separator?' Rod asked.

'The separator cleans itself automatically,' Herby answered. 'Look!'

Rod noticed for the first time that the rubber sheet was moving very slowly, it was also an endless belt running round two rollers. As the belt inverted, so fine jets of water washed the gold from the corrugations into a collection tank.

'I'm the only one who has access. We change the collection tanks daily,' said Herby.

It looked foolproof, Rod had to admit.

Rod turned and glanced down the row of four Bantu attendants. They were all intent on their duties, and Rod knew that each of them had a high security rating. They had been carefully selected and screened before being allowed into the reduction works.

'Satisfied?' Herby asked.

'Okay,' Rod nodded, and the two of them went out through the door in the far wall. Locking it behind them.

Immediately they had gone the four Bantu attendants reacted. They straightened up, the scowls of concentration smoothed out to be replaced by grins of relief. One made a remark and they all laughed, and opened the waist bands of their tunics. From inside each trouser leg they drew a length of quarter-inch copper wire and began probing them through the steel screen.

It had taken Crooked Leg, the photographer, almost a year to work out a means of milking gold from the heavily screened and guarded separators. The method which he had discovered was, like all workable plans, extremely simple.

Mercury, quicksilver, absorbs gold the way blotting paper sucks up moisture. It will suck in any speck of gold that comes in contact with it. Mercury has a further property, it can be made to spread on copper like butter on bread. This layer of mercury on copper retains its powers of absorbing gold.

Crooked Leg had devised the idea of coating lengths of copper wire with mercury. The wire could be inserted through the apertures in the steel mesh and the wire laid across the corrugated rubber sheet, where it set about mopping up every speck of gold that flowed over it. The lengths of wire could be quickly slipped down the trouser leg at the approach of an official, and they could be smuggled in and out of the reduction works the same way.

Every evening Crooked Leg retrieved the gold-thickened wire, and issued his four accomplices with newly coated lengths. Every night in the abandoned workings beyond the ridge he boiled the mercury to make it release its gold.

'Now,' Herby could speak normally in the blessed quiet of the cyanide plant, 'we have skimmed off the free gold – and we are left with the sulphide gold.' He offered Rod a cigarette as they made their way between the massive steel tanks that spread over many acres. 'We pump this into the tanks and add cyanide. The cyanide dissolves the gold and takes it into solution. We tap it off and run it through zinc powder. The gold is deposited on the zinc, we burn away the zinc and we are left with the gold.'

Rod lit his cigarette. He knew all this but Herby was giving him a Cooks' tour for visiting VIPs. He flicked his lighter for Herby. 'There is no way anyone could swipe it when it's in solution.'

Herby shook his head, exhaling smoke. 'Apart from anything else, cyanide is a deadly poison.' He glanced at his watch. 'Three-twenty, they'll be pouring now. Shall we go across to the smelt house?'

The smelt house was the only brick building among all the galvanized iron. It stood a little isolated. Its windows were high up and heavily barred.

At the steel door Herby buzzed, and a peephole opened in the door. He and Rod were immediately recognized and the door swung open. They were in a cage of bars which could only be opened once the door was closed behind them.

'Afternoon, Mr Ironsides, Mr Innes.' The guard was apologetic. 'Would you sign, please?' He was a retired policeman with a paunch and a holstered revolver on his hip.

They signed and the guard signalled to his mate on the steel catwalk high above the smelt room floor. This guard tucked his pump action shotgun under one arm, and threw the switch on the walk beside him.

The cage door opened and they went through.

Along the far wall the electric furnaces were set into the brickwork. They resembled the doors of the bread ovens in a bakery.

The concrete floor of the room was uncluttered, except for the mechanical loader that carried the gold crucible in its steel arms, and the moulds before it. The half dozen personnel of the smelt house barely looked up as Rod and Herby approached.

The pour was well advanced, the arms of the loader tilted and a thin stream of molten gold issued from the spout of the crucible, and fell into the mould. The gold hissed and smoked and crackled, and tiny red and blue sparks twinkled on its surface as it cooled.

Already forty or fifty bars were laid out on the rubber-wheeled trolley beside the mould. Each bar was a little smaller than a cigar box. It had the knobby bumpy look of roughly cast metal.

Rod stopped and touched one of the bars. It was still hot and it had the slightly greasy feeling that new gold always has.

'How much?' he asked Herby, and Herby shrugged.

'About a million rand's worth, perhaps a little more.'

So that's what a million rand looks like, Rod mused, it's not very impressive.

'What's the procedure now?' Rod asked.

'We weigh it, and stamp the weight and batch number into each bar.' He pointed to a massive circular safe deposit door in the near wall. 'It's stored there overnight, and tomorrow a refinery armoured car will come out from Johannesburg and pick it up.' Herby led the way out of the smelt house. 'Anyway, that's not the trouble. Our leak is sucking off the shine before it ever reaches the smelt house.'

'Let me think about it for a few days,' Rod said. 'Then we'll get together again, try and find the solution.'

He was still thinking about it now. Lying in the darkness and smoking cigarette after cigarette.

There seemed to be only one solution. They would have to plant Bantu police in the reduction works.

It was an endless game involving all the mining companies and their reduction plant personnel. An inventive mind would devise a new system of sucking off the shine. The Company would become aware of the activity by comparison of estimated and actual recovery and they would work on the leak for a week, a month, sometimes a year. Then they would break the system. There would be prosecutions, stiff gaol sentences, and the Company would circularize its neighbours, and they would all settle back and wait for the next customer to appear.

Gold has many remarkable properties, its weight, its non-corruptibility and, not least, the greed and lust it conjures up in the hearts of men.

Rod stubbed his cigarette, rolled onto his side and pulled the bedclothes up over his shoulders. His last thought before sleep was for the major problem that, these days, was never very far from the surface of his mind.

The Delange brothers had driven almost 1,500 feet in two weeks. At this rate they would hit the Big Dipper seven weeks from now, then even the theft of gold would pale into insignificance.

At the time that Rod Ironsides was composing himself for sleep, Big King was taking a little wine with his business associate and tribal brother Philemon N'gabai, alias Crooked Leg.

They sat facing each other in a pair of dilapidated cane chairs with a lantern and a gallon jug of Jeripigo set between them. The bat stench of the abandoned workings did little to bring out the bouquet of the wine, which was of small concern to either man, for they were drinking not for taste but for effect.

Crooked Leg refilled the cheap glass tumbler that Big King preferred, and as the wine glug-glugged from the jar he continued his attack on the character and moral fibre of José Almeida, the Portuguese.

'For many months now I have had it in my heart to speak to you of these matters,' he told Big King, 'but I have waited until I could set a deadfall for the man. He is like a lion that preys upon our herds, we hear him roar in the night and in the dawn we see his spoor in the earth about the carcasses of our animals, but we cannot meet him face to face.'

Big King enjoyed listening to the oratory of Crooked Leg and while he listened he drank the Jeripigo as though it were water, and Crooked Leg kept refilling the tumbler for him.

'In counsel with myself I spoke thus: "Philemon N'gabai, it is not enough that thou should suspect this white man. It is necessary also that you see with your own eyes that he is eating your substance".'

'How, Crooked Leg?' Big King's voice was thickening, the level of the jug had fallen steadily and now showed less than half. 'Tell me how we shall take this man.' Big King showed a fist the size of a bunch of bananas. 'I will . . .'

'No, Big King.' Crooked Leg was scandalized. 'You must not hurt the man. How then would we sell our gold? We must prove he is cheating us and show him we know it. Then we will proceed as ever, but he will give us full measure in the future.'

Big King thought about that for some time, then at last he sighed regretfully. 'You are right, Crooked Leg. Still, I would have liked to . . .' He showed that fist again, and Crooked Leg went on hurriedly.

'Therefore, I have sent to my brother who drives a delivery van for SA Scale Company in Johannesburg, and he has taken from his Company a carefully measured weight of eight ounces.' Crooked Leg produced the cylindrical metal weight from his pocket and handed it to Big King who examined it with interest. 'Tonight, after the Portuguese has weighed the gold you take to him, you will say, "Now, my friend, please weigh this for me on your scale," and you will watch to see that his scale reads the correct number. Each time in the future he will weigh this on his scale before we sell our gold.'

'Hau!' Big King chuckled. 'You are a crafty one, Crooked Leg.'

Big King's eyes were smoky and blood-shot. The Jeripigo was a raw rough fortified wine, and he had drunk very nearly a gallon of it. He sat opposite the Portuguese store-keeper in the back room behind the concession store, and watched while he poured the gold dust into the pan of the jeweller's scale. It made a yellow pyramid that shone dully in the light from the single bare bulb above their heads.

'One hundred and twenty-three ounces.' Almeida looked up at Big King for confirmation, a strand of greasy black hair hung onto his forehead. His face was pale from lack of sun so that the blue stubble of beard was in heavy contrast.

'That is right,' Big King nodded. He could taste the

liquor fumes in the back of his throat, and they were as strong as his distaste for the man who sat opposite him. He belched.

Almeida removed the pan from the scale and carefully poured the dust back into the screw-top bottle.

'I will get the money.' He half rose from his chair.

'Wait!' said Big King, and the Portuguese looked at him in mild surprise.

Big King took the weight from the pocket of his jacket. He placed it on the desk.

'Weigh that on your scale,' he said in Portuguese.

Almeida's eyes flicked down to the weight, and then back to Big King's face. He sank back into his seat, and pushed the strand of hair off his forehead. He began to speak, but his voice cracked and he cleared his throat.

'Why? Is there something wrong?' Suddenly he was aware of the size of the man opposite him. He could smell the liquor on his breath.

'Weigh it!' Big King's voice was flat, without rancour. His face was expressionless, but the smoky red glare of his eyes was murderous.

Suddenly Almeida was afraid, deadly, coldly afraid. He could guess what would happen once the error in his balance was disclosed.

'Very well,' he said, and his voice was forced and off key. The pistol was in the drawer beside his right knee. It was loaded, with a cartridge under the hammer. The safety-catch was on, but that would only delay him an instant. He knew it would not be necessary to fire, once he had the weapon in his hand he would have control of the situation again.

If he did have to fire, the calibre was .45 and the heavy slug would stop even a giant like this Bantu. *Self-defence*, he was working it out feverishly. A *burglar*, I surprised him and he attacked. *Self-defence*. It would work. They'd believe it.

But how to get the pistol? Try and sneak it out of the drawer, or make a grab for it?

There was a desk between them, it would take a few seconds for the Bantu to realize what he was doing, a few more for him to get around the desk. He would have plenty of time.

He snatched the handle of the drawer, and it flew open. His fingernails scrabbled against the woodwork as he clawed for the big black U.S. Navy automatic, and with a surge of triumph his hand closed over the butt.

Big King came over the top of the desk like a black avalanche. The scale and the jar of gold dust were swept aside to clatter and shatter against the floor.

Still seated in his chair, with the pistol in his hand, Almeida was borne over backwards with Big King on top of him. Many years before, Big King had worked with a safari outfit in Portuguese East Africa, and he had seen the effect of gunshot wounds in the flesh of dead animals.

In the instant that he had recognized the weapon in Almeida's hand, he had been as afraid as the Portuguese. Fear had triggered the speed of his reaction, it was responsible for the savagery of his attack as he lay over the struggling body of the Portuguese.

He had Almeida's pistol hand held by the wrist and he was shaking it to force him to drop the firearm. With his right hand he had the Portuguese by the throat, and instinctively he was applying the full strength of his arms to both grips. He felt something break under his right hand, cracking like the kernel of a nut, and his fingers were suddenly without strength, and the gun skittered across the floor to come up against the far wall with a thump.

Only then did Big King begin to regain the sanity that fear had scattered. Suddenly he realized that the Portuguese was lying quietly under him. He released his grip and scrambled to his knees. The Portuguese was dead. His neck was twisted away from his shoulders at an impossible angle. His eyes were wide and surprised, and a smear of blood issued from one nostril over his upper lip.

Big King backed away towards the door, his gaze fixed in horror on the sprawling corpse. When he reached the door, he hesitated, fighting down the urge to run. He subdued it, and went back to kneel beside the desk. First he picked up the controversial cylindrical weight and placed it in his pocket, then he began sweeping up the scattered gold dust and the shattered fragments of the screw-topped container. He placed them into separate envelopes that he found among the papers on the desk. Ten minutes later he slipped out through the back door of the concession store, into the night.

– 49 –

At the time Big King was hurrying back towards the mine hostel, Rod Ironsides thrashed restlessly in a bed in which the sheets were already bunched and damp with sweat. He was imprisoned in his own fantasy, locked in a nightmare from which he could not break away. The nightmare was infinite and green, quivering, unearthly, translucent. He knew it was held back only by a transparent barrier of glass. He cowered before it, and he knew it was icy cold, he could see light shining through it, and he was deadly afraid.

Suddenly there was a crack in the glass wall, a hairline crack, and through it oozed a single drop. A large, pear-shaped drop, as perfect as though it had been painted by Tretchikoff. It glittered like a gemstone.

It was the most terrifying thing that Rod had ever seen in his life. He cried out in his sleep, trying to warn them, but the crack starred further, and the drop slid down the glass, to be followed by another and another. Suddenly a jagged slab of glass exploded out of the wall, and Rod screamed as the water burst through, in a frothing jet.

With a roar the entire glass wall collapsed, and a mountain high wave of green water hissed down upon him, carrying a white plume of spray at its crest.

He awoke sitting upright in his bed, a cry of horror on his lips and his body bathed in sweat. It took minutes for him to steady the wild racing of his heart. Then he went through to the bathroom. He ran a glass of water and held it up to the light. 'Water. It's there!' he muttered. 'I know it's there!' He drank from the tumbler.

Standing naked, with his sweat drying cold on his body, the tumbler held to his lips, the idea came to him. He had never heard of anyone trying it before, but then nobody he knew would be crazy enough to drive into a death trap like the Big Dipper.

'I'll drill and charge a matt of explosive into the hanging wall of the drive. I'll get the Delange boys on to it right away. Then at any time I choose I can blast the whole bloody roof in and seal off the tunnel.'

Rod was surprised at the strength of the relief that flooded over him. He knew then how it had been worrying him. He went back to the bedroom and straightened out his bedclothes. However, sleep would not come easily to him. His imagination was overheated, and a series of events and ideas kept playing through his mind, until abruptly he was presented with the image of Terry Steyner.

He had not seen her for almost two weeks, not since their meeting just after Manfred Steyner's return from Europe. He had spoken to her twice on the telephone, hasty, confused conversations that left him feeling dissatisfied. He was increasingly aware that he was missing her. His one attempt to find solace elsewhere had been a miserable failure. He had lost interest halfway through the approach manoeuvres and had returned the young lady to the bosom of her family at the unheard-of hour of eleven o'clock on a Saturday night.

Only the unremitting demands of his new job had prevented him from slipping away to Johannesburg and taking a risk.

'You know, Ironsides, you'd better start bracing up a little, don't lose your head over this woman. Remember our vow – *Never Again!*'

He punched the pillow into shape and settled into it.

Terry lay quietly, waiting for it. It was after one o'clock in the morning. It was one of those nights. He would come soon now. As never before she was filled with dread. A cold slimy feeling in the pit of her stomach. Yet she had been fortunate. He had not been near her since his return from Paris. Over two weeks, but it could not last. Tonight.

She heard the sound of the car coming up the drive and she felt physically ill. I can't do it, she decided, not any more, not ever again. It wasn't meant to be like this, I know that now. It's not dirty and furtive and horrible, it's like . . . like . . . it's the way Rod makes it.

She heard him in his bedroom, suddenly she sat up in bed. She felt desperate, hunted.

The door of her room opened softly.

'Manfred?' she asked sharply.

'It's me. Don't worry.' He came briskly towards her bed, a dark impersonal shape and he was undoing the cord of his dressing-gown.

'Manfred,' Terry blurted. 'I'm early this month, I'm sorry.'

He stopped. She saw his hands fall back to his sides, and he stood completely still.

'Oh!' he said at last, and she heard him shuffle his feet into the thick pile of the carpet. 'I just came to tell you,' he hesitated, seeking an excuse for his visit, 'that . . . that I'll be going away for five days. Leaving on Friday. I have to go to Durban and Cape Town.'

'I'll pack for you,' she said.

'What? Oh, yes – thank you.' He shuffled his feet again. 'Well, then.' He hesitated, then stooped quickly and brushed her cheek with his lips. 'Good night, Theresa.'

'Good night, Manfred.'

Five days. She lay alone in the darkness and gloated. *Five whole days alone with Rod.*

– 50 –

Detective Inspector Hannes Grobbelaar of the South African Criminal Investigation Department sat on the edge of the office chair with his hat tipped onto the back of his head and spoke into the telephone, which he held in a handkerchief-covered hand. He was a tall man with a long sad face and a mournful-looking moustache that was streaked with grey.

'Gold buying,' he said into the receiver, and then in reply to the obvious question, 'There's gold dust spilled all over the place and a jeweller's scale, and a .45 automatic with a full magazine and the safety-catch still on, dead man's prints on it.' He listened. 'Ja. Ja. All right, ja. Broken neck, looks like.' Inspector Grobbelaar swivelled his chair and looked down at the corpse that lay on the floor beside him. 'Bit of blood on his lip, but nothing else.'

One of the finger-print men came to the desk and Grobbelaar stood up to give him room to work, the receiver still held to his ear.

'Prints?' he asked in disgust. 'There are finger prints on everything, we have isolated at least forty separate sets so far.' He listened a few seconds. 'No, we will get him, all right. It must be a Bantu mine worker and we have got all the finger prints of the men from outside the Republic. It's just a matter of checking them all out and then questioning. Ja, we'll have him within a month, that's for sure! I'll be back at John Vorster Square about five o'clock, just as soon as we finish up here.' He hung up the receiver, and stood looking down at the murdered man.

'Ugly bastard,' said Sergeant Hugo beside him. 'Asked for it, buying gold. It's as bad as diamonds.' He drew attention to the large envelope he carried in his hand. 'I've got a whole lot of glass fragments. Looks like the container the gold was in. The murderer tried to clean up, but he didn't make a very good job. These were under the desk.'

'Prints?'

'Only one piece big enough. It's got a smeary print on it. Might be of use.'

'Good,' Grobbelaar nodded. 'Get cracking on that, then.'

There was a feminine wail from somewhere in the interior of the building, and Hugo grimaced.

'There she starts again. Hell, I thought she'd exhausted herself. Bloody Portuguese women are the end.'

'You should hear them having a baby,' grunted Grobbelaar.

'Where did you hear one?'

'There was one in the ward next door to my old girl at the maternity home. She nearly brought the bloody roof down.'

Grobbelaar's moustache took on a more melancholy droop as he thought about the work that lay ahead. Hours, days, weeks of questioning and checking and cross-checking, with a succession of sullen and uncooperative suspects.

He sighed and jerked a thumb at the corpse. 'All right, we've finished with him. Tell the butcher boys to come and fetch him.'

It had taken Rod almost two days to design his dropblast matt. The angle and depth of the shot holes were carefully placed to achieve maximum disruption of the hanging wall. In addition he had decided to drill and charge the side walls of the drive with charges timed to explode *after* the hanging wall had collapsed. This would kick in on the rubble filling the tunnel and jam it solid.

Rod was fully aware of the power of water under pressures of 2,000 pounds per square inch and more and he had decided it was necessary to block at least 300 feet of the tunnel. His matt blast was designed to do so, and yet he knew that this would not seal off the water completely. It would, however, reduce the flow sufficiently to allow cementation crews to get in and plug the drive solid.

The Delange brothers did not share Rod's enthusiasm for the project.

'Hey man, that's going to take three or four days to drill and charge,' Johnny protested when Rod showed him his carefully drawn plan.

'Like hell it will,' Rod growled at him. 'I want it done properly. It will take at least a week.'

'You said ultra-fast. You didn't say nothing about drilling the hanging wall with more holes than a cheese!'

'Well, I'm saying it now,' Rod told him grimly. 'And I'm also saying that you will drill, but you won't charge the holes until I come down and make sure that you've gone in as deep as I want them.'

He didn't trust either Johnny or Davy to spend time drilling in twenty feet, when he could go in six feet, charge up and nobody would know the difference. Not until it was too late.

Davy Delange spoke for the first time.

'Will you credit us bonus fathomage while we fiddle around with this?' he asked.

'Four fathoms a shift.' Rod agreed to pay them for the removal of fictitious rock.

'Eight?' said Davy.

'Hell, no!' Rod exclaimed. That was robbery.

'I don't know,' Davy murmured, watching Rod with sly ferrety little eyes. 'Maybe I should talk to Brother Duivenhage, you know, ask his advice.'

Duivenhage was No. 1 shaft shop steward for the Mine Workers' Union. He had driven Frank Lemmer to the edge of a nervous breakdown and was now starting on Rodney Ironsides. Rod was pleading with Head Office to offer Duivenhage a fat job in management to get him out of the way. The last thing in the world that Rod wanted was Brother Duivenhage snooping around his drive on the Big Dipper.

'Six,' he said.

'Well . . .' Davy hesitated.

'Six is fair, Davy,' Johnny interrupted, and Davy glared at him. Johnny had snatched complete victory from his grasp.

'Good, that's agreed.' Quickly Rod closed the negotiations. 'You'll start drilling the matt right away.'

Rod's design demanded nearly 1,200 shot holes to be filled with two and a half tons of explosive. It was 1,000 feet down the drive from the main haulage on 66 level to where the matt began.

The drive now was a spacious, well lit and freshly ventilated tunnel, with the vent piping, the compressed air pipe, and the electrical cable bolted into the hanging wall, and a set of steel railway tracks laid along the floor.

All work on the face ceased while the Delange brothers set about drilling the matt. It was light work that demanded little from the men. As each hole was drilled, Davy would insert his charging rod to check the depth and then plug the entrance with a wad of paper. There was much time for drinking Thermos coffee and for thinking.

There were three subjects that endlessly occupied Davy's mind as he sat at ease, waiting for the completion of the next shot hole. Sometimes for half an hour at a time Davy would hold the image of that 50,000 rand in his mind. It was his, tax paid, painstakingly accumulated over the years and lovingly deposited with the local branch of the Johannesburg Building Society. He imagined it bundled and stacked in neat green piles in the Society's vault. Each bundle was labelled 'David Delange'.

Then his imagination would pass automatically on to the farm that the money would buy. He saw how it would be in the evenings when he sat on the wide stoep, with the setting sun striking the peaks of the Swart Berg across the valley, and the cattle coming in from the paddocks towards the homestead.

Always there was a woman sitting beside him on the stoep. The woman had red hair.

On the fifth morning Davy drove home in the dawn, he was not tired. The night's labours had been easy and unexacting.

The door of Johnny and Hettie's bedroom was closed. Davy read the newspapers with his breakfast; as always the cartoon strip adventures of Modesty Blaise and Willie Garvin intrigued him completely. This morning Modesty was depicted in a bikini and Davy studied her comparing her to the big healthy body of his brother's wife. The thought of her stayed with him as he rolled onto his bed, and he lay unsleeping, daydreaming an adventure in which

174

Modesty Blaise had become Hettie, and Willie Garvin was Davy.

An hour later he was still awake. He sat up and reached for the towel which lay across the foot of his bed. He wrapped the towel around his waist as he went down the passage to the bathroom. As he reached for the handle of the bathroom door, it opened under his hand and he was face to face with Hettie Delange.

She wore a white lace dressing-gown with ostrich-feather mules on her feet. Her face was innocent of make-up and she had brushed her hair and tied it with a ribbon.

'Oh!' she gasped with surprise. 'You gave me a fright, man.'

'I'm sorry, hey.' Davy grinned at her, holding the towel with one hand. Hettie let her eyes run quickly over his naked upper body.

Davy was muscled like a prizefighter. His chest hair was crisp and curly. On both arms the tattoos drew attention to the thickness and weight of muscle.

'Gee, you *are* built,' Hettie murmured in admiration, and Davy sucked in his belly reflexively.

'You think so?' His grin was self-conscious now.

'Yes.' Hettie leaned forward and touched his arm. 'It's hard too!'

The movement had allowed the front of her dressing-gown to gape open. Davy's face flushed as he looked down into the opening. He started to say something, but his voice had dried up on him. Hettie's fingers stroked down his arm, and she was watching the direction of his eyes. Slowly she moved closer to him.

'Do you like me, Davy?' she asked, her voice throaty and low, and with an animal cry Davy attacked her.

His hands ripping at the opening of her gown, pinning her to the wall of the bathroom with his mouth frantically hunting hers. His body pressing hard and urgent, his eyes wild, his breathing ragged.

Hettie was laughing, a breathless gasping laugh.

This was what she loved. When they lost their heads, when they went mad for her.

'Davy,' she said, jerking loose his towel. 'Davy.'

She kept wriggling away from his thrusting hips, knowing that it would inflame him further. His hands were tearing at her body, his eyes were maniacal.

'Yes!' she hissed into his mouth. He threw her off balance and she slid down the wall onto the floor.

'Wait,' she panted. 'Not here – the bedroom.'

But it was too late.

Davy had spent the afternoon locked in his bedroom, lying on his bed in an agony of black all-pervading remorse and guilt.

'My brother,' he kept repeating. 'Johnny is my brother.'

Once he wept, each sob tearing something in his chest. The tears squeezed out between burning eyelids, leaving him feeling exhausted and weak.

'My *own* brother,' he shook his head slowly in horrified disbelief. 'I cannot stay here,' he decided miserably. 'I'll have to go.'

He went to the washbasin and washed his eyes. Stooping over the basin, water still dripping from his face, he decided.

'I will have to tell him.' The burden of guilt was too heavy. 'I'll write to Johnny. I'll write it all, and then I'll go away.'

Frantically he searched for pen and paper, it was almost as though he could wipe away the deed by writing it down. He sat at the table by the window and wrote slowly and laboriously. When he had finished it was three o'clock. He felt better.

He sealed the four closely written pages into an envelope and slipped it into the inside pocket of his jacket. He dressed quickly, and crept out of the house, fearful of meeting Hettie, but she was nowhere about. Her big white Monaco was not in the garage, and with relief he turned out of the driveway and took the road out to the Sonder Ditch. He wanted to reach the mine before Johnny came off shift.

Davy listened to his brother's voice, as he kidded and laughed with the other off-duty miners in the company change house. He had locked himself in one of the lavatory closets to avoid meeting his brother, and he sat disconsolately on the toilet seat. The sound of Johnny's voice brought his guilt flooding back in its full strength. His letter of confession was buttoned into the top pocket of his overalls, and he took it out, broke open the flap and reread the contents.

'So long, then.' Johnny's voice sang out gaily from the change room. 'See you bastards tomorrow.'

There was an answering chorus from the other miners, then the door slammed.

Davy went on sitting alone for another twenty minutes in the stench of stale bodies and urine, dirty socks and rank disinfections from the foot baths. At last he tucked the letter away in his pocket and opened the closet door.

Davy's gang were at their waiting place at the head of the drive. They were sitting along the bench laughing and chatting. There was a holiday spirit amongst them for they knew it would be another shift of easy going.

They greeted Davy cheerfully, as he came down the haulage. Both the Delange brothers were popular with their gangs and it was unusual that Davy did not reply to the chorused greeting. He did not even smile.

The Swazi boss boy handed him the safety lamp, and Davy grunted an acknowledgement. He set off alone down the tunnel, trudging heavily, not conscious of his surroundings, his mind encased in a padding of guilt and self-pity.

177

A thousand feet along the drive he reached the day's work area. Johnny's shift had left the rock drills in place, still connected to the compressed air system, ready for use. Davy came to a halt in the centre of the work area, and without a conscious command from his brain his hands began the routine process of striking the wick of the safety lamp.

The little blue flame came alight behind the protective screen of wire mesh, and Davy held the lamp at eye level before him and walked slowly along the drive. His eyes were watching the flame without seeing it.

The air in the tunnel was cool and refrigerated, scrubbed and filtered, there was no odour nor taste to it. Davy walked on somnambulantly. He was wallowing in self-pity now. He saw himself in a semi-heroic role, one of the great lovers of history caught up in tragic circumstances. His brain was fully occupied with the picture. His eyes were unseeing. Blindly he performed the ritual that a thousand times before had begun the day's shift.

Slowly in its wire mesh cage the blue flame of the safety lamp changed shape. Its crest flattened, and there formed above it a ghostly pale line. Davy's eyes saw it, but his brain refused to accept the message. He walked on in a stupor of guilt and self-pity.

That line above the flame was called 'the cap', it signified that there was at least a five per cent concentration of methane gas in the air. The last shot hole that Johnny Delange's gang had drilled before going off shift had bored into a methane-filled fissure. For the previous three hours, gas had been blowing out of that hole. The ventilation system was unable to wash the air fast enough and now the gas had spread slowly down the drive. The air surrounding Davy's body was heavy with gas, he had breathed it into his lungs. It needed just one spark to ignite it.

Davy reached the end of the drive and snapped the snuffer over the wick, extinguishing the flame in the lamp.

'All safe,' he muttered, not realizing that he had spoken. He went back to his waiting men.

'All safe,' he repeated, and with the Swazi boss boy leading them the forty men of Davy Delange's gang trooped gaily into the mouth of the drive.

Moodily Davy followed them. As he walked he reached into his hip pocket and took out a pack of Lexington filter tips. He put one between his lips, returned the pack and began patting his pockets to locate his lighter.

Davy went from team to team of his machine boys, directing them in the line and spot to be drilled. Every time he spoke, the unlit cigarette waggled between his lips. He gesticulated with the hand that held his cigarette-lighter.

It took twenty minutes for him to set all his drills to work. And he stood and looked back along the tunnel. Each machine boy and his assistant formed a separate sculpture. Most of them were stripped to the waist. Their bodes appeared to be carved and polished in oiled ebony, as they braced themselves behind the massive rock drills.

Davy lifted his cupped hands, holding the cigarette-lighter near his face, and he flicked the cog wheel.

The air in the tunnel turned to flame. In a flash explosion, the flame reached the temperature of a welding torch. It seared the skin from the faces and exposed bodies of the machine boys, it burned the hair from their scalps. It turned their arms to charred stumps. It roasted their eyeballs in their sockets. It scorched their clothing, so as they fell the cloth smouldered and burned against their flesh.

In that instant, as the skin was licked from his face and hands, Davy Delange opened his mouth in a great gasp of agony. The flame shot down his throat into his gas-drenched lungs. Within the confines of his body the gas exploded and his chest popped like a paper bag, his ribs fanning outward about the massive wound like the petals of a sunflower.

Forty-one men died at the same moment. In the silence

after that whooshing, sucking detonation, they lay like scorched insects along the floor of the drive. One or two of them were moving still, an arched spine relaxing, a leg straightening, charred fingers unclenching, but within a minute all was absolutely still.

Half an hour later Doctor Dan Stander and Rodney Ironsides were the first men into the drive. The smell of burned flesh was overpowering. Both of them had to swallow down their nausea as they went forward.

– 52 –

Dan Stander sat at his desk and looked out over the car park in front of the mine hospital. He appeared to have aged ten years since the previous evening. Dan envied his colleagues the detachment they could bring to their work. He had never been able to perfect the trick. He had just completed forty-one examinations for issue of death certificates.

For fifteen years he had been a mine doctor, so he was accustomed to dealing with death in its more hideous forms. This, however, was the worst he had ever encountered. Forty-one of them, all victims of severe burning and massive explosion trauma.

He felt washed out, exhausted with ugliness. He massaged his temples as he examined the tray of pathetic possessions that lay on the desk before him. This was the contents of the pockets of the man Delange. Extracting them from the scorched clothing had been a filthy business in itself. Cloth had burned into the flesh, the man had been wearing a cheap nylon shirt under his overalls. The fabric had melted in the heat and had become part of his blistered skin.

There was a bunch of keys on a brass ring, a Joseph Rogers pen-knife with a bone handle, a Ronson cigarette-lighter which had been clutched in the man's clawed and charred right hand, a springbok skin wallet, and a loose envelope with one corner burned away.

Dan had already passed on the effects of the Bantu victims to the agent of the Bantu Recruiting Agency, who would send them on to the men's families. Now he sighed with distaste and picked up the wallet. He opened it.

In one compartment there were half a dozen postage stamps, and five rands in notes. The other flap bulged with paper. Dan glanced through salesmen's cards, dry-cleaning receipts, newspaper cuttings offering farms for sale, a folded page from the *Farmer's Weekly* on the planning of a dairy herd, a JBS savings book.

Dan opened the savings book and whistled when he saw the total. He fanned the remaining pages.

There was a much-fingered envelope, unsealed and tucked behind the cardboard cover of the savings book. Dan opened it, and pulled a face. It contained a selection of photographs of the type which one found offered for sale in the dock area of the Mozambique port of Lourenço Marques. It was for this type of material that Dan was searching.

When the man's possessions were returned to his grieving relatives, Dan wanted to spare them this evidence of human frailty. He burned the photographs and the envelope in his ashtray and then crushed the blackened sheets to powder before spilling it into his waste-paper bin.

He went across to the window and opened it to let the smell of smoke escape. He stood at the window and searched the car park for Joy's Alfa Romeo. She had not arrived as yet and Dan returned to his desk.

The remaining envelope caught his eye and he picked it up. There was a smear of blood upon it, and the corner was burned away. Dan removed the four sheets of paper and spread them on the desk:

Dear Johnny,

When Pa died you were still little – and I always reckoned you were more like my son, you know, than my brother.

Well, Johnny, I reckon now I've got to tell you something . . .

Dan read slowly, and he did not hear Joy come into the room. She stood at the door watching him. Her expression fond, a small smile on her lips, shiny blonde hair hanging straight to her shoulders. Then she moved up quietly behind his chair and kissed his ear. Dan started and turned to face her.

'Darling,' Joy said and kissed him on the mouth. 'What is so interesting that you ignore my arrival?'

Dan hesitated a moment before telling her.

'There was a man killed last night in a ghastly accident. This was in his pocket.'

He handed her the letter and she read it slowly.

'He was going to send this to his brother?' she asked, and Dan nodded.

'The bitch,' Joy whispered, and Dan looked surprised.

'Who?'

'The girl – it's her fault, you know.' Joy opened her purse and took out a tissue to dab her eyes. 'Damn it, now I'm messing my make-up.' She sniffed, and then went on. 'It would serve her right if you gave that letter to her husband.'

'You mean I shouldn't give it to him?' Dan asked. 'We have no right to play God.'

'Haven't we?' asked Joy, and Dan watched quietly as she tore the letter to tiny shreds, screwed them into a ball, then dropped them into the waste bin.

'You are wonderful,' he said. 'Will you marry me?'

'I've already answered that question, Dr Stander.' And she kissed him again.

53

Hettie Delange was in a turmoil.

It had started with the phone call that had roused Johnny from their bed. He had said something about trouble at the shaft as he pulled on his clothes, but she had come only briefly awake and then drifted off again as Johnny hurried out into the night.

He had come in hours later and sat on the edge of the bed, his hands clasped between his knees and his head bowed.

'What's wrong, man,' she had snapped at him. 'Come to bed. Don't just sit there.'

'Davy's dead.' His voice had been listless.

There was a moment's shock that had convulsed the muscles of her belly, and brought her fully awake. Then, immediately, she had felt a swift cleansing rush of relief.

He was dead. It was as easy as that! All day she had worried. She had been stupid to let it happen. Just that moment of weakness, that self-indulgent slip and she had been dreading the consequences all that day. She had imagined Davy trailing after her with puppy eyes, trying to touch her, making it so obvious that even Johnny would see it. She had enjoyed it but just the once was enough. She wanted no repeat performance and certainly no complications to follow the original deed.

Now it was all taken care of. He was dead.

'Are you sure?' she had asked anxiously, and Johnny heard the tone as concern.

'I saw him!' Johnny had shuddered, and wiped the back of his hand across his mouth.

'Gee, that's terrible.' Hettie had remembered her role, and sat up and put her arms about Johnny. 'That's terrible for you.'

She had not slept again that night. Somehow the

thought of Davy going directly from her to his violent death was exciting. It was like in the movies, or a book, or something. Like he was an airman and he had been shot down, and she was his girl. Perhaps she was pregnant and all alone in the world, and she would have to go to Buckingham Palace and get his medal for him. And the Queen would say . . .

The fantasies had played out in her mind until the dawn, with Johnny tossing and muttering beside her.

She woke him when it was first light in the room.

'How was he?' she asked softly. 'What did he look like, Johnny?'

Johnny shuddered again, and then he started to tell her. His voice was husky, and the sentences broken and disconnected. When he stumbled into silence, Hettie found herself trembling with excitement.

'How terrible,' she kept repeating. 'Oh, how awful!' And she pressed against him. After a while Johnny made love to her, and for Hettie it was better than she had ever known it to be.

All that morning there were phone calls, and four of her friends came over to drink coffee with her. A reporter and photographer from the *Johannesburg Star* called and asked questions. Hettie was the centre of attraction, and again and again she repeated the story with all its grisly details.

After lunch Johnny came home with a little dark-haired man in a charcoal suit and black Italian shoes, with a matching black briefcase.

'Hettie, this is Mr Boart. He was Davy's lawyer. He's got something to tell you.'

'Mrs Delange. May I convey to you my sincere condolences in the tragic bereavement you and your husband have suffered.'

'Yes, it's terrible, isn't it?' Hettie was apprehensive. Had Davy told this lawyer about them? Had this man come to make trouble?

'Your brother-in-law made a will of which I am the executor. Your brother-in-law was a wealthy man. His estate is in excess of fifty thousand rand.' Boart paused portentously. 'And you and your husband are the sole beneficiaries.'

Hettie looked dubiously from Boart to Johnny.

'I don't – what's that mean? Beneficiary?'

'It means that you and your husband share the estate between you.'

'I get half of fifty thousand rand?' Hettie asked in delighted disbelief.

'That's right.'

'Gee,' exulted Hettie. 'That's fabulous!' She could hardly wait for Johnny and the lawyer to go before she phoned her friends again. All four of them returned to drink more coffee, to thrill again and to envy Hettie the glamour and excitement of it.

'Twenty-five thousand,' they kept repeating the sum with relish.

'Hell, man, he must really have liked you a lot, Hettie,' one of the girls commented with heavy emphasis, and Hettie lowered her eyes and contrived to look bereft and mysterious.

Johnny came home after six, unsteady on his feet and reeking of liquor. Reluctantly Hettie's four friends left to rejoin their waiting families, and almost immediately after that a big white sports car pulled up in the driveway and Hettie's day of triumph was complete. Not one of her friends had ever had the General Manager of the Sonder Ditch Gold Mining Company call at their home.

She had the front door open the instant the doorbell rang. Her greeting had been shamelessly plagiarized from a period movie that had recently played at the local cinema.

'Mr Ironsides, how good of you to come.'

When she led Rod through into the over-furnished lounge, Johnny looked up but did not get to his feet.

'Hello, Johnny', said Rod. 'I have come to tell you that I'm sorry about Davy, and to . . .'

'Don't give me that bull dust, Tin Ribs,' said Johnny Delange.

'Johnny,' gasped Hettie, 'you can't talk to Mr Ironsides like that.' And she turned to Rod, laying a hand on his sleeve. 'He doesn't mean it, Mr Ironsides. He has been drinking.'

'Get out of here,' said Johnny. 'Get into the bloody kitchen where you belong.'

'Johnny!'

'Get out!' roared Johnny, rising from his chair, and Hettie fled from the room.

Johnny lurched across to the chrome and glass liquor cabinet that filled one corner. He sloshed whisky into two glasses and handed one to Rod.

'God speed to my brother,' he said.

'To Davy Delange, one of the best rock hounds on the Kitchenerville field,' said Rod, and tossed the drink back in one gulp.

'The best!' Johnny corrected him, and emptied his own glass. He gasped at the sting of the whisky, then leaned forward to speak into Rod's face.

'You've come to find out if I'm game to finish your bloody drive for you, or if I'm going to quit. Davy didn't mean nothing to you and I don't mean nothing to you. Only one thing worrying you — you want to know about your bloody drive.' Johnny refilled his glass. 'Well, hear this, friend, and hear it well. Johnny Delange don't quit. That drive ate my brother but I'll beat the bastard, so you got nothing to worry about. You go home and get a good night's sleep, 'cos Johnny Delange will be on shift and breaking rock tomorrow morning first thing.'

54

A Silver Cloud Rolls-Royce was parked amongst the trees in the misty morning. Ahead was the practice track with the white-painted railings curving away towards the willow-lined river. The mist was heavier along the river and the grass was very green against it.

The uniformed chauffeur stood away from the Rolls, leaving its two occupants in privacy. They sat on the back seat with an angora wool travelling rug spread over their knees. On the folding table in front of them was a silver Thermos of coffee, shell-thin porcelain cups, and a plate of ham sandwiches.

The fat man was eating steadily, washing each mouthful down with coffee. The little bald-headed man was not eating, instead he puffed quickly and nervously at his cigarette and looked out of the window at the horses. The grooms were walking the horses in circles, nostrils streaming in the morning chill, blankets flapping. The jockeys stood looking up at the trainer. They wore hard caps and polo-necked jerseys. All of them carried whips. The trainer was speaking urgently, his hands thrust deep into the pockets of his overcoat.

'It's a very fine service,' said the little man. 'I particularly enjoyed the stop in Rio. My first visit there.'

The fat man grunted. He was annoyed. They shouldn't have sent this agent out. It was a mark of suspicion, distrust, and it would seriously hamper his market operation.

The conference between trainer and jockeys had ended. The diminutive riders scattered to their mounts, and the trainer came towards the Rolls.

'Good morning, sir.' He spoke through the open window, and the fat man grunted again.

'I'm giving him a full run,' the trainer went on. 'Emerald Isle will make pace for him to the five, Pater Noster will take over and push him to the mile, I've Tiger Shark to pace him for the run in.'

'Very well.'

'Perhaps you'd like to keep time, sir.' The trainer proffered a stop-watch, and the fat man seemed to recover his urbanity and charm.

'Thank you, Henry.' He smiled. 'He looks good, I'll say that.'

The trainer was pleased by the condescension.

'Oh! He's red-hot! By Saturday I'll have him sharpened down to razor edge.' He stood back from the window. 'I'll get them off, then.' He walked away.

'You have a message for me?' asked the fat man.

'Of course.' The other wriggled his moustache like a rabbit's whiskers. It was an annoying habit. 'I didn't fly all this way out here to watch a couple of mokes trotting around a race-track.'

'Would you like to give me the message?' The fat man hid his affront. What the agent had called a moke was some of the finest horseflesh in Africa.

'They want to know about this gas explosion.'

'Nothing.' The fat man dismissed the question with a wave of his hand. 'A flash explosion. Killed a few men. No damage to the workings. Negligence on the part of the miner in charge.'

'Will it affect our plans?'

'Not one iota.'

The two horses had jumped away from the start, shoulder to shoulder, with the wreaths of mist swirling in their wake. The glossy bay horse on the rails ran with an easy floating action while the grey plunged along beside it.

'My principals are very concerned.'

'Well, they have no need to be,' snapped the fat man. 'I tell you it makes no difference.'

'Was the explosion due to an error of judgement on the part of this man Ironsides?'

188

'No.' The fat man shook his head. 'It was negligence of the miner in charge. He should have detected the gas.'

'Pity.' The bald man shook his head regretfully. 'We had hoped it was a flaw in the Ironsides character.'

The grey horse was tiring, while the bay ran on smoothly, drawing away from him. From the side rail a third horse came in to replace the grey, and ran shoulder to shoulder with the bay.

'Why should the character of Ironsides concern you?'

'We have heard disturbing reports. This is no pawn to be moved at will. He is taking the job of General Manager by the throat. Already our sources indicate that he has reduced running costs on the Sonder Ditch by a scarcely believable two per cent. He seems to be tireless, inventive – a man, in short, to reckon with.'

'Well and good,' the fat man conceded. 'But I still fail to see why your – ah, principals – are alarmed. Do they expect that this man will hold back the flood waters by the sheer force of his personality?'

The second pacemaker was faltering, but still the big bay ran on alone. A far figure in the mist, passing the mile post, joined at last by the third pacemaker.

'I know nothing about horses,' said the bald man watching the two flying forms. 'But I've just seen that one,' he pointed with his cigarette at the far-off bay. 'I've just seen him run the guts out of the other two. One after the other he has broken their hearts and left them staggering along behind him. We would call him an imponderable, one who cannot be judged by normal standards.' He puffed at his cigarette before going on. 'There are men like that also, imponderable. It seems to us that Ironsides is one of them, and we don't like it. We don't like them on the opposing team. It is just possible that he could upset the entire operation, not, as you put it, by sheer force of personality, but by suddenly doing the unexpected, by behaving in a manner for which we have not allowed.'

Both men fell silent watching the galloping horses come round the last bend and hit the straight.

'Watch this.' The fat man spoke softly, and as though in response to his words the big bay lengthened his stride, reaching out, driving strongly away from the other horse. His head was going like a hammer, twin jets of steam shot from wide flaring nostrils, and thrown turf and dirt flew from his hooves. Five lengths clear of the following horse he went slashing past the finish line and the fat man clicked his stop watch.

He scrutinized the dial of the watch anxiously and then chuckled like a healthy baby.

'And he wasn't really being extended!'

He rapped on the window beside him, and immediately the uniformed chauffeur opened the driving door and slid in behind the wheel.

'To my office,' instructed the fat man, 'and close the partition.'

When the sound-proof glass panel had slid closed between driver and passengers, the fat man turned to his guest.

'And so, my friend, you consider Ironsides to be an imponderable. What do you want me to do about him?'

'Get rid of him.'

'Do you mean what I think you mean?' The fat man lifted an eyebrow.

'No. Nothing that drastic.' The bald head bobbed agitatedly. 'You have been reading too much James Bond. Simply arrange it that Ironsides is far away and well occupied when the drive holes through the Big Dipper Dyke, otherwise there is an excellent chance that he will do something to frustrate our good intentions.'

'I think we can arrange that,' said the fat man and helped himself to another ham sandwich.

55

As he had promised, Manfred caught the Friday evening flight for Cape Town. On the Saturday night Rod and Terry took a wild chance on not being recognized and spent the evening at the Kyalami Ranch Hotel. They danced and dined in the Africa Room, but were on their way back to the apartment before midnight.

In the dawn a playful slap with the rolled-up Sunday papers which Rod delivered to Terry's naked posterior as she slept triggered off a noisy brawl in which a picture was knocked off the wall by a flying pillow, a coffee table overturned and the shrieking and laughter reached such a pitch that it called down a storm of indignant thumping from the apartment above them.

Terry made a defiant gesture at the ceiling, but they both subsided gasping with laughter back onto the bed to indulge in activity every bit as strenuous if not nearly so noisy.

Later, much later, they collected Melanie and once again spent the Sunday at the stud farm on the Vaal. Melanie actually *rode* a horse, a traumatic experience which bade fair to alter her whole existence. After lunch they launched the speedboat from the boat house on the bank of the river and water-skied down as far as the barrage, Terry and Rod taking turns at the wheel and on the skis. It occurred to Rod that Terry Steyner looked good in a white bikini. It was dark before Rod delivered his sleeping daughter to her mother.

'Who is this *Terry* that Melanie talks about all the time?' demanded Patti; she was still sulking about Rod's promotion. Patti had a memory like a tax collector.

'Terry?' Rod feigned surprise. 'I thought you knew.' And he left Patti glaring after him as he went back down the stairs.

Terry was curled up in the leather bucket seat of the Maserati, just the tip of her nose protruding from the voluminous fur coat she wore.

'I love your daughter, Mr Ironsides,' she murmured.

'It would appear that the feeling is reciprocated.'

Rod drove slowly towards the Hillbrow ridge, and Terry's hand came out of the wide fur sleeve and lay on his knee.

'Wouldn't it be nice if we had a daughter of our own one day?'

'Wouldn't it,' Rod agreed dutifully, and then found to his intense amazement that he really meant it.

He was still investigating this remarkable phenomenon as he parked the Maserati in the basement garage of his apartment and went round to open Terry's door.

Manfred Steyner watched Terry climb out of the Maserati and lift her face towards Rodney Ironsides. Ironsides stooped over her and kissed her, then he slammed and locked the door of the Maserati, and arm in arm the two of them crossed to the elevator.

'Peterson Investigations always delivers the goods,' said the man at the wheel of the black Ford parked in the shadows of the garage. 'We will give them half an hour to get settled in comfortably, then we will go up and knock on the door of his apartment.'

Manfred Steyner sat very still and unblinking on the seat beside the private detective. He had arrived back in Johannesburg three hours previously in answer to the summons from the investigation bureau.

'You will leave me here. Drive the Ford out and park at the corner of Clarendon Circle. Wait for me there,' said Manfred.

'Hey? Aren't you going to . . . ?' The detective was taken aback.

'Do as I tell you.' Manfred's voice stung like thrown vitriol, but the detective persisted.

'You will need evidence for the court, you need me as a witness . . .'

'Get out,' Manfred snapped, and opening the door of the Ford he climbed out and closed the door behind him. The detective hesitated a moment longer, then started the engine and drove out of the garage leaving Manfred alone.

Manfred moved slowly towards the big shiny sports car. From his pocket he took a gold-plated pen-knife and opened the large blade.

He had recognized that the car was of special significance to the man. It was the only form of retaliation he could make at the moment. Until Rodney Ironsides completed the drive on the Big Dipper Dyke, he could not confront him nor Theresa Steyner. He could not let them know he even suspected them.

Such human emotions as love and hate and jealousy Manfred Steyner seldom experienced, except in their mildest manifestations. Theresa Hirschfeld he had never loved, as he had never loved any woman. He had married her for her wealth and station in life. The emotion that gripped him was neither hatred nor jealousy. It was affront. He was affronted that these two insignificant persons should conspire to cheat him.

He would not rush in blindly now with threats of physical violence and divorce. No, he would administer an anonymous punishment that would hurt the man deeply. This would be part payment. Later, when he had served his purpose, Manfred would crush him as coldly as though he were stepping on an ant.

As for the woman, he was aware of a mild relief. Her irresponsible behaviour had placed her completely at his mercy, both legally and morally. As soon as the strike beyond the Big Dipper had made him financially secure and independent, he could throw her aside. She would have served her purpose admirably.

The journey which he had interrupted by this hurried return to Johannesburg was connected with the purchase of Sonder Ditch shares. He was touring the major centres arranging with various firms of stock brokers that on a given date they would commence to purchase every available scrap of Sonder Ditch script.

As soon as he had completed this business he would tell the private detective to drive him out to Jan Smuts Airport where he had a reservation on the night plane to Durban where he would continue his preparations.

It had all worked out very well, he thought, as he slipped the knife blade through the rubber buffer of the triangular side window of the Maserati. With a quick twist he lifted the window catch, and pushed the window open. He reached through and turned the door handle. The door clicked open and Manfred climbed into the driver's seat.

The blade of the pen-knife was razor sharp. He started on the passenger seat and then the driver's seat, ripping the leather upholstery to shreds before moving to the back seat and repeating the process there. He slid the panel that concealed the tray of tools each in their separate foam rubber padded compartment, and selected a tyre lever.

With this he smashed all the dials on the dashboard, broken glass tinkling and falling to the carpeted floor. With the point of the tyre lever he dug into the rosewood panelling and tore out a section, splintering and cracking the woodwork into complete ruin.

He climbed out of the Maserati and struck the windshield with the tyre lever. The glass starred. He rained blows on it, unable to shatter it but reducing it to a sagging opaque sheet.

Then he dropped the tyre lever and groped for his pen-knife again. On his knees he slashed at the front offside tyre. The rubber was tougher than he had allowed. Annoyed, he slashed again. The knife turned in his hand, the blade folding against the blow. It sliced the ball of his

194

thumb, a deep stinging cut. Manfred came to his feet with a cry, clutching his injured thumb. Blood spurted from the wound.

'Mein Gott! Mein Gott!' Manfred gasped, horrified by his own blood. As he staggered wildly from the basement garage, he was wrapping a handkerchief around his thumb.

He reached the waiting Ford, hauled the door open and fell into the front seat beside the detective.

'A doctor! For God's sake, get me to a doctor. I'm badly hurt. Quickly! Drive quickly!'

– 56 –

Terry's husband is due back in town today, Rod thought, as he sat down at his desk. It was not a thought that gave him strength to work through a day he knew would be filled with hectic activity.

The quarterly reports were due at Head Office tomorrow morning. In consequence the entire administration was in its usual last-minute panic. Already there was a mob in the waiting-room outside his office that Lily Jordan would soon need a stock whip to control. At three o'clock he was due at a consultants' meeting at Head Office, but before that he wanted to go underground to check the drop-blast matt that Johnny Delange had now completed and charged up.

The phone went as Lily led in his first visitor, a tall, thin, sorrowful-looking man with a droopy moustache.

'Mr Ironsides?' said the voice on the phone.

'Yes.'

'Porters Motors here. I've got an estimate on the repairs to your Maserati.'

'How much?' Rod crossed his fingers.

'Twelve hundred rand.'

'Wow!' Rod gasped.

'Do you want us to go ahead?'

'No, I'll have to contact my insurance company first. I'll call you.' He hung up. That act of unaccountable vandalism still irked him terribly. He realized that he would be reduced to the Company Volkswagen for a further indefinite period.

He turned his attention to his visitor.

'Detective Inspector Grobbelaar,' the tall man introduced himself. 'I am investigating officer in the murder of José Almeida, the concession store proprietor on this mine.'

They shook hands.

'Have you any ideas on who did it?' Rod asked.

'We have always got ideas,' said the Inspector, so sadly that for a moment Rod had the impression that his name was on the list of suspects. 'We believe that the murderer is employed by one of the mines in the district, probably the Sonder Ditch. I have called on you to ask for your co-operation in the investigation.'

'Of course.'

'I will be conducting a great number of interrogations amongst your Bantu employees. I hoped you might find a room for me to use on the premises.'

Rod lifted his phone and while he dialled he told Grobbelaar, 'I'm calling our Compound Manager.' Then he transferred his attention to the mouthpiece. 'Ironsides here. I am sending an Inspector Grobbelaar down to see you. Please see that an office is placed at his disposal and that he receives full co-operation.'

Grobbelaar stood up and extended his hand.

'I won't take up more of your time. Thank you, Mr Ironsides.'

His next visitor was Van der Bergh, his Personnel Officer, brandishing his departmental reports as though they were a winning lottery ticket.

'All finished,' he announced triumphantly. 'All we need is your signature.'

As Rod uncapped his pen, the telephone squealed again.

196

'My God,' he muttered with pen in one hand and telephone in the other. 'Is it worth it?'

It was well after one o'clock when Rod fled his office, leaving Lily Jordan to hold back the tide. He went directly to No. 1 shaft where he was welcomed like the prodigal son by Dimitri and his old Line Managers. They were all anxious to know who would be replacing him as Underground Manager. Rod promised to find out that afternoon when he visited Head Office, and changed into his overalls and helmet.

At the spot where Davy Delange had died, Rod found a gang fixing a screen of wire mesh over the hanging wall to protect the fuses of his drop-blast. The electric cable that carried the blasting circuit to the surface was covered with a distinctive green plastic coating and securely pegged to the roof of the drive.

In the concrete blast room at the shaft head, his electrician had already set up a separate control for this circuit. It would be in readiness at all times. He could fire it within minutes. Rod felt as though a great weight had been lifted from his shoulders as he passed through the swinging ventilation doors and tramped on up the drive to speak to Johnny Delange.

Halfway to the face he met the gigantic figure of Big King coming back towards him with a small gang of lashing boys under his command. Rod greeted him, and Big King stopped and let his gang go on out of earshot before he spoke.

'I wish to speak.'

'Speak then.' Rod noticed suddenly that Big King's face was gaunt, his eyes appeared sunken and his skin had the dusty greyish look of sickness so evident in an ailing Bantu.

'I wish to return to my wives in Portuguese Mozambique,' said Big King.

'Why?' Rod was dismayed at the prospect of losing such a valuable boss boy.

'My blood is thin.' This was as non-committal an answer as any man has ever received. In essence it meant, 'My reasons are my own, and I have no intention of disclosing them.'

'When your blood is thick again, will you return to work here?' Rod asked.

'That is with the gods.' An answer signifying no more than the one preceding it.

'I cannot stop you if you wish to go, Big King, you know that,' Rod told him. 'Report to the Compound Manager and he will mark your notice.'

'I have told the Compound Manager. He wants me to work out my ticket, thirty-three more days.'

'Of course,' Rod nodded. 'You know that it is a contract. You must work it out.'

'I wish to leave at once,' Big King replied stubbornly.

'Then you must give me your reason. I cannot let you break contract except if there is some good reason.' Rod knew better than to set a dangerous precedent like that.

'There is no reason.' Big King admitted defeat. 'I will work out the ticket.'

He left Rod and followed his gang down the drive. Since the night he killed the Portuguese, Big King had slept little and eaten less. Worry had kept his stomach in a turmoil of dysentry, he had neither danced nor sung. Nothing that Crooked Leg nor the Shangaan Induna could say comforted him. He waited for the police to come. As the days passed, so the flesh melted from his body, he knew that they could come before the thirty-three days of his contract expired.

His approach to Rod had been a last despairing effort. Now he was resigned. He knew that the police were inexorable. One day soon they would come. They would lock the silver chains on his wrists and lead him to the closed van. He had seen many men led away like that and he had heard what happened to them after that. The white man's law was the same as the tribal law of the Shangaans. The taking of life must be paid for with life.

They would break his neck with the rope. His ancestors would have crushed his skull with a war club, it was the same in the end.

Rod found Johnny Delange drinking cold tea from his canteen while his gang barred down the face.

'How's it going?' he asked.

'Now we have finished messing about, it has started moving again.' Johnny wiped cold tea from his lips and recorked the canteen. 'We have broken almost fifteen hundred feet since Davy died.'

'That's good going.' Rod ignored the reference to the methane explosion and the drop-blast matt.

'Would have been better if Davy were still alive.' Johnny disliked Campbell, the miner who had replaced Davy on the night shift. 'The night shift aren't breaking their fair ground.'

'I'll chase them up,' Rod promised.

'You do that.' Johnny turned away to shout an order at his gang.

Rod stood and stared at the end of the drive. Less than a thousand feet ahead lay the dark hard rock of the Big Dipper – and beyond it . . . ? Rod felt his skin creep as he remembered his nightmare. That cold green translucent thing waiting for them beyond the dyke.

'All right, Johnny, you are getting close now.' Rod tore his imagination away from that green horror. 'As soon as you hit the serpentine rock you are to stop work immediately and report to me. Is that understood?'

'You'd better tell that to Campbell also,' said Johnny. 'The night shift may hit the Big Dipper.'

'I'll tell him,' Rod agreed. 'But you make sure you

remember. I want to be down here when we hole through the dyke.'

Rod glanced at his watch. It was almost two o'clock. He had an hour to get to the consultant's meeting at Head Office.

'You are late, Mr Ironsides.' Dr Manfred Steyner looked up from the head of the boardroom table.

'My apologies, gentlemen.' Rod took his seat at the long oak table. 'Just one of those days.'

The men about the table murmured sympathetic acknowledgement, and Dr Steyner studied him for a moment without expression before remarking, 'I would be obliged for a few minutes of your time after this meeting, Mr Ironsides.'

'Of course, Dr Steyner.'

'Good.' Manfred nodded. 'Now that Mr Ironsides has graced the table with his presence, the meeting can come to order.' It was the closest any of them had ever heard Dr Steyner come to making a joke.

It was dark outside when the meeting ended. The participants shrugged on their coats, made their farewells and left Manfred and Rod sitting at the table with its overflowing ashtrays and littered pencils and note pads.

Manfred Steyner waited for fully three minutes after the door had closed on the last person to leave. Rod was accustomed to these long intent silences, yet he was uneasy. He sensed a new hostility in the man's attitude. He covered his awkwardness by lighting another cigarette and blowing a series of smoke rings at the portrait of Norman Hradsky, the original chairman of the Company. Flanking Hradsky's portrait were two others. One of a slim blond man, with ravaged good looks and laughing blue eyes. The caption read: 'Dufford Charleywood. Director of CRC from 1867–1872.' The other portrait in its heavy gilt frame depicted an impressively built man with mutton-chop whiskers and black Irish features. 'Sean Courtney' said the caption, and the dates were the same as Charleywood's.

These three had founded the Company, and Rod knew a little of their story. They had been as pretty a bunch of rogues as would be found in any convict settlement. Hradsky had ruined the other two in an ingenious bear raid on the stock exchange, and had virtually stolen their shares in the Company.*

We have become a lot more sophisticated since then, thought Rod. He looked instinctively towards the head of the long table and met Dr Steyner's level, unblinking stare. *Or have we?* he wondered. Just what devilment has our friend in mind?

Manfred Steyner was examining Rod with detached curiosity. So remote from any emotional rancour was Manfred, that he intended using the relationship that had developed between this man and his wife to further the instructions he had received that morning.

'How far is the end of the drive from the dyke?' he asked suddenly.

'Less than a thousand feet.'

'How much longer before you reach it?'

'Ten days. No more, possibly less.'

'As soon as the dyke is reached, all work on it must cease immediately. The timing of this is important, do you understand?'

'I have already instructed my miners not to hole through without my specific orders.'

'Good.' Manfred lapsed into silence for another full minute. Andrew had called him that morning with instructions from the man. Ironsides was to be well away from the Sonder Ditch when they pierced the dyke. It was left to Manfred to engineer his absence.

* Read *When the Lion Feeds*.

'I must inform you, Mr Ironsides, that it will be at least three weeks before I give the order to drill through. When you reach the dyke, it will be necessary for me to proceed to Europe to make certain arrangements there. I will be away for at least ten days during which time no work of any type must be allowed in the drive to the Big Dipper.'

'You will be away over Christmas?' Rod asked with surprise.

'Yes,' Manfred nodded, and could read Rod's mind.

Terry will be alone, Rod thought quickly, she will be alone over Christmas. The Sonder Ditch goes onto *essential services only* for a full seven days over Christmas. Just a skeleton crew to keep her going. I could get away for a week, a whole week away together.

Manfred waited until he knew that Rod had reached the decision to which he had been steered, then he asked: 'You understand? You will await my order to hole through. You need not expect that order until the middle of January.'

'I understand.'

'You may go.' Manfred dismissed him.

'Thanks,' Rod acknowledged drily.

There was a coffee bar in the ground-floor shopping centre of Reef Building. Rod beat a bearded hippie to the telephone booth, and dialled the Sandown number. It was safe enough, he had just left Manfred upstairs.

'Theresa Steyner,' she answered his call.

'We've got a week to ourselves,' he told her. 'One whole glorious week.'

'When?' she demanded joyously.

And he told her.

'Where shall we go?' she asked.

'We'll think of somewhere.'

At 11.26 a.m. on December 16th, Johnny Delange blasted the face of the drive, and went forward in the fumes and dust.

In the beam of his lantern, the new rock blown from the face was completely different from the blueish Ventersdorp quartzite. It was a glassy, blackish green, veined with tiny white lines, more like marble than country rock.

'We are on the dyke.' He spoke to Big King, and stooped to pick up a lump of the serpentine rock. He weighed it in his hand.

'We've done it, we've beaten the bastard!'

Big King stood silently beside him. He did not share Johnny's elation.

'Right!' Johnny tossed the lump of rock back onto the pile. 'Bar down, and make safe. Then pull them out of the drive. We are finished here until further orders.'

'Well done, Johnny,' applauded Rod. 'Clean her up and pull out of the drive. I don't know how much longer it will be till we get the order to hole through the dyke. But take a holiday in the meantime. I'll pay you four fathoms of bonus a day while you are waiting.' He broke the connection with his finger, keeping the receiver to his ear. He dialled and spoke to the switch-board girl at Head Office. 'Get me Dr Steyner, please. This is Rodney Iron-sides.' He waited a few seconds and then Manfred came on the line.

'We've hit the Big Dipper,' Rod told him.

'I will leave for Europe on tomorrow morning's Boeing,' said Manfred. 'You are to do nothing until I return.' Manfred cradled the receiver and depressed the button on his intercom.

'Cancel all my appointments,' he told his secretary. 'I am unavailable.'

'Very well, Dr Steyner.'

Manfred picked up the receiver of his unlisted, direct-line telephone. He dialled.

'Hello, Andrew. Will you tell him that I am ready to discharge my obligations. We have intersected the Big Dipper.' He listened for a few seconds, then spoke again. 'Very well, I will wait for your reply.'

Andrew replaced the telephone and went out through the sliding glass doors onto the terrace. It was a lazy summer's day, hushed with heat, and the sun sparkled on the crystal clear waters of the swimming-pool. Insects murmured languidly in the massed banks of blooms that surrounded the terrace.

The fat man stood before an artist's easel. He wore a blue beret and a white smock that hung like a maternity dress over his jutting stomach.

His model lay face down on an air mattress by the edge of the pool. She was a dainty, dark-haired girl with a pixy face and a doll-like body. Her discarded bikini lay in a damp bundle on the flags of the terrace. Drops of water caught the sun and bejewelled her creamy buttocks, giving her a paradoxical air of innocence and oriental eroticism.

'That was Steyner,' said Andrew. 'He reports that they have hit the Big Dipper.'

The fat man did not look up. He went on laying paint upon the canvas with complete concentration.

'Please lift your right shoulder, my dear, you are covering that utterly delightful bosom of yours,' he instructed, and the girl obeyed him immediately.

Finally he stepped back and regarded his own work critically.

'You may have a break now.' He wiped his brushes while the naked girl stood up, stretched like a cat and then dived into the pool. She surfaced with the water slicking her short dark hair against her head like the pelt of an otter, and swam slowly to the far end of the pool.

'Cable New York, Paris, London, Tokyo and Berlin the code word "Gothic",' he instructed Andrew. This was the word which would unleash the bear offensive on the financial markets of the world. On receipt of those cables, agents in the major cities would begin to sell the shares of the companies mining the Kitchenerville field, sell them by the millions.

'Then instruct Steyner to get Ironsides out of the way, and hole through the dyke.'

Manfred answered Andrew's return call on the unlisted line. He listened to, and acknowledged, his instructions. Afterwards he sat still as a lizard, running over his preparations. Reviewing them minutely, examining them for flaws. There were none.

It was time to begin the purchase of Sonder Ditch shares. He called his secretary on the intercom and instructed her to place calls to numbers in Cape Town, Durban and Johannesburg itself. He wanted the purchase orders to come through a number of different brokers, so that it would not be obvious that there was only one buyer in the market. There was also the question of credit; he was not covering the purchase orders with banker's guarantees. The stock brokers were buying for him simply on his name and reputation and position with CRC Manfred could not place too large a buying order with any one firm lest they ask him to provide surety. Dr Manfred Steyner had no surety to offer.

So, instead, he placed moderate orders with dozens of different firms. By three o'clock that afternoon Manfred had ordered the purchase of three quarters of a million rand's worth of shares. He had no means of paying for those shares but he knew he would never be called upon to do so. When he sold them again in a few weeks' time they would have doubled in value.

A few minutes after his final conversation with the firm of Swerling and Wright in Cape Town, his secretary came through on the intercom.

'SAA have confirmed your reservation on the Boeing to Salisbury. Flight 126 at nine a.m. tomorrow. You are booked to return to Johannesburg on the Rhodesian Airways Viking at 6 p.m. tomorrow evening.'

'Thank you.' Manfred grudged this wasted day but it was imperative that Theresa believed he had left for Europe. She must see him depart on the SAA flight. 'Please get my wife on the phone for me.'

'Theresa,' he told her, 'something important has come up. I have to fly to London tomorrow morning. I am afraid I will be away over Christmas.'

Her display of surprise and regret was unconvincing. She and Ironsides had made their own arrangements for the time he was away, Manfred was convinced of this.

It was all working out very well, he thought as he cradled the receiver, very well indeed.

– 58 –

The Daimler drew up under the portico of Jan Smuts Airport and the chauffeur opened the door for Terry and then for Manfred.

While the porter removed his luggage from the boot of the Daimler, Manfred swept the car park with a quick scrutiny. So early in the morning it was less than half filled. There was a cream Volkswagen with a Kitchenerville number plate parked near the far end. All the line and senior members of the Sonder Ditch had cream Volkswagens as their official vehicles.

'The bee has come to the honeypot,' thought Manfred, and smiled bleakly. He took Terry's elbow into the main concourse of the airport.

Terry waited while Manfred went through his ticket and immigration formalities. On the outside she was a demure and dutiful wife, but she also had seen the Volkswagen and inside she was itching and bubbling with excitement. Darting surreptitious glances from behind her sunglasses, looking for that tall broad-shouldered figure among the crowds.

It seemed a lifetime until she stood alone on the observation balcony with the wind whipping her piebald calfskin coat around her legs, and blowing her hair into a snapping, dancing tangle. The long shark-like shape of the Boeing jet crouched at the far end of the runway and as it started forward Terry turned from the balcony rail and ran back into the main building.

Rod was waiting for her just inside the doors, and he swung her off her feet.

'Gottcha!'

With her feet dangling, she put her arms around his neck and kissed him.

The watchers paused and then smiled, and there was a minor traffic jam at the head of the stairs.

'Come on,' she entreated, 'let's not waste a minute of it.'

He put her on her feet, and they ran down the staircase hand in hand. Terry paused only to dismiss the chauffeur, and then they ran through the car park like children let out of school, and clambered into the Volkswagen. Their luggage was on the back seat.

'Go,' she said, 'go as fast as you can!'

Twenty minutes later Rod pulled the Volkswagen to a tyre-squealing halt in front of the hangars at the private airfield.

The twin-engined Cessna stood on the tarmac. Both engines were ticking over in readiness, and the mechanic climbed down from the cockpit when he recognized Terry.

'Hello, Terry, right on time,' he greeted her.

'Hello, Hank. You've got her warmed up already. You are a sweety!'

'Filed your flight plan also. Nothing too good for my most favourite customer.' The mechanic was a chunky grizzled little man, and he looked at Rod curiously.

'Give you a hand with the bags,' he said.

By the time they had the luggage stowed away in its compartment, Terry was in the cockpit speaking to the control tower.

Rod climbed up into the passenger seat beside her.

Terry switched off her radio and leaned over Rod's lap to speak to Hank.

'Thanks, Hank.' She paused delicately, and then went on with a rush. 'Hank, if anyone asks you, I was on my own today, okay?'

'Okay.' Hank grinned at her. 'Happy landings.' And he closed the cockpit door, and Terry taxied out onto the runway.

'Is this yours? Rod asked. It was a 100,000 rand's worth of aircraft.

'Pops gave it to me for my birthday,' Terry replied. 'Do you like it?'

'Not bad,' Rod admitted.

Terry turned upwind and applied the wheel brakes while she ran the engines up to peak revs, testing their response.

Suddenly Rod realized that he was in the hands of a woman pilot. He fell silent and his nerves began to tighten up.

'Let's go,' said Terry and kicked off the brakes. The Cessna surged forward, and Rod gripped the arm rests and froze with his gaze fixed dead ahead.

'Relax, Ironsides,' Terry advised him without taking her eyes off the runway, 'I've been flying since I was sixteen.'

At 3,000 feet she levelled out and banked gently onto an easterly heading.

'Now that didn't hurt too much did it?' She smiled sideways at him.

'You are quite a girl,' he told her. 'You can do all sorts of tricks.'

'You just wait,' she warned him. 'You ain't seen nothing yet!'

They flew in silence until the Highveld had fallen away behind them, and they were over the dense green mattress of the Bushveld.

'I'm going to divorce him.' She broke the silence, and Rod was not surprised that they were experiencing the mental telepathy of closely attuned minds. He had been thinking about her husband also.

'Good,' he said.

'You think I'd have a chance with you if I did?'

'If you played your cards right, you might get that lucky.'

'Conceited swine,' she said. 'I don't know why I love you.'

'Do you?' he asked.

'Yes.'

'And I you.'

They relapsed into a contented silence, until Terry put the Cessna in a shallow dive.

'What's wrong?' Rod asked with alarm.

'Going down to have a look for game.'

They flew low over thick olive-green bush broken by veils of golden brown grass.

'There,' said Rod, pointing ahead. A line of fat black bugs moving across one of the open places. 'Buffalo!'

'And over there.' Terry pointed left.

'Zebra and wildebeeste,' Rod identified them. 'And there

is a giraffe.' Its long stalk of a neck stuck up like a periscope. It broke into an awkward stiff-legged run as the aircraft roared overhead.

'We have arrived.' Terry indicated a pair of round granite koppies on the horizon ahead. They were as symmetrical as a young girl's breasts, and as they drew nearer Rod made out the thatched roof of a large building standing in the hollow between the koppies. Beyond it a long straight landing-strip had been cut from the trees, and the fat white sausage of a wind sock flew from its pole.

Terry throttled back and circled the homestead. On the lawns half a dozen tiny figures waved up at the Cessna, and as they watched, two of the figures climbed into a toy Land Rover and set off for the landing-strip. A ribbon of white dust blew out from behind it.

'That's Hans,' Terry explained. 'We can go down now.'

She lined the Cessna up for its approach, and then let it sink down with the motors bumbling softly. The ground came up and jarred the undercarriage, then they were taxiing to meet the racing Land Rover.

The man who piled out of the Land Rover was white-haired, and sunburned like old leather.

'Mrs Steyner!' He was making no attempt to conceal his pleasure. 'It's been much too long. Where have you been?'

'I've been busy, Hans.'

'New York? What the hell for?' said Hans surprisingly.

'This is Mr Ironsides.' Terry introduced them. 'Rod, this is Hans Kruger.'

'Van Breda?' asked Hans as they shook hands. 'You related to the van Bredas from Caledon?'

'I don't think so,' Rod muttered weakly and looked at Terry appealingly.

'He is stone deaf,' Terry explained. 'Both his ear drums blown out by a hangfire in the 1930s. He won't admit it though.'

'I'm glad to hear it,' Hans nodded, happily. 'You always

were a healthy girl. I remember when you were a little piccaninny.'

'He is an absolute darling though, so is his wife. They look after the shooting lodge for Pops,' Terry told Rod.

'Good idea!' Hans agreed heartily. 'Let's get your bags in the Land Rover and go up to the house. I bet Mr van Breda could use a drink also.' And he winked at Rod.

The lodge had thatch and rough-hewn timber roofing, stone-flagged floors covered with cured animal skins and Kelim rugs. There was a walk-in fireplace flanked by gun racks on which were displayed fifty fine examples of the gunsmith's art. The furniture was massive and masculine, leather-cushioned and low. The Spanish plaster walls were hung with trophies, horned heads and native weapons.

A vast wooden staircase led up to the bedrooms that opened off the gallery above the main room. The bedrooms were air-conditioned, and after they had got rid of Hans and his fat wife, Rod and Terry tested the bed to see if it was suitable.

An hour and a half later the bed had been judged eminently satisfactory, and as they went down to pass further judgement on the gargantuan lunch that fat Mrs Hans had spread for them, Terry remarked, 'Has it ever occurred to you, Mr Ironsides, that there are parts of your anatomy other than your flanks which are ferrous in character?' Then she giggled and added softly, 'And thank the Lord for that!'

Lunch was an exhausting experience and Terry pointed out that there was little sense in going out before four o'clock as the game would still be in thick cover avoiding the midday heat, so they went back upstairs.

After four o'clock Rod selected a .375 magnum Holland and Holland rifle from the rack, filled a cartridge belt with ammunition from one of the drawers, and they went out to the Land Rover.

'How big is this place?' Rod asked as he turned the Land

Rover away from the gardens and took the track out into the virgin bush.

'You can drive for twenty miles in any direction and it's all ours. Over there our boundary runs against the Kruger National Park,' Terry answered.

They drove along the banks of the river, skirting sandbanks on which grew fluffy-headed reeds. The water ran fast between glistening black rocks, then spread into slow lazy pools.

They saw a dozen varieties of big game, stopping every few hundred yards to watch some lovely animal.

'Pops obviously doesn't allow shooting here,' Rod remarked, as a kudu bull with long spiral horns and trumpet-shaped ears studied them with big wet eyes from a range of thirty feet. 'The game is as tame as domestic cattle.'

'Only family are allowed to shoot,' Terry agreed. 'You qualify as family, however.'

Rod shook his head. 'It would be murder.' Rod indicated the kudu. 'That old fellow would eat out of your hand.'

'I'm glad you feel like that,' Terry said, and they drove on slowly.

The evening was not cool enough to warrant a log fire in the cavernous fireplace of the lodge. They lit one anyway because Rod decided it would be pleasant to sit in front of a big, leaping fire, drink whisky and hold the girl you love.

– 59 –

When Inspector Grobbelaar lowered his teacup, there was a white scum of cream on the tips of his moustache. He licked it off carefully, and looked across at Sergeant Hugo.

'Who have we got next?' he asked.

Hugo consulted his notebook.

'Philemon N'gabai.' He read out the name, and Grobbelaar sighed.

'Number forty-eight, only sixteen more.' The single smeary fingerprint on the fragment of glass from the gold container had been examined by the fingerprint department. They had provided a list of sixty-four names any one of which might be the owner of that print. Each of them had to be interrogated, it was a lengthy and so far unrewarding labour.

'What do we know about friend Philemon?' Grobbelaar asked.

'He is approximately forty years old. A Shangaan from Mozambique. Height 5' 7½", weight 146 lb. Crippled right leg. Two previous convictions. 1956: 60 days for bicycle theft. 1962: 90 days for stealing a camera from a parked car,' Hugo read from the file.

'At one hundred and forty-six pounds I don't see him breaking many necks. But send him in, let's talk to him,' Grobbelaar suggested and dunked his moustache in the tea cup again. Hugo nodded to the African Sergeant and he opened the door to admit Crooked Leg and his escort of an African constable.

They advanced to the desk at which the two detectives sat in their shirt sleeves. No one spoke. The two interrogators subjected him to a calculated and silent scrutiny to set him at as great a disadvantage as possible.

Grobbelaar prided himself on being able to sniff out a guilty conscience at fifty paces, and Philemon N'gabai reeked of guilt. He could not stand still, he was sweating heavily, and his eyes darted from floor to ceiling. He was guilty as hell, but not necessarily of murder. Grobbelaar did not feel the slightest confidence as he shook his head sorrowfully and asked, 'Why did you do it, Philemon? We have found the marks of your hand on the gold bottle.'

The effect on Crooked Leg was instantaneous and

dramatic. His lips parted and began to tremble, saliva dripped onto his chin. His eyes for the first time fixed on Grobbelaar's face, wide and staring.

'Hello! Hello!' Grobbelaar thought, straightening in his chair, coming completely alert. He sensed Hugo's quickening interest beside him.

'You know what they do to people who kill, Philemon? They take them away to . . .' Grobbelaar did not have an opportunity to finish.

With a howl Crooked Leg darted for the door. His crippled gait was deceptive, he was fast as a ferret. He had the door open before the Bantu Sergeant collared him and dragged him gibbering and struggling back into the room.

'The gold, but not the man! I did not kill the Portuguese,' he babbled, and Grobbelaar and Hugo exchanged glances.

'Pay dirt!' Hugo exclaimed with deep satisfaction.

'Bull's eye!' agreed Grobbelaar, and smiled, a rare and fleeting occurrence.

– 60 –

'You see it has a little light that comes on to show you where the keyhole is,' said the salesman pointing to the ignition switch on the dashboard.

'Ooh! Johnny, see that!' Hettie gushed, but Johnny Delange had his head under the bonnet of the big glossy Ford Mustang.

'Why don't you sit in her?' the salesman suggested. He was very cute really, Hattie decided, with dreamy eyes and the most *fabulous* sideburns.

'Ooh! Yes, I'd love to.' She manoeuvred her bottom into the leather bucket seat of the sports car. Her skirt pulled up, and the salesman's dreamy eyes followed the hem all the way.

'Can you adjust the seat?' Hettie asked, innocently looking up at him.

'Here, I'll show you.' He leaned into the interior of the Mustang and reached across Hettie's lap. His hand brushed over her thigh, and Hettie pretended not to notice his touch. He smelled of Old Spice after-shave lotion.

'That's better!' Hettie murmured, and wriggled into a more comfortable position, contriving to make the movement provocative and revealing.

The salesman was encouraged, he lingered with his wrist just touching a sleek thigh.

'What's the compression ratio on this model?' Johnny Delange demanded as he emerged from the engine, and the salesman straightened up quickly and hurried to join him.

An hour later Johnny signed the purchase contract, and both he and Hettie shook the salesman's hand.

'Let me give you my card,' the salesman insisted, but Johnny had returned to his new toy, and Hettie took the cardboard business card.

'Call me if you need anything, anything at all,' said the salesman with heavy significance.

'Dennis Langley. Sales Manager,' Hettie read out aloud. 'My! You're very young to be Sales Manager.'

'Not all that young!'

'I'll bet,' Hettie murmured, and her eyes were suddenly bold. She ran the tip of a pink tongue over her lips. 'I won't lose it,' she promised, and placing the card in her handbag, walked to the Mustang, leaving him with a tantalizing promise and a memory of swaying hips and clicking heels.

They raced the new Mustang as far as Potchefstroom; Hettie encouraging Johnny to overtake slower vehicles with inches to spare for oncoming traffic. With horn blaring he tore over blind rises, forking ringed fingers at the protesting toots of other drivers. They had the speedometer registering

120 mph on the return run, and it was dark as they pulled into the driveway and Johnny hit the brakes hard to avoid running into the back of a big black Daimler that was parked outside their front door.

'Jesus,' gasped Johnny. 'That's Dr Steyner's bus!'

'Who is Dr Steyner?' Hettie demanded.

'Hell, he's one of the big shots from Head Office.'

'You're kidding!' Hettie challenged him.

'Truth!' Johnny affirmed. 'One of the real big shots.'

'Bigger than Mr Ironsides?' The General Manager of the Sonder Ditch was as high up the social ladder as Hettie had ever looked.

'Tin Ribs is chicken feed compared to this joker. Just look at his bus, it's five times better than Tin Ribs's clapped-out old Maserati.'

'Gee!' Hettie could follow the logic of this line of argument. 'What's he want with us?'

'I don't know,' Johnny admitted with a twinge of anxiety. 'Let's go and find out.'

The lounge of the Delange home was not the setting which showed Dr Manfred Steyner to best advantage.

He sat on the edge of a scarlet and gold plastic-covered armchair as stiff and awkward as the packs of china dogs that stood on every table and shelf of the show cabinet, or the porcelain wild ducks which flew in diminishing perspective along the pale pink painted wall. In contrast to the tinsel Christmas decorations that festooned the ceiling and the gay greeting cards that Hettie had pinned to strips of green ribbon, Manfred's black homburg and astrakhan-collared overcoat were unnecessarily severe.

'You will forgive my presumption,' he greeted them without rising. 'You were not at home and your maid let me in.'

'You're welcome, I'm sure,' Hettie simpered.

'Of course you are, Dr Steyner,' Johnny supported her.

'Ah! So you know who I am?' Manfred asked with satisfaction. This would make his task so much easier.

'Of course we do.' Hettie went to him and offered her hand. 'I am Hettie Delange, how do you do?'

With horror Manfred saw that her armpit was unshaven, filled with damp ginger curls. Hettie had not bathed since the previous evening. Manfred's nostrils twitched and he fought down a queasy wave of nausea.

'Delange, I want to speak to you alone.' He cowered away from Hettie's overwhelming physical presence.

'Sure.' Johnny was eager to please. 'How about you making us some coffee, honey,' he asked Hettie.

Ten minutes later Manfred sank with relief into the lush upholstery of the Daimler's rear seat. He ignored the two Delanges waving their farewells, and closed his eyes. It was done. Tomorrow morning Johnny Delange would be on shift and drilling into the glassy green rock of the Big Dipper.

By noon Manfred would own quarter of a million shares in the Sonder Ditch.

In a week he would be a rich man.

In a month he would be divorced from Theresa Steyner. He would sue with all possible notoriety on the grounds of adultery. He no longer needed her.

The chauffeur drove him back to Johannesburg.

It began on the floor of the Johannesburg Stock Exchange.

For some months nearly all the activity had been in the industrial counters, centring about the Alex Sagov group of companies and their merger negotiations.

The only spark of life in the mining and mining financials had been Anglo American Corporation and De Beers Deferred rights issues, but this was now old news and the prices had settled at their new levels. So it was that nobody was expecting fireworks when the call over of the gold mining counters began. The brokers' clerks crowding the floor were quietly spoken and behaved, when the first squib popped.

'Buy Sonder Ditch,' from one end of the hall.

'Buy Sonder Ditch,' a voice raised.

'Buy!' The throng stirred, heads turned.

'Buy.' The brokers suddenly agitated swirled in little knots, broke and reformed as transactions were completed. The price jumped fifty cents, and a broker ran from the floor to confer with his principal.

Here a broker thumped another on the back to gain his attention, and his urgency was infectious.

'Buy! Buy!'

'What the hell's happening?'

'Where is the buying coming from?'

'It's local!'

The price hit ten rand a share, and then the panic began in earnest.

'It's overseas buying.'

'Eleven rand!'

Brokers rushed to telephone warnings to favoured clients that a bull run was developing.

'Twelve fifty. It's only local buying.'

'Buy at best. Buy five thousand.'

Clerks raced back onto the floor carrying the hastily telephoned instructions, and plunged into the hysterical trading.

'Jesus Christ! Thirteen rand, sell now. Take your profit! It can't go much higher.'

'Thirteen seventy-five, it's overseas buying. Buy at best.'

In fifty brokers' offices around the country, the professionals who spent their lives hovering over the tickers regained their balance and, cursing themselves for having been taken unawares, they scrambled onto the bull wagon. Others, the more canny ones, recognized the makings of a sick run and off-loaded their holdings, selling industrial shares as well as mining shares. Prices ran amok.

At ten-fifteen there was a priority call from the offices of the Minister of Finance in Pretoria to the office of the President of the Johannesburg Stock Exchange.

'What are you going to do?'

'We haven't decided. We won't close the floor if we can possibly help it.'

'Don't let it go too far. Keep me informed.'

Sixteen rand and still spiralling when at eleven o'clock South African time, the London Stock Exchange came in. For the first fifteen wild minutes the price of Sonder Ditch gold mining rocketed in sympathy with the Johannesburg market.

Then suddenly and unexpectedly the Sonder Ditch shares ran head-on into massive selling pressure. Not only the Sonder Ditch, but all the Kitchenerville gold mining companies staggered as the pressure increased. The prices wavered, rallied a few shillings and then fell back, wavered again, and then crashed downwards, plummeting far below their opening prices.

'Sell!' was the cry. 'Sell at best!' Within minutes freshly-made paper fortunes were wiped away.

When the price of the Sonder Ditch gold mining shares

fell to five rand seventy-five cents, the committee of the Johannesburg Stock Exchange closed the door in the interests of the national welfare, preventing further trading.

But in New York, Paris and London the investing public continued to beat South African gold mining shares to death.

In the air-conditioned office of a skyscraper building, the little bald-headed man was smashing his balled fist onto the desk top of his superior officer.

'I told you not to trust him,' he was almost sobbing with anger. 'The fat greedy slug. One million dollars wasn't enough for him! No, he had to blow the whole deal!'

'Please, Colonel,' his chief intervened. 'Control yourself. Let us make a fair and objective appraisal of this financial activity.'

The bald-headed man sank back into his chair, and tried to light a cigarette with hands that trembled so violently as to extinguish the flame of his lighter.

'It sticks out a mile.' He flicked the lighter again, and puffed quickly. 'The first activity on the Johannesburg Exchange was Dr Steyner being clever. Buying up shares on the strength of our dummy report. That was quite natural and we expected it, in fact we wanted that to happen. It took suspicion away from us.' His cigarette had gone out, the tip was wet with spit. He threw it away and lit another.

'Fine! Everything was fine up to then. Dr Steyner had committed financial suicide, and we were on the pig's back.' He sucked at his new cigarette. 'Then! Then our fat friend pulls the big double-cross and starts selling the Kitchener-ville shares short. He must have gone into the market for millions.'

'Can we abort the operation at this late date?' his chief asked.

'Not a chance.' The bald head shook vigorously. 'I have

sent a cable to our fat friend ordering him to freeze the work on the tunnel, but can you imagine him obeying that order? He is financially committed for millions of dollars and he will protect that investment with every means at his disposal.'

'Could we not warn the management of the Sonder Ditch company?'

'That would put the finger squarely on us, would it not?'

'Hmm!' the chief nodded. 'We could send them an anonymous warning.'

'Who would put any credence on that?'

'You're right,' the chief sighed. 'We will just have to batten down our hatches and ride out the storm. Sit tight and deny everything.'

'That is all we can do.' The cigarette had gone out again, and there were bits of tobacco in his moustache. The little man flicked his lighter.

'The bastard, the fat, greedy bastard!' he muttered.

– 62 –

Johnny and Big King rode up shoulder to shoulder in the cage. It had been a good shift. Despite the hardness of the serpentine rock that cut down the drilling rate by fifty per cent, they had been able to get in five blasts that day. Johnny reckoned they had driven more than half-way through the Big Dipper. There was no night shift working now. Campbell had gone back to the stopes, so the honour of holing through would be Johnny's. He was excited at the prospect. Tomorrow he would be through into the unknown.

'Until tomorrow, Big King,' he said as they reached the surface and stepped out of the cage.

They separated, Big King heading for the Bantu hostel, Johnny to the glistening new Mustang in the car park.

Big King went straight to the Shangaan Induna's cottage without changing from his working clothes. He stood in the doorway and the Induna looked up from the letter he was writing.

'What news, my father?' Big King asked.

'The worst,' the Induna told him softly. 'The police have taken Crooked Leg.'

'Crooked Leg would not betray me,' Big King declared, but without conviction.

'Would you expect him to die in your place?' asked the Induna. 'He must protect himself.'

'I did not mean to kill him,' Big King explained miserably. 'I did not mean to kill the Portuguese, it was the gun.'

'I know, my son.' The Induna's voice was husky with helpless pity.

Big King turned from the doorway and walked down across the lawns to the ablution block. The spring and swagger had gone from his step. He walked listlessly, slouching, dragging his feet.

– 63 –

Manfred Steyner sat at his desk. His hands lay on the blotter before him, one thumb wearing a turban of crisp white bandage. His only movement was the steady beat of a pulse in his throat and a nerve that fluttered in one eyelid. He was deathly pale, and a light sheen of perspiration gave his features the look of having been sculptured from washed marble.

The volume of the radio was turned high, so the voice of the announcer boomed and reverberated from the panelled walls.

'The climax of the drama was reached at eleven forty-five South African time when the President of the Johantruck, bounded over the far kerb and swung back into the road.

Dan watched it tear away towards Kyalami.

He let the truck pass and then swung into the traffic behind it. He had to wait until the road was clear ahead before he could overtake the truck, and by that time the Alfa was a dwindling cream speck ahead of him.

Dan settled back in the leather bucket seat, and gave the Jaguar its head. He was furious, outraged by the treatment he had seen Manfred meting out to Terry. Her swollen and bruised face had shocked him and his feet were firmly set upon the path of vengeance.

His hands gripped the steering-wheel fiercely, he was muttering threats of violence as the speedometer moved up over the hundred mile per hour mark and he began relentlessly overhauling the cream sports car.

Steadily he moved up behind the Alfa until he was driving almost on its rear bumper. The Alfa was held up by a green school bus. Dan could not pass, however, for there was a steady stream of traffic coming in the opposite direction.

He fastened his attention on the back of Manfred's head, still fuming with anger.

Dan dropped down a gear, ready to pull out and overtake the Alfa when the opportunity arose. At that moment Manfred looked up into his rear view mirror. Dan saw the reflection of his white face with disordered damp hair hanging onto the forehead, saw his expression change immediately he recognized Dan and the Alfa shot out into the face of the approaching traffic.

There was a howl and blare of horns, vehicles swerved to make way for Manfred's wild rush. Dan glimpsed frightened faces flicking past, but the Alfa had squeezed around the green bus and was speeding away.

Dan dropped back, then sent the Jaguar like a thrown javelin through the gap between bus and kerb, overtaking on the wrong side and ignoring the bus driver's yell of protest.

The Jaguar had a higher top speed, and on the long straight Pretoria highway Dan crept up steadily on the cream Alfa.

He could see Manfred glancing repeatedly into his driving-mirror, and he grinned mirthlessly.

Ahead of them the highway rose and then dipped over a low rounded ridge. A double avenue of tall blue gum trees flanked each side of the road.

Travelling in the same direction as the two high performance sports cars was a Mini of a good vintage year. Its elderly driver was triumphantly about to overtake an overloaded vegetable truck. Neck and neck they approached the blind rise at twenty-five miles per hour, between them they effectively blocked half the road.

The horn of the Alfa wailed a high-pitched warning, and Manfred pulled out to overtake both slower vehicles. He was level with them, well out over the white dividing line, when a cement truck popped up over the blind rise.

Dan stood on his brake pedal with all the strength of his right leg, and watched it happen.

The cement truck and the Alfa came head on towards each other at a combined speed of well over a hundred miles per hour. At the last moment the Alfa began to turn away but it was too late by many seconds.

It caught the heavy cement truck a glancing blow and was hurled across the path of the two slower vehicles, miraculously touching neither of them; it skidded sideways leaving reeking black smears of rubber on the tarmac, and hurdled the low bank. It struck one of the blue gums full on, with a force that shivered the giant tree trunk and brought down a rain of leaves.

Dan pulled the Jaguar into the side of the road, parked it, and walked back.

He knew there was no hurry. The drivers of the Mini

her hair falling forward in wild disorder, kneeling as though for the headsman's stroke. Manfred felt a flood of disappointment. He did not want it to end so soon, he wanted to savour this sadistic elation, this sense of power.

At the last possible moment he yanked the wheel over and the car slewed violently. It shot past Terry with six inches to spare, and its rear wheels pelted her with clods of turf and thrown dirt.

Laughing aloud, wild-eyed, Manfred held the wheel hard over, bringing the Alfa around in a tight skidding circle, crackling sideways through another protea bush.

Terry was up and running again. He saw immediately that she was heading for the changing rooms of the swimming-pool among the trees on the bottom lawn and she was far enough ahead to elude him, perhaps.

'Bitch!' he snarled, and crash-changed into third gear, with engine revs peaking. The Alfa howled in pursuit of the running girl.

Had Terry thrown the bulky report aside, she might have reached the brick change rooms ahead of the racing sports car, but the report hampered and slowed her. She still had twenty yards to cover, she was running along the paved edge of the swimming-pool, and she sensed that the car was right on top of her.

Terry dived sideways, hitting the water flat on her side, and the Alfa roared past. Manfred trod heavily on the brakes, the Michelin metallic tyres screeched against the paving stones, and Manfred leapt out of the driver's seat the moment the Alfa stopped.

He ran back to the pool side. Terry was floundering towards the far steps. She was exhausted, weak with exertion and terror. Her sodden hair streamed down over her face, and she was gasping open-mouthed for air.

Manfred laughed again, a high-pitched, almost girlish giggle, and he dived after her, landing squarely between

Terry's shoulder blades with his full weight. She went under, sucking water agonizingly into already aching lungs, and when she surfaced she was coughing and gagging, blinded with water and her own wet hair.

Almost immediately she felt herself seized from behind and forced face down into the water. For half a minute she struggled fiercely, then her movements slowed and became weaker.

Manfred stood over her, chest deep in the clear water, gripping her around the waist and by a handful of her sodden hair, forcing her face deep below the surface. He had lost his spectacles, and he blinked owlishly. The wet silk of his shirt clung to his upper body, and the water had slicked his hair down.

As he felt the life going out of her, and her movements becoming sluggish and slow, he began to laugh again. The broken, incoherent laughter of a madman.

'Dan!' Joy pointed off through the trees. 'That's my car down there, parked by the swimming-pool!'

'What the hell is it doing there?'

'There's something wrong, Terry wouldn't drive through her beloved garden, unless there was!'

Dan braked sharply and pulled his Jaguar to the side of the driveway.

'I'm going to take a look.' He slid out of the car and started off across the lawns. Joy opened her own door and trotted after him.

Dan saw the man in the water, fully dressed, intent on what he was doing. He recognized Manfred Steyner.

'What the hell is he up to?' Dan started running. He reached the edge of the pool, and suddenly he realized what was happening.

'Christ! He's drowning her,' he shouted aloud, and he sprang into the water.

He did not waste time struggling with Manfred. He hit him a great open-handed, round-armed blow, that cracked against the side of Manfred's head like a pistol shot and sent him lurching sideways, releasing his grip on Terry.

Ignoring Manfred, Dan picked Terry from the water like a drowned kitten and waded to the steps. He carried her out and laid her face down on the paving. He knelt over her and began applying artificial respiration. He felt Terry stir under his hands, then cough and retch weakly.

Joy came up at the run and dropped on her knees beside him.

'My God, Dan, what happened?'

'That little bastard was trying to drown her.'

Dan looked up from his labours without interrupting the rhythm of his movement over Terry. She spluttered and retched again.

On the far side of the pool Manfred Steyner had dragged himself from the pool. He was sitting on the edge with his feet still dangling into the water, his head was hanging and he was fingering the side of his face where Dan had hit him. On his lap he held a wet pulpy mess that had been the geological report.

'Joy, can you take over here? Terry's not too far gone, and I want to get my hands on that little Hun.'

Joy took Dan's place over Terry's prostrate form, and Dan stood up.

'What are you going to do to him?' Joy asked.

'I'm going to beat him to a pulp.'

'Good show!' Joy encouraged him. 'Give him one for me.'

Manfred had heard the exchange and as Dan ran around the edge of the pool he scrambled to his feet, and staggered to the parked Alfa. He slammed the door and whirred the engine to life. Dan was just too late to stop him. The car shot forward across the lawns, leaving Dan running, futile, behind it.

'Look after her, Joy!' Dan shouted back.

By the time Dan had run up the terrace to his Jaguar and reversed it to point in the opposite direction, the Alfa had disappeared through the white gates with a musical flutter of its exhaust.

'Come on, girlie,' Dan spoke to his Jaguar. 'Let's go get him.'

The rear wheels spun as he pulled away.

Without his spectacles Manfred Steyner's vision was blurred and milky. The outlines of all objects on which he looked were softened and indistinct.

He instinctively checked the Alfa at the stop street at the bottom of the lane. He sat undecided, water still streaming from his clothing, squelching in his shoes. Beside him on the passenger seat lay the sodden report, its pages beginning to disintegrate from its soaking and the rough handling it had received.

He had to get rid of it. It was the shred of incriminating evidence. That was the only clear thought Manfred had. For the first time in his life the crystalline clarity of his thought processes was interrupted. He was confused, his mind jerking abruptly from one subject to another, the intense pleasure of inflicting hurt on Terry mingled with the sting and smart of his own injuries. He could not concentrate on either sensation for overlying it all was a sense of fear, of uncertainty. He felt vulnerable, hunted, hurt and shaken. His brain flickered and wavered as though a computer had developed an electrical fault. The answers it produced were nonsensical.

He looked in the rear view mirror, saw the Jaguar glide out between the white gates and turn towards him.

'Christ!' he panicked. He rammed his foot down on the accelerator and engaged the clutch. The Alfa screeched out into the main highway, swerved into the path of a heavy nesburg Stock Exchange declared the floor closed and all further trading suspended.

'Latest reports from the Tokyo Stock Exchange are that Sonder Ditch gold mining shares were being traded at the equivalent of four rand forty cents. This compares with the morning's opening price of the same share on the Johannesburg Stock Exchange of nine rand forty-five cents.

'A spokesman for the South African Government stated that although no reason for these extraordinary price fluctuations was apparent, the Minister of Mines, Doctor Carel De Wet, had ordered a full-scale commission of inquiry.'

Manfred Steyner stood up from his desk and went through into the bathroom. With his flair for figures he did not need pen and paper to compute that the shares he had purchased that morning had depreciated in value by well over one million rand at the close of business that evening.

He knelt on the tiled floor in front of the toilet bowl and vomited.

– 64 –

The sky was darkening rapidly, for the sun had long ago sunk below a blazing horizon.

Rod heard the whisper of wings, and strained his eyes upwards into the gloom. They came in fast, in V-formation, slanting down towards the pool of the river. He stood up from the blind and swung the shotgun on them, leading well ahead of the line of flight.

He squeezed off both barrels. Wham! Wham! And the duck broke formation and rocketed upwards, whirring aloft on noisy wings.

'Damn it!' said Rod.

'What's wrong, dead-eye Dick, did you miss?' asked Terry.

'The light's too bad.'

'Excuses! Excuses!' Terry stood up beside him, and Rod pushed a balled fist lightly against her cheek.

'That's enough from you, woman. Let's go home.'

Carrying the shotguns and bunches of dead duck, they trudged along the bank in the dusk to the waiting Land Rover.

It was completely dark as they drove back to the lodge.

'What a wonderful day it's been,' Terry murmured dreamily. 'If for nothing else, I will always be grateful to you for teaching me how to enjoy my life.'

Back at the lodge, they bathed and changed into fresh clothes. For dinner they had wild duck and pineapple, with salads from Mrs Fat Hans' vegetable garden. Afterwards, they sprawled on the leopard-skin rugs in front of the fireplace and watched the log fire without talking, relaxed and happy and tired.

'My God, it's almost nine o'clock.' Terry checked her wristwatch. 'I fancy a bit of bed myself, how about you, Mr Ironsides?'

'Let's hear the nine o'clock news first.'

'Oh, Rod! Nobody ever listens to the news here. This is fairyland!'

Rod switched on the radio and the first words froze them both. They were 'Sonder Ditch'.

In horrified silence they listened to the report. Rod's expression was granite-hard, his mouth a tight grim line. When the news report ended, Rod switched off the radio set and lit a cigarette.

'There is trouble,' he said. 'Big trouble. I'm sorry, Terry, we must go back. As soon as possible. I have to get back to the mine.'

'I know,' Terry agreed immediately. 'But Rod, I can't take off from this landing-strip in the dark. There is no flare path.'

'We'll leave at first light.'

Rod slept very little that night. Whenever she woke, Terry sensed him lying unsleeping, worrying. Twice she heard him get up and go to the bathroom.

In the very early hours of the morning she woke from her own troubled sleep and saw him silhouetted against the starlit window. He was smoking a cigarette and staring out into the darkness. It was the first night they had spent together without making love. In the dawn Rod was haggard and puffy-eyed.

They were airborne at eight o'clock and they landed in Johannesburg a little after ten.

Rod went straight to the telephone in Hank's office and Lily Jordan answered his call.

'Miss Jordan, what the hell is happening? Is everything all right?'

'Is that you, Mr Ironsides. Oh! Thank God! Thank God you've come, something terrible has happened!'

– 65 –

Johnny Delange blew the face of the drive twice before nine o'clock, cutting thirty feet further into the glassy green dyke.

He had found that by drilling his cutter blast holes an additional three feet deeper, he could achieve a shatter effect on the serpentine rock which more than compensated for the additional drilling time. This next blast he was going to flout standard regulations and experiment with double-charging his cutter holes. He would need additional explosives.

'Big King,' he shouted to make himself heard above the roar of drills. 'Take a gang back to the shaft station. Pick up six cases of Dynagel.'

He watched Big King and his gang retreat back down the drive, and then he lit a cigarette and turned his attention to his machine boys. They were poised before the rock face, sweating behind their drills. The dark rock of the dyke absorbed the light from the overhead electric bulbs. It made the end of the drive a gloomy place, filled with a sense of foreboding.

Johnny began to think about Davy. He was aware suddenly of a sense of disquiet, and he moved restlessly. He felt the hair on his forearms come slowly erect, each on a separate goose pimple. *Davy is here.* He knew it suddenly, and surely. His flesh crawled and he went cold with dread. He turned quickly and looked over his shoulder. The tunnel behind him was deserted, and Johnny gave a sickly grin.

'Shaya, madoda,' he called loudly and unnecessarily to his gang. They could not hear him above the roar of the drills, but the sound of his own voice helped reassure him.

Yet the creepy sensation was still with him. He felt that Davy was still there, trying to tell him something.

Johnny fought the sensation. He walked quickly forward, standing close to his machine boys, as though to draw comfort from their physical presence. It did not help. His nerves were shrieking now, and he felt himself beginning to sweat.

Suddenly the machine boy who was drilling the cutter hole in the centre of the face staggered backwards.

'Hey!' Johnny shouted at him, then he saw that water was spurting in fine needle jets from around the drill steel. Something was squeezing the drill steel out of its hole, like toothpaste out of a tube. It was pushing the machine boy backwards.

'Hey!' Johnny started forward and at that instant the heavy metal drill was fired out of the rock with the force of a cannon ball. It decapitated the machine boy, tearing his head from his body with such savagery that his carcass was thrown far back down the drive, his blood spraying the dark rock walls.

From the drill hole shot a solid jet of water. It came out under such pressure that when it caught the machine boy's assistant in the chest it stove in his ribs as though he had been hit by a speeding automobile.

'Out!' yelled Johnny. 'Get out!' And the rock face exploded. It blew outwards with greater force than if it had been blasted with Dynagel. It killed Johnny Delange instantly. He was smashed to a bloody pulp by the flying rock. It killed every man in his gang with him, and immediately afterwards the monstrous burst of water that poured from the face picked up their mutilated remains and swept them down the drive.

Big King was at the shaft station when they heard the water coming. It sounded like an express train in a tunnel, a dull bellow of irresistible power. The water was pushing the air from the drive ahead of it, so that a hurricane of wind came roaring from the mouth of the drive, blowing out a cloud of dust and loose rubbish.

Big King and his gang stood and stared in uncomprehending terror until the head of the column of water shot from the drive, frothing solid, carrying with it a plug of debris and human remains.

Bursting into the T-junction of the main 66 level haulage, the strength of the flood was reduced, yet still it swept down towards the lift station in a waist-deep wall.

'This way!' Big King was the first to move. He leapt for the steel emergency ladder that led up to the level above. The rest of his gang were not fast enough, the water picked them up and crushed them against the steel-mesh barrier that guarded the shaft. The crest of the wave burst around Big King's legs, sucking at him, but he tore himself from its grip and climbed to safety.

Beneath him the water poured into the shaft like bath

227

water into a plug hole, forming a spinning whirlpool about the collar as it roared down to flood the workings below 66 level.

– 66 –

Leaving Terry at the airfield to solicit transport from Hank, the mechanic, Rod drove directly to the head of No. 1 shaft of the Sonder Ditch. He jumped from the Volkswagen into the clamouring crowd clustered above the shaft head.

Dimitri was wide-eyed and distracted, beside him Big King towered like a black colossus.

'What happened?' Rod demanded.

'Tell him,' Dimitri instructed Big King.

'I was at the shaft with my gang. A river leaped from the mouth of the drive, a great river of water running faster than the Zambesi in flood; roaring like a lion the water ate all the men with me. I alone climbed above it.'

'We've hit a big one, Rod,' Dimitri interrupted. 'It's pouring in fast. We calculate it will flood the entire workings up to 66 level in four hours from now.'

'Have you cleared the mine?' Rod demanded.

'All the men are out except Delange and his gang. They were in the drive. They've been chopped, I'm afraid,' Dimitri answered.

'Have you warned the other mines we could have a burst through into their workings?'

'Yes, they are pulling all their shifts out.'

'Right.' Rod set off for the blast control room with Dimitri trotting to keep up with him. 'Give me your keys, and find the foreman electrician.'

Within minutes the three of them were crowded into the tiny concrete control room.

'Check in the special circuit,' Rod instructed. 'I'm going to shoot the drop-blast matt and seal off the drive.'

The foreman electrician worked quickly at the control panel. He looked up at Rod.

'Ready!' he said.

'Check her in,' Rod nodded.

The foreman threw the switch. The three of them caught their breath together.

Dimitri said it for them: 'Red!'

On the control panel of the special circuit the red bulb glared balefully at them, the Cyclops eye of the god of despair.

'Christ!' swore the foreman. 'The circuit is shot. The water must have torn the wires out.'

'It may be a fault in the board.'

'No.' The foreman shook his head with certainty.

'We've had it,' whispered Dimitri. 'Goodbye the Sonder Ditch!'

Rod burst out of the control room into the expectant crowd outside.

'Johnson!' He singled out one of his mine captains. 'Go down to the Yacht Club at the dam, get me the rubber rescue dinghy. Quick as you can, man.'

The man scurried away, and Rod turned on the electrician foreman as he emerged from the control room.

'Get me a battery hand-operated blaster, a reel of wire, pliers, two coils of nylon rope. Hurry!'

The foreman went.

'Rod.' Dimitri caught his arm. 'What are you going to do?'

'I'm going down there. I'm going to find the break in the circuit and I'm going to blast her by hand.'

'Jesus!' Dimitri gasped. 'You are crazy, Rod. You'll kill yourself for sure!'

Rod completely ignored his protest.

'I want one man with me. A strong man. The strongest there is, we will have to drag the dinghy against the flood.' Rod looked about him. Big King was standing by the banksman's office. The two of them were tall enough to face each other over the heads of the men between them.

'Will you come with me, Big King?' Rod asked.

'Yes,' said Big King.

– 67 –

In less than twenty minutes they were ready. Rod and Big King were stripped down to singlets and bathing-trunks. They wore canvas tennis shoes to protect their feet, and the hard helmets on their heads were incongruous against the rest of their attire.

The rubber dinghy was ex-naval disposal. A nine-foot air-filled mattress, so light that a man could lift it with one hand. Into it was packed the equipment they would need for the task ahead. A water-proof bag contained the battery blaster, the reel of insulated wire, the pliers and a spare lantern. Lashed to the eyelets along the sides of the dinghy were two coils of light nylon rope, a small crowbar, an axe and a razor-sharp machete in a leather sheath. To the bows of the dinghy were fastened a pair of looped nylon towing lines.

'What else will you need, Rod?' Dimitri asked.

Rod shook his head thoughtfully. 'That's it, Dimitri. That should do it.'

'Right!' Dimitri beckoned and four men came forward and carried the dinghy into the waiting cage.

'Let's go,' said Dimitri and followed the dinghy into the cage. Big King went next and Rod paused a second to look up at the sky. It was very blue and bright.

Before the onsetter could close the shutter door, a Silver Cloud Rolls-Royce came gliding onto the bank. From the rear door emerged first Hurry Hirschfeld and then Terry Steyner.

'Ironsides!' roared Hurry. 'What the hell is going on?'

'We've hit water,' Rod answered him from the cage.

'Water? Where did it come from?'

'Beyond the Big Dipper.'

'You drove through the Big Dipper?'

'Yes.'

'You bastard, you've drowned the Sonder Ditch,' roared Hurry, advancing on the cage.

'Not yet, I haven't,' Rod contradicted.

'Rod.' Terry was white-faced beside her grandfather. 'You can't go down there.' She started forward.

Rod pushed the onsetter aside and pulled down the steel shutter door of the cage. Terry threw herself against the steel mesh of the guard barrier, but the cage was gone into the earth.

'Rod,' she whispered, and Hurry Hirschfeld put his arm around her shoulders and led her to the Rolls-Royce.

From the back seat of the Rolls, Hurry Hirschfeld was conducting a Kangaroo Court Trial of Rodney Ironsides. One by one he called for the line managers of the Sonder Ditch and questioned them. Even those who were loyal to Rod could say little in his defence, and there were others who took the opportunity to level old scores with Rodney Ironsides.

Sitting beside her grandfather, Terry heard such a condemnation of the man she loved as to chill her to the depths of her soul. There was no doubt that Rodney Ironsides, without Head Office sanction, had instituted a new development so risky and contrary to company policy as to be criminal in concept.

'Why did he do it?' muttered Hurry Hirschfeld. He seemed bewildered. 'What could he possibly achieve by driving through the Big Dipper? It looks like a deliberate attempt to sabotage the Sonder Ditch.' Hurry's anger began to seethe within him. 'The bastard! He has drowned the Sonder Ditch and killed dozens of men.' He punched his fist into the palm of his hand. 'I'll make him pay for this. I'll break him, so help me God, I'll smash him! I'll bring criminal charges against him. Malicious damage to property. Manslaughter. Culpable homicide! By Jesus, I'll have his guts for this!'

Listening to Hurry ranting and threatening, Terry could keep silent no longer.

'It wasn't his fault, Pops. Truly it wasn't. He was forced to do it.'

'Ha!' snorted Hurry. 'I heard you at the pithead a few minutes ago. Just what is this man to you, Missy, that you spring to his defence so nobly?'

'Pops, please believe me.' Her eyes were enormous in her pale face.

'Why should I believe you? The two of you are obviously up to mischief together. Naturally you will try and protect him.'

'Listen to me at least,' she pleaded, and Hurry checked the run of his tongue and breathing heavily he turned to face her.

'This better be good, young lady,' he warned her.

In her agitation she told it badly, and halfway through she realized that she wasn't even convincing herself. Hurry's expression became more and more bleak, until he interrupted her impatiently.

'Good God, Theresa, this isn't like you. To try and put the blame for this onto your own husband! That's despicable! To try and switch the blame for this . . .'

'It's true! As God is my witness.' Terry was almost in tears, she was tugging at Hurry's sleeve in her agitation. 'Rod was forced to do it. He had no option.'

'You have proof of this?' Hurry asked drily, and Terry fell silent, staring at him dumbly. What proof was there?

– 68 –

The cage checked and slowed as it approached 65 level. The lights were still burning, but the workings were deserted. They lugged the dinghy out onto the station.

They could hear the dull waterfall roar of the flood on the level below them. The displacement of huge volumes of water disturbed the air so that a strong cool breeze was blowing up the shaft.

'Big King and I will go down the emergency ladder. You will lower the dinghy to us afterwards,' Rod told Dimitri. 'Make sure all the equipment is tied into it.'

'Right.' Dimitri nodded.

All was in readiness. The men who had come down with them in the cage were waiting expectantly. Rod could find no reason for further delay. He felt something cold and heavy settle in his guts.

'Come on, Big King.' And he went to the steel ladder.

'Good luck, Rod.' Dimitri's voice floated down to him, but Rod saved his breath for that cold dark climb downwards.

All the lights had fused on 66 level, and in the beam of his lamp the water below him was black and agitated. It poured into the mouth of the shaft, bending the mesh barrier inwards. The mesh acted as a gigantic sieve, straining the floating rubbish from the flood. Amongst the timber and planking, the sodden sacking and unrecognizable objects, Rod made out the water-logged corpses of the dead pressed against the wire.

He climbed down and gingerly lowered himself into the water. Instantly it dragged at his lower body, shocking in its power. It was waist-deep here, but he found that by bracing his body against the steel ladder he could maintain his footing.

Big King climbed down beside him, and Rod had to raise his voice above the hissing thunder of water.

'All right?'

'Yes. Let them send down the boat.'

Rod flashed his lamp up the shaft, and within minutes the dinghy was swaying slowly down to them. They reached up and guided it right side up to the surface of the water, before untying the rope.

The dinghy was sucked firmly against the wire mesh, and Rod checked its contents quickly. All was secure.

'Right.' Rod tied a bight of the nylon rope around his waist, and climbed up the wire mesh barrier until he could reach the roof of the tunnel. Behind him Big King was paying out the nylon line.

Rod leaned out until he could get his hands on the compressed air pipes that ran along the roof of the tunnel. The pipes were as thick as a man's wrist, bolted securely into the hanging wall of the drive; they would support a man's weight with ease. Rod settled his grip firmly on the piping and then kicked his feet free from the barrier. He hung above the rushing waters, his feet just brushing the surface.

Hand over hand, swinging forward with feet dangling, he started up the tunnel. The nylon rope hung down behind him like a long white tail. It was 300 feet to where the water boiled from the drive into the main haulage, and Rod's shoulder muscles were shrieking in protest before he reached it. It seemed that his arms were being wrenched from their sockets, for the weight of the nylon rope that was dragging in the water was fast becoming intolerable.

There was a back eddy in the angle formed by the drive and the haulage. Here the flood swirled in a vortex, and

Rod lowered himself slowly into it. The water buffeted him, but again he was able to cower against the side wall of the haulage and hold his footing. Quickly he began tying the rope onto the rawlbolts that were driven into the sidewall to consolidate the rock. Within minutes he had established a secure base from which to operate, and when he flashed his lamp back down the haulage he saw Big King following him along the compressed air piping.

Big King dropped into the waist-deep water beside Rod, and they gripped the nylon rope and rested their burning arm muscles.

'Ready?' asked Rod at last, and Big King nodded.

They laid hold of the rope that led back to the dinghy and hauled upon it. For a moment nothing happened, the other end might just as well have been anchored to a mountain.

'Together!' grunted Rod, and they recovered a foot of rope.

'Again!' And they drew the dinghy inch by inch up the haulage against the rush of water.

Their hands were bleeding when they at last pulled the laden dinghy up to their own position and anchored it to the rawlbolts beside them. It bounced and bobbed with the water drumming against its underside.

Neither Rod nor Big King could talk. They hung exhausted on the body lines with the water ripping at their skin and gasped for breath.

At last Rod looked up at Big King, and in the lamp light he saw his own doubts reflected in Big King's eyes. The drop-blast matt was 1,000 feet up the drive. The strength and speed of the water in the drive was almost double what it was in the haulage. Could they ever fight their way against such primeval forces as these that were now unleashed about them?

'I will go next,' Big King said, and Rod nodded his agreement.

The huge Bantu drew himself up the rope until he could reach the compressed air pipe. His skin in the lamplight glistened like that of a porpoise. Hand over hand he disappeared into the gaping black maw of the drive. His lamp threw deformed and monstrous shadows upon the walls of rock.

When Big King's lamp flashed the signal to him, Rod climbed up to the pipe and followed him into the drive. Three hundred feet later he found Big King had established another base. But here they were exposed to the full force of the flood, and they were pulled so violently against the body lines that the harsh nylon smeared the skin from their bodies. Together they dragged the dinghy up to them and anchored it.

Rod was sobbing softly as he held his torn hands to his chest and wondered if he could do it again.

'Ready?' Big King asked beside him, and Rod nodded. He reached up and placed the raw flesh of his palms onto the metal piping, and felt the tears of pain flood his eyes. He blinked them back and dragged himself forward.

Vaguely he realized that should he fall, he was a dead man. The flood would sweep him away, dragging him along the jagged side walls of the drive, ripping his flesh from the bone, and finally hurling him against the mesh surrounding the shaft to crush the life from his body.

He went on until he knew he could go no farther. Then he selected a rawlbolt in the side wall and looped the rope through it. And they repeated the whole heart-breaking procedure. Twice as he strained against the dinghy rope Rod saw his vision explode into stars and pinwheels. Each time he dragged himself back from the brink of unconsciousness by sheer force of will.

The example that Big King was setting was the inspiration which kept Rod from failing. Big King worked without change of expression, but his eyes were bloodshot with exertion. Only once Rod heard him grunt like a gut-shot lion, and there was bright blood on the rope where he touched it.

Rod knew he could not give in while Big King held on.

Reality dissolved slowly into a dark roaring nightmare of pain, wherein muscles and bone were loaded beyond all endurance, and yet continued to function. It seemed that for all time Rod had hung on arms that were leadened and slow with exhaustion. He was inching his way along the compressed air pipe for yet another advance up the drive. Sweat running into his eyes was blurring his vision, so at first he did not credit what he saw ahead of him in the darkness.

He shook his head to clear his eyes, and then squinted along the beam of his lamp. A heavy timber structure was hanging drunkenly from the roof of the drive. The bolts that held it were resisting the efforts of the water to tear it loose.

Rod realized abruptly that this was what remained of the frame which had held the ventilation doors. The doors were gone, ripped away, but the frame was still in position. He knew that just beyond the ventilation doors the drop-blast matt began. They had reached it!

New strength flowed into his body and he swung forward along the pipe. The timber frame made a fine anchor point and Rod secured the rope to it, and flashed back the signal to Big King. He hung in the loop of rope and rested awhile, then he forced himself to take an interest in his surroundings. He played the beam over the distorted timber frame and saw instantly why the blasting circuit had been broken.

In the lamp light the distinctive green plastic-coated blasting cable hung in festoons from the roof of the drive; clearly it had become entangled in the ventilation doors and been severed when they were ripped away. The loose end of the cable dangled to the surface of the racing water.

Rod fastened his eyes on it, drawing comfort and strength from the knowledge that they would not have to continue their agonized journey down the drive.

When Big King came up out of the gloom, Rod indicated the dangling cable.

'There!' he gasped, and Big King narrowed his eyes in acknowledgement; he was unable to speak.

It was five minutes before they could commence the excruciating business of hauling the dinghy up and securing it to the door frame.

Again they rested. Their movements were slowing up drastically. Neither of them had much strength left to draw upon.

'Get hold of the end of the cable.' Rod instructed Big King, and he dragged himself over the side of the dinghy and lay sprawled full-length on the floor boards.

His weight forced the dinghy deeper, increasing its resistance to the racing water, and the rope strained against the wooden frame. Rod began clumsily to unpack the battery blaster. Big King stood waist-deep clinging with one arm to the wooden frame, reaching forward with the other towards the end of the green-coated cable. It danced just beyond his fingertips, and he edged forward against the current, steadying himself against the timber frame, placing a greater strain on the retaining bolts.

His fingers closed on the cable and with a grunt of satisfaction he passed it back to Rod.

Working with painstaking deliberation, Rod connected the crocodile clips from the reel of wire to the loose end of the green cable. Rod's plan was for both he and Big King to climb aboard the dinghy, and, paying out the nylon rope, let themselves be carried back down the drive. At the same time they would be letting the wire run from its reel. At a safe distance they would fire the drop-blast matt.

Rod's fingers were swollen and numbed. The minutes

238

passed as he completed his preparations and all that while the strain on the wooden frame was heavy and constant.

Rod looked up from his task, and crawled to his knees.

'All right, Big King,' he wheezed as he knelt in the bows of the dinghy and gripped the wooden frame to steady the dinghy. 'Come aboard. We are ready.'

Big King waded forward and at that instant the retaining bolts on one side of the heavy timber frame gave way. With a rending, tearing sound the frame slewed across the tunnel. The beams of timber crossed each other like the blades of a pair of gigantic scissors. Both Rod's arms were between the beams. The bones in his forearms snapped with the loud crackle of breaking sticks.

With a scream of pain Rod collapsed onto the floorboards of the dinghy, his arms useless, sticking out at absurd angles from their shattered bones. Three feet away Big King was still in the water. His mouth was wide open, but no sound issued from his throat. He stood still as a black statue and his eyes bulged from their sockets. Even through his own suffering Rod was horrified by the expression on Big King's contorted features.

Below the surface of the water the bottom timber beams had performed the same scissor movement, but this time they had caught Big King's lower body between them. They had closed across his pelvis and crushed it. Now they held him in a vicelike grip from which it was not possible to shake them.

The white face and the black face were but a few feet apart. The two stricken companions in disaster looked into each other's eyes and knew that there was no escape. They were doomed.

'My arms,' whispered Rod huskily. 'I cannot use them.' Big King's bulging eyes held Rod's gaze.

'Can you reach the blaster?' Rod whispered urgently. 'Take it and turn the handle. Burn it, Big King, burn it!'

239

Slow comprehension showed in Big King's pain-glazed eyes.

'We are finished, Big King. Let us go like men. Burn it, bring down the rock!'

Above them the rock was sown with explosive. The blaster was connected. In his agitation Rod tried to reach out for the blaster. His forearm swung loosely, the fingers hanging open like the petals of a dead flower, and the pain checked him.

'Get it, Big King,' Rod urged him, and Big King picked up the blaster and held it against his chest with one arm.

'The handle!' Rod encouraged him. 'Turn the handle!'

But instead Big King reached into the dinghy once more and drew the machete from its sheath.

'What are you doing?' Rod demanded, and in reply Big King swung the blade back over his shoulder and then brought it forward in a gleaming arc aimed at the nylon rope that held the dinghy anchored to the wooden frame. Clunk! The blade bit into the wood, severing the rope that was bound around it.

Freed by the stroke of the machete, the dinghy was whisked away by the current. Lying in the dancing rubber dinghy, Rod heard a bull voice bellow above the rush of the water.

'Go in peace, my friend.'

Then Rod was careening back along the drive, a hell ride during which the dinghy spun like a top and in the beam of his lamp the roof and walls melted into a dark racing blur as Rod lay maimed on the floor of the dinghy.

Then suddenly the air jarred against his ear drums, a long rolling concussion in the confines of the drive and he knew that Big King had fired the drop-blast matt. Rodney Ironsides slipped over the edge of consciousness into a soft warm dark place from which he hoped never to return.

Dimitri squatted on his haunches above the shaft at 65 level. He was smoking his tenth cigarette. The rest of the men waited as impatiently as he did; every few minutes Dimitri would cross to the shaft and flash his lamp down the hundred-foot hole to 66 level.

'How long have they been gone?' he asked, and they all glanced at their watches.

'An hour and ten minutes.'

'No, an hour and fourteen minutes.'

'Christ, call me a liar for four minutes!'

And they lapsed into silence once more. Suddenly the station telephone shrilled, and Dimitri jumped up and ran to it.

'No, Mr Hirschfeld, nothing yet!'

He listened a moment.

'All right, send him down then.'

He hung up the telephone, and his men looked at him enquiringly.

'They are sending down a policeman,' he explained.

'What the hell for?'

'They want Big King.'

'Why?'

'Warrant of arrest for murder.'

'Murder?'

'Ja, they reckon he murdered the Portuguese store-keeper.'

'Jeez!'

'Big King, is that so!' Delighted to have found something to pass the time, they fell into an animated debate.

The police inspector arrived in the cage at 65 level, but he was disappointing. He looked like a down-at-heel under-taker, and he replied to their eager questions with a sorrowful stare that left them stuttering.

For the fifteenth time Dimitri went to the shaft and peered down into it. The blast shook the earth around them, a long rumbling that persisted for many seconds.

'They've done it!' yelled Dimitri, and began to caper wildly. His men leapt to their feet and began beating each other on the back, shouting and laughing. The police inspector alone took no part in the celebrations.

'Wait,' yelled Dimitri at last. 'Shut up all of you! Shut up! Damn it! Listen!'

They fell silent.

'What is it?' someone asked. 'I can't hear anything.'

'That's just it!' exulted Dimitri. 'The water! It has stopped!'

Only then did they become aware that the dull roar of water to which their ears had become resigned was now ended. It was quiet; a cathedral hush lay upon the workings. They began to cheer, their voices thin in the silence, and Dimitri ran to the steel ladder and swarmed down it like a monkey.

From thirty feet up Dimitri saw the dinghy marooned amongst the filth and debris around the shaft. He recognized the crumpled figure lying in the bottom of it.

'Rod!' he was shouting before he reached the station at 66 level. 'Rod, are you all right?'

The floor of the haulage was wet, and here and there a trickle of water still snaked towards the shaft. Dimitri ran to the stranded dinghy and started to turn Rod onto his back. Then he saw his arms.

'Oh, Christ!' he gasped in horror, then he was yelling up the ladder. 'Get a stretcher down here.'

Rod regained consciousness to find himself covered with blankets and strapped securely into a mine stretcher. His arms were splinted and bandaged, and from the familiar rattle and rush of air he knew he was in the cage on the way to the surface.

He recognized Dimitri's voice raised argumentatively.

'Damn it! The man is unconscious and badly injured, can't you leave him alone?'

'I have my duty to perform,' a strange voice answered.

'What's he want, Dimitri?' Rod croaked.

'Rod, how are you?' At the sound of his voice Dimitri was kneeling beside the stretcher anxiously.

'Bloody awful,' Rod whispered. 'What does this joker want?'

'He's a police officer. He wants to arrest Big King for murder,' Dimitri explained.

'Well, he's a bit bloody late,' whispered Rod, and even through his pain this seemed to Rod to be terribly funny. He began to laugh. He sobbed with laughter, each convulsion sending bright bursts of pain along his arms. He was shaking uncontrollably with shock, sweat pouring from his face, and he was laughing wildly.

'He's a bit bloody late,' he repeated through his hysterical laughter as Dr Dan Stander pushed the hypodermic needle into his arm and shot him full of morphine.

– 70 –

Hurry Hirschfeld stood in the main haulage on 66 level. There was bustle all around him. Already the crews from the cementation company were manhandling their equipment up towards the blocked drive.

These were specialists from an independent contracting company. They were about to begin pumping thousands of tons of liquid cement into the rock jam that sealed the drive. They would pump it in at pressures in excess of 3,000 pounds per square inch, and when that concrete set it would form a plug that would effectively seal off the drive for all time. It would also form a burial vault for the body of Big King, thought Hurry, a fitting monument to the man who had saved the Sonder Ditch.

He would arrange to have a commemorative plaque placed on the outer wall of the cement plug with a suitable inscription describing the man and the deed.

The man's dependants must be properly taken care of; perhaps they could be flown down for the unveiling of the plaque. Anyway he could leave that to Public Relations and Personnel.

The haulage stank of wetness and mud. It was dank and clammy cool, and it would not improve his lumbago. Hurry had seen enough; he started back towards the shaft. Faintly he was aware of the muted clangour of the mighty pumps which in a few days would free the Sonder Ditch of the water that filled her lower levels.

The laden stretchers with their grisly blanket-covered burdens stood in a row under the hastily rigged electric lights along one wall of the tunnel. Hurry's expression hardened as he passed them.

'I'll have the guts of the man responsible for this,' he vowed silently as he waited for the cage.

Terry Steyner rode in the rear of the ambulance with Rod. She wiped the mud from his face.

'How bad is it, Dan?' she asked.

'Hell, Terry, he'll be up and about in a few days. The arms of course are not very pretty, that's why I'm taking him directly to Johannesburg. I want a specialist orthopaedic surgeon to set them. Apart from that he is suffering from shock pretty badly and his hands are superficially lacerated. But he will be fine.'

Dan watched curiously as Terry fussed ineffectually with the damp hair of the drugged man.

'You want a smoke?' he asked.

'Light me one, please Dan.'

He passed her the cigarette.

'I didn't know that you and Rod were so friendly,' he ventured.

Terry looked up at him quickly.

'How very delicate you are, Dr Stander,' she mocked him.

'None of my business, of course.' Hurriedly Dan withdrew.

'Don't be silly, Dan. You're a good friend of Rod's and Joy is mine. You two are entitled to know. I am desperately, crazily in love with this big hunk. I intend divorcing Manfred just as soon as possible.'

'Is Rod going to marry you?'

'He hasn't said anything about marriage but I'll sure as hell start working on him,' Terry grinned, and Dan laughed.

'Good luck to you both, then. I'm sure Rod will be able to get another job.'

'What do you mean?' Terry demanded.

'They say your grandfather is threatening to fire him so high he'll be the first man on the moon.'

Terry relapsed into silence. Proof was what Pops had asked for, but what proof was there?

'They'll be waiting on the X-ray reports.' Joy Albright gave her opinion. Since her engagement to Dan, Joy had suddenly become something of a medical expert. She had rushed down to the Johannesburg Central Hospital at Dan's hurried telephonic request. Dan wanted her to keep Terry company while she waited for Rod to come out of emergency. They sat together in the waiting-room.

'I expect so,' Terry agreed. Something Joy had just said had jolted in her mind, something she must remember.

'It takes them twenty minutes or so to expose the plates

and develop them. Then the radiologist has to examine the plates and make his report to the surgeon.'

There, Joy had said it again. Terry sat up straight and concentrated on what Joy had said. Which word had disturbed her?

Suddenly she had it.

'The report!' she exclaimed. 'That's it. The report, that's the proof.'

She leapt out of her chair.

'Joy! Give me the keys of your car,' she demanded.

'What on earth?' Joy looked startled.

'I can't explain now. I have to get home to Sandown urgently, give me your keys. I'll explain later.'

Joy fished in her handbag and produced a leather key folder. Terry snatched it from her.

'Where are you parked?' Terry demanded.

'In the car park, near the main gate.'

'Thanks, Joy.' Terry dashed from the waiting-room, her high heels clattered down the passage.

'Crazy woman.' Joy looked after her bewildered.

Ten minutes later Dan looked into the waiting-room.

'Rod's fine now. Where's Terry?'

'She went mad—' And Joy explained her abrupt departure. Dan looked grave.

'I think we'd better follow her, Joy.'

'I think you're right, darling.'

'I'll just grab my coat,' said Dan.

There was only one place where Manfred would keep the geological report on the Big Dipper that Rod had told her about. That was in the safe deposit behind the panelling in his study. Because her jewellery was kept in the same safe, Terry had a key and the combination to the lock.

Even in Joy's Alfa Romeo, taking liberties with the traffic regulations, it was a thirty-five-minute drive out to

Sandown. It was after five in the evening when Terry coasted down the long driveway and parked before the garages.

The extensive grounds were deserted, for the gardeners finished at five, and there was no sign of life from the house. This was as it should be, for she knew Manfred was still in Europe. He was not due back for at least another four days.

Leaving the ignition keys in the Alfa, Terry ran up the pathway and onto the stoep. She fumbled in her handbag and found the keys to the front door. She let herself in, and went directly to Manfred's study. She slid the concealing panel aside and set about the lengthy business of opening the steel safe. It required both key and combination to activate the mechanism, and Terry had never developed much expertise at tumbling the combination.

Finally, however, the door swung open and she was confronted by the voluminous contents. Terry began removing the various documents and files, examining each one and then stacking them neatly on the floor beside her.

She had no idea of the shape, size nor colour of the report for which she was searching, it was ten minutes before she selected an unmarked folder and flicked open the cover. 'Confidential Report on the geological formations of the Kitchenerville gold fields, with special reference to those areas lying to the east of the Big Dipper Dyke.'

Terry felt a wonderful lift of relief as she read the titling for she had begun doubting that the report was here. Quickly she thumbed through the pages and began reading at random. There was no doubt.

'This is it!' she exclaimed aloud.

'I'll take that, thank you.' The dreaded familiar voice cut into her preoccupation, and Terry spun around and came to her feet in one movement, clutching the file protectively to her breast. She backed away from the man who stood in the doorway.

She hardly recognized her own husband. She had never

seen him like this. Manfred was coatless, and his shirt was without collar or stud. He appeared to have slept in his trousers, for they were rumpled and baggy. There was a yellow stain down the front of his white shirt.

His scanty brown hair was dishevelled, hanging forward wispily onto his forehead. He had not shaved, and the skin around his eyes was discoloured and puffy.

'Give that to me.' He came towards her with hand outstretched.

'Manfred.' She kept moving away from him. 'What are you doing here? When did you get back?'

'Give it to me, you slut.'

'Why do you call me that?' she asked, trying for time.

'Slut!' he repeated, and lunged towards her. Terry whirled away from him lightly.

She ran for the study door, with Manfred close behind her. She beat him into the passage and raced for the front door. Her heel caught in one of the Persian carpets that covered the floor of the passage, and she staggered and fell against the wall.

'Whore!' He was on her instantly trying to wrestle the report out of her hands, but she clung to it with all her strength. Face to face they were almost of a height, and she saw the madness in his eyes.

Suddenly Manfred released her. He stepped back, bunched his fist and swung it round-armed into her cheek. Her head jerked back and cracked against the wall. He drew back his fist and hit her again. She felt the quick warm burst of blood spurt from her nose, and staggered through the door beside her into the dining-room. She was dizzy from the blows and she fell against the heavy stink-wood table.

Manfred was close behind her. He charged her, sending her sprawling backwards onto the table. He was on top of her, both his hands at her throat.

'I'm going to kill you, you whore,' he wheezed. His thumbs hooked and pressed deep into the flesh of her throat. With the frenzied strength of despair, Terry clawed at his eyes with both hands. Her nails scored his face, raking long red lines into his flesh. With a cry Manfred released her, and backed away holding both hands to his injured face, leaving Terry lying gasping across the table.

He stood for a moment, then uncovered his face and inspected the blood on his hands.

'I'll kill you for that!'

But as he advanced towards her, Terry rolled over the table.

'Whore! Slut! Bitch!' he screamed at her, following her around the table. Terry kept ahead of him.

There were a matched pair of heavy Stuart crystal decanters on the sideboard, one containing port, the other sherry. Terry snatched up one of them and turned to face Manfred. She hurled the decanter with all her remaining strength at his head.

Manfred did not have time to duck. The decanter cracked against his forehead, and he fell backwards, stunned. Terry snatched up the report and ran out of the dining-room, down the passage, out of the front door and into the garden. She was running weakly, following the driveway towards the main road.

Then behind her she heard the engine of an automobile roar into life. Panting wildly, holding the report, she stopped and looked back. Manfred had followed her out of the house. He was behind the steering wheel of Joy's Alfa Romeo. As she watched he threw the car into gear and howled towards her, blue smoke burning from the rear tyres with the speed of the acceleration. His face behind the windscreen was white and streaked with the marks of her nails, his eyes were staring, insane, and she knew he was going to ride her down.

She kicked off her shoes and ran off the driveway onto the lawns.

Crouched forward in the driver's seat of the Alfa, Manfred watched the fleeing figure ahead of him.

Terry ran with the full-hipped sway of the mature woman, her long legs were tanned and her hair flew out loosely behind her.

Manfred was not concerned with the return of the geological report, its existence was no longer of significance to him. What he wanted was to completely destroy this woman. In his crazed state, she had become the symbol and the figurehead of all his woes. His humiliation and fall were all linked to her, he could exact his vengeance by destroying her, crushing that revolting warm and clinging body, bruising it, ripping it with the steel of the Alfa Romeo's chassis.

He hit second gear and spun the steering-wheel. The Alfa swerved from the driveway, and as its rear wheels left the tarmac, they skidded on the thick grass. Deftly Manfred checked the skid and lined up on Terry's running back.

Already she was among the protea bushes on the lower terrace. The Alfa buck-jumped the slope, flying bird-free before crashing down heavily on its suspension. Wheels spun and bit, and the sleek vehicle shot forward again.

Terry looked back over her shoulder, her face was white and her eyes very big and fear-filled. Manfred giggled. He was aware of a sense of power, the ability to dispense life or death. He steered for her, reckless of all consequences, intent on destroying her.

There was a six-foot-tall protea bush ahead of him, and Manfred roared through it, bursting it asunder. Scattering branches and leaves, giggling again, he saw Terry directly ahead of him. She was still looking back at him, and at that moment she stumbled and fell onto her knees.

She was helpless. Her face streaked with tears and blood,

and the vegetable truck were there before him. They were attempting to talk each other down, both of them excited and relieved by their own escapes.

'I'm a doctor,' said Dan, and they fell back respectfully.

'He doesn't need a doctor,' said one of them. 'He needs an undertaker.'

One look was sufficient. Dr Manfred Steyner was as dead as Dan had ever seen anybody. His crushed head was thrust through the windscreen. Dan picked up the sodden bundle of paper from the seat beside the huddled body. He was aware that some particular importance was attached to it.

Dan's anger had evaporated entirely, and he felt a twinge of pity as he looked into the wreckage at the corpse. It appeared so frail and small – of such little consequence.

– 71 –

The sunlight was sparkling bright, broken into a myriad eyestinging fragments by the rippling surface of the bay.

The breeze was strong enough for the Arrow class yachts to fly their spinnakers as they came down on the wind. The sails bulged out blue and yellow and bright scarlet against the sombre green of the great whale-back bluff above Durban Bay.

Under the awning on the afterdeck of the motor yacht it was cool, but the fat man wore only a pair of white linen slacks with his feet thrust into dark blue cloth espadrilles.

Sprawled in a deck-chair, his belly bulged smooth and hard over the waistband of his slacks; he was tanned a dark mahogany colour and his body-hair grew thick and curly from chest to navel.

'Thank you, Andrew.' He extended his empty glass, and the younger man carried it to the open-air bar. The fat man watched him as he mixed another Pimms No. 1 cup.

A white-clad crew member clambered down the companion way from the bridge. He touched his cap respectfully to the fat man.

'Captain's respects, sir, and we are ready to sail when you give the order.'

'Thank you. Please tell the captain we will sail as soon as Miss du Maine comes aboard.' And the crew man ran back to the bridge.

'Ah!' The fat man sighed happily as Andrew placed the Pimms in his outstretched hand. 'I have really earned this break. The last few weeks have been nerve-racking, to say the least.'

'Yes, sir,' Andrew agreed dutifully. 'But, as usual, you snatched victory from the ashes.'

'It was close,' the fat man agreed. 'Young Ironsides gave us all a nasty fright with his drop-blast matt. I was only just able to make good my personal commitments before the price shot up again. The profit was not as high as I had anticipated, but then I have never made a habit of peering into the mouths of gift-horses.'

'It was a pity that our associates lost all that money,' Andrew ventured.

'Yes, yes. A great pity. But rather them than us, Andrew.'

'Indeed, sir.'

'In a way I am glad it worked out as it did. I am a patriotic man, at heart. I am relieved that it was not necessary to disrupt the economy of the country to make our little profit.'

He stood up suddenly, his interest quickening as a taxi cab came down onto the Yacht Club jetty. The cabby opened a rear door and from it emerged a very beautiful young lady.

'Ah, Andrew! Our guest has arrived. You may warn the captain that we will be sailing within minutes; and send a man to fetch her luggage.'

He went to the entry port to welcome the young lady.

Hettie's eyes flew wide with delight.

'Gee!' she gasped. 'That's *fabulous*!'

– 74 –

Hurry's original intentions had expanded considerably. Instead of a plaque on the cement plug at 66 level, the monument to Big King had become a life-sized statue in bronze. He sited it on the lawns in front of the Adminstrative offices of the Sonder Ditch on a base of black marble.

It was effective. The artist had captured a sense of urgency, of vibrant power. The inscription was simple, just the name of the man – 'King Nkulu' – and the date of his death.

Hurry attended the unveiling in person, even though he hated ceremonies and avoided them whenever possible. In the front row of guests facing him his granddaughter sat beside Doctor Stander and his very new blonde wife. She winked at him and Hurry frowned lovingly back at her.

From the seat beside Hurry, young Ironsides stood up to introduce the Chairman. Hurry noted the expression on his granddaughter's face as she transferred all her attention to the tall young man with both his arms encased in plaster of Paris and supported by slings.

'Perhaps I should have fired him, after all,' thought Hurry. 'He is going to cut one out of my herd.'

Hurry glanced sideways at his General Manager, and decided with resignation, 'Too late'. Then he went on to cheer himself. 'Anyway he looks like good breeding stock.'

His line of thought switched again. 'Better start making arrangements to transfer him up to Head Office. He will need a lot of grooming and polishing.'

Without thinking he fished a powerful-looking cigar from his breast pocket. He had it halfway to his mouth when he caught Terry's scandalized glare. Silently her lips formed the words: 'Your doctor!'

Guiltily Hurry Hirschfeld stuffed the cigar back into his pocket.

In mid-summer in the Zambesi Valley the heat is a solid white shimmering thing. In the noonday nothing moves in the merciless sunlight.

At the centre of the native village grew a baobab tree. A monstrous bloated trunk with malformed branches like the limbs of a polio victim. The carrion crows sat in it, black and shiny as cockroaches. A score of grass huts ringed the tree, and beyond them lay the tilled fields. The millet stood tall and green in the sun.

Along the rude track towards the village came a Land Rover. It came slowly, lurching and jolting over the rough ground, its motor growling in low gear. Printed in black on its sides were the letters ARC, African Recruiting Corporation.

The children heard it first, and crawled from the grass huts. Naked black bodies, and shrill excited voices in the sunlight.

They ran to meet the Land Rover and danced beside it, shrieking and laughing. The Land Rover came to a halt in the meagre shade under the baobab tree. An elderly white man climbed from the cab. He wore khaki safari clothes and a wide-brimmed hat. Complete silence fell, and one of the oldest boys fetched a carved stool and placed it in the shade.

The white man sat on the stool. A girl came forward, knelt before him and offered a gourd of millet beer. The white man drank from the gourd. No one spoke, none would disturb an honoured guest until he had taken refreshment, but from the grass huts the adult members of the village came. Blinking into the sunlight, winding their loin clothes about their waists. They came and squatted in a semi-circle before the white man on his stool.

He lowered the gourd and set it aside. He looked at them.

'I see you, my friends,' he greeted them, and the response was warm.

'We see you, old one,' they chorused, but the expression of their visitor remained grave.

'Let the wives of King Nkulu come forward,' he called. 'Let them bring each their first-born son with them.'

Four women and four adolescent boys left the crowd and came shyly into the open. For a moment the white man studied them compassionately, then he stood and stepped forward. He placed a hand on the shoulder of each of the two eldest lads.

'Your father has gone to *his* fathers,' he told them. There was a stirring, an intake of breath, a startled cry, and then, as was proper, the eldest wife let out the first sobbing wail of mourning.

One by one each wife sank down onto the dry musty earth and covered her head with her shawl.

'He is dead,' the white man repeated against the background of their keening lament. 'But he died in such honour as to let his name live on forever. So great was his dying that for all their lives money will each month be paid to his wives, and for each of his sons there is already set aside a place at the University that each may grow as strong in learning as his father was in body. Of Big King there will be raised up an image in stone.

'The wives of Big King and his sons will travel in a flying machine to I'Goldi, that their eyes also may look upon the stone image of the man who was their husband and their father.' The white man paused for breath, it was a lengthy speech in the midday heat of the valley. He wiped his face and then tucked the handkerchief into his pocket.

'He was a lion!'

'Ngwenyama!' whispered the sturdy twelve-year-old boy standing beside the white man. The tears started from his eyes and greased down his cheeks. He turned away and ran alone into the millet fields.

Dennis Langley, the Sales Manager of Kitchenerville Motors who were the local Ford agents, stretched his arms over his head luxuriously. He sighed with deep contentment. What a lovely way to spend a working-day morning.

'Happy?' asked Hettie Delange beside him in the double bed. In reply Dennis grinned and sighed again.

Hettie sat up and let the sheet fall to her waist. Her breasts were big and white, and damp with perspiration. She looked down on his naked chest and arm muscles approvingly.

'Gee, you're built nicely.'

'So are you,' Dennis smiled up at her.

'You're different from the other chaps I've gone out with,' Hettie told him. 'You speak so nicely – like a gentleman, you know.'

Before Dennis Langley could decide on a suitable reply, the front door bell shrilled, the sound of it echoing through the house. Dennis shot into an upright position with a fearful expression on his face.

'Who's that?' he demanded.

'It's probably the butcher delivering the meat.'

'It may be my wife!' Dennis cautioned her. 'Don't answer it.'

'Of course I've got to answer it, silly.' Hettie threw back the sheet, and rose in her white and golden glory to find her dressing-gown. The sight was enough to momentarily quiet Dennis Langley's misgivings, but as she belted her gown and hid it from view he urged her again.

'Be careful! Make sure it's not her before you open the door.'

Hettie opened the front door, and immediately drew her gown more closely around her with one hand, while the other she tried to pat her hair into a semblance of order.

'Hello,' she breathed.

The tall young man in the doorway was really rather dreamy. He wore a dark business suit and carried an expensive leather briefcase.

'Mrs Delange?' he enquired. He had a nice soft dreamy voice.

'Yes, I'm Mrs Delange.' Hettie fluttered her eyelashes. 'Won't you come in?'

She led him through to the lounge, and she was pleasantly aware of his eyes on the opening of her gown.

'What can I do for you?' she asked archly.

'I am your local representative of the Sanlam Insurance Company, Mrs Delange. I have come to express my company's condolences on your recent sad bereavement. I would have called sooner, but I did not wish to intrude on your sorrow.'

'Oh!' Hettie dropped her eyes, immediately adopting the role of the widow.

'However, we hope we can bring a little light to disperse the darkness that surrounds you. You may know that your husband was a policy-holder with our Company?'

Hettie shook her head, but watched with interest while the visitor opened his briefcase.

'Yes, he was. Two months ago he took out a straight life policy with double indemnity. The policy was ceded to you.' The insurance man extracted a sheaf of papers from his case. 'I have here my company's cheque in full settlement of all claims under the policy. If you will just sign for it, please.'

'How much?' Hettie abandoned the role of the bereaved.

'With the double indemnity, the cheque is for forty-eight thousand rand.'